Julian Symons, *The Sunday Times*

'Emotion is handled with the old classical
assurance of the nineteenth-century novel, and
stays in the mind with appalling force'

Richard Holmes, The Times

'The finest work of fiction to come out of
Ireland in the last fifty years'

Patrick Boyle

'A masterpiece'

Sunday Express

STRUMPET CITY

James Plunkett

ARROW BOOKS

To
Valerie

Arrow Books Limited
20 Vauxhall Bridge Road, London SW1V 2SA

An imprint of the Random Century Group

London Melbourne Sydney Auckland
Johannesburg and agencies throughout
the world

First published by Hutchinson 1969
Arrow edition 1978
13 15 16 14 12

Printed and bound in Great Britain by
Cox & Wyman Ltd, Reading

ISBN 0 09 918750 7

CONTENTS

BOOK ONE 1907–1909
page 11

BOOK TWO 1910–1912
page 175

BOOK THREE 1913–1914
page 367

SPEAKER: Shall we sit down together for a while? Here on the hillside, where we can look down on the city . . .

> Strumpet city in the sunset
> So old, so sick with memories
> Old Mother;
> Some they say are damned
> But you, I know, will walk the streets of Paradise
> Head high, and unashamed.

The Old Lady Says 'No' DENIS JOHNSTON

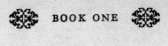

BOOK ONE

1907—1909

CHAPTER I

A T 3.15 a.m., with spectral quiet, His Majesty's yacht *Victoria and Albert* approached the harbour mouth and lay to. And at half past six, with the first light, the workmen had finished. They looked with some pride on the result of their labours. The floral arch was ready for the disembarkation. It stood mute and beautiful at the harbour mouth, its green leaves stirring a little in the dawn breeze, its crimson and gold banner announcing the warm welcome of the citizens with the words,

'Come Back To Erin
God Bless Our King'

From the gardens by the shore and from the garlands entwined about railings and lamp-posts throughout the town of Kingstown the wind stole the sweet breath of thousands of flowers. It had been a tender July night, calm at sea, warm on shore. Now that dawn had come they could see the fluttering pennants of the battleships, the three-stringed bunting about the clubs on the waterfront, the greenery and flowers entwined about the masts of the private yachts, the crimson and gold banners overhanging the sides. In contrast, the landing stage was dressed in St. Patrick's Blue and Cream.

They went up through the town, under bunting and streamers, Japanese lanterns and fairy-lights, thousands of coloured gaslamps. The workmen were tired. Their boots made an early-morning din. Their tongues were silent. They wanted their breakfasts.

Mary peeped from her bedroom window and saw them pass.

13

Then she looked down the street and felt a thrill of excitement. She hoped to have the day off, because Mrs. Bradshaw had said either she or Miss Gilchrist, the cook, could take a free day in honour of the occasion. Miss Gilchrist had said she would refuse. She had political views and did not approve of British royalty. Mary's difficulty would be to contact Fitz and tell him. They could look at the procession to the Viceregal Lodge and perhaps visit the prison ship which was lying at Custom House Dock. The advertisements said it was one hundred and seventeen years old, with cells on it and lifelike wax figures of prisoners. Mary was not sure that she would care much for that. But if Fitz was with her she might chance the visit.

She dressed quickly. She was not quite sure what shift Fitz was on, but she had left a note at the sweetshop to say that she would be off if Miss Gilchrist did not change her mind. They used the sweetshop as a post office. Fitz called out from the city when he was free and if there was no note he went off swimming at Seapoint. It had been hard to arrange meetings at first, because Fitz worked six twelve-hour shifts a week. Sometimes he was on night work and other times on day work. She had found it necessary to pretend that she had an aunt in the city in order to get out more frequently to see him. It was easy enough to deceive Mrs. Bradshaw about it. She was kind and prepared to be lenient if it helped Mary to make occasional visits, especially as Mary had said that the lady was old and delicate. She had not so far asked why Mary's father, in his occasional letters about his daughter's progress and welfare, had never mentioned the aunt, but the possibility that it might one day occur to her to do so had to be considered. The thought sometimes troubled Mary, but never for long. She was young, she was learning a job, she was happy to have swopped her father's small farmhouse in County Cork for the luxury of serving in a large residence in the fashionable township of Kingstown. The Bradshaws were not demanding.

Mary knocked at the door of the Bradshaws' bedroom at seven o'clock. They wished to breakfast early and to view the proceedings from their window. She prepared the breakfast room and was drawing the curtains when the door handle turned and a gentle voice said:

'Good morning, my dear.'

It was Mrs. Bradshaw.

'Good morning, ma'am.'

'Tell Cook to have the tea especially strong this morning. Mr. Bradshaw had a most restless night.'

'Yes, ma'am,' Mary said. As she turned, the light fell full on her face, so that Mrs. Bradshaw smiled and remarked:

'You look very pretty this morning. And such a lovely colour in your cheeks. I expect it is the excitement.'

Mary inclined her head modestly, letting her dark hair swing down against her cheeks.

'Have you and Cook decided between you who is to have the day off?'

'I think it's me, ma'am.'

' "I", dear.'

'I, ma'am.'

Mrs. Bradshaw acknowledged the correction. She was a short, grey woman of about fifty. The one child of her marriage had died when he was three. Nature had refused to repeat the experiment, which was a great blow. But it had taught her what it was to suffer and it had given her patience and understanding in her dealings with others. She said:

'I'm glad it's you. You're young and will enjoy it. Besides, you will probably find time to visit your aunt.'

Mary coloured a little but Mrs. Bradshaw did not notice. She was peering through the window. Mary slipped out. Mrs. Bradshaw found that the sky was overcast. That was a pity. If it rained it would be such a disappointment to the Kingstown Decoration Committee.

The kitchen had a large window to compensate for the fact that it was a little below the level of the garden. Miss Gilchrist, the cook, prepared two portions of fresh fruit while Mary waited. In addition there was a liberal dish of liver and bacon and eggs for Mr. Bradshaw, who had the habit of dining more heartily than his thinnish frame would lead one to suppose. For Mrs. Bradshaw, who had never taken meat on Wednesdays since the death of her child, there was toast to go with her lightly boiled egg.

'She was asking again about which of us was taking the day,' Mary said, while she waited.

'I told you last night,' Miss Gilchrist said, 'I've more to do than stand gawking at King Edward.'

'But are you sure?'

'Or Queen Alexandra.'

'The decorations are wonderful,' Mary said. 'I was looking down at them from the bedroom window.'

'And you can tell herself that if she doesn't know my feelings on the subject of King and Empire by this time she damn well ought to, seeing I'm over thirty years with her.'

'I couldn't very well say that to her,' Mary said, laughing. 'He's not Ireland's king, anyway.'

'What difference does it make, whether he is or not?'

'You call yourself an Irishwoman, and you ask a question like that.'

'Ah, it's only a bit of excitement,' Mary said, because she saw that Miss Gilchrist's hands were trembling and her cheeks flushed with suppressed rage.

'God be with my poor father and the brave Fenian brotherhood. There was men for you. Not like what's going nowadays.'

Taking the tray and trying to ignore the old woman's anger, Mary said:

'Don't forget that they'll be firing off the guns at eight o'clock. They make a terrible noise, I'm told.'

Miss Gilchrist cocked her head as she squinted through the window at the overcast sky. With great satisfaction she said:

'I'm glad to hear it. I hope it brings the bloody rain down on them.'

At breakfast Mr. Bradshaw betrayed his agitation several times by laying down his paper to consult his watch. He felt that the whole business of the visit was being overdone. He was not opposed in principle to honouring the royal visitors. As a retired civil servant he knew where his duties and his loyalty lay. He approved, for instance, of municipal decorations. In the paper he was trying to read, under the heading Kingstown Decoration Committee, the Chairman Arthur E. Mills, Esq., J.P., and the secretary M. A. Manning, Esq., Town Clerk, jointly acknowledged several subscriptions, including one of one guinea from R. A. Bradshaw, Esq. And, although neither he nor Mrs. Bradshaw would, for the life of them, venture that day into the crowded and confused streets, they had arranged to watch the procession from a window on the second floor, from which he had already hung a large banner with the words 'God Save Our King' picked out in gold letters. The evening would be marked by a special meal followed by an intimate musical party.

But Mr. Bradshaw had to look at the arrangements in a dual capacity. In addition to being a retired civil servant and a substantial shareholder in a number of well-established companies, he was the owner of five houses in an alley very close to the harbour. A family occupied each room. What would happen to these five infirm shells of tottering brick and their swarms of poverty-stricken humanity when His Majesty's Navy blasted off a battery of heavy guns Mr. Bradshaw trembled to think. The nearby railway line had already caused damage enough.

'You're not eating, my dear,' Mrs. Bradshaw said.

'I keep thinking of this damned salute.'

'I'm sure the houses will be quite safe.'

'I wish I had your confidence. Why can't they blow bugles or something.'

'I expect they'll do that as well.'

'Or pipe him ashore.'

'I think that's only for admirals.'

'They have decorations, floral arches, addresses of welcome, military bands. I'm as loyal as the next, I hope, but surely to goodness that ought to be enough without the criminal waste of useful and probably expensive ammunition. It is vulgar, apart from anything else. What time is it?'

'It must be almost eight.'

Mr. Bradshaw consulted his watch again.

'I make it five minutes to,' he said, 'but I may be fast.'

'You must think of something else, something pleasant. We'll have a lovely evening of music. Think forward to that.'

'If all goes well in the meanwhile,' Mr. Bradshaw said, in a tone which betrayed his grave doubt.

'Young Father O'Connor is coming. He has a beautiful tenor voice.'

'Too much wobble in it for my fancy,' Mr. Bradshaw said, again consulting his watch.

'And Mr. Yearling is bringing his 'cello. I'll always remember the night you and Father O'Connor sang "The Moon Hath Raised". Mr. Yearling extemporised beautifully by just looking at the piano score over my shoulder. I thought that very accomplished. It's a great gift of his.'

'He makes heavy inroads on my whiskey,' Mr. Bradshaw said sourly, 'that's another great gift of his.'

Mrs. Bradshaw knew it was useless to talk to him when he had anything on his mind; he simply refused to be cheered. He had always been like that, easily worried and plunged into gloomy humours. Not indeed that she herself looked forward to the noise. It was all very well for soldiers, or young people with strong nerves. Still, she was certain there was nothing whatever to worry about. She noted that his cup was empty and reached across for the teapot.

'Tea?' she asked gently.

He put aside his paper and held out his cup.

'Don't quite fill it,' he requested.

She began to pour. Suddenly a thundering salvo shook the room. The windows rattled and the tableware danced. Mr. Bradshaw jumped and let his cup and saucer slip from his fingers. Mrs. Bradshaw, in her efforts to stifle a scream, continued to pour strong tea over the tablecloth for some seconds. The royal party were coming ashore. Mr. Bradshaw's watch had not been fast. It was, in fact, three minutes slow.

About an hour later the royal cortège left Kingstown. Mr. and Mrs. Bradshaw, recovered from their upset, waved loyally from the upstairs window. Mary stood behind them, her heart beating with excitement. The procession moved into Crofton Road, turned into Monkstown and paused at Blackrock for yet another address of welcome. The King had been informed of

Kingstown's determination to supply small cottages for the labouring classes and gave the scheme his unqualified approval. The health and efficiency of the labourer depended to a great extent, he said, on a happy home life. He was much touched by their warm and generous welcome. Thousands lined the royal route. They waved flags and bantered good-humouredly with the police. It was the same all the way along Rock Road, Ailesbury Road and Donnybrook. At Morehampton Road a series of venetian masts had been erected on both sides of the broad central avenue which divided Herbert Park and the route leading from there to the central bandstand quivered under gay bunting. Slender flag-staves with suitable banners had been affixed to the ornamental light standards. There was a wealth of flowers and plants. A journalist, recording their Majesties arrival at the exhibition, observed that the people raised lusty cheers of loyal welcome. He noted something further, something which might be interpreted as a manifestation of Divine approval. Just as the Anthem was being played the clouds dispersed, the July sun blazed out, the watching thousands cheered afresh. There had been some doubt about the sky's intentions. Now they smiled at one another in relief. 'King's weather,' they remarked.

At the speech of welcome there was a little incident which did not escape the attention of the onlookers. His Majesty, having replied, called for his sword. Lord Aberdeen spoke *sotto voce* to the organising chairman, Mr. Murphy. He was then obliged in turn to speak *sotto voce* to His Majesty, who moved on to other business with characteristic composure. A few astute onlookers tumbled to it that a knighthood had been refused.

It was the second small cloud to trouble the minds of those who were responsible for the King's content during his short stay. The man directly concerned was Sir Arthur Vicars, Ulster King-at-Arms and custodian of the jewelled Royal Order of St. Patrick. These had mysteriously disappeared from Dublin Castle only a few days before. They were valued at over £50,000. Worse still, they were the jewels worn on state visits by the reigning Monarch of England. The King would have to do without them. Mr. Birrell, the Chief Secretary, was openly of the opinion that the Chief Herald and Ulster King-at-Arms had stolen them himself. Social opinion was divided between those who endorsed his view and those who deplored his lack of restraint. Meanwhile the Treasury, in a practical frame of mind, offered £1,000 reward for information leading to the recovery. And the King, imperceptibly diminished in splendour, went, unbejewelled, to the Viceregal Lodge.

Rashers Tierney rose that morning about the same time as King Edward. First the dog barked and then a hand reached down and shook his shoulder. It was very dark in the basement. The form above him could have been Death, or a ghost, or the hangover figure from a nightmare. Rashers was lying on straw. It was no cleaner than it could be in the damp and dirt of the almost windowless cellar. Recognising the figure at last as that of Mrs. Bartley, he threw aside the nondescript rags which covered him. There was no need for any modest precautions. He was fully dressed.

'I boiled you a can of water,' Mrs. Bartley said, 'you'll want it for to make tea.'

Rashers gurgled to dislodge the sleep phlegm from his throat and spat on the floor.

'The blessings of God and His Holy Mother on you for the kind thought,' he said.

'You're welcome,' Mrs. Bartley said. She looked around the hovel. It distressed her. She lived herself in the front parlour with her husband and five children. There were ten rooms in the house and ten families. Nobody regarded Rashers' room as being in the house. It was under it. It cost him one shilling and threepence a week—when he could pay it.

'Did you see me little flags,' Rashers asked, stretching his hand behind his pillow and dragging out a board for Mrs. Bartley's inspection. They were home-made favours with four ribbons apiece.

'They're gorgeous, Mr. Tierney,' she said.

'Red, white and blue,' Rashers said, 'the colours of loyalty.'

'My husband doesn't hold with England,' Mrs. Bartley said.

'That's been catered for,' Rashers explained, showing her a sample, 'the green ribbon is for Ireland.'

'It doesn't match-up, somehow.'

'It never did, ma'am,' Rashers said. 'Isn't that what all the bloody commotion is about for the last seven hundred years?'

'Wet your tea before the water's gone cold for you.' Rashers reached behind his pillow and brought out a tin from which he took part of a loaf, a tin of condensed milk and a jampot. He took out a cold potato too, but put it back. The rest he left on the straw beside him.

'I brought you some bread.'

'I have some,' Rashers said.

'It's as hard as the rock of Cashel,' Mrs. Bartley pronounced, having felt it.

'It'll soften up when I dip it in the tea,' Rashers explained. 'I'll keep yours for afterwards.'

Mrs. Bartley sighed and handed him the spoon. He put in the tea.

'What's it doing out or what?' he asked conversationally as he drank. He meant the weather.

'It's dull. I wouldn't say it was a bit promising.'

'Let's hope to God the rain keeps off,' Rashers said. 'They're more given to buying favours and things when it isn't raining.'

'Are you taking the dog?'

'And have him walked on?' Rashers asked.

'If you're not I'll give him a little something later on.'

'You're a jewel.'

'So long as he doesn't take the hand off me in the process.'

'Is it Rusty?' He called the dog to his side.

'That's Mrs. Bartley,' he explained to the dog, 'and if you don't know her by now you bloody well ought to. She's to come and go as she pleases.' He patted the dog and looked around at the empty floor.

'He thinks you have your eye on the furniture,' Rashers added. Mrs. Bartley laughed aloud.

'Is the husband working again?' Rashers asked.

'All last week, four days this week and a bit promised for next.'

'Look at that now,' Rashers approved, 'isn't he having the life of Reilly.'

Mrs. Bartley said the children might be calling for her so she would leave the spoon and the can and get them when she was bringing down the scraps for Rusty. She hoped God would give him good luck with his selling.

'I'll be rattling shilling against shilling when I get home,' Rashers said, 'and the first thing I'll buy is a tin whistle.'

'You never found the one you lost?'

'Never,' Rashers said, 'neither sign nor light of it from that day to this.'

'Bad luck to the hand that took it.'

'May God wither it,' Rashers said. He had lost his tin whistle after a race meeting nearly a year before.

'It was the drink, God forgive me,' Rashers confessed.

'It's a very occasional failing with you,' Mrs. Bartley said indulgently.

'Drink and the sun. After the few drinks I lay down in the sun and it overpowered me. When I woke up the whistle was gone.'

'The children miss it most of all,' Mrs. Bartley said, 'they loved you to play for them.'

'Rusty too. I used to play to the two of us and we were never lonely.'

'The best music you ever had is the bit you make yourself. It's a great consolation.'

'For man and beast alike, ma'am,' Rashers assented. Mrs. Bartley had a very proper understanding of the whole thing.

When Mrs. Bartley had gone he got up and began to pull on socks, thinking of the whistle he had lost. It had been given to him by Mrs. Molloy, the woman who had reared him. It had earned him coppers at football matches and race meetings. His ambition was to replace it when he had the money to spare. He looked down at his socks and for the moment he forgot about the tin whistle. Both socks had holes in the toes and heels. He thought about that and took them off again. Then he put on his boots. They felt hard and uncomfortable for the amount of walking he would have to do. He took off his boots again, put on the socks and then put on his boots once more. He stood up and stretched. When he yawned, the few rotten teeth seemed very long because the gums had shrunk back almost to the roots.

He took his overcoat from among the rags on the bed, tied it about his middle with a piece of cord and took his board with the coloured favours. He put a bottle and the bread into a short sack which he secured so that it hung from his waist. He shut the door on the dog, which whined, went up the decaying stairs, past the pram in the hallway and down the steps into the street.

The children in Chandlers Court jeered after him, but Rashers was used to that and scarcely heard them. He had already mapped out his journey in his mind. He would go over the iron bridge, through Ringsend and out the Strand Road to Merrion Gates. There would be a crowd there and on the way he could root in the ashbins of the big houses facing the strand. There were always scraps to be found that way. He could use the side streets to contact the crowds at various points along the route. It would be a long walk. By the time he got back from the procession to the Viceregal Lodge he would have covered ten to fourteen miles. But if he sold all his favours he would earn ten shillings. Rashers kept his mind on that. He deviated only once from his planned route and that was to look for some minutes into the window of McNeill's music shop. It was still closed, a dingy little shop, with one dusty window and a small entrance door which needed painting. In the window, among instruments of a more aristocratic kind, there was a board displaying tin whistles. It said:

'Superior toned Italian Flageolets.
Price: One Shilling'

They were masterly looking instruments, and ought to be, Rashers decided, at such an outrageous price. He stared at them for some time. Then he caught sight of his own face and the reflection of his favours in the glass window. He turned away.

The morning air had a sulphur smell about it, a compound of mist from the river, smoke from the ships, slow-drifting yellow fumes from the gas works. It was like the look on Rashers' face. Hungry, dirty and, because so many things conspired to kill him, tenacious. His beard straggled. His gait was uncertain. He dragged his fifty years in each step forward through the streets of his city. She had not denied him her unique weapons. Almost from birth she had shaped his mind to regard life as a trivial moment which had slipped by mistake through the sieve of eternity, a scrap of absurdity which would glow for a little while before it was snatched back into eternity again. From her air, in common with numberless others about him, he had drawn the deep and unshakable belief that the Son of God loved him and had suffered on earth for him and the hope that he would dwell with Jesus Christ and His Blessed Mother in Heaven. His city had never offered him anything else. Except her ashbins.

At the sweetshop Mary found her note had been collected and that one from Fitz has been left in its place.

'He called last night,' Mrs. Burns said, handing it to her.

'At what time?'

'It must have been about nine.'

Mary tried to remember what she had been doing at nine o'clock the previous evening. She remembered that she had been talking to Miss Gilchrist over a cup of cocoa. She remembered the scrubbed surface of the table, the sad, evening light outside, Miss Gilchrist's talk of Fenians.

'He was on his bicycle,' Mrs. Burns volunteered.

'Had he been swimming?'

'He must have been. He had his togs wrapped about the handlebars.'

'He was probably at Seapoint. Thank you, Mrs. Burns,' she said, and went out into the street. She was suddenly shy of Mrs. Burns. The note read:

Dear Mary

I'm going on at twelve tonight, finishing at twelve tomorrow. I'm hoping you will be free. You remember you said you might. I'll be at the usual place from two o'clock. Even if it is much longer than that before you are free don't feel it would be too late. I'll wait.

What do you think of the decorations?

Fitz

P.S. Give my regards to King Ed.

She folded the note and saw that it was almost half past one by the town hall clock. Fitz would be waiting at the Liffey Wall, where Butt Bridge let the heavy traffic cross from the South Wall into Beresford Place. The sun was now full and warm in the cloudless July sky, so she travelled on the top section of the tram. It was open to the heat and the light. There was hardly anybody else. The trolley sang and rattled in front of her, bucking and sparking when the wires above it crossed at junctions, its great spring stretching and contracting like a concertina. She would be late, but Fitz would not mind. It was over a year now since their first meeting. It had happened at Seapoint too. She had gone down to the strand, passing close to a young man who was sitting on the rocks and who smiled at her. She ignored him. Down at the water's edge she removed her shoes and began to paddle, holding her skirts away from the water but as little as possible because of the young man. He was watching her. Although there was no one else on the beach the situation did not trouble her. It had been a nice smile. She felt quite sure there was nothing to worry about and that the young man meant nothing more dangerous than gentlemanly admiration. It was nice to be admired from a respectful distance, to feel the water cool about her ankles and look down through it at the wrinkled sand. She paddled for half an hour and was on her way across the sand to find a spot where she could sit and put on her shoes again when she walked on the shell. It cut deeply into the sole of her foot and when she felt the pain and saw the gush of red blood she cried out and stumbled. Tears clouded her eyes so that when eventually the young man bent over her she felt his presence for quite a while before she could see him clearly.

'That's a bad gash,' he said, 'let me help you.'

It was embarrassing to sprawl with bare feet on the damp sand under the eyes of a complete stranger. She felt foolish and undignified. But when she rose and tried to walk by herself she was unable.

'Look, I know something about this,' the young man said.

She made a rapid appraisal of him. He had a very pleasant face with dark hair and eyes which reflected kindness and concern. It was a good face. Everything was all right.

'You're very kind,' she said.

He drew her arm around his shoulder and put his other arm about her waist. That shocked her for a moment until she realised that it was necessary. He was half lifting her and his grip was firm. She could feel his body against hers. The sensation was pleasant. He released her when they reached the rocks and examined the cut.

'Have you a handkerchief?' he asked. His own was coloured and they thought it might be dangerous. She produced one which was too small to be of use. He went away some distance and returned with his towel which he tore into strips.

'This'll do the job,' he said.

Mary who found destruction of any kind unbearable, protested.

'Your good towel, it's a shame.'

'What's a towel,' he said carelessly, and went on bandaging. It was a neat job. She found she could get her shoe on.

'That's wonderful,' she said.

He smiled at her.

'I look after the first-aid box and that sort of thing on the job,' he explained.

'You're quite an expert.'

'You'd better rest it for a while,' he said.

They sat together, silent.

'I'm on shift work in Morgan's Foundry,' he said.

'Are you long there?'

'Three years constant. Of course I was casual before that.'

'Casual?'

'You stand at the gate every morning and at eight o'clock the foreman comes out and says "I want you, you, you and you".'

He gave an imitation of the foreman singling out the lucky ones.

'What happens if he doesn't select you?'

'You drift round to the quays and see if you can get work discharging. If you can't you go home and hope for better luck the next time.'

'But you don't have to stand at the gate now?'

'No. I'm constant in No. 3 house—a stoker.'

He pulled up the left sleeve of his jacket. There was a long red weal on his arm.

'That was a present from No. 3 furnace I got the other day. It empties hot ash on you if you don't keep your eyes skinned.'

'Did it burn through your jacket,' she asked. She found it hard to believe.

He hesitated. He put it as delicately as he could.

'We don't usually wear very much when we're stoking,' he said.

She realised that he meant they worked stripped.

'Well,' she said, glossing it over, 'I'm lucky you weren't stoking today.'

'So am I,' he said.

There was no mistaking what he meant.

She was pleased but was careful not to betray it.

'I think it's time I tried to get home,' she said, rising.

He rose with her. Again she found it painful to put very much weight on her foot.

'Let me help you,' he said.

She consented, but this time she managed by allowing him only to link her. They reached his bicycle and after some persuasion she agreed to let him take her on the carrier. When they reached Kingstown she made him bring her to Mrs. Burns' shop, where they parted, Mrs. Burns undertaking to see her home. He said his name was Bob Fitzpatrick and he would like very much to meet her again. But she was doubtful.

The next day, much to her relief, he left a note for her at Mrs. Burns'. And the next day again. The little sweetshop became a sort of private post office. It had continued so as their meetings became more frequent and their love grew.

The tram stopped short of the city centre and Mary had to get off. The royal procession had just passed, or was passing, or was about to pass, on its way to the Viceregal Lodge. The conductor was not sure. Mary forced her way through the crowd, which grew larger and less penetrable the further she went. Eventually she found herself jammed and immobilised. She thought of Fitz waiting at Butt Bridge and looked around desperately for a way out. There was none. She held tightly to her purse, remembering the newspaper warning about pick-pockets. The royal occasion had drawn them in hundreds to the city. There were gentlemen in bowler hats, younger men in caps and knickerbockers, an odd policeman here and there keeping sharp eyes on the crowd. A ragged man with a beard was singing out a rigmarole to draw attention to the favours on his board.

'One penny each the lovely ribbings. Red for royalty, white for fraternity, blue for Britannia and green for the beam of the fair isle of Erin. Buy your emblems of honour.'

It was Rashers Tierney. He came towards Mary. It was part of his technique to be able to move in the densest gathering.

'Buy a favour, miss,' he said to her.

She shook her head. She was thinking about Fitz.

'For luck, lady,' Rashers persisted. He held one up to her.

There was something hungry in his face which moved her. She gave him a penny. He pinned the ribbons in her coat.

'God bless and reward you,' he said, moving on.

She tried to do so too but made little progress.

A band was approaching, unseen but faintly heard. Horses stamped and pennants, at a great distance, tossed in orderly file above the heads of the crowd. A cheer began, travelling through the street until those around Mary joined in. It was overpoweringly warm as the heat of packed bodies augmented the blaze of the sun. Yet there was a communicated excitement too which drew Mary to her toes. She found it hard to understand Miss Gilchrist's bitterness against the King. Patriots had been put in gaol and banished into penal servitude, of course, but you could not expect a king or a queen to do nothing to people who openly threatened to take over the country themselves. They made beautiful speeches, the patriots. They defied their judges and said they preferred English chains or even the gallows to an English king ruling over Ireland. Yet when all was said and done what great difference would it make, whether King Edward or the others ruled over Ireland. Would the patriots come back and live in Cahirdermot, scratching for a living like her father and her father's people? Kings built great cities and that was why there were aristocrats and gentry and after them business people and then shopkeepers and then tradesmen and then poor people like Fitz and herself. Who would give work if there were no kings and gentry and the rest? No one ever said anything about that.

The band was now directly in front, so that now and then, between shoulders and heads, she caught the sudden flash of sun on the instruments. The roar of the people became louder and everybody said the King and Queen were at that moment passing. The men took off their hats, the crowd tightened and tightened. Mary looked behind and saw students clinging to the railings of Trinity College. They wore striped blazers and whirled their flat straw hats over their heads. Some of them were skylarking, of course, as young gentlemen always did on such occasions. One of them even had a policeman's helmet wherever he had managed to get it. Mary felt the pressure easing and heard the notes of the band growing fainter, but the rhythmic chorus of carriage wheels over paving setts continued. People stopped cheering and talked to each other. Mary looked about once again for a way of escape. She frowned and bit her lip in perplexity, her thoughts so fixed on her purpose that at first the disturbance passed unnoticed. She felt the movement in the crowd for some time before the shouting of a raucous voice drew her eyes to her right. They rested on Rashers, who was pushing in her direction once more. There was a startling change in his face. It was working curiously and his arms were jerking with excited movements.

'Come back, you bloody hill-and-dale robber,' he was shouting, 'come back with my few hard-earned ha'pence.'

He stopped close to Mary and appealed to the crowd.

'Why couldn't youse stop him? What ails the world that youse let a lousy pickpocket past youse?'

The people near him smiled. It maddened Rashers.

'That's right,' he howled, 'laugh. That's all you were ever good at. A lousy lot of laughing loyalists. By Jasus, if I get my hands on that slippery fingers I'll have his sacred life.'

Rashers pushed violently to force a passage. He swore at those in his way. His struggles and his curses attracted a widening circle of attention, until a section of the crowd opened and a policeman appeared. Rashers in his excitement gripped him by the tunic. The policeman pulled his hand away and caught him by the collar.

'What's all the commotion?' he asked. Rashers squirmed.

'I've been rooked by a bloody pickpocket,' Rashers said, 'while you and your like were gaping at his shagging majesty.'

'You'd better come with me,' the policeman said, twisting up Rashers' coat.

'What for?' Rashers bawled, 'for being bloodywell robbed, is it?'

'And watch your language,' the policeman said.

Rashers turned in his grip to fix a vicious eye on him.

'That's all you and the likes of you were ever good at,' he said, 'manhandling the bloody poor.' He clawed at the policeman's uniform, dislodging a loose button. The policeman's face became thunderous.

'Shut your mouth,' the policeman said.

'Shut your own,' Rashers yelled. There was a line of foam about his lips. The policeman slapped him hard on the side of the mouth and twisted his arm. Rashers yelled with pain. Then the policeman began to hustle him through the crowd. They parted respectfully. Mary followed. The policeman was making a road for her which would lead eventually to Fitz. As she walked she caught glimpses now and then of Rashers. The blood on his mouth increased the pallor of his skin. His eyes were half closed and his teeth were clenched tight. Yet in the line of his jaw there was something unbreakable and defiant, a spirit which could bear with suffering because from experience it knew that it must eventually, like everything else, have an end. At the edge of the crowd Mary stood and stared after the policeman, wanting to do something for Rashers, to help in some way. But she could think of nothing to say that would be of any use. After a while she gave up and turned in the direction of Butt Bridge.

Rashers was brought to College Street station, where the duty sergeant glanced at him over a sheaf of reports.

'What's this?' he asked the policeman.

'Obscene language and conduct likely to lead to a breach of the peace.'

30

The policeman wiped sweat from his face. The day was too warm for even mild exertion.

'Drink, I suppose?'

'Drink how-are-you,' Rashers said. 'I was lifted of nine and fourpence by some louser of a pickpocket.'

The sergeant looked at the policeman.

'That's as may be,' the policeman said, 'but what about this?' He pointed to his uniform where the button was missing.

'I see,' the sergeant said, 'another George Hackenschmidt.' The policeman smiled at the reference to the popular wrestler.

'The real thing, Sergeant,' he confirmed.

The sergeant relished his joke again.

'What else?' he asked.

'For one, the use of an inflammatory expression.'

'To wit?' asked the sergeant.

'Lousy loyalists.'

'Better and better,' said the sergeant.

He turned furiously on Rashers.

'So you're a bit of a Republican too,' he said. Rashers made no answer.

'Name?' the sergeant barked.

'Tierney.'

'Christian name?'

'Rashers.'

The sergeant put down his pen.

'They never poured holy water on the likes of that,' he said. The policeman took a hand.

'Give the sergeant your proper Christian name,' he ordered.

'I haven't got a Christian name.'

'Then you'd better bloodywell find one,' the sergeant said. He had grown red and angry. He turned to the policeman and added, 'Lock him up inside there for a while. Maybe it'll jog his memory.'

Rashers was put in a cell. It had a rough bed which he sat down on gratefully. The socks were cutting into his feet. He ached all over. At intervals they came to demand his Christian name. He was afraid to invent one because that would convince them that he had been stubborn in the first instance. He kept answering 'Rashers'. They determined to be as stubborn as he was.

Mary saw Fitz from a distance. He was leaning on the wall of the river. At the sight of him she hurried her step.

'You got away,' he said, looking down at her.

She smiled up at him and touched his hand lightly.

'I very nearly didn't. The tram was held up and then I got mixed up with the crowds.'

She wondered why he was staring at her coat. She looked down and saw the ribbons.

'Oh, those,' she said. 'I bought them from an old man. He looked hungry.'

She wondered if Fitz had been waiting long.

'Did you see the procession?' she asked.

'I stayed here in case I'd miss you. I heard the bands, though.'

'It was impossible to see anything. The crowd was frightening.'

'Where would you like to go?'

'I don't mind. Somewhere quiet.'

'The prison ship? It's just down beyond the Custom House.'

'No—not that.'

'You've changed your mind.'

'The old man who sold me the ribbons was hit on the mouth by a policeman and his arm twisted until it was nearly broken. I don't want to see anything today that would remind me of that.'

'Poor Mary,' Fitz said, taking her arm gently.

They decided against going to Phoenix Park because the garden party at the Viceregal Lodge was bound to attract numerous sightseers. Fitz suggested a walk along the sandbanks beyond Pigeon House Fort. They took the tram as far as Irishtown and when they reached the seafront they took off their shoes and began to walk together across the ebbed strand. It was a mile or more to the sandbanks. They waded through pools in which the water had grown warm from the strong sun and crossed swift-flowing rivulets which had worn deep channels in the sand. Behind them the houses along the front grew tiny with distance. Far out in front of them they could discern the thin white edge of foam and beyond it the calm water of the open sea. The sky was high and blue and immense.

'Watch out for shells,' Fitz said over his shoulder.

She smiled to let him know that she remembered.

He took her hand. At the touch of his fingers on hers they both stopped. In a moment he had come close to her. His face, above hers, was dark against the sun, but hers was radiant and expectant, her mouth half open, her eyes closed. Alone in the centre of the sun-filled strand they kissed. Her own love frightened her. She said:

'What is going to become of me if I keep on loving you like this.'

He held her to him, repeating her name. After a while she released herself gently and they walked on again, hand in hand, until the sand became dry and after that fine and shot through with silver specks which clothed their feet. They climbed among the hillocks of strong, sparse grass and sat down. Behind them the narrow breakwater reached out a further mile into the sea, dividing the river at their backs from the strand in front of them, keeping navigable depth for the shipping traffic of the Port of Dublin. The strand they had just crossed was sunlit and empty. They were quite alone.

'Were you waiting a long time?' Mary asked.

'Not very long, but I was a bit afraid Miss Gilchrist had taken the day herself and left you stuck in the house.'

'She wouldn't look at the King. She's a Fenian.'

'All the Fenians are dead and gone.'

'Not for her. She keeps a picture of one of them in her room. They used to call at her house when she was a child in Tipperary. She told me she once saw the watchfires lit on the hills and it was a signal for a rising against the British.'

'I'd like to have seen them myself,' Fitz admitted.

'It does no good,' Mary said.

She had brought some sandwiches with her, which she had filled with left-over meat. Fitz had a bottle with milk and also some oranges. They began to eat. The walk across the strand and the salt flavour of the air lent an edge to their appetites.

'Ham,' Fitz remarked appreciatively. He bit into the sandwich.

'Pity it's not tomorrow,' Mary said. 'They'll have chicken to-night, for Father O'Connor and Mr. Yearling.'

As Fitz took another, a thought struck him.

'If they ever want a butler, let me know.'

He broke a piece of bread and threw it lazily across the sand towards a gull which had been resting, its head tucked in tight against its shoulders. The gull was awake immediately. It stalked across and began to eat.

'It's beautiful here,' Mary said.

'As nice as Cahirdermot?' Fitz asked.

'Different. We had only mountains and fields. There was a river too, of course, but only the boys used to swim.'

They finished their meal and walked across to where firmer sand began beyond the tide-mark. At a pool left by the tide they knelt close together and peered among the rocks and sea-weed. A dead crab, tangled in a frond of seaweed, swayed gently beneath the surface. It was a small, green crab, its up-turned belly showing the V-shaped cut in its shell. Fitz pointed at this.

'That's where he keeps his money.'

Mary saw his face reflected in the pool, so close to her own that they might have been painted together on a medallion, against a background of blue sky and barely discernible wisps of white cloud. Fitz, she knew, was telling her something he had believed as a child. She had often wondered about his child-hood, about his growing up in the noise and bustle of the city, about his work among trundling carts and swinging cranes and furnaces so huge that when he told her of them she thought of hell and its fire. How had he remained gentle and kind through all that? Perhaps it was because of the sea and the strand, the beautiful summer strands where even the poorest child could wander and hunt in the pools for crabs, hoping some day to find one that carried money in its purse. She rested her head against his shoulder, linking her arm through his.

'You believed the funniest things when you were a child. You must have been happy.'

'I'm happier now,' Fitz pushed her hair back from her face.

They rose and began to walk again. Far away, near the Martello Tower at Sandymount, tiny figures on horseback moved to and fro. The young ladies from the riding schools of Tritonville Road were exercising on the sands. They went back again among the coarse grasses of the sandbanks. When they were seated a moment Fitz drew her down until they were lying side by side.

After what seemed a long time he said :

'You love me?'

He had withdrawn a little to ask her and she could see his face. Its tenderness brought her near to tears. She nodded.

'Say it.'

She paused a moment and then said :

'I love you.'

'And you'll marry me?'

'I'll marry you.'

He drew something from his pocket and held it towards her. It was a ring.

'I know you can't wear it yet about the house, but I'd like you to take it and keep it with you.'

She put it on her finger.

'It's not a very dear one,' he said humbly. Again the tears gathered because of the way she felt.

'It's beautiful,' she said.

She wanted to give him something in exchange, a memento which would stand ever afterwards for the happiness of the day. She had nothing with her.

They delayed until the edge of the incoming tide was less than a hundred yards away. It approached slowly over the flat sands, rimmed by an edge of white foam. Here and there streamlets, like the scouts of an approaching army, crept forward in advance of the main body. It was time to go. They left the sandhills and climbed up on to the breakwater which was as wide as a road but unevenly surfaced, for the foundations had moved and the great granite blocks which comprised it had angled in places. Sand and fragments of shells, the remnants of winter storms and furious seas, filled the gaps where the granite had parted.

They stopped to watch a coal boat moving up river towards the bay. It glided full of peaceful purpose. The waves in its wake rolled towards them and broke at last against the stonework, a commotion about nothing. Screaming and swooping, the white gulls followed the ship.

'How soon do you think we could manage?' Fitz asked.

Mary wasn't sure. They would have to save money. She told him she would not care to live in a house with others and of her hope that the Bradshaws would help them to get a cottage.

'I have some money saved,' she said.

Fitz had none. But his job was steady and, compared with most of the others, not badly paid. They talked until Mary, thinking once more of the time, said urgently :

'Fitz, we must hurry.'

They began to walk again. In an hour they were back in the streets of the city and Fitz was waiting to see her on to the tram. She was pensive, thinking of the day they had spent together.

'A penny for them,' Fitz offered.

'I'm feeling sad.'

'About what?'

'Our lovely day—all gone.'

'There'll be others,' Fitz said.

'Will you think about it—I mean tonight when you're working?'

'Nearly all the time.'

'Here's my tram,' she said. On and off she had been wishing for something to give him and now the solution occurred to her. She took Rashers' ribbons from her coat and pushed them into his hand. He looked at them, puzzled.

'To remember,' she said.

She was afraid he might laugh, or that he might think she was mad. Or, because he was not in favour of the King, that he might be angry.

He took them gravely and said :

'I'll keep them, always.'

Her heart quickened. She was filled with happiness.

He helped her on to the tram, waved, and was gone. She sat

once more on the outside, hearing the trolley's conversational humming and feeling the wind against her cheeks and hair as the tram battled its sturdy way towards Kingstown.

When the night sergeant came in at fifteen minutes past eight he put his helmet on the desk and looked around the office without a word of greeting for the young policeman who had risen behind his desk. The sergeant was a burly man with a very red face. He breathed heavily and mopped his brow. The policeman said:

'Good evening, Sergeant.'

The sergeant looked at the coat-rack and then at the fireplace which was littered with cigarette stubs and empty cartons.

'Has Dunleavy gone?'

'Sergeant Dunleavy left sharp at eight.'

'I see,' the night sergeant said.

He loosened the neck of his tunic and, turning his back on the policeman, stared out of the barred window.

'You were up at the hospital?' the policeman asked.

The sergeant sighed heavily. 'Aye. And Dunleavy knew that.'

'He said he was in a bit of a hurry this evening.'

'He might have waited the few minutes. I did it for him often enough.'

The policeman did not want any part in the quarrels of his superiors. So he said:

'How was the youngster?'

The sergeant turned away from the window and looked at him.

'It's what we suspected. Meningitis.'

'The poor little scrap,' the policeman said, seeing the red face was tight with pain.

'They'll send for me here if there's a change.'

'Please God it'll be for the better.'

'No,' the sergeant said, 'he'll die. They always do.'

'Is he the youngest?'

'The second youngest.'

'It's a heavy cross for you, Sergeant,' the policeman said.

'It's bad for a father, but worse again for the mother,' said the sergeant.

'It's hard on the two of you.'

The sergeant went to his desk. He wrote *Sergeant J. Muldoon* on top of the duty sheet and then with an effort began to examine the papers in front of him. The policeman worked in silence. He could not think of anything to say.

'What's in?' the sergeant asked him. He was finding it difficult to read the reports for himself. The policeman gave him particulars. Then he said:

'We have a guest in cell No. 3.'

'What's he there for?'

The policeman told him about Rashers.

'How long is he there?'

'Since early afternoon.'

'I'll go and see him.'

Activity helped. The sergeant took the heavy key and went down a passage. The cell was in gloom. Rashers was stretched on the bed, asleep. The sergeant stood over him. Rashers' heavy breathing reminded him of the child in the hospital, struggling for the life that minute by minute was being prised from his grasp. In an hour or two they would send for him to say that the end was near. He would stand and watch helplessly. There were no handcuffs to hold Death at bay. You could not lock Death up in a cell or let it off with a caution. It was the biggest thief of all.

The sergeant shook Rashers by the shoulder.

'Wake up,' he commanded.

Rashers stirred and sat up. He blinked at the strange sergeant.

'A new one, be God,' he said.

'What's this about refusing to give your name?'

'I gave the only name I ever knew of,' Rashers said. 'Is it lies you want me to tell?'

'What name was that?'

'Rashers Tierney.'

'Who christened you Rashers?'

'The first woman I remember.'

'Your mother?'

'I don't remember her.'

38

'Who then?'

'A little woman by the name of Molloy that lived in the basement of 3 Chandlers Court. I came to her at the age of four.'

'From where?'

'They never found out. Maybe God left me under a dustbin lid.'

'Where do you live now?'

'In Chandlers Court. When Mrs. Molloy died she had to leave it. They carried her out. That was when I was fifteen or so. They'll do the same with me when my time comes.'

Rashers reflected on what he had said.

'They'll do it with us all, for that matter,' he added, 'you and the sergeant before you, King Edward and Rashers Tierney. We're all booked for the same trip.'

'Don't talk so much,' the sergeant commanded.

'It was always my failing,' Rashers admitted.

'Did you get anything to eat?'

'Damn the scrap.'

The sergeant went out, locking the door. A little while later he returned with a mug of tea and roughly cut bread.

'Take that,' he said.

Rashers took it and began to eat. The sergeant sat on the bed too, in the warm gloom locked up, a prisoner within himself, his thoughts pacing around and around in his skull. For much of the time they were not thoughts at all, just the name of the child being repeated to him over and over again by some voice which he had no power to silence. The names of Jesus, Mary, and Joseph also went through his mind and he prayed to these because he too, like Rashers, had been taught to look to them in trouble. He did not expect a miracle from them. The child was doomed to die. But he wanted comfort, he wanted to feel there was a Court of Appeal, that there was a world beyond this one, a world untouched by sorrow and disease and death, to which the child would go. His child must not cease to exist.

'I'm going to let you out,' he said when Rashers had finished.

'Thanks be to God,' Rashers said. 'The oul dog at home will be demented.'

'Have you money?'

'Every penny was lifted off of me. Isn't that what has me where I am?'

The sergeant took a shilling from his pocket and gave it to Rashers.

'Take that,' he said.

Rashers looked at it suspiciously. A charity from a police sergeant was one of the impossibilities of his world.

'Go on, take it,' the sergeant commanded. Rashers put it in his pocket.

'Now get on home.'

Rashers collected his bag and his board with the few remaining favours. He found it hard to walk. The sweat had dried on his socks. His feet were numb. He took a set of colours from the board and offered them to the sergeant.

'You're a loyal servant who'll appreciate them,' he said.

'I've no use for them. Say a prayer for me.'

'I'll say a rosary,' Rashers promised warmly.

They went to the door of the station. The streets were bright still, but the sky had the evening look of waiting. At some invisible point night was mustering to invade it. Rashers pressed the colours into the sergeant's hand.

'Take them home for one of the kids,' Rashers insisted generously.

He hobbled down the street. The sergeant clutched the colours tightly and stared at the street without seeing it. He went back into his office and let the colours fall into the fireplace, to take their place among the dust and the cartons and the pile of cigarette stubs.

'They returned by motor,' Mr. Belton Yearling informed the company.

'I was fortunate enough to see them. At a distance, of course,' Father O'Connor volunteered.

'Are they dining aboard the royal yacht?' asked Mrs. Bradshaw.

'Yes. With his Excellency the Lord Lieutenant and Lady Aberdeen.' Mr. Yearling's tone was tinged a little with disrespect.

'Such a strenuous day for the Queen and the young princess.'

'I hope we have finished with salutes, anyway,' Mr. Bradshaw said grumpily. 'I can't abide them.'

Mrs. Bradshaw smiled at everybody. The meal had been excellent. Young Father O'Connor, though normally abstemious, had consented to a glass of port after it, in honour of the occasion, and when they retired for music Mr. Yearling's first request had been for Sinding's 'Rustle of Spring', a piece she was just a little bit afraid of, but which she had managed to play surprisingly well. She flushed with pleasure at their compliments, the more so because, in all modesty, she felt them at that moment to be well deserved. Mr. Yearling had responded on the 'cello with Mendelssohn's 'On Wings of Song' and she accompanied with exquisite sympathy. He played beautifully so that even Mr. Bradshaw was moved at the end to say:

'Dammit, Belton, you have wonderful warmth and tone tonight. You surpassed yourself.'

Mr. Yearling was refreshing himself with a glass of whiskey.

Although the evening was warm she had had a fire lit, not only as a courtesy to the company but because a room without a fire made her restless. She loved to see its light flickering on the walls and shining on the glasses and glowing deeply in the rich varnish of Mr. Yearling's 'cello. Through the french windows she watched the last light lingering on the lawn, giving the grass a reddish tint and picking out the contrasting colours of the flowers. The laburnum at the end, in full flower, glowed deeply yellow, its base encircled by fallen blossoms. She had remarked that it had been a beautiful day for the royal pair and that had drawn the information from Mr. Yearling about the manner of their return.

'Let's hope they don't go to Belfast,' Mr. Yearling added, when he had finished his whiskey.

'Why not, Belton?' Mr. Bradshaw asked.

'This fellow Larkin has the city in a state of revolution.'

'Of course,' Mr. Bradshaw admitted. He had questioned without thinking very deeply about what he was saying.

'The military are camped in the main streets,' Father O'Connor contributed.

'They mean business too. They fired on the strikers the other day.'

'There have been deaths,' Father O'Connor reminded them. 'It is so very regrettable.'

'Hope he keeps away from Dublin,' Mr. Bradshaw said.

'He will, because he'll be broken,' Mr. Yearling assured him. 'If our chaps don't do it his own people will. Sexton has threatened to expel him.'

'Who's Sexton?' Father O'Connor asked.

'The general secretary of the union Larkin represents. Apparently Larkin called this strike without the sanction of the union executive. From his speeches he seems to be a law unto himself.'

'It's a pity it should be necessary,' Father O'Connor said.

The company looked at him curiously. Father O'Connor flushed. He was quite young.

'Don't misunderstand me—I am totally against Mr. Larkin's outrageous methods. He seems to me to be little better than a socialist. But I understand conditions are very, very bad in Belfast.'

Mr. Yearling surprised everybody by saying:

'They are very bad in Dublin too.'

'Nonsense,' Mr. Bradshaw said, rudely.

'Ralph,' Mrs. Bradshaw reproved him.

'Sorry. But you surprise me, Belton.'

'Facts,' Mr. Yearling insisted, sticking to his guns.

'I think we should have a little music,' Mrs. Bradshaw suggested. She smiled at Father O'Connor. 'You haven't done anything for us, Father.'

'Of course,' the others agreed.

Father O'Connor opened his music case and selected a piece which he handed to Mrs. Bradshaw. She went to the piano.

'What is it, Father?'

' "Ave Maria",' Mrs. Bradshaw answered, smoothing the sheets.

'Schubert or Gounod?'

'Actually,' Father O'Connor said, a little apologetically, 'it's by Locatelli.'

Behind Father O'Connor's back Mr. Yearling's bushy eye-brows arched enquiringly at Mr. Bradshaw. Mr. Bradshaw shrugged his ignorance of the piece and Mr. Yearling acknowledged with a nod. Neither was enthusiastic. They felt the priest's selection was in dubious taste. A social evening should be kept strictly secular. Besides, Mr. Yearling was a Protestant.

Father O'Connor sang pleasantly, if a little bit too sweetly. His voice had a touch of vibrato, poorly controlled. Still, he knew something about music generally: he could sight read quite well too.

'Bravo,' Mr. Bradshaw said, when he had finished.

'I'm not of your persuasion, Father, but I think the "Ave Maria" is a very beautiful prayer,' Mr. Yearling contributed.

Everybody thought it uncommonly handsome of him, a further proof of his offhanded generosity and tolerance. Mr. Bradshaw pressed him to another liberal measure of whiskey. Father O'Connor declined a glass of port; Mr. Bradshaw helped himself instead.

'You've had the training, Father,' he said.

'In the seminary we were allowed to study music.'

'One can hear it in the voice. It's unmistakable.'

'The training, yes,' Father O'Connor said, 'but not the equipment.' He laughed. He was a genuinely modest man.

'I know now what keeps you in Kingstown,' Mrs. Bradshaw said, smiling affectionately at him. 'You love training our church choir.'

'Have you chaps a choice?' Mr. Yearling asked. 'I mean, about where you are going to be stationed?'

'Oh no,' Mr. Bradshaw explained, 'a priest must go where he's sent. It's part of the rule of obedience.'

'We can apply for special work,' Father O'Connor added.

The friendly interest of the company focussed on him and he responded to it before he quite realised it.

'As a matter of fact, I may be leaving Kingstown shortly.'

'Oh no,' Mrs. Bradshaw said.

'I've asked to be transferred to a poor parish. I'd like to work among the poor.'

He discovered too late that he had embarrassed the company. He became embarrassed himself. He plunged on.

'My mother had a great devotion to St. Vincent de Paul, you see, and she encouraged it in me too.'

'Is that why you were christened . . .?'

Mr. Yearling, not certain of the propriety of mentioning a priest's Christian name, left his sentence unfinished.

'Yes. I was called Vincent,' Father O'Connor said.

'We would be very sorry to lose you,' Mrs. Bradshaw said.

'Perhaps you won't,' Father O'Connor said, 'perhaps I have not the ability.'

It was obvious that he was not anxious to say any more. He looked across at Mr. Bradshaw.

'Isn't it time our host obliged?' he suggested generally.

Mr. Bradshaw rose and looked for suggestions to his wife. She said:

'The policeman's song from *The Pirates.*'

Mr. Yearling laughed and said:

'Well, that's topical enough anyway. I see Mr. Larkin has the police going on strike in Belfast too.'

Everybody enjoyed the joke except Mrs. Bradshaw, who did not follow the reference. Mr. Yearling explained to her that Larkin had spoken to the policemen who were keeping his strikers in order and had told them that they were not being paid enough for their heavy duties. He had roused them to such a pitch of resentment that the police were threatening to go on strike too.

'That's why the Chief Secretary asked for the help of the military,' Mr. Bradshaw put in.

Mrs. Bradshaw said Larkin must be a remarkable strike leader. It all sounded fantastic.

'Gilbertian,' Mr. Yearling roared, in sudden inspiration. Everybody laughed aloud and as a result of his aptness Mr. Bradshaw's rendering of 'A Policeman's Lot' was punctuated all the time by smiles and laughter.

'We really must be serious,' Mrs. Bradshaw said when it was over.

'Very well,' said Father O'Connor, 'Why not something from *The Yeomen of the Guard*.'

'Yes,' Mr. Yearling said, 'why shouldn't we too introduce the military.'

But Father O'Connor, having acknowledged the quip, went on to deal seriously with the opera he had mentioned. He said he had always felt that *The Yeomen of the Guard* contained Sullivan's best music. The rest agreed. Mr. Yearling praised Sullivan's setting for 'Onward Christian Soldiers'. Mr. Bradshaw drew attention to the musical excellence of 'The Lost Chord'.

'How long is it since he died?' Mr. Yearling tried to remember.

'Seven years,' Mrs. Bradshaw said.

'It doesn't seem that long, really.'

'Florence is right,' Mr. Bradshaw said. 'It was in 1900. I remember now.'

'We can be proud that he was an Irishman,' Father O'Connor said.

Mr. Bradshaw liked strict accuracy. 'Well, the son of an Irishman—an Irish bandsman.'

When he died he was Sir Arthur Sullivan. Mrs. Bradshaw said she thought it wonderful that a humble youth should reach such heights.

'He had the divine gift,' Mr. Yearling pronounced solemnly. 'The gift of music. What are we others, after all, but pen-pushers. Directors, property owners, public servants, nothing but glorified nonentities. One of us dies and the world is still the same. Sullivan dies—and the world is the poorer until God permits another genius to come and walk among us.'

This time he helped himself to the whiskey decanter uninvited and poured a large measure.

'The song,' Mr. Bradshaw said, uneasily.

Mr. Yearling suggested the introduction to the second act which contained a sombre opening for the 'cello, but little else that the company could manage satisfactorily, because of the disposition of the voices and the fact that it required a chorus too. Father O'Connor came out best, with a moving interpretation of 'Is Life a Boon?' Mr. Bradshaw remained silent but

Mr. Yearling supplied an obbligato on the 'cello. Then Mrs. Bradshaw, knowing how much her husband enjoyed singing and not wishing him to feel neglected, closed the score and produced a volume of Moore's melodies which contained duets which occupied everybody, the priest and Mr. Bradshaw on the voice parts, accompanied by piano and Mr. Yearling's clever 'cello improvisations. Then she asked if it was time for soup. The men searched for their watches. As Father O'Connor produced his, Mr. Bradshaw thought he heard something fall.

'Have you dropped something, Father?'

'I don't think so,' Father O'Connor replied. They scanned the carpet mutually but could see nothing. Mrs. Bradshaw rang and Mary served them with soup. They sat around, informally conversing.

'Your "Is Life a Boon?" revived some happy memories for me tonight, Father,' Mr. Yearling said sadly. They looked at him with polite interest.

'I was at one of the first performances of *The Yeomen* in the Savoy. George Grossmith sang Jack Point and Courtice Pounds was Fairfax. That was nearly twenty years ago.'

'Is it so long?' Mr. Bradshaw said.

'It is, Ralph, October 1888. I was a young dog on my first visit to London. Wonderful. And a pretty girl with me too.' He turned particularly to Father O'Connor. 'All very correct and everything in order, Father, no wild oats or that sort of thing.'

'Of course,' Father O'Connor said quickly, but modulating his tone to convey a reminder of Mrs. Bradshaw's presence.

'Truth is, I was madly in love with her.'

'But you didn't marry her?' Mrs. Bradshaw asked, allowing herself to betray a woman's curiosity.

'She wouldn't have me, ma'am,' Mr. Yearling confessed. He turned to Mr. Bradshaw. 'You know, Ralph, we Irish chaps don't stand much chance against the fellows over there. We think we have polish, poise, elegance, but in thirty minutes at the smallest social gathering the British fellow has us completely outclassed.'

'Oh, I don't know,' Mr. Bradshaw protested.

'It's true, Ralph. And I'll tell you why. Gentility, manners, social behaviour, they're all part of a game, a sort of national game which is played to different rules in different countries. The British play their own game best because they've made the rules to suit the British temperament and the British climate.'

'I don't see the difference,' Mr. Bradshaw said. He had taken up the decanter again and was handing Mr. Yearling his glass. Mr. Yearling raised it and looked around at everybody.

'There's part of the difference,' he said sadly, indicating the golden spirit. 'I won't embarrass your good wife with the grisly details.'

Mrs. Bradshaw smiled her gentle smile as he threw back his head and swallowed. She knew his weakness and could guess that it had once, perhaps, been a wildness. She thought, a little wistfully, that a touch of human weakness in her husband would have been nice, her husband who was so good but at times so meticulous, at times so grumpy with rectitude. She rang for Mary to take the plates and said : 'You may go to bed as soon as you have cleared away. Leave whatever is inessential until morning.'

The company rose and Mr. and Mrs. Bradshaw accompanied them into the garden. The night air was mild and perfumed with mown grass and flowers. A rocket sailed upwards in a bright parabola and burst brilliantly above their heads. They gasped with surprise. 'What on earth . . . ?' Mr. Bradshaw exclaimed.

Mrs. Bradshaw remembered.

'It's the firework display at the Pavilion.'

'Ah, of course,' Mr. Yearling said.

She remembered the notice in the paper that morning which had advertised the attractions.

Grand Illumination of the Bldgs & Gardens by Brock. Grand Display of Fireworks. Portraits of Their Majesties. Bands, pipers, sword dancing. Torchlight procession in the gardens. Illuminations of The Fleet. Russell Rosse and company were playing *Arabian Nights.*

They looked up at the sky for some time. Now and then one or the other made an exclamation of admiration. The multicoloured fireworks traced elaborate patterns above the garden. Now and then one burst with a brilliant blooming and sent a joyful cascade of light pouring through the sky, lighting up the garden and picking out the upturned faces of the men: Father O'Connor, young, almost childish, frankly enjoying it; Mr. Yearling, with his great, bushy eyebrows, his long neck, his tall, spare figure and greying hair, smiling; her husband, thin, not quite as tall as Mr. Yearling, interested but unsmiling. There was something boyish about the three of them. Mrs. Bradshaw felt the moment keenly, felt the night about her, felt the soft dark air of the garden, felt the extra touch of excitement which had become part of the day itself. She sighed. The moment filled her with an oppressive sense of mortality. She wanted to leave the garden and get back into the house, to feel its four walls putting comfortable bounds to a world which was too wide and careless to hold intact for any certain period the happiness it now and then offered. She shivered and the others noticed.

'We mustn't detain you,' Mr. Yearling said.

They took their leave and went out through the gate. Mr. Bradshaw put the heavy chain on the hall door and began his nightly task of winding each of the clocks.

The rockets made a playground of the sky for an hour on end, while Mary watched from her bedroom window, thinking of Fitz, speaking silent messages to him, living again the moments of their day together. As they burst and drew successive cheers from the watching crowds, Death kept its ordained appointment with the little boy in his strange hospital bed. The night sergeant suffered the news quietly. He had been expecting it since early evening. Rashers, exhausted by the day, sat on his straw bed in the dark and told the dog about him.

'He was kind, Rusty,' he said. 'Imagine that. I met a kind sergeant today, the first kind policeman in history.'

The dog raised itself in response to Rashers' voice, placed its paws on Rashers' knees and, sniffing delicately, began to lick the dried blood on the side of his face.

ON Thursday, the eleventh day of July 1907, King Edward honoured the races at Leopardstown with his royal presense and on Friday 12th he sailed away, leaving behind him a genteel glow of goodwill and friendliness, marred only by a piece of gossip which turned out eventually to be true. Mr. William Martin Murphy, Chairman of the Exhibition Committee, owner of Independent Newspapers, a large drapery business and a hotel, controlling director of the Dublin Tramway Company and several other large-scale ventures, had refused a knighthood at the opening of the Exhibition. Yearling, who was in intimate contact with the business gossip of the city, being a director himself, told Father O'Connor about it when they met one day along the harbour front. Father O'Connor was reading his office. Yearling, looking spruce and smart in a grey suit with a flower in his buttonhole, tapped him on the shoulder.

'And how are things spiritual, Father?' he asked.

Father O'Connor closed his missal, marking the place carefully with a red silk tab. He matched Yearling's light-hearted humour.

'That is a difficult question to answer. If I say they are satisfactory I may be guilty of presumption, and if I say they are bad I am opening the door to Despair.' He settled his missal under his armpit. 'Perhaps my best answer is that we continue to trust in God.'

Yearling swung his cane and pointed out to sea.

'Before you came along I was watching that small boat. The thought occurred to me that there was something which has changed little in two thousand years. The boat, the fishermen, their nets.'

Father O'Connor's eyes followed the pointing stick. The boat moved gently with the motion of the water. Behind it a series of cork floats, spread in a wide semi-circle, marked the line of the net. He had not noticed before.

'The humblest of men,' he said, 'yet when He called to them, they followed.'

Yearling's heavy eyebrows went upwards. He was in an impish mood.

'Not quite, Father. He had to put on a little bit of magic for them. Didn't He walk on the water?'

'That was later,' Father O'Connor corrected. Yearling's scepticism did not disturb him. He was, after all, only a Protestant.

'He did something,' Yearling insisted. 'Let me think now.'

'After a night spent catching nothing, He filled their nets with fish.'

'Ah,' Yearling said. That was his point.

'We must remember who they were. Poor fishermen, ignorant and illiterate. How else was He to win them to Him?'

'Could He not simply inspire them with Faith?'

'He wanted them to know their vocation. Remember what He said to them?'

'What was that?' Yearling asked, unable to remember.

'Henceforth you shall be fishers of men.'

Yearling looked sceptical.

'It's too damned literary to be true,' he objected. 'I feel somebody made it up.'

Father O'Connor pursed his lips and then articulated carefully. 'The substance of your complaint seems to be that Christ could be graphic and direct. But aren't these the marks of leadership always?'

'I don't expect parlour tricks from God. And why fishermen?' Yearling mused as they went. 'Why not start at the top?'

'Perhaps because it is easier to get the fisherman to leave his net,' Father O'Connor said.

'Yes. It takes more than a parlour trick to get a banker to leave his gold.'

'Quite,' Father O'Connor agreed.

'The poor are generally regarded as being more religious than the rich,' Yearling continued, 'but of course that isn't true. They are simply more impressionable and have less to lose.'

Father O'Connor considered for a moment and before speaking pitched his voice so that it would sound polite.

'Your Church believes that worldly success is a measure of spiritual worthiness; you believe that material well-being and good fortune are marks of God's favour and that ill fortune is a manifestation of His disapproval. Do you know the story of Dives and Lazarus?'

'I do,' Yearling said firmly, 'and I regard it as the mad creation of some socialist fancy.'

Then he broke out into a loud peal of laughter which brought both of them to a standstill.

'Forgive me, Father,' he said contritely, 'I am presuming too much on our friendship.'

Father O'Connor said: 'It is better to explore an idea than to keep a polite silence.'

'You are not offended?'

'Who am I to be offended?' Father O'Connor asked.

'Well then, you must prove it by having coffee with me,' Yearling insisted.

Father O'Connor accepted graciously. They strolled up the town together, Yearling with a happy spring in his step, his light cane swinging joyfully, his tall, tweed-clad figure with its gay buttonhole matching the sunshine of the morning. Father O'Connor, shorter and more sombre in his black clerical garb, acknowledged at intervals the salutes of his parishioners. Some were old women, some were carters and delivery men, some were little boys who touched their forelocks respectfully. To all he raised his hat and smiled.

'I'll concede this,' Yearling commented, 'you chaps keep the honour and respect of your flock.'

'It ought to act as a reminder of our unworthiness,' Father O'Connor said.

'Nothing to be ashamed of,' Yearling said, holding open the glass door of the coffee lounge for him. 'Society is hierarchical. If they stop saluting you they'll find something else to salute. And it might not be as worthy.'

They walked across luxurious carpet and joined Mr. Yearling's colleagues. Father O'Connor recognised Mr. Harrison, a member of the Decorations Committee. The aromas of coffee and cigar smoke, blending pleasantly in the sun-filled room, made him feel urbane and important. He was a young curate in a rich parish, welcomed for his office and his pleasant manners by the important men of the town. He stirred his coffee with careful elegance. Yearling's bubbling energy had not abated. He beamed over his cup at Harrison and said:

'Congratulations on an excellent job of work.'

'In what respect?' Harrison asked.

'The decorations. Magnificent. Didn't you think so, Father?'

'A credit,' Father O'Connor said.

'We all did our share,' Harrison acknowledged, modestly.

'Better show here than in Herbert Park. I suppose you heard . . .'

'I know what you're going to say: That Murphy refused to be knighted. It sounds incredible.'

'It's perfectly true. I had the whole story from an official source. The King called for his sword, but the Lord Lieutenant had to whisper that it was no dice.'

'With everybody looking on?'

'In front of a galaxy of gapers.'

'Good God!'

'What is Mr. Murphy?' Father O'Connor asked.

'One of our own—a Catholic,' someone blundered.

'No . . . I mean, politically speaking,' Father O'Connor hastened to explain.

'A Constitutional Nationalist,' Yearling said. 'The crown for Ireland and West African concessions for William Martin.'

Everybody laughed. Yearling continued:

'But you must not think it was a question of politics, Father. It was rumoured beforehand that Murphy had organised the exhibition and asked for chairmanship simply to get a knight-

52

hood. It so happens that organisers of exhibitions elsewhere had been honoured in that way. When Murphy heard the rumour he told Aberdeen that on no account would he accept such an honour. It appears that the message was not transmitted in time to the King, with the result that William had to say no in public. What do you think of that, Father?'

'I think Mr. Murphy demonstrated that he is a strong-minded man and a man of principle,' Father O'Connor said.

'After the event he sent a letter to His Excellency asking him to explain his refusal to the King. It was delivered at Leopardstown races. I happen to know that it contained this.'

They looked at him expectantly. Yearling, their attention securely held, changed his voice and articulated with great emphasis.

'I would not wish that His Majesty should leave Ireland thinking that he had left one churlish man behind him.'

Harrison voiced the feelings of the rest.

'That was well said.'

Yearling looked derisive, but the rest agreed with Harrison. Father O'Connor reflected on the incident and felt admiration for the man, as much for his show of moral courage as for his gracious expression of regret. He felt that with men of like character at the head of Ireland's business affairs the country must surely prosper. It was an added satisfaction to have gathered that the man concerned was a Catholic as well.

Harrison, not to be outdone in the matter of inside information, put down his cup with a compelling clatter and said:

'Of course you know what happened at the Viceregal Lodge. I mean about Vicars and the Crown Jewels?'

'I'd forgotten Vicars would be there.'

'When Vicars was presented the King shook him by the hand —most warmly, I believe—and held a cordial and cheerful conversation with him. So what price Birrell now?'

'A handshake and a smile won't deflect our friend Birrell,' Yearling said. 'By God, no!'

The others raised their eyebrows, disapproving of his language in front of the priest. Father O'Connor smiled and waved his hands to convey that he was not put out by full-blooded talk.

They went on to discuss the theft, a subject on which each had a theory. When Father O'Connor rose and excused himself they stood politely and bowed him out. Then they resumed more freely.

Father O'Connor went into the church to pray a little before lunch. There was a man in front of him whose ragged coat was tied about the middle with a piece of cord. He had a dirty beard and his remaining teeth stood up like cartridges in his hungry face. Father O'Connor's mind wandered from his prayers. The face particularly held his attention. A scavenger's bag swung from his waist. The man left almost immediately. Father O'Connor, alone now in front of the altar, reproached himself for the pride he had felt a little while before. He was not endowed with a talent for bringing Christ's word to the men of business or for living according to Christ's wish while among them. He was not clever enough, nor was he strong enough to endure the small temptations to worldliness and conceit without becoming their tool instead of being their master. And it was not only the respect of the prominent which would corrupt him. There was corruption in the submissiveness of the ladies' committees, in the deference to his superior musical knowledge on the part of the humble organist and the choir, in the assumption of his genteel parishioners that to have good breeding, a clean person and unremitting politeness was to honour Christ as He had commanded.

Father O'Connor left the centre aisle and knelt before the shrine of St. Anthony to continue his novena for the recovery of his mother's rosary. She had given him the beads when he was a young student, a Galway rosary of amber and silver which had belonged to her mother before her. They were the only memento he had of her, a cherished link with the love he had lost when she died. Perhaps, thought Father O'Connor, their loss was part of God's plan to chasten him, a trial to take his mind from the vanities of the genteel world around him, so that this grief would be with him to draw his thoughts back to the verities. Their disappearance was mysterious enough. At first he had thought the beads must be in the Bradshaw's house, because he had first missed them after their musical evening. But they searched thoroughly and found nothing. They were not in his rooms or in the vestry. Father O'Connor prayed fervently and humbly. It remained now with St. Anthony, in whom he placed his last hope.

He rose after a while and left the church, finding it a relief now to close the door of the Parish House and leave the sunshine to those whose moods were a better match for it. His room was high up in the house, a quiet, carpeted retreat with two devotional pictures from which the faces of Christ and the Madonna brooded over the well-bound volumes that lined each wall. A letter lay on the table which had not been there when he left. He picked it up and read it, then he put it down and sat for a long time in thought. The letter promised him the transfer he had asked for. He would be posted to work among the poor in the first months of the New Year. God, he was now certain, was truly intervening to shape his life for him. Father O'Connor, sitting alone in the quiet, sunless room, felt his eyes pricking with tears of gratitude, and his heart being filled to overflowing with love of Christ.

CHAPTER 3

FATHER O'CONNOR'S parishioners marked the change.
There was a quietness about him in the weeks that
followed, an abstracted dedication which marked his attitude to even the most unrewarding and inconvenient of his parish
duties. In private he practised small privations, which included
doing without lunch on each Friday. His devotion during his daily
mass had the effect of making it unduly long, so that his parish
priest had to remind him that those attending it had worldly
duties and must not be detained unduly. Only in his sermons did
he seem to become aware of the living church arrayed dutifully
beneath his pulpit. On the second Sunday in Advent his vehe-
ment condemnation of worldly show and snobbery set a number of critical tongues wagging. Mr. Bradshaw was greatly
offended.

'That man O'Connor gave another most extraordinary sermon today,' he said. 'I wonder the parish priest doesn't speak
to him.'

'Whatever for?' Mrs. Bradshaw asked. 'Wasn't he speaking
on the day's gospel? I'm sure he didn't say anything that wasn't
in it.'

'It's not that,' Mr. Bradshaw said, 'it's the construction he
puts on things. You'd think it was a crime to wear a coat without a hole in it.'

'He was only reminding us of our duty,' Mrs. Bradshaw said,
'and I'm very glad too, because it's bound to help our collection
for the poor at Christmas.'

She finished the letter she was writing and sealed the envelope.

'Thank goodness that's done,' she said.

'Who is it for?'

'Mary's father. I undertook to tell him of her progress at least twice in the year. He is a strict and good man.'

'You surprise me. I didn't know he could read,' Mr. Bradshaw said, returning to his paper.

Mary met Fitz and they looked at the Christmas displays in the shops. The evening was cold and overcast, the Liffey wrinkled at intervals as the sharp breeze drove down it from the mountains. Gaslight from the busy shops shed a mellow glow on damp pavements. At Westland Row the jarveys in worn caps loitered beside their cabs, waiting for incoming trains and their laden passengers. In the lamplight a white mist hovered above the bodies of their horses, harness clanked at each movement of the patient heads or the stamping of metal-shod feet. They stopped for a moment at a shop window. There were long red and yellow Christmas candles, which reminded Mary of her home, where in childhood they would stand in all the windows on Christmas night. There were iced cakes with sugar robin redbreasts on marzipan logs; there were boxes of candied peel and raisins and nutmeg packets and glasses filled with cloves. Turkeys and geese dangled from a gallows by the legs.

'This time next year,' Fitz said, 'we'll have Christmas together.'

'It's hard to believe,' Mary said. She would put up paper chains and mottoes saying 'Merry Christmas' or 'Adeste Fideles' or 'Christus Natus Est' done on glossy paper with coloured letters.

They left the main thoroughfare and found themselves among tall tenements. Children were playing on the streets and on the steps. All the doors stood open. The smells from the hallways were heavy and unpleasant.

'There he is,' Mary said suddenly, pointing. A man with a beard was hobbling along on the opposite path. He had half a dozen balloons strung from his left hand.

'Who?' Fitz asked.

'The man I saw being beaten by the policeman.' She followed

him with her eyes. Rashers had an unmistakable gait, a way of stooping his shoulders and pushing his neck forward so that his face and pendulant beard had an aggressive tilt. It took Fitz a little time to recollect what she was referring to. When he did he said:

'They had little to do.'

They went through back streets to the cottage where Fitz lodged with Mr. and Mrs. Farrell, who were expecting Mary and had the table set for tea for both of them. Farrell was at the fire, smoking a pipe and spitting now and then into the flames.

'That's a nice way to receive anybody,' Mrs. Farrell chided him.

'How?' he asked.

'Sitting there in your stocking feet.'

'The girl knows us all by now,' Farrell said, amicably.

'I do indeed,' Mary agreed.

'We'll leave them to themselves just the same,' Mrs. Farrell suggested to her husband.

'Anything strange at the foundry?' Farrell asked, ignoring her.

'Not a thing,' Fitz said. He sat down opposite Mary while Mrs. Farrell, having failed to move her husband, covered her defeat by picking up the pot and pouring tea for them.

'I thought you might. I heard talk myself of a strike with the carters.'

'They were working up to twelve.'

'Ah—it didn't come off so.'

'It's a bit near Christmas for anything like that,' Fitz suggested.

'Not when I tell you who's in town.'

Fitz looked at him enquiringly.

Farrell spat into the fire before replying.

'Jim Larkin.'

'Larkin,' Fitz repeated.

'He had a meeting with the carters and with a crowd from the purifier sheds in the Gas Company. He had a word with us too.' Farrell was a docker.

'When was that?'

'After the morning read.'

'Did you speak to him yourself?'

'I told him what had happened to me and about the stevedores paying us in pubs,' Farrell said. 'He says he'll put a stop to it.'

After almost a year of constant work, Farrell, in a moment of stubbornness, had refused to put up a drink for the stevedore. He had not been jobbed by him since. It was hard on Mrs. Farrell, especially with Christmas so near.

'You can talk to Fitz tonight,' Mrs. Farrell hinted once again.

This time her husband grunted and heaved himself from his chair. 'Right,' he said.

The Farrells retired into their bedroom. It was an understood thing by now.

After tea they sat a little while by the fire, then it was time to leave. She rose and Fitz took her in his arms.

'I hate having to go,' she told him. He held her tightly. It was a rare happiness to be together in a warm room, in the intimacy of firelight and lamplight. He kissed her. They went out into the street once again. The air was moist. The raw wind smelled and tasted of fog.

Later it rolled in from the sea, creeping across sandbanks and fingering its way up the river, curling across the sea-wall and fanning out lazily about houses and streets. It trapped the light from each lamp-post in turn and held it inescapably in a luminous tent. The foghorns at regulated intervals intoned their melancholy warnings. Rashers, returned to his cellar, drank tea in the light of a candle and shivered because of the rising damp. Fitz on his way to the foundry blinked constantly to remove its cobweb breath from his eyes.

On her way to bed Mary brought a glass of warm milk to Miss Gilchrist, who had been told to go early to her room because she had not been feeling well. The old woman was sitting at the fire which Mary had been allowed to light for her earlier. She gestured to Mary to sit.

'We have plenty of work before us tomorrow,' Miss Gilchrist said. 'There's the drawing room to do and every stick of furniture to move for the sweeping.'

'You won't be able for it,' Mary said.

'I'll be right in the morning. It's only a little turn.'

But Mary felt she would not be right. She looked drawn and wan.

'Drink your milk,' she said gently.

'I was thinking to myself that I'm the lucky woman,' Miss Gilchrist said, 'with my own little room and my own fire. There's many a one this night that's cold and hungry.'

Mary wondered that she could be contented. She had spent her life giving to others what she could have spent on a home and children and she would die without one to mourn for her. But she said nothing of that. The lonely old woman was on the brink of uselessness. What would happen when that time came? Who would care for her.

'Be a wise girl and stick to service,' Miss Gilchrist continued, 'it's a great safeguard against poverty.'

Mary said, shyly :

'There are some would say to go for a house and a husband.'

'And hardship,' Miss Gilchrist said. 'They say nothing about the hardship. That's what house and husband mean for people of our rearing and family. Take an old woman's advice and don't be led astray by a fancy.'

Mary, thinking of Fitz, knew she would follow her fancy wherever it led. Whatever hardship might come it would be better than loneliness. It would be better to share cold and want than have food and fire in a house that must always be a stranger's. She said nothing of that either. How could she?

'When I was a child,' said Miss Gilchrist, 'I saw the famine. They ate the grass out of the ditches and the leaves off the trees and when I walked as a little girl down the length of a lane the corpses I saw had the green juice still on their lips. That's what I remember as a child. That and the smell of the potato blight.'

'I heard about it from my own people,' Mary said.

'And those that tried to raise the people out of poverty were hanged or sent off in chains to Australia.'

Mary looked at the drawing on the mantelpiece, Miss Gilchrist's Fenian; the handsome young rebel who had sheltered

60

in her father's house when she was a young girl. Miss Gilchrist followed her eyes.

'That was one of them,' she said gently, 'the flower of them all.'

It occurred to Mary that Miss Gilchrist may have loved him. Had she watched him slip out into the dark one night, watched the bonfires on the hills, heard of the miserable failure of yet another rebellion?

'Stick to service,' Miss Gilchrist repeated. 'In this country the ones that don't fight are not worth your attention and the ones that do bring nothing but heartbreak.'

'You should go to bed now,' Mary prompted. 'The rest will do you all the good in the world.'

Miss Gilchrist handed her the glass and rose with difficulty.

'That's what I'll do,' Miss Gilchrist agreed.

Mary went to sleep with the sound of foghorns still vibrating at intervals through the room. It was past midnight. Outside the fog spread and deepened, curling around the well-kept houses of Kingstown, creeping along the deserted roads of Blackrock and Booterstown, stealing along the quays and the crowded slums of the city where rooms became damper and more evil-smelling and the great tide of destitute humanity settled down to the familiar joys and miseries of its lot; in the stink of terrible houses quarrelling, loving, sinning, sleeping, cohabiting, praying and dying. The fog rolled over all with ever-shifting movements, so that the city lay submerged and paralysed and the foghorns had it all to themselves. They sang all night to the great and the little, telling them life was vanity and Death the only certainty.

MARY had told Mrs. Bradshaw she had an aunt in the city for one reason only. There was no other way in which she could be free to visit Fitz. As a servant in training she was practically the property of the Bradshaws, dependent on their kindness for every occasional release from duty. She had no fixed day off and no agreed arrangement of work. To her parents, as to society, the condition was customary and there-fore beyond questioning. She hated the deceit which, in the face of Mrs. Bradshaw's gentleness and trust, made her feel un-worthy. Yet what was she to do? She was one of a class without privilege and like most of the others she had found her own means to filch a little freedom from time to time. When it was discovered, as it had to be, she suffered in a way which puzzled and terrified her.

Mrs. Bradshaw suffered too. She felt that Mary had justified Mr. Bradshaw's frequent criticisms of her indulgence.

'This is what comes of sentiment when dealing with ser-vants,' he said, 'how many times have I spoken to you about it?'

'It's a great disappointment,' was all she could offer in de-fence.

The lie had been discovered through her innocent reference to the visits in her letter to Mary's father. His reply that there was no relative in Dublin and his anxiety to know what exactly could be going on made Mrs. Bradshaw regret her mention of the matter. She was fond of Mary. She felt there could be nothing seriously wrong.

'It was terribly wicked of you,' she said, 'your father is so upset. I'm quite certain he thinks we have been lax.'

'I'm very sorry,' Mary offered. There was nothing else she could say.

'And what necessity was there for it?' Mrs. Bradshaw asked. 'I never refused you permission to go out.'

Mary remained silent. She could not have asked permission week after week to see Fitz. People refused to trust young servants with young men. It was a part of their thinking to expect the worst. So she would have had to tell lies anyhow. There was no way out. Mrs. Bradshaw, in the absence of a reply, asked the question which her world considered unavoidable in such situations.

'Have you been meeting any people? . . . I mean people of the opposite sex?'

Mary flushed at the implication which, however delicately Mrs. Bradshaw strove to push it into the background, remained in the question itself. She determined on this occasion not to lie. It was better to be punished than to go on with the deceit.

'I've been meeting a young man . . . the same young man,' Mary said.

The next question framed itself automatically, but Mrs. Bradshaw decided against asking it. She saw that Mary was suffering. Pity was always stronger in Mrs. Bradshaw than anger or anxiety.

Mary, who understood the hesitation, said: 'There's been nothing wrong between us.' She was glad that the lies had ended.

'I believe you,' Mrs. Bradshaw said.

But Mr. Bradshaw was not so easily satisfied. His mind was quite made up and his conversation on the matter was punctuated by frequent raising and lowering of his perpetual newspaper.

'She must go,' he insisted.

'The poor girl has done nothing wrong.'

'We have only her word for it.'

'I believe her.'

The newspaper was lowered.

'You also believed her about this ridiculous aunt.'

Mrs. Bradshaw had no reply. She changed her voice and her tactics.

'It seems such a pity to dismiss her.'

'I fail to see why.'

'I was thinking of the girl herself. We can't give her a clear reference and without that she'll find it impossible to get another position.'

'She should have thought of that before she picked up with some young blackguard.'

'They don't have very much freedom. I'm sure it was all quite innocent.'

'Innocent,' Mr. Bradshaw repeated, bringing his newspaper down on his knees with a loud noise. 'You mustn't think these young girls are like yourself. They breed like rabbits. My God, woman, do you want her having babies all over the place?'

Mrs. Bradshaw changed colour. He noticed. Mistaking the reason, he apologised.

'Forgive me if I sound crude, but we must face facts.'

It was not the crudeness which had upset Mrs. Bradshaw. In a small, dry voice she said: 'I really don't think it would arise.'

'While there are hundreds of strong, willing and reliable girls to choose from, am I to sit by and see you saddled with an impressionable trollop. We pay for trustworthiness, my dear. We must make sure that we get it.'

Mrs. Bradshaw said, quietly: 'I liked her. She suited me.'

'You are being sentimental again. It is a constant fault of yours.'

'Perhaps I am,' Mrs. Bradshaw admitted. 'I don't think it so wrong to want to forgive.'

'Nonsense. She goes back to her parents. A servant is not like an ordinary employee. One has moral responsibilities in the case of a servant.'

But Mary's departure was delayed by the illness of Miss Gilchrist. The old woman's collapse was gradual. In the course of the Christmas cleaning Mary helped her to shift the heavy furniture and noted the toll it took of her strength. She refused to rest on the grounds that the work had to be done. One day when they had moved the sideboard near the piano they discovered Father O'Connor's beads, an amber and silver rosary in a worn purse. Miss Gilchrist put them in her apron pocket, saying she would return them personally later. Father O'Connor had become a favourite of hers and she recognised his property at once. She regarded him as something of a saint and never missed going to him for her monthly confession.

Less than an hour later she collapsed. Mary shouted for Mrs. Bradshaw and together they managed to take her to her room. They got her to bed. Mary lit the lamp and drew the curtains, cutting out the gloom of the December evening. The pallor of Miss Gilchrist's face and her heavy breathing frightened her. They stayed watching her for a while until Mrs. Bradshaw said : 'I think it would be as well to go for the doctor.'

During the next few days Mary, in between frequent errands, found an opportunity to contact Fitz again. She asked him to be near the gate at midnight on the following Sunday. Sunday was an early night in the Bradshaw household. When the rest had retired she would somehow get out to see him.

She made it a habit to sit with Miss Gilchrist during the night until after midnight. The old woman recovered a little, but remained too weak to be allowed up. On Sunday evening Father O'Connor called to see her. She had asked Mary to summon him. Mary left everything ready for the priest and withdrew. He gave no sign of being aware of the pending dismissal. When Miss Gilchrist had confessed to him he removed his purple stole, kissed it and folded it. He looked round the room. Miss Gilchrist smiled.

'Haven't I the height of comfort, Father,' she said.

'You have indeed,' Father O'Connor said. 'You're the lucky woman.'

'That shows you that I'm highly thought of.'

'Are you long here?' Father O'Connor asked.

'Over thirty years.'

'Then why wouldn't you be highly thought of?' he bantered, not without difficulty. He found it difficult to be easy and natural with a servant.

'It isn't always so,' she said. 'There's some would dump you in an attic without fire or comfort.'

'And who would have the heartlessness to do that?' Father O'Connor reproved.

'Many's the one. I seen it and I know. Or pack you off to the Union the minute you showed a sign of feebleness. And why not, I suppose, when a poor body is not of their blood.'

'Mr. and Mrs. Bradshaw are good people,' he said.

'That's what I'm saying, Father.'

'And most people are good too, but gossip doesn't give them credit.' He felt it might be no harm to slip in a few words about the danger of uncharitable talk. But he got no chance.

The old woman said next: 'Hand me across my apron, Father.'

He looked around, searching, and saw it draped on a chair. A tiny wave of irritation at being commanded by the old woman moved inside him but was suppressed. He handed it to her. She rooted for the pocket and gave him the purse.

'I found them for you when we were cleaning,' she said, with wonderful pleasure.

He opened the purse and let the beads fall into his hands. To have them again choked him with happiness.

'My rosary,' was all he could say, 'how can I thank you . . .?'

'You can say a little prayer for me.'

'They were my mother's. I'd rather lose anything than these.'

Miss Gilchrist lay still, taking in his happiness, smiling in sympathy with it.

'God bless you,' he said. On an impulse he placed his hand lightly on her head and murmured his formal blessing. She closed her eyes and barely opened them when he bid her good night.

'What do you make of her?' Bradshaw asked.

He had made a point of meeting the priest in the hallway.

'I think she should be all right,' Father O'Connor said. Priests, he knew, had the reputation of being good judges, but as yet he had had very little experience of the sick-room.

'Can you step in here a moment,' Bradshaw invited. He held open the door of the drawing room. They sat down.

'The doctor,' Bradshaw began, 'thinks it may have been a little . . . stroke.'

They always said little, Father O'Connor thought, remembering the old woman's closed eyes and tired face. It was a little weakness, a little turn, a little upset.

'The trouble is,' Bradshaw continued carefully, 'that it seems to have affected one of the legs.'

'In what way?' the priest asked.

'Paralysis—at least partial. Of course, it may pass.'

'Please God it will.'

'On the other hand it may not.' Bradshaw fixed his gaze on the far corner. 'What are we to do if she is no longer able to work?'

He waited for the priest to answer. Father O'Connor, drawn suddenly into the problem by the use of the word 'we', felt he should answer that the Christian thing would be to look after the old woman. But no matter how he tried to formulate the sentence it sounded incredibly impracticable. He decided to play for time and, if possible, to put forward his view obliquely.

'She has been a very long time in service with you,' he began.

'She's been paid for her trouble, every penny.'

'Of course. It was not my intention . . .'

'And been treated with every consideration.'

'I have personal evidence of that,' Father O'Connor said, in a conciliatory voice.

'Indeed, if Mrs. Bradshaw has a shortcoming, it is her indulgent nature, as I have bitter cause to know.'

Father O'Connor, intimidated by Bradshaw's commanding tone, nodded his head.

'It's not that I mind her growing old,' Bradshaw continued, 'provided she can potter around and get her work done. But what if she is incapable? We can't employ a servant to dance attendance on a servant. The thing would be absurd.'

'Has she no relatives?'

'None at all.'

'That makes it very difficult,' Father O'Connor found himself saying.

'And worrying, very worrying,' Bradshaw added. He sighed

deeply, thinking that he was never quite free from ill fortune; troubles trailed him everywhere like kittens after a cat.

'God knows I'm fond of the old woman, she is quite devoted,' Bradshaw continued. 'If she remains as she is and we have to part with her it will be a terrible upset.'

Father O'Connor wanted to speak for her. The suggestion that she should be kept in the house no matter what the outcome of her illness came several times to the tip of his tongue. He could not say it. He told himself it would do no good. It would only make Bradshaw regard him as an incorrigible fool.

'We can only pray,' Father O'Connor said. 'Prayer works wonders.'

The dilemma haunted him as he walked home. It seemed insoluble. If the old lady remained incapable, only Bradshaw's generosity would stand between her and the workhouse; and Bradshaw, Father O'Connor knew, was incapable of charity in so large a measure. Indeed, Father O'Connor reminded himself, God did not demand it of his children. And yet, given certain circumstances, was not something required, in all justice, over and above the meticulous discharge of a contract? St. Thomas had somewhere discussed the matter. Father O'Connor tried but failed to remember specifically.

The streets were deserted, the bulk of the church looked black and forbidding, the wind was cold and burdened with rain. Father O'Connor went through the side gate and heard it groan as it shut behind him. What he could have said on the old woman's behalf he did not know. He only knew that he had not said it. He walked along the narrow, tree-lined approach, his shoulders hunched, feeling like Judas.

'What time is it?' Miss Gilchrist asked.

'Almost midnight.'

'You should get to your bed.'

'Presently,' Mary said, 'when you've had your milk and settled down for the night.'

The wind was making a great noise outside, bullying the trees and driving the rain against the windows. Sometimes the lamp dimmed and then brightened again, sometimes a gust beat down on the fire and sent a puff of smoke into the room. Mary watched the saucepan of milk, which for convenience she was heating at the bedroom fire. Miss Gilchrist returned to her chosen topic, Father O'Connor's visit.

'Did he say anything to you?'

'About what?'

'About your trouble.'

That was the phrase she had found for Mary's loss of favour.

'Not a word. Perhaps he didn't know.'

'Nonsense,' Miss Gilchrist said, 'of course he knew.' She lay staring at the ceiling, a whitewashed one on which the beaded lamp-shade cast restless patterns. They were faces, flowers, animal shapes.

'He's kind. If you'd mentioned it to him he would have put in a word with the boss about you.'

'I don't want him to.'

'But what will you do?'

Mary did not know as yet. First she must see Fitz. The milk bubbled around the edges and she took it away from the fire. Fixing Miss Gilchrist's pillows, Mary sat down at the bedside and they both drank. The room was cosy, yet in some subtle way it had changed. It was no longer a place in which she was accepted and approved. The furniture, the sick-room utensils, Miss Gilchrist's rebel, were no longer part of her life. They surrounded her like enemies. She had a home no longer. Even outside the house everything had changed. At mass on Sundays she saw people she knew and thought they looked strangely at her. It made her hate them and brought her several times to the verge of tears.

'What *can* I do?' she said at length. Except get away. That meant home. She would feel unwanted at home too. And neighbours would gossip in the small townland.

'Father O'Connor is the man to go to,' Miss Gilchrist said again, just before Mary settled the clothes about her and she began to fall asleep. 'He won't let you down.'

Mary turned down the lamp. The clock said midnight. She took the glasses and left on tiptoe, pausing for a moment on the stairs to assure herself that the house was sleeping. It was hard to unbolt the kitchen door without making a noise, but she succeeded at last. She closed it behind her, hoping the latch, which often slipped, would hold against the wind. The cold sting of the rain made her catch her breath as she hurried down the length of the garden. She opened the garden gate and stared into the darkness. Coming from the lighted house made it impossible to see anything. She started with fright when Fitz stood suddenly close to her.

'Mary,' he said.

She turned to him and he folded her tightly in his arms. After a moment she said: 'Not here. Come inside.'

They went up the garden together until they found cover under a tree. It was no longer much protection against the driving rain, but it held off the wind a little and hid them from the roadway. Fitz took her in his arms again and she said: 'My darling, I kept you waiting, and you're soaked.'

'It doesn't matter,' Fitz said.

She kissed him in sudden abandon, his lips, his cheeks, his forehead, finding them cold and soaked with rain. Then she began to cry.

'Tell me what has happened.'

She told him. For the first time in many days she found love offered to her in place of hostility. Under a dark tree, in the wind and the rain of a December midnight, there was the feeling of home. She had been exiled from that for longer than she could bear. She clutched him desperately and said: 'What am I to do?'

He held her for a moment in silence. Then in a voice which was unexpectedly calm and firm he said: 'You mustn't go home.'

'No.'

'Because if you do they'll keep you there. We might never see one another again.'

'Where else can I go?'

'You can stay with the Farrells and I can find some other place for a while.'

'Will they agree?'

'Of course they'll agree.'

She had never had a problem of any importance to put to him before. His assurance was a new quality at which to marvel.

'You can stay there until we can arrange to be married.'

'I'll do it,' she said, 'but how?'

'Give me just a little time to arrange it,' he said, 'I'll leave word for you and when I do all you'll have to do is walk out as you did tonight.'

'What about my father?'

'You can write to him to tell him you're safe. We'll be married before they can do anything about it.'

She said: 'It all seems simple now when you are with me. But when you're not here I'm going to be afraid.'

'Don't you want to come with me?'

'How can you ask?'

'Then there's nothing to be afraid of. From the moment you leave here I'll be with you.'

The leaves above them shook furiously and the dislodged drops soaked both of them. Mary shivered and said: 'I must go. They might miss me.'

'I'll send word,' he said.

'Tell me you love me.'

'I love you.'

'Think of me later and say it too.'

'I'll say it all the way home,' he answered.

He waited until she had gone into the house and the candle-light showed in her window. Then he went off. She thought of him battling his way back to the city, his head down against the rain. His confidence had reassured her. The future no longer filled her with dread and uncertainty.

In the first days of the New Year Mary left the Bradshaw's home for ever. She met Fitz once again in the garden and closed the gate quietly, this time from the outside. She had a small case of belongings and sixteen pounds, the fortune she had managed to save. They walked all the way to the city, a journey which took over two hours. When they reached the Farrells' house

Mrs. Farrell was waiting with tea for them. She asked no questions.

The next day Fitz moved to a room elsewhere and Mary wrote two letters. The one to her father assured him that she was safe and that he must not worry about her. The one to Mrs. Bradshaw found the house in chaos for want of servants, a troublesome situation which continued for a couple of weeks, when suitable new recruits were eventually found. Miss Gilchrist's partial paralysis remained, until in the end Mr. Bradshaw made up his mind. Her removal to the workhouse upset Mrs. Bradshaw for several months.

CHAPTER 5

WINTER was always the worst time in that city. In autumn the trees along suburban roads were venerable but elegant; in winter they were gnarled and ragged ancients, with rheumatic knuckles and bones. The large houses became draughty and hard to heat; the young children on their way to Miss Tieler's ballet and dancing class in Molesworth Hall wore gaiters over thick stockings and top-coats over jerseys and shawls, so that when they alighted from trams and cabs they were recognisable because of their enormous size. In the mornings just at the breakfast hour the poor searched diligently in the ashbins of the well-to-do for half-burnt cinders and carried sacks and cans so that as much as possible of the fuel might be salvaged. The ashbin children were pinched and wiry and usually barefooted. They lived on the cast-offs. They came each morning from the crowded rooms in the cast-off houses of the Rich; elegant Georgian buildings which had grown old and had been discarded. The clothes they wore had been cast-off by their parents, who had bought them as cast-offs in the second-hand shops in Little Mary Street or Winetavern Street. If the well-to-do had stopped casting-off for even a little while the children would have gone homeless and fireless and naked. But nobody really thought about that. These things Were.

It was a bad time for the carters, rising by candlelight, shivering on their way to work before six o'clock, wondering would there be ice on the streets to keep the horses in the stables. And for the building trade, where every other day the weather became ugly and there was broken time. The dockers hated winter. They huddled in groups on the quayside and waited through interminable mornings for ships that had been delayed.

It was a bad time all round. The east wind beat in from the sea and drove under the arches of the river, so that when the gulls rose with a cry from the water it hurled them backwards in a high, swift curve. The Farrells' house, where Mary continued to stay, quivered often at night because of the great beating of the sea. She had grown used to its sound while with the Bradshaws, but here it was nearer and more violent. Frequently, when she walked along the front in the mornings, she found the beach strewn with driftwood and debris. After a while she began to join others in collecting what could be used for fuel. At times, when she sat listening to the sea and the wind, her thoughts turned to the house in Kingstown and she wondered if Mrs. Bradshaw still complained of the draughts from the folding doors.

On one of the bleakest nights the great coal-stack in the foundry went on fire. Fitz, who was on duty, was called out a little after midnight by Carrington the foreman. At first there were no flames and the smoke could not be seen in the pitch darkness. But both recognised the smell, a particular odour which left a thick taste on the tongue. They traced it to the lower yard, after much uncertain groping and guessing. The smoke was heavy in the yard and hit them so suddenly that they both swallowed it and coughed. From the darkness beside Fitz, Carrington's voice said: 'It's the coal-stack.'

It had happened before. Carrington, wondering if he should put the emergency routine into operation, hesitated.

'I wonder how bad it is?'

'We won't know until we disturb it,' Fitz said, 'and when we do that it may be too late.'

'I'll see about getting the brigade,' Carrington decided. 'Take out enough of the furnace crew to rig up the lighting set and see about mustering extra help.'

A little later the city, huddled behind drenched housefronts, stirred to hear the clangour of bells in the empty streets. As the first engine swung into the yard the men were already moving the lighting set into position. A cloud of smoke, bent at an angle by the wind, showed up blackly.

'Why the hell wouldn't it happen in summer,' one of the men said.

They had shovels ready and were crouching in the meagre shelter of the lamp supports. Sleet slanted intermittently, a curtain between the darkness and the lamps. The brigade men were in position with hoses ready.

The foreman had some words with the chief before he ordered the labourers forward. They dug gingerly, testing for the source of the fire and leaving small mounds of coal about the main stack. After a while one of the men, digging deeper than the rest, sprang aside and called out. A small tongue of flame licked upwards. Carrington said to Fitz:

'You'd better call out help. We'll need carters and more men to dig.'

Fitz found the list in the time office, where the timekeeper, half asleep over the fire, jumped up in alarm at his entrance.

'Blast you anyway,' he said. 'I thought for a minute you were Carrington.'

'I've come for the emergency list,' Fitz said, 'the main coal-stack is on fire.'

The timekeeper produced it from a drawer.

'We use the carters from Doggett & Co.,' he said. 'Barney Mulhall is the man to see first.'

'Have you his address?'

'Chandlers Court,' the timekeeper said, his eyes searching down the list. 'Here you are—number three.'

Fitz took his bicycle and headed out into the streets. He was the only traveller. The city was dead and dark and windswept. In addition to the carters there would be labourers needed. He decided to call on Pat Bannister, with whom he had been sharing a room since Mary had gone to the Farrells. Pat was out of work because for the moment the storage yard of Nolan & Keyes was packed to capacity. He decided to call on Farrell too: he was still being ignored by the stevedores. There was at least a night's work in it for each of them. The double line of tram-tracks gleamed wetly as he turned across them into Chandlers

Court and found number three with difficulty. The hall door was closed over, but there was no lock and he pushed it in with his shoulder. A dog barked from the basement as he entered the hall. He climbed two flights. It was impossible not to make a noise on the bare boards and to stumble now and then on the uneven stairs. The walls in the dim light of the oil lamp he had taken from his bicycle were greasy and peeling. The smell of communal living lay heavily and unpleasantly on the landing. He knocked at the door of the two pair back and noticed that the paint was cracking and blistered as though there had been a fire.

After a while there were movements and a deep voice asked:
'Who is it?'

'Emergency call,' Fitz answered, 'Morgan's Foundry.'

'Hold your horses,' the voice acknowledged.

Fitz waited patiently. Somewhere above a baby had begun to cry. It was remote yet it transformed everything. There was more here than darkness, than decay, than evil smells. Behind each of these peeling doors, from the ground to the top, there was a home. A man who was naked except for a pair of trousers which he held in position with one hand, opened the door and said: 'Step in.'

Fitz hesitated.

'Do as you're told,' the man insisted. He was obviously used to laying down the law. Fitz noticed his bulk and height. But there was a pleasant note in his voice. He was not a bully.

Mulhall made way for him and he entered the room. The atmosphere was close, but snugly so. The only illumination was the red glow of a lamp which stood on the mantelpiece before a statue of the Sacred Heart. A yellow circle of light wavered on the ceiling above it. As Mulhall pulled on his shirt there were movements in the far corner. A match gleamed and a gas ring threw a blue light. Mulhall, having pulled his braces over his huge shoulders, lit a candle and said:

'What the hell are you at now?'

'Keep your voice quiet,' the woman whispered. She was elderly. Fitz knew by the voice and by her stooping movements in the combined light of candle and gas ring.

'That's herself,' Mulhall said to Fitz, pulling on his socks. The woman said: 'You'll waken the child.'

Mulhall chuckled deeply and said to Fitz: 'The child is in the bed beyond there. He's fifteen and nearly as big as I am.'

Fitz guessed at, rather than saw, a single bed in the far corner.

'What's your name?' Mulhall asked.

'Fitzpatrick,' Fitz said.

There were sounds near the gas ring; the thump of a kettle, the rattle of cups.

'She's making tea,' Mulhall confided. He was having trouble with one of his boots.

'It won't take a minute,' the woman said, 'and you'll be glad you had it when you face the street outside.' Then she said: 'You might ask the young man to take the weight off his legs.'

Fitz could see them better now. Mulhall had thick grey hair above a heavy forehead. The woman, a coat thrown about her shoulders, had once been tall. Her movements were gentle. In the candlelight her shadow bobbed from wall to wall as she put cups on the table and cut bread.

'Sit over,' she said.

'Dear God,' Mulhall protested, 'a bloody coal-stack on fire—and she makes tea.'

'Take it in your hand and swallow it.' She listened to the wind for a moment and added: 'It's a terrible night.'

The second bed was in the angle between a small window and the far wall. Fitz could see it better now. There were movements from it and a boy sat up, blinking. He had a handsome face with dark hair tumbled about the forehead.

'What's wrong?' he asked.

'Emergency call,' Mulhall answered.

'I knew you'd wake him,' the woman said. She turned to Fitz and explained: 'The child is in the parcels department in the Tramway. He has a six o'clock start.'

The tea was sweet and hot—too hot. Mulhall emptied his into a saucer and drank it that way.

'Do you need extra help?'

'We could do with some,' Fitz said.

'Glory be to God,' his wife said, 'you're surely not thinking of the child?'

Mulhall said to her, 'Will you let me talk, woman.' He glared at her for a moment over his shoulder. Then he spoke to Fitz.

'There's a poor divil upstairs with a wife and a couple of children. He could do with a night's work.'

'Is it Mr. Hennessy?' his wife asked. Again Fitz noted that she was a quiet-spoken woman.

'The Toucher Hennessy,' Mulhall confirmed.

'Then they've four children,' his wife corrected.

'Holy God,' Mulhall said, 'that woman is like a rabbit.'

'I'll go up and get him,' Fitz agreed.

They left down their cups and while Mulhall set off to alert the carters Fitz climbed the remaining stairs. He was now in the attic, on a narrow landing where the ceiling was so low that he stooped. The baby was crying again when he knocked. A woman's voice responded.

'Who is it?'

'We have a night's work in the foundry, if Mr. Hennessy will take it,' Fitz shouted.

There was a long interval. He heard whispering inside. Then the woman shouted: 'He wants to know what kind of work it is.'

Fitz explained and there was another interlude. Then the door opened and a small skinny man looked up into his face.

'I hope you'll pardon the preliminary enquiry,' he said with great politeness, 'but what class of work is involved?'

'Digging coal,' Fitz said.

'Aw God, wouldn't that vex you now. I've no shovel.' Fitz thought there was a note of relief in the voice.

'They'll give you a shovel,' the woman shouted, 'won't youse, mister?'

'That's right,' Fitz said, 'we can supply a shovel.'

The man considered this. Then he asked cautiously:

'Is there any climbing?'

'What has that to do with it?' Fitz asked.

'I've no head for heights,' Hennessy said.

'Don't listen to a bloody word he says, mister,' the woman screamed, 'he's only acting the old soldier.'

'There's no climbing,' Fitz said.

With obvious lack of enthusiasm for the prospect of facing the raw and laborious night, Hennessy turned up the collar of his coat and cast a despairing glance back at the room.

'All right—I'll go,' he said.

He followed Fitz on to the street and set off in the direction of the foundry. His figure was huddled against the cold, his pace reluctant. Fitz went to his own place to rouse Pat Bannister and then to Farrell's. He waited in the kitchen while Farrell dressed, all the time conscious that behind the door to the left of the fireplace Mary lay sleeping. He was torn between his desire to speak to her and his reluctance to disturb her. Before he could make up his mind Farrell had joined him and they went down to the foundry together.

As they walked Farrell said: 'I won't forget it to you for coming down for me.'

'Who else would I call on?' Fitz said, easily.

But he was shocked at the change in Farrell. He had not seen much of him since moving out to make room for Mary. Most of the time Farrell had been out searching for work. Or, if he was in, he had remained in his own room. He was not simply out of work. He was a marked man, barred by one stevedore after another, a man who had tried on his own to break a highly organised system of petty extortion.

'You haven't had any luck?' Fitz asked.

'Nor won't,' Farrell said.

'What about Larkin?'

'There's been no word.'

'Maybe there will be, soon.'

'What can Larkin do, when the rest didn't stand by me?'

Very little, Fitz thought. The shipowners gave each unloading job to the stevedore on contract. Who the stevedores employed after that, or how they paid them, was not the shipowners' concern. The custom of paying the dockers in public houses had been accepted for years. It seemed impossible to Fitz that the lonely, elderly man walking beside him could alter it. There were too many who were jobless and willing to take his place. Farrell was beginning to look at it that way too. It had been painful to see his eyes light up at the prospect of a casual night's work.

Farrell walked in silence for a while. Then he said, more hopefully:

'What's the foreman at the foundry like?'

'Carrington is his name. He's as hard as nails, but he has no favourites. All he cares for is a good worker.'

'Does he job casuals often?'

'Two or three times a week, usually for a day at a stretch.'

'I'll go out of my way to bring myself to his notice tonight,' Farrell said. 'I'm finished as a docker, anyway.'

They worked without rest through a night of continuing sleet and wind; the labourers digging and hauling, the carters loading, dumping, re-loading. Steam rose in dense clouds beneath the water from the hoses and fanned about the yard so that the sleet itself tasted of cinder and ash and the clothes of the labouring men smelled strongly and sourly. At last it became so dense that the men digging on the leeward side could work no longer. It had become impossible to breathe as the wind bent it downwards in an impenetrable fog.

Carrington, who was directing the carters, left off and came over to Fitz. It was a habit of his. Fitz was his unofficial deputy.

'What now?' he asked.

Fitz had been thinking about it. They had tried taking the hoses off for intervals and digging when the steam cleared. But when the hoses stopped the strong wind fanned the fire into life again.

'We could try screening the fire and see if we can dig it out.'

There were large screens in No. 2 house, which were used in summer to cut off the heavy draught when both ends of the house had to be left open because of the heat.

Carrington felt it was worth trying.

Fitz gathered some labourers and half a dozen carters, one

of whom was Mulhall. He set the furnace hands disassembling the screens so that the carts could carry them to the yard. While they were working Mulhall said to him:

'Are you deputy gaffer here?'

'No. Just senior hand.'

'Union man?'

'National Union of Dockers,' Fitz said.

'Same as us. Is the whole job union?'

'Half and half.'

'Ever met Larkin?'

'No,' Fitz said.

'He fixed an overtime rate some time ago—ninepence an hour. It's in the carters' agreement.'

'I wouldn't know about that,' Fitz said. He was a furnace hand. The carters had their own set of conditions. Lately, one section or another of the carters was always in trouble.

'Maybe you'd ask the head bottle-washer,' Mulhall said, then backed up and drove off. They got the screens into position and after a while they shut off the hoses. The wind no longer had direct access to the fire, but it bundled over the top and caught the coal at its higher level. The steam too, was clear of the ground and the men could work in the lee of the stack. They loaded the carts without respite. Meanwhile other workmen had begun to dig towards the ignited coal. Fitz saw Farrell among them, working steadily and easily, the relaxed technique of the docker showing in every movement of his body. He was one of the small number selected by Carrington for a special and difficult operation. Fitz was glad. It would give Farrell hope—and for the moment hope had become his desperate need. Pat Bannister was among them too, working steadily, absorbed as he always was, in the job that confronted him. Further away, in among the general collection, Hennessy stood idle, with a long-handled trimmer's shovel which was almost as tall as himself.

'Don't kill yourself,' Fitz said as he passed him.

'I'm a delicate framed man,' Hennessy said, 'and I'm crucified with rheumatism of the back.'

'You'd better look as though you were working,' Fitz advised him. 'If Carrington puts his eye on you he'll give you your papers.'

Hennessy sighed and dug his shovel into the coal.

The night passed slowly. As they grew exhausted it took on a dreamlike quality; the figures of men bent under the lamps; the sleet thickened and slackened, died and found new reserves; the scrape of shovels and the creaking of carts filled the darkness incessantly. For a while Fitz found himself beside Carrington and remembered Mulhall's enquiry.

'The carters want to know what's the freight?'

Carrington thought and then said :

'Sixpence an hour, I suppose.'

'They seem to expect overtime rate.'

'What's that?'

'Ninepence.'

'My bloody eye,' Carrington said.

His tone angered Fitz, but it did not seem to be the moment for argument. In the upper end of the yard a new coal-stack was rising as the men moved more and more coal.

'Better keep them hosing as they build the new stack,' Carrington said, 'otherwise we may have another bloody fire on our hands.'

'We'll need the reserve water supply,' Fitz said.

'That's all right. Go ahead and turn it on.'

'Who'll look after the hosing?'

'There's a couple of likely looking casuals. I'll get one of them to take charge.'

Carrington's eyes searched among the working figures. He walked over towards the group near him and singled out Farrell.

'You,' he said, 'what have you worked at?'

'Docker,' Farrell said.

'Name?'

'Jim Farrell.'

'Out of work?'

'This past few months.'

Carrington hesitated. Then he said, dismissing Farrell, 'All right, carry on.'

When Farrell had gone Carrington turned to Fitz.

'I know who he is now. I couldn't use him.'

'Why not?'

'Dangerous. That's the fellow who tried to start some trouble with the stevedores.'

Carrington shouted again. 'Hey, you,' and another man approached.

'I'll turn on the reserve water cock,' Fitz said.

Fitz climbed into the top gallery of No. 4 house where in a wing overlooking the river the reserve pump was located. The bare metal was painfully cold to touch and the wind, bullying fiercely through the glassless apertures, had almost scoured the floor clear of coal-dust. Fitz threw his weight against the release wheel. It was an unreliable piece of mechanism at the best of times.

He had carried the image of Farrell with him and the words of Carrington remained in his head as he waited. Farrell's moment of rebellion was known now along the length of the dockside. They were going to hound him, even people like Carrington, who had no conscious determination to do so. It was a comfortless city.

Below the catwalks and weblike ladders the men still on duty sweated over the furnaces. Here there was a forsaken, steel-cold emptiness, a half-lit gloom. To his right the river was grey and wrinkled under the wind, the waiting ships as yet not clearly discernible. Fitz noted with surprise that it was almost dawn. He imagined he could smell it: a distinctive odour of metal and river and many cargoes, the cold and hungry smell of the dockside. A ship hooted, getting up steam. That meant an early tide. The sound hit the iron roof above him, then drifted off across streets and alleyways, startling the sleepy gulls and foraging cats. It had barely died away when the pipes near Fitz lurched suddenly and began to dance. The pump was working. He took his time negotiating the ladders. They were narrow and dangerous for someone who had been eighteen hours on duty.

When Fitz reported to Carrington again it was morning. The lighting set had been dismantled, the men looked haggard and hungry. Looking at them as they worked, Fitz was filled suddenly with pity. The wind and the cold had been an unremitting hardship, the steam and ash had attacked their eyes and added their own brand of torture. Yet except for Mullhall's enquiry they continued to work without questioning what they were to get at the end of it. For most of them, anyway, anything earned would be regarded as a godsend.

'How about payment?' he asked Carrington.

'I'll leave the list with the pay clerk before I go home. Tell them to call back about four o'clock.'

'What am I to tell them about the overtime rate?'

'Up in Nellie's room,' Carrington said.

'There'll be trouble.'

'The casuals don't matter—they'll take what they're given. The carters are more dangerous. But they have no case. They're only entitled to overtime if they've worked for us during the day. These didn't. They were working for Doggett & Co.'

'I hope they understand that piece of reasoning,' Fitz said.

'There's nothing they can do about it, anyway,' Carrington said. 'They're not employed normally by us, so they can't very well go on strike.'

Fitz went home with Pat Bannister. They made tea, washed, and lay down to sleep. Meanwhile the rest of the city got into the swing of yet another day.

'You wished to see me?' Father O'Connor said.

His new parish priest, Father Giffley, looked around and said testily: 'Please don't stand with the door knob clasped in your fist—it's a habit I detest.'

He saw Father O'Connor's flush of embarrassment and added: 'It lets the raw air into the room. Come in and sit down.'

He was seated in a leather armchair with a high back, his feet stretched out to the fire. On a table, which for comfort he had drawn over to the fireplace, the remains of his breakfast lay scattered: the peeled skin of an orange, a porridge bowl with its milky residue; a plate with egg stains and the stringy rinds of bacon.

Father O'Connor sat down facing him. Through a high window opposite he could see the walled yard at the back of the church and a section of railway line. The Church of St. Brigid lay near the railway and the canal. It was an unattractive view which the overcast sky and the spattering sleet did nothing to improve. The glass wore a thick grime, the inescapable grime of the neighbourhood.

'Yes,' Father Giffley said. 'I wanted to see you—would you care for some whiskey?'

'No, thank you,' Father O'Connor said.

'A follower of Father Mathew?'

'No, Father.' He was about to add that eleven o'clock in the morning seemed a little on the early side for heavy spirits, but realised in time that that might be interpreted as a reflection on his superior's habits. He found them disturbing.

'Then you might pour some for me,' Father Giffley ordered. 'The bottle is at your elbow.'

He had grey, spiky hair and a red face which the heat of the fire had roused to a steaming glow. Father O'Connor poured the whiskey and shuddered at the smell. In a few weeks he had grown to associate the smell of whiskey and the smell of peppermint sweets. His superior's breath was always heavy with one or the other—or both.

'You treat it very gingerly, very gingerly indeed,' Father Giffley boomed at him. 'Liberality, man. Don't stint it.'

Father O'Connor withdrew the glass he had been in the act of extending to his superior and poured in a further supply.

'That's better,' Father Giffley said. 'That's a more likely looking conqueror of a raw morning.' He screwed up his eyes, regarding the glass with approval. He had water beside him with which he diluted the sizable measure. Then he drank, made an approving sound with his lips and pursued :

'You have been with me for some weeks, Father . . .'

'Six,' Father O'Connor supplied.

'Six,' Father Giffley repeated. The number seemed to give him material for reflection. He gazed for quite a while into the fire, his eyes bulging and bloodshot. He had the habit, when thinking, of grunting and breathing laboriously.

'The thing that puzzles me is how you came here.'

'It was my own wish, Father.'

'So I have been told—but why?'

'I felt the life in a rich parish too easy. It was not what God called me to the priesthood for.'

'Do you find the work here more . . . elevating?'

'It is more arduous, Father. It requires more humility.'

Father Giffley stared at him over his whiskey and left it down without tasting it.

'Ah—I see. Humility. So that's the coveted virtue.'

'I beg your pardon, Father?'

Father Giffley made a sound of impatience. This time he compensated for his previous abstinence and almost emptied the glass.

'You are full of polite catch-phrases. You beg my pardon; you ask may you come in; I offer you whiskey and you act as though I had told you a bawdy story. I asked you to see me this morning because, frankly, I found it quite impossible to understand what brought you here.'

'I don't follow you, Father.'

Father O'Connor was trembling, not with rage, but confusion. His superior terrified him.

'I am bound to tell you that if you think you've come to a good place for the exercise of your priestly office you've made a stupid mistake. It is my duty as your parish priest to put you on the right track.'

'I was not aware that I was displeasing you,' Father O'Connor said.

'Displeasing me? Not a bit. Thank God I have not lived in the stink of one slum parish after another without finding ways and means of insulating myself. I am merely warning you of the situation. You have met Father O'Sullivan?'

Father O'Connor had. It was Father O'Sullivan, not Father Giffley, who had instructed him in the parish routine, shown him where vestments and vessels were kept, wished him a happy stay in the parish and hoped he would like the parish priest. He had said that with a sad, shy smile which betrayed that he found Father Giffley just a little bit odd. He was a stout, grey-haired man himself, much given to vigils at the Altar of Our Lady of the Immaculate Conception. After that first, routine exposition of the workings of St. Brigid's his conversations with Father O'Connor, though pleasant and friendly, were few.

'You must study Father O'Sullivan,' Father Giffley said. 'While you are here you must follow his example, not that of your parish priest.'

Father O'Connor failed to hide his embarrassment.

'Really . . . Father,' he managed.

'I am trying to help you.'

Screwing up his courage, Father O'Connor faced his superior and said: 'There is one way in which you could help me very much.'

'I could?'

'If you could try to like me a little,' Father O'Connor said. 'You make me feel useless and unwanted.'

How true it was came freshly to his mind as he said it. Father Giffley had treated him with contempt from the very first day. He had treated him unfairly too, giving him the seven o'clock mass to say each morning without a single respite and taking the ten o'clock mass himself. Father O'Connor had accepted it in a spirit of self-abasement and obedience. The conscious act of submission bore him up as he rose morning after morning in the raw, high-ceilinged bedroom.

'Is it merely politeness you want? The work here demands slightly different accomplishments.'

'I had hoped for your guidance in that.'

'Guidance,' Father Giffley repeated. He had sat down again and this time he addressed the word to the fire.

'I had hoped so.'

'You are a hypocrite, Father.'

Wondering, not for the first time, if his superior was mad, Father O'Connor said:

'I don't know why you should say so.'

'Because you consider me a drunkard.'

'Oh no, Father.'

'Yes, indeed, Father.'

Father Giffley took his glass to the whiskey bottle and this time he poured for himself.

'It's almost thirty years since I first came to the slums. I didn't come like you, looking for the dirty work, I came because I was sent. They knew of my weakness for good society and good conversation. I suppose they thought they'd cure me by giving me the faces of the destitute to console me and the minds of the ignorant to entertain me. And the tenements to drink tea in. Have you any idea, Father, how many tenements there are in this gracious city?'

'Too many, Father, I realise that.'

'Too many is a generalisation which is good enough for the pious horror one expresses in the pulpit. There are almost six thousand of them and they accommodate about eighty-seven thousand people. I have lived in the centre of that cesspool for thirty years.'

Father Giffley sat on the edge of the table and gave a smile which was a spontaneous flash of triumph.

'I have at least been able to minister to them without feelings of pious condescension.'

'Are you suggesting that I . . .'

'I am drawing your attention to a possibility and reminding you that your office is to serve all equally, right down to the most illiterate poor gawm at my altar rails.'

Father Giffley, having used the possessive pronoun with intent, rose and banged the bell, summoning the housekeeper to clear the table.

'That is all I wanted to see you about.'

He went to the window and transferred his interest to the railway signals.

At four in the afternoon a new night had almost begun. The sky outside the bedroom which Fitz was sharing with Pat Bannister was already dark. In the half-light Fitz saw Pat's shoulder above the bedclothes. He got up and shook him.

'Four o'clock.'

Pat squinted at him and realised the significance of what he had said.

88

'Thanks be to God,' he answered, throwing back the clothes, 'we've a few bob to collect.'

They went down to the foundry and found Hennessy and Farrell at the gate. There had been an argument. They had been paid at sixpence an hour. Mulhall was in the office demanding ninepence. Pat went to the pay office and was given six shillings for his twelve-hour stretch. Fitz, being on the regular payroll, was not due to draw his wages until the following day.

'Overtime rate will be paid to our regular men,' the pay clerk assured him, 'it's only the casuals who are in dispute.'

'Our agreement is ninepence,' Mulhall said.

'I've already been into that,' the pay clerk answered.

'So has Jim Larkin,' Mulhall said. 'He negotiated ninepence. I'm going to report this.'

'You mustn't threaten me with Mr. Larkin. We have nothing to say to him.'

'Maybe he'll have something to say to you,' Mulhall said. Then he took the six shillings which the clerk had already set before him and walked out.

'What about a drink?' Pat suggested while they were still arguing at the gate.

'Not for me,' Farrell said.

Fitz said : 'Come on. I owe you money.'

'What about you?' Pat said to Mulhall.

'I was thinking of reporting to Larkin . . .' Mulhall said, tempted.

'Have a jar and then report to him.'

'Larkin hates the smell of drink,' Pat said. 'He told me once I'd live to see the grass growing over the ruins of Guinness's Brewery.'

The thought seemed to depress Hennessy.

A little drink is no more than our modest due, gentlemen,' he urged.

They went together, striding purposefully along the tram-rattling streets, conscious of the fact that they had money enough for once to meet the needs of the occasion. Only Hennessy lagged behind.

'Gentlemen,' he said, 'have a little mercy on a man with a rheumaticky back.' They slowed down and he joined them again. Mulhall guffawed and said:

'If you left the woman alone now and then you'd find the walking easier.'

'It's the only amusement available to the penniless,' Hennessy said good-humouredly.

As they turned off the main street Fitz slipped some money to Farrell so that he would not be embarrassed when his turn came to buy a drink. They walked between tall decaying houses. Candlelight and lamplight predominated in the tenement windows, with here and there a gas mantle distinguishable by its whiter glow. A lamplighter just ahead of them went methodically about his work, reaching upwards with his long, light cane and leaving a glowing chain of lamps in his wake. The iron railings which bordered the houses took on a wet sheen. Fitz watched him. The lighting of lamps always fascinated him. He said generally:

'When I was a youngster I always wanted to be a lamplighter.'

'Does he work for the Gas Company?' Pat asked.

'No, the Corporation,' Hennessy answered knowledgeably. 'It's a pensionable job. He nearly lost it once.'

'Who is he?' Mulhall asked.

'Baggy Conlon,' Hennessy supplied. 'He's very fond of a sup and one night after he lit the lamps he went into a pub and fell into company. After a few hours he got stupid drunk and forgot he was after lighting the lamps already. He kept saying he had his work to do and they mustn't detain him. At last when he came out and saw the lamps were lighted he gets the mistaken notion that it's putting them out he should be. So off he starts and has half the bloody city in darkness before he's arrested on a charge of public mischief.'

Then they turned into Cotter's public house and called for hot whiskeys.

The rags and the beard arrested Father O'Connor's attention. The travelling sack and the cord about the waist reminded him of pictures of pilgrims in some childhood book. He touched Rashers on the shoulder. Rashers, absorbed in his search of the large ashbin, straightened slowly and looked around. When he saw it was a priest he raised his hat. Father O'Connor fumbled in his pocket and gave him a shilling.

'The blessings of God and His Holy Mother on you,' Rashers said.

'And on you,' Father O'Connor returned.

He looked down the street. The public clock told him it was a little early for his return to St. Brigid's, so he lingered.

'Did you salvage anything of value,' he asked, 'a piece of clothing, perhaps?'

'Not in this lot,' Rashers said. 'I wouldn't be looking here for clothes.'

'Not . . . food?' Father O'Connor asked, the thought upsetting him.

'Sometimes you'd find food,' Rashers said, 'but very seldom.'

'And why not?'

Father O'Connor's dullness of imagination shocked Rashers, but the shilling claimed indulgence.

'Because this is a theatrical bin,' Rashers explained. For a moment Father O'Connor was lost. Then he realised that the windowless side wall behind him belonged to the Royal Theatre and, presumably, the bin was an extra-mural property.

'I understand,' he said, looking skywards, so as to hide his smile.

The grey sky, unsmiling, looked back at him. It was only the merest strip above the narrow street, yet it was big enough to contain all the despair of the winter city. Father O'Connor lowered his eyes quickly. The sky, the long, wet, unrelieved wall, the cramped street, the forsaken cobbles, they combined about this ragged figure and turned him suddenly into a denial of God. Should a man smell of filth and scrape in bins?

He said, 'And what has a theatrical bin to offer?'

'Cigars and cigarette butts, half smoked at the intervals,' Rashers said. 'They light them up and the bell goes and they throw them half finished away. There's good smoking in a theatrical bin.' He dug into his pockets.

'There's a sample collection,' he said, displaying his goods.

Father O'Connor pretended interest. He felt the muscles about his mouth tightening and turned his head quickly. Perhaps Father Giffley was right. Perhaps he should not look too closely at things until he had learned the trick of controlling his face.

'You did well,' he said.

'I did better, Father,' Rashers added. He fumbled and displayed another find.

'What's that?' Father O'Connor asked.

'It's a broken 'cello string,' Rashers said, 'which is a class of musical instrument.'

Yearling came to mind, smelling of whiskey and with red cheeks. Father O'Connor thought of conversation and smiling, well-mannered people. He tried to dismiss them. It was a world he had turned his back on.

'Is it useful?' he asked.

Rashers extended the string to its full length.

'That's the best cure for rheumatism in the land,' he said. 'I know many a carter will give me twopence for it. Have a look at it.'

But Father O'Connor moved a pace away, declining. The string had come from a dustbin and the hands which offered it for scrutiny were filthy. Rashers, noting the refusal, continued:

'The carter humps thirty-five tons of coal a week, up and down stairs, in every weather. After a while he gets a dose of rheumatism from the wet sacks. And the only good cure for it is to tie a 'cello string around your waist, right against the skin.'

An older man might have smiled. Father O'Connor did not.

'They should have more sense,' he said reprovingly.

'It's some virtue in the gut,' Rashers explained. 'It's not there when it's new, but when the sweat of the fingers has soaked into it it has the power to draw out the poison. That's why only used strings is any use.'

'Nonsense,' Father O'Connor said. Rashers said nothing. But he took care putting the string back in his pocket. The wind caught the two of them, fluttering Rashers' coat and causing Father O'Connor to grasp at his hat.

'We'll both have rheumatism if we stand here,' Father O'Connor said. Rashers, realising he was being dismissed, touched his forehead and shuffled away.

Father O'Connor went in the direction of the main thorough-fare, distressed by the poverty which reached out to him from every side, and wondering again what he could do to relieve those who suffered it. The obvious thing was to form a charit-able society. Father Giffley had never done so—why, it was hard to understand. Furthermore, Father Giffley would be hard to approach. It would be necessary to beg permission.

That consideration, he determined, must not stop him. He must not let human pride undermine him; he must suffer re-buffs in a spirit of complete humility. But he would need advice and counsel. It occurred to Father O'Connor that the Bradshaws could help him. He considered the problem carefully, weighing his resolve to keep away from comfort and gracious company against his need for guidance and help, a little fearful as he wrestled with it that he might be merely seeking a justification for a visit that was bound to be refreshing and enjoyable. Father O'Connor walked and thought for some time until at last, al-most without knowing how it happened, he found himself sit-ting in the Kingstown tram.

'About our ninepence an hour,' Mulhall said, as they were having their second drink.

'Carrington says you can do nothing,' Fitz said.

'Neither can we,' Farrell said. 'We don't work for the foundry. They have us by the short hairs.'

'I have an idea,' Mulhall said quietly. 'They tried it in Bel-fast.'

'I wouldn't be gone on anything they try in Belfast,' Hen-nessy said.

The hot whiskey had brought a glow to his cheeks. His eyes were brighter. They searched the public house as he spoke, a pair of magpie eyes that gathered all the scraps and gossip of living.

'I heard tell of a raffle someone ran once,' Hennessy explained. 'The first prize was a week's holiday in Belfast. And do you know what the second prize was?'

He paused long enough to fix their attention. Then he said:

'The second prize was two weeks' holiday in Belfast.' They laughed, all except Farrell, who said to Mulhall:

'How do you propose to get the ninepence out of them.'

'This way. The foundry crowd take coal from Doggett & Co. Very well. The next time I'm told to deliver to the foundry, I'll refuse.'

'What good will that do?' Hennessy asked. 'They'll only sack you.'

'Not if everyone else in Doggett & Co. stand by me.'

'They could get it from us,' Pat said.

'Not if the Nolan & Keyes men do the same thing,' Mulhall said.

They thought over this. It sounded impracticable at first, but gradually its possibilities suggested themselves.

'You stand by us—we stand by you?' Pat said. He was beginning to consider the idea.

'Simple,' Mulhall said.

'Suppose they sack someone,' Pat offered. 'Suppose a carter is told to deliver and he refuses and he's sacked. What then?'

'Everybody downs tools,' Mulhall said.

'We get some of the coal direct from our own boats in the foundry,' Fitz pointed out.

'When they start doing that we'll call on your fellows not to unload,' Mulhall said.

'You'd have the whole bloody city tied up in a week, at that rate,' Pat put in, worried.

'Why not?' Mulhall urged. 'That's what they did in Belfast.'

'For three shillings?' Hennessy asked, sceptical.

Farrell banged the table suddenly and roared at him.

'For principle.'

His face had become thunderous. Hennessy shrank back.

'No offence,' he said, in a startled voice.

'That's what's wrong with this city,' Farrell said. 'There isn't a man of principle in it. I was steady on the quays until I refused to buy the stevedore a drink when he brought us into his brother's pub to pay us. And I haven't got a job on the quays since.'

Fitz put his hand on Farrell's shoulder.

'What Hennessy says makes sense,' he said. 'The issue is only three shillings for about twelve hands. No union would tie up a whole dockside for that.'

'Larkin would. We have an agreement,' Mulhall insisted.

'With the carting firms, but not with the foundry.'

'Larkin fixed the carters' rate. It applies to everybody.'

'Larkin might risk tying up the docks the way you suggest,' Fitz said, 'but Sexton and the British Executive won't. It's too costly.'

'If Larkin agrees to do it,' Mulhall said, 'I don't care a damn what the Executive says or thinks. And I'm going to see him about it tomorrow when we knock off.'

'I'll go with you,' Pat said.

'What about you?' Mulhall asked Fitz.

Pat said: 'Fitz can't. He's on shift work tomorrow.'

'You can tell him we'll stand by you if we're needed,' Fitz said, 'but it's mad.'

'That's the stuff,' Mulhall said, satisfied.

'What about you?' Pat asked Hennessy.

Hennessy sighed and said:

'The unfortunate fact is that I've never been in any job long enough to join a union.'

The voice of a singer drifted in through the closed doors, a hard yet tuneful sound, which distracted Mulhall's attention.

'I know who that is,' he said.

A shadow appeared on the glass, fumbled with the knob and shuffled in. It was Rashers. He blinked in the light. The dog beside him gave a short bark, recognising Mulhall before Rashers did.

'Are you looking for money or drink?' Mulhall asked.

'Either or both,' Rashers said, agreeably.

The damp air had condensed on his beard and made his rags

smell. Mulhall introduced him and invited him to sit down. Rashers did so gratefully.

'What brings you round this way?' Hennessy asked.

'Money or drink,' Rashers said. Mulhall bought a pint for him and Rashers shook sawdust from a saucer spittoon and poured some of the drink into it for the dog. The dog lapped greedily. Rashers drank to the company.

'Here's my special blessing to you,' he said.

'Take the porter but keep the blessing,' Mulhall said. 'God knows what way a blessing from Rashers Tierney would work.'

'Have the blessing,' Rashers said, 'There's great virtue in it today.' He put his pint down and addressed them generally.

'I had the height of luck today. A young clergyman gave me a shilling. So I had a feed of soup and spuds in the St. Francis Dining Hall and a cup of cocoa with a cut of bread. I could hardly waddle from there to here.'

He fumbled under his coat.

'Any one of you gentlemen want to see today's paper?'

Hennessy held out his hand.

'Where did you get that?'

'In one of the bins.'

'It's escaped the weather,' Hennessy said, turning over the pages critically and noting that they were crisp and dry.

'This was a very classy kind of bin, with a lid on it. And so big you'd be able to take shelter from the rain in it. That's what I said to the priest who gave me the shilling.'

Hennessy, who had put on his spectacles, now lowered the paper and said to the company:

'It says here there's a thousand pounds reward for anyone who gives information or finds the Crown Jewels.'

Mulhall said:

'Now we know why Rashers spends his days looking in dustbins.'

'I'll give you another bit of information to save you the trouble of reading it,' Rashers said. 'There'll be no more paying in pubs.'

He found he had drawn the full attention of the company. Hennessy lowered the paper; Mulhall put down his drink;

Fitz looked first at Rashers and then at Farrell. Farrell leaned across the table.

'What was that?' he asked.

Surprised at the interest he had aroused, Rashers explained.

'The shipowners agreed with Larkin last night to bar the stevedores from paying the dockers in public houses.'

Everybody looked at Farrell.

'You ought to slip down to the hall,' Mulhall said.

'I'd do it right away,' Pat urged.

There was a great happiness in Mulhall's face. He had not expected that the belief he expressed in Larkin would be so quickly justified. Farrell rose uncertainly.

'If you'll excuse me . . .' he began.

He was torn between the importance of the news and the fact that he was proposing to leave before taking his turn to buy the company a drink.

'Go on,' Fitz urged, 'don't be standing on ceremony.'

Farrell went, and Rashers, staring after him and scratching his head, asked:

'What the hell have I done on your friend?'

'You've earned your pint, Rashers,' Mulhall answered.

Fitz smiled. He, too, felt the stirring of a new, slightly incredulous hope.

Hennessy and Rashers were the last to leave. They were both unsteady. At Chandlers Court Rashers sat down on the wet steps, cleared his throat and began to sing. Hennessy remembered his wife.

'For God's sake—stop it,' he appealed.

'All right,' Rashers agreed, 'but sit down beside me and we'll have a chat.'

'I daren't—not with this rheumatism.'

'I've offered you the cure.'

'I'm not giving you tuppence. I've spent more than enough already.'

'Please yourself. There's many a carter will be glad to get a good 'cello string for tuppence.' A thought struck Rashers.

'Who was the young fellow that was with us?'

'The dark young fellow?'

'Certainly,' Rashers said.

'Fitzpatrick. He's thinking of tying the knot.'

'Ah. Getting married. It's a contagious notion between two opposites.'

'He works in the foundry.'

'He stood me a pint, so God give him luck.'

'And do you know where he hopes to live?'

'Tell me.'

Hennessy jerked his thumb over his shoulder at the hall of 3 Chandlers Court. Rashers looked unbelieving.

'No,' he challenged.

'When the Kennys move out.'

This was news to Rashers.

'They're off to America in a fortnight. I'd like to go myself.' Another thought struck him.

'Suppose you found the Crown Jewels or something—would you go to America?'

'I'd often a wish to go to France.'

'The French have a queer way of living,' Rashers said. 'Very immoral, by all accounts.'

'I'd like to see the vineyards.'

'Isn't porter good enough for you?'

'It's the grapes. Lovely green clusters.'

'Some of them is black.'

'Did you ever taste grapes?'

'Every morning at breakfast,' Rashers said, putting on a grand accent, 'and twice of a Sunday.'

'Grapes is the loveliest things you ever tasted,' Hennessy said.

'Wasn't I reared on them,' Rashers insisted.

'I worked on a job in a kitchen in Merrion Square,' Hennessy explained, 'and the oul wan there was never done eating grapes. For a fortnight I had grapes every day because I used to lift a few off the table. I've always had a wish for grapes since then.'

'Were they black or green?'

'Black.'

'Them is for invalids,' Rashers said, knowledgeably.

'I'd better go up,' Hennessy said.

But Rashers was in a mood for conversation.

'Sit down, can't you,' he appealed.

'I wouldn't risk it. The pain in me back is desperate.'

Rashers fumbled under his coat and took out the 'cello string. He screwed up his face until the beard covered it completely and said in sudden love of all mankind:

'Here, you can have it.'

'I couldn't take it,' Hennessy said.

'Amn't I offering it to you for nothing.'

'No. I couldn't deprive you.'

Rashers cursed violently.

'You're a contrairy bloody man,' he shouted. 'I proffered it to you for tuppence and you wouldn't venture the money. Then I offer it to you for nothing, for the sake of neighbourliness and friendship, and begod, you say you couldn't take it. Have you rheumatism at all?'

Hennessy looked behind nervously.

'Keep your voice down,' he pleaded.

'If you didn't eat so many bloody grapes,' Rashers said loudly, 'you wouldn't have rheumatism.'

Hennessy panicked and said:

'All right. I'll sit down to please you.'

The steps felt wet. After a while Hennessy shivered and drew his coat about him with his hands. They sat talking in low voices, Hennessy to sober up a little before facing his wife, Rashers because it was hardly less comfortable than his room and had the advantage of company of a kind. The dog sat with them too, its head turning from one side to the other as occasional footsteps approached and passed.

'The first thing you'd do if you found the Crown Jewels is buy grapes, isn't that right?' Rashers asked.

'And go to France,' Hennessy agreed.

'The first thing I'd do is buy a tin whistle,' Rashers said, 'and stay where I bloody well am and play it.'

The belligerent note disappeared. His voice became gloomy. 'And it's not a lot to ask for, is it?' he added. They were silent. Then Rashers looked up into the rain at the darkness of the sky.

'Do you think Jesus Christ is up there?' he asked.

'And His blessed Mother,' Hennessy affirmed, touching his hat.

'Can he see us?'

'That's what the Penny Catechism says.'

'Through the rain?'

'I don't think the rain makes any difference.'

They rose and faced the hallway. Above their heads all the windows, spaced out evenly in the flat face of the tenement, showed their late lamps. As they moved forward the dog stiffened and barked. They looked around. A tall figure approached, paused to pet the dog and said:

'Good night, men.'

Each said good night in turn. The man passed on. Hennessy, his magpie eyes alight with information once again, gazed after the retreating figure. Then he turned to Rashers.

'Do you know who that was?'

'He was polite, anyway,' Rashers said, pleased about the dog.

'It was Jim Larkin,' Hennessy said, delighted that he had so easily identified someone who was becoming the talk of Dublin.

CHAPTER 6

THE city faced the winter as best it could. It had its days of good weather, the freakish out-of-season days that always came to surprise it, as though a piece of summer had fallen from heaven out of its turn, days when the gulls looked whiter and the river wore a blue, chilled sparkle.

It was on such a day that Fitz took Mary to view the flat in Chandlers Court. He was uncertain how she would take it. She had hoped so much for a place of their own. But she realised it was best to make definite plans as soon as possible. Her own small capital was almost exhausted.

The hallway, even on so good a morning, looked grim enough. The staircase and the worn steps sagged and creaked as they climbed. But the rooms themselves were better. A large window overlooking the street gave glimpses of the mountains, now blue and bare, and admitted plenty of sunlight. Children at play in the street made sounds that were happy and tolerably distant. The large fireplace, with its marble surround left over from better days, gave plenty of room for cooking. A bedroom and a kitchenette completed the flat which, at four shillings and threepence a week was dearer, but then bigger, than average. The Kennys would be leaving in a week. When they reached the street again Mary said:

'Well, what do you think?'

'It suits me.'

She tightened her arm on his and said: 'It's a nice room but I wonder about the house.'

'The people across the landing are all right.'

'And above?'

'I wouldn't know.'

Mary considered. Then she said: 'Let's take it, Fitz.'

'Good,' he said, 'we'll take it next week.'

'How can we do that?'

'I can move in with Pat,' Fitz said.

'Won't he mind?'

'I don't think so. It's a bit dearer, but he isn't happy about the place we're in.'

Joe Somerville was with Pat when Fitz made the suggestion. Pat had lit the fire and was drying a pair of drawers.

'It's a dearer room,' Fitz said, 'but I'll stand the extra.'

'Why don't you move in with the girl right away?' Pat asked.

Fitz smiled and said: 'Some people regard that as immoral.'

'It wouldn't deter me,' Pat said.

'We all know your tastes in the matter,' Joe said sourly.

'What do you mean?'

'Down in Mabbot Street with Lily Maxwell.'

'It isn't in Mabbot Street.'

'Then wherever it is. Fitz thinks more of himself than that.'

'I don't see what's wrong with Lily Maxwell.'

'Visiting the kip shops,' Joe said, 'When you get a skinful.'

'It's a very natural class of an occupation.'

'It's not Christian,' Joe said.

'I've never laid claim to being a Christian,' Pat said, in a reasonable tone.

The steam from the drawers rose about his wrists and face and upwards towards the oil lamp on the box beside him.

'You'll crack the funnel of the lamp!' Joe shouted.

He was low-sized and squat and worked for Nolan & Keyes with Pat. Pat moved the lamp back.

'As a socialist,' he explained, 'I don't regard marriage as necessary.'

'The union of decent Christians has to be blessed by a priest,' Joe insisted.

'Who blessed the union of Adam and Eve, then,' Pat asked. 'Don't tell me there was a priest.'

'God did.'

'Very well,' Pat said, 'let Fitz ask God to bless the union and go ahead. It won't do any harm, and he'll save a few bob.'

'It was all right for Adam and Eve,' Joe said, 'but now the Church has the sacrament of marriage.'

'A class of modern convenience,' Pat said, 'like the electric tram. If you want to know, it was the capitalists who invented marriage in order to protect the laws of inheritance.'

'You're too bitter altogether against religion,' Joe said.

'Maybe you'd have me like Keever, asking the office clerk to give him the stamps to save for the black babies.'

'I suppose if he was collecting stamps for Karl Marx he'd be a hero,' Joe snarled.

'I'd be satisfied for a start if he began paying his subscription to the union.'

'He's only trying to help the missionaries.'

'The missionaries do more harm than good.'

Exasperated, Joe appealed to Fitz.

'There's not a charitable drop in him,' he accused.

'Charity begins with my own class,' Pat insisted.

'And isn't Keever your own class?' Joe shouted.

'No,' Pat shouted back. 'Because he's against us. He that is not with me is against me.'

'Now he has the bloody nerve to quote the Bible at me,' Joe protested.

Fitz said: 'For God's sake stop talking like a pair of public meetings.'

They both glared at each other in silence.

'I'm getting married at Easter,' Fitz said, 'and I'm asking if you'll move in with me so that I can hold on to the flat when it's left empty. If you don't want to do that, say so.'

'Of course I'll move in with you,' Pat said, 'if you haven't got the courage to go against the institutions of capitalist society.'

'I haven't. Does that satisfy you?'

'It doesn't,' Pat said, 'but I'll have to put up with it, I suppose.'

He felt the drawers and judged them to be dried out enough to hang on a line that stretched from the bedpost to the corner of the fireplace. He drew the legs down so that they hung at full length.

'They're nearly as holy as Keever himself,' he remarked.

Joe opened his mouth but had to close it again. He could think of nothing to say.

Winter took a heavy toll of life in the parish of St. Brigid, where the old succumbed to the usual diseases. Parish duties kept Father O'Connor busy. People asked for the priest, were anointed, and left the overcrowded rooms for whatever place God and their way of living had prepared for them. He found the dirt and the poverty hard to get used to. Even the room he slept in joined forces with the weather and fell in league with the district that surrounded it. There were damp spots on the wall and damp patches on the painting of Our Lady of Sorrows. When the window was open the noise of trains and traffic was unbearable; when it was closed the room became musty and unpleasant. The iron-framed bed was a double one, unpriestly and lonely. Father Giffley continued to be boorish and unfriendly.

'A charitable society,' he repeated, 'I am more interested in your finding me another boilerman.'

The boilerman who had tended the unreliable contraption which heated the water system for the church, had been one of the winter's victims. His body was due to arrive at the church that evening.

Father O'Connor said: 'I have been enquiring about a deserving case.'

'You want a charitable society,' Father Giffley said with a snort, 'yet you are unable to find a deserving case.'

'The poor man is only dead two days.'

'Throw a stone from any window in the parish of St. Brigid. You're bound to hit a hungry wretch.'

'He must be trustworthy.'

'For ten shillings a week—impossible.'

'I'll do my best,' Father O'Connor submitted. If his superior did his share of the duties there might be more time to attend to the matter he was complaining of. Father O'Connor resisted the temptation to say so.

'Hanlon was a gentle poor old dodderer,' Father Giffley brooded.

'His chest was bad, I understand.'

'He didn't die of a surfeit of piety, anyway, the poor soul.'

'His language was sometimes objectionable.'

Father Giffley was surprisingly tolerant. 'It's their physic against ill health,' he said. 'As for charitable societies—charity in this parish must remain the monopoly of the Protestants. They have the money. We haven't.'

'We lost a family to them last week,' Father O'Connor said, using an argument that Father Giffley, he felt certain, could not dare to ignore. But his superior took it as a necessary part of the pattern.

'A bowl of soup, a hot bath—and then they wash them in the Blood of the Lamb,' he said. 'Do you know, I've heard them singing in the streets a thing that goes: "Yes, we shall gather at the River". Grown adults warbling about gathering at the river is beyond me.'

'I think the river is figurative, representing the flow of grace . . .'

Father Giffley sat upright.

'Do I need explanations of what is obvious and elementary?' He left down his whiskey glass.

'What family has apostasised?'

The word startled Father O'Connor. It fell into the room with an evil and terrible sound.

'People named Conlan. Keever, one of my confraternity men, told me. I've tried to trace them but they seem to have moved into another parish.'

'They always do,' Father Giffley said.

'It happens often, then . . . ?'

'No, not often. Our parishioners keep the Faith. It is the only thing most of them have.'

'That is why I am anxious to start some kind of relief fund.'

'Without money?'

'The ladies of the parish . . .'

'There are no ladies in the parish of St. Brigid; except, of course, a few ladies of light virtue. And even they find it difficult to live.'

'I was going to say—the ladies of the parish of Kingstown. Some of them are very interested.'

'Have you asked them?'

'I have described the conditions here. They seemed anxious to help.'

Father Giffley looked at the young man for some time, his eyes reflective, his cheeks veined and swollen. He hated the fair hair and pale, unlined face. He hated the humble manner and the bowed head, the zeal for good works which he was convinced was an outlet for a strange form of snobbery. Father Giffley, while his junior waited patiently for a decision, let his mind wander through the parish he had spent so many lonely years in. He hated it too, and made no effort to do otherwise. In his own way he pitied the people. He had no contempt for them. It was not their fault that they were born into poverty or that the rooms they inhabited were overcrowded. The filth they lived in was unavoidable. And this self-centred young fool wanted to scratch at the surface.

Father Giffley said :

'Some form of relief fund? Very well. You have my permission, Father.'

He held up his glass and regarded it through half-closed eyes. There would be words of gratitude.

'I am deeply grateful, Father.'

That was the phrase Father Giffley had anticipated. He smiled at his glass, as though it, too, had guessed aright.

'When will you start?'

'At the earliest moment . . . with your permission?'

There it was again. Deeply grateful. With your permission.

'Do you think, Father, that the widow who gave her mite may have had it from the ladies of Kingstown?'

Father O'Connor flushed. He did not know what his superior meant, except that he intended to be insulting.

'I don't know what you mean, Father.'

He was embarrassed and unhappy.

'Your charitable efforts will be a cover for hypocrisy, because you know you can do nothing for these people by throwing them a blanket or giving them a hot meal.'

'A family left our church for that.'

'You see. You are worried exclusively about souls, Father. You must worry now and then about human beings. Ask the ladies of Kingstown and their husbands to give back what they have taken.'

Father Giffley began to laugh. It was not the sort of laughter that was meant to be shared. Father O'Connor remained silent. The fact that one of his cloth should be a drunkard distressed him unbearably. He looked pointedly at the clock.

'I have the funeral to receive,' he said. He rose.

Father Giffley fixed his eyes on the young, hurt, disapproving face.

'Let me tell you something before you leave,' he said, in a kindlier tone. 'It may help you—it may not.' Father O'Connor sat down again.

'You have seen a Mrs. Bartley from time to time?'

Father O'Connor had. Before first mass, or very late at night, he had seen her on her knees, scrubbing the floors, scraping candle-grease from the sanctuary carpet with the broken blade of a knife. She was one of a number of casual cleaners.

'Mrs. Bartley had a child who was very ill once. He was on the point of death,' Father Giffley continued. 'I sat in her room throughout the whole of a winter's night and watched the child. I don't know why I did it. I prayed some of the time. Some of the time I wiped the sweat from the child's forehead. The woman sat with me and so did the father. She made tea for me throughout the night, but they spoke to me hardly at all. They had never heard before of a priest sitting all night with a child. When I left in the morning the child had not died. He was sleeping easily and by the next day it was obvious that he was going to live.'

Father Giffley sighed and added:

'For some months I was highly edified by my priestly conduct. Mrs. Bartley believed there had been a miracle. In fact she is probably the only parishioner who, whenever she salutes this poor, drunken oddity, feels she is in the presence of a saint. You see—she thinks I have a harmless fondness for peppermints.'

'Father . . . please.'

'And, oddly enough, I should not like her to learn the truth.'

'You feel there was a miracle?'

'The child? No. But in me there was. For one isolated night I had found the true disposition, so that even if the child had died they would still have drawn comfort and peace from me.'

'It was a privileged experience.'

'Your ladies of Kingstown will never teach you how to find it. They'll do worse. They'll draw you away, into self-satisfied almsgiving. But if you can find it for yourself you will be the comforter of the destitute, even when your pocket and your belly are as empty as theirs.'

Father O'Connor hardly knew what to say. He looked at the purple-veined face, the bulging eyes, the strong nose with the sprouting hairs marking each nostril. This heavy-breathing boor was trying to show him the road to sanctity. At last he said :

'I appreciate what you have told me.'

'It is the only piece of truth I have ever learned,' Father Giffley said.

Father O'Connor guessed he was being challenged. If so, organising charity was an excellent beginning. Some of the poor, at least, could be fed. Not them all, because there were too many. One started with the most deserving. And, of course, with those who seemed tempted to apostasise, even though the apostate could never be said to be deserving.

'I will give thought to what you've told me, Father,' he said.

In the presbytery the clerk had Father O'Connor's black cape and biretta laid out for him and beside it the brass bowl and the sprinkler for the holy water. He was rubbing his hands with the cold. Hanlon's labours, though inefficient at the best of times, were missed. The boilerman was dead, and the pipes out of action. A damp cold had gripped every part of the church.

'He went off very sudden, Father,' the clerk said.

'He did, poor man.'

'The oul chest was very poorly,' the clerk said. Father

O'Connor took the book and marked the appropriate section with a purple-coloured tab. He did not answer the clerk. Recognising that the priest had no desire to talk about the dead boilerman, the clerk turned to business.

'There are two people in the outer room wishing to see you,' he said.

'They must wait,' Father O'Connor told him.

He vested reluctantly and went down the church to the porchway, where he paused and saw that the funeral had arrived and was marshalled on the far side of the street. In the light of the gas-lamps the leading horses waited, their black plumes stiff and upright. On each side of the hearse a candle flame wavered in its little glass tomb. Behind stood the mourners: the women with shawls over their heads, the men—now that the church door had been reached—uncovered. Traffic passed slowly to show respect and stopped on either side when the hearse and followers began to cross the street. They held the coffin at the church door while Father O'Connor, about to admit it, sprinkled it with holy water, welcoming what was left of Hanlon back to the church he had spent some winters working in. Under his aloft hand the fittings became marked with blobs of holy water. The leading women began to weep loudly. One of the men, grey-haired and shabby, nodded a greeting to Father O'Connor, who did not know him but placed him as a brother of Hanlon's because there was a clear resemblance. Without acknowledging him Father O'Connor turned and walked down the echoing church. It amplified the sounds of grief and the sharp contact of boots on marble. In the mortuary chapel he stood at the head of the coffin once again and read the prayers, four candles in front of him. The people were poor, yet the coffin was a good one. It was a point of honour with them to bury their dead decently. He led them in a decade of the rosary, his voice unhurried but efficient, his mind quite detached from his surroundings. He found it impossible to feel anything about his congregation. Here, in a shadowed chapel, dismal with cold, where the air was unpleasant because of the corpse and the close-packed mourners, another one of the obscure thousands was poised between the anonymity of his life and the anonymity of the grave. Day after day he said the same prayers and went through the same ceremonial. There were particular deaths no longer, only Death in general.

He concluded and was approached by the grey-haired man.

'I was his brother,' he said in a whisper. Father O'Connor realised that he expected formal sympathy.

'I see,' Father O'Connor said. He handed the sprinkler back to the clerk.

'Good evening, Andy,' the man said to the clerk.

'I'm sorry for your trouble, Pat,' the clerk said.

'You were a good friend, Andy.'

Father O'Connor took the man's hand.

'I will pray for your brother at my masses,' he said.

'Thank you, Father, you're very kind.'

It seemed to be enough. The grip on Father O'Connor's hand tightened for a moment and was withdrawn. He returned to the sacristy.

Father O'Connor unvested. There was a void inside him, as though Jesus Christ himself were a lie and there was no Church, no Belief, nothing but the dominion of darkness and mortality. He wondered that he should want to help anybody, least of all the poor. They came carrying their stinking corpses to be blessed and despatched. They were uncouth and ill-clad and rough of tongue. They had faces and forms that were half animal. The clerk whispered:

'The two people is still inside, Father. A young couple. They want to arrange to get married.'

To get married. To sleep in the sweat of one bed and deposit in due time a few more animal faces among the dirt and the dilapidation.

'They must wait,' Father O'Connor snapped, and turned away.

He felt he must clean himself, change his clothes, wash. He thought of his mother and ached for her presence, for her comforting voice and lovable fingers. Taking the Galway rosary from his pocket, he went to the prieu-dieu and knelt for a long time, not so much in prayer as in thought, his mind reliving what remained with him of childhood, the favourite memories he had guarded passionately against annihilation. They helped as they always did.

The clerk, returning, found him still on his knees and was about to withdraw again when Father O'Connor rose and said in a voice which betrayed his tiredness:

'Please tell the two people I am coming.'

'It won't be necessary now,' the clerk said, 'Father Giffley is already with them.'

'I thought Father Giffley was in his room.'

'He came down a while ago and found them waiting. He said he would deal with it.'

'Thank you,' Father O'Connor said, wondering bitterly if Father Giffley was in a condition to talk to anybody. He decided he did not care, and went out again to the church, where he stood for some time in the mortuary chapel. The coffin plate bore the name 'Edward Hanlon' and was still damp from the sprinkler. The Christian name looked out of place. It had never been used when Hanlon was referred to about the church. The shrine in front of the small altar was ablaze with candles, which the mourners had lit before leaving. For each candle a halfpenny had been dropped into the donation box, a small sum which called, nevertheless, for self-sacrifice. They made an occasion of death, giving it its due in candles and coffins.

At the high altar he tried to pray again, but still the emptiness dragged at him, his feeling of depression and purposelessness increased. He abandoned the attempt after a while and moved down the almost empty church to the porchway, where he clasped his hands behind his back and stared dismally at the traffic. His immediate need, he knew, was companionship. In Kingstown he could have muffled up and walked briskly between rows of elegant houses to the seafront, where one could pace away depression and the air was always fresh and invigorating. He could have called on one of his parishioners and spent an hour or so in pleasant conversation. There was no one to talk to in that way here.

A voice beside him said: 'Good evening, Father.'

It was Rashers Tierney. He was about to let him pass with a formal nod when an idea occurred to him.

'Just a moment,' he said.

Rashers, who had put on his hat in the porch, removed it again. Father O'Connor took in the shabby clothes and the hungry-looking face. Why not? Surely here was a deserving case, a poorer one than the poor themselves.

'Have you been in the church?'

'I showed a young couple the way to the presbytery. Then I went in to say a prayer or two for the late lamented.'

'You knew Hanlon?'

'A decent poor skin,' Rashers said.

'Could you do his work?'

'Stoking a little bit of a boiler wouldn't be beyond me, Father. Sure what's in it?'

'If you are free tomorrow call to me after the eight o'clock mass. I'll give you a week's trial.'

'As boilerman?' Rashers asked, not sure that he understood aright.

'As temporary boilerman,' Father O'Connor qualified.

He went back into the church. He was satisfied to feel he would be able to tell Father Giffley that he had engaged a boilerman. If the fellow proved unsuitable he could be easily replaced. It was one duty disposed of for the moment. Still restless, he climbed the side stairs to the organ loft. Below him the pews, divided into geometrical sections by the centre and side aisles, moved in rows to the altar rails. Above them in its funnel of red glass, the sanctuary lamp displayed its tiny flame. Father O'Connor sat on the stool at the large harmonium which did service instead of an organ and leaned his elbows on the manual. The keys were yellow and cracked, like practically everything else in St. Brigid's. When he rested his foot on one of the foot pumps a thin note sounded. He sat upright, startled. Realising that one of the keys must be stuck he made a laborious search in the half-dark of the gallery until he found it. He prised it gently back into position with his fingernail until the sound stopped. Then he pumped with his feet and pressed the note again. This time it released when he removed the pressure of his finger. He pressed it again, listened, built a chord on it, moved to a related chord and completed a phrase which reminded him of the

'Ave Verum'. He began to play it, softly at first and then, as the music engaged him, more loudly and purposefully. He switched to a secular tune and then to a march by Handel which he remembered from his student days. It filled the church with a cracked and wheezy grandeur, so that the three or four of the faithful scattered in the pews below turned their heads and looked up. Father O'Connor played for some time, until the gallery door opened and the clerk stood waiting for his attention.

'What is it now?' Father O'Connor said. The small mirror in front of him, used by the organist so that ceremonies could be followed without it being necessary to turn the head, reflected the rose-coloured sanctuary lamp and caught the effulgence of unseen shrine candles against a velvet darkness.

'It's Father Giffley. He wants to speak with you immediately.'

Wondering what piece of urgent unimportance his superior had fastened on this time, Father O'Connor accompanied the clerk to the vestry. He was in time to see the young couple as they left and recognised the girl immediately.

'Were they the callers about the marriage?' he asked the clerk.

'They are, Father.'

'I think I know what Father Giffley wants. Where is he?'

'He went back to the house.'

That was quite typical of Father Giffley, to send for a person and then expect to be followed to his rooms.

'I'll go immediately,' Father O'Connor said. He tried not to betray his annoyance.

He crossed the courtyard with its grimy Calvary set against the high stone wall and climbed the stairs. Father Giffley was entering details of something in a black book.

'You had one of my former parishioners with you I see,' Father O'Connor said.

'You recognised her?'

'She was a servant girl in the house of friends of mine—the Bradshaws.'

'What do you know about her?'

'She left her employment, presumably to take up with a young man.'

'The young man was with her. They explained to me.'

'I hope she is not in trouble. Mrs. Bradshaw would feel responsible.'

Father Giffley put down his pen and stared.

'You sometimes shock even me,' he said at last.

'I don't understand,' Father O'Connor protested.

'If the unfortunate girl is in trouble, as you term it, don't you think that her plight is more worthy of your sympathy than the delicacy of Mrs. Bradshaw's feelings.'

'That is not what I meant.'

'The girl is not in trouble, unless you consider wanting to get married to a decent young man a trouble.'

'I am sorry. I thought you might wish to question me about her background.'

'Don't be a fool,' Father Giffley said and returned to his writing.

Father O'Connor stared at the bowed head and struggled to control his temper. At last he said: 'You mustn't speak to me like that.'

Father Giffley looked up as though surprised to hear the voice and find someone still there.

'You must not speak to me as though I were a servant.'

'I see,' Father Giffley said. He laid his pen aside and folded his arms.

'And what are you—if not a servant?'

'I am a priest.'

'A priest. And what is a priest?'

'He is not to be spoken to like a dog,' Father O'Connor said.

'Are you questioning my authority?'

'Not your authority. Your manner. Your cruelty.'

'Do you wish to make a complaint?'

'Very much so.'

'Then make it to any quarter you think fit,' Father Giffley challenged. 'As for me, I will go on treating you as I feel you deserve.'

'You have no right to humiliate me.'

'I am trying to teach you that social disease cannot be cured with buns and cocoa. Until you condescend to live in the world of the parish you serve I will continue to chastise your pride.'

'I have made my protest,' Father O'Connor said, 'and I will leave it at that for the moment.'

He put his hand on the door handle and was about to leave when Father Giffley snapped: 'One moment, Father.'

He turned round.

'You have not yet heard what I wanted to speak to you about.'

'I am sorry,' Father O'Connor said, 'I thought you had finished.'

'You were playing on that foul instrument in the organ loft.'

'Is that forbidden too?' Father O'Connor asked bitterly.

'Tonight it was not fitting.'

'May I ask why not?'

'Any of my respected parishioners could tell you why not. The body of the poor boilerman who served us well is lying in the church. Was he too lowly to qualify for your respect?'

Father O'Connor's face changed.

'You had forgotten?' Father Giffley suggested.

Father O'Connor said nothing. He was trapped. It was true. He had forgotten.

'That is what I wanted to say,' Father Giffley concluded.

CHAPTER 7

O N Easter Tuesday evening Mary and Fitz moved into 3
Chandlers Court. Their feet on the unfamiliar stairs made
an echoing noise and they had to pick their way carefully
until a figure holding an oil lamp appeared on the landing above
them and addressed her for the first time as Mrs. Fitzpatrick.

'This is Mrs. Mulhall,' Fitz introduced.

'I've taken the liberty of laying down a bit of a fire,' Mrs.
Mulhall explained. 'I thought it would make the room cosy.'

The elderly woman before her looked quiet-natured and
good-hearted. There would be a new life, with new friends.

'You'll come over later?' Mary invited.

'For a little while,' Mrs. Mulhall agreed, 'when you're both
rested.'

The living room was bare except for a table, a cupboard,
some chairs and a long couch Fitz had bought and repaired in
his spare evenings.

They drew this over to the fire.

'It's a bit bare, isn't it?' Fitz said.

'It's home.'

They sat down. The fire in the half-light cast friendly
shadows. It was theirs, at least. There would be no more part-
ings, no more reluctant goodbyes, no more being the only person in the whole world. On impulse she kissed Fitz, surprising him. He knew something had moved her deeply and said:

'Why did you do that?'

'I thought of a lonely old woman.'

'Who?'

'Miss Gilchrist. I wonder if she is still with Mrs. Bradshaw.'

'What made you think of her?'

'Just before I left them she was sick and I often sat in front of the fire in her room. She told me to stick to service.'

'Why did she want you to do that?'

Mary smiled. 'I think she loved someone years and years ago. And because she never married she consoled herself that being in service in a good house was the best thing, after all.'

'Have you missed it?'

'What was there to miss?'

'Practically everything people fight each other for: good food and comfortable houses.'

Mary looked about her at the room.

'I think I like this place better.'

'The pay isn't quite so good,' Fitz said.

Mary smiled and said:

'The duties are lighter.'

'That's true. Not so much silver to be polished.'

'And the meals won't be such a problem.'

'No.'

'But I'll make up by brushing your clothes every morning.'

'That won't be much of a problem either.'

'Then I'll mend your broken socks.'

'That might take longer.'

'And answer the door.'

'That seems to settle everything.'

'You're satisfied?'

He took her in his arms.

'How long are you likely to stay?'

'Until I'm as old as Miss Gilchrist,' she answered.

After a while he released her and she rose, made a paper spill and began to light the lamp. He watched her. She removed the globe, trimmed the wick and touched it with the flame. Then she replaced the globe. He wondered, as she leaned over to set the lamp on the table, how often in the course of their life together she would go through the same routine. How often would he sit and admire without speaking her dark hair showing its lustre in the lamplight and worship her face that was fine-boned and beautiful. It made him sad to have so little to offer to her, to think even that little should be so insecure.

'Your friend Pat is comical,' he heard her saying. Fitz noticed that they had reversed moods and thought of the two figures on some novelty clocks he had seen in Moore Street. When one came out the other went in; he remembered from childhood that they were fine-weather-and-foul-weather-never-seen-to-gether.

'He has great heart,' he agreed.

Pat had acted as best man. He paid for a cab from the church to the Farrell's cottage and after breakfast he had pressed a sovereign into Fitz's hand. Fitz, wondering at his sudden wealth, guessed that he had had a stroke of unusually good luck at the horses. But he had found no opportunity to ask.

'Is he wild?' Mary asked.

'A bachelor and fancy free.'

'He seemed to have plenty of money.'

'It's some windfall or other,' Fitz said, 'most of the time he hasn't a cigarette.'

'He needs a woman's hand,' Mary said. 'You'd think he'd have a girl friend.'

'He has,' Fitz said. And then, as an afterthought he added, 'A sort of a one.'

'Who is she?'

'A girl named Lily Maxwell. When Pat knocks himself about in a spree he usually ends up in her room. She looks after him.'

At eight o'clock the Mulhalls arrived and by nine they had been joined by Mr. and Mrs. Farrell. Joe came later and later still Pat surprised them by arriving in presentable shape. He had a heavy parcel which he immediately deposited in a corner, and a bottle of whiskey which he pressed into Fitz's hands.

'There's my welcome,' he whispered. The local publican had loaned glasses. Fitz offered port to the women. The men played their expected part by pressing them and coaxing them. Mrs. Farrell gave in first, remarking that she would be a long time dead. Mrs. Mulhall also agreed, on condition that Mary did likewise. When everybody had a full glass Pat proposed the toast of the bride and groom and after that there was no further reluctance.

An hour later Rashers paused on the steps and looked up at the lighted windows. Pat's voice drifted into the dark street, his song winding past gas-lamps and growing faint and being swallowed altogether in other sounds. He was singing 'Comrades'.

> 'Comrades, comrades ever since we were boys
>   Sharing each other's troubles, sharing each other's joys.'

Rashers, conscious suddenly of the emptiness of the street, looked down sadly at his dog and petted it before going in. Mrs. Mulhall, troubled by some memory or other, wept a little as she listened.

'That was lovely,' she said, when Pat had finished.

'Hasn't he a grand voice altogether,' Mrs. Farrell remarked.

'He'd draw tears from a glass eye,' Joe said.

'A few bars from yourself, ma'am,' Pat invited. But Mrs. Mulhall said she had no voice.

'You've voice enough when it comes to giving out the pay to me,' Mulhall assured her.

Everybody took a hand in encouraging her and at last she gave in and began to sing 'If I were a Blackbird'. Her voice was thin and had a quiver in it, but Mulhall regarded her with a proud look. They were a kindly couple, Fitz thought, unbroken by hardship. He hoped he would reach Mulhall's age with as much of his courage and his world intact.

When the song finished Fitz raised his glass and said : 'Here's to ninepence an hour.'

Mulhall, delighted, repeated 'Ninepence an hour' and drank.

'How is it going?' Farrell asked.

'They're marking time,' Pat said. He was elaborately complacent.

'Larkin wrote and said we won't deliver to the foundry,' Mulhall explained. 'We've heard nothing more since.'

'They haven't paid,' Joe put in.

'Any day now they'll load us and tell us to deliver to the foundry. We'll all refuse.'

'Amen,' Pat said.

'If they lock you out we'll stand by you on the quays,' Farrell said.

'I wonder,' Mulhall said, challenging him.

'It's a certainty,' Farrell assured him.

'That's worth drinking to,' Pat declared.

'I'm sure Mrs. Fitzpatrick doesn't want to begin married life with a session about strikes,' Mrs. Farrell protested.

'I'm not listening,' Mary said lightly.

She was making tea. There was something about her which set her apart from the others, a way of moving, of lifting things, of using her features and varying her intonation when she spoke.

'That's the proper way to treat them,' Mrs. Farrell agreed, 'don't listen.'

The women were having tea and cake when Hennessy tapped at the door. Fitz invited him in. He stood uncertainly and said to Mrs. Mulhall:

'I was knocking at your room ma'am, this while back. Then I chanced to hear the voices and guessed you might be here.'

'Is there something I can get you?'

'Herself was wondering if you'd oblige her with the loan of a cup of sugar.'

Mrs. Mulhall rose, but Fitz looked at Mary and she went to the cupboard.

'I hesitate to trouble you . . .' Hennessy protested.

'We have it to spare,' Mary assured him.

Fitz invited Hennessy to drink and he sat down.

'My respects and wishes for a long and happy life,' he toasted.

'How is the work with you?' Mulhall asked.

'Not too bad,' Hennessy said. 'I've landed a bit of a watching job. Three nights a week.'

'You're a great man at the watching.'

'I've a natural gift for it,' Hennessy said. Then he added: 'I suppose you all heard about Rashers and his stroke of fortune?'

'What was that?'

'He swears he owes it all to yourself, ma'am.'

Mary, finding the voice directed at her, put down the cup of sugar.

'The night of poor Hanlon's funeral he showed the two of you the way to the presbytery and on the road out he dropped in to say a few prayers. He met the curate and landed the boilerman's job. Ten bob a week. Wasn't that a stroke of good fortune?'

'It's only seasonal,' Joe said.

'It'll keep him going through the winter.'

'Ten bob is a scab rate,' Pat said, with disgust.

Mary said: 'The curate is Father O'Connor. I knew him in Kingstown.'

'Is that a fact?' Hennessy said, happy to gather a further piece of information.

Pat, with obvious satisfaction, remarked: 'St. Brigid's must be a bit of a change for him.'

'It was his own wish to work here,' Mary said.

'Imagine that now,' Hennessy was greatly impressed.

'Only a saintly soul would make such a change,' Mrs. Mulhall said.

'Every man to his taste,' Pat said.

Hennessy noted there was full and plenty and lingered. He accepted a second drink and agreed to sing a song. Later he recited a ballad about a young man who gambled away his inheritance and died all alone in the Australian bush, where he was found with a locket in his hand containing a lock of golden hair. Was it his own, a relic of the lost innocence of his childhood, or had it been cut from a sweetheart's golden hair before sin sullied the hopes of youth? Or was it, perhaps, a sweet mother's tresses, carried to the ends of the earth by an erring son and fondled with remorse when Death laid its chill hand on his brow? The poet was unable to say and Hennessy, having posed the question and moved everybody by the light, nasal style of his recital, let his eye rest on the cup of sugar and suddenly remembered his wife.

'She'll think I'm lost,' he said, springing to his feet.

'That's the greatest oddity in Dublin,' Mulhall remarked.

'He has the gift, mind you,' Joe said. The rest had been equally impressed and agreed with him.

Mrs. Mulhall, thinking of the peaky face with its short moustache and small chin, and the far-away look in the eyes during the recital, sighed and said: 'The poor soul.'

'I think it's time we all went,' Farrell suggested. He had a long walk home before him and a six o'clock start the next morning.

'That's a thought,' Joe said.

They gathered their belongings and began to renew their wishes for happiness and good fortune. They were halfway down the stairs when Mary, who had gone back into the room to tidy up, noticed the parcel in the corner and called to Fitz.

Fitz shouted down the stairs: 'Pat—your parcel.'

'Never mind it.'

'You've left it behind you.'

Pat returned a little from the rest and said: 'It's for herself—a bit of a wedding present. There's no need to waken the house over it.' He was gruff and embarrassed.

'Did you rob a bank or something?' Fitz said, smiling.

'Never mind what I robbed,' Pat said. He turned and went down to join the rest.

'Thanks,' Fitz shouted after him, but he got no reply and went in and closed the door.

Mary was still tidying. Already, he noticed, she had given the room a touch of home.

'What was ninepence an hour?' she asked, working busily.

'I told you about it. The job I called Farrell for.'

'The night I was asleep and you didn't waken me?'

Something had happened to him that night that had nothing to do with their love. He remembered the sharp morning wind and, far off, the shouts of the men. Isolated in the top gallery of the house, just before the water pipes rattled into life, he had felt the inward drag of compassion and responsibility, linking him with the others below. Some part of him had become theirs. It was a moment he had no way of explaining to anybody, not even to Mary. He said, 'It may mean trouble for us.'

'But it's so long ago.'

'So far we've been able to keep going at the foundry by drawing from stock. But if the carters don't deliver to us soon we'll have to close down. And if non-union men deliver to us we'll have to refuse to handle the coal.'

'Maybe they'll give in and pay them.'

'That's what we're hoping for.'

She had finished her work and was removing her apron. He remembered.

'The parcel Pat left is a wedding present.' He took it from the corner and put it on the table. It was heavy. He unwrapped it. It was a marble clock, with the figure of a wolfhound on either side. The gilt on the hands had worn thin in places, but when they wound it and moved the hands it had a low, musical chime.

'It's lovely,' Mary said. They set it on the mantelpiece and stood back to admire it.

'It's a bit on the elegant side for the rest of the room,' Fitz said.

'It's beautiful.' Her pleasure touched Fitz.

'That's two beautiful things to look at every day,' he said.

'I'm sure he spent a fortune on it, it's too much to give.'

'In a way it's just as well,' Fitz said, 'he'll have less to act the tin elephant with.'

'Does he never try to save?'

'He'd rather give it away.'

'You have generous friends,' Mary said. She stood back to look at it once more.

'Let me hear it chime again,' she asked.

Fitz moved the hands and the clock responded.

'It has a happy sound,' she pronounced.

Fitz took the lamp and they went into the bedroom together. They undressed. Everything had gone well: the ceremony, the breakfast, the afternoon expedition around Howth Head, the customary wedding party. They lay together in the darkness, two lovers in a dilapidated world, knowing each other for the first time. They were near enough to the river to hear, faintly, the siren of a ship. The city grew quiet. Before they slept the clock in the outer room chimed once again.

'Listen to it,' Mary whispered.

They listened together. Fitz covered her mouth with his. They forgot the clock and the plaintive siren and the house which was peopled above and below them.

Pat left the rest at Ringsend Bridge and watched them go down past the Catholic church. Its back wall overhung the Dodder. From the bridge he saw the masts of the sailing ships that lay close against the church. They had a derelict look. The water about them gleamed faintly, gathering what light reached it from the few, scattered stars. The stars had a misty look of imminent rain. Under the great hump of the bridge the river, already swollen, moved towards the intricate system of docks and canals which would conduct it deviously to the Liffey and so to the sea. The breeze carried the taint of salt water, a forlorn smell.

As he walked back towards the city the rain began. It was late. The last trams were arriving at Ringsend Depot. They swung into the sheds with a great rattling and clanging, with trolleys that hissed and sparked as they crossed the wire intersections. They left a taste of metal in the street. Machinery vibrated behind the grey walls of Boland's Mills, and the little, lighted cabin of the overhead telpher made a blurred circle above the foundry yard before it disappeared into the awning of one of the furnace houses. Pat turned into Townsend Street and crossed Butt Bridge. The rain began to seep through his clothes. He had been sharing with Fitz and had neglected to make provision for a bed now that the arrangement had come to an end. But he was contented with drink. He knew what he was going to do.

In the shelter of Amiens Street Bridge he uncorked a bottle of whiskey, drank and went on. The streets were badly surfaced. Already muddy pools were beginning to form. There were lights in occasional windows and once he heard a piano playing

> 'For in his bloom
> He met his doom
> Tim Kelly's early grave.'

A policeman with his cloak fully buttoned and the great collar covering his ears turned to stare at him as he passed. Pat went on, changing the song.

> 'O girl of my heart you are waiting for me
> Mora, my own love
> Mora, my true love
> Will you be mine through the long years to be.'

He turned into a narrower, muddier street and climbed the stairs, still singing, his boots and his voice making a rowdy din. Someone jerked open a door.

'I thought so,' Lily Maxwell cried.

'Lily, my own.'

'Come in out of that,' she grumbled at him.

'Lily, my true love.'

'Do you want to bring the whole bloody Metropolitan Constabulary in on top of me?' she shouted at him.

Pat held out his arms to her and begged, 'Will you be mine through the long years to be?'

She pushed him in and closed the door.

'Will you look at the cut of him?' she said, appealing to one of the pictures on the wall.

Water was running from his hat. His coat was sodden and shapeless. She took it off him. She sat him down at the fire. Lily's room was small. An enormous iron bed with brass fittings took up most of the floor space. The fireplace, which was deep, was well filled with glowing coals, in spite of the general shortage. Lily had friends among the humble. Intimate garments were scattered haphazardly, as though Lily had been unable to make up her mind about what she was going to wear and had given it up.

'I was at a wedding,' Pat explained.

'You needn't tell me. I can smell the confetti,' Lily said.

'We'll have a drink.'

'Not any of mine, you won't,' Lily assured him, 'it's strictly for the paying guests.'

Pat produced the bottle of whiskey.

'Out of this, Lily my own love.'

She took it. 'Where did you find it?'

'I bought it.'

Lily looked astounded. 'There'll be a blue moon tomorrow night.'

'Will you pour the drink and not have so much bloody oul guff,' Pat said.

The steam was rising from his trousers.

'Take them off you,' Lily advised.

'Don't be impatient.'

'You're full of smart answers, wherever you were.'

'I told you, I was at a wedding.'

'I suppose they gave you this to get shut of you,' she said, taking the cork from the bottle.

'You never say anything agreeable to me,' Pat complained. 'All the time you keep nagging.'

He was taking off his trousers.

'Here,' she said, throwing him a towel. He began to dry his legs.

'Nag, nag, nag.'

'For all the good it does. Just look at you.'

She hung his wet trousers near the fire and handed him a drink.

'You're not bad, after all,' he said, sampling the whiskey. 'How is business?'

'Bloody terrible,' Lily said. 'How would you expect it to be of an Easter Tuesday. They're all after making their Easter duty. Finishing up their retreats and mending their souls.'

'What about the Protestants?'

'It seems this is a Roman Catholic area.'

'The Army?'

'On leave. Or blew it all of an Easter Monday.'

'And the students?'

'They only come to be seen, most of them.'

'Lily—you shouldn't be in this game. I told you so.'

'Maisie persuaded me there would be good money in it. She exaggerates a bit, the same Maisie.'

'Then don't settle to it. Get out of it.'

'Back to what? To making biscuits or something for five bob a week? I had enough of that, thank you.'

'You'd be happier.'

'I wasn't any happier. I was bloody well miserable, if you want to know.'

She consoled herself with a long slug of whiskey. She was sitting opposite to him at the fire, a thin, dark-haired girl with a slight figure. She had small features and neat hands that Pat liked to touch. His own had broken nails from humping sacks and coal-dirt which had settled permanently in the pores. She got up and began to twist the ends of his trousers. A stream of water fell from them.

'You'll wind up with pneumonia,' she said.

'I have money, Lily.'

'That's two blue moons tomorrow.'

'The horses,' Pat said. 'Give me another drink and I'll tell you about it.'

'I can't wait,' Lily said. But she gave him the drink. While she squeezed his trousers she said to him: 'Are you not staying?'

He had been about to tell her the story of his luck. Her remark surprised him.

'What do you mean?'

'You could take off your hat,' she said. He groped and was surprised to find it poised on the back of his head. He dropped it at his feet.

'I brought off a sixpenny treble at Fairyhouse: Axle Pin at sevens in the Farmers Plate, Lord Rivers in the Irish National at tens and all on to Little Hack the Second in the King's Cup. He came up at sevens.'

'What did you make?'

'Fifteen pounds eight shillings,' Pat said.

'Out of sixpence?' Lily asked.

'Out of a little crooked sixpence,' Pat said. He found it hard to believe himself. He held his glass up in front of him and nodded his head at it several times.

'What have you left?' Lily asked.

'Count it,' Pat invited. 'It's in my back pocket.' She took the trousers down and emptied the contents on to the table.

'I declare to God!' she exclaimed. She counted eight pounds and some odd shillings.

'What happened to the rest?'

'I bought a wedding present for five pounds. A clock.'

'You should have your head examined with what's left,' Lily said, outraged.

'It was for a friend,' Pat said.

'Who's the friend?'

'Bob Fitzpatrick. They were married this morning and after breakfast they went out to Howth.'

A thought struck him.

'Were you ever in Howth, Lily?'

'What would I be doing in Howth,' Lily answered.

'It's a beautiful place. It sticks right out into the sea. You can see the whole Bay from the cliffs, and the Dublin mountains all around it.'

'I was there once or twice,' Lily said. 'The cliffs made me dizzy.'

'Then the gardens,' Pat said, 'with the dandderodents, the rhodadandins . . . what the hell do you call them . . . the flowers.'

'I've seen them,' Lily said, 'but it must be years ago.'

'Come with me tomorrow.'

'Are you retiring from business?'

'There may be a bit of a lock-out tomorrow.'

'You'd better wait and see,' Lily suggested sensibly.

'Or the day after. Or the day after that again.'

'Or next Christmas,' Lily prompted. She saw he was full of drink.

'I'll tell you what,' Pat said, 'hold four pounds out of that for me and we'll go to Howth next Sunday.'

Lily took the four pounds.

'I'll keep it for you,' she said.

'If you have to spend some of it it's all right. Give me another drink.'

'You're crooked already.' But she poured it.

'I've no bed for tonight.'

'You can stay here. But no monkey business.'

'You don't love me any more,' Pat accused.

'I don't love anyone any more,' Lily said, suddenly weary. 'I feel bloody awful.'

'Have another drink.'

'Two is enough. Any more kills me.'

This was unusual. Pat looked at her unbelievingly. Then he shrugged and said: 'Please yourself.' He began to take his own. The heat of the fire helped the effect of the alcohol. Lily was sitting opposite again. He was becoming drowsy and found it hard to keep her in focus. They had grown up together, played together, found out the usual things together. The boys liked Lily. She wandered around with them and when they dared her she stood on her hands for them. The boys shouted 'I see Paris' when her bloomers showed and the other girls tried to be scandalised. They both came from a world where very little ever remained to be known after the age of twelve or thirteen.

'What's the strike?' Lily asked.

'For a proper rate—three shillings.'

'Three shillings a week?'

'No—three shillings they owe us for overtime.'

'A strike for three shillings?'

'For principle.'

'It takes a lot of principle to fill a pint,' Lily said.

'You never think of the world you live in, Lily,' Pat said, 'that's what's wrong with you.'

'I know what's wrong with me,' Lily said, 'but it isn't that.'

'You never ask yourself why the poor are poor. You see the quality going off to balls at the Castle and receptions in the Park. Will Lily Maxwell ever do that?'

'I'd look well, wouldn't I?'

'You'd look as well as the next and better if you had their advantages.'

'That's the way God made the world,' Lily said. 'You'd better lodge your objections with Him, not with me. I have my own troubles.'

'All that is going to be changed. We'll have a revolution about that.'

Pat's eyes were closing. Lily, watching the drunkenness slowly mastering his body and his thoughts, felt affection for him and asked: 'Had you any definite date in mind?'

He opened his eyes and was puzzled. 'What date?'

'For all the changing you're going to do.'

'They're going to lock us out. That'll be a start.'

'But no novelty,' Lily said, thinking of the other strikes.

'It'll be changed. The expropriators are to be expropriated. Did you ever listen to that Connolly chap?'

'Who's he?'

'Come to think of it,' Pat said, 'I haven't seen him around this past couple of years. He wanted votes for women. That's something should interest you.'

'What would I do with a vote?' Lily asked.

'Vote for the socialists. I'm a radical socialist. I believe we should hold everything in common, even our women.'

'Is your friend Fitzpatrick a socialist?'

'Fitz is all right. He's going to stand by us.'

'For your three shillings? He must be as mad as the rest of you.'

'He's the heart of the roll—the flower of the flock.'

'Try holding his woman in common and see what happens,' Lily invited. 'God, that's an explosion I'd love to watch!'

'Give me another drink,' Pat said.

'If you go to bed,' she promised.

He was agreeable. She helped him to undress. When he had stretched out beneath the covers she made an elaborate show of pouring whiskey into a glass. But she kept it in her hand while she sat at the bedside and made no move to give it to him.

'It's a bitch of a city, Lily,' he said to her.

'It's no great shakes,' Lily agreed.

'More babies die in Dublin than anywhere else in Europe—did you know that, Lily?'

'All babies die,' Lily said, 'when they reach the right age.'

'More men and women too. Does the Lord Lieutenant care? No. Does the Government? Do the employers? Does God?'

'I'd leave Him out of it,' Lily said.

'All right. Leave Him out of it. Do the others?'

'You should go asleep.'

'If you get in beside me.'

'I told you there's something wrong with me,' she half shouted it at him.

'Where's my drink?'

'I have it here for you.' But she kept it in her hand.

'Take Lord Aberdeen. Does *he* care?'

'I'll ask him the next time I bump into him,' Lily said.

'You haven't got into bed, Lily.'

'Take your hour, can't you.'

She was watching him, watching the sleep stealing over and through him. She was reckoning the moment of its victory. His speech became thick and blurred.

'We're going to tear it all down,' he said, 'tear it all down. Like that.'

He tried to make a descriptive movement with his hands. They barely stirred. Lily looked at him for some time with lonely affection. She said: 'You couldn't tear down wallpaper.' He was asleep. The stupor had won. He lay stretched with his mouth wide open. She drew the covers to his chin and bowed her head against the bulk of his body.

'Jesus help me,' she whispered. 'Jesus help me.' She was crying.

CHAPTER 8

M R. DOGGETT, of Doggett & Co., found himself with a problem. A letter, signed by James Larkin, Irish Organiser of the National Union of Dockers, warned him that if he instructed his carters to deliver coal to Morgan's Foundry there would be a strike. A letter from Morgan & Co demanded delivery immediately and warned him that the long-standing contract which he shared with Nolan & Keyes would be cancelled and given solely to Nolan & Keyes, if supplies were not despatched. He rightly guessed that his rivals had received a similar letter but had no way of finding out what they intended to do. He had no desire to face a strike. He had no desire either to lose the contract. It was a situation which kept his thoughts fully occupied. It was obvious that Nolan & Keyes shared his dilemma. For some weeks neither accepted the challenge by attempting delivery.

The situation troubled Timothy Keever too, but for a different reason. He worked for Nolan & Keyes and felt there was a moral issue. He decided to put it before Father O'Connor. His opportunity arose when the priest visited him as part of his parish work. Mrs. Keever spent more than she could afford in entertaining him to tea. After the meal Keever brought Father O'Connor into the yard at the back of the cottage to show him the shrine to St. Finbar he had built in his spare time. Father O'Connor seemed impressed.

'Very beautiful,' he said.

The shrine occupied the right-hand angle of the back and side walls. The statue was a small one, the tiny grass plot in front accommodated three jamjars with artificial flowers.

Keever had distempered the wall behind in yellow and white and had contrived a kneeling board out of a packing case.

'Maybe you'd say a prayer,' Keever invited, diffidently.

The idea of kneeling in such surroundings horrified Father O'Connor. Tea with the Keevers, in itself, had been something of an ordeal.

'Later, perhaps,' he evaded.

The rest of the yard, he noted, was occupied by a manhole cover and the pathway to the outdoor toilet. There was a large box.

'What is this?' Father O'Connor asked. It was an alternative topic to the shrine.

'It's for the dog,' Keever explained. 'He keeps the cats away. Especially at night.'

'Ah,' Father O'Connor said.

The back wall, which was enormously high, puzzled him, until he recognised it as part of the railway embankment. The railway line seemed to be everywhere in the parish of St. Brigid.

'You have a comfortable home,' Father O'Connor said. He was not quite sure, now that he had seen the shrine, what was expected of him next.

'It was my father's home,' Keever said, 'he was a carpenter.'

'I see.'

'In his time he was senior prefect.'

There was a strong tradition in favour of the skilled worker in parish activities.

'Isn't our present senior prefect a carpenter too?'

'No, Father, Mr. Hegarty is a bricklayer.'

'Of course,' Father O'Connor said.

'My own father intended me for a trade,' Keever explained, 'but God took him at an early age, so I became a carter. In fact I'm in a difficulty at the moment that Mr. Hegarty told me to ask your advice on.'

'By all means,' Father O'Connor agreed. He examined the box, found there was no dog present and sat down on it.

While Keever explained the situation in Nolan & Keyes Father O'Connor listened with half a mind. The man before him was, he thought, a model of what the Christian worker should be, accepting his social position with humility and making up for his lack of formal education by his persistence in good works of various kinds. He collected used stamps for the missions from the office staff of Nolan & Keyes and went among the carters on paydays gathering halfpennies for the same purpose. He carried a notebook in which he recorded each subscription as he received it and he handed over the total to Father O'Connor each week. He was constantly seeking recruits for the Church sodality among the men with whom he worked.

'You are being asked,' Father O'Connor summarised when he had finished, 'to refuse your own employer's instructions in order to force a point against another employer?'

'That's what I'm being asked, Father.'

'And you've no grievance against your own employer?'

'None at all, Father.'

'It seems to me,' Father O'Connor said, 'there can be no moral justification whatever for injuring your own employer in his business because of the supposed shortcomings of some other employer.'

'That's how Mr. Hegarty put it.'

'Mr. Hegarty is perfectly right.'

'You've taken a weight off my mind, Father,' Keever assured him. He turned again to the statue of St. Finbar, then looked questioningly at Father O'Connor, who hesitated. The shrine and the kneeling board were obviously sources of deep pride. Father O'Connor crossed himself. Despite the dog box, the outdoor toilet, the monstrous, grimy wall, he attempted to pray. He would have liked to gratify Keever's wish, but the thought of kneeling defeated his will. He crossed himself but remained standing. After a while he crossed himself again and followed Keever back into the kitchen, consoling himself with the thought that at least he was visiting in his parish, and ministering in foul rooms compared with which Keever's kitchen was a palace. As they went in, a train passed with such a thunderous commotion that the yard and its contents shuddered and seemed to hover on the brink of disintegration.

They had a glass of plain porter each in Mulligan's snug.

It was almost noon. Sunlight caught the edge of the table. The wood was worn. Near where Lily's glass rested someone had tried to carve initials but they were indecipherable.

'You shouldn't have come into this business, love,' Maisie said. 'You haven't the temperament.'

'I know that now,' Lily confessed.

'And this fellow I was talking about,' Maisie said. 'Mind you, it's not everybody he'll take on, because he's afraid of gossip. But I think I could persuade him to see you.'

'Three pounds is a lot of money.'

'Three guineas, sweetheart, he's sti'l got his professional pride.'

'Maybe it isn't *It* at all.'

'Maybe it is. Do you want your teeth going bad and your nice hair . . .'

'Shut up, for Jaysus' sake.'

Lily moved her glass until it covered the indecipherable initials.

'I'm near distracted, Maisie.'

Maisie drained her drink and punched the bell behind her.

'You don't want to go to the Locke, do you, with all the ditch-and-doorway element?'

'God forbid,' Lily said.

'How are you for money?'

'Desperate, but I've four quid . . .'

'I wouldn't call that very desperate,' Maisie said.

'. . . which isn't mine.'

'Matter-a-damn who's it is.'

'I'm minding it for a fella.'

'Get yourself looked after, girl.'

A panel opened and a man acknowledged Maisie's gesture by inclining his bald dome at them. They both waited. He returned and placed two more glasses on the ledge. Maisie paid him and took the drinks to the table.

'Well . . . ?' she said to Lily.

'Give me the address.'

'That's the ticket.' Maisie beamed with relief. 'He never qualified because of the drink and he'll have a booze with your three guineas as soon as you leave him. But he won't let you down if treatment is wanted.'

'I hope to God he's good.'

'Liz and Agnes Benson swear by him. And many another.'

Maisie rooted in her handbag. She found a pencil, but neither of them had a piece of paper.

'To hell with it,' Maisie said, 'I'll bring you to him myself.'

'You're an angel,' Lily said. 'When?'

'This evening.'

They both drank.

'Here's hoping,' Maisie said, smiling encouragement. There was no need to name the hope. Lily remained subdued.

'I'm sorry about this chap's four pounds,' she explained. 'He's not a customer, he's a friend.'

Maisie said she was a queer girl.

The news that Nolan & Keyes had made up their minds to attempt delivery to Morgan & Co. reached Doggett through channels of his own. He had no option but to act himself. The men he employed knew of his presence almost as soon as they reported for work. They, too, had their own channels.

'Doggett's up above,' the nearest carter whispered to Mulhall. They both interrupted yoking-up to look at the window of the superintendent's office. It was long and overlooked the yard. The early-morning air, pungent and misty, forecast an uncertain day.

'It's not the weather brought him down so early,' Mulhall said.

To Doggett, who was looking down at the activity in the marshalling yard, they were two men among a score or so of others. He smoked and watched.

'You've instructed the foreman?' Doggett asked.

'I have, sir. They get the dockets as they pass the scales.'

The superintendent was nervous.

'All the dockets are for Morgan & Co.?'

'All the one destination, sir.'

'That's the idea,' Doggett said. 'No word yet of the situation at Nolan & Keyes?'

'Not yet, sir.'

Doggett moved nearer to the window. He said, conversationally, 'We've been busy, you know—very busy.'

'It'll slacken soon, with the summer coming on, sir.'

'Seasonal. Still, I anticipate we'll do better than average.'

'I hope so, sir.'

'We all hope so,' Mr. Doggett said. He was watching each move below him, his mind working coolly. He saw the carts loaded and the marshalling procedure beginning.

Mulhall lay about twelfth in line. He lit his pipe and spat from his plank seat. He kept his eyes on the men nearer the scales. They had agreed, but they might break just the same. It would be a new kind of strike, if it came off. The first man drove on to the scales and waited while the clerk weighed. He accepted the destination docket, read it carefully and put it in his pocket. Doggett, his hands behind his back, watched from the window. This, he knew, was the crucial moment. The line of carters watched too. The leading carter drove clear of the scales and towards the gate. Everybody wondered. They saw him rein in as he approached the gate, which was narrow. Then he gave a check to the reins. While still in the yard the horse and cart swung to the right of the gate and the carter dismounted. The second carter did likewise but more decisively. So did the rest, until the whole line was at a standstill and the cart in front left no room to cross the scales. Mulhall, seeing the foreman going over to the men, left down his reins and went to them also. He took the delivery docket from one of the men who had crossed the scales, read it and signalled to the others. They dismounted, some with a leap, some clambering down laboriously or reluctantly. Doggett saw them forming into a circle for consultation. Some time later the foreman reported to the superintendent in the outer office, who brought the decision to Doggett.

'They refuse to deliver to Morgan & Co., sir.' Mr. Doggett had already discussed the procedure with him.

'Very well,' he instructed, 're-consign everything as we pre-

pared it. And try to find out what the situation is in Nolan &
Keyes.'

'It'll take some time, sir. Where can I contact you?'

'Right here,' Doggett said in a tone which made the superintendent jerk nervously. Before he moved away from the
window he saw the men being despatched one by one to the
alternative destinations. It took time, because their loads had to
be adjusted. But it was accomplished without a hitch.

Nolan & Keyes reported a split. At first the refusal seemed
unanimous, but after bickering and argument Timothy
Keever, fortified by Father O'Connor's advice, followed his
conscience and persuaded some of the others that he was right.
They delivered to the foundry. The rest of the men in Nolan
& Keyes persisted in their refusal. They were locked out. Doggett took the news coolly, although it placed him in an extremely
dangerous position. If word got out to Morgan's that he had
given in to the carters' threat and that Nolan & Keyes had stood
firm his contract would be in danger. But he had laid his plans.
Now that Nolan & Keyes had attempted delivery there was only
one safe course open.

'Work out an afternoon consignment for Morgan's,' he told
the superintendent. 'Supervise the loading personally and lock-
out immediately if we have a second refusal.'

'Yes, sir.'

There was a chance, Doggett felt, that the men might weaken
under the pressure of a renewed instruction. Meanwhile there
was another precaution to be taken, in case the news that he
had surrendered early that morning got about.

'I've forgotten the yard foreman's name.'

'O'Connor, sir.'

'Please send him to me.'

The foreman was a small man in his fifties. Coal grime had
settled permanently in the pores of his face. A black sweat
beaded his forehead and streaked his temples.

'You're O'Connor?'

'That's right, sir.'

'The men refused your instructions this morning?'

138

'They did, sir. They said they were standing by Larkin's agreement.'

'Are you a member of that gentleman's organisation?'

'No, sir.'

'Do you know anything about it?'

'Only what I hear the men saying, from time to time.'

'For instance?'

'It's the National Union of Dockers, sir. Mr. Sexton is general secretary but Mr. Larkin is Irish organiser. Sexton doesn't like him. He won't recognise the strikes engineered by Mr. Larkin and he may stop strike pay.'

'How do they propose to finance themselves?'

'They'll collect around the docks and all over the country. Larkin is collecting in Cork at present.'

'You know quite a lot about Mr. Larkin.'

'Only what I hear, sir. The men have a good deal of talk about him.'

'Too much, it appears,' Doggett said. He rose and left the desk.

'How long are you with us?'

'About thirty years, sir—since Mr. Waterville's time.'

'How long have you been yard foreman?'

'Fifteen years, sir.'

'Fifteen years is a long time.'

'It is, sir,' O'Connor's face betrayed a moment's pleasure.

'Long enough,' Doggett continued, 'to have learned the art of handling men in.'

O'Connor hesitated. Doggett's tone had changed suddenly. He became confused.

'It isn't easy these days, sir, with so much agitation going on.'

'We had evidence of that this morning, hadn't we?'

'Yes, sir.'

'That's all for the moment,' Doggett said. He called the superintendent.

'I have been speaking to O'Connor.'

'Yes, sir.'

Doggett looked steadily at the superintendent.

'O'Connor is unsatisfactory,' he said, 'pay him off this evening.'

The superintendent took a little while to grasp what was meant.

'Dismiss him—sir?'

'Yes. I expect my foremen to be competent.'

The next day the men in the foundry, standing by their promise, refused to handle the coal that had been delivered by Keever and his followers. The Board met briefly to decide to lock-out. Only Yearling expressed hesitation.

'Our insistence hasn't done much good, has it?' he remarked

'What do you suggest?' the chairman asked.

It was a question Yearling had answered over and over again. Now he merely shrugged.

'We have no option,' the chairman insisted, 'unless we are prepared to encourage anarchy.'

'I thought Doggett might fail us,' someone said, 'He's been trick-o'-the-looping.'

'Not this time,' the chairman said.

'He diverted the first load, I've been told.'

'There is an explanation,' the chairman answered. 'He had trouble with a foreman. It appears the fellow was in the pay of Larkin and diverted the load on his own initiative. Doggett tells me he has dismissed him.'

'The only medicine,' someone approved. 'Good for Doggett.'

In May the carters of Nolan & Keyes and of Doggett & Co. were joined by all the other carters of the city who went on strike against the masters' rejection of a general wage demand. New pickets appeared. The coal-carrying trade came to a standstill. Father O'Connor paid off Rashers and closed down the boiler-house for the summer. He wondered if his advice to Keever had been responsible, however indirectly, for closing down the foundry. Whenever he passed a picket throughout the months of June and July the thought came freshly into his mind. He had spoken with a conscientious regard for justice, yet there was another side to it that troubled him, something in the faces of the

men : tiredness, the dark lines of hunger, the way they saluted
him and the speculative look with which their eyes regarded him
as he passed. When he went the rounds of his parish there were
hungry children in the strikers' homes. Poverty might disgust
him, but that was some uncontrollable reaction in himself. It
was not that he had lost his pity for it.

'Do you think they would have locked out if all of you had
refused delivery?' he asked Keever.

'I don't know, Father. They didn't at first in Doggett's.'

'I see,' Father O'Connor said.

'The men are blaming me.'

'You must tell them . . .' Father O'Connor began. He had
been about to add 'that Father O'Connor advised you.' But he
had second thoughts. The Church had its own work. He must
keep clear of conflicts in a world he did not altogether understand. He had been asked for a moral judgment. He had given
it. The rest was not his business.

'Tell them the Christian workman must at all times acknowledge certain principles to be above the claims of man-made
organisations.'

Keever decided not to mention that he had already done so.
He had been told what to do with his principles. It hurt him
but had no persuasive effect whatever. Finding no outlet for
ambition or reason for hope on earth, Keever had long ago fixed
heaven with acquisitive and unflinching eyes.

'At the same time we have a duty to help the wives and children,' Father O'Connor said. 'I want you to make a list of families
for me—not more than ten for a start—whom you think are
most in need of relief. You and Mr. Hegarty and the members
of the Confraternity Committee can make up some food parcels
for distribution.'

'I'll do that, Father.'

Father O'Connor thought Keever looked uneasy.

'Do you not agree?'

'Certainly, Father, of course,' Keever said.

'Very well. Let me have the list as soon as you can.'

There was a large press in Father O'Connor's bedroom, which
was quite empty. He decided that tins of cocoa would be easiest

to store and more nourishing than tea. Sugar and tins of milk would be no problem. He ordered these in quantity. While he was at it he decided to stock in some blankets. They would be cheaper now that summer was coming and could be held against the winter. He found room for these in the press also. Drawing the money by cheque, visiting shops, consulting with the two prefects, kept him busy and contented. They spent three evenings in the room behind the vestry making up parcels. Each contained a packet of flour, a tin of cocoa and a tin of milk. It was good to work so humbly for others.

The rumours of disagreement between Sexton and Larkin persisted. Fitz was certain that sooner or later the Liverpool Executive would stop their strike pay.

'Isn't Larkin collecting in Cork?' Joe pointed out.

'I'd feel happier with a little cash in reserve, just the same,' Fitz said.

They were resting on a piece of waste ground near the river, a favourite site for games of pitch and toss. Nettles and weeds wrestled for possession of the few feet of soil. A mane of grass, reaching upwards through the broken bottom of an upturned bucket, had the gloss of health.

'If you need it badly I can lay hands on a couple of pounds for you,' Pat offered.

'Where?'

'From Lily.'

'The fancy woman,' Joe put in.

'It's my own money,' Pat added, ignoring him. 'She's minding four pounds for me.'

Joe looked up at the blue sky and joined his hands across his belly.

'Minding it for him,' he said, addressing his scepticism directly to God.

'When do you want it?' Pat asked Fitz.

Joe remained in isolated communion with the Powers above him.

'There's no great hurry,' Fitz said.

The Angelus bell sounded from a nearby church. When they

had taken off their hats and crossed themselves Joe asked:

'Did you hear it was the curate in St. Brigid's advised Keever to carry on?'

'I didn't hear that,' Fitz admitted.

'We're a priest-ridden race,' Pat declared, 'but we'll get rid of them.'

'When?' Joe asked.

'When we organise and establish a Workers' Republic.'

'With Lily Maxwell in the chair.'

'Leave Lily Maxwell alone.'

'That's what you should do,' Joe said, goading him.

'You'll have your money tomorrow,' Pat assured Fitz.

But though he tried throughout the week to find Lily she seemed to have disappeared. There was no answer when he knocked at her room. Maisie, when he met her, said she had no idea where Lily could be. He met her again and was told the same thing. The second time he got the impression that she was lying.

Chandlers Court looked out on the summer evenings and waited for whatever might choose to happen. There was a tension in the streets, a promise of action which seemed each day to be on the point of materialising, but which never did. The weather, mercifully, made heating unnecessary, but fires were still needed for cooking. In No. 3 a communal system helped the economy. They pooled their resources and took it in turns to use each other's fireplace. Mary began to know the lives of those about her. The Mulhalls lived best. They had a table with a cover, good chairs, a dresser well stocked with crockery. Mrs. Mulhall was a woman who polished and scrubbed. The Bartleys below were clean people too, but the room was poorly equipped because Mr. Bartley never seemed to be able to find anything except casual work. The little boy at whose bed Father Giffley had watched some years before was now a messenger with one of the grocery shops. He earned half a crown a week, which helped to pay the rent. Most of all she hated going to the Hennessys, who were desperately poor. They drank out of tins and jamjars and spread covering on the floors at night for their numerous children.

The first ten families listed by Keever received their food parcels with gratitude. They were all, in one way or another, intimates of his. With the second ten he ran into trouble. After an evening of successive calls he returned to Father O'Connor. Hegarty and he placed the parcels on the table.

'What's this?' Father O'Connor asked.

'We had trouble,' Keever said.

'They refused to take the parcels,' Hegarty explained.

'They refused . . .'

'They called me a scab,' Keever said.

'And they didn't leave your name altogether out of it either, Father,' Hegarty added.

Father O'Connor flushed deeply. 'All of them refused?'

'Every one of them.'

'In one of the houses they tried to empty water over us from the windows.'

'Blackguardism,' Father O'Connor said.

'It's Larkin and the union, Father. They're boycotting Keever and myself.'

'I see,' Father O'Connor said. He had betrayed anger. That was a mistake. He should be calm. He should receive the information as though it was of no importance.

'Well—leave the parcels back in the press. Tomorrow evening we'll have a committee meeting.'

But the next evening only Keever and Hegarty and one very old man turned up.

'If you'd send someone else with the parcels they'd take them,' Keever suggested. He was humble. It would not matter to him.

'Certainly not,' Father O'Connor decided. 'We are not going to be dictated to.'

The parcels remained in the press. He owed a duty to Keever. More important still, he owed a duty to himself. Or, rather, to his cloth and the Church which had been offered a blackguardly insult. It was an indication of the evil disposition which was gaining ground, even among the lowly and illiterate.

Rashers had his own campaign to fight in the daily battle to survive and he fought it with his own weapons. Circumstances were making it more than usually difficult. The city was either curtailing its charity in the belief that that would kill the new tendency among its lower orders to strike and perhaps do worse, or reserving its coppers for the collecting boxes of the locked-out men. It was a new partisanship which left no place for Rashers. The idea of cashing in on this sympathy occurred to him, and he got as far as painting the words 'Help the Lock-Out' on the side of a home-made box. But while he waited for the lettering to dry he changed his mind. It would be wrong, his conscience suggested, and he gave in to its reproaches. The idea of writing a ballad about the strikes seemed better and more honest. Hennessy found him sitting on the steps one afternoon, already at work on it. He had the first two lines on the back of a cigarette packet, but its composition was a laborious process. He welcomed the interruption.

'Is Fitzpatrick above? Hennessy asked.

'He went out about twenty minutes ago,' Rashers said.

'That's most unfortunate,' Hennessy remarked. The cigarette packet intrigued him.

'What's the writing about?'

'It's a ballad about the strike.'

Rashers handed him the packet. Hennessy, screwing up his eyes, read:

> 'Come all ye gallant Dublin crew and listen
>   to my song
> Of working men and women too who fight the
>   cruel wrong.'

'What comes after that?'

'Damn the bit of me knows,' Rashers confessed, 'it has me puckered.'

'What are you going to do with it?'

'Sing it at meetings and outside public houses.'

'In the hope of making a few coppers?'

'What else?'

'Not a chance now,' Hennessy said.

'Why not?'

'The tide has gone out, oul skin. That's why Mulhall sent me looking for Fitzpatrick.' Henessy handed back the cigarette packet.

'The Liverpool Executive stopped the strike pay this morning.'

Fitz was already down at the committee rooms, where Mulhall had been waiting in the hope of seeing him. The doors were still closed and the crowd grew as they talked. Men who would not normally have come until later in the evening arrived early because the story of the stoppage of the relief money had spread from street to street. There were carters, shipping workers, a number of hands from factories that had become involved in the spread of the stoppages. The rumour went that there would be no money at all. Mulhall was more optimistic.

'Larkin collected in Cork,' he said, 'and as well as that the committee built up a relief fund through the collection boxes. There's bound to be something.'

'It'll want to be a lot,' Fitz said, looking at the crowd, 'to go anywhere among this mob.'

Joe joined them and after an hour Pat came along.

'Trouble in our native land,' he said.

'The strike pay has been stopped,' Fitz confirmed. There was still no sign of the doors being opened, so they moved over to the river wall. Down towards the sea, on the South Wall, cranes swivelled above ships.

'It's at times like this I wish I was a docker,' Fitz said.

'Or a sailor,' Pat said. 'Plenty of money and a wife in every port.'

Joe, who had been brooding about the matter on and off, saw his opportunity and said:

'What about the four pounds you left with Lily Maxwell?'

Mulhall looked mildly curious. Fitz, glancing quickly at Pat's face, knew that Joe had gone too far. It was one of those things which should never have been said.

'I haven't been able to see her,' Pat said. Joe began to explain to Mulhall.

'Imagine giving four pounds to mind to a . . .'

But Fitz, his tone sharp and violently angry, cut him short.

'Give it a rest.'

Pat, who had been leaning on the wall, straightened and faced the three of them.

'I promised Fitz two pounds of it and he'll have it. I'll pick her up.'

'The girl might need it,' Fitz said, 'don't go trailing her.'

He was sorry for Pat, whose face showed pain and humiliation.

'There's no question of trailing her,' Pat said, 'the girl never wronged me of a penny piece. You'll have two pounds tonight.'

He left them abruptly. Mulhall looked after him and then asked: 'What's the matter with him?'

'His sweetheart let him down,' Joe said, beginning to laugh.

'Give it over, I told you,' Fitz said, rounding on him.

They went back to the hall and found it open, but the crowd outside seemed as dense as before. Someone Mulhall knew said: 'They're paying out inside.'

'What's the damage?'

'It's reduced to five bob.'

'Better than nothing,' Mulhall remarked. He began to elbow his way in. Fitz and Joe followed. Inside they produced their cards to the first man of three sitting at a table. With a shock Fitz realised that he was looking at Jim Larkin.

He was bigger than Fitz had imagined him and was smoking a black cheroot. The thumb of his left hand was stuck into the docker's belt which he wore loosely about his waist. The man next to him made a quick entry in a book, the third man counted out five single shillings and handed them to Fitz, together with a printed notice which said:

'Meeting This Evening At Parnell Square 5 p.m. sharp.
Jim Larkin Will Speak
Scabs Arriving
Muster For Action
Unity Is Strength'

They reached the sunlight again.

'It was Jim Larkin,' Fitz said. The encounter had excited him. It was as though he had just seen personalised all the slogans and half-conceived ideas that had been the common currency of the past two months. Mulhall, more experienced in such matters, found it less remarkable.

'How's the time?'

'I've no notion.'

They walked together towards the city centre to consult the public clocks. It was half past four. All three were more or less hungry, yet they passed the bread shops and walked across restaurant gratings and were unaware for the moment of their drifting odours.

'What's that about scabs arriving?' Joe asked, looking again at the badly printed notice.

'That's more of their dirty play.'

'They did it in Belfast, didn't they?' Mulhall reminded them.

They went on towards the square, where they found a few men with banners building a temporary platform against the ornamental railings. Four or five hundred men were spread about in loose groups, waiting. From the windows of Vaughan's Hotel guests were watching curiously.

'Anyone a cigarette?' Fitz asked.

Men were still arriving and the scattered groups began to move forward into a mass. After a while Fitz found himself hemmed in on either side and then, quite suddenly it seemed, the pressure of people jammed his shoulder tight against Mulhall's. He looked towards the platform and saw that Larkin had mounted it. He began to address them.

At first the accent was strange. Part Liverpool, part Irish, it produced immediate silence. The voice, flung back again from the high housefronts on the other side of the road, was the strongest Fitz had ever heard. From time to time the hands moved with an eloquence of their own. The strike pay had been withdrawn, he was saying, because the British Executive were indifferent to the sufferings of people in Dublin. For two months they had given them half-hearted support and now, the fight was proving too big. The Executive were afraid. It was

148

laughable, he said, that trade union leaders with the broad waters of the Irish Sea between them and the field of action should be afraid, while the Dublin trade unionists were still full of courage and fighting fit. If they intended to withhold strike pay why was it not done at the beginning, before men had sacrificed themselves and their families throughout two long and bitter months?

They answered with a cheer. Fitz found himself joining in. He saw Larkin's hand upheld for silence and stopped. They were going to carry on, Larkin continued, with or without money. A sum had been collected which would keep them going for a while. The weekly payment would be even less than in the past, but they must see themselves as soldiers in the field, holding a position against odds, surrounded and cut off and ready to continue on short rations. He had information that a shipload of free labourers would arrive at the South Wall that evening. The answer to that would be to call out the dockers. He intended to address meetings on the South and the North Wall and hoped to bring work there to a standstill. In that way they would close the port of Dublin. The Government might then take a hand in persuading the employers to see reason.

The meeting lasted almost an hour. At the end of it Fitz found himself in a column of marching men, headed by Larkin. As they rounded the corner of Parnell Square he looked back. A few hundred men in ranks of four stretched behind. They passed the Rotunda and met the first heavy traffic. Horse-drawn cabs pulled in to one side, trams came to a standstill, people on the footpaths stood to stare. After two months of doubt and idleness to have control of a city street, however briefly, was an exhilarating experience. They strode out strongly, turning left before crossing O'Connell Bridge. They found the approach to the North Quays blocked by a cordon of police in plenty of time to swing confidently to the right and across Butt Bridge, then left again along the approach to the south bank of the river. As they passed the closed gates of the marshalling yards men who had worked in them before the strike cheered derisively. Mulhall pointed out Doggett & Co. to Fitz. The gate was red and the firm's name stood out on it in white painted letters. About two hundred yards below that they came to a second cordon of police and halted. At a distance behind the police the first gang of dockers were unloading and behind that they could see the masts of ships that were lying to and crane arms swinging backwards and forwards against the sky-line.

The police inspector stepped forward and Larkin went over on his own to meet him. In the centre of the few yards of dock-side dividing the police from the strikers they parleyed for some minutes. The police were about sixty strong and the strikers, Fitz knew, had drawn too close. Anything would spark off a clash.

'They won't let us through,' Mulhall predicted, while they waited.

'Not a hope,' Fitz said.

'We could burst our way through,' Joe said.

'I'm on,' Mulhall agreed.

'Better wait and see what Larkin wants to do,' Fitz advised.

The pressure of body against body in the crowd behind him generated an excitement of itself which was already reckless and dangerous. The police inspector rejoined his column and Larkin returned. For a while nothing happened. Then the police, turning about, withdrew some yards and about-faced again. This time they drew their batons. Larkin pushed through the ranks of the strikers, reached one of the quayside capstans and mounted it. He began to address them.

The police, he said, had closed the quays. They said it was to avoid disturbances but that was not the truth. It was to aid and abet the employers in their plan to import free labour. The Government had made its police force the minions of the employers instead of the servants of all the citizens. The answer to that was to close the port, not for a day or two days, but until such time as the demands of the men on strike had been conceded. He was going to address the dockers, despite employers and governments and police, and he would do so within the hour. Meanwhile he appealed to them to have trust in him and to promise that in his absence their demonstration would continue to be orderly and disciplined. He was helped down from the capstan and struggled towards the back of the crowd.

'What do we do now?' Joe asked generally.

'How is he supposed to talk to the dockers,' Mulhall wondered, 'both sides of the river are cordoned off.'

'He might get through on his own over on the North Bank.'

The men had broken rank and were gathered in a crowd. With Larkin gone there was no longer a focal point. Some of them lined up against the gates of the marshalling yards and shared cigarettes. The police, seeing the situation losing its tension, put away their batons.

'Come on,' Mulhall said. Fitz and Joe followed him over to the wall and they stood with their backs to Doggett & Co.'s gate.

'If there's a heave we don't want to end up in the river,' Mulhall explained, looking over at the unprotected quayside.

There was no sign of any slackening of work along the river. The cranes continued to swing, the rattle of horse-drawn floats and distant shouts mingled and drifted; it was the familiar voice of the riverside. A man who knew Mulhall came across and said:

'What are we going to do?'

'We were instructed to wait,' Mulhall said.

'Some of the lads at the back want to get on with it.'

'That's what I think too,' Joe said.

'We could easily break through. What do you say?' He was speaking to Fitz, who said:

'I say we should hold tight, but I'm willing to do what Mulhall thinks best.'

Mulhall looked across at the police.

'We'd break through all right,' he said, 'because they'd let us. But you'd find they've reserves up every side street. And when they got us between them they'd let us have it.'

'I don't think we should be afraid of the police,' the man objected.

'There's your answer,' Fitz said, pointing towards the police. A second column had approached from behind and was spreading out in formation behind them.

'That's what I mean,' Mulhall said.

A cheer began from behind. At first they thought the men

were jeering at the reinforcements, but after a moment they realised that all heads were turning in the direction of the river. They could see nothing because of the crowd in front.

'Up here,' Mulhall said, turning to the wall. They climbed up after each other.

Fitz, who reached the top first, shouted 'Look' and pointed.

A rowing boat was moving downriver, manned by four oarsmen. Standing in the centre and waving to the men on shore was Larkin. The boat drew level with the police cordon, passed it and went on towards the unloading docks. A detachment of police left the main body and moved down the quayside, keeping pace with it.

Mulhall, deflated, said: 'They'll get him when he tries to land.'

But Larkin's intention came suddenly to Fitz. He gripped Mulhall's arm tightly and shouted:

'He won't land. He'll speak to them from the boat.'

A hush fell on the crowd and they heard, after what seemed an age, the distant but still recognisable tones. What he was saying was lost, but the effect soon became clear. The nearest crane arm completed its semicircle and remained still. So did the next. Then, at intervals that grew shorter as the word spread from gang to gang, crane after crane became immobilised. They watched in silence as the paralysis spread. Yard by yard and ship by ship, the port was closing down. The cordon of police opened to form a narrow laneway, and through this the first contingent of striking dockers filed to join the demonstrators. Their arrival started a movement in the crowd which spread through it rapidly.

'Let's get down,' Fitz suggested.

'Stay put,' Mulhall warned.

The cheering had grown wilder and the movement, reaching the rear, stopped for a moment and then began to surge forward. The front lines moved nearer to the police, hesitated, then surged forward once again. The police, deciding the moment of initiative, drew their batons and charged.

The mass of bodies shuddered as it took the impact, gave ground a little, but held, Fitz, looking down on the swaying

152

bodies, wondered at the foolishness of the police action. Caught on one side by the wall and threatened by the river on the other, the crowd tightened and became impenetrable. There was no room to scatter and therefore no option but to stand firm. Already a number of men had been forced over the quayside into the water. Some of the police, detached from their colleagues, went down and were left behind, while the main body, finding the pressure irresistible, retreated and tried to hold together. The struggle continued back along the quays until the first side street offered a channel of escape, through which men streamed thickly from the main body. Fitz saw the mass thinning, and the police, the pressure at last released, stopping to regroup. Up the road from where they sat were three or four casualties of the charge. He climbed down and walked towards them. One man, with a deep gash along the side of his head, needed help urgently. Fitz turned and called to Mulhall.

'Have a look at this.' The man was barely conscious. His shirt and the collar of his coat were stained heavily with blood.

'Can we lift him?' Mulhall asked, when he had reached them.

'I wouldn't like to.'

'There's a stretcher in the first-aid room back in Doggett's,' Mulhall remembered.

'I'll go with you,' Joe offered.

'Will there be someone there?'

'There's bound to be a watchman,' Mulhall said. It seemed the best thing. Doggett's was only a short distance away. Fitz agreed.

'Does he know how to use the telephone?'

'I imagine so.'

'Get him to call the ambulance while you're there.'

When they had gone he lifted the injured man gently so that his arm made a rest for his head. It helped to slow down the flow of blood. Beyond that there was little he could do. The area immediately around them was deserted, but further along the riverside men still hung around in groups. Fitz, wondering uneasily where the police had got to, wished that Joe and Mulhall would hurry. The man in his arms was unconscious and breathing heavily, the wound was open and ugly, about him the painted gateways and dusty cobbles wore an air of brooding menace. He looked behind him and there was no sign of help.

'Mulhall,' he shouted, hardly knowing why. There was no answer. The injured man began to moan. It seemed to Fitz that the others had been gone for an hour. His arm under the head began to ache unbearably, the evening light bathed the cobbles about him with an oppressive light that seemed to press on him physically. At last he caught sight of Mulhall and Joe. They moved towards him for a short distance and stopped. He waved his free arm at them to hurry, but they signalled wildly to him and shouted. He looked downriver again and froze. The isolated groups had formed into a crowd again and were racing towards him. It was another baton charge, this time with the police in control. He heard Mulhall shouting to him to run, but the head on his arm, helpless and bloody, held him fixed where he was. He hugged the injured man tighter, until the bedlam of legs and bodies milled about him on all sides, cutting out the light, tripping over him, throwing him to the ground with his broken burden now lying beneath him. A heavily booted foot caught him on the forehead as it passed and he lost consciousness.

He woke up again in the timekeeper's office of Doggett & Co. There were keys about the wall, each with a number chalked beneath its hook. Mulhall and Joe were drinking tea with the watchman.

'We've been keeping an eye on you,' Mulhall said, when he sat up. Fitz felt his head.

'Don't mind the bandage,' Mulhall reassured him, 'the ambulance man said you'd be as right as rain.'

Fitz remembered. 'Where's the other chap?'

'They carted him off with them,' Joe said.

'Is he bad?'

'Fractured skull—they think. You probably saved his life.'

'Give me a cup of that,' Fitz asked. Mulhall took a can from a gas ring in the corner and poured.

'We were keeping it hot for you,' he said. He grinned at

154

Fitz, a kindly and approving grin that made Fitz feel happy. He sipped the tea. He realised as he did so that he was ravenously hungry.

Pat searched for Lily until the heat of airless streets brought him to a standstill. He leaned against a lamp-post and wondered what likely place was left. He had stood on the narrow landing outside her room for almost an hour, thinking she must surely return for a meal. He heard the Angelus bell striking and nodded to other occupants as they passed up and down the uncarpeted stairs until it became embarrassing to be seen standing so long in the same place. He went out again into the streets, tried the pubs and the usual shops all over again and met Maisie for the second time that evening. She treated him this time like a harmless lunatic.

'There's no sign of Lily anywhere,' he reported.

'Maybe she's gone off with a soldier,' Maisie said, laughing at him.

'I want to see her urgently.'

'You must be in a bad way,' Maisie sympathised, 'and it only half past six of a summer's evening.'

'Do you know where she is?'

'I know where you'll find as good as her.'

'It's important, Maisie,' Pat appealed.

'I haven't seen sight nor light of her,' Maisie said, 'and that's the gospel truth.'

She was lying. He was convinced of it. Lily, for whatever reason, was avoiding him.

Hunger and thirst made him wish now that he had waited to see if there was any strike pay. The thought that Lily did not want to see him began as a puzzling suspicion and became a gnawing pain. They had been warm to each other for so long.

He decided to abandon the search for the moment. His immediate need was a drink. He set off purposefully until he reached a shop with three brass balls hanging outside it.

'Are we doing business, Patrick?' Mr. Donegan said pleasantly. He had been writing in his accounts book. Pat removed his jacket.

'This,' he said putting it on the counter.

Mr. Donegan adjusted his glasses and held it up to examine it.

'Your coat?' he questioned.

'How much?' Pat asked.

'How much did you want?'

'Half a crown.'

Mr. Donegan made a clicking noise with his tongue. Pat was well known to him, a regular and reliable client. But he liked to make a business point.

'It's not worth half that,' he said.

'Two shillings,' Pat compromised.

Mr. Donegan wrote a docket and handed him half a crown.

'We'll leave it the half-crown,' he said easily. 'Any sign of the work resuming?'

'Not yet,' Pat said, 'but I'll be back to you, whether or aye.'

'Of course you will,' Mr. Donegan said. A thought occurred to him. 'Anything in the pockets?' He ran his hands through them absentmindedly.

'You might find a few holes.'

'For ventilation,' Mr. Donegan smiled. Then he frowned. 'Don't go getting drunk. There's no nourishment in porter.'

'There's other things in porter,' Pat suggested.

'No,' Mr. Donegan denied. 'Drink, like women, is a snare and a delusion. God bless you.'

'God bless us all,' Pat said.

He met Rashers on his way across town, recognising first the voice and then the bearded figure with the hand cupped against the side of the face and its feet planted in the gutter. The dog sat patiently, as though adjudicating.

'Come all ye gallant neighbours come, and listen to my song
Of working men and women too who fight a cruel wrong
How sad their plight, this bitter night, deserted and let
   down
Their cause betrayed by foreign knaves which serves the
   British crown
O, do not trust unless you must the men that serves the
   crown.'

Pat slapped Rashers on the shoulder.

'Come on. I'll buy you a pint.'

'I'd rather you forked out the tuppence.'

'I'll do both. Come on.'

'You're a decent Christian gentleman,' Rashers said, following him, 'and may you have the life of Reilly and a large funeral.'

He gave a jerk to the lead, bringing the dog reluctantly to its feet.

They went into the public house and ordered. Sunlight slanted through the windows and the air was warm and smelled a little of urine.

'Where did you get the ballad?'

'I made it up.'

'Out of your head?'

'Out of my heart,' Rashers said, correcting him. 'A ballad made out of the head is worse than useless. Here's my best respects.'

He raised his pint.

'A happy Christmas,' Pat said.

'We'll see that too,' Rashers predicted, 'when the working class comes into their own.'

'We'll have a statue put up to you in years to come,' Pat promised, 'and the people will gather from near and far to see the words spelled out on it in golden letters: Rashers Tierney, Bard of The Revolution.'

They both fell silent, picturing in their mind the stone tribute of Pat's fantasy.

'The only thing is,' Pat amended, 'they'd have to leave the bloody oul dog out of it.'

'I seen a statue to a dog once,' Rashers volunteered. 'It was put up by a rich oul wan in memory of a pet terrier.'

'And why not?'

'It didn't look right. I often wondered had she the priest to pronounce over it, sprinkling holy water and wishing it eternal rest, *in secula seculorium*.'

'Maybe she believed in that thing about souls.'

'What thing?'

'When you pass on you come back as an animal.'

'You mean Rusty here mightn't be a dog at all? He might only be somebody looking like a dog?'

'Rusty could be Napoleon. Or Julius Caesar.' Rashers looked down at the dog. It cocked its head at him, wondering if they were about to leave.

'Poor Rusty,' Rashers said, 'it's a bit of a come-down for you, whatever the hell you were.'

He patted the dog on the head. Pat looked for the public house clock and saw that it was half past eight.

'There's your tuppence,' he said. 'I have to be off.'

He finished his pint and went out. There seemed very little point in going to Lily's room again, so he decided to kill time by walking down towards the quays. There were policemen everywhere in the streets, moving along in groups. He changed his mind about going to the quays and went in again to drink, this time with a man who was full of talk about the disturbances. When he came out it was half past nine. The streets had the late evening odour of dust, and an old man in a long black soutane was closing over the entrance doors to the Pro-Cathedral. One scraped its lock along the stone paved threshold, the other collided roughly with it and set up a thunder roll of sound that escaped from the church and echoed along the street. Pat, the drink moving in him, hurried his pace and headed directly for Lily's favourite pub, where the curate said yes, she had been there on and off. His expression conveyed his conclusions about Pat's reason for asking, but he went off polishing a glass and whistling. His customers' business was their own, provided they conducted it in an orderly fashion. Pat took his drink and sat down to wait.

The pain inside him, which he had managed to forget in his talk with others, attacked him more fiercely now that he was alone. He looked at the fly-blown mirror with its lettered advertisement and recollected a night when Lily had asked to have it brought into the snug so that she could fix her hair. The curate did it for Lily, although he would have refused any of the others. Pat remembered her small, pretty face in it and the hands shaping the hair about it with movements that he loved. He had money that night after a lucky break with the horses, and they had gone to the Empire Palace Theatre afterwards to see James Fawn, the comedian.

Pat pushed the memory from his mind and was raising his glass when he heard the voice from the snug. He took his drink with him and walked down with it.

'Lily,' he said.

She started when she saw him at the door. He noted that too. It upset him. She stood waiting for her drink, drumming her fingers on the ledge of the service hatch, unable to think of something to say that would be ordinary and usual. At last she managed, lamely, 'Hello, Pat.'

She took her drink and sat down. He joined her.

'I want to ask you something, Lily.'

'You don't have to sound like a bloody funeral about it.'

'Why have you been avoiding me?'

She laughed falsely and said: 'Are you getting ideas about yourself?'

'For weeks I've been looking for you. You even got Maisie to put me off.'

She flushed angrily and he could see that her rage, too, was false. She was working it up purposely, a weapon of defence.

'That's something I want to have out with you, Pat Bannister. You've been following me around and asking every Tom, Dick and Harry about me, getting me talked about and making a holy show of me. What the hell ails you?'

'I wanted to see you. About the few pounds you were holding for me.'

'Four lousy pounds. Is that the extent of your trouble?'

'Did you spend it?'

He said it casually, knowing now that she had.

'You said I could.'

'All of it?'

'All of it he says. Four lousy pounds.' Her vehemence surprised him. She looked tired and overwrought. In her eyes and on her face he saw the months of anguish and fear. They puzzled and touched him. He put his hand on hers.

'It doesn't matter if you needed it, Lily.'

'I needed it,' Lily said. 'I bloody well needed it all right.'

Her voice was bitter, but it was more like her own. He had got nearer to the Lily he had always known.

'All right,' he said, 'I'll buy you a drink and we can talk.'

He rapped on the counter.

'What's the use of talk?'

'What did you need it for?'

She froze again and said shortly: 'Never mind what I needed it for.'

'All right,' he said, pacifying her, 'it doesn't matter. I didn't know you'd spent it—not all of it.' He paused and added, 'You never did that before.' He meant it as an explanation, but Lily chose to take it as a reproach. She turned quickly on him.

'I needed it. I've told you already.'

'And I said that's all right. But you shouldn't have avoided me.'

'Who avoided you?' Lily demanded, raising her voice.

The curate, coming for the order, said soothingly, 'Now, now, lady, keep the voice down—no commotion.'

'You shut up,' Lily snapped at him.

He grinned at her and went off to get the drinks. Pat, the hurt of it goading him, persisted.

'All those weeks you were avoiding me. And you had Maisie and her likes laughing at me.'

'What the hell do you think they were doing at me?'

Pat touched her hand again, but she drew it quickly away from him. Her hostility was harder to bear than anything else. He had not realised before how much he cared for her; not her body only, that she had denied to him when they had last met, but Lily herself, Lily who was quick to gibe but quick also to comfort and generous also in giving. Lily who could touch him with a slender hand and evoke a memory of childhood. Painfully he asked:

'Are you in trouble, Lily?'

His warmth and concern undermined her anger.

'Was I ever in anything else?' she said, her lip trembling and her eyes filling with tears, 'since the day I came into the world.'

160

'And you won't tell me what it is?'

'Please don't ask me, Pat,' she pleaded. 'I needed your few pounds and I spent it. And for all the good it done I might as well have flung it into the Liffey.' She turned to face him, a desperate honesty in her voice. 'I played square with you always, didn't I. You trusted me with many a thing and I never once let you down. This time it couldn't be helped.'

'You don't have to explain anything, Lily.'

'That's what I used to think. But you kept looking for me.'

'Is there any harm in that? Am I not to look for you?'

'You were asking everybody. I knew it was the money you wanted.'

'The others had me upset. I said I could get two pounds and when I told them how one of them jeered at me for a fool.'

He saw her stiffen and wondered what he had done now.

'What others?' she asked, in a tight, agonised voice.

'Joe—Fitz. I told them I could get two pounds.' The curate came and put their drinks on the table. Lily ignored him.

'So you've been talking to them about me . . .'

'I haven't been talking to anybody.'

'You blazoned it to the world and its wife that Lily Maxwell spent four pounds that didn't belong to her.'

'You have it all wrong, Lily.'

He had half risen in his effort to explain away her misunderstanding, but she brushed past the curate and stopped at the door.

'After that you can keep your drink. I don't want you crying it around the city that I drank your money on top of spending a bloody fortune on you.'

Pat stood up. Everything he tried to say had come out wrong. He struggled for more words, the right words. They didn't come and he felt he was going to burst.

'Lily . . .' he shouted. He loved her. He wanted to shout that too. But the curate was standing by, grinning, taking it all in. She pushed open the door and went out. It banged hard behind her, sending a cloud of sawdust inwards along the floor. The curate, large, red-faced, amiable, said to Pat:

161

'That's women for you—never know when you have them.'
He was greatly amused.

'Will I take back the second drink?'

'Leave it where it is,' Pat told him.

He tried to match the curate's mood—to sound offhand and undisturbed. It was painfully difficult, with his world in bits about him.

She was gone. He lingered over the drink Lily had left behind her until the loneliness became unbearable. He was back in the street and wondering what direction to take, when the idea of approaching Mr. Donegan again suggested itself. He had nothing to pledge that was worth anything and anyway Mr. Donegan was bound to have put up the shutters for the night, but he made up his mind to try what was a forlorn hope.

It was quite dark now. Along Mr. Donegan's street, the gas-lamps, spaced widely apart, threw a circle of soft light about themselves. The shutters of Mr. Donegan's shop caught and reflected the ghost of their glow, the three brass balls shone dimly. A light escaped from the chink in the blind which covered the window above the gold lettered name. Pat began to knock at the door, producing a sound that startled the deserted street. It took Mr. Donegan some time to descend the stairs and when he opened the door he was not in the best of humour.

'What's all this?' he demanded, peering out.

'It's me,' Pat said.

'Either that or your twin brother,' Mr. Donegan agreed.

'I want to see you about a little matter.'

'I open in the morning,' Mr. Donegan pointed out.

'For the love of your mother, Mr. Donegan, as an old and loyal customer.'

Mr. Donegan sighed.

'Come in.'

He led the way down a narrow passage until they came to a side door which let them into the shop. It was in darkness. Mr. Donegan found the portable ladder, struck a match and grunted elaborately as he stretched up to light the gas.

'Now look what I've done,' he said. He had touched the mantel with the head of the match. A blue flame, escaping through the puncture, tried like a tongue to lick the side of the glass.

'It's a favour,' Pat began, when Mr. Donegan had climbed down.

'So I feared.' He looked again at the mantel, as though it was at fault.

'I want two pounds.'

'Tonight?'

'At once, if I can have it.'

'Are you in trouble?'

'Of a kind.'

'If it's to bribe a policeman don't be a fool. He'll either list it in the charges or he'll take it and tip off one of his pals to pick you up tomorrow.'

'It's not that sort of trouble.'

'What have you to pledge?'

'Nothing,' Pat said.

It took Mr. Donegan some moments to find words.

'Nothing,' he repeated.

'If you give me two pounds now, I'll have it back with you before three o'clock tomorrow.'

'Where will you get it?' Mr. Donegan asked, putting his elbows on the counter and leaning forward, confident that there was no satisfactory answer.

'From a moneylender who knows me well.'

'And what guarantee have I that I'll ever see you again?'

'My good name.'

'You've a good name,' Mr. Donegan agreed, 'but that's not a good business basis. We must be reasonable.'

Pat bent down. Mr. Donegan, leaning forward still further, saw with growing surprise that he was unlacing his boots. He took them off with difficulty and placed them on the counter under Mr. Donegan's nose.

'These,' he said.

Mr. Donegan lifted one of the boots, and, looking hard at the sole, spoke his mind.

'Is it these . . . ?'

'Them.'

'You'd buy five pairs of these for two pounds.'

'I could. But I wouldn't,' Pat said.

'You wouldn't,' Mr. Donegan agreed. 'I know you well enough to believe that.'

'Then take the boots. A man can't do without his boots very long and they'll be your warrant that I'll be back with the money.'

Mr. Donegan thought hard. Then he went to the back of the shop. He reappeared with two sovereigns, which he gave to Pat.

'Are you satisfied,' Pat asked, before he accepted them.

'I'm satisfied,' Mr. Donegan said, 'but take the boots. I can't have you going around naked.'

'A bargain is a bargain,' Pat insisted.

Mr. Donegan, noting the barefooted, coatless, ridiculously dogged cut of him, gave it up. He had found the measure of his man. His confidence was unprofessional, but complete.

'All right,' he said, shrugging his shoulders, 'if it pleases you, it pleases me.'

Pat put the money in his pocket and made immediately for Chandlers Court. He could not bear to have them think her dishonest, a common tart who took whatever she could get. The night was warm, the side streets almost deserted, a sickle moon poised gracefully above them and touched the roof-tops with silver. He climbed the stairs without meeting anybody and tapped at the door. It took Fitz some time to recognise his caller.

'Where were *you* all day?' he asked.

'I went to see Lily,' Pat said. He was searching in his pockets. Fitz felt on his palm the tiny weight of the two sovereigns. He was moved, by loyalty, by generosity, by that superb quality in Pat's love for others which made his personality something of a riddle.

'You're far too generous. And, besides, I told you there was no hurry.'

'They're safer with you than lying about in Lily's place,' Pat said. He was elaborately offhand.

'You're a real friend in need,' Fitz said, touched.

'For nothing,' Pat said.

'Aren't you coming in for a minute?'

'No—it's a bit on the late side. How did things go?'

'Larkin addressed the dockers. We think the port is completely closed—but we can't be sure until tomorrow.'

'I heard there was trouble.'

'A bit. I got a clatter myself.'

'So I see,' Pat said, acknowledging the bandage. 'Sorry I wasn't there.'

Fitz wondered at this apparent lack of curiosity.

'Come in and we'll talk.'

'No,' Pat said, 'I have to get along. See you sometime tomorrow.' He turned to go, then turned back.

'Just one little favour.'

'Of course,' Fitz said.

'I didn't like what Joe said today.'

'Neither did I. I told him off.'

'Would you let him know when you see him that Lily was all right.'

Fitz knew what he meant. He said he would.

'And Mulhall?'

'I'll tell both of them.'

'Thanks,' Pat said. 'She's a straight girl—and I want them to know that. Good luck.'

'Thanks,' Fitz said Pat waited until he had closed the door. Then he went down the stairs and out again into the streets. He passed under a gas-lamp and into the shadows. A passerby stared after him, puzzled by his noiselessness, but the night hid his want and left him wondering.

On the following day the dockers continued their strike. Stevedores read out names to knots of men who listened in silence and then moved away, ships tied up and remained idle and untouched in calm water under a lazy sun. For over a week nothing moved along the port. There were policemen everywhere, or so it seemed, parading in groups and looking grim and businesslike, but finding very little to do. Even the mass meeting of dockers at which they had pledged themselves to remain out until the carters' grievances had been dealt with remained orderly. Fitz heard Larkin again that night and wondered at the magnetism of the man as the crowd cheered and the flares of the torch-bearers tossed about the platform, painting shadows on hungry faces that peered under peaked caps. Most of them had empty pockets, bare rooms to return to, bread and tea to kill hunger with and no assurance of strike pay or any kind of relief. Yet they cheered when he said he could promise them nothing except hardship, and felt that somewhere at the end of the road there was a better world waiting. Like heaven, it was very far away, and like heaven it would be very hard to reach. Yet where before the only certainty had been obscurity and want, now at least there was that hint of hope. Hope for what, Fitz in the calm after the speechmaking, could not quite remember. He could only remember that it had been there, that it had infected him in company with thousands of others crushing and jostling and listening; perhaps it was a feeling of movement that remained, a journey beginning, a vague but certain purpose.

Whatever it was, it served Rashers well. People parted with pennies and halfpennies when he moved among the gatherings, singing in his cracked voice before the speakers mounted the platform. He had a fortnight of unusual prosperity. Then the Government, alarmed at a situation for which there was no precedent, intervened by calling a meeting of the interested parties at Dublin Castle and setting up a board of conciliation to examine and recommend new conditions for wages and hours of work. Mr. Sexton, seeing the moment ripe to reassert his authority, crossed over from Liverpool and decided to represent the union in his capacity as general secretary. On his advice the men agreed to return to work pending the outcome. Rashers found the ballad still good for a few pence on Saturday nights, until his clients learned that Sexton, not Larkin, would carry on the negotiations. The disappointment had its effect on Rashers' income and the ballad, though useful, ceased to be the money-earner it had been.

Mr. Doggett, having met the general wage demand, was anxious to clean the slate of the other outstanding irritation. He informed the foundry that he would accept responsibility for the few shillings overtime pay that had caused the dispute. Nolan & Keyes did likewise. The whole transaction cost less than five pounds and the men concerned received three shillings each. Mulhall, meeting Fitz on the stairs, offered him a drink on the strength of it.

'I want to talk to you,' he said.

It was August. The trams were bringing back visitors from the Horse Show at Ballsbridge, the streets were beginning to breathe again after the drenching sun of the afternoon.

Mulhall paid and said immediately: 'It's about Sexton taking over the negotiations. Most of us feel Larkin should have been allowed to carry it on.'

Fitz felt the same way, but he knew there was little they could do.

'Sexton is general secretary. He can overrule Larkin anytime he likes. At the same time I don't see why he should come into it now.'

'Because Larkin's tactics don't suit,' Mulhall said, 'they cost too much money. And it's going to remain that way until we break away and form a union of our own.'

'I've heard that being talked about,' Fitz said.

'With Larkin as general secretary,' Mulhall added. He paused and drank. 'What do you think about that?'

Fitz hesitated.

'I agree that we should start on our own,' he said carefully, 'but not just yet. We'll need money. After the knocking around we've taken during the past few months we need time to find our feet again.'

'I know, but we can make a beginning. Will you do your bit on the organising end?'

'In the foundry—yes.'

'That's enough for a start. Myself and a few others will be moving around the jobs generally. We may have to be ready quicker than you think—and I'll tell you why. Larkin may be prosecuted by the union—for misappropriation of funds.'

It took Fitz some time to grasp his meaning.

'What funds?'

'The money he collected in Cork.'

'But that was paid out.'

'It was paid out to us in Dublin. Their case is that it was

collected for the National Union of Dockers and should have been sent on to Liverpool first. It's a legal wrangle, but they've written to the committee about it.'

'What's their reason?'

'It's clear enough to me,' Mulhall said. 'He's called too many strikes without consulting them. They'll move heaven and earth to stop him doing it.'

Mulhall finished his pint.

'So we need a union of our own. Are you still backing us?'

Fitz, remembering the meetings, put aside his other doubts and said : 'I'm with Larkin—all the way.'

'Good,' Mulhall said. He indicated the empty glass.

'Have another.'

'No thanks,' Fitz declined. 'I'm on shift at twelve. But we'll talk again.'

'I'm glad you're with us,' Mulhall said, 'you're important.' He reached out his hand. It was a formality Fitz had not expected.

'Thanks,' he said, taking it warmly.

'I beg your pardon, Father.'

The paper lay on the breakfast table between them. Father O'Sullivan had the right to pick it up first, but the headlines had roused Father O'Connor's curiosity. He reached out his hand.

'Certainly,' Father O'Sullivan said. He had a large, benevolent face.

'Just the headlines.'

Father O'Sullivan motioned with a large benevolent hand to explain that it didn't matter.

'*Strikes in Cork and Derry: Larkin's Answer to exclusion from Conciliation Board. Expulsion Certain, confirms Sexton.*'

It was everywhere, this unheaval, a symptom of materialistic thinking spreading through the whole of Irish society. He would give warning from the pulpit.

'Thank you, Father,' he said, not bothering to read further.

He saw now that it would have been a mistake to distribute the food to the strikers. It was as well they had refused. Relief would only prolong their miseries and strengthen the hold of their

168

leaders. There were others who could be served, neglected and harmless creatures who were hungry too. The old. He should have thought in the first place of the old.

Near Christmas he told Hegarty and Keever to dispose of the parcels to the aged of the parish, provided they were not mixed up with the troublemakers. Keever made out his list. He was more prudent this time. The parcels were accepted gratefully. One learned, Father O'Connor reflected, however painfully, to separate the sheep from the goats. Some months earlier the true meaning of the phrase would not have been clear to him. Now he saw that it applied even to charity. It was sad. It was painful. It was true.

THEY sheltered in the gateway while the east wind, beating up the river, brought a sudden flurry of snow with it. Many of the gateways facing on to the river were closed. Once again, at intervals of a hundred yards or so, groups of carters were picketing.

'A white Christmas,' Fitz said, ironically.

Mulhall, looking at the cold, white spray that broke along the water said : 'And a hungry one.'

It was rough, being on strike for the second time within a few months. But the carters were a determined crowd. Larkin's expulsion from the Liverpool union had left the road open for the formation of a union of his own. He had taken it. The carters were his first members.

'Are you getting strike pay regularly?'

'It hasn't failed yet.'

'Where does Larkin get it from?'

'A mystery,' Mulhall admitted, 'but he always finds it somehow. Maybe the clergy are right. He's in league with oul Nick.'

'We had a meeting at the foundry last night,' Fitz told him. 'We're all transferring to the new union.'

'You had a hand in that, I'd say.'

'I gave you a promise.'

'That's what I meant,' Mulhall acknowledged.

'It was easy. They all want to be with Larkin.'

'When is it to happen?'

'Tomorrow evening. We're going over in a body.'

'Good,' Mulhall said, 'we'll all be together again.'

'We can levy right away to help the strike fund for you fellows.'

Mulhall nodded. The curtain of snowflakes had thinned. The air became clear. They began to walk home together. It was a desolate walk, with the east wind freezing their limbs and putting an edge on appetites they could not hope to satisfy. The streets were muddy and scattered with puddles. One stretched almost the entire width of a laneway. Mulhall waded straight through but Fitz picked a passage around the edges. His boots were leaking.

Mary was almost certain she was going to have a baby. It was another strong reason for avoiding trouble. The savage militancy of the new movement had bothered him throughout the whole of the autumn. Many a time, while the city slept and he broke off stoking to eat the supper Mary had made up for him, he had stared at the glowing frames of the furnace openings which spread in line down No. 2 House, feeling the bond between himself and that glowing gallery of fires. When he fed them they in turn fed him; if he let them go out there would be nothing for the home and nothing for the table. Sooner or later Larkin would call on him again to starve them and starve in turn himself. Sometimes, when turning to say goodbye to Mary in the evenings he would see through the large windows behind her the roofs of houses on the far side, their broken slates a dark blue under a sky that was taking a long time to get rid of the day, and she would seem so lonely and unprotected that it felt like the act of a traitor not to grasp tightly for her sake to the little bit of security that offered. But he had come to see that the security itself was a mirage; people he did not know and would never meet decided its extent and continuance for reasons that suited only themselves. He and the others did not count.

On Christmas Day Mary gave half of what they had to the Mulhalls; Mrs. Bartley thought of Rashers and saved a piece of cake for him; Rashers, in turn, invited Hennessy to the boiler house of St. Brigid's Church on the Feast of the Epiphany. Father O'Connor had re-employed him as boilerman for the season and the housekeeper had promised to give him his breakfast in the kitchen, a privilege of boilermen, which had become traditional in the parish. Hennessy waited for him in the boiler house itself. It lay under the back of the church, down stone steps that were surrounded by iron railings. A small furnace stood in the centre, and there was enough room to accommodate the couple of broken chairs between it and the coke from which Rashers fed it. He opened the door of the furnace and extended his hands to the warmth. Then he lit the candle which stood on a ledge in the stonework. The wavering light showed up walls that were thickly coated with black dust and ancient webs so encrusted that they hung like rags from the corners of the ceiling. He jumped when Rashers came suddenly behind him.

'You took a start out of me,' Hennessy confessed.

'Sit where you are,' Rashers ordered.

It was only a dirty hole under the church, but it was warm and dry and for a season it was his. The fact gave him the right to play host.

'Did you hear the bell ringing?' he asked.

'I did. I'd want to be deaf not to.'

The bell of St. Brigid's stood in the church grounds, a great bronze affair supported by bars which were imbedded in a stone pedestal.

'That was me,' Rashers said, modestly.

'You rang it?'

'The clerk said I could. Hanlon used to do it for him of a Sunday.'

'And now it's your privilege,' Hennessy said. 'Isn't that a great honour—to be summoning near and far to the house of God.'

'I knocked a bloody fine clatter out of it,' Rashers boasted. 'Got my feet against the stonework, took the rope in my hand and lay back.'

He gave Hennessy a rough demonstration.

'It sounded very impressive,' Hennessy confirmed. 'Every clang caught me at the back of the throat.'

'Here's something else for the same place,' Rashers said. He opened a newspaper and displayed slices of chicken and ham, which he had managed to hide away in the course of breakfast.

When he had divided them with Hennessy he took a bottle from his pocket, removed the cork and passed it under Hennessy's nose.

'Port wine,' Hennessy breathed.

'Pinched it from a bottle on the dresser.'

'They'll miss it and you'll be in trouble.'

'There were three half-finished bottles in a row. They'll never guess.'

'Somebody must be partial to the cup that cheers.'

'Father Giffley, I imagine. The other man is a bit prejudiced in that direction. He doesn't like the smell of drink at all.'

'God bless the thought, anyway,' Hennessy said. He drank deeply.

'What do you think of my little place here?' Rashers asked, as they feasted.

'If I was you I'd bunk down here at nights instead of in that bloody oul basement in Chandlers Court.'

'I would, only for the dog. I can't very well leave him on his own.'

'Bring him with you,' Hennessy suggested generously.

'That would be a class of a sacrilege,' Rashers objected, 'bringing an unbaptised animal into a church.'

'This isn't the church.'

'It's all sanctified ground.'

'Not the boiler house,' Hennessy argued. 'Sanctifying the boiler house would be a bit Irish. You might as well say the toilet at the back of the vestry was sanctified.'

The point impressed Rashers.

'You might be right,' he conceded.

'Of course I'm right.'

'Maybe I'll chance bringing him down an odd night,' he agreed. Again he passed the bottle to Hennessy. He thought in silence for a while.

'A bit of music mightn't be out of place.'

'What music?' Hennessy asked.

'This,' Rashers said. He rooted in his inner pockets and drew out a tin whistle. It was a superior toned Italian Flageolet.

'I got a present of a shilling at Christmas from Father Giffley,' he explained, 'and I squandered it on this.'

'Are you not afraid they'd hear you above?'

'Divil the bit.' He held the whistle towards Hennessy. 'What do you think of it?'

It's slender column took on the rosy hue of the firelight. They both regarded it, Rashers affectionately, Hennessy, his mouth full of food, with an expression of bulbous curiosity.

'You spent a shilling on that?' he asked when it was physically possible.

Rashers turned it about and about in the firelight and said: 'I often spent a shilling on less.' He took a swig from the bottle and passed it to Hennessy.

'Isn't this the life of Reilly?' Hennessy exclaimed. They bent forward together to let the fireglow play on their bodies, unaware of the antics of their gigantic shadows in the flickering candlelight.

'I knew you'd like the wine,' Rashers said. 'It's made out of grapes.'

'Play the oul whistle,' Hennessy invited. He disposed himself comfortably to listen.

Rashers began to do so. The notes came out sweetly and slowly. Hennessy, listening politely, now and then gathered food crumbs from the paper on his knee with fingers that courteously avoided noise. Rashers thrust his chin forward and found again a simple consolation he had lost months before in race crowds and drink.

Celebrating late mass in the church above them, Father Giffley bent down to the altar and breathed the *Domine Non Sum Dignus*. The act of stooping sent a stab of pain shooting from his neck to his throbbing eyes. The server struck the altar gong three times with the felt-headed hammer and the worshippers bent low also and beat their breasts.

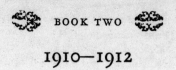

BOOK TWO

1910—1912

CHAPTER I

A T fifteen minutes to midnight on the sixth day of May
1910, in the presence of Her Majesty Queen Alexandra,
the Prince and Princess of Wales, the Princess Royal and
the Duke of Fife, Princess Victoria, Princess Louise and the
Duchess of Argyll, Edward VII breathed his last.

The Archbishop of Dublin had called for prayers for his
recovery. When these were seen to have gone unanswered, the
city did the next best thing. It went into deep mourning. Pres-
cott's, the cleaners, who claimed to have enormous facilities
for such work, offered to dye all articles of clothing black at the
shortest notice. Mrs. Bradshaw availed of their services and
during his lying-in-state she began to read the newspapers
closely, keeping her husband well informed on the day-to-day
events. The report of a storm, particularly, caught her interest.
It occurred on the Wednesday and involved the historic scene
at Westminster in a wild splendour. It broke about the heads of
his loyal subjects who waited hour after hour to pay their last
tribute. Vivid flashes of lightning streaked the sky and thunder
crashed above the hall in which the King lay, guarded by his
silent and motionless watchers. He was the least troubled of
them all. The Liberals had threatened to abolish his house of
peers; they could do so now without causing him the least pain.
John Redmond had urged his Irish followers to hasten Home
Rule by supporting the Liberal policy; he could now lean over
to bawl it in the King's ear and no flicker of the royal eyelids
would reprove or admonish him. For months his subjects had
wondered if in such a crisis the King could remain above poli-

177

tics. Death, with an unexpected gesture, had assured them that he would.

'What a terrible storm last night,' Mrs. Bradshaw said to her husband, when he had returned from his morning walk along the front.

'A fog,' he corrected. 'I'd hardly call it a storm.'

'I mean in London.'

'Oh—that.'

'It's all here in the paper.'

'I'm not surprised,' he said, 'the Kish was going all night.'

She had heard it too. All night the boom of the fog signal had disturbed her rest, a regular, disembodied moan that made the night restless.

'There's a thick mist at sea,' he reported.

'I felt there would be. How I pity the poor sailors.'

'Didn't stop the Navy. Part of the Home Fleet have anchored down below—I could make out the *Lord Nelson*.' Bradshaw was very good at ships. He knew their names and could tell the difference between battleships and cruisers, gunboats and destroyers. The gentlemen of Kingstown, of course, took a very special pride in such things. Naturally so.

'It's a beautiful name—the Peacemaker.'

Bradshaw looked puzzled. Then he understood.

'You mean the King?'

'Of course. That is what they are calling him.'

'Ah. For a moment I thought you meant one of the battle-ships,' he explained.

The next day public departments, banks and business establishments closed. The Most Reverend Dr. Walsh, Archbishop of Dublin, presided at Votive Mass in the Pro-Cathedral.

Yearling, who was staying at a remote hotel in Connemara for the mayfly fishing, forgot the significance of the day until very late that night. He was drinking whiskey, not in the hotel, but unobtrusively in a little public house. One of the local people was playing a fiddle and Yearling had the seat beside the turf fire. There was a smoky oil lamp hanging from the ceiling which gave the room a small, shadowed look, and the men near him, to his delight, were speaking quietly together in Gaelic. Their voices, unaccountably, reminded him that this had been the day of the royal funeral. He thought of William Martin Murphy and, with the merest ghost of a smile, he remembered his refusal to be tapped on the shoulder by the dead king's sword.

The high grey walls of the workhouse shut out almost everything; they were a fortification against the life of the city, a barrier against time, which passed yet did not seem to pass. The visitors who came weekly were few; the inmates were many. Carts passed in and out on stated days with a jingling of harness and a creaking of shafts and a stumbling of hooves on the uneven cobbles, but these meant little to the old women who hobbled about the grounds in shapeless grey dresses, and nothing at all to those lying in the close-packed wards, their eyes fixed on the high ceilings for hours of silence. Here, too, Death came most frequently and with no noise at all. From where, Miss Gilchrist sometimes wondered: through the great arched gateway whether closed or open, up from the deep earth or down from the insubstantial sky? Three times it had come for her in the space of almost three years: once in daylight, when from beyond the screens about her bed the voices of the others and the clatter of crockery told her it was tea-time; once in the small hours when the candle in the hand of the sister lit the priest's bending face; once when a giantlike thumb stretched down to anoint her from a limitless absence of either light or darkness. Yet she struggled back to the world again and at breakfast time the old woman whose turn it was to be on ward duty said:

'We thought you were gone on us for certain yesterday, Gilchrist.'

She was unable to speak. After a while she managed to assemble her surroundings once more; the rusted iron beds side by side, the high window, the bare uneven boards of the ward.

'You'll be off your feet for good this time, Gilchrist,' the old woman said, coming back, 'and you're a lucky oul bitch in that. You won't have to empty any more bedpans.'

Miss Gilchrist smiled again. She had a sharp tongue, once

well stocked for use. But now she kept to herself the answers that occurred so readily. They were no longer worth making. In a day or in a week, or in another three years, it would be all the same, whatever had been said or unsaid.

She was content now to lie quietly and know nothing of what passed outside. She would not, she knew, ever again take her turn at emptying the slops or the bedpans, or scrub the walls down, or sweep the floors or attend at the morgue where Death laid out his conquests before they were carted off to the grave. Miss Gilchrist had taken her turn at washing them for their journey. One day in winter she had entered to do her work and screamed because there were seven dead babies on one of the slabs. She was to be reprimanded severely for her conduct, but nothing further was said to her because near dawn the next morning she had her second attack. After considerable thought she decided to speak to Father O'Connor about it. It was his habit now to make occasional visits. He had come first because Mrs. Bradshaw, her conscience still troubled about the servant she had been fond of, asked him. Then, seizing the opportunity for the exercise of Christian virtue, he decided to continue, because he suffered each time he had to enter among the miserable and the destitute and it seemed good to him to offer it to God for salvation's sake, for his own soul and that of his superior. It might be the means of saving Father Giffley from alcoholism; if not it was still part of his duty to practise the corporal works of mercy—to clothe the naked, to feed the hungry, to visit the sick and imprisoned and to bury the dead.

The thought of seven naked babies, side by side on the slab of the dead, was a terrible one. But, then, everything about the workhouse was terrible; poverty and illness and loneliness and senility were its four guardian angels.

'You must think of them as seven innocent souls,' he told Miss Gilchrist, 'seven new angels praising God in heaven.'

Without changing her expression she said: 'I want you to speak to Mrs. Bradshaw for me.'

'Certainly.'

'I want her to know what will happen to me when I die here.'

'You're distressing yourself . . .' Father O'Connor said.

'They'll take me with the rest and bury me in a pauper's grave. I want her to claim my body and save me from that.'

He tried to say something, but it was difficult. Her face was grey and very small, her lips were colourless and ringed with dried spittle which cracked when she spoke. Her mind was fixed firmly now on what she wanted to say.

'I've seen too many of them, Father, laid out there to be whipped off without a tear from a friend or a solitary soul to say goodbye. Do you know what I seen once?'

She turned her face away and for a moment he thought she was wandering back to the incident of the babies again. But it wasn't that.

'Sometimes they forget to lock the back door of the morgue —the one that leads into the laneway. Once when I went in there was a scattering of little boys. Do you know what they were up to, Father? They were stealing the pennies from the eyes of the dead.'

He had learned enough these past few years to feel only regret. The children of need were capable of deeds far worse.

'I would like to think that when I go someone will claim my poor body.'

'I'll speak to Mrs. Bradshaw,' he promised. As always, his temptation to run away almost mastered his will to help. He fought it; for over two years it had been the same battle, trying not to surrender to disgust.

'You mustn't give way to morbid fancies,' he insisted. 'You can be sure you'll see many and many a long day yet.' He looked over at the high window. He saw, at a great distance it seemed, the Dublin mountains. They were, as always, fresh and beautiful. In surroundings such as that, among fields and hills, the old lady near him had been born. He looked back at the bed. She was shaking her head from side to side, denying something he had said.

It was through Miss Gilchrist that he paid his first visit to Mary. He did so to ask Mary to visit the old woman. The meeting was embarrassing at first. Mary had been two years in his parish yet he had made no attempt to contact her, partly because of what had happened on the night she had called to the vestry with Fitz to arrange their marriage, partly because it was difficult to avoid reference to the world they had met in first. Mary offered him tea but he refused.

'And have you children?' he asked, letting his attention fix itself on his surroundings while he questioned her. He noted a table, a sideboard and some butter boxes. The clock on the mantelpiece seemed out of place.

'Two, Father.'

He had to think hard to connect her answer and his question. 'Two boys?' he asked, relieved to remember.

'A boy and a girl. The girl is only four weeks old.'

He had noticed she was looking unwell and had blamed poverty. Now he knew it was the usual combination of hunger and childbirth. The women had it hard. To ease the feeling of constraint he said : 'I'd like to see them.'

It was morning. Mary led him into the bedroom. Everything was clean. And they had two rooms. That was quite unusual.

'Your husband is working?'

'At the foundry.'

'A blessing,' he approved.

This made the extreme poverty hard to understand. Father O'Connor, turning the matter over in his mind as he talked, remembered there was an explanation. Mr. Larkin. Was this one of the homes that had refused the food parcels?

The children were wholesome and neat too. He put it down to the beneficial effect of training in a good house. The baby was sleeping, but the older child smiled at him. Father O'Connor crossed to the bed and then formally, gravely, he gave his blessing to both of them, touching each forehead lightly in turn, and murmuring the formula quietly but audibly. Mary moved to one side, knelt and crossed herself.

'I must tell Mrs. Bradshaw you have a thriving family,' he said, smiling and stretching out his hand to help her to rise. They were both suddenly at ease.

'Give her my best respects,' Mary said. Her voice trembled. At his blessing of the children she had felt a pang of emotion, an inexplicable happiness. For a moment, in a long barrenness, a vague hope filled her.

'Of course.' Her gratitude was moving.

'I'll visit Miss Gilchrist on Sunday.'

'She'll be delighted, I assure you.' He held up his hand to prevent her when she moved to see him to the door.

He went down the stone steps and into the sunlight. The streets he passed through were familiar now; it was satisfactory to be able to name the side turns, to remember here and there a family to which he had ministered personally.

Father O'Connor paused to take a paper from a newsboy, who touched his hat and said 'God bless you, Father' when he waved aside the change. He put the paper in his pocket. The woman was unwell. As he walked he wondered what sting of the flesh could tempt a young girl to exchange service in a good house for a couple of rooms and a few butter boxes. He had been told something about Fitzpatrick. By Timothy Keever, was it? He could not remember what.

At lunchtime he said to Father O'Sullivan: 'Would you oblige me in something, Father?'

Father O'Sullivan had been eating in silence, his eyes fixed more or less continuously on a devotional booklet. It was his mealtime habit. It took him a while to realise he had been spoken to, but when it penetrated he looked up and smiled pleasantly.

'Certainly.'

'I'd rather Father Giffley were here . . . I should really ask him, but it's urgent and quite important.'

'Father Giffley is still unwell.'

Father O'Connor, immediately suspicious, regarded the other closely. Then he said, casually, 'Really. Today again?'

'I went to his room to enquire, but he said he would rather be left alone.'

'Was the door locked?' Father O'Connor asked.

'I didn't try,' the other said, looking surprised.

Father O'Connor paused. Then he said, in a confiding tone: 'It might have been wiser to do so.'

'I asked him if he would like a doctor, but he assured me it was unnecessary.'

Remembering other sessions behind locked doors and other

refusals of his superior to leave his room, Father O'Connor pushed his plate roughly aside.

'Are you so blind, Father,' he asked, 'do you not know as well as I do what is wrong with our parish priest?'

'He is not strong, the poor man,' Father O'Sullivan said. Then, in almost the same tone, he added: 'But you wanted my assistance, Father?'

This large, guileless man was either a saint or a humbug, Father O'Connor decided.

'I would like you to take benediction for me this evening,' Father O'Connor said, controlling himself, 'I have some personal business.'

'I shall be glad to, Father.'

Father O'Sullivan smiled. His soutane, with its faded, green-streaked sheen, its frayed cuffs and buttonholes that gaped loosely from long use, might have been the parish clerk's second best, the one he did the heavy work in and from which he removed the dribbles of candle grease by scraping them with a knife. The booklet propped against the sugar bowl irritated Father O'Connor too. It was a gaudy-covered production dealing with the devotion to the Sacred Heart. But it intrigued him.

'May I trouble you for the sugar, Father?'

'Forgive me—how selfish.'

The Faith for The Family: 'A series for the instruction of the Faithful simply rendered by "A Catholic Priest", and approved by . . .'

As he had guessed, a popular concoction, aimed at the uneducated. But perhaps Father O'Sullivan was preparing a simple sermon. Or was he—at the unexpected thought Father O'Connor almost upset the sugar bowl—was he, perhaps, the anonymous priest who wrote them?

Yearling left his luggage at Westland Row Station and went across the street to the Grosvenor. There was a barmaid there he admired. In his hand he carried his two fishing rods, a green-heart and a split cane, both too precious to be left out of sight. After the serene quiet of Connemara, with its reed-grown lakes and blue, remote hills, the streets seemed more than usually airless. He dodged a hackney cab, winced at the rattle of trams and found the pavement. Almost immediately a hungry wretch thrust a collecting box under his nose. Yearling examined the letters on the side. They said: 'Jim Larkin Defence Fund'. Mr. Yearling, with a magnanimous flourish, dropped in a shilling. He bowed when the man raised his cap.

Feeling much better, he entered the hotel and rang the bell. It was answered by an unfamiliar female. Disappointed, he asked her for a large Irish.

'Yes, sir. Will you be wanting soda as well?' He decided she was bulgy and unprepossessing.

'Good God, no.'

The startled girl withdrew. She came back with whiskey and a small, stone jug containing water.

'Where's Rose?' Yearling asked. He measured carefully the quantity of water.

'Gone, sir.'

'What do you mean—gone? Has she left?'

'More or less, sir.'

The reply displeased him.

'How much more than less?' he snapped.

'I beg your pardon, sir?'

'Was she sacked?' Yearling barked.

The girl jumped and said: 'She was, sir.'

'And why?' He bunched his bushy eyebrows at her, terrifying her.

'Miss Harrigan thought she made a bit free with the gentlemen, sir.'

'I wouldn't call that a fault—would you?'

'I don't know, sir.'

Yearling sighed.

'Never mind. Please bring me the morning paper. And another whiskey.'

'Yes, sir.'

The girl went off. Yearling sipped his drink and listened in a melancholy mood to the constant clip-clop of hooves outside the wide uncurtained window, missing the pretty face of Rose and the pleasure of making her laugh with his drolleries. He opened his paper and read it over his second whiskey until it seemed time to go back to the station for his train to Kingstown. When he was paying her he asked her name.

'Alice, sir.'

'That's a song,' Yearling told her. ' "Alice, Where Art Thou". Pretty air. I hope you won't disappoint the respected Miss Harrigan.'

She laughed and delighted him by venturing, shyly. 'Sure what harm is a bit of gas, sir.'

'That's the ticket,' he boomed at her. As they laughed together he began to see that she was pretty, after all. For her show of spirit he tipped her a shilling and went out in better humour.

At the entrance to the station he stood courteously aside to let a figure in clerical dress go first and discovered, with an exclamation of pleasure, that it was Father O'Connor.

'My dear friend.'

Startled by the bellow, Father O'Connor swung round. He came to a standstill.

'This is unexpected . . .' he began.

Yearling pumped inordinately at his extended hand while he asked: 'Are you going to Kingstown?'

Father O'Connor was.

'Excellent,' Yearling said. 'So am I.'

Father O'Connor found it necessary to excuse himself while he went to the booking office. They rejoined each other and when the gateman had checked each ticket and raised his cap with great respect to Father O'Connor they searched out an empty carriage and took their seats. Conversation proved difficult. Clouds of steam, hissing upwards, coiled and were trapped under the great glass awning. Father O'Connor saw Yearling's lips moving, but could not catch what he was saying. He had to raise his voice as though he were in the pulpit and say: 'I beg your pardon?'

'Milkcans,' Yearling shouted.

Father O'Connor looked puzzled.

Yearling shouted: 'I said I have never entered this station yet but they were shifting milkcans—millions of damned milkcans.'

Father O'Connor leaned towards the window, smiled and nodded. Porters were rolling the empty cans from one end of the platform to the other. The din was ear-splitting. It was a relief when the coaches jerked and bumped and the train moved slowly towards open day. Sunshine came leaping into the carriage, the backyards with their lines of washing slipped past, there was motion and peacefulness. In the basin by Boland's Mill, an old-time schooner lay to. Near one bank, where green reeds leaned in delicate clusters above their own reflections, three swans rested.

'What a beautiful picture,' Father O'Connor said.

'A serene and beguiling lie,' Yearling answered. Father O'Connor looked surprised. Yearling, with unexpected gravity, said:

'I sometimes despair of this city of ours.'

'Its poverty?'

'Its contradictions.'

'I work in its back streets every day and when I lie down to sleep I am conscious of its squalor being on my doorstep. But I don't despair.'

'You have one eye fixed on heaven,' Yearling said, 'try looking at it with both eyes sometimes.'

'I assure you I've looked at it closely,' Father O'Connor spoke the truth. He did not despair. But there were days after days of depression, of feeling lost in a nightmare. The excuse of business or good manners brought him now and then to the Bradshaws. They were welcome retreats.

'What do you think of Larkin's sentence?'

A little confused at what appeared to be a sudden change of subject, Father O'Connor hesitated before asking: 'Has he been sentenced?'

'To twelve months with hard labour, it's in today's paper.' Yearling held out the paper he had been reading over his whiskey.

Father O'Connor, remembering having bought a paper himself at some stage, searched vaguely and found it stuck in his pocket, unopened and, until now, completely forgotten.

'I hadn't seen it,' he explained.

'Savage,' Yearling pronounced.

Father O'Connor spread out his hands.

'If he was dishonest . . .' he began.

'He collected money from one city and gave it to the wretches who were on strike in another. The only case against him is that the money should have been sent on first to Liverpool. Where's the dishonesty?'

'It was irregular . . .' Father O'Connor suggested.

'If it was, who are collecting for his defence? The very people he's accused of defrauding. One of them shook a box under my nose less than an hour ago.'

That was what Timothy Keever had told him. Fitzpatrick had been collecting for Larkin—he remembered now. 'I haven't followed the trial very closely.' As he said so he remembered a detail which had shocked him early on. It was a newspaper interview in which Mr. Sexton, the general secretary who had come over from Liverpool to give evidence against Larkin, confessed that he had had to go through the streets armed with a revolver.

'They've bungled,' Mr. Yearling said, 'and bungled badly. First they delay the trial for two years. Now they convict him on a technicality and give him twelve months' hard. They're determined to make a popular martyr of the most dangerous man of our time. They'll have the dregs of the city flocking to him.'

'They seem to be flocking to him already,' Father O'Connor said.

'That is no reason why the law should become his recruiting sergeant.'

'Is that what you meant when you said you despair of the city?'

'I despair of the law and the Government,' Yearling confessed, 'and of the men who are supposed to be my business colleagues. They're fools—all of them.'

They had stopped at Booterstown. On their left the tide was advancing towards the wall, a thin edge of foam along its border. A light breeze found its way into the carriage. It tasted of salt. Looking across towards Howth Hill, Father O'Connor said: 'Men bungle and make mistakes. But you must at least agree that the city is beautiful.'

'It depends on where you live and how much you earn, doesn't it?'

'I think we are talking of different things.'

'What is your answer to poverty?' Yearling challenged. He was not yet prepared to leave the subject alone.

Father O'Connor sighed and after a moment of reflection said: 'From those who have wealth, charity for the sake of God; from those who suffer poverty, resignation for His sake also.'

'Marx has a different answer. He says the expropriators must be expropriated. That means me,' Yearling pointed out.

'We condemn socialism, of course.'

'I have read your condemnations, Father. But for all their hat-raising to you, I am beginning to doubt that they will always listen to you. Does that sound offensive?'

'Not at all. We've pointed out already that Larkin is a dangerous man; he's a self-professed socialist. He doesn't hesitate to criticise the priests, yet the people still help him and listen to him.'

'And you will leave it like that?'

'I am not the Hierarchy,' Father O'Connor said, with a modest smile. 'My duty is to be obedient.'

'You broke Parnell,' Yearling suggested.

'I wonder did we?' Father O'Connor said. 'Do you not think it was his own party that broke him? After all, many of the people continued to follow him.'

'You condemned him,' Yearling insisted. 'Yet, as you say, many of the people remained loyal to him. They didn't listen to you—that's my point.'

Did Yearling speak with sympathy of Parnell because he, like the fallen chief, was a Protestant. Why was he questioning about Larkin? Did he wish the Church to condemn openly and at once? Or was it possible that Larkin's methods had his sympathy? Surely not. If the Church commanded absolute obedience Yearling would say the country was priest-ridden; if it did not he would taunt the Church for its failure. A note of sadness crept into Father O'Connor's voice as he answered, generally:

'There are other, more important matters in which they some-times do not listen to us either. That is why we have to spend so much of our time hearing confessions.'

To his surprise Yearling began to laugh.

'Have I said something amusing?'

'You are like all the others of your cloth,' Yearling explained. 'I point out the very real threat of social revolution to you and you are only concerned about it because it may, perhaps, be a sin.'

'Surely,' Father O'Connor said earnestly, 'that is the only thing which is worth being concerned about.'

At Kingstown Father O'Connor was persuaded to agree to drop in on Yearling when he had concluded his visit to the Bradshaws. They parted. Father O'Connor allowed himself the pleasure of a walk along the front. The elegance of the houses pleased him, the frequent carriages, the manifestations of polite living. It was a world in which he had once held an honoured place. He turned into the back streets, where the passage of a couple of years had left their less kindly traces. Mr. Bradshaw's set of houses near the harbour, he discovered, were now in need of support and had great beams slanting against them to prop the front walls. But their poverty was not like that of the central city; their squalor kept itself to itself. The township remained elegant.

He refused Mrs. Bradshaw's invitation to stay for dinner, and explained that he was already committed. As an alternative she was happy to have him accept tea and scones. She hoped he was contented still in his parish and wondered why he seemed to have abandoned the relief fund idea. She had thought it such an excellent one. Father O'Connor explained that it had not proved so straightforward a matter as, in his early en-thusiasm, he had believed it to be. He would not vex her with details. She thought his uneasiness was a sign that their efforts had fallen short of his expectations. He assured her that that was not the case.

'Our help was so small it wasn't worth while,' she suggested.

'Everything is worth while,' Father O'Connor insisted, 'even the smallest thing we do.'

'I've often thought of visiting myself,' Mrs. Bradshaw confided, 'but my husband is very much against it.'

'He is right,' Father O'Connor said.

'And Miss Gilchrist. I'd like to speak to her even for half an hour.'

Father O'Connor insisted that it was out of the question. He told her again about the kind of place it was, about the inmates, their coarseness, the overpowering combination of age and ignorance and illness. Mrs. Bradshaw would find it too distressing.

'Is she very ill?' Mrs. Bradshaw asked.

'Last week there seemed little hope for her. But on Sunday she seemed as well as ever.'

'She was always very strong,' Mrs. Bradshaw said. She seemed to be considering something. In order not to intrude, he took his time putting milk and sugar in his tea, stirring it, tasting it. He was glad he did so. Her next question led without embarrassment towards the topic he had come to discuss.

'When they die,' Mrs. Bradshaw asked, 'what are the arrangements?'

He chose his sentences carefully.

'The relatives are notified—if there are any. If there are and they claim the body they have the option of making the customary funeral arrangements—at their own personal expense, of course.'

'And if there are no relatives?'

'In that case, I'm afraid, it's an institutional burial in a pauper's grave.'

'I shouldn't like that to happen to Miss Gilchrist,' Mrs. Bradshaw said.

Father O'Connor saw that the moment had come when he should be frank.

'She spoke to me about it last Sunday. The thought seems to be constantly at the back of her mind. It has made her very unhappy—so unhappy that she asked me, as a great favour, to mention it to you.'

His words so affected Mrs. Bradshaw that he wondered for a moment if he had been too brutal and direct, if he had assaulted her feelings instead of appealing to her charity. She set his mind at rest almost at once.

'I'm very glad you told me this. Please let Miss Gilchrist know that if I've failed the living I'll at least do my duty by the dead.'

She began to weep. They were the tears of a kind-hearted woman and they distressed him greatly. It was not her fault that Miss Gilchrist had been cast off.

'You are very generous,' he offered. It was the best he could think of.

'We should have looked after her ourselves. She was such a loyal poor soul—and she was with us so long.'

'Your husband had to be practical.'

'Do we fulfil our obligations by being practical all the time?' she asked.

Her bitter tone caught him on the wrong foot. He had only meant to console, not to begin a discussion on the morality of a dismal affair. The main thing was she was prepared to meet Miss Gilchrist's wishes.

'I'll tell Miss Gilchrist. It will make her very happy. And grateful.'

'For so little?'

'It is not by any means little,' he said, earnestly.

'It seems so to me.'

'I assure you it isn't. You are a generous woman. You must stop reproaching yourself. And you must not blame your husband.'

'He is not to know,' she interrupted quickly. 'Please don't mention anything to him.'

This mild woman surprised him. He had thought her incapable of bitterness, an imperturbable woman at the centre of a small, smoothly enamelled world. Yet she criticised her husband and was prepared to disobey him because in her heart she felt a greater power at work. He knew how hard that must be for her, a woman shaped—to the raising of a teacup—by the conventions of her class.

'You need have no fear,' he told her, in his quietest and most reassuring tone.

Then, to ease her mind further, he told of his call on Mary. She questioned him about Mary's circumstances, her husband, her children. He began to understand how lonely and unhappy she was, this woman without children of her own who brooded too much over the misfortunes of those for whom she felt the tug of responsibility. She did not brush shoulders often enough with reality to know that these were commonplace hardships. There was nothing to be done about them that Father O'Connor could see, except to suffer them with patience and to offer, where possible, some negligible but well-intentioned relief. Her kindness impressed him, but he was glad, nevertheless, when he could look at the clock and say, without lying, that it was really time to go if he was to spare a little while for Mr. Yearling before getting back to the duties of his parish.

Hennessy, about to climb the steps to 3 Chandlers Court, heard the tin whistle and cocked his head to listen. The notes, creeping from behind the basement window, shaped a slow air that was barely audible, although the street was enjoying one of its rare interludes of quietness. Where were the men? Hennessy wondered. Where were the women, the children, the dogs that should have been searching the gutter with noses nursing the remote hope of something edible? Off to gape at some moment's diversion, he decided; off to follow a German band, maybe, or a parade of military passing on its way to join a ship. It was disappointing. There was no one to pass on his news to, no one standing on any of the steps, no one leaning against a lamp-post; only a street in the evening sunlight and a melancholy air meandering down its emptiness. The basement window had no glass in it. Instead, pieces of cardboard filled in its frame, leaving a small panel at the top for light and air.

'Rashers,' he shouted.

The air continued. It was slow; it was a personal, unorganised kind of air that could meander on for ever. Hennessy saw a stone, stooped for it, then let it fly at the window. It made a sharp sound on the cardboard. For a moment the melody broke off, then started again. Irritated, Hennessy searched once more. He found a larger stone which hopped back off the cardboard and fell into the area space with a thud. The music stopped abruptly and a voice from inside yelled in anger.

'Who flung that?'

'Rashers,' Hennessy shouted again.

'Go home, you little bowsie. Flinging stones at a decent man's window. I know you. I'll tell your mother—honest to God I will.'

'It's me, Hennessy.'

'Who?'

'Hennessy.'

'Wouldn't you think you'd have more sense at your age,' Rashers yelled.

'I want to talk to you.'

'You could knock at the bloody door.'

'A bit of news.'

'Like a bloody Christian. That cardboard cost money.'

'Come on up,' Hennessy invited, 'I want a word with you.'

He sat on the steps. The stone under his skinny behind felt warm. The day had been good. He had spent it travelling between the office of Bates & Sons, Contractors, in Merchants Lane and a gang of men who were working in Phoenix Park. Twice he had pushed a handcart across the city to them with supplies. But he had taken his time, pausing when he wanted to watch anything of interest, enjoying the sunlight, happy to have a few weeks' work as a runner. Two rosy spots on his normally sallow face showed the benefit of good weather and exercise. He took a cigarette from his waistcoat pocket, lit it with an air of luxury and waited. When Rashers joined him he had the tin whistle still in his hands.

'What's the commotion?' Rashers asked, taking a seat beside him.

'Where's everybody gone?'

'To hell, for all I know.'

'Not even a stray cat . . .'

'Or out of their minds for the want of sense.'

Rashers absentmindedly raised the tin whistle to his lips.

'Don't start on that again,' Hennessy appealed.

'You're unmusical as well as being a bowsie,' Rashers commented.

'It was a sad sort of tune you were playing.'

'I was thinking,' Rashers said. He laid the whistle aside.

'Have a cigarette,' Hennessy invited. He drew one from a packet of Woodbines and passed it over to Rashers, who said:

'Thanks be to God someone's earning,' and lit it.

'Are you in a bad way?'

'Bloody terrible.'

'I'll get the missus to send down one of the kids with a few cuts of bread and a cup of tea,' Hennessy promised.

'You're earning, then?'

'A few weeks.'

'It makes all the difference,' Rashers said.

Summer was now his bad time. Father O'Connor no longer needed a boilerman. There were too many beggars. People like the Gaelic League and the Larkinites, the St. Finbar's Hurling and Football Club or the charitable societies were all joining in the competition for stray pennies. Besides, he was not as good at the walking as he had been. It was his chest. Sometimes in the heat he found it hard to get air into his lungs. Often he had to stop, his hand against a wall for support, while he struggled to breathe.

'That's what I was thinking about,' Rashers said, not knowing that so far he had said nothing to Hennessy of what he was thinking about.

'What was that?'

'I'm getting the bronchitis bad.'

'The weather will soon fix that up.'

'I wouldn't be too sure. Look at King Edward. Weather or no weather, it bloodywell killed him.'

'His heart was bad,' Hennessy consoled.

'And what's to stop my heart getting bad?' Rashers asked in a reasonable tone. Finding he had silenced Hennessy, Rashers dragged the cigarette and offered:

'If a fellow only had a bit of capital he could set himself up comfortable enough.'

'That's right,' Hennessy said. 'I often thought myself if I had enough to buy an old ass and cart I'd be made.'

'What would you do?'

'Removals. Or selling coal blocks—there's good profit in coal blocks.'

'You'd have to hump all them sacks up all them stairs. Up and down and up and down all day. What I'd do is buy a barrel-organ and a monkey,' Rashers said. 'There's great money in it and only a modicum of exertion.'

'Monkeys is very hard to rear. I knew a man was put out of business by it. Three of them in a row kicked the bucket on him.'

Mary, sitting at the open window above them, heard the exchange and leaned out to identify them. She recognised Rashers first. He came in and out at such odd hours and kept so much to himself that she seldom saw him. Whenever she did she thought of the coloured favours and the blood on his mouth.

'There's a catch in everything,' Rashers said, when he had considered the triple tragedy.

Nothing ever worked out. You went up with your tin whistle to a polo match in the Park, expecting a crowd, and found there was a reception at the Castle or cricket in Trinity College. The theatre queues were overworked and, worse still, overwatched by policemen.

'There's nothing but bloody beggars in this misfortunate town,' he complained, 'and, what's more, the half of them is illegitimate beggars, a crowd of amateurs with boxes for the Jim Larkin Defence Collection. It makes shocking inroads on the Rashers Tierney Fund.'

'You won't be troubled much longer from that quarter,' Hennessy told him. 'Larkin got twelve months' hard today. That's the news I had for you.'

'Holy God—you're codding me.'

'Here's the very man will tell you.'

Fitz had turned the corner. They watched his approach, but when he came abreast of them and climbed the steps he passed them with a nod. He had a collection box under one arm.

'That's another that's in on the collection box act,' Rashers said.

'If I was you,' Hennessy advised, 'I'd make up another ballad. About Larkin going to gaol.'

'Do you think they'd like it?'

'They've gone so mad about Larkin now,' Hennessy assured him, 'they'd get down on their knees to lick it off the streets. That's what I wanted to suggest to you.'

'You're a man of unusual sagacity,' Rashers told him, admiringly. He began to finger the tin whistle again. Already his mind was at work. He was thinking hard. Hennessy, catching sight of Mulhall and Pat Bannister, rose and went down the street to join them.

Mary arranged a meal of bread and stew on the table while Fitz left the collection box on the dresser and went into the kitchenette to wash. When he was working she could manage, with difficulty, to provide three meals a day. They had tea and bread for breakfast and supper. The main meal followed a pattern she had picked up from the wiser among the older women —meat on Sundays, cold scraps on Monday, stew on Tuesday. On Wednesdays and Fridays she got herrings cheap. She usually managed to have bread and potatoes. Several times in their few years of marriage they had gone to bed hungry. It took a long time to recover from a strike, to pay off grocers, to clear themselves with moneylenders. She herself was always the first to go short and the arrival of the children made it harder. She watched them as carefully as she could. Whatever else suffered she had tried to give them fresh milk all the time, but once or twice she had found it necessary to water down the condensed milk for them, despite the advice of the doctor in the hospital. Advice was one thing—finding money another. When Fitz returned and sat down she took a little of the food herself and said to him: 'I had a visitor today.'

'Not Mrs. Hennessy again?'

Every other day Mrs. Hennessy came to borrow something— a sprinkle of salt, a few spoons of tea or sugar.

'You'll never guess,' she challenged.

It was seldom she had news. She smiled, waiting for him to question her.

He thought and then said: 'His Excellency, the Governor General.'

'You're not even trying.'

Because she wanted him to guess he made an effort, but after some further thought he said: 'I give up.'

'Father O'Connor.'

The news was unexpected. With satisfaction she saw him lay down his knife and fork. Then he said, critically, 'It's taken him long enough to find his way.' He had never forgotten Father O'Connor's advice to Keever.

'He came about Miss Gilchrist. She's in the workhouse.'

'So that's where they put her.' He said it grimly. They had often wondered about her.

'How long is she there?'

'Over two years, he tells me. He wants me to visit her. I was thinking of going on Sunday.'

'Of course,' he said. 'I'll mind the youngsters.'

'You won't have a meeting or anything?'

'I'll mind them whether I have or not,' he promised.

'She always liked a pinch of snuff,' Mary remembered, 'I'll bring her some.'

He nodded. She wondered what he had been doing all day. Walking the main streets with a box in his hand, sticking it under people's noses, being told to move on by policemen, who were always ready to make trouble? She found it hard to understand what attracted him in the speechmaking and the upheavals or to see the sense in strikes which always lasted too long and brought too little in the end. It seemed more sensible to take the steady work when it was going and leave the quarrels to others. There were children now to suffer. But she said nothing of that to him either. He knew his own mind and she trusted him to do what was best. It was not her business. She took her empty plate to the dresser and as she shifted the collection box she noticed its weight.

'You did well today,' she remarked.

'They sentenced him to twelve months this morning,' he said. 'The whole city is on our side since the news came out—even the silk hats. We're having a protest march tonight.'

She heard his plate being pushed aside and went over to take it.

'Are you going?'

'I couldn't miss it.'

That meant he would go on straight to the job. He was on night work.

'I'll make up your supper for you before I wash the dishes,' she said, accepting his decision without comment.

He went over to sit at the window, which she had opened at the bottom. On summer evenings they often sat there together, watching the skies growing darker, listening to the life of the street. It was not possible any more to go walking on the strand or swimming together, because of the children. They had tried to get a pram, but there was always something else to be bought first. She tried not to mind. In a way it brought them closer together. While she was making up his supper parcel he said:

'It was very quiet when I came in. What happened to everybody?'

'Two policemen were taking a drunken sailor down to his ship. The whole street went off to gape.'

'I'm surprised Hennessy wasn't with them.'

'He was late for it,' she said, laughing.

He rose again and went into the bedroom, opening the door quietly so as not to waken the children. Almost immediately the room became lonely. He had left his cap beside the collection box and she touched it gently for no conscious reason. She hoped Mulhall was going with him to the protest march. Mulhall was huge and capable. If they stayed together Fitz would be safe. She heard him entering again and found she was holding his cap. He was amused.

'Are you going out?' he asked.

'The dresser is no place for it,' she said, pretending annoyance. He took it from her and pushed it into his pocket.

'Nor your pocket,' she added. He took it out again and placed it solemnly on her head.

'Maybe you'd like to wear it yourself.' He kissed her lightly and drew her over to the window.

'I'm sorry to be going out tonight,' he said. His voice was tender.

'Will Mulhall be with you?'

'He's to call across for me.'

She said she didn't mind.

They had half an hour together before Mulhall knocked at the door. Pat was with him. They had slogans painted on sheets of cardboard which they had mounted on sticks. Mulhall's read: 'Release Larkin'. Pat's was general. It said: 'Arise, Ye Slaves'.

'What do you think of it?' he asked, holding it up for inspection.

'It has a Salvation Army smack about it,' Fitz criticised.

'We'd better hurry,' Mulhall advised.

'Onward Christian soldiers,' Pat said.

'I'll be after you,' Fitz promised.

They left. Mary gave him his supper parcel and pressed her cheek against his.

'Watch yourself,' she said, earnestly, 'don't go where there might be trouble.'

She looked down at the three of them from the window. They stepped out strongly together and were joined on their way by another neighbour. The boards with their painted slogans lent them an air of unfamiliarity. She felt a distance growing between her and them that was greater than the street's. She stood, the loneliness creeping out from every part of the room. In the flat above a door banged, sending a tremor through the floorboards. She heard the baby beginning to cry and went in to it.

'Won't do you a bit of harm,' Yearling assured him. He left his 'cello lying on one side, placing the bow carefully along it.

'Well, then . . . but very little.'

It would be his third glass of port, an unpredecented gluttony for Father O'Connor. But Yearling was persuasive and, besides, the evening had been pleasant. Rising from the piano, he went over to the window while Yearling found the bottle of port. The windows looked out on a long, well-kept garden.

'I'll have whiskey myself,' he heard Yearling say, from somewhere behind him. 'It goes better with the last of the day.' Then he heard him say, 'Do, please sit down.'

'I mustn't delay too long,' Father O'Connor answered. He sat down, just the same. The piano was an excellent instrument. It had been such a pleasure to play on it. There was none in St. Brigid's and he had not gone near the harmonium there since his difference with Father Giffley. Yearling, too, had acquitted himself admirably.

'You play very well,' he said, still looking at the garden. Shadows lay across it and the night dew was already settling. If he walked down it the grass would keep the imprint of his feet. A good dinner, an hour's music, a little wine. He was far away now from Father Giffley's hostility, Father O'Sullivan's frayed soutanes and common-or-garden mind, from the straw on the floor and the candles in bottles. Here summer came to shed grace and beauty where houses and gardens received her condescendingly, as they would a favoured entertainer. The windows wore tasselled shades, the doors had gay canvas covers to protect their paintwork; ladies with parasols welcomed her as they strolled along the front. Father O'Connor, made daring by the wine, remembered their earlier discussion and put his mood into a question.

'I omitted to ask what was *your* answer to poverty?' He heard the clink of a glass as Yearling moved something and almost immediately his good-natured laugh.

'Man will conquer poverty just as he will conquer the problems of disease and war—by his own determination and intelligence.'

'Without Christianity?'

'I don't know what you mean by Christianity,' Yearling said, 'There are too many brands of it.'

'Without God, shall I say.'

'The spirit which informs mankind may be of God—I think it probably is; but what God I cannot say.' Yearling handed him his glass of port and sat opposite to him. 'Can you?' he added.

'Without any shadow of doubt.'

'It doesn't seem to make you any happier.'

'Because I am not happy about what I see,' Father O'Connor confessed suddenly.

He had not meant to say it. The sentiment surprised himself. It was the port, perhaps; it was the shadowed garden and its gathering in to itself all the sadness of the fading evening; it was the music, the Bach Arioso Yearling had played so tenderly on his 'cello, and the profound deliberation of the accompaniment which had sounded so well on the excellent piano.

'You have a hard life,' Yearling said, with uncharacteristic gentleness.

'At this moment an old lady who is dying is unhappy because she does not know how she is to be buried. Tomorrow, thank God, I'll be able to set her mind at rest.'

'That, at least, is a reason for happiness.'

'She is only one. What of the others?'

Yearling shrugged at that and said: 'I don't care a damn who buries me.'

'You were never so destitute that the only piece of property you ever owned was your poor body.'

'If I died,' Yearling said, 'I'd be going where the needs of the body didn't matter any more. Certainly I'd rather not know who was going to bury me than wonder how I was going to live.'

'There are so many like that too.'

'And you feel sorry for them?'

'Don't you?'

Yearling's moment of gentleness had passed.

'Every time I think about them,' he said, 'Which on average is about once every two years.'

'You thought about them today.'

'In times of upheaval. They may yet come out of their hovels in search of a better living—all together, a visitation from the locusts.'

'After Larkin, perhaps?'

'Very likely, if today's sentence is indicative of the enlightened medicine we can expect the law to prescribe.'

'I've been thinking a little about that since you spoke to me.'

Yearling was pleased.

'So. You see the danger—I mean the social danger, not the spiritual.'

'I walked past Mr. Bradshaw's houses today. He has propped them up with wooden supports.'

'You mustn't blame him,' Yearling said. 'His tenants don't earn enough to pay an economic rent, unless he crams them six in a room. Even that doesn't leave him enough for major repairs.'

'I haven't blamed him at all,' Father O'Connor said, 'he's not exceptional.'

Yearling tasted his whiskey and, in the half-light that lay about them, took in the sad, white face of the man he had been playing music with. In spite of the tired lines and the pallor, the face was ridiculously young. Did celibacy keep them that way. Or holiness. They read a lot of intellectual stuff which ought at least to give the eyes the set of learning. It had left no mark on this man. Nor had music. He was certainly musical. Tomorrow morning, the fingers that had been so competent on the keyboard and were now white about the stem of the wineglass would break the wafer that they believed was the Body of Christ. If it was, how could they bear to break it. Cr-a-a-ck. Just like that. Yearling knew. The girl he had known in London had been a Catholic. He had seen for himself.

'Shall we play some more music?'

'There's nothing I'd love more, but I really must watch the time.'

'You're not drinking your wine.'

'I'm not used to it.'

'Don't you have it every morning?'

Father O'Connor's understanding grasped the point slowly.

'It's not quite the same thing,' he said. He spoke with difficulty. A great gap had opened between them, of which only he was aware; Yearling, faintly smiling in the twilight, relished his whiskey. It was loneliness, then. And for ever. No company in the Bradshaws, whom he admired only for good taste and smooth manners, none in Father Giffley, whom he tried hard not to despise or Father O'Sullivan who had a dull mind, none in the ragtag and bobtail of his parish, for whom he had a dutiful love which shrank at every physical contact. And in Yearling, below a now more clearly understood level, no companionship. No real understanding between himself and the poor, or between the world of poverty and the world of comfort. He had left a gracious way of life to do what his heart told him was God's will, and all he had found so far was disrespect, humiliation, an inner disgust. The devil worked more successfully than he, and the people looked to agitators for deliverance. He had been on the point of telling Yearling about that, of expressing a little of his aloneness and disappointment. Now it was impossible. His unhappiness grew until it became physically painful.

'I'll play for thirty minutes,' he said. It would stop the ache, a temporary sedative. Unintentionally he emptied his third glass of wine.

'Excellent,' Yearling said, moving for his 'cello. On his way he rang for lamps. He was nervous of gas and electricity had not yet attracted his consideration.

They jammed the street in front of the station, a jumble of torches and banners, a tightly packed array that had generated a soul and a mind of its own, capable of response only to simple impulses, able to move itself, to emit a cry, to swing right or left, to stop altogether. They had come out *en masse* from the hovels and tenements, disrupting traffic, driving the respectable off the sidewalks. Their sudden arrogance was astonishing. Here and there Father O'Connor recognised a face. He stood on the steps leading down to the exit, knowing it was useless to try to pass through. The dizzy feeling which had made him so uncomfortable in the train attacked him again. It was dark, yet the street seemed unusually bright and certain faces seemed larger than others. He recognised Fitzpatrick, whom he had known for a long time, without pretending to; he knew the big man who walked by his side; he knew Rashers and the sickly little man

204

who kept him company. 'Release Larkin' the banners said. 'Arise, Ye Slaves'. They turned confusingly this way and that above the shoulders that bore them. The flaring torches were a melodramatic touch and, he thought, dangerous. He wondered how they were made. He stood with the other passengers on the steps—behind him the station where gas-lamps with pendant chains spread a sickly light between the platform and the soot-blackened canopy—in front of him the mob, the torches, the banners.

'Stick close to me,' Rashers advised.

Hennessy, already pressed painfully against him by the pressure of bodies, his arms pinioned and his hat coming down over his eyes, answered obscenely. It was a rare thing in Hennessy.

'I'm surprised at you,' Rashers said. He had the whistle under his coat and wrapped around it the paper with the words of his new ballad.

'Wait'll I sing my song for them,' he said.

'You'll never be able to sing in this mob.'

'Passed unanimously.'

'Then what the hell are we getting walked on for?'

'To be ready with the song when they reach Beresford Place before the speechifying starts.'

'Did you see who was on the station steps?'

'Give over gasbagging. I'm putting the words through my mind.'

'Father O'Connor.'

Rashers, disturbed by the information, hesitated for a moment and was trampled on immediately. When he had released his feelings in a flow of bad language he asked :

'Did he see us?'

'How do I know?'

'If he did I'll never get the job back.'

'Of course you'll get the job back.'

'The clergy is always giving out the pay about us socialists.'

This was news to Hennessy.

'I never knew you were a friend of the cause.'

'In times of crisis,' Rashers said, 'I'm a stalwart.'

'When there's a bit of money to be made out of trials and tribulations, I suppose.'

'As Bard of the Revolution,' Rashers said, remembering Pat's phrase.

They reached a street junction and the pressure eased. Those at the sides held back, then fell in in ranks behind the main body, five or six abreast.

'It's a great turn-out,' Mulhall said to Fitz. He was a mountain of satisfaction.

'Half of them are gapers.'

'Some of them will join up.'

'How many?'

'Enough for our purpose.'

At least there had been a swing in public opinion. It was easy to judge that in the suddenly increased response to the collection boxes.

'Maybe,' Fitz said.

Mary would be by herself, looking down on the quiet back street, the room in half light about her because she would be saving oil by doing without the lamp. For him there was the excitement to keep the anxieties from growing too powerful. Tonight, when he felt the drag of the loaded shovel on his shoulders and the sweat trickling down his body, there would be the roar of the furnaces and at break times the conversation of his mates. She would be alone, with the two children of their marriage near at hand to keep doubt and fear in her heart.

'They've been slow enough about joining,' he added.

'After this they'll flock to us,' Mulhall said. He was smiling and full of confidence.

At Beresford Place they formed into a meeting before the derelict block of buildings that had once been the Northumberland Commercial and Family Hotel. The torches went out one by one, night crept up the river and spread over the city. People in trains that passed from time to time across the loopline bridge leaned out of windows to look down at the packed street while for some moments the speaker gesticulated and was unheard because of the trundling carriages. At half past eleven Fitz said to Mulhall:

'I'd better move. I'm due in at twelve.'

Mulhall nodded.

Fitz worked his way slowly through the crowd, which was still dense. He was tempted to go home, to pick up on the sleep he had cut short in the daytime in order to walk the streets with his collection box, but he could not afford to lose a night's pay.

Touching his pocket to feel if his supper was still there, he began to cross the bridge. To his left there were berthed ships, lying idle and deserted on the low tide. At the far end of the bridge a figure leaned on the parapet. At first he paid no attention, thinking it was a down-and-out or a drunk, using the parapet to rest against, but when he came abreast he realised that it was a priest. He went over and touched the shoulder.

'Can I help you, Father?'

After a moment the other raised his head and looked around at him.

'It's nothing,' Father O'Connor said, 'a little turn.' He had never spoken to Father O'Connor before. He thought it strange that he should meet him like this on the day the priest had decided to call on Mary.

'I could get a cab for you.'

'No . . . please.' He hesitated. 'I know you, I think—a parishioner.'

'Fitzpatrick, Father.'

'That's it. Your wife, I think . . .'

Fitz made no offer to fill in the long pause.

'I followed your meeting from the station and listened for a while. I began to feel unwell . . . the heat, probably.'

'You should let me call a cab.'

'No—I feel better in the air.'

Fitz hesitated.

'Then let me walk back with you to the church.'

It would mean being late for work, and for a moment he hoped the other would refuse. But Father O'Connor accepted and said :

'Thank you, that's very kind of you.'

Fitz took his arm lightly. They walked in silence until they had left the river behind and were in the main thoroughfare once more. Father O'Connor released his arm and said he felt much better. Yet his face was drained of colour and he walked with a slight uncertainty.

'I followed your meeting because I thought I might catch a glimpse of Mr. Larkin.'

'He's in gaol, Father.'

'Yes, I know,' Father O'Connor said, attempting a smile. 'The extraordinary thing is I've known that since early afternoon.'

'We're trying to get him released.'

'It's an extraordinary thing,' Father O'Connor said again. 'I knew that and yet I followed with the idea . . .' He stopped.

'It was being unwell, I suppose. I was unwell and didn't realise it. However, I'm much better now—thanks to you.'

'You're more than welcome, Father,' Fitz said. They had reached the iron railings which cut off the courtyard of the church from the footpath. Fitz tried the side gate and found it open. He held it for the priest.

'I've kept you from your home.'

'Not at all, Father,' Fitz said.

'Do you often attend meetings of this kind?'

'Whenever I can.'

Father O'Connor appeared to make a great effort of will.

'You must be careful,' he said. 'There are men who pretend to have sympathy with the working men and the unemployed in order to win power for themselves—power for the socialists.'

'I don't know very much about these things, Father,' Fitz said. He wanted to avoid an argument.

'It's an evil doctrine. You must be careful who you set up as your leaders.'

'It isn't difficult, Father. We haven't had many to choose from,' Fitz said. He was already late for work. The delay would cost him a quarter—three hours' pay.

'Guard your faith and listen only to those who honour it,' Father O'Connor said. He spoke gently and, to Fitz, like one who was hearing his own voice from a distance. He looked very ill.

'You should go in, Father,' he urged.

'Thank you,' Father O'Connor said. His tone was warm. 'Thank you very much indeed.'

Fitz raised his cap. His feet sounded loudly in the street. It was after midnight.

They arrived back at Chandlers Court within minutes of each other—first Rashers and Hennessy, then Mulhall alone.

'You did well,' Hennessy said in the hallway, 'you did magnificent.'

'One and threepence,' Rashers agreed, with modesty.

'I mean the ballad,' Hennessy corrected. 'It was a great success.'

'Success is one thing,' Rashers reminded him, 'money is another.'

'You got both.'

'For once,' Rashers allowed. He fumbled. 'Have a cigarette.'

'It's too late.'

'I took one from you out of your plenty. Now you take one of mine.'

'I'll take it upstairs with me.'

'Bring it to bed with you if the fancy takes you that way.'

Hennessy pushed the cigarette behind his ear. It was pitch dark in the hall and there was an evil smell. Hennessy wrinkled his nose and sniffed.

'Some bowsie did his what-you-know', he complained.

Rashers wasn't squeamish.

'It's an old Dublin custom—there must have been a queue for the jakes.'

'I can't stand that,' Hennessy said. 'It's the one thing I can't abide.'

'You worked in too many high-falutin' houses—feeding yourself on grapes and delicacies.'

'They were right at that meeting tonight. We live and die like animals. I'll go on up. I can't stick it.' Rashers chuckled. As he was going, he said:

'Mind you don't walk in it.'

209

Hennessy, his foot feeling out for the first rung of the stairs, froze for a moment. He picked his way delicately.

The door of Father Giffley's bedroom opened and his voice called: 'Father O'Sullivan ...'

The corridor seemed unfamiliarly long. A gas-lamp at the far end, turned low, cast a blue half-light. Father O'Connor stopped.

'It's Father O'Connor,' he managed after a while.

'Oh—you.' The voice changed. 'Isn't it rather late?'

With a great effort of will Father O'Connor pushed aside the temptation to ignore the question, to walk on to his bedroom and leave his superior standing there. For the moment he felt physically unable to bear up to criticism.

'I was delayed.'

'Please step into my room.' Father Giffley had a dressing gown over his nightshirt and, incongruously, his priest's biretta perched on his head. He seemed to have been reading. A black-covered book lay open, but face downwards, on a bedside chair.

'Father O'Sullivan was obliged to go out on a sick call,' he reproved. Father O'Connor should have been available. It was his duty period.

'I felt unwell when I got off the train and did something quite unaccountable.'

'Indeed.'

'There was a protest march—banners, slogans, torches; the street in front of the station was packed with them.'

'Until this hour?' Father Giffley commented. He smiled humourlessly.

'They were demanding Larkin's release. I followed them to their meeting place. There were socialists on their platform and they listened with respect and cheered them. I heard a vile diatribe from one of them against the Church. They cheered him. Later—I don't remember how—I found myself standing on Butt Bridge.'

Father Giffley stared at him and then, knitting his brows, asked: 'Have you been drinking?'

'I haven't that habit,' Father O'Connor said. The contemptuous phrase escaped him before he could stop it. It stung his conscience. Besides, it was a lie. He cast around for some way to correct himself, to say he had taken a little wine, but had not been drinking in the sense implied by Father Giffley. It was too difficult. The room, like the corridor, had a bluish tint which made his stomach unwell. He narrowed his eyes so that he would see as little of it as possible. A wave of nausea made him tremble.

'May I sit down?' he asked.

Father Giffley, detecting the tremor, waved towards a chair and peered at him.

'A bilious attack. You have a very bad colour,' he pronounced.

'Please forgive me if I . . .'

'A small drop of brandy is what you need.'

Father O'Connor shook his head.

'You look as though you could do with it.' The voice had grown a shade kinder.

'No—I think if I lie down . . .'

'As you please.' Father Giffley turned his back. The movement was formal, deliberate.

'So you followed the rabble. That's interesting. And singularly unlike you.'

The voice was no longer kind. There was a glass-fronted bookcase in front of Father Giffley. He stared at it, as though trying to locate something. Father O'Connor kept silence.

'Why?' his superior asked.

Quietly, the emotion of an earlier moment moving in him again, Father O'Connor said: 'They are being led away from us.'

'Did you imagine you could bring them back—even if they were?'

'Please,' Father O'Connor pleaded. 'I must go to bed.'

'By threatening to change them into goats. That day has passed. Do you know whose fault that is?'

'I am not well enough to discuss . . .'

'Ours,' Father Giffley answered, swinging about suddenly, 'because we've watched in silence while the others turned them into animals.'

'The devil is at work among them.'

'The devil is busy everywhere, always; at work on them and at work on the others. He was busy here all day too.'

Father Giffley paused. Then he said: 'For once his efforts were not very profitable.'

Father O'Connor wondered was he speaking of himself. But he was too sick to care. 'May I go to bed?' he asked.

'Don't let me detain you,' Father Giffley replied, lifting the black book from the chair and sitting down. As Father O'Connor closed the door he said, raising his voice slightly: 'If you need help during the night, call out for me.'

At first it was a relief to get inside his own bedroom, but when he closed the door he began to feel he had walked into a tomb. The curtains were drawn, the window closed, it was completely dark. He crossed and opened a press, the wrong one. Some left-over tins of cocoa fell about the floor. He left them there. He felt unable to stoop. He found he had to stand quite still to remember where he was. He saw the placards twisting this way and that, white against the darkness, he saw the torches sparking and swaying, lurid red against the pitch darkness. He bumped against the bed, leaned heavily on it, heard the noise of its springs and groped with his free hand. He reached the chamber-pot in time to be violently and repeatedly sick. Then he knelt, his cheek against the coverings, until the trembling of his body ceased.

When he felt stronger he removed his collar and went over to draw the curtains and open the window. The sky above the church was a vast, night blue field, stars grew wild all over it, the breeze from the window touched his face with healing and cool-ness. It was a mild night of June, month of the Sacred Heart. The gardens of Kingstown would smell sweetly at this hour, full of flowers and leafy quiet. Along the coast, on miles and miles of fine· wet shingle, about crusted rocks, against the wooden beams of piers, the sea was making night sounds, the tides building and turning in time with the laws of God who was the maker and regulator of all things. He had a sense of sin.

Casting back over the day he remembered his lack of humility with the young woman who had once been a servant; the impatience that caused him to turn down Mrs. Bradshaw's offer of hospitality; his three glasses of wine which, in him, might well count as intemperance; his delight in Yearling's praise when he played well on the beautiful piano.

Troubled, he fingered his rosary and, leaning against the window jamb, his eyes fixed on the night sky, he began to pray —for his mother's soul, for Miss Gilchrist, for each face that looked out at him from moment to moment as he examined his conscience and lived in retrospect through the events of the day. He remained so for almost half an hour until, his attention wavering, he became aware of the odour in the room. It was the smell of puke, of half-digested food and sour wine. Away from the window it was worse, an offensive and choking manifestation of infirmity, of uncleanness, of corruption. It was the wine then, that had made him sick.

He shrank from the ordeal of lifting the pot, but there was no help for it. Gingerly he opened the door and stole past Father Giffley's room once again to the toilet on the upper landing. His stomach turned as he emptied the foul contents and rinsed out the remaining traces. He returned and got into bed, relieved that the unpleasant task was over and done with, relieved too that Father Giffley had not come into the corridor to investigate these late-night comings and goings. There were tins of some kind lying on the floor, he now remembered. Let them stay there.

He lay exhausted, yet sleepless. The retort he had made to Father Giffley returned several times to his mind: 'I haven't that habit, Father.' He regretted it. He wished he could recall and erase it. He had been wrong in his earlier suspicions about the locked room. Father Giffley had been perfectly sober. As he watched the narrow strip of sky between the partly drawn curtains, accusing himself, asking for forgiveness, the meaning of Father Giffley's phrase about the devil's efforts not being very profitable—for once, suggested itself. Had he locked his door to shut out temptation? Had he called out for Father O'Sullivan because, at the end of the long day, from that simple, unnoticing man, there would flow the springs of consolation? 'I haven't that habit, Father.' Had he asked for bread, and been given a stone?

Father O'Connor closed his eyes tightly, not in an effort to sleep, but the better to bear the self-accusation which desolated him.

CHAPTER 2

In October, whenever he walked along the Vico Road, the hills rising at the back of the city reminded Yearling of Connemara. They were turning brown now under evenings of long, yellow sunsets. Often the green sea below him set him thinking of the miles and miles of water and waste; of England; of the too-faraway years of youth. One day, when Father O'Connor strolled with him, he said: 'I am getting old.'

He stopped to lean for a moment on his cane. It was growing dusk. The sea had a strong, autumn smell. The air was damp.

'Everybody does,' Father O'Connor said, agreeably.

'I begin to think that times are changing, that soon the world we knew will be finished and done with.'

'There are new ideas,' Father O'Connor admitted, 'disturbing ideas, abroad. I feel it too and I'm younger than you are.'

'And I begin to look back—to remember; that's a bad sign.' He knitted his heavy eyebrows and looked sharply at Father O'Connor.

'Do you think I should have married?' he asked.

'There's still time.'

'I don't think so—ah no.'

He sighed and began to walk again.

'Still,' he said, after a while, 'celibacy was never suited to me. I don't understand how you fellows manage.'

'We win it by our own means. For some it is easy; for others —it is painfully hard.'

'Is it the same with drink?'

'You are confusing what is sinful and what may only be unseemly.'

'Yes,' Yearling admitted, 'you are more broadminded about drink than our crowd. Still, I was jilted for drinking—did I ever tell you that? She was a Catholic too.'

'Once, when we were playing music with Mr. and Mrs. Bradshaw, you hinted at something. It happened in England, I think?'

'A long, long time ago. The sea there reminded me of it. I must tell you about it some time.'

'If you are unhappy at times there are other ways of considering life. There may be a plan, or a reason . . .'

Yearling looked at him sharply.

'Are you thinking of trying to convert me?'

Father O'Connor did not return the look. But he said: 'If I thought I could I would not hesitate.'

'And do you?'

'It is God who converts . . . not bunglers such as I am.'

A little later Father O'Connor said: 'When I spoke of drink as being unseemly I didn't mean that it could not be sinful. It can. I've seen it become sinful and I've seen it lead to much human tragedy.' He spoke generally. But he was thinking of Father Giffley.

October brought work for Rashers once again. He piled paper on the cold bars of the furnace, spread sticks and a dressing of coke. Then he lit the first fire of another season, building it to give a slow heat which he could control. For the first week it required attention at night-time, so he decided to sleep in the boiler house. On the Saturday night, when there was a corpse in the mortuary chapel above, he brought the dog and played music on the flageolet to keep himself company. The dog was a mistake. In the morning, when Father Giffley passed near the entrance, it gave a warning bark.

'In the first week of the season I have to sleep here at night, Father,' he said. 'I keep a slow fire so as not to do damage to the pipes.'

'And is the . . . dog . . . very useful?'

'In the matter of company, Father.'

'St. Francis and yourself would get on well together, I can see that.'

Father Giffley peered into the corners beyond the ring of candlelight. They were grimed with dust. The cobwebs looked solid.

'Do you sleep on the coke?'

'With a sack underneath.'

'And it is comfortable?'

'It could be worse.'

Father Giffley noted the familiar phrase. Everything could be worse.

'It could, indeed.'

'Only I noticed it's inclined to bring on the bronchitis.'

'That would be the dust,' Father Giffley said.

'I hope you don't think bad of me bringing the dog, Father.'

'We could deduct something for its board and lodging,' Father Giffley suggested, smiling to himself. 'What's his name?'

'Rusty, Father.'

Father Giffley bent down to the dog and said: 'Here, Rusty, that's the fellow, that's the good doggie.'

The dog wagged its tail. It was a mangy-looking specimen, he thought, like its lord and master. Father Giffley wrinkled his forehead. He thought of a religious picture which had hung somewhere, of a saint who wept for his ox. The picture he remembered clearly—a great, bearded human face pressed in fellowship against the hairy face of the beast—but the saint's name evaded him. Or—after all, was it called 'The Peasant Weeps Over His Ox'? Father Giffley was unsure. He patted the dog's head. Then he straightened and said:

'You shouldn't spend too much time in this place. The air is foul. Call into the housekeeper later—I'll tell her to give you some breakfast, and some scraps for Rusty. Do you drink?'

'Whenever good luck pushes a drop under my nose.'

'I'll tell her to give you a little something to take home.'

'God bless you, Father.'

'For your bronchitis, you understand,' Father Giffley added.

He climbed the steps and went out into the air, which was

mild. When he had seen the housekeeper he came back again, circled the courtyard a couple of times and then went out into the street. With his hands behind his back and his head bowed forward he pushed through the people who were on their way to mass. They parted for him. Some of them who greeted him were acknowledged with an inclination of the head, others he did not see. He passed under the railway bridge, through side streets which were so far from the church that people wondered to see a priest dressed only in his soutane. Here and there he stopped to talk to children who were playing hopscotch and skipping outside the tenements which occupied so large a part of his parish. He came to the riverside at last and remained leaning against a capstan for some time. To the right and left of him ships lay to. Sunday ships, deserted, he would believe, were it not for the smoke streaming up from the galleys. The cranes were still and the buckets empty. Behind him the bells of Sunday were clamouring throughout the city, marking the arrival of each half-hour. Men passed him and saluted. One of them, a young man of average height, well built, had a grimy and unsabbath like face.

'Good morning,' Father Giffley said.

'Good morning, Father.'

'Have you been working?'

'At it all night, Father,' Fitz said. He pushed his cap on to the back of his head and now that he had stopped, let his eyes travel with the river to the point where the north and south walls widened, disappeared and left it to the sea. It was sluggish and grey, but with a sheen here and there that acknowledged the sunshine.

'Shift work, I suppose?' Father Giffley questioned.

'At the foundry, Father.'

'How do you get to mass?'

'Our mates come in an hour earlier on Sundays—we do the same for them in our turn.'

'You're a good bunch of men,' Father Giffley said. 'You'll be off to a football match after the dinner, I suppose?'

Fitz smiled and said: 'No such luck today—I'm minding the kids.'

'Letting herself out?'

'For a change,' Fitz said easily. Father Giffley, he realised, did not remember him.

'You've a button in your coat,' Father Giffley remarked, 'and I haven't seen one like it before.'

Fitz said it was a trade union button.

'Will they release Larkin, do you think?'

'There's great talk of it, Father.'

'So they should,' Father Giffley said. 'Have you ever been on strike?'

'Which of us hasn't?'

'Of course,' Father Giffley said, 'everybody in my parish has been, I suppose. They don't treat you very fairly, do they?'

It was not a question that needed answering. Father Giffley rose and put his hands behind his back once more.

'No, indeed,' he said as he went off, 'they do not.'

He went back again through the side streets. People who knew him thought it strange, not because he was walking in his soutane—he was odd and had peculiar ways—but because he was seldom known to stroll through his parish.

The high windows let in the afternoon sun behind the girl at the bedside, giving lights to her smooth, black hair, leaving her pale face in shadow. She was the girl with the two children who so often brought her snuff, who in fact had just given her a small packet of snuff, which was now under the pillow somewhere, if she could find it. She quested with the fingers of one hand.

'I'll get it for you.'

The lights in the hair went out as the girl who had left a good place to marry some poor chap or other leaned nearer the bed. Mary . . . that was the name she was searching for.

'What were you saying, love?' Miss Gilchrist asked.

'I said I'll get it for you.'

The young face smiled. A pleasant girl, she now remembered, who always brought her snuff. Mary.

'I mean before that.'

'I was saying the days are growing short already.'

'What day is it?'

'Sunday.'

Of course it was Sunday. It was on Sundays she got the snuff. If she used it carefully and watched that it wasn't stolen it would last a week. Almost.

'When I was a young bit of a thing in Dublin at first I never liked Sundays.'

'Why was that?'

'The bells. I never liked the sound of them.'

'Yes. They make you lonely when there's only yourself.'

'Our own bells making a din the whole of the morning. And then the Protestant bells going in the afternoon. And the bells for devotion at seven or eight o'clock. They made such a commotion from morning till night I used to be glad when it was Monday.'

'I was like that myself too, at first.'

'When you looked out the window and saw everyone else parading it in their finery?'

'Meeting each other and going to each other's houses.'

'That was it.'

Lonely, that was it. In the winter it had not been so bad, though. There were more musical evenings. You got used to it. Sometimes, even, you enjoyed it. Guests got to notice you, gradually. They enquired after your health. They said, 'Miss Gilchrist, you're a treasure—you really are.'

'Is it very warm out?'

'It's lovely—for October.'

'Is it October . . .? Well, well.'

She made a noise of disbelief.

'That's what I was saying. About the days growing short.'

They always began to grow short in October, the days did. The leaves began to come down on the lawn; a bit of wind and you spent the day sweeping, unless Mrs. Bradshaw saw you and said leave them; a woman that liked leaves lying about, the colours beautiful, the sound as your feet brushed through them on the walks, a sentimental woman. If there was a sup of rain you could slip and break your ankle. Small comfort in the swish and colour then.

The girl handed her the packet and said, 'Take a little of your snuff.'·

It blurred the outer world with water, making the lungs larger inside and the air that entered them weighty and nourishing. She put it back carefully under her pillow.

'They steal it on me when I'm sleeping,' she confided, 'the nurses do it or one of the patients.'

'Perhaps you mislay it,' the girl said in a gentle tone.

'No fear—it's stolen. If I find out who I'll crucify her for it. Time and time again I reach under my pillow and it's gone—spirited away—vanished.'

'It's a shame for them,' Mary said. As she did so the dismissal bell began in a nearby ward. The sound came nearer. She rose, promising to come next Sunday.

'If I'm still here,' Miss Gilchrist said.

'Of course you'll be here.'

Miss Gilchrist smiled a little and closed her eyes.

They let her sleep through the evening meal. When she awakened she reached for the snuff immediately. It had gone. She raised herself with a great mustering of willpower and looked about her at the other beds.

'Who took my snuff?' she shouted. 'Which of youse thieving trollops made love to my snuff.' Nobody answered. When she shouted again a nurse came to quieten her.

'Where did you put it?' the nurse asked.

'Here—under my pillow.'

The nurse searched. 'There's no snuff,' the nurse said finally, 'you must have been dreaming.'

'I wasn't dreaming. It was brought to me today.' The nurse patted the pillow into shape and arranged the bedclothes. Her face was stern.

'Now, now,' she said, firmly.

Father Giffley took afternoon devotions. They consisted of rosary, sermon and benediction. While Father O'Sullivan preached the sermon Father Giffley, who sat to one side of the altar, his hands palms downwards on his knees, his head inclined forward, saw the altar boy with ginger hair nod off to sleep—as usual. After tea they sat together in a room on the ground floor which the three priests sometimes shared. Father O'Sullivan, writing at the table, found the matter difficult. He frowned frequently and bit the handle of his pen. At the fireside Father Giffley rested his black book on his knee. He wrote easily but slowly, pausing often to search his memory. He wrote: 'Thomas A Kempis instructs us as follows: "*I had rather feel compunction than know the definition thereof*". Father O'Sullivan, who is still trying to write a devotional booklet, if I recognise the signs, and I ought to be able to by now, is an illustration of what it means. "*If thou knowest the whole Bible by heart, and the sayings of all the philosophers, what would it profit thee without love of God and without grace.*"

That hits at me, of course. Except that I don't know very much by heart.

"*It is Vanity to desire to live long and not to care to live well.*"

My trouble is that I care to live too well. A Kempis means something quite different. There we are—the difficulty of communication. You do not care to live well. You only care to live well.

"*Call often to mind the proverb—The eye is not satisfied with seeing, nor the ear filled with hearing.*"

That's the best thing he has said. We see and we hear. But it is the thing beyond the eye that we immediately wish to see. We hear and there is still something unheard even in what we hear. And it tempts us to seek a more complete satisfaction. What kind of satisfaction? Society, Power, Eminence—what? I do not know. We seek it, just the same. Of course it doesn't exist, this S-A-T-I-S-F-A-C-T-I-O-N. Only the craving. Of course, a drop from the B. kills it. Temporarily.

"*For they that follow their lusts stain their own consciences and lose the grace of God.*"

Me again. The drop from the B. Lust of the Belly. He closed the book.

'You are very quiet, Father,' he said.

Father O'Sullivan looked up vaguely. After a painful knitting of the brows he succeeded in relating the remark to himself.

'Yes, indeed,' he said.

'What is the subject this time?'

Father O'Sullivan left down his pen. He was diffident.

'The Holy Family as a model for the ordering of the humble Catholic home.'

'It's always the humble Catholic home we dare to order, isn't it?' Father Giffley remarked. 'Well, I'm glad you're still trying.'

'No longer very hopefully,' Father O'Sullivan confessed.

'Oh, I don't know. In the world of—ah—literature' (Father Giffley stumbled unintentionally over the word) 'I'm told it's quite usual to fail, over and over again.'

Father O' Sullivan smiled and looked embarrassed.

'You mustn't call it literature—that would frighten me off altogether.'

'Pamphlets, religious exhortations, devotional booklets—they all have to be written, haven't they? Though, having read my fill of them I must confess that frequently I fail to see why.'

'They serve a very great need.'

'Do you think so?'

'I have no doubt about it. That's why I keep trying to write them.'

'Thousands are written. Are they not enough? Why should you try to add to them?'

'I can never answer that question when I put it to myself. When I sit down to write it comes so terribly hard with me that I feel I'm the last one in the world who should attempt it. And yet, whenever I stop trying, I become desperately unhappy.'

Father Giffley grunted impatiently. Yet his face, turned fully now on Father O'Sullivan, was gentle with sympathy and companionship.

'Some day, never fear, you'll write one that will be approved. You'll see it among the others on the bookstand at the door of the Church. *The Holy Family, A Devotional Booklet for the Catholic Home.* With a nicely coloured cover. Your lifelong ambition available to the world at the popular price of one halfpenny. Does the thought make you happy?'

Father O'Sullivan considered. Then he said :

'I am not quite sure, Father, whether you are saying that to encourage me or to amuse yourself.'

'Both,' Father Giffley confessed. He looked into the fire. His mood changed.

'How long are you here, John?'

He very rarely used Christian names. He hardly noticed now that he had done so.

'I came three years after yourself.'

'And you are contented with St. Brigid's?'

'It's much the same as anywhere else.'

'In some ways, yes. We baptise, we marry, we minister to the sick, we bury the dead. And that's all you have to say.'

'I think so.'

'Does it never trouble you, John, to think that there are parishes where faces are not hungry and where rooms are not bare and children are not dirty? Don't you wish, every now and then, that you could hear confessions without having to endure the smell of badly nourished bodies?'

'I have never thought about it.'

'Never?'

Father O'Sullivan frowned in his effort to give a precise answer.

'Perhaps at times I *have* noticed. . . . I honestly can't say.'

'Don't misunderstand me,' Father Giffley said. 'I don't blame the people. I blame those who are responsible for a deplorable state of affairs; hypocrites and windbags—all of them pious, and all of them pitiless.'

'Would you agree with Mr. Larkin, then?'

Father Giffley hit the book on his knee with the flat of his hand.

'I do—by the Lord Harry. He'll do what our respected colleagues haven't the stomach to attempt—he'll put the fear of God into all of them.'

He stared at the opposite wall. Father O'Sullivan, watching his face, began to fear for him. His eyes gleamed too brightly, his mouth was rigid. Once again the eyes turned to Father O'Sullivan.

'We seem to be missing the pleasure of Father O'Connor's company.'

Anxiety made Father O'Sullivan's voice unsure.

'It's his evening free.'

'I am aware of that. Does he visit in the parish?'

'No. In Kingstown, I think. He has friends out there.'

'Ah yes, his comfortable friends. I thought he had given up all that to work among the poor.'

Father O'Sullivan attempted an explanation.

'They give him money from time to time, I understand, which he distributes through the Confraternity Committee.'

'Hmm. He doesn't distribute it himself, of course.'

'He doesn't wish to have the credit.'

'You mean he hasn't the stomach for it,' Father Giffley said. 'I may not know the sayings of all the philosophers, but I know something about character. St. Brigid's has taught me.'

Father O'Sullivan lowered his eyes, embarrassed.

'You think I should keep a bridle on my tongue—eh, Father?'

Father O'Sullivan did not reply.

'The tongue was made to speak truth and do battle,' Father Giffley insisted. 'I'll risk the occasional sin of uncharity.'

He went abruptly back to his book, fidgeted about, then wrote the letters of the word *Satisfaction* under each other from the top to the bottom of the page. He began to make a poem. It was an old device of his. Sometimes it worked. He roughed out the lines on one sheet of paper and then, when each seemed right, he put it after its appropriate letter in the black-covered book. As he struggled with his task the night grew older. An hour, two hours, passed. Father O'Sullivan completed what he was writing and excused himself. The servant restocked the fire twice. At last Father Giffley re-read what he had written:

Sun on the river spreads peace in this Sabbath of stillness
After the season of toil, the sorrow of labour
The children of bondage have straightened and flung
*   away tiredness*
In parks and at pastimes escaped from their tyrant the
*   harbour*

Seagull, you skim on white feathers where old ships are
  sleeping
Fleeing the stain that pursues on the face of the water
All who are born, all under Heaven's strange keeping
Carry the stain and drag the same shadow after.
Teach me O symbol, Sing of the Holy Spirit
I am in dread and seek to outstrip the shadow
Oh, lead Thou to God and His Presence—lead, through
  Christ's Merit
Not to His Feet, but Their Print in the dews of His
  Meadow.

It disappointed him. He did not like it very much, although
he had struggled manfully with it and it had taken a long, long
time, so long that he was stiff and his eyes ached. Still, it had
served its purpose. He went up to his room, undressed wearily
and got into bed. He felt tired in a dull way, all his interest
spent. He was no poet, yet he had accomplished something better than a poem. He had resisted the urge to open the press, to
feel with trembling fingers for the neck of the bottle. Once more
he had won a victory. It would be only temporary, he knew that.
But each temporary triumph would stave off a little longer the
eventual collapse. It would come, that collapse. Father Giffley
did not try to fool himself. It was a disease—this appetite of
his. He had seen others. Unless by a miracle of grace . . . and
he was unworthy of that.

They were lighting the lamps in Chandlers Court. The children still played in the street. They were used to Rashers and his
dog by now and let both pass without stopping to jeer at them
as was once their habit. Rashers paid no attention either. He
was tired and unwell. But he had food in his bag and the
whiskey Father Giffley had said he was to get. It was a generous
measure—nearly half a bottle. That was something. The housekeeper was glad to give away as much of it as she could. It
would leave all the less for the parish priest, God help him. It
was not right in a priest to . . . And then his face, purple all the
time. The smell of peppermints from his breath too. She had

226

seen it begin and she had seen it become a habit and then more
than habit. She had seen . . . Well, there were strange things in
the world and indeed if everybody was made the same it would
be a very dull place indeed. It wasn't always the virtuous and
the temperate who were the most forbearing and considerate of
those in a lowlier station. Not by a long chalk. Father Giffley
was a harsh man with his equals and his superiors, more power
to him, but he was seldom cross with those who had the menial
place. He took everything from them as it came. There were
certain others now . . . no names—no pack drill.

Rashers hoped Hennessy might be about, but there was no
sign of him. He could have shared some of the whiskey with
him and he would have welcomed his chat. Hennessy had an
interest in things. Hennessy had suggested staying in the boiler
house. It seemed to have done his rheumatism good, but not
his bronchitis. He wanted to tell Hennessy that. Hennessy
would be interested. And now this dark damp hall, these rickety
stairs and the wave of cold, wet air and the smell of clay as he
opened the door to the basement room.

'Like a grave, Rusty,' he said, groping about for the bottle
with the candle butt. It gave a wavering light. His bedding was
still as he had left it, the rags lying in a heap at the bottom of
the straw. The biscuit box had another coat of rust and the
jamjars were stained with stale tea.

'No fire to cock your behind to tonight, Rusty,' he said. The
dog sat down on the clay floor, first to scratch itself, then to
sniff at the accumulated odours, his nose detecting and defining
delicately the week's trespassers.

'Have they been here?' Rashers questioned. He was taking
off his clothes.

'You're not to go eating them,' he warned. 'Chase them if
you want to—kill them with my full licence and leave; but don't
devour them. Don't even taste them. The rats in this bloody
place would poison you.'

He lay back on the bedding and adjusted the rags about him.

'Anyway, we have some tasty morsels here.'

From the sack near his head he selected food, giving portion of it to the dog. Both began to eat. For tonight, at least,

there was enough and plenty. He put a little of the meat aside to give to Mrs. Bartley and the children. It would be nourishing for them and there would be luck in the eating of it, since it had come from the table of the priest. Good luck and bad luck wandered the streets outside, invisible, so that you never knew until afterwards which of the pair you had been meeting up with. Above the streets were God and His Mother, His saints, His angels. Sometimes, if the luck was too persistently bad, one or other of them might intervene to help you out. They had done so for Rashers. Brushing the crumbs from his beard, he gave thanks. He was stretching out his hand to put out the candle when someone knocked at the door.

'Who is it?'

'Hennessy.'

'Come in.'

Hennessy was wearing an unfamiliar bowler and a coat that was too large for him.

'Style—begod,' Rashers commented.

'I was given them from a house in Nutley Lane,' Hennessy said. 'What are you lying there for?'

'I'm in bed—a most respectable place to be.'

'You should be above in the streets singing ballads. Such excitement. Did you not meet up with any of it? There was a procession and speeches.'

'I declare to God the Parnell anniversary parade. And I never thought of it.'

'That's not until next week.'

'It's no use anyway,' Rashers said, 'they're not very givish with the money.'

'They've released Larkin,' Hennessy explained. 'The Viceroy himself ordered it. The Irish flag and the stars and stripes is flying outside 10 Beresford Place and there's a meeting going on this past hour. Get up and come round to it with your ballad.'

Rashers shook his head. He had eaten; he had drawn his ten-shillings wages. Besides, he was not feeling too well.

'I'm not up to the mark,' he said. 'The oul chest. And the leg is giving me hell.'

The bowler was too big for Hennessy. He pushed it up off his forehead.

'It's the opportunity of a lifetime.'

'No,' Rashers said, 'sing it for them yourself.'

Hennessy wondered would he. It would earn money. There were thousands crammed in the street outside the union hall. They would be there for about an hour more; longer, if Larkin decided to speak again. But he had never yet, in the extremes of his neediness, tried singing as a livelihood. It would be a step nearer to beggary. It surprised him to find that there was a step still below him. He would work at anything, he would scrounge and borrow; he would not stand in the street and sing. With tact, he said :

'I wouldn't have the voice.'

'I've heard to the differ—that you're a great hand at a song or a recitation.'

'I haven't the right kind of voice for the outdoor stuff.'

'Try the pubs.'

'No,' Hennessy said, 'it's your ballad. I wouldn't make use of it.'

'Please yourself,' Rashers said.

Disappointed, Hennessy moved towards the door.

'Before you go,' Rashers said, 'take a swig of this.'

'Glory be to God!' Hennessy exclaimed, when he saw the bottle. He took out the cork and swallowed.

'You're welcome to your half—if you care to stay.'

Tempted, Hennessy hesitated. But he thought of the crowds, the speeches, the excitement. Something might happen, something that had never happened before and, as like as not, would never happen again.

'No. I'll get back. I wouldn't care to miss what's going on.'

'Please yourself,' Rashers said again.

'Well . . . I hope your chest improves. A good night's rest works wonders.'

The door closed. Rashers, disappointed in his turn, reached once more for the candle, smothering the flame between his finger and thumb. The dog whimpered. Rusty would stay with him, anyway.

When Rashers lay down he fell asleep, but after an hour or less he woke up coughing. He groped again for the whiskey. At the first gulp his cough got worse. At the second it stopped. Now that he knew where the housekeeper kept it, there was always the chance of acquiring a little from time to time. They sent him to the kitchen on and off for messages. Quite often there was nobody there. A drop now and then for medicine, to help him sleep. There wouldn't be any great harm in that. 'Well —we'll see,' he said aloud to the dog. He took a third swig for good measure. He lay back then and slept right through until the morning.

While he did so the submerged city continued to gather at Beresford Place. They were coming out *en masse* once again, as Father O'Connor had seen them do only a few months previously, coming from hovels and tenements, flaunting their rags and their destitution, disrupting traffic and driving the respectable off the pavements. Once again their arrogance astounded the press, which brought the whole story to Father O'Connor at breakfast the next morning. He was disturbed, for it appeared now that some of the well-to-do class had spoken from Larkin's platform congratulating him on his release, describing it as a victory for the workers of Dublin.

'Can you tell me who Countess Markiewicz is, Father?' he enquired, over his paper.

Father O'Sullivan thought very hard but had to acknowledge that he did not know. He was not greatly interested in such things. Father Giffley, who was also at table, did. However, he did not feel like enlightening Father O'Connor; instead, he held out his cup to him, requesting more tea with an aloof movement of his eyebrows.

For brief moments over an endless day it was the iron end-piece of a bed, the rough boards of the ward, a nurse, an old woman in a shapeless grey dress. It was a face filling the whole of the visible, bending. But for long periods it was the laneway at home, winding between ash and sycamore, with blue sky and white cloud above the branches of trees, so dizzily bright that when you stared too long it all swung upside down and you fell in. In the house it was evening with shadows already in the corners and the fire burning high on the hearth. You took food on a tray to the loft where among sacks and oddments two bearded faces turned towards you when you entered. They took the food and said 'Thank you' in very good voices indeed. Once, one of them, the younger one who was very manly and handsome said:

'How old are you, Sara?'

'Seventeen, sir.'

'You mustn't call me sir—I'm only twenty. Do you think we will escape?'

'I pray for it—I keep praying.'

'You're very kind, Sara. And you're terribly pretty.'

'No, indeed.'

'But yes, Sara. I hope you don't mind my saying so.'

'I don't mind.'

Why would you mind? It was forward but not when a young man was about to be captured and to die maybe, not then. Or the evening when he came down to the kitchen and asked if he might speak to you for a little while. Or the morning the soldiers came and his eyes, the way they looked at you as they took him away. You walked again among the ash and the sycamore and in the terrible silence that would never more be broken it was the look in the eyes you remembered. She would never breed men like that again, Ireland of the heroes and the songs and the great deeds. It was strange you could remember forever a young face and strong fingers reaching to take bread from a platter and a voice saying 'You're terribly pretty' and a look in a pair of going-away eyes. It was ash and sycamore, it was shadows and a fire, it was bare boards and a nurse and the end-piece of an iron bed.

She stirred and felt she must sit up. Just once, before she gave in finally to the weariness and the sickness. It was hard though, to overcome it. Several times she tensed the muscles and levered on her elbows and thought at last she was sitting up; yet when she shook her head to clear it she was still lying down and had not stirred at all. Was she, then, powerless? For ever? She tried again and again, until at last she found she was really and truly off her back. Not sitting up, she discovered, but raised, supported by her elbows, seeing the beds about her, some empty, some occupied. It was morning, she thought. Those not in bed were busy with small tasks. None of them seemed to notice her. She tried to talk to the woman in the bed beside her but succeeded only in making noises. She persisted, searching for speech until at last the head turned towards her. The eyes stared at her and the voice called out:

'Nurse... Nurse... come quickly.'

The rest stopped what they were doing to turn and stare. Then she saw the whole face clearly, a grey, alarmed face with a single brown snot oozing down in a thin line from one nostril to the mouth. She thought of her snuff and knew that she had found out at last. Her speech came back to her suddenly, in a storm of shock and anger.

'It was you, you bitch,' she screamed, 'it was you that robbed me.'

The nurse had reached her and was about to push her back. There was no need. Her elbows slid gently under her of their own accord, her body, of its own accord, settled back again on the mattress. There was no further movement in the face and, when the nurse took the wrist, no further movement discernible in the pulse. She went for the doctor. He took his time about coming. When he arrived it was only to draw the coarse sheet over Miss Gilchrist's face.

THE morning was bright, the sky high and blue, on the walls of gardens not yet reached by the sun the frost was a black gleam. The carriage, as it swayed on the cobbles past the grounds of Blackrock College, gave views of the sea on the right, a wide sweep of water, a great chilled sparkle. Mrs. Bradshaw found it cold. She wrapped her furs more closely about her, reconsidering their itinerary. First to Father O'Connor, to tell him what she proposed to do. He had sent word to her immediately, asking for her instructions. He would do everything for her, of course, he would arrange all from beginning to end. But she did not want it that way. There were some things which must be attended to personally. This was one of them, a matter of individual responsibility, a question of conscience. If Mr. Bradshaw found out he would fume and rant. If necessary, that would have to be faced. For too long now the fate of her one-time servant had haunted her mind. In the little service that was left to be done to Miss Gilchrist she would not fail.

Father O'Connor, summoned to the waiting room, was surprised, she could see that. It was early. Outside, the bell was still being run for the ten o'clock mass. A deformed and bearded creature had been dragging fiercely on the rope when she entered the church grounds. She knew what she was going to say to Father O'Connor when he protested—as he would. He would not think it fitting that she should visit Mary Fitzpatrick. She prepared herself to be inflexible.

'Mrs. Bradshaw . . .' Father O'Connor said, advancing to greet her.

233

'You're surprised to see me, Father?'

'I intended to call out to you this morning. You shouldn't have troubled to come all the way in . . .'

'I've made up my mind what should be done. Miss Gilchrist will have a funeral.'

'But of course, I've notified the authorities already that there must be no question of a pauper's grave.'

'I mean a proper funeral, with some carriages following.'

'Carriages?' he asked, puzzled. 'Is that necessary?'

'I feel it is.'

'But—who will travel in them?'

'She had one friend—Mary Fitzpatrick. If Mary and her husband and perhaps one or two of their friends went, it would be perfect.'

'But . . . unnecessary, surely?'

'For me,' Mrs. Bradshaw said, 'it is very necessary that this should be done as I know Miss Gilchrist would wish. Now—I want you to give me Mary Fitzpatrick's address.'

'Do you intend to call on her?'

'I do.'

The answer left Father O'Connor without words. He had been standing. Now he walked to the corner of the room, took a chair and brought it to the table. He sat down.

'Have you any idea of the surroundings you are going to visit?'

'A tenement room?' Mrs. Bradshaw said. 'My husband owns several housefuls of them. There are, I understand, thousands of them. Aren't they part of our city?'

'They are part of our city, but not necessarily fitting places to be visited.'

Mrs. Bradshaw bowed her head. She looked down at the gloved hands which lay joined on her lap.

'You, of all the people I know, should recognise this feeling, this absolute necessity . . .'

She stopped and looked up suddenly at him. Her eyes appealed for his understanding. He knew what she meant. No words of his would clear her of the guilt that she felt. Only restitution, given in the form which seemed to her to be fitting, would do that.

'You are not responsible,' he said to her. 'You did not decide the matter. Besides, in all the circumstances—what else was there to do?'

'I've asked myself that many times.'

'And you still don't know—isn't that so?'

'I know what should be done now,' she said with decision. 'For the moment that will be sufficient.' Her determination impressed him.

'Very well. I'll give you the address. Meanwhile, let me call for some tea.'

The carriage took her back past the railway station again, under the gloomy iron bridge, past a public house on a corner where men stood in a group, talking, spitting, waiting for something to happen, for a cart to pass that was shy a helper, for someone to come along who would stand a drink, for the sun to climb a bit higher, the day to grow a bit warmer.

'Number 3 Chandlers Court,' she said again to the driver, raising the leather flap to project her voice to where he was sitting.

'That's where we're headed ma'am,' he assured her.

They went down a long street, took a turn right and slowed to a walk.

'Chandlers Court, ma'am,' he shouted in to her, 'Number 3.'

He drew back on the reins and the carriage came to a standstill. He opened the door.

'Wait here for me,' she instructed. He nodded. The steps that led up to the hall were uneven, the fanlight was broken, the door stood wide open. The area showed a basement window stuffed with cardboard. From each window of the four storeys above her poles stuck out and carried ropes which supported drying clothes. It was, she could see, wash day. She went uncertainly through the gloomy hall, climbed the stairs to the front room on the first landing and knocked.

At first Mary did not recognise her. She stood, staring, until at last Mrs. Bradshaw had to say, gently :

'May I come in for just a moment, Mary?'

'Mrs. Bradshaw . . .'

Mary opened the door wide and her guest went through. The room was clean, Mrs. Bradshaw noticed. There was very little in it. A table and a couple of rough kitchen chairs, a dresser of sorts, a long couch with a clumsy, home-made look about it and on the mantelpiece, incongruously, a large, ornamental clock.

'Please sit down,' Mary invited. She chose a kitchen chair. There was a fire in the grate, warm enough to keep the cooking pot and kettle simmering but not big enough to heat satisfactorily the large room. Mrs. Bradshaw saw another door to the left and surmised a bedroom. Mary sat opposite. It was the first time she had ever been seated in the presence of Mrs. Bradshaw. She sat straight and still, waiting for the other to speak.

'You are wondering why I've come,' Mrs. Bradshaw said. 'It's about Miss Gilchrist. She . . . died yesterday.'

'Oh,' Mary said. The news was a shock. Death always was. Week after week you saw it in the eyes, yet week after week they opened and looked when your footsteps sounded across the floor of the ward. Recognition, a smile. Until you came to believe that it was going to go on that way, a part of the world, like making a bottle for the baby, or washing on Mondays and shopping on Saturdays. Mary nodded and said :

'Poor Miss Gilchrist.'

'You were very good to her.'

'There was so little I could do.'

'You visited her . . .' Mrs. Bradshaw continued.

'So little . . .' Mary repeated, not listening, and found herself crying.

Mrs. Bradshaw waited a while and then said :

'I've come to ask you to do something more.'

'Now?'

'Miss Gilchrist will be taken from that terrible place. She will be put to rest in a proper and dignified way, with those who knew her in attendance. Father O'Connor will make the funeral arrangements. If it can be done at all, I would like you and your husband to attend. Would you do so?'

'I'd like to,' Mary said, 'but we haven't . . .'

'Where does your husband work?'

'With Morgan & Co.—the foundry.'

'I'll send a carriage for you. If your husband can't be free, perhaps a neighbour would go with you.'

'When will it be?'

'In the morning to Glasnevin cemetery. I'll go myself with Father O'Connor.'

'I'm sure we'll be able to manage,' Mary said.

'You were always a good girl,' Mrs. Bradshaw said. She rose. Mary remembered that she had not been offered hospitality.

'May I make you some tea?'

'You have your children to attend to . . .'

'They're both asleep. It's no trouble.'

Mrs. Bradshaw wondered what would be the right thing to do. What could this bare home offer without hardship to those who lived in it? The pale, pretty face with its dark hair waited uncertainly for her answer.

'A cup of tea would be nice,' Mrs. Bradshaw decided, 'but in my hand—and, please, nothing else whatever.'

She saw Mary stirring the fire under the kettle and wondered what Mr. Bradshaw would have to say if he knew she was preparing to drink tea in a tenement room. And with the servant he had dismissed. Yet she was such a civil, warm-hearted girl. And clean. Everything was clean. That was a sure sign of character, one she had always looked for when engaging.

She was handed a cup and saucer. She reached her spoon for sugar and then waited. Mary hesitated and said:

'I beg your pardon—milk.'

She went to the sideboard. She seemed to have trouble finding what she wanted. Mrs. Bradshaw, sensing a crisis, watched. She saw her empty some from a baby's bottle into a jug. Mrs. Bradshaw was shocked. Mary returned, smiling and said, 'Here it is.'

Mrs. Bradshaw pretended not to have noticed. But she took as little as possible.

Mary took up a tin of condensed milk from the table and said: 'I'd rather have this myself.' She was apologetic.

'Of course,' Mrs. Bradshaw said.

They drank tea in silence for some moments. At last Mrs. Bradshaw said:

'You keep everything very nice, Mary.'

'We haven't much, indeed.'

'You've two little children. Isn't that a great deal?'

'Yes,' Mary said. 'Children are a blessing.'

'Of course they are. Your husband is working with Morgan & Co. I do believe Mr. Yearling is a director. What's your husband's first name?'

'Robert,' Mary said, 'he's a shift worker.'

'I see,' Mrs. Bradshaw said. 'I may find an opportunity to speak to Mr. Yearling about him—that's why I ask.'

'It's very kind of you,' Mary said.

Mrs. Bradshaw left her cup down and said she really must go. Before going to the door she opened her purse and fumbled in it. She put a pound on the table. Mary was embarrassed.

'Please, Mrs. Bradshaw—I couldn't.'

'There may be little expenses to meet tomorrow which neither Father O'Connor nor I will be able to attend to for you. Your husband must not be out of pocket.'

Mary held open the door for her. A group of children had gathered about the cab. Many of them, Mrs. Bradshaw remarked, were in rags. Most of them were barefooted. They cleared a passage for her and stared after the cab as it turned in a wide circle and departed. Mary, from her window, watched it go. She took the jug from the table and returned what remained of the milk to the child's bottle. It was all the fresh milk she had. But there would be no shortage. The pound note on the table was almost a week's wages. The clock on the mantelpiece chimed, telling her it was noon already and that Fitz would soon be returning. 'And what is your husband's first name?' If Mrs. Bradshaw was interested, even a little bit, God knows what good might come of it.

The cab took them at a smart pace to the workhouse. The morning was bright again, but mild. Mary thought they might have a window open.

'Just a little,' she suggested to Fitz.

He unhooked the leather strap from its brass stud, eased the frame down and re-secured it. He was wearing his stiff collar and a tie. It made him look stouter, somehow, but very handsome, she thought. Pat, who was off work, had come with them for company. She was glad. The children of the neighbourhood had gathered about the cab when it called for them. It was less embarrassing to step into it when there were three of them. Pat, she thought, looked very neat too, with his serge suit and butterfly collar and bowler hat. It was such a pity he was a bit wild at times, because underneath he had a warm, kind nature. Mrs. Mulhall, who was minding the children, had waved goodbye from the window and for a moment it had felt like setting off on a day's outing. But she reminded herself that it was to see the very last of poor Miss Gilchrist, who had been so kind to her when she had no Fitz and no children. It would be unseemly to treat it like an excursion.

At the mortuary chapel they stood for a little while beside the coffin to pray. Mrs. Bradshaw was in the grounds, but did not go into the mortuary. It was not the custom among well-to-do ladies. Father O'Connor came in, took his stole from his pocket, kissed it, placed it around his neck and prayed. He sprinkled holy water from a tiny bottle which he also carried. He acknowledged their presence with a nod, then rejoined Mrs. Bradshaw. They got into a coach together. When the hearse was ready both cabs followed it, slowly as far as the gates, more briskly as they began the journey across the city. In the second coach Pat offered Fitz a cigarette.

'Where are we off to?' he asked.

Fitz looked at Mary. She looked blankly back at him.

'I never thought of asking,' she confessed.

'Glasnevin, probably,' Pat decided.

'We'll soon know,' Fitz said, unconcerned.

In a minute or so the cab driver confirmed their guess by turning left. They reached the quays and travelled towards the city centre. Men stopped to raise their hats as the hearse passed, women crossed themselves. People searching through the shelves outside second-hand bookshops turned to pay their respects. At the rattle of their wheels the gulls loitering along the river wall rose lazily with outstretching necks and glided down to the safety of the water.

'It's such a fine morning,' Mrs. Bradshaw said, leaning forward for a moment to peer through the window.

'It would be so unpleasant if it rained,' Father O'Connor agreed.

'I'd no idea how truly destitute most of your parishioners were. Even your poor clerk . . .'

'The clerk of the church can hardly be described as destitute,' Father O'Connor suggested. But politely. Mrs. Bradshaw's ideas of destitution and his own were bound to be different.

'He seemed to me to be in rags,' she answered.

Father O'Connor was puzzled.

'When did you meet him?'

'When I arrived yesterday morning he was ringing the bell—a bearded, very odd-looking poor creature.'

That was not the clerk. Father O'Connor wondered who it could have been. He remembered the boilerman.

'It must have been Tierney, our boilerman.' The discovery irritated him. What an impression to give a lady visitor.

'He shouldn't have been ringing the bell,' he explained, 'his place is in the boiler room. I must speak to the clerk about it.'

A green wreath, the ribbons bedraggled, lay at the plinth which would soon support the Parnell monument, a tribute, now several days old, from the Parnell anniversary parade. What inscription did the pedestal carry? Something about the onward march of a nation. Something to the effect that no one had the right to say—this far shalt thou go and no further?

'A tragic poor man,' Mrs. Bradshaw remarked, surprisingly.

An adulterer. Nevertheless, a great leader. Unfortunate entanglement. Could he not foresee—probably not. A Protestant and a patrician. Outlook quite different. Behind the euphemisms and the sentimentalities Catholic Ireland had not failed to discern the real horror. They were laying wreaths just the same. Yearling had remarked on that. *De mortuis nil nisi bonum.*

'Ah yes, indeed,' Father O'Connor said, as the laurelled sinner slipped behind.

The passers-by continued to raise their hats to Miss Gilchrist.

She had joined the ranks of the dead, and commanded now their unanimous and ungrudging respect. Miss Gilchrist R.I.P. She was ennobled.

A hearse and mourning coaches stood empty outside the Brian Boru House waiting, while the mourners, their kinsman already buried, consoled themselves with alcohol. It was a custom deplored by Father O'Connor. They were talking about the dead one, praising him, exchanging remembrances of him. Sometimes they sang—an odd vehicle for the expression of grief. 'The drunken funerals of Ireland.' He shook his head, deploring it.

'We are a strange people,' Mrs. Bradshaw answered. Again her tolerance surprised him.

Inside the cemetery another funeral was in possession of the mortuary chapel. He bore the delay patiently, leaning on his umbrella as he waited. Mrs. Bradshaw beckoned Mary to come to her and enquired if everything had been as arranged. It had. She was pleased. She drew her apart and said: 'I've been waiting to give you this note.' She passed an envelope to Mary. Mary, knowing it would not be seemly at that moment to open it, put it in her pocket. Father O'Connor, turning his head for a moment, met her eyes and nodded in vague acknowledgment of her smile, which he thought had been meant for him.

Some distance away, Pat pointed out to Fitz the huge round tower which marked the resting place of Dan O'Connell.

'Do you know what that is?' he asked Fitz.

'The tomb of the Liberator.'

'They say in Kerry that you couldn't throw a stone over a work house wall without hitting one of Dan's bastards.'

'They buried his heart in Rome, just the same,' Fitz said. 'It was his own request.'

Pat, who did not care for O'Connell, grunted and said: 'I wonder where they buried his cockalorum.'

They found that the body of Miss Gilchrist was being moved into the chapel and followed. There were prayers. Then they followed the coffin down an avenue of trees, until they reached the new dug grave. The diggers passed their ropes under it and lowered it skilfully into the earth. Father O'Connor prayed, so quietly that all the time he did so they could hear the birds in the nearby trees. Soon there would be hardly any birds at all, Mary thought, soon the dead of winter would strip every remaining remnant. There would be no leaf and no wing. She wept when the first clod of earth bumped on the coffin. Then it was time to go back to the waiting coach.

They seated themselves.

'The Brian Boru House,' Pat suggested.

'Please,' Mary asked, 'I wouldn't like Father O'Connor and Mrs. Bradshaw to see you.'

'We'll let them go first then,' Pat said.

He got out and spoke to the driver, who began to examine the harness inch by inch, as though tracing a fault. Mrs. Bradshaw's coach passed them and went rattling down the road. The driver looked up and Pat shouted to him, 'Coast clear.'

The driver climbed up, settled himself in the driving seat and cracked his whip. He looked very dignified.

Mary waited outside. She lay back against the padded leather and thought that she had not been in a coach since her childhood. It had been the funeral of an aunt, she remembered, on a day in summer when there were poppies spread through the grass in the country churchyard. She had been given biscuits and lemonade by her father. That was all she could remember, red poppies in long grass, worn headstones warm to touch, dust on the nettles and poppies red in the long grasses. Where was that day now? Where was the little girl in laced boots, a cousin of some sort, who had waited with her and played in the hot sun and got sick on the way home? She could not even remember her name. It was a strange thing, growing up and changing a little day by day, so slowly that you never noticed, so surely moving to maturity and old age and the front place at the funeral, having children to take in their turn the biscuits and the lemonade, to play in the sun and be sick in the evening. If you could be sure of heaven . . . She leaned towards the window and looked up at the sky. It was so high and blue it made her dizzy. One day she would close her eyes and fall into it. If she was spared to see the children reared and settled—that's all she would ask of God.

When that was done He could take her.

She pressed back against the leather, alone in the cab, alone, for a moment, in the world. If she got out and strolled up and down it would make no difference. If she went in and sat with the men and drank port wine it would still make no difference. She was trapped by life and by mortality. She began to wish Fitz would come out. When he did she leaned forward to welcome him, as though he had been away for some days. The driver climbed into his seat. Fitz shouted 'Go ahead' and closed the door.

'Where's Pat?' she asked.

'He's not coming.'

She frowned.

'He met someone he knew inside.'

'Does that mean he'll spend the day drinking?'

'No,' Fritz said, 'he has other plans. Do you remember Lily Maxwell?'

Mary did. The girl who, from all accounts, was no better than she should be.

'He hasn't seen her for ages. While we were inside he met someone who knows where she's living.'

'Any man would be better away from women like that.'

It was a woman's view. Fitz did not share it. He knew Lily meant much to Pat.

'Not always,' Fitz said.

Mary touched his hand and he turned to her. She asked: 'Do you love me?'

The question surprised him. Something had upset her. He wondered what it could be.

'Of course I love you.'

It was both an answer and a question. She left it unanswered. His reply had satisfied a need in her that she no longer tried to understand. She was content to leave her hand in his, to feel her reassurance return slowly as the cab travelled through the bright streets of the city, towards their couple of rooms and the insecure world in which her children waited. Thinking of her home, she remembered for the first time the note Mrs. Bradshaw had left with her. She took it from her pocket and opened it. It contained three one-pound notes. She drew them out.

'Where did this come from?' Fitz asked.

'Mrs. Bradshaw gave me the envelope in the cemetery.' There was a letter, which she passed to Fitz. He read aloud :

'My dear Mary

This will help you and your husband to provide something in the way of a special treat for your children. Accept it on their account.

Since I called to you I have been clearing out some old furniture and some floor coverings which I propose to send to you within a few days. You will be able to make use of them, I feel sure.

I have had the full story of your visits to Miss Gilchrist and consider your kindness to that old and friendless poor soul does you very great credit. God will reward you for that, as He promised long ago "one hundredfold".

Believe me when I say that your goodness has been most praiseworthy indeed.

Florence Bradshaw'

Fitz handed back the letter.

'That should make you happy.'

'The furniture will be wonderful, won't it,' she said.

Father O'Connor, having sent the housekeeper to fetch the clerk, watched at the window for their arrival. Sunlight lay on the courtyard outside and slid past the brass flower bowl in the window to fall on worn linoleum. It was a pleasant room which at the moment smelled of polish—a clean and agreeable smell. If his own room caught the sun for even an hour or two of the day it would have been entirely transformed. As it was it remained dark and damp and almost always depressing.

Sunlight meant so much. At the funeral today, for instance, it had been so pleasant: the earth dry and firm, the breeze mild and agreeable, a perfect setting for an extremely edifying occasion. Miss Gilchrist had received a fitting reward for faithful service; Mrs. Bradshaw had performed a quite singular act of

244

charity. People like Yearling might laugh and say they did not care a fig where they were buried or by whom; but then Yearling, for all his unusual perceptiveness, did not understand the poor. The Fitzpatricks, too, had behaved very well—neither too forward nor too awkward. He seemed a respectable type of man to be mixed up with Larkin and strikes. But that was part of the tragedy—the good and the bad alike were being drawn in. If people of title were now choosing to associate with such things, was it fair to blame the ordinary workman for being misled? Mrs. Bradshaw might take an interest there. He might speak to her. The man had gone out of his way to help him on that dreadful night.

The housekeeper and the clerk crossed the courtyard. There was a light tap on the door.

'Come in.'

The clerk was wearing a frayed and faded soutane that reminded him, like everything else in the parish, of a rag-and-bone shop.

'Have you no better soutane than that?'

'I have indeed, Father.'

'Is the good one very uncomfortable or something?'

'I was cleaning the novena lamps—a dirty job.'

'I see.'

There was always some excuse.

'You wouldn't want me getting oil stains up to me elbows, would you?'

The voice was not what it should be.

'I would have you moderate your tone,' Father O'Connor suggested, coldly.

The clerk frowned, making it plain that he was annoyed. Clerks everywhere were the same, Father O'Connor reflected. They grumbled, they disapproved, they argued back. He would not do it with Father Giffley though. Indeed no. Afraid.

'It was reported to me this morning that Tierney the boilerman was ringing the bell for the ten o'clock mass.'

'I let him do it when I'm busy,' the clerk said. He was offhanded—deliberately so.

'You mustn't allow it in future.'

'He thinks it a great privilege.'

'What he thinks about it doesn't matter in the least,' Father O'Connor insisted. 'It isn't seemly.'

'Seemly,' the clerk repeated. 'I declare to God, Father, I don't follow you at all. What's unseemly about a poor man pulling a bell-rope to give me a hand.'

It was always so. Nothing was accepted simply. Everything had to be argued in St. Brigid's.

'Tierney is the boilerman. He is not very clean. His appearance—to say the least about it—is extremely odd. We mustn't let the bell-ringing become a music-hall turn for the parish gapers.'

'Father Giffley never objected.'

'I am quite sure Father Giffley knows nothing about it or he would. Anyway, kindly attend to the bell-ringing yourself in the future.'

'Whatever you say, Father.'

Once again the tone of voice was disrespectful.

'That will be all.'

'I see.'

The clerk, stern-faced, angry, withdrew. Some hours later, when the three priests were at the evening meal, Father Giffley said: 'You were speaking to the clerk about the ringing of the bell.'

'I see, the clerk has complained to you.'

'He has the excellent habit,' Father Giffley said, 'of referring such matters to his parish priest.'

'The boilerman was ringing the bell. It looks most unseemly.'

'You saw him?'

'Not personally. It was reported to me.'

'It didn't occur to you to consult my views.'

'I was certain they would be the same as mine.'

'I am still your parish priest,' Father Giffley said. The deep, red colour was in his cheeks and forehead. Father O'Connor lowered his eyes.

'It seemed such a small matter—I am sorry.'

'I have already issued instructions. In the future—as in the past—Tierney may help the clerk whenever it is required.'

'Very good, Father.'

Father O'Connor knew he was being humiliated. It was deliberate. It was putting him in the wrong with the clerk and the boilerman, placing him below the ragtag and bobtail. That hurt almost unbearably—that and the contempt which was now unconcealed. He beat down anger and rebellion, kept them from showing in his face, guarded each movement of hands and head, pushed them back when they sought other means of entry. He did so by fixing his thoughts inflexibly on obedience. To be obedient was everything. Humiliation, the sting of wounded pride, the knowledge of being unloved and unrespected by another, these things did not matter at all, if one could become truly as nothing, if one could empty the house of Self and be stripped utterly.

Over a cup of tea and a half-eaten egg, Father O'Connor fought to possess Christ.

Pat stopped to check the name of the road. It was as the man in the Brian Boru House had informed him. There were parallel rows of small, two-storey houses with tiny gardens in front. It was quiet, respectable. Closed doors kept each household to itself, curtained windows gave away no secrets. A door opening and closing somewhere down the cul-de-sac startled Pat and sent the air trembling. He looked down the road and recognised Lily immediately, although as yet she was too far away for him to see her face. She was coming towards him. It was a piece of luck he had not bargained for. Watching her, he began to tremble a little. She might still not want to speak to him. He waited. She came forward, unsuspecting, with easy, unconcerned movements. When she was some yards from him he shouted: 'Lily.'

She faltered. The serge suit, the butterfly collar, the bowler hat did not seem to match the voice. Then she recognised him and stopped.

'My God,' she said, 'have they made you Lord Mayor or something?'

Delight made his heart jump. She was herself. She was accepting him in the old way.

'Lily,' he repeated. To say her name helped to release the pressure of tenderness inside him and made speech easier.

'Where did you spring from?'

'I found out at last where you were living.'

'And you were coming to see me?'

'I was hoping to see you, Lily.'

'Is that why you're wearing the regimentals?'

'No. I was at a funeral.'

'I might have guessed. It's a bit of a hobby of yours, isn't it, going to weddings and funerals.'

She was smiling at him. He thought she looked more lovely than ever, her eyes lively, her face quick with banter. He said suddenly:

'Come with me somewhere, anywhere. I want to talk to you.'

She laughed at him.

'Please . . . Lily.'

'All right. Where?'

'The Park?'

She hesitated. Then with an odd air of decision said: 'I don't mind—I'm free today.'

'We'll get a tram at the bottom of the road. Come on.'

He was glad now to be wearing the bowler and the serge suit. They fitted the occasion. The day was still mild enough to make it pleasant on top of the tram. When they passed by Nelson's Pillar, Lily said: 'This is the first time I've been down here in two years.'

He saw his opportunity to question her.

'I know that. But why?'

He was sorry almost immediately. She stiffened.

'How did you know?'

'I enquired about you. I couldn't help asking after you. No one had seen you.'

For the first time since their meeting he saw the old look of hurt in her eyes.

'I'll tell you later,' she said.

She slipped her arm through his, a gesture that reassured him and filled him with an intense pleasure.

They walked the hill of the Phoenix Park. The trees,

exposed on its height, were stripped almost bare; in the valley below, a silver gleam between green slopes, the Liffey flowed towards Islandbridge and the city. They had walked here many times in the past; in the season of hawthorn, when the air was full of white petals and fragrance; in the season of lilac and laburnum; in the dying of the year when the paths, as now, were thick with fallen leaves. Sometimes they had listened to the military band which played on Sundays in The Hollow. Pat remarked that.

'I wish there was a band.'

She said : 'No bands today, Pat.'

But the air was better than any band, and the light, streaming down from behind high clouds, picked out isolated green patches on the slopes of the Dublin mountains. They found a seat that was sheltered and sat down. Pat took a paper bag from his pocket and handed it to her.

'What's this?'

She opened the bag and looked.

'God—it's a long time since anyone bought me sweets. When did you get these?'

'When I was on my way across to look for your house.' She took one and offered him the bag, but he refused.

'You were at a funeral this morning. Had you anything to eat?'

'I had a sandwich in the Brian Boru.'

She dismissed that.

'A sandwich for a grown man,' she said, 'that's no way to look after yourself.'

He waited, not quite sure if this was the moment to plunge. He made up his mind.

'Maybe you'd do the looking after for me.'

She selected another sweet with exaggerated care and fixed her eyes on the glen below. It was damp in its lower reaches; the branches of the tangled hawthorns were black against the light.

'Meaning what, Uncle Pat?' Her tone was light. But lines of caution moulded her face.

'I want you to marry me.'

She threw back her head.

'God, will you listen to him.'

'What's wrong with that?'

'You used to say you didn't believe in marriage.'

'I don't. But everyone else does. Well . . .'

She continued to be interested in the black branches near the bottom of the glen.

'Not a chance,' she said.

He took it without protest and remained silent. She held the bag towards him without looking at him.

'Have a sweet,' she invited. She was matter-of-fact, off-hand. He made no movement. When she looked around his face was full of suffering. She let down the bag, leaned her hands on his knee and kissed him on the cheek.

'I'm sorry,' She had dropped her matter-of-factness. He put his hand on her shoulder, turning her towards him.

'I love you, Lily.'

'When did you find that out?'

'The night you walked away from me.'

'I'm glad.'

'Glad?'

'Glad you love me—not glad I walked off on you.'

He kissed her. He held her against him, letting the hurt and loneliness of two years find what release it could. He knew, for the moment anyway, that she wanted him to hold her.

'I've been thinking about you all the time, Lily.'

'Dear Pat.'

'Why did you walk off like that. You weren't as angry as you let on to be, I know that. Were you just fed up with me and all of us?'

'Not with you, Pat.'

'With the others?'

'With the others and with myself.'

'Why? What happened? Tell me—please, Lily.'

'I'll tell you,' she promised, 'just give me a minute or two.'

She released herself and sat thinking. He waited. It seemed to him that everything else, the stripped trees, the green slopes, the damp mist in the hollow, the black branches, the whole world waited with him. He looked at her face and it was unhappy again. It tempted him to tell her not to answer, to say it was all right. He could not. He must know where he stood.

'Well,' he asked, after an interval.

'If you want to know,' she said at last, 'I got a dose of something.'

He knew what she meant. There was no need to ask questions. He thought carefully.

'That wouldn't make any difference to me.'

'You're daft,' she said.

'Did you go anywhere? Did you get treatment?'

'I went to a fellow that Maisie knew. That's how I came to spend your money.'

'And you wouldn't tell me.'

'I was ashamed.'

Her own admission surprised her. She tried to laugh at it.

'Imagine Lily being ashamed,' she said.

'Did he do any good?'

'I think he did the trick, all right. Maisie swears by him. But you can never be sure, can you?'

'I don't know,' Pat said. It was a subject he knew very little about. One thing he was quite certain of. It made no difference.

'I'm still asking you, Lily.'

'But I couldn't, Pat. Supposing something happened to you.'

'It doesn't matter.'

'Or supposing there were children. Jesus—imagine that! Children brought into the world and *that* already rotting them.'

She began to cry. He took her to him and held her fiercely. He was angry now, with the green slope and the black boughs, with everything that dared to remain aloof from Lily's suffering.

'Lily. We needn't have children. We needn't do anything like that at all. We can marry and be with each other.'

'You think that would be enough?'

'I do.'

'I wouldn't do that on you,' she said, gently. She took his hand and pressed it against her cheek.

'But if I'm the one who wants it that way?'

She shook her head. She was staring again at the hawthorn

boughs. He knew it would be no use to go on. For the present, anyway, there was no purpose to it. She was in his arms willingly, gratefully. For the moment that was sufficient happiness.

'After you left me, did you think of me at all?'

She said: 'At first I thought about nothing except *it*. I got work in a place in Glasnevin and never went near town except to see this doctor fellow. I hated everybody. Then, when it seemed to clear up, I knew I'd never go back to the old places. I was a fool to think that sort of life would suit. The funny thing was, when I made up my mind about that, I began to think about you. I thought quite a lot about you.'

'What did you think?'

'That I hadn't been very fair to you. It was the way I felt at the time. I'm sorry, Pat.'

'It doesn't matter, now. Do you think you could love me, Lily?'

She did not answer immediately. When she spoke it was to say: 'It'll be dark very soon. We should think of getting home.'

'Lily . . .?'

She looked up at him for some time, her eyes wide and beautiful.

'Yes I think I might.'

That was sufficient. The rest could wait. He kissed her again and they got up. Behind the mildness of the air there was a chill, the evening damp rising from earth and grass. Night was moving stealthily among the bushes and the branches, treading warily after the vanished sun, flowing noiselessly over the stripped trees and the heights, spreading unresisted across the plains of Ireland.

They walked back towards the city with the river below them still luminous in the twilight, the trees ghostly, the air chilled and earthy. At the Park gate the river broadened and became defiled and smelled like a slum. The tramcars passed them, twinkling with lights.

THERE were few days left of sunshine and mildness. The evenings drew in, fog drifted across the city, sometimes thickly, sometimes light and noticeable only because each lamp along the street wore a shimmering corona. Mary, thinking of Christmas, looked about a living room that had been transformed. There was a fine oval table in the centre with a tasselled covering and four good chairs about it. There was a sideboard with a mirror and a rug which she put before the fireplace when the day's cooking was done. There was an easy chair for Fitz and a matching one for herself. They were well worn, but decent looking. The clock which Pat had given them on their wedding night still stood on the mantelpiece. It added an elegant touch to the room. Sometimes she looked at the furniture as it was reflected in the mirror of the sideboard. For some reason the reflection made it more real. They had sold some odd pieces and bought a second-hand pram. It was not much use just then, with the days so cold and short. But there would be spring and summer. Time would pass quickly. They could walk out together to Sandymount and Merrion again. They could bathe and then sit on the sands and look out to Howth with the sea around it. Everything seemed easy and worth while now. It would have taken them years to build up such a home. It had come to them in a single afternoon, in a delivery van drawn by two horses, about which the children of the street had gathered to gape.

Father O'Connor saw it and admired it. He praised Mrs. Bradshaw's generosity. He said he knew they appreciated their good fortune. He hoped her husband would be able now to put everything else out of his mind and work steadily for the good home that was theirs. He had in mind, he said, the labour troubles that were bringing misery and want into homes that could enjoy that peace which was the hallmark of the Catholic family. As he went down the street afterwards he passed Rashers Tierney, who took off his hat and said, with irritating energy:

'There's yourself, Father.'

'Good evening,' Father O'Connor answered.

His voice had a cold edge to it. That was unintentional. He wished to have no grudge against this poor, limping oddity. That would be a strange way for a priest to behave. Indeed it would. What had the poor old man done, except what he had been told to do—and told to continue doing. Naturally, he would see nothing unfitting in a bundle of galvanised rags tolling the church bell.

There were other things to be thought about. Winter and cold rooms. Hunger and empty stomachs. The sting of pride which had almost mastered him when Father Giffley rejected his decision about Tierney could be chastised by taking up again the thankless task of providing a little relief for want and misery. He had given in too easily. The time to put into practice his resolution to make amends had come. The job of distribution would be one for Timothy Keever and the Confraternity Committee. Strictly speaking, Mr. Hegarty should supervise the arrangements, but the head prefect, he had noticed, was not so familiar with the deserving cases and did not seem to have much relish for that kind of work. It would be quite wrong to blame the man. Hegarty was a tradesman, and tradesmen were careful to keep themselves aloof from the ragtag and bobtail.

Once again they brought down the foodstuff from his bedroom and spread it out in the room behind the vestry. They made out a list. Some would receive money; others, who might put money to the wrong use, would receive parcels. The procedure was to be the same.

'I want you to avoid any who are on strike—as far as seems reasonable.'

That was painful, perhaps, but absolutely necessary. In all justice.

'When I say reasonable I mean that you will not give out parcels indiscriminately to strikers, because for one thing, it is a disservice to themselves to encourage them and, in addition, we must not appear to seek charity from well disposed people in order to make it possible for their employees to hold out against them—that would hardly be a just arrangement.' Father O'Connor wondered if they understood.

'On the other hand, if there is extreme want or sickness in a home or some factor of that kind you could overlook the fact that one of the victims may also, incidentally, be involved in a labour dispute.'

'We'll consult you, Father,' Keever said.

Father O'Connor frowned. He did not want to be set up as an arbitrator in such things.

'That shouldn't be necessary if you use your own judgment,' he decided.

They went around the streets again each evening after work, a small band of devoted workers. Keever wore the long, black overcoat and the bowler hat which was his Sunday uniform. It was easy to help the old. They crouched over small fires or lay in rough beds and took the smallest kindness with gratitude. But with men who were only destitute because there was no one to hire the labour of their bodies it was different. They watched their wives accepting charity and gave none of the usual signs of gratitude. Their attitude made him cautious. It showed they had not forgotten. Once, he ran into trouble. He had a parcel to spare at the end of a long night of visits. Thinking he would leave it in the house with someone and get home, he said to the woman he was dealing with:

'Is there anyone else in the house that's out of work?'

'Mrs. Moore's husband has been idle this while back.' That seemed all right. He was very tired and the room depressed him. It was practically bare of furniture. All he could see was the rough table. There was a candle burning on that, which threw more shadows than light. The woman's husband was over by the uncurtained window, watchful, a silhouette.

'And where does she live?'

'Just above us—on the next landing.'

He decided to go up. The two men with him were already making for the door when the woman added:

'Her husband is on strike, God help her.'

Keever stopped and turned. There was a note of genuine disappointment in his voice.

'In that case, ma'am, I'm afraid I'll have to go further.' He turned again to find that her husband had come between him and the door.

'What's wrong with being on strike?'

Keever, careful not to shoulder full responsibility, said: 'I have my instructions.'

'Who's instructions?'

'Father O'Connor's.' Immediately he regretted it. It was indiscreet. Father O'Connor would certainly think so. The man took the family's parcel from the table and pushed it into Keever's arms.

'If Father O'Connor thinks he's going to beat Jim Larkin with cocoa and sugar,' he said, 'you can tell him what to do with his parcel.'

Timothy Keever backed away. Burdened now with both parcels, he struggled clumsily to open the door.

'There you are—that's the thanks you get,' one of his helpers said, as they trooped down the stairs. The voice was disgruntled and lacking in conviction. Was there yet another waverer in the Confraternity? That was the way Larkinism spread and grew, even among the selected workers of the Church. He felt no personal grudge; all he wished was to get to heaven. If the road to travel was through obedience and good works only it would hold little hardship. It looked now, though, that it would be through suspicion, unpopularity, insult, as well.

'We are not working just to be thanked,' he pointed out.

He told his wife about it that night as they sat over supper in his cottage by the railway line. She agreed that it might have been a mistake. They worried about it together, listening to the occasional thundering of trains that passed by their back garden, where the now weathered statue watched with joined hands and the surrounding railings creaked in the rigours of wind and winter.

The news reached Mulhall and from him it went to Fitz.

'I'm going to see this Father O'Connor,' Mulhall decided. Fitz thought that unwise.

'What does it matter?' he said.

But Mulhall had made up his mind.

'I'll deal with Keever too,' he said.

'O'Connor will fling you out.'

'Let him try,' Mulhall said.

Mulhall was a big man with iron-grey hair and a sure way of walking that inspired confidence in those who worked with him. He liked the new movement well. It was direct and simple. Demand, refusal, strike. He worked for Doggett & Co. under constant threat of dismissal. One slip and he was out of his job, with little hope of being jobbed elsewhere. He was well known as a troublemaker. In the eyes of Doggett he thrived on trouble. Where others bent, Mulhall bloomed. The shoulders straightened, the chest stuck out, the face settled into firm lines of confidence and composure. His demands were conveyed simply—to the yard foreman, to the superintendent, even to Doggett himself.

'No work after four o'clock on Saturdays, Mr. Doggett.'

'You'll work when you're told, Mulhall.'

'Mr. Larkin wrote to you. Why didn't you answer him?'

'I don't have to reply to Mr. Larkin.'

'That's gameball. We don't have to work after four on Saturdays either.'

'I'll get rid of you, Mulhall, if this nonsense continues.'

'Right. I'll let the men know.'

'You'll let them know what?'

'That you're getting rid of me.'

'That's enough. You'll hear more about this.'

But Mulhall remained in his job. Doggett knew better. Strike fever had hit the city. One ended, another began. It was better to settle up. For the moment. Later on the cure for the epidemic would be found. Already more powerful and more resourceful minds were at work on the problem.

Father O'Connor received Mulhall in the visitors' room and began the interview at a disadvantage. He had expected one of the usual enquiries; an appeal for spiritual advice, a request for help. It took him some time to grasp that this huge, rough-looking working man was taking him to task. It was quite an incredible situation. He tried at first not to look at it that way.

'You have some objection to our distributing relief?'

His voice was controlled.

'We've an objection to Timothy Keever.'

'You have . . .? May I ask why?'

'He goes about making fish of one and flesh of another.'

'In what way?'

'Asking women if their husbands are on strike and telling them they'll get nothing if they are.'

'Those are my instructions.'

'If they are they're no instructions for a priest to give.'

'You are being insolent now.' The tone had changed.

'Mr. Doggett's fond of saying that too.'

'Mr. Doggett?'

'The boss. He locked us out twice in the past twelve months. We gave him his bellyful.'

'You keep saying "we". Who are "we"?'

'Myself, the other carters, Jim Larkin.'

So it had come into the room to him. All that he had read, all that he had heard from the platform when on impulse he had followed the procession, was standing in the room with him. He should have recognised it earlier.

'If you follow Mr. Larkin, you have no business coming to me.'

'I'm a Catholic. I don't want to be made ashamed of my Church.'

The voice had grown angry. Father O'Connor's first impulse was to order the man to go. He changed his mind. He had learned that he was unable to do such things without losing dignity. He could never impress or terrify as Father Giffley could.

'You are the one who should be ashamed,' Father O'Connor said. 'You are turning your back on the Church to follow her enemies.'

'I thought the Church should be on the side of the poor.'

This was no ordinary workman.

'And so we are,' Father O'Connor said, gently.

'You couldn't be. You backed Mr. Doggett. You back the landlords. You told Timothy Keever to see that anyone on strike was left to stew.'

'Socialism is an evil doctrine and Mr. Larkin is one of its propagandists. It attacks property and the Church Herself. If you are a Catholic you should do what the Church tells you. You must trust the wisdom of your priests.'

'In their proper sphere, Father.'

Father O'Connor recognised the phrase. It came from the platforms. This illiterate man was beginning to consider himself competent to determine the sphere of the Church's influence, to place bounds to the radiation of a wisdom that was nineteen centuries old. How could he explain the arrogance of that.

'You are misled and I am sorry for you. Now I must ask you to leave.'

The man went quietly, too quietly. He closed the door behind him without another word. Father O'Connor remained in the visitors' room for some time. The bishop had spoken out clearly about this new movement. Priests all over the city had preached on its evils. There could be no misunderstanding. But something was going wrong. Humble people were no longer listening. Were they beginning to believe the Reformers, to think that a world without God could be turned into an Utopia? He took out his pocket book and wrote carefully: '*What shall it profit a man if, gaining the whole world, he suffereth the loss of his own soul.*' He would use it as the text for a future sermon.

It was raining. Cabs and occasional motor cars splashed through muddy streets. The gas-lamps steamed lightly. Mulhall pulled his cap down on his forehead and turned up the collar of his jacket. He felt warm inside him, in spite of the chill of the rain. It was the battle glow. It showed in the line of his jaw and the set of his shoulders. He was the father of the old women who passed him with shawls drawn tight over their heads. He was brother to the old men who sheltered against public house fronts and waited, hopefully, for someone who would bring them in for a drink and maybe a smoke. He was God, and the small boy who passed pushing a battered pram was his creature. Rain had plastered the boy's hair about his face and the pram was piled with rain-soaked firewood. It was his creature and all his creatures were wet, cold, hungry, barefooted.

They would change that. Not by talk though. Do something. Keep on all the time doing something. Even if it led to trouble. Trouble attracted attention. People you wanted to rouse always took an interest when you did something. There were ways of dealing with Keever. Put the fear of God into others who might feel like following his example.

Mulhall went in for a drink. He wanted to think and he wanted to consult the clock. It was nearly half past eight. He said to the curate: 'Your clock right?'

'Ten minutes.'

'I'll have a half of malt,' he decided.

He was in Keever's district. A turn off the main street and he would be among the warren of cottages that ended with their backs against the railway line. The trouble was, he was not quite sure of the address. The curate, bringing the whiskey, remarked: 'That's a bit of a sprinkle.'

Mulhall looked round at the long windows. Rain was beating against them.

'A good night,' he said, 'for ducks.'

'Keeps the customers indoors.'

Keever was likely to be at home. It would be worth trying.

'Do you know Timothy Keever? He works for Nolan & Keyes?'

'I've heard talk of him.'

'I'm looking for his address.'

'Hold on,' the curate said. He went off into the back of the shop. After a while he came back.

'The basket boy works in the grocery end during the day,' he said. 'He knows the house.'

He gave Mulhall directions, tracing out the turns on the counter with a finger he had moistened in porter dribbles.

'Number 43,' he said at last, 'here.' He drew a circle on one of the lines.

'Thanks,' Mulhall said.

He went out into the street again. The rain drove hard against him. He bent a little towards it. Otherwise he did not mind it. All his life he had faced the weather from the seat of his cart. Wind, cold, rain, snow, they were enemies he had long mastered. Only children he pitied. And old people. Weather, among other things, killed both. One thing you couldn't change. The weather. But you could protect them against it. Proper clothes would do it. Boots for the feet, coats for the body. The poorer and hungrier they were, the less fitted to stand up against weather. The poorer and the hungrier, the more often they had to face it. To chop up and sell firewood. To go out gathering the debris of the city. Who would stop that? Larkin would, with Mulhall doing his part in all the ways that he could.

He was among the cottages now. He looked out for street names. There was a lamp at each corner, but the name plates were hard to make out in the driving rain. He knocked at several doors for directions and went down street after street where cottages huddled under the downpour and overfull gutters splashed noisily. At last, in a cul-de-sac that the wall of the railway line sealed off, he found the house. Keever himself answered the door. Mulhall recognised him. He gripped him by the lapels and dragged him quickly into the street.

'I want you,' he said.

The cottage door, caught by the wind, moved slowly, gathered pace, closed with a loud bang.

'Mulhall.'

'You're a scab, Keever.'

'Let me go.'

'Not until I show you and every other scab in this town what happens to strike-breakers.'

'I'm breaking no strike. Let me go.'

They were against the railway wall. High, featureless, blackened with soot and rain, it rose above both of them. Keever braced himself against it.

'You're using charity parcels to break a strike.'

'I'm serving the poor.'

'You're a liar. You're selling them.'

Keever twisted but failed to free himself.

'You'll do six months' hard if you touch me.'

'Gladly,' Mulhall said.

Keever pushed forward. Mulhall gave ground, then swung hard and connected. He dragged Keever to his feet again. They struggled together until Mulhall landed again. Then he began to beat up Keever, on the body, on the head, until Keever lay against the railway wall, rain and blood mixing together on his swollen face. He fixed Mulhall with eyes that were only half open. He struggled for breath.

'Six months,' he said.

Mulhall turned and left him. Halfway up the street he heard a door opening and a woman's voice calling. Then he heard the woman scream out. He continued to walk at the same pace. He reached the corner, turned it, continued his deliberate stride.

In the morning the police came for him. They hammered on the door while he and his son were getting ready for work. They entered without ceremony.

'I'll go with you,' he said.

Mrs. Mulhall sat on the bed. She was crying. His son looked on but said nothing.

'Who's this?' the police said.

'My son. He's a messenger in the Independent.'

'Where was he last night?'

'In his bed. He'd nothing to do with it.'

They accepted that. Mulhall walked between them down the stairs and out on to the street. The sky was still dark, but the early-morning lamps shone out from windows above and about them.

'You'll be locked up for this,' one of the policemen told him.

'I'm not the first,' Mulhall said, 'and I won't be the last.'

The lighted windows above and about him filled him with tenderness and smouldering anger. He was God and all his creatures were in bondage. He had been cruel, as God often seemed to be. But he had served them. When he came back he would serve them again. That was what his birth had been for. It was a good thing, in middle age, after years of despondency and search, to know why he had been born. He did not mind walking up the street, his arms pinioned by police; he would not mind the stares of the city as he was being dragged for trial. It did not matter, because he was entirely certain now about everything, about who he was and what God had made him for.

The justice said it was a disgraceful charge. He had beaten a man whose only sin was to work in Christian charity for the welfare of others. He had insulted, by his conduct, the person of a priest. His conduct was an example of what could be expected in the future from an anarchical movement, if decisive steps were not taken to suppress it. Mulhall said nothing in defence. He was sentenced, as Keever had predicted, to six months' imprisonment with hard labour.

Father O'Connor mounted the steps to the pulpit and looked at the congregation for some moments with unusual gravity. He had already assisted Father Giffley with the distribution of holy communion, because it was the monthly mass of the men's sodality and there were many communicants. Behind him Father Giffley sat to the side of the altar, his biretta on his head, his hands resting palms downwards on each knee, his head slightly bowed. Father O'Connor read the notices and the names of those who had died recently or whose anniversaries occurred. Then he signed himself in the name of the Father and of the Son and of the Holy Ghost and began to speak.

'My dear brethren: For some time I have had it in mind to talk to you on a subject which has been a source of ever-increasing distress, not only to me, but to those in Holy Orders who are far above me in holiness, in wisdom, in experience. I might have continued to hesitate in the hope—indeed, in the confident belief—that the advice of your priests would triumph over the promptings of evil men. I refer to those who have been working among you for some years now to spread discontent and a godless creed.'

He stopped to assess their measure of attention. It was not

great. The hour was early, they had come without breakfast to receive holy communion, the church was damp and unusually cold. The odour of tightly packed bodies made the air unpleasant. Throughout mass someone had been coughing persistently. It began again now in the silence. A chorus of coughs and snuffles responded. Father O'Connor found it necessary to raise his voice.

'Our hopes have not been fulfilled and our advice has gone unheeded. Only a few days ago, in this parish of ours, a good and conscientious man suffered a brutal assault.'

The coughing stopped. He had their attention.

'The hand of the law has reached out to the perpetrator of this outrage; he is now paying the penalty. With him—we need not concern ourselves any further. But what must concern us very deeply indeed is the reason given for the attack I have just mentioned. The reason put forward was that the unfortunate victim was attempting to interfere against a strike engineered by professional exploiters of discontent. The allegation, of course, was not true. The man was simply performing a christian duty, distributing charity in Christ's name, offering a little relief to the destitute. But the incident serves well to illustrate the attitude of these self-styled Reformers towards any activity of religion. It shows their hatred of it, their anger at it, their determination to oppose the work of God at any cost and in any shape or form.'

That rang effectively. He paused, but it was spoiled again by the long rasping coughs of one man. Before the rest began unconsciously to join him, Father O'Connor spoke.

'It is a wet morning, my dear brethren, you have risen early to fulfil your duty to God, I will not detain you now by speaking at length on this subject. I only ask you to keep it in mind for what it is—an insult to God and an insult to those who were ordained to preach His gospel. When next these men urge you to extreme courses, when they try to win your support and your confidence, when they declare—as they have done—that they respect religion and seek only the order that is God's—when they do this recall the incident I have referred to, and the many others that have occurred throughout our city. You will know then where they really stand. You will be able to see that for all their fair words and protestations of concern for poverty and hunger, they are enemies of God and of His Church. In that way you will keep to Truth. And you will ensure that no more unfortunate victims will suffer physical assault at the hands of God's enemies.'

That seemed to be enough. Father O'Connor allowed his eyes to rest steadily on the upturned faces for some seconds. Then he signed himself very deliberately, saying again: 'In the Name of the Father, and of the Son, and of the Holy Ghost.'

They answered 'Amen'.

Rashers got up to leave as Father O'Connor did. The cough phlegm in his throat thickened and refused to be dislodged. He struggled so hard for breath that he almost fell. A neighbour grasped him by the shoulders and led him outside. Rashers nodded his thanks, then leaned against the arch of the porch on his own. The rain clung to his unkempt beard but the air was cool and moist and easier to breathe. He gulped at it until he felt its cold bulk in his lungs. He rested, coaxing his heart to find a slow, regular beat. Soon mass would be over, the people would come crowding about him. They would look at him, some of them with pity. That was something he never sought and did not like. If he had a drop of whiskey it might do the trick, straighten him out for the job of stoking the furnace which he had been unable to tackle early that morning. As the first trickle of the congregation began to move about him, he stirred himself and decided that he must ask the housekeeper. She was a kind enough woman.

He managed to get as far as the basement door. While she was opening it another spasm seized him. She found him doubled up and breathless. He stopped, his eyes streaming, unable to ask her. She took his arm and led him into the kitchen. It was spick and span. The red gleam of the fire behind the range reminded him that the furnace would go out if he did not get well quickly enough to attend to it. As it was, the pipes were almost cold. He made a tremendous effort.

'For the love of God, woman, spare me a thimble of whiskey.'

'Sit down,' she said, helping him. He looked about him and recognised the press it was usually kept in. He saw her opening it. When she came back she poured him a stiff measure. He took it slowly, coughing and spluttering over it at first, but becoming easier after a while, until at last he felt he could talk to her.

'God reward you,' he offered.

'I'll give you a cup of tea.'

'No, no. The whiskey did the trick. It always does.'

'The tea will cap it,' she said.

She prepared it and with it he took some bread and butter. He felt warmer and better after it. Drowsy, too. He had slept very brokenly the night before.

'I'll go now and attend the furnace.'

'You're a man that shouldn't be out at all,' she warned him. Even now his face was a deadly colour. She wondered should she tell Father Giffley.

'If Rashers stays out, the furnace is out too.'

'What matter about the furnace.'

'Am I to let it out and lose my job.'

'You're in no condition to be abroad.'

'It's only a little turn,' Rashers said. 'I'm right as rain now.'

He got up with difficulty and went to the door. It was a pity to have to leave the warm, dry air of the kitchen. It would have been good to curl up and sleep on its flagged floor. He had slept on less comfortable beds.

'Wait now,' she called to him.

She put the cork back in the bottle, which was still almost half full of whiskey, and gave it to him.

'Put it under your coat,' she warned him.

He looked at it doubtfully.

'They'll surely miss it.'

'Divil the miss.'

'You're a good-hearted woman.'

'I'll not have your death on my conscience, and that will be the story if you don't watch yourself.'

Rashers held up the bottle and measured it with his eye.

'If I die it'll be of free drink,' he said. It was an effort. He did not feel in the mood to joke.

The rain had found its way under the broken door and down the first two steps of the boiler house. Beyond that it was dry and dark. He groped for the candle butt, lit it and opened the furnace gate. A thick white ash was all that remained of the coke-dressing he had spread the previous night. He raked it gently, bringing the live coke to the surface. He threw a shovel full of fresh coke to the back of the furnace. The white ash, disturbed, burst upwards in a dense cloud and flowed into the furnace room. In the light of the candle, against the background darkness, countless white particles began to dance and jostle. Rashers breathed deeply as he lifted the shovel a second time. The dust caught him at the back of the throat and the muscles of his chest convulsed. He threw the spade aside, knelt suddenly on the coke and began another fight for air that seemed endless and doomed to defeat. But it passed. He lay down trembling. There was sweat on his face and under his clothes. Everything had withdrawn to a great distance. The candle flame was a luminous petal which shed no light at all. He remembered the whiskey and drank. The cork fell when he fumbled as he tried to replace it. He drank again, a long slug, for comfort this time, not for medicine. It felt better. With his eyes closed and lying still, it was possible to think a little. If it was Edward VII he would be surrounded by doctors. It did no good, in the heel of the hunt. Maybe a high-up like him wouldn't chance a drop of whiskey. Champagne or a high-class foreign wine. That was their dish. Rashers slugged again at the bottle and burrowed deeper into the coke stack. Drowsiness crept over him, a murmur in his ears and in his limbs. He dozed while the furnace shared the misfortune of many another in St. Brigid's and starved to death.

The church suffered. At afternoon devotions, during the recitation of the rosary, the cold and damp penetrated Father Giffley to the bone. On his way into the vestry he touched the pipes with his hand and confirmed his suspicions. In the house he summoned Father O'Connor.

'Have we a boilerman?'

'Of course.'

'The heating system contradicts it.'

'I beg your pardon?'

'The church is like an icebox.'

'I'll see what is wrong.'

'You should have done that four or five hours ago.'

Father Giffley went to the press, groped in it and took out a bottle. He half filled a glass.

'I'm petrified,' he grumbled.

Father O'Connor, with a sinking heart, saw him take it over to the fireside chair where he swallowed most of it with the first mouthful.

'I'll find out what has happened,' he promised.

The courtyard was dark and rain was still falling. He turned up his collar. The image of Father Giffley raising the yellow liquid and swallowing remained vividly with him. It had been so long since that had happened. Was it about to start again: the whiskey after breakfast, the inflamed afternoon face, the sickly and perpetual odour of peppermints? There would come a time when Father Giffley's weakness could no longer be ignored.

He reached the boilerhouse and pushed in the broken door. It was pitch dark. Stale coke fumes hung unpleasantly in the cold air. The sound of heavy breathing came from the darkness. It startled him. He called out.

'Tierney.'

The breathing continued, its rhythm uninterrupted. He picked his way gingerly down the remaining steps, struck a match and found a stump of candle. Beside it the earlier one had guttered to death. Its grease dribbles clung to the ledge and spread in knuckled streams down the side of the wall.

'Tierney,' Father O'Connor called again.

He held the candle above the sleeping figure and bent down. The sight horrified him. Rashers' mouth had fallen open. The teeth in it were yellow and rose crookedly from the narrow gums. The empty whiskey bottle was in his right hand. He had been incontinent in his sleep. Father O'Connor recoiled from the strong smell of urine. He prodded Rashers with his foot.

'Tierney,' he called.

He was tempted to kick at the prostrate horror. Was the whole of Ireland possessed by Drink; had it become an unwashed wretch on a slag-heap, grasping an empty bottle by the neck? What right had any creature to spurn God's gifts of mind and health in this way, to put out God's sun—quench His stars and obliterate the lovely face of His Creation. Father O'Connor felt fury blazing in the arteries of neck and temple.

'Tierney!' he roared.

Rashers opened his eyes and identified his visitor.

'It's yourself, Father.'

'Get on your feet.'

'All in good time, Father.'

Rashers spoke soothingly. It was all very well to say get on your feet. It was another thing to have complete confidence in their ability to obey.

'The furnace is out.'

'Bloody end to it,' Rashers said. Then he recollected himself and apologised.

'Saving your presence, Father.'

'You're a drunken disgrace,' Father O'Connor exploded at him. Rashers looked puzzled. He thought. He became conscious of the empty bottle about which his fingers were still curled.

'A drop for my chest,' he said.

'A good deal more than a drop. The furnace has been out all day. You should be ashamed of yourself.'

'First it was contrary with me. Then I went up to mass. Then I got a little turn. The chest . . .'

'Do you buy and consume a bottle of whiskey every time you have trouble with your chest?'

'I didn't buy it.'

'You stole it, then.'

Rashers made an effort and raised himself on one elbow. In the candlelight, with the black beard merging into the background of piled coke, he was little more than a pair of eyes. They were suddenly focussed and scornful.

'That's a strange conclusion for a man of your cloth to jump to.'

'Who gave it to you?'

Rashers, with both elbows under him now, found his full voice and shouted his anger: 'Ask my arse.'

'How dare you use obscenity in my presence?'

'I never asked for your presence,' Rashers yelled. 'So bad cess to you and to hell with you and God's curse on you for labelling me a robber. Now get to hell out of here.'

He scrabbled at the coke about him and flung a fistful in Father O'Connor's direction. Father O'Connor dodged backwards. Some pieces hit the skirts of his soutane and fell harmlessly to the floor. The attack astounded him. He stood wordlessly, the candle held above his head. They faced each other with hatred. Rashers made a final effort and found his feet. He pulled his clothes down about him. He continued to hold the empty bottle by the neck.

'Tomorrow,' Father O'Connor said, controlling his voice. 'the clerk will have whatever wages is due to you. You're dismissed.'

'Sacked?' Rashers cocked his head at an angle.

'That is what I have just said.'

Rashers brushed past him and mounted the steps. He took them slowly, controlling his limbs.

'Then good riddance,' he said, when he had reached the top. He went out into the courtyard and on into the street, still holding the empty bottle by the neck.

Father O'Connor retired to his room. He was deeply upset. The poverty of St. Brigid's parish was bad; its ingratitude was appalling. His efforts to help the poor had led to assault and bad blood. A useless, crippled old man he had picked off the streets had flung his kindness back in his face. His parish priest was likely to take the side of the boilerman. He had done so before. It seemed to give pleasure to Father Giffley to humiliate him. If that was to happen again, then the sooner they had it out and over with the better.

Father Giffley was not in the room on the ground floor—a bad sign. Had he retired to his own room to drink himself stupid? If so, that too would have to be faced. Father O'Connor climbed the stairs again. He knocked on the door.

'Come in.'

The fire was piled high in the way that Father Giffley liked. It added its own light to that of the buzzing gas mantle. The bookcase in the corner gleamed orange and red where the wood and the glass reflected its glow. Father Giffley was seated in a deep armchair. A tumbler with whiskey stood near him.

'Am I disturbing you, Father?'

'Please close the door. I am just beginning to feel warm again.'

Father O'Connor did so.

'That is what I came to see you about. I found the furnace completely out.'

'Did you find the boilerman? That's the essential thing.'

'He was lying on a pile of coke—asleep.'

'Asleep?'

Father O'Connor decided to call a spade a spade.

'He was dead drunk.'

The other, about to raise the tumbler to his lips, replaced it. The eyes examined Father O'Connor closely, noting his agitation, interpreting it.

'And where is he now?'

Father O'Connor steeled himself.

'I dismissed him. That's what I came to tell you.' Father Giffley continued to regard him closely. He spoke very calmly.

'And why do you come to me?'

'On a previous occasion you reproached me for not having done so.'

'It appears you didn't on this occasion either.'

'I acted on impulse. The furnace was out. The man was lying on the coke heap. He had been . . .'

It would be indelicate to refer to that—the smell of urine, the unwashed smell.

'His language was obscene and he threw things at me.'

Father Giffley gave some moments of consideration to that. At last he said: 'Do your respectable friends never drink?'

'In moderation . . .'

'Always?'

The emphasis on the word communicated his disbelief. He

looked sadly at the tumbler in his hand.

'If you found your parish priest drunk would you try to have him sacked?'

'Please, Father . . .'

'Why don't you answer?'

'There is no answer. You are complicating something that is quite simple. The boilerman was drunk. He neglected his duty. He . . .'

'Complications? Is there one law for Kingstown and another for the clergy and another for the boilerman?'

Father O'Connor did not answer.

'Well?'

It was no use answering. Any attempt of his would be twisted by the other to suit his purpose. His parish priest hated him. It was, he could only hope, part of the man's mental sickness.

'This morning I listened to you speaking about the Larkinites. You were quite wrong—as usual. The reformers have a better case than we have. They are trying to destroy this dung-heap. I wish I had the strength of will to help them.'

'That is not the generally accepted view.'

'No. Yet one day, when they have succeeded in spite of us, it will be.'

It was a surprising speech and Father O'Connor had nothing to say about it. He wondered what bearing it could have on the boilerman.

'Have I done wrong in sacking the boilerman?'

'You took that step without consulting me,' Father Giffley said. 'And now you ask me did you do wrong. Am I to take responsibility for your decisions? This time I leave the matter in your own hands. You feel you have been insulted. If you wish to punish, it is your sole responsibility.'

'It was not a question of punishment.'

'No?'

'One has a right to expect decency and good behaviour.'

'Quite so,' Father Giffley agreed.

The words should have reassured, but instead they disturbed. What was the use of discussing decency and good behaviour with a man who was himself about to offend against both. Irritated by the whiskey, the swollen face, Father O'Connor snapped :

'I never know what you mean.'

He stopped short, alarmed at the sound of his own voice. It was loud, it was almost contemptuous. Father Giffley turned fully about, fixing his eyes squarely on Father O'Connor.

'You have that look again now,' he said.

'I spoke loudly. I am sorry.'

'That look on your face. It comes quite often. I saw it earlier today. Shall I tell you when?'

Goaded beyond endurance by the tone, Father O'Connor said : 'I am not here to be insulted.'

Father Giffley rose from his chair and left down his glass with a bang.

'This morning,' he continued, his hands clasped behind him, his head inclined pugnaciously towards Father O'Connor, 'I watched you distributing holy communion. The old men—and the young men too, thronged to the altar rails—in this parish they always have on sodality Sunday. You were distributing holy communion. It had been raining. Nothing unusual in that, of course. It is never done raining in the parish of St. Brigid. You have probably had time to notice that—in between your visits to Kingstown. The rain makes them smell quite badly. And when they are packed together, row on row, that smell can be more than a little distressing.'

Father Giffley took his hands from behind his back and leaned his weight on the table.

'You were faced with a line of assorted tongues, all thrust forward to receive the Body of our Lord from your hands. You kept as far off as possible from the assorted breaths they were exhaling at you. And in all my days I have never seen a priest's face that wore such a look of loathing and disgust.'

'It's a lie,' Father O'Connor shouted. The denial broke from him before he could attempt to control it. The sound of his voice reverberating through the room shocked him. He trembled as Father Giffley resumed his seat by the fire. Then, with a feeling of loneliness and despair which reduced him almost to tears, he added:

'I can only assume that you have already had too much whiskey to drink. It will ruin you. If you do not respect yourself I cannot expect you to respect me.'

Father Giffley was unmoved. He folded his arms and gave his attention entirely to the fire. It burned clearly and brightly. In it were coloured scenes of ethereal beauty. In it were no dead born babies, no lice-infested heads, no worn-out creatures, no malformed bodies. Soul and imagination could wander down its galleries for ever, in peace, in contemplation without end.

He heard the door close. He did not associate it with Father O'Connor leaving. Already, it seemed to him, Father O'Connor had left a long time ago.

Rashers went back once more among the old women and the children who searched the dustbins. There was nothing much to be got elsewhere. A dock strike spread and involved the railway workers; there was a partial stoppage in the timber trade. Throughout the city, jobs closed, men picketed, homes went short of food and firing. Among themselves the poor had nothing to spare. At night Rashers played his tin whistle for the theatre queues. Everywhere the competition proved formidable. A man with a barrel-organ and a monkey was a frequent rival. Another pair, with fiddle and full-size harp, outdid him in both sound and spectacle. There was an unusual number of casuals, from broken-voiced ballad-singers to outright beggars wheedling for the price of a cup of tea and a night's lodging.

Often enough he lost heart. His limp had grown worse, his chest constantly gave him trouble.

'Why don't you go round and apologise to Father O'Connor?' Hennessy urged him more than once throughout the long winter.

'Because Rashers Tierney isn't that class of a man,' he always answered.

'After all—he's a priest.'

'If he is he shouldn't want an apology.'

'And what should he do?'

'He should turn the other cheek.'

Hennessy, with a grunt of impatience, sat down beside him.

'Ah—talk sense.'

'Sense be damned.'

Finding him immovable, Hennessy offered a cigarette. They smoked and watched the children swinging about a lamp-post on the opposite pavement.

'You're a stubborn and cantankerous bloody oul oddity,' Hennessy decided.

Rashers shrugged the rebuke away. His job was filled. Apologising would get him nowhere. Never again would he go next or near St. Brigid's. Mass was available elsewhere; God and His Blessed Mother and St. Joseph and St. Anthony and anyone else he cared to address a prayer to would listen to him without asking Father O'Connor's permission. That was one good thing about religion. No one owned it. No one could put a wall around it and lock the gate on you. If he was sorry for his sins God would smile and say, 'Come on in Rashers—I knew your knock.' If he was not, all the Father O'Connors in the world could do nothing to put him back into favour.

'I'll creep in through a little hole or behind the little children,' Rashers said aloud.

He screwed up his face defiantly.

Hennessy, wondering what he was wandering in his mind about, looked at him but said nothing. For once he was incurious, his thoughts returning to his own plight. Another of his temporary jobs had come to an end. There were too many idle men now to compete for what might be left. Like Rashers, he stood little chance in open competition. Unlike Rashers, his accomplishments did not include a command of the tin whistle. He sighed and said:

'One of the chisellers is sick.'

'Which of them?'

'The second youngest. It's some class of a bowel complaint. I'd like to get a bit of decent nourishment for her.'

'The poor little morsel,' Rashers said.

'But with all the strikes, it's hard to know where to turn to earn a crust.'

'It always was,' Rashers agreed, 'in this glorified kip of a city.'

They both fell silent again.

IT was summer when Mulhall left prison. He had to stand for some moments to adjust himself to the space and noise of the early-morning streets. Even the sunlight seemed loud. Then he began to head towards the centre of the city, where the crowded pavements bewildered him, until he remembered again that he was a leader among all the people. He had been in gaol for them. He would be in gaol again. He squared his shoulders when the floats and carts rattled past him. While he had been in gaol for them they had not let him down. The dockers had tied-up the port rather than work with non-union labour. The Viceroy had invited Larkin to Dublin Castle to discuss ways and means of settling with the men. That was a new measure of recognition. Now the railway men were on strike in sympathy with their comrades in England.

Mulhall saluted the pickets as he passed and was saluted in turn. They knew him as a leader too. These were part of his great army, an army that would grow and grow until wealth and eminence would bow to its banners. There would be no more slums, no more rickety children, no more hunger and cold. Because he, and others like him, would refuse to be defeated.

'I declare to God,' Rashers said, 'will you look who's here?'

Mulhall paused to greet Rashers on the steps. Rusty the dog sniffed at his trouser legs. That, more than anything so far, assured him that he was back in the world again. Mulhall patted the dog.

'All present and correct,' he said.

As he went into the house Rashers stared after him. So did the dog.

'I might do worse than go to gaol myself,' Rashers said to the dog, 'but if I did what the hell would happen to you?'

The dog flexed his ears and sat down again. Neither of them had very much to do.

Mulhall found his wife making their son's bed. She turned round slowly when the door opened. He stood for a moment, waiting for her to overcome her surprise. The room was familiar and yet new. The chairs and the table, the statue and its lamp, the pictures on the wall, seemed to turn with her to regard him.

'You're back,' she said.

'Like a bad ha'penny.'

She let the blanket fall from her hands and came to him. He embraced her.

'We missed you, Bernie.'

He knew they had—his wife, his son, the statue and the lamp, the pictures and the furniture. He was a leader in a great army, but he was king also here, in a little world where everything was moulded to serve him.

'I know,' he said. While he had been dreaming of conquering a city, they had been lonely for him and wishing him home. He released her and found tears covering her face. It was her way. She cried for sorrow and for joy, a tender, ageing woman easily moved. She wiped her face with her apron as she went over to the stove.

'I'll make you a cup of tea.'

That was her answer to every visitation of woe and joy, her response to an unexpected call, the preliminary to all departures.

'No hurry,' he said. He was over at the window and looking down at the street. The sight gave him pleasure. It was sunny and quiet. He saw Rashers and the dog turning the corner, two inseparable questors. Then he looked at his pipe-rack. There were four pipes stuck in it, all old, acquired over a lifetime. He kept them clean with methylated spirit which the watchmen in Doggett & Co. saved for him from time to time. He went over and took one down. He was examining it when she came over to give him the plug of tobacco.

'I've a head like a sieve,' she complained.

'Where did this come from?'

'I bought it to keep for when you came out. I knew it'd be the first thing you'd want.'

'God bless the thought,' he said. He sat down and began to cut it. As he filled his pipe he asked:

'And how's Willie?'

'He missed you.'

'Damn the miss,' he said gruffly, to hide his pleasure. The smell of his tobacco drifted about the room.

'I've a job for Willie,' he said presently, when they were sitting at table, 'and that's to get them messengers and parcel boys organised in the union.'

'You've got thin in the face,' she said, when she had scrutinised him closely. 'Did they treat you bad?'

'I didn't mind it.'

'It used to worry me all the time, thinking of you locked in there with rogues and robbers.'

He had known that would worry her. She could not be expected to understand what it had taken himself a long time to find out. There were worse rogues.

'Gaol isn't so bad,' he said; 'the real criminals are outside.'

After a while he went out again, roaming for an hour or so at will. He walked the docks and saw, piled along the quayside and outside the sheds, the accumulation of goods that the rail workers and the dockers had refused to handle. At the gates of Doggett & Co. some of the carters reined in and greeted him.

'When are you starting back, Barney?' they asked him.

'That's what I'm here to see about.'

'If there's any mullarkey, let's know.'

They took pains to show him they would stand by him if Doggett made any difficulties. He waved them on and went through the gate, pausing for a moment in the yard as affection stirred in him for the familiar coal-heaps and the black dust which formed odd patterns on the ground. He had worked here a long time and knew every corner of it. He could recognise every horse in an instant and recall its name. Horses, when you worked with them for a long time, he thought, were like any other working mate. Some were lazy and forgetful, some had good humours and bad, some were inexhaustible and patient and long suffering, pulling loads without flinching until the great heart inside them burst.

The timekeeper said Mr. Doggett would see him. He was to wait. They talked about gaol and what it was like. The timekeeper told him of small changes.

'Who took over my horse?' Mulhall asked.

'Gibney,' the timekeeper said.

'Gibney is a butcher, not a carter,' Mulhall said, 'he'll pull the mouth off her.' The timekeeper took a delivery docket off the table and stuck it on a hook behind him, over a key that was numbered fourteen.

'Who the hell gave her to him?' Mulhall demanded.

'You seem to forget,' the timekeeper said, when he had completed his business, 'that his nibs Gibney is related to the foreman.'

'Since when?'

'Married to the daughter, less than six weeks ago.' Then, as though Mulhall ought to have known, he added: 'That's been going on a long time.'

A clerk came in and said Mr. Doggett would see Mulhall. They went together through the door at the back of the office and up a carpeted staircase. Doggett was standing at the window overlooking the yard. He turned and said to the clerk: 'You may go.' Then he sat at his desk.

'I expect you've come for your job back.'

'I've come to find out when do I start,' Mulhall corrected. There was a difference.

'And if I say you can't start?'

'Why should you say that?'

Doggett paused before answering. He was alert and cool. If what stood before him was simply a man, he could smash him by merely deciding to do so. But he was not confronted by a man. He was face to face with a movement. He did not want Mulhall back. On the other hand, it would not be worth facing a strike to get rid of him. The thought ran through Doggett's mind that things had changed. Three years ago it would have been a simple matter.

'I don't know if you're aware of it,' he said, 'but there is a railway strike and several smaller strikes too. We haven't the work for a full staff.'

'No one's been laid off.'

'Not yet—but the situation changes day by day.'

'And what about Gibney?'

'Gibney?'

'He's got my horse and he isn't a carter at all. He hasn't twelve months' service.'

'And what service had you?'

'I was jobbed in Mr. Waterville's time,' Mulhall said, 'and that was neither today nor yesterday.'

'In the meanwhile,' Doggett suggested quietly, 'you've been in gaol—on a criminal charge.'

Mulhall smiled. They were getting down to brass tacks. He went over to the window and looked down. Three carts had pulled up in a line and were waiting their turn to ride on to the tare scales.

'Those men below wouldn't consider it criminal,' he answered.

Behind his back irritation had brought Doggett to his feet. His workmen did not usually behave so casually in his presence. He mastered his ill humour. There would be a time to put this man back in his place. To do so too obviously now would be a mistake. He went over quietly and they both stood shoulder to shoulder. Below them lay the yard, peaceful in the sunlight. To Doggett it was not unlovely. Anything he had he owed to it. For Mulhall it meant bread and butter and, now that he had been away from it for half a year, something more. It was a familiar plot, as much a part of him as the street he had played in when he was a child, or the school he had gone to for so short a while, or the walks he had walked with his father when he was still small enough to be led by the hand.

'You'd like to own it, wouldn't you,' Doggett said.

Mulhall looked round in surprise. It was a thought that had never entered his head.

'I only want to work in it.'

'You must understand that there may not be room—not at present.'

'Because I've a criminal record?'

'Not at all,' Doggett said, 'we'll forget that part of it.' He went back to his desk and thought carefully for some moments. Then he said:

'You can enquire later in the week. It will give us an opportunity to see how things are going.'

He began to arrange the articles on his desk. Mulhall went to the door, but Doggett's voice again stopped him.

'You mustn't think I am holding anything against you.'

'No,' Mulhall said.

He closed the door and went down the stairs. The timekeeper asked him if he was starting, but Mulhall shook his head. He did not stop to talk.

Mulhall walked with his hands tucked in his belt and his hat tilted forward over his eyes to protect them from the sun. He went thoughtfully. The meaner streets smelled badly because of the heat; all the doors stood open, revealing, down hallways that were foul and dark tunnels, the small sunlit yards, each with its communal lavatory. At first he thought he would go to the union office, but the idea of stating a case for himself put him off. It would come better from the men themselves. He decided to see Fitz and turned down the quays again. At Morgan & Co. the gateman told him Fitz was on shift.

'I'd like to see him, if I could.'

The gateman said he would ask Mr. Carrington, the foreman.

'Fitzpatrick is well got with him,' he explained. 'I don't think there'll be any objection.'

'Thanks,' Mulhall said.

The gateman delayed. He knew Mulhall, who often delivered coal to Morgan & Co.

'How are you after your spell away?'

'Gameball,' Mulhall assured him.

'We cleaned up a few scabs ourselves the other night,' the gateman confided.

'Where was that?'

'In Tobin's of Thorncastle Street. Four of them were drinking together. There's not a pane of glass left in the place after it.'

'What about the police?'

'They didn't show up until it was all over—like sensible men.'

The gateman rubbed his hands briskly together and said with relish: 'By God, we gave them a bellyful.' Then his attention fixed on a distant figure crossing the yard.

'There's Carrington going into the house now. I'll ask him.'

Mulhall lit his pipe and waited. Men were unloading coal into an endless chain of buckets which rose in procession up an open tower before moving along a belt and into one of the furnace houses. It was the newest house, machine fed. A few more of these, Mulhall thought, and there would be less work for furnace hands. It was one of the things he had given thought to while in gaol. Machinery would improve and replace labour. The motor car would replace the horse, and do the work of three carters. What would happen then? He had argued about it with another prisoner.

'The motor will never be a success,' the prisoner said, 'because they can't invent a wheel to suit the roads.'

Mulhall knew better than that.

'If the wheel won't suit the road,' he said, 'they'll make the roads suit the wheel.'

After some time Fitz came out to him. He smiled broadly and held out his hand.

'Welcome home,' Fitz said.

Mulhall shook his hand and then gestured towards the tower and the moving buckets.

'That's new, isn't it?' he asked.

'They put it up about two months ago.'

'Has it done away with labour?'

'It's servicing the new house, so no one's been laid off. But more would have been taken on if the furnaces were hand fed,' Fitz admitted.

'Suppose they start feeding the old houses in the same way?'

'Too bad for some of us,' Fitz said.

But you couldn't stop them using machinery. Machinery meant more profit, and profit was the beginning and the end of everything. Roads and bridges and buildings would be reduced to rubble wherever they impeded profit. Men would be laid off and children would go hungry. For the sake of the machines families would know want.

'We've got to keep a watch on new machinery,' Mulhall warned. Then he told Fitz about his interview with Doggett.

'Have you seen Larkin?'

'I'd rather someone else saw him for me.'

'I'll go down with Joe Somerville tonight,' Fitz promised. 'We'll call a meeting and state your case.'

'What's Joe Somerville got to do with it?'

'He's acting secretary for the carters' section,' Fitz explained.

'That's a new one,' Mulhall said.

Things had changed in his short absence.

The next day, before knocking-off time, there was a notice scrawled on the gate of Doggett & Co. which read;

'Stand by Bernad Mulhall
No Victimisation'

It was in white chalk. Doggett, who read it on his way out, instructed the gateman to clean it off. He noticed, without surprise, that the name Bernard had been misspelled. Neither was he very much perturbed. If the pressure became dangerous he could settle it by reinstating Mulhall. He had consulted with the manager of Nolan & Keyes, with the Chairman of Morgan & Co. Foundries, with a number of other employers. There were wider issues than that of Mulhall. There was the question of curbing Mr. Larkin himself. Doggett's colleagues were evolving machinery for doing so.

Later that night Joe Somerville, acting secretary of the carters sub-section, settled down by candlelight and began the labour of composing the minutes of the meeting.

Minutes of Meeting of Carters' No. 3 section re Bernard Mulhall, held in Beresford Place . . .

He paused and consulted Pat, who was stretched on the bed in the far corner.

'What was yesterday's date?'

Pat, glancing first at the top of the newspaper he was studying, told him.

Joe continued:

Opening the meeting, J. Somerville explained that R. Fitzpatrick was a Foundry worker who was here only to deliver a message about the position of B. Mulhall, who was speaking to him. The meeting agreed there was no objection to a Foundry member being present for this purpose. R. Fitzpatrick and J. Somerville then reported how B. Mulhall had applied for reinstatement to the firm of Doggett & Co., he had been released from gaol that day where he served six months hard labour for his class. The answer he got was to say the least evasive and the question arose what further action was to be taken to secure his rights as he was a carter with long service.

J. Brady said there should be an immediate heel-up, that Comrade Mulhall was a solid trade union member, one of the first in Doggetts', and it was up to each and all to stand by him now. T. Williams asked who was it chalked the message on the front gate, this was no use to anyone and only showed our hand to Mr. Doggett. The general secretary asked what message and when he was told he said he would do the talking to Mr. Doggett and the men must await his instructions. J. Brady said everyone had confidence in Mr. Larkin and they were sure he would call out the men when the time came. After further discussion it was agreed unanimously to call out the men if his talk with Mr. Doggett did not bring quick results.

This business being completed P. Forde said he wished to raise the question of a collection for the railway men who were on sympathetic strike with their comrades across the water. It was agreed there would be a weekly collection, P. Forde to collect from the men in Doggetts and P. Bannister to look after the levy from Nolan & Keyes men. The meeting concluded.

Joe read over the minutes to Pat, who listened with half an ear. He was thinking of Lily. He had met her a few times since their walk in the Park, but although she was friends with him once again it was always hard to persuade her to come out with him. When she did it was never into the city. She was afraid to meet people she had once known.

'I think the cupboard will stretch to a cup of tea for the supper,' Joe suggested. He had laboured hard in the literary field. It was up to Pat to look after the menu. Pat left down his paper and began to prepare the tea without enthusiasm.

'I wish it was as easy to make a pot of porter,' he said, when the water had boiled at long last and he began to pour it over the two spoons of tea that lay on the bottom of the blackened can.

Doggett met Yearling at a special employers' meeting. It was a large meeting, representative of most of the industrial and manufacturing firms in the city. The objective was to form a combination to fight the continuous strikes and threats of strikes. One of the speakers described it as an effort to form an Association of Employers to present a united front to Larkinism. The speeches bored Yearling but Doggett gave them his shrewd attention. On a number of occasions over the past three years he had succeeded in keeping his coal-carting concern open when others were closed down. It had paid off well in increased profit, but it had cost him much in goodwill. In the case of Morgan & Co. it had almost cost him an important contract. It became clear from the tone of the meeting that his technique of settling demands and then sweeping the market while the other coal concerns remained stubbornly closed would not work much longer. The leaders were appealing for consultation and concerted action. When the proposition was put 'that a Company, to be called the Dublin Employers' Federation Limited, be formed, with the object of affording mutual protection to and indemnity of all employers and employees', Doggett raised a reluctant hand in favour of its adoption. He felt it only politic to do so and wondered when the man beside him kept his arms folded.

After the meeting Doggett went out alone into the summer evening. The red glow of sunset was in the sky and the odour of evening flowers accompanied him as he passed the railings of St. Stephen's Green. It was a little bit early as yet to take a cab home; on the other hand the clubs and hotels in the area were almost certain to be occupied by groups of employers, some of whom he had no great desire to meet. Doggett turned down Grafton Street and then left into the snug of a public house. It was a place he knew well, with pictures of royalty and racing prints on the wall.

'A baby Power,' Doggett ordered, when the shutter in the partition opened.

'I'll have the same,' a voice behind him said. He turned to find himself in the company of Yearling. Yearling smiled at him and said : 'Interesting meeting.'

'Very,' Doggett answered.

'The name is Yearling.'

'Mine is Doggett.'

'How do you do.'

'How do.'

The curate brought the drinks.

'Allow me,' Yearling said, and paid for both.

'Thank you.'

'You're Doggett & Company?'

'That's right,' Doggett said. 'And you?'

'Morgan & Company—on the Board.'

'Oh,' Doggett said. This was the very thing he had tried to avoid. He still held his contract with the foundry, but his conscience was not altogether clear. He remembered that Yearling had not voted for the proposition. Yet the chairman of Morgan & Co. had been on the platform.

'I've two minds about this combination business,' Yearling confessed.

Mr. Doggett agreed, but waited a while for the other to give reasons. He was not quite sure where he stood. When Yearling failed to say anything further he decided to chance a sentiment that had been expressed at the meeting.

'In a way,' Doggett said, 'I suppose if the rabble of the city can combine there's nothing wrong in principle if we employers do the same thing.'

'Nothing at all—if you want industrial warfare,' Yearling said grimly.

'We seem to have that already.'

'We'll have more of it.'

'It may make Larkin draw in his horns.'

Yearling grunted in disbelief.

'He's more likely to paralyse the whole country,' he pronounced. That was Doggett's own assessment.

'Personally,' he confessed, 'I've had to decide between Mr. Larkin's threats and the threats of my own colleagues. That's why I voted for the resolution. I wonder who's behind all this.'

'Can't you guess?'

'I've thought it might be Sibthorpe or Jacob. It's hard to know.'

'A certain gentleman who refused to be knighted?' Yearling hinted.

Doggett thought for a moment until the name and the association joined somewhere in his shrewd skull.

'William Martin Murphy.'

'I may be wrong,' Yearling conceded, but only out of politeness.

Doggett nodded.

'He's certainly the strongest,' he said.

In the morning he sent for the yard superintendent.

'We could do with an extra carter,' he said. 'Send for Bernard Mulhall and tell him he can start in the morning.'

Doggett was prepared, under pressure of self-interest, to combine, but he was damned if he was going to be the first in the firing line.

Joe Somerville had the pleasure of reporting to a meeting of carters that Bernard Mulhall had been reinstated unconditionally. For Doggett it meant only temporary respite. He read with sinking heart of the general rail strike in England, of riots and bloodshed and the interruption of Irish supplies. Then the Irish rail workers brought the trouble to his doorstep by walking out in sympathy. Doggett saw this with his own eyes. They marched past him in the street, singing 'Fall in and Follow Me', a ditty which, being a music-hall fan, he recognised as George Lashwood's. That evening the police patrolled the city in unprecedented numbers. They guarded railway stations, they stood in strong formations at the entrances to principal streets. Their presence filled the city with uneasiness. Yet beyond the rallies and the speeches nothing much happened. Three days later a general settlement in England put an end to the dispute. The trains began to run again.

Yearling, travelling from Kingstown to the Imperial Hotel, was glad. He liked travelling by train, especially on the Kingstown line. He liked the yachts with coloured sails in the harbour, the blue shape of Howth Hill across the waters of the bay, the bathers and the children digging sandcastles. These were pleasant to look at in the last hours of an August evening. Yearling loved his city, her soft salt-like air, the peace of her evenings, the easy conversation of her people. He liked the quiet crossings at Sydney Parade and Lansdowne Road, simply because he had swung on them as a schoolboy. The gasometers near Westland Row were friends of his. He could remember passing them many a time as a young man making amorous expeditions to the city. When he looked at these things they in some way kept the presence of loved people who were now dead or in exile; his father and his mother, a favourite aunt whose eccentricities once delighted him; a sister long married and settled in the colonies, a brother killed in childhood. These were melancholy thoughts, but for him melancholy had a rare flavour. It united him with his childhood and his youth. It gave him a reason for continuing to explore life with interest. It was like repeating the part of a story one had already read, in order to savour the more the part that was about to happen.

'It makes it easier to abide the end,' he explained to Father O'Connor, with his large eyebrows lifting upwards a little in self-mockery.

He had been explaining his mood after their meal together. The windows of the Imperial Hotel overlooked Sackville Street. Opposite them, when they averted their heads to look, the fronts of buildings were tinged with the orange glow of evening.

'I think often of childhood myself,' Father O'Connor confessed, 'and the person I remember most is my mother. The love of a good mother is the most precious experience granted to man.'

'The other kind of love is not to be sneezed at either,' Mr. Yearling said robustly.

'Of course not. The love of a good wife is precious too.'

'Wife or lover, good, bad or indifferent, false or true, it's a damned exciting experience. I've known a few of them and I wouldn't have missed one.'

Father O'Connor looked at him curiously. These were loves he had never experienced and to which he had given little personal thought. But he knew the pitfalls. Sometimes in the confessional he had to warn against ill-advised matches, to put the brake on too passionate responses, to sound warnings against immoderate love-making, whether casual or in serious courtship. Penitents had wept in the darkness next to him because of love and its entanglements, because of shame at the sins it led to, because, when he refused absolution unless there was a sincere promise to abandon an association, the penitent struggled between the desire for forgiveness and the human frailty that made the promise impossible. The world of passion could be dark and terrible. Surely the man next to him must know it.

'Surely all love is not the same,' he suggested. 'Surely what is bad leads to sin and shame and suffering?'

'I did not mean it was all the same. I said that even the bad was exciting.'

Yearling smiled sadly at the street. It, too, reminded him of adventures long past. He had once, with some other students, stolen a horse tram, filled it with young ladies and driven it to Howth. They were bad young ladies, no doubt, but extremely agreeable. They shouted at passers-by and cheered at puzzled policemen. Ralph Bradshaw, he remembered, had refused to be involved.

'Love,' he added, 'is a much misused word. It ranges emotionally from the boy and girl skylarking behind the haystack to the extravagances of Héloïse and Abélard.'

It had been worth it, pinching that tram. He could still feel the traces in his hand and hear the clip-clop of hooves. That was something—after God knows how many years. He could feel the sunshine too. He could smell the warm salt air of the sea. He could taste the tea and the sticky buns they had bought on the hill. He could remember a young man's appetite.

'I hope Mr. and Mrs. Bradshaw are enjoying the theatre,' Father O'Connor offered. They had gone to the Abbey to see Mr. Yeats's *Kathleen ni Houlihan* and a play called *The Eloquent Dempsey* by a Mr. Boyle. Later they would call to the Imperial for a light supper with Yearling and Father O'Connor. Father O'Connor's cloth forbade him to enter a playhouse. Yearling had been disinclined.

'They're welcome to my share of Mr. Yeats,' he said, rising to look more closely at the street and to remember more clearly the affair of the horse tram. What he saw drove the thought from his mind. There was no traffic to be seen in the street below. At the end near the bridge a cordon of police stood with batons drawn.

'Come and look,' he said to Father O'Connor. They both stood and watched. Yearling opened the window a little. From the streets to their right came the sounds of people shouting and glass breaking.

'My God,' Yearling said, 'a riot.'

Father O'Connor, peering over his shoulder, saw the advance guard of the crowd moving steadily down the street. They were brandishing sticks and shouting. A plate-glass window on the far side quivered under a barrage of stones and gave way with an ear-splitting crash. Glass tumbled out on to the pavement. Under Father O'Connor's alarmed eyes, men and women and urchins clambered over the glass and began to strip the shop of its contents. While the looters did their work the front ranks kept the police at bay with a bombardment of stones. Lamps along the sidewalks shattered and went out one by one.

Yearling, opening the windows wider, drew Father O'Connor with him as he stepped out on to the balcony.

'Bradshaw should have come here,' he remarked, pointing to the milling crowd below, 'There's the real Kathleen ni Houlihan for you.'

The police, moving in close formation, advanced against the mob. Bottles and stones rattled and fell short of their targets as the crowd retreated. Then the hand to hand fighting started and for fifteen or twenty minutes police and people struggled for possession of the street. Already the roadway was strewn with injured rioters. Yearling, turning to address a remark to Father O'Connor, noticed that his face was white and sick looking. He took him by the arm and led him back to his chair.

'You must have something to drink.'

'No . . . please.'

'Something to settle the nerves.'

Father O'Connor shook his head.

'I'll be better in a moment.'

Yearling went out on the balcony once more, delayed a little, then re-entered.

'The mob has gone back up the side streets,' he said.

'Perhaps I should go down,' Father O'Connor said, 'Somebody might be dying in the street, in need of the priest.'

He half rose, but Yearling pushed him back. 'You are not well enough,' he advised. 'There is plenty of help for anyone who needs it. The ambulances are looking after the injured.'

Father O'Connor gave in. Unruly crowds terrified him. The sight of violence made him weak and useless. He remembered the night he had followed the marchers to Beresford Place and the weakness which had overcome him when the speeches and the cheering had reached their climax. It had not been the wine, after all. It had been the near presence of evil. Agitators were working on the diseased parts of the city, spurring obscure poor souls to hatred and bloodshed. Yearling went over and closed the window.

'All quiet once more,' he announced cheerfully, and rang for the waiter, who brought two stiff brandies.

'This will settle it,' he said in a kindly way, 'and then I'll drive you home.'

Father O'Connor accepted the glass, but said he ought to wait to see Mr. and Mrs. Bradshaw.

'I wouldn't venture abroad yet, sir,' the waiter advised.

There were rioting mobs in a ring about the principal streets and the situation was likely to get worse as darkness descended.

'It's very bad, sir,' the waiter assured them. 'I'd stay put until the police have got things under control. I'll keep you advised.'

Father O'Connor thanked him and said to Yearling: 'Is this more of Mr. Larkin's handiwork?'

'Hardly,' Mr. Yearling said.

The strike had been fixed the day before. What was there to riot about? They settled back in their chairs and after half an hour the waiter came to attend to the lights. It was dusk now outside the windows. The situation in the city was very bad, he told them. There were pitched battles raging in the side streets near at hand. Yearling opened the window again. The noise of fighting could be heard, far-off, but unmistakable.

'They are coming out of their hovels,' Yearling announced. 'Listen to them.'

Father O'Connor did so. He heard glass breaking and knew they were still looting. In the streets he had seen little children clambering with bare feet across broken glass. He said: 'What can they hope to gain?'

'That is the mob,' Yearling said, still standing by the window. 'They are searching for justice.'

'Hooligans,' Father O'Connor protested.

But Yearling did not agree. They were ignorant, uncouth, deplorably unwashed. They were also miserably poor and down-trodden, despised by the articulate city. Yet they had minds to judge injustice and hearts to be broken by the contempt of their fellows. Yearling did not waste pity on them. But he could see their point.

'Let's hope they confine their search to the side streets,' was all he said.

Then he came over to finish his brandy and order another.

In the streets behind them, Pat, trying to return to Nolan & Keyes after delivering a late load, ran into the thick of the trouble. It caught him unawares. The unusual quietness of the street puzzled him. The metal-shod dray made more noise than usual. He drove on into a section of complete darkness and heard the splintering of glass under the wheels. As he reined in to investigate, a piece of iron crashed against the wooden side of the dray. He looked behind him and there was nobody; he peered ahead and made out at last the glint of police helmets about a hundred yards away. Something thudded beside him, then the air became thick with missiles. He jerked the reins to make a turn away from the police and found dark figures surrounding him. Voices shouted obscenities. From the windows on either side stones and broken bottles descended on the advancing police. They began to retreat. The rioters, crushed about the dray, dragged the reins from his hands. When he tried to resist he was pulled from his seat and went down struggling. The horse and dray moved up the street, a new piece of equipment in the onslaught. People loaded it with the ammunition that lay scattered about. Pat, fighting and swearing, struggled to his feet and tried to follow it. Somebody struck him from behind with a bottle and he went down once more. He felt warm blood on his head and neck. The noise of the rioting receded to a distance although legs and bodies still milled about him. He felt behind him and touched a low stone step. Guessing a doorway, he dragged himself backwards and crouched between the pillars. He remained there, unable to see or hear anything now except a roaring noise that he knew was in his own head.

When he became conscious again the ambulances were clearing the street. They searched the darkness with their lamps while the running motors echoed against the dark houses. Pat tried to call out but found it made the pain in his head unbearable. After a while he saw the lamps go out one by one, heard feet receding and the slam of ambulance doors and the revving of engines. The cars lumbered away one by one.

'They'll never get here,' Father O'Connor said, 'the whole city must be in chaos.'

Yearling looked at his watch.

'Not time yet,' he said, 'they are still watching Mr. Yeats.'

Once again the rioters had invaded Sackville Street. The sounds of fighting could be heard distinctly. Father O'Connor refused to look. Yearling, although he would have liked to indulge in a balcony-seat view, remained in his armchair out of sympathy.

'We were talking earlier about love,' he remembered. Father O'Connor, unsure of the absolute propriety of the theme, acknowledged uneasily.

'Have you seen the Parnell statue, Father?'

Father O'Connor, wondering what that could have to do with it, confessed that he had not.

'It was put in place a few weeks ago, and I went specially to see it.'

'You were a follower of Parnell?'

'Not at all. It amused me to see our principal street dedicated so entirely to love.'

Father O'Connor's pale eyebrows shot up.

'Parnell at the top—an adulterer,' Yearling explained. 'Nelson in the middle—another adulterer. And at the end O'Connell—a notorious wencher.'

The thought amused Yearling afresh. He chuckled agreeably to himself. Father O'Connor indicated polite disapproval by shaking his head and assuming a deliberately unamused expression. Parnell's sin had split the Irish Party. Nelson was English —an outsider and unrepresentative. O'Connell may have been all Yearling said—a young man given to wenching and duelling. But in maturity he had become the instrument of Catholic emancipation. Yet it did seem odd. Three of them—all solemnly pedestalled. Trust Yearling to remark the coincidence. Frowning, Father O'Connor said:

'They are honoured for their worthy acts, not for their human frailty.'

'A pity it's not the other way round,' Yearling speculated. 'The inscriptions would make more interesting reading.'

Father O'Connor, feeling the limit had now been reached, held up his hand and begged him not to pursue the subject.

Yearling apologised. 'Forgive me,' he said, 'I meant no disrespect to your office.'

They fell silent. For Father O'Connor it was difficult. Beside him a man made light of a sacred matter, refusing the distinction between lust and love. Love was capable of being blessed, a stimulus, the natural end of which was to produce souls for Christ, souls that would fill in heaven the places left vacant by the angels who had fallen from grace and were now among the legions of the devil. Lust led also to hell. It was the flesh; lewd flesh, lascivious flesh, unbridled, passionate, self-destroying flesh. Love too, if unsanctified. Paolo and Francesca, betrayed by a book.

Having stopped the conversation, he felt obliged to introduce the next topic. But nothing occurred. The room became oppressive. Outside the shouting seemed to have died away.

'I must look through the window,' he said.

'You'll distress yourself.'

But he rose. From the window nothing could be seen and from the balcony only occasional patches of the street, where the few lamps not quenched by the rioters threw their weak circles of light. Was somebody lying down there in the darkness, dying. There had been so much tumult.

'I feel I should go down.'

'Nonsense. Everything is over.'

Yearling was now at his side. The breeze from the river was cool and came fitfully. Peaceful. No more dreadful oaths, thuds of stones and sticks, that black milling tide tossing and shrieking. Had they fought to exhaustion or was it still going on in the side streets, in the smelling alleyways, men and women and little children transformed into obscene beasts?

'What a dreadful night,' he said. His distress was so obvious that it moved Yearling.

'I am sorry if my remarks have upset you,' he said.

'Not at all. I meant the fighting and the looting.'

Yearling knew that. But his broadness on the subject of love had not helped.

'What I said was prompted by a very genuine and beautiful memory,' he explained. 'May I tell you?'

'Of course.'

'I've met many women in my time—and the least said now the better. But there was one in London—I mentioned this before.'

'I remember,' Father O'Connor said. 'You met her at the first performance of *The Yeoman of the Guard*.'

Yearling smiled. It was Father O'Connor's tone, meticulously interested. It was his face, so young, gravely composed, moulded to convey sympathy. He remembered clearly and wanted to tell about it, realising that indeed there was nothing to tell.

'Yes. Or rather afterwards, while at supper with some friends.'

Father O'Connor nodded, waiting.

Now—what was there to say. That she was beautiful? That she had golden hair? There were millions with golden hair. That she turned to him frequently during the meal, smiling, sympathetic, favouring him? He could remember the face so well, bending towards him in the light of the table lamps, the clear eyes and delicately toned skin. And her first question: 'You are Irish—aren't you?' put flatteringly, as though to be Irish was to be special and exclusive. That had been in October 1888, and yet he could remember vividly, with a sensation that was like the throbbing of an old wound.

'For some months we went about together. We got on like a house on fire, except on the subject of drink. She had a set against drink, I think because her father had been an alcoholic, and we used to argue about that. Or, rather, we used to talk about it—the English are too polite to argue. To tell you the truth, I was always pretty expert at hitting the bottle, and I never tried to hide it from her. She cared enough for me to try like the devil to be tolerant about it, but it was no use. Drink frightened her—she couldn't help it. We had good fun, just the same. We went three or four times to the *Yeoman,* we liked it so much, and when we were together we sang it for one another. We did rather more serious things too, of course—but I won't distress you with the details. Then, on the evening I was leaving, quite suddenly she told me she was engaged—some chap on foreign service. She hadn't mentioned this before and it was quite a shock. I asked her to break it off and marry me and she said she'd let me know. I was sure she would, because she wept a lot. She even pleaded with me to stay on longer while she thought about it, but that was impossible. Anyway, I got a letter some weeks later to say she was going to marry this other chap after all. And that was the end of it.' Yearling smiled. 'I wonder why I should tell you such a remote little piece of autobiography.'

'I am honoured,' Father O'Connor said with sincerity. Then, groping to phrase the question delicately, he asked:

'Would it have been so difficult, to meet her wishes—to give up . . . ?'

'I had an instinct about that,' Yearling said, 'and the years have proved me right. For me, memories and alcohol are necessary defences. This is a dunghill of a world.'

It was a surprising sentiment from Yearling, who so seldom betrayed pessimism.

'Perhaps if you had married this girl,' Father O'Connor suggested gently, 'the defences would be unnecessary. You would have had her companionship.'

'There is no such thing as companionship,' Yearling said, 'when it comes to coping with the melancholy intimations of Anno Domini.'

His voice had the familiar note of self-mockery, and, as he spoke, he put his arm companionably about Father O'Connor's shoulder. As they turned to re-enter the room the waiter approached.

'Father O'Connor?' he enquired.

Father O'Connor nodded.

'A telephone call.' The waiter led the way.

It was Bradshaw. He was very agitated. There was uproar in the streets about the theatre, he said, and it would be quite impossible to risk travelling to the Imperial. The cabman had advised strongly against it. They would have to be excused.

'Of course,' Father O'Connor said. 'I hope Mrs. Bradshaw is not too upset.'

'Please explain to Yearling.'

'He is here beside me.'

Father O'Connor handed the earpiece to Yearling, who shouted: 'You missed a grandstand seat.'

'I beg your pardon?'

'At the riots.'

'I am entirely surrounded by rioters,' Bradshaw shouted back, 'blackguards and hooligans who are looting and destroying. I daren't risk bringing Mrs. Bradshaw across.'

'Of course not,' Yearling agreed.

'Where ·are the military?—that's what I'd like to ask Asquith,' Bradshaw added. He sounded outraged, as though it had all been arranged for his sole inconvenience. Then he repeated that he was sorry to disappoint them.

'Don't worry about that. We had quite a pleasant evening. Do you remember the horse tram?'

'The what?'

'The horse tram. Do you remember the time I stole the horse tram. You refused to come with me.'

'I am not interested in damned horse trams at the moment. I am entirely occupied with the problem of getting Florence and myself home in safety.'

'Sorry,' Yearling explained. 'I've been thinking about it on and off all evening. Well—safe journey.'

'And to you. Wish the same to Father O'Connor.'

'I'll do that,' Yearling assured him

Bradshaw rang off. His wife, who had heard only one side of the conversation, was curious.

'What did he say?' she asked.

'I think it typical of Yearling,' Bradshaw complained. 'I tell him the city is in the throes of a revolution and he asks me if I remember the time he stole a horse tram.'

'What horse tram?' Mrs. Bradshaw asked.

Bradshaw went purple.

'Damn it, Florence,' he exploded, 'you are every bit as bad as he is.'

Pat found himself after an unreckonable time at the door of Lily's house. At first the rioting stopped him from crossing to the south side of the city. He wandered northwards instead, dazed and without any particular goal. His horse and cart had disappeared altogether, the blood had caked hard on his collar. At some point he took off his scarf and wound it tightly about his head, hoping in that way to stop the flow of blood. He was weak, his wound throbbed, but for most of his journey he felt light and happy. The streets he passed gave him the idea that he was calling on Lily to take her somewhere, to a music-hall, or to the Park—he could not quite remember where. He would apologise for the blood and the dirt on his clothes. She would understand. Lily nearly always understood. Yet when he reached her door he stood for a long time, undecided whether he should knock or go away again. The feeling of lightness and happiness left him. There was something wrong. She was not expecting him. He was not dressed to take her out. He had forgotten his money. He should be back at Nolan & Keyes, to unyoke and stable his horse, to collect and sort his delivery dockets for the next day. He leaned his back against the door and began to think it out.

The street was dark and untrafficked, the air soothing and warm. A cat, methodically investigating the line of refuse bins, took a long time to approach and pass him. It moved with great stealth, a furry silence, strangely soothing to watch. When it had gone he made up his mind and knocked on the door.

At first Lily thought he had been drinking. She warned him to be quiet and led him into the parlour.

'Give me a match,' she said.

She lit the gas and turned to take stock of him.

'Jesus,' she said, 'you're destroyed!'

At her words his hands went automatically to the scarf on his head.

'You've been in a fight. Was it a policeman?'

'Not a policeman, Lily. It happened down the city.' He looked around.

She took his arm and said: 'Sit here—you look terrible.'

He began to tell her what had happened. The throbbing made it difficult. She undid the scarf as he spoke and gently lifted the matted hair away from the wound. It was long and jagged. Blood oozed very slowly from it.

'Come down to the kitchen, I'll wash and dress it for you.'

'Where's the household?'

'The landlady is in bed. I'll have to tell her you're here.'

'Give me ten minutes. Then I'll go.'

'Don't be daft,' Lily said, 'you can't go travelling home with that.'

She cleaned the wound and washed the blood from his neck. For the hundredth time he noted how small and delicate her hands were. They were the hands he had always loved. They soothed more than the mere physical pain. Because they were Lily's hands he closed his eyes, the hurt that had nothing to do with bottles and broken flesh dying away under their compassionate movements.

'I'm only getting you into trouble,' he said.

'I'll go up and explain to her. She can't turn you out the way you are. Wait here.'

Lily was gone a long time. When she came back she had a couple of blankets on her arm. She led him into the parlour again.

'She says you can sleep here.'

Lily arranged the blankets about him and settled cushions under his head.

'Now I'll make tea.'

'Lily . . .' he began.

'Don't stir.' She went back down to the kitchen.

He found a cigarette and lit it. Lying on the carpeted floor did not bother him. He had slept on harder beds. The room was heavily furnished. There was a picture of Queen Victoria on one wall and photographs of uniformed groups. Souvenirs and trophies in the china cabinet recorded domestic comings and goings that had finished with the Boer War.

He sat up when Lily brought him tea and bread and butter. In an effort to conceal how he felt he asked. 'How do you stick that oul wan?'

Lily, thinking he meant the landlady, said sharply: 'I like that. She's been good enough to let you stay.'

'I mean her nibs,' Pat said, indicating Queen Victoria.

Lily dismissed the picture with a shrug.

'That oul wan let Ireland starve,' Pat insisted.

'She's dead and Ireland is still starving,' Lily said, 'so I don't see that you can put all the blame on Her Majesty.'

'Ireland will be free one day. Royalty will go and the employers will go.'

'You should have explained all that to your comrades-in-arms that gave you the clatter with the bottle.'

He gave up pretending.

'God, Lily,' he said, 'I feel awful.'

'Then lie back,' she advised.

She took away the tea things and settled him comfortably.

'I'll take away your jacket and wash the collar.'

He took her hand and said: 'Don't go, Lily.'

She hesitated. Her face became sad. Then she disengaged her hand and touched his cheek.

'I must,' she told him gently, 'you know I must.' She put out the light and closed the door. Some time later he heard footsteps moving back and forth on the floor above his head. He knew it was Lily going to bed. He listened until at last they ceased. Then he lay thinking about her. It was hard to sleep, knowing her to be so near. It was hard not to rise and go searching in the darkness. His love for her had been like that for a long time, a lonely desire searching vainly for a room. When he closed his eyes the air became heavy and hard to breathe. He dreamed fitfully, knocking on door after door in search of Lily. Each in turn was opened by Queen Victoria.

'This will do me,' Father O'Connor said.

The cab stopped and he got out.

'Sleep well,' Yearling said, lowering the window.

'Thank you for a most hospitable evening.'

'A great pleasure,' Yearling assured him and waved benevolently as the cab jolted forward again.

The night was mild and starless. In front of Father O'Connor the railings of the church were faintly visible and behind them the bulk of the church rose darkly. It had been a distressing journey through streets that looked as though they had been hit by a hurricane. Shop windows had gaping holes, lamp-posts were shattered and bent, the wheels crunched over scattered glass and skidded against bricks and debris. In Father O'Connor's memory nothing like it had happened before. Yearling had refused to agree that it was the handiwork of the strikers. If not, then it was an indirect effect. The lowest elements of the city were prepared now to engage the police, challenging the law and social order in pitched battles. It was a sign that revolt had percolated to the degraded depths of slumland. Here was proof, if indeed proof were needed, of the evil fruits one must be prepared to expect. The challenge to God and religion would not be long delayed

Opening the hall door he let himself in quietly and turned up the gas light. He put his hat on the hallstand and arranged his umbrella, taking care that it would not fall during the night, as Father Giffley's so often did. As he turned the hall door opened and Father O'Sullivan stepped in. With a shock he saw that there was blood on his face and his hands and on the white band of his collar.

'Father,' he said, 'you are hurt.'

'Hush,' Father O'Sullivan said, 'don't waken Father Giffley.'

Father O'Connor lowered his voice.

'You were caught in the riots?'

'Not at all,' Father O'Sullivan said. 'I've been out seeing what I could do. There were some who were badly hurt. A little soap and water will clean it all away.' When Father O'Connor continued to look doubtful, he became concerned and said apologetically.

'I assure you, Father, that I haven't a scratch. Please don't worry.'

He went past and down the hall. The shoulders of his coat were stained and there was dust on its skirt. Father O'Connor stared after him. He stood in the hallway for some minutes after Father O'Sullivan had gone. It was very quiet and he could hear the buzzing of the gas mantle. His face, reflected in the mirror of the hallstand, was suddenly haggard, his jaw tense with pain.

CHAPTER 6

O N Thursday, sixth of June 1912, Feast of Corpus Christi, white being the liturgical colour, Father Giffley took the eight o'clock mass. That evening, during the procession of the Blessed Sacrament, the Introit kept recurring to him. It had been his intention to speak briefly on it at mass, but at the last moment he had changed his mind. He could not bring himself to say:

'In the name of the Father and of the Son and of the Holy Ghost.

'He fed them on the fat of wheat, alleluia; and filled them with honey out of the rock!'

To address metaphors of wheat and honey to unfortunates who were spending most of their time on strike seemed inappropriate. Father O'Connor, however, had found no such difficulty. During the ten o'clock mass his voice had penetrated to Father Giffley through the partly open door of the vestry. He told his listening congregation that however much they might lack for material comforts in comparison with the more well-to-do, as Catholics they had access to a daily Banquet which was nothing less than the Body and Blood of our Lord Jesus Christ Himself. Here was a spiritual food, necessary to salvation, which was the daily right of the poorest Catholic in the world, but forbidden to the non-Catholic, however rich in worldly goods he might be. Here truly, said Father O'Connor, was no mere bodily fare, but the fat of wheat referred to in the Introit of the mass, here was the honey out of the rock. For these riches, the gift of the Father, let them join the psalmist in rejoicing to God our Helper on this great feast of the Body of Christ.

Father Giffley walked rigidly and angrily as the procession moved about the church grounds. Under the canopy, borne by four Confraternity men, Father O'Connor held the monstrance aloft, the chasuble draped about his shoulders and upheld hands. He had been celebrant at solemn benediction. Father Giffley, dressed only in surplice and soutane, assisted by holding his cope on the right-hand side; Father O'Sullivan assisting in the same manner on his left. Before them, walking backwards with occasional wary glances behind, a young altar boy offered incense from the Thurible. Three puffs of aromatic smoke rose at each incensing, accompanied by the threefold tap of the Thurible against its silver coloured chain. Behind the priests walked the little children. Some with surplices or white veils, some even with bunches of cheap flowers, sang 'O Sacrament Most Holy, O Sacrament Divine' and kept glancing about to locate their parents among the onlookers. Their voices reached out beyond the church grounds into the streets, which were hot and stuffy under the evening sunshine.

Where had the children got the flowers? Father Giffley wondered. Some had come from wasteland plots, for he himself had told them to gather the humble flowers that were free to all—the daisies, the buttercups, the wild, unnameable growths that for all he knew might be weeds. But some had the more cultivated kind. Father Giffley did not take much note of flowers. The wild kind that spread along grasslands and ditches were pleasant enough, but the gardens of the well-to-do he despised as so many useless acres of multi-coloured vegetation. Father O'Connor had suggested buying a supply of flowers to distribute to the first few ranks of processionists.

'It is merely a suggestion,' Father O'Connor had said.

'We should distribute onions and turnips and cabbages to them to carry,' Father Giffley said, 'then we might have some right to admonish them to rejoice to God their Helper.'

Father O'Sullivan, who heard the exchange, left the room, remembering that he must make ready the surplices and veils which Father Giffley kept for distribution among the children, most of whom were too poor to supply their own. Father O'Connor had made no reply.

Anger accompanied Father Giffley through the length of the journey, anger at the plight of the children, anger at his own powerlessness, anger, most of all, at the pale face of Father O'Connor the celebrant, whose cope he held in apparent priestly brotherhood. This man was content (Father Giffley reflected) in the thought that the fat of wheat and the honey out of the rock were safely stored in the strongrooms of his middle-class friends, to be distributed to the destitute in small doses from time to time. Under the auspices of the good ladies of Kingstown, no doubt. The time had come when these outcasts were demanding something more than figurative nourishment. Walking in the sunshine, with the voices of the children in his ears, the Thurible tapping its three-beat praise in front of him, the cope of his hated curate held ceremoniously outward by his hand, Father Giffley, without any feelings of pity, but with an anger that was not altogether sane, wished them well. If they could succeed in toppling the society this insensitive young fool believed in, he would listen with joy to the crashing and the pandemonium.

Some distance away, out of earshot of the children's singing, Rashers leaned on the parapet of the bridge. The iron was hot and comforting under his elbows. When he looked down the water of the basin showed him the bridge with his own image planted in the centre. To his left, rising out of the water, was the grey stone wall of Boland's granary, with great open doors where ships had been unloading some time earlier in the afternoon. Inside he could see the sacks of grain piled one on the other. Weeds grew at intervals from ancient cracks in the wall and these too were reflected in the water, profuse, colourful, without movement in the June evening. A pigeon which had discovered a hole in one of the grain bags at the bottom of the pile was pecking patiently at it to make it bigger, so that the grain would spill out. Rashers had seen them at it often; it was a trick that was part of the granary pigeon's inheritance. Pigeons had it easy, Rashers reflected, as the bridge trembled under the wheels of the traffic and dislodged dust made tiny whirlpools in the water beneath it.

When he looked down the street, Rashers could see the front of the bakery, a greystone building with lines of windows, granary floors, hoists and platforms. Somewhere near the top the pigeons had their nests. They came and went as he watched. They were sleek and fat with glossy coats. They exercised above the roof and watched the comings and goings of carts. In the wake of each load grain littered the cobbles and the pigeons flew down to search. The grain in the evening sunlight was golden, the green and purple feathers about the necks of the birds had a healthy sheen.

Rashers was hungry. The warm odour of the bakery set up an aching in his mouth and his belly. Mrs. Bartley, if he asked her, would give him a cup of tea and a slice of bread when he got home, but his hunger was for more than that. He watched the pigeon still at work on the sack and thought of crisp, freshly baked loaves. It seemed a long way back to Chandlers Court. All day he had worked moving rubble from the garden of a woman in Sandymount, in the hope that she would offer him an evening meal as part of his payment. But when he finished she had left to attend benediction for the feast, leaving word that he should call back for his money tomorrow. Now the dog would be waiting for him and he would have nothing to give it. It was well for the pigeons flying high above the streets, mating, resting, pilfering grain. Tonight Rusty could be let out to root in the bins, with the chance of picking up God knows what class of poison. He himself could impose on Mrs. Bartley, a thing that troubled him, for she had not much more than himself. He stared at his own reflection, trying to think of an alternative.

The pigeon at the sack had been joined by three others. They knew what was afoot and stood waiting for the hole to grow and the grain to spill. They were patient. It was part of their way of existence and had happened many times before.

Father Giffley, when the procession was over, called the clerk from the vestry to his study so that Father O'Connor had to disrobe without the assistance which was his due as celebrant. Father O'Sullivan collected the veils and the surplices from the children and put them away in the wickerwork hamper. Father O'Connor knelt for some time in private prayer in the vestry, which smelled of incense and flowers. The odours and the hush were pleasant at first. Later they made him lonely, so that he longed for companionship. But he continued to pray, in thanksgiving to God for the gift of priesthood, the power of his hands to change bread and wine into the Body and Blood of the Lord. There was a moment when his realisation of the mystery of it raised his thoughts into ecstasy. He continued to pray until all was as usual again and the vestry and the flowers and the lingering incense existed once more about him.

Very quiet and still, Rashers thought the evening was. For the moment the pigeon had given over his work at the sack and stood with the other three, as though in consultation. Bob Fitzpatrick, crossing the bridge on his way home, waved a greeting. His face was black from the furnaces. Easy knowing the wife and the children were away. He would have washed his face before leaving the job if they were at home. A man who knew Rashers slightly stopped to stand beside him and together they watched as the pigeon resumed its work.

'I've seen them at that a hundred times,' the man commented.

'You'd wonder at it,' Rashers said, 'you wouldn't think a pigeon would have the brains.'

'More brains than many a Christian,' said the man, 'like the rat.'

'The rat is sagacious.'

'Highly sagacious. I believe the crowd in the College of Surgeons would rather have a rat to experiment on than a guinea-pig. More like the human.'

'I can believe that,' Rashers said. 'Some humans is remarkably like the rat.'

'Now you're talking,' the man agreed.

They considered the pigeon's activity for a while longer.

'Did you back anything in the Derby?' the man asked.

'I gave that up a long time ago,' Rashers said.

'You're wise. I had two bob on Sweeper myself and he's still running. Are you stepping up the road?'

'No,' Rashers said, 'I may as well rest here a while longer.'

He wanted to see the result of the pigeon's labour. There was nothing better to do. The man lingered a while longer out of politeness, then he went off.

Father O'Sullivan noted in the *Irish Catholic* that a new publication had been issued from the office of the Messenger of the Sacred Heart. He went off to consult Father Giffley about it, finding him in his study.

'What is the title of this latest evidence of religious fervour?' he was asked. Father O'Sullivan, reading from the paper said:

'The Litany of the Sacred Heart, with commentary and meditations.'

'By whom?'

'By Father Joseph McDonnell, S.J.'

'Ah—an S.J. Don't you think it might be a bit on the intellectual side for St. Brigid's?'

Father O'Sullivan smiled, knowing that he was not being asked a question.

'I would like a few copies for the church pamphlet box.'

'And why not,' Father Giffley said. He closed his eyes and spoke aloud the verses of the Litany that came to his mind. 'Heart of Jesus, filled with reproaches: Heart of Jesus, bruised for our crimes: Heart of Jesus, made obedient unto death.'

He stopped and gestured to a chair.

'Sit down, John.'

Father O'Sullivan took the chair. He was always at ease in his parish priest's presence, even when Father Giffley used him as the butt of his humour.

'I want to tell you that I am going mad, John. Will you join me in a glass?'

'Not now, thank you,' Father O'Sullivan said. He looked to one side, not to evade, but to hide the sadness which he knew might show itself.

'Why don't you look at me, John?'

'I took back the veils and the surplices from the children to-

309

night,' Father O'Sullivan said gently. 'All the surplices were returned, but two of the veils were not.'

'The boys' surplices are always fully accounted for, aren't they?' Father Giffley said. 'The veils are more uncertain. The little girls steal them. They woo men as they woo God—with raiment. I am not disturbed. Buy two more.'

Father O'Sullivan watched as the other rose and took whiskey from a cabinet. He saw him pour a measure and then add a little water from the jug on the table. As he did so, Father Giffley said:

> 'Heart of Jesus, desire of the everlasting hills
> Heart of Jesus, patient and full of mercy.'

He drank. He regarded Father O'Sullivan over his glass with amused affection. 'You have no pamphlet of your own published yet?'

'When I finish them they are never good enough.'

'Will you be here during the evening, John?'

'All of it.'

'Then go and bring me your last effort and I'll read it and send for you and we'll discuss it. I'll give you a frank opinion.'

Father O'Sullivan was surprised. Father Giffley had never offered to read anything of his before. Pleased, he went to his room and returned with the neatly written pages, to find Father Giffley pouring himself another glass. His mood had changed. He was staring through the window at the bunting which decorated the path about the church which the Corpus Christi procession had followed.

'Leave it with me,' he said. Father O'Sullivan placed the manuscript on the table beside him and withdrew.

Fitz washed when he got home, made tea for himself, then attended a meeting of his section that had been called to organise support for a strike in one of the timber yards. Mulhall took the chair, while Joe sat beside him on the platform making notes. It was becoming a routine now: the resolution of support, the decision not to pass pickets and not to handle goods moved from the yard by non-union labour. There were three further resolutions of sympathy and pledges of support for comrades on strike in England. Then they retired to Tobin's of Townsend Street, because Pat had backed the winner of the Derby and offered to treat them.

'Tagalie,' Pat said, when they were sitting with pints of porter in front of them, 'it was a certainty.'

'The only filly in the race,' Joe pointed out.

'What price?' asked Mulhall.

'One hundred to eight,' Fitz supplied. He had read the results on the job.

1.	Tagalie	100—8
2.	Jaegar	8—1
3.	Tracery	66—1

Sweeper, an American horse, had been favourite at two to one.

'You had courage, anyway,' Mulhall said, 'backing the filly.'

'He has a weakness for fillies,' Joe commented.

'The jockey was J. Rieff,' Pat challenged, 'and I wonder if the name conveys anything to any of you?'

They thought about it but eventually had to admit that they could find no particular significance in it.

'What was the winner of the 1907 Derby?' Pat asked.

'Boss Croker's horse, Orby,' Mulhall answered. Then he clapped his fist against his knee and added: 'Begod, I remember—it was ridden by J. Rieff.'

It came back to the rest of them then. Joe said it was only a fluke that a filly should win against nineteen others—all colts.

'Fluke or no fluke,' Mullhall said, raising his glass again to Pat, 'we're all having a drink out of it.'

He looked over to Fitz for approval. Increasingly now, Fitz had noted, Mulhall, who took the lead in most of their discussions and decisions, looked to him for support and approval. They began to talk about the court of inquiry which was investigating the *Titanic* disaster of the previous April. Joe said the captain had brought the curse of God on his ship by boasting that even God couldn't sink the *Titanic*. The Orangemen who built it had let loose the most terrible blasphemies against the Catholic Church. It was a well-known fact that the *Titanic* job was labelled No. 3909. If you held the number 3909 up to the mirror it read POPE. That was done deliberately so that the *Titanic* would be built under the slogan of 'No Pope'. Mulhall said they were a notorious anti-Catholic crowd, the mob up in the North.

They were beginning to discuss this when a man who was not of their company intervened and said: 'I hope I'm not interrupting...'

Then he said he had heard their talk about the *Titanic* and asked if anyone of them could say how many people had been drowned. When no one could remember precisely, he told them the number had been one thousand five hundred and ninety-four.

'And here's a very interesting thing a man showed me,' he said. Taking out a cigarette packet, he wrote on the back the figures 1594 and showed it to them.

'Now,' he asked, 'what's the first, fifth, ninth and fourth letters of the alphabet?' Without waiting he wrote them down under the numbers.

1594
AEID

Then he said that by a remarkable coincidence these letters spelled out an answer to the pro-British attitude and anti-Nationalist sentiments of the Orange shipwrights. 'A.E.I.D.,' he said. 'All England Is Damned.'

They agreed that it was an extraordinary coincidence.

'It ties in with your friend's information about the "NO POPE" slogan,' he said. 'I thought I'd show you.'

When he had gone Mulhall said there was something very queer about the whole business of the *Titanic*; pride always went before a fall. Fitz smiled quietly. Joe said the owners and the workers flew in God's face. Pat looked at him pityingly and said:

'All England is Damned. Do you believe that nonsense?'

'It may be nonsense,' Joe insisted, 'but it's a very extraordinary coincidence.'

'That fellow made it all up out of his head,' Pat said. 'He's one of Arthur Griffith's mob—a bloody Sinn Feiner.'

'What's wrong with Sinn Fein?'

'They're against you and against Larkin!' Pat shouted at him. 'That's what's wrong with them.'

Mulhall intervened.

'If you don't keep your voices down,' he warned them, 'you'll get us all flung out.'

Mrs. Bradshaw attended the Corpus Christi procession at Kingstown Church and after it she had a number of the children for a little party. She had sandwiches and cakes and jellies for them, all prepared by herself. Making such things for children gave her great pleasure. At first she meant to have fruit as well, but decided against it on the advice of her husband, who reminded her that fruit was golden in the morning, silver in the afternoon, but lead at night. It had been a maxim of his mother's, he said. Yearling had agreed to take them all home afterwards in his motor car. Games were in progress in the garden when he arrived and as he opened the gate a small boy tumbled out of a tree above him and landed at his feet. Yearling picked him up, made sure he was undamaged, and gave him a shilling to be good in the future. He found Mrs. Bradshaw trying very hard to supervise the proceedings.

'If you don't watch them all the time,' she said to him, 'they get quite out of hand.'

Bradshaw greeted him from a porchway and invited him to have a drink.

'Florence loves this sort of thing,' he said, as he poured whiskey, 'but what happens if there's an accident?'

Yearling laughed and said children and animals had charmed lives.

'Did you see the procession?'

Yearling had not. It would be enough to shepherd two or three carloads home.

'I walked by the seafront,' he explained. The activities down there had been more to his taste—the yachts in the harbour, the promenaders, the pier fishermen, a gull resting on the water which had stayed all the time in the same place, bobbing gently up and down and up and down. He had watched it a long time and now he could recall the scene vividly. The water had been green and sluggish, the seaweed clinging to the wooden supports of the landing stage moved perpetually, the water made lapping sounds all the time. It had been pleasantly hypnotic to stand quite still and watch, to feel that Time, trapped between him and the seagull, had been unable for some moments to move forward.

It would be useless, however, to try to convey anything of that to Bradshaw who, with thumbs in the waistcoat pockets that accommodated the twin strands of his watch-chain, awaited conversation.

'I walked by your houses on the way back,' he said instead, 'you should do something about them.'

The houses were now supported by great timber props, their hall doors open, their fanlights broken. From each window a pole protruded, displaying the tenants' laundry. The props and the poles and the laundry gave the place a military air and reminded Yearling of medieval drawings of beleaguered cities. If the tenants had poured boiling pitch on the passers-by it would not have surprised him.

'It's the damned railway,' Bradshaw complained. 'The trains going past all these years have loosened the foundations. I've written to the company several times but they disclaim responsibility.'

'If you don't do something soon,' Yearling warned, 'the authorities will take a hand in it. They are threatening action in the city.'

'They've been sending me letters. I've told them it's the railway's responsibility,' Bradshaw said. Then he smiled tightly and added: 'However—they won't get very far with me.'

The smile conveyed that he had influence in the right quarter. Local politicians were vulnerable and yielded to pressure. Yearling did not like the smile. Placing his glass on the table, he joined his hands and asked:

'How many tenants are in them?'

'God knows,' Bradshaw said. 'Certainly not enough to make

an economic proposition of them. Why do you ask?'

'When I passed by this evening,' Yearling said, 'I wondered how many would be killed if they collapsed.'

Bradshaw looked surprised.

'What a damned peculiar notion,' he began.

But Yearling stood up. 'I must see that the children get home,' he said. He went to the door. It was an extremely abrupt departure. Bradshaw saw him crossing the lawn and a little later he was shepherding the first group of children towards the garden gate. Mrs. Bradshaw was waving after him and calling out something which made him wave back reassuringly. The glass of whiskey on the table beside Bradshaw was untouched. That was damned unusual.

Fitz arrived home late. Mary and the children were staying at her father's small farm in the country, so there was nothing to bring him home early. As he mounted the steps he heard Rashers' dog barking in the basement. He knew by its loneliness and persistence that Rashers was still out. The windows of the empty flat were letting in the last of the evening light. The air was warm, a cup and saucer and teapot remained on the table as he had left them. Through the windows he could see the mountains, dark now but still visible in the distance. A jumble of roofs and chimney-pots spread out on all sides, angled and broken and awry, a battered brotherhood enduring with the city the incurable disease of old age. These bricks were returning once more to dust, one by one these walls would bulge outwards, crack, collapse into rubble. They were despised and uncared for, like the tenants they sheltered, who lived for the most part on bread and tea and bore children on rickety beds to grow up in the same hardship and hunger. Larkin was thundering his message of revolution, organising strikes, leading assaults on a shocked society, but the immediate gains, where they came at all, made little difference. The comfort that Mary and himself were beginning to enjoy had come by accident, through the regard of a wealthy woman, who bestowed on them the furniture and clothes she would otherwise have thrown out. Patronage, not organisation, had given them anything they possessed. Watching in silence the jumble of roofs under the darkening air, he thought again of countless people in drab rooms. The trouble was there would never be enough patrons to go round.

He brought the tea things to the basin and began to wash them, using cold water. In some strange bedroom many miles to the south, in a house surrounded by fields, his children were asleep. Mary too, perhaps. It was odd not to know. Later, as he lay in bed waiting for sleep, he continued for a long time thinking gravely about Mary, their children, the world they would live in, their future together.

Tagalie had won the Derby, Rashers knew. At a hundred to eight. If you had a shilling on that you'd collect—what would it be? A hundred to eight that was twelve and a half to one—twelve and sixpence. But you never had luck like that anyway. Once in a blue moon, maybe, after you'd lost ten times over.

That was why he gave it up. When you were destitute nothing lucky ever happened. The more you were in want, the more you'd go without. Mrs. Molloy, the only mother he had ever known, used to say that. The more you're in want, the more you'll go without. And she used to say to him: Rashers, me heart, if it was raining soup, you'd have nothing but a fork.

That was a long time ago now, and somehow the sunset colours in the water and on the stone of the granary wall and on the distant railway bridge brought it all sadly back to him. In the open doorway of the granary the pigeon, after a long respite, was again at work. Fine dust floated in the shaft of light that struck the floor beside it and coloured it like a rainbow. It was a hard way to gather food. And unnecessary. Further down the street, near the entrance to the bakery, grain in plenty lay scattered on the cobbles. Perhaps thievery was a sauce.

'More power,' a voice said behind him. It was the man who had spoken about the horses earlier on, the man who had backed the favourite. Rashers remembered the sum he had worked out.

'I was thinking,' he said, 'if a body had a shilling on the filly he'd win twelve and sixpence.'

'Damn nearly a week's wages,' the man agreed.

If wishes were horses, beggars would ride.

'And I was wondering,' Rashers continued, 'why you'd want to back the favourite.'

'Putting it where the big money is—taking a lead from the crowd with the information.'

'What information—wasn't he beaten?'

'Something went wrong,' the man said. 'There's many a slip —if you follow me.'

He sounded as though he had personal knowledge of some piece of trickery that had failed to come off. Then, dismissing his bad luck, he slapped Rashers on the back and went off.

'There'll be another day,' he said, with a great show of confidence.

Rashers turned away from him in time to see the pigeon being killed. It happened very simply. First the pigeon hopped back as the break in the sack became wide enough to let a trickle of grain fall on to the floor. As it began to eat, three of four companions joined it. The breach in the sack widened under the weight of the sacks which were piled above it. The trickle of grain became a steady stream. As the broken sack emptied, those relying on it for support began slowly to shift position. The movement, beginning at the bottom, travelled upwards. Rashers saw those on the top tilting. The movement was very slow. For some seconds he waited, knowing what was going to happen. Then, quite suddenly, the whole pyramid collapsed. The floor shuddered as sacks tumbled about it, a cloud of dust filled the granary and cut out the sunlight. Somewhere beneath the tumble of sacks the pigeon and his companions lay crushed and dead.

When the dust had cleared and the workmen had begun to rebuild the sacks Rashers turned for home. It was one of those never-ending June evenings, with long reaches of sky from which the light seemed unable to ebb. Rashers moved slowly. The rumble of the collapsing sacks and the great cloud of dust had set his heart beating in a way that now made him breathless. His bad leg made movement very difficult, his chest pained him. He began to curse the pigeon, for its thievery, its unnecessary death, the shock that was making the road home interminable, the delay that would send him hungry to bed. It was too late now to ask Mrs. Bartley for bread. Rusty would go hungry too. At Chandlers Court he stopped to get his breath and to look up at the sky. It was never ending, with never fading light. He thought of Death and felt it was waiting for him somewhere in the sky's deeps, cold Sergeant Death, as the song said, Death the sad smiling tyrant, the cruel and remorseless old foe. He listened to his heart and heard it speaking to him of Death, not in words, but with a sound like sad music. He listened for some time. Then he stepped into the hallway, where his feet echoed on the wooden floor. At the third footstep the dog below in the basement began to bark.

At about eleven-thirty Father O'Sullivan, having waited all evening to be summoned by Father Giffley, decided to go to his parish priest's room and knock. At first he had been anxious because of the promised discussion on his pamphlet, but now he was uneasy only because something might have happened. 'I want to tell you that I am going mad, John,' Father Giffley had said. The words had upset him, because he regarded his parish priest with compassion and because he feared in his heart that they were true.

He remembered them again as he waited for a reply to his knock. There was none. When he had tried several times without success he opened the door gently and went in. Father Giffley was snoring in his chair. The manuscript lay on the table beside him. It had not been opened. A water jug rested beside it and a drinking glass had left circular stains on it. The whiskey bottle beside it was almost empty.

He hesitated, wondering what to do.

'Father,' he whispered. 'Father Giffley.' When he had repeated the name several times his superior opened his eyes.

'Go away,' he said.

'But, Father . . .'

Father Giffley turned away and closed his eyes once more. After a moment, while Father O'Sullivan waited, he said:

'Heart of Jesus patient and full of mercy, Heart of Jesus, desire of the everlasting hills.'

Father O'Sullivan remained very quiet. In the twilight of the room the words seemed for a little while to have physical presence, to repeat of themselves, clearly at first, then fading gradually into silence. Father Giffley's breathing became heavy. After a while he began to snore.

Father O'Sullivan, knowing there was nothing he could do, withdrew, closing the door very gently.

CHAPTER 7

YEARLING, back in the city for the first time in six weeks, re-marked anew its characteristic odours; the smell of soot and hot metal in Westland Row station, the dust-laden air in streets, the strong tang of horse urine where the cabbies had their stand, the waft of beer and stale sawdust when a public house door swung open. If the fishing in Connemara had been poor this season, at least the open spaces had given him back his nose.

He stood at the corner, a jaunty figure in Norfolk jacket and knickerbockers, with a walking-stick which he wagged content-edly to and fro as he considered his surroundings. He liked to smell things. Smell was part of place. It was more. It seeped into forgotten storerooms of the mind and unlocked hidden memories. Smell, like music, could produce the latchkey to pain and pleasure.

He looked down Brunswick Street to read the clock above the fire brigade station. Twenty-five minutes to three. That gave him an hour before his appointment with the chairman of Morgan & Co. He was glad. The October afternoon was fine. There were plenty of pleasant, inconsequential things to do.

Wondering if there was anything of interest going on at the Antient Concert Rooms, he crossed the road and turned left down Brunswick Street. He found the place was locked and the notice board outside blank. Too early yet, he remembered, for any of the concerts of the Dublin Orchestral Society. He had played with the orchestra some years before, when they presented all the Beethoven symphonies. They had to leave out the last movement of the Ninth, though, because there was no choir.

Michele Esposito had conducted, an accomplished musician, Yearling considered, unanimously respected by musical citizens. Pity they were also unanimous in mispronouncing his name.

In the graveyard of St. Mark's Church an old man was sweeping up the leaves. The trees that had shed them were covered with grime from the nearby railway bridge, as black as the coal carters who lived in the surrounding tenements. Yet they budded in spring and decked themselves in summer, with a gnarled and grimy courage which moved Yearling to admiration. The old man swept the leaves into little heaps along the paths. From time to time he exchanged his sweeping brush for a barrow and brought them to the fire that smouldered by a stone wall. There was no flame visible, only a plume of blue smoke rising steadily towards the sky. On all sides were tombstones, upright, angled, grimy as the trees. The iron railings of the graveyard ran parallel with the street, a barrier to divide the kingdoms of the living and the dead.

The metal-shod wheels of a dray ground on the cobbles behind Yearling's back. The noise was deafening. He turned impatiently to shake his stick at the driver and put his fingers in his ears. The driver, unabashed, winked to convey his good humour. As the dray passed Yearling saw the board on the back. It read: 'Morgan & Co.'

The reminder of his appointment was unwelcome. His mother had been Cecilia Morgan and from his grandfather, George Morgan, he had inherited an aptitude for music and his influential place on the Board. His brother-in-law, John Bullman, was now chairman. Neither approved of the other.

As Yearling turned to resume his walk, a man passed him with a barrel-organ and a monkey on a chain. One of Signor Esposito's fellow-countrymen, a twin soul, a musician. The man was thin and famished looking and the monkey, in its red flannel jacket, clung to the organ and scrutinised the passers-by with quick, continuous movements of its head. When a group of children waved and shouted to it, the monkey responded by leaping up and down several times. Showing-off, Yearling thought.

He crossed the road. The children had now gathered about a

shop window. They were ragged and poor. The boys wore trousers that had been cut down to fit, the girls' dresses were made of oddments run clumsily together by their mothers. All of them were barefooted. For the moment the window held their unanimous interest. It displayed drumsticks and liquorice pipes, toffee apples, jelly babies, cough-no-mores, aniseed balls, conversation lozenges.

Yearling, aware suddenly of a conglomeration of appetites, tapped the nearest shoulder and asked: 'Who'd like sweets?'

The faces turned in unison to look up at him. They examined in unison the knickerbockers, the Norfolk jacket, the cane.

'Come,' Yearling encouraged, 'first in gets the most.'

He went into the shop. There were bundles of firewood in one corner and a large drum with tin measures beside it. The tap, dripping occasionally, filled the air with the smell of paraffin. The shelves behind the counter supported trays of money balls, potato balls, peggy's legs, jaw stickers, bull's-eyes and lemon drops. There was a closed box which contained something called Kruger's Soothers. Slices of snow cake and plum pudding were stacked on the counter itself and a tumbler stood for a measure beside a basin of cooked peas.

Yearling, aware now that the small space about him was crammed, wondered where to begin. A middled-aged woman faced him. She was smiling.

'Give them what they want,' he said, smiling back at her.

For some minutes there was chaos, until the woman said no one would get anything until they were all quiet and waited their turns. Then she began to select from the boxes, counting sweets and measuring out peas. The snow cake and plum pudding disappeared altogether. When all had been served he paid her. It was a modest amount. Never, Yearling thought, had a mob been so economically mollified. He dismissed them and they went whooping out the door.

'Thank you,' he said to the woman who had served him.

'You're welcome, sir.'

He was about to remark on their appetites, their excitement, the bewildering combination of poverty and high spirits. He changed his mind. What seemed remarkable to him was everyday to her. Raising his hat ceremoniously, he left.

The traffic in Townsend Street, preponderantly horse-drawn, displayed the familiar names—the Gas Company, the Glass Bottle Company, Boland's Bakery, Tedcastle McCormack, Palgraves, W. & R. Jacob, the Foundry of Morgan, the Dublin United Tramway Company. Most of the drivers had sacks pinned about their shoulders. Many of them wore moustaches that made them look curiously alike. All of them seemed lost in some slow-minded afternoon reverie. Yet these were the revolutionaries and the Larkinites, Yearling reflected, patiently revolving God knows what plans for further mischief behind short clay pipes.

The thought gave him zest for his appointment which, his watch informed him, was now imminent. He began to swing his cane again, in time with a jingle which had begun to repeat itself in his head.

> 'Edward Carson had a cat
> It sat upon the fender
> And every time it caught a rat
> It shouted : No Surrender.'

Carson, arming his Ulster volunteers in the Northern counties of Ireland, wanted a Protestant parliament for a Protestant people. Home Rule is Rome Rule.

> 'Ulster will Fight
> And Ulster will be Right.'

'The men of Ulster, loyal subjects of King George V, will use all means which may be found necessary to defeat the present conspiracy to set up a Home Rule parliament in Ireland, and in the event of such a parliament being forced upon them, will refuse to recognise its authority.'

Edward Carson signed the Solemn Covenant, and immediately after him came the pillars of Northern society; Lord Londonderry, the Bishop of Down, the Moderator of the General Assembly. It would be a fight between John Redmond and

Edward Carson, Dear-Harp-of-my-Country-In-Darkness-I-found-Thee against the Protestant Boys and the Ould Orange Flute.

There would be excitement, whatever way the cat jumped. Was it this that had his brother-in-law worried? Or was it the labour unrest? He turned in by the works gate and stood for a while to wonder at the endless belt of buckets which groaned and rattled as they climbed the mechanical hoist. He would soon know.

Rashers, summoned urgently into the street, examined the monkey and the barrel-organ at Hennessy's request.

'Where the hell did you get it?'

'This little Italian collapsed in front of my eyes. I know him well and went over to him. When they were taking him away in the ambulance he asked me to mind the monkey for him.'

'How can you mind a monkey?'

'Take him into the room with the rest of the brood, I suppose. I'm wondering what he'll eat.'

'One of your misfortunate kids, the minute you turn your back.'

Hennessy looked worried for a moment. Then he said: 'Monkeys is vegetarians.'

'I wouldn't be sure. That fellow there has the look of a bloody cannibal.'

Hennessy scrutinised the monkey closely. It frowned at him and gave an unexpected leap. He jerked away.

'What did I tell you?' Rashers said.

'Ah no,' Hennessy said, 'I frightened him. They don't like to be stared at.' They sat down on the steps.

'What am I to do?' Hennessy asked again.

The barrel-organ and the monkey, overshadowing both of them, cut off the rest of the street and for a long time seemed quite insoluble.

Rashers, applying his mind to the matter, began at the beginning. Anything that lived; men, women, children; dogs, pigeons, monkeys; even lesser things like cockroaches, flies and fleas, had to eat. He had been of their company for long enough to sympathise with them all—the child rooting in the ashbin, the cat slinking along the gutter, the cockroach delicately questing along the wooden joins of the floor, its grey-blue body corrugated with anxiety. These were sometimes his competitors, but more often his brothers. He could never watch a dog nosing in a bin without a feeling of sympathy and fellowship. The monkey, too, was a questor, who could pick out fortunes for the curious and collect their pennies in his little black bag. They could work together, the monkey and himself.

Rising from the steps, he began to investigate the handle of the organ. He moved it slightly.

'Don't touch it,' Hennessy warned him.

'What do you mean—don't touch it?'

'You might break it.'

Rashers became angry.

'Break, me arse,' he said.

He took a firm grip of the handle and turned it rapidly. The organ, galvanised into action, began at a breathtaking tempo to emit a waltz.

'For the love of God, will you stop?' Hennessy appealed. 'You'll banjax it.'

But Rashers continued. The burst of music at the turning of the handle astonished him. He cocked his head to it and tried it at different speeds.

' "Over the Waves",' he announced finally.

'Over what waves?' Hennessy asked. 'What the hell are you talking about?'

'It's a waltz called "Over the Waves".'

Rashers found the right speed at last. The tune rattled out beneath roofs and window and flowed down the length of the street, past broken fanlights and open hall doors. Rashers, his head to one side, listened with delight.

'Elegant,' he said.

As he turned to invite approval, the behaviour of the monkey caught his attention.

'Look,' he said to Hennessy.

The monkey had taken the little black bag in his paw. Its body trembled a little, its eyes were alive and full of intelligence.

The head, moving constantly from one side to the other, left no doubt about it thoughts. It was watching for the approach of a client to beg from.

'Come on,' Rashers decided, 'if we don't make a few bob, we'll have a damn good try.'

Hennessy agreed to push the barrel-organ from place to place, a task Rashers found impossible because of his bad leg. He was persuaded to try the handle too, but after the terrifying burst of music which answered his first attempt he refused to have anything further to do with it. It was decided that Rashers, who had a more professional understanding of music anyway, should be solely responsible for performance. He became expert at it in the course of the afternoon and learned to vary the tempo to suit his mood. Turn the handle rapidly and the air was lively. Turn it more slowly and the effect was pensive—even melancholy.

'It's more impressive than the tin whistle,' Hennessy remarked.

'More orchestral,' Rashers agreed.

By evening they had arrived at their last stand, a vantage point at the corner of Bachelor's Walk and Sackville Street. It was here that Pat and Lily, on their way to one of their rare walks in Phoenix Park, saw them.

'There's some friends of mine,' Pat said. She looked around her. People were passing continuously. She searched.

'Where?'

'Over there.'

'The barrel-organ?'

'The thin fella is Hennessy. The one with the beard is Rashers.'

'And the monkey . . . ?'

'I don't know. I haven't yet had the pleasure,' Pat said.

He took her over to introduce her. Hennessy was polite and raised his hat. Rashers stared for some moments until he recognised Pat as the friend of Fitz and Mulhall.

'Have you gone into partnership?' Pat asked him.

Hennessy explained about the Italian who had collapsed.

Then, because he was by nature gallant, he insisted that the monkey should draw Lily's fortune. He refused to hear of any payment. The monkey selected a card from the fortune box. Lily took it.

'Let's see,' Pat asked her.

'Fortunes are private,' she said, keeping it out of his reach. He shrugged. They walked all the way to the Park, following the river to Kingsbridge and entering at last by the main gate. The trees were rich with the colour of autumn, grassland and paths were strewn with fallen leaves. It was their habit to be together once a week. Lily would not agree to meet him more often and he had given up his earlier attempts to persuade her. A string of horses, returning from exercise, went by at a distance. Riders and animals made beautiful silhouettes against the autumn sky.

'There goes the Quality,' Pat commented.

'Are you jealous?' Lily asked.

'Why should I be jealous?'

'Because the gentry have horses.'

'I have a horse of my own,' Pat said, 'the one I drive for Nolan & Keyes.'

Lily laughed and reached out her hand to him. He took it gently. She was wrong if she thought he coveted any of the things the Quality enjoyed. He would fight them only because people of his own class were hungry and in want and those who were taking too much must give something back. And because he would refuse any longer to cringe before their lackeys or fawn on them for his livelihood. When a banner swaying above a meeting said 'Arise, Ye Slaves' the words stirred him like the sound of a great band. He would not be a slave for the sake of livelihood, and he would not tolerate the company of slaves. Riders and animals passed by in silhouette, far away and beautiful in the autumn evening.

When he had been silent for some time Lily said to him: 'Don't you want to know my fortune?'

'You said it was private.'

She took from her bag the card the monkey had given her and said: 'There's a Dark Man and a Fair Man in my life and I'm supposed to fall in love very soon with one or the other of them. Oh—and I'm to go on a journey by water too.'

'If I'm the Dark Man,' Pat said, 'who's this fair fella?'

'I don't care for fair fellas,' Lily told him.

'Neither do I,' Pat decided.

The horsemen had gone and the Park all about them was empty.

From time to time the telpher circled above the works yard, a small cabin suspended from a rail, with a trolley which crackled now and then and threw out a cascade of blue sparks. It was almost level with the windows of the boardroom, which occupied the top storey. Watching it as it passed, Yearling wondered what it would be like to drive. What purpose it served he could not remember, although he had been watching it during Board meetings since his youth. Sometimes it broke down, and the driver would climb out on to the roof to adjust the trolley. Some years ago a man had been blown off the roof by a sudden squall of wind. Yearling, who had been watching him throughout a particularly boring meeting, saw him fall and rushed down to help. He found a knot of workmen gathered about a mangled and unrecognisable body. The telpher had remained driverless for most of the afternoon, tiny and inaccessible on its rail above the yard, marooned in mid journey until the riggers worked out a plan to lift another driver to it by means of a hoist chair. The wind tore at the ropes and tossed the chair about, until Yearling stopped watching because apprehension was making him sick. But the new man got there and after an hour or so the telpher was moving about its business once again. Yearling sent twenty pounds to the widow—anonymously. How long ago was that? Twenty years, perhaps.

'You haven't been listening,' his brother-in-law said. Mr. Yearling shifted his gaze from the window. He had been conscious of the voice in the background.

'You joined the Employers' Federation several months ago,' he said. 'There's nothing very new in what you've been saying.'

'I feel it my duty to bring you up to date. There were several important meetings of the Board while you were away shooting.'

'Fishing,' Yearling corrected.

Bullman, controlling his irritation, said: 'I beg your pardon —fishing.'

He was well named, Yearling thought. Deep voice, thick neck, heavy shoulders that were beginning to stoop. When he had married into Morgan & Co. he was already a man of influence in other fields, particularly shipping. The indiscipline of the working class of the city, after years of docility, confused and frightened him. The world of industry, so long stable, so entrenched in its authority, was sliding on its foundations.

'We are going to make a stand against Larkinism,' he said.

'You said that several months ago.'

'A determined stand,' Bullman insisted. 'You see, you haven't been listening. The shipping crisis brought matters to a head.'

'You were beaten by Larkin in the shipping business,' Yearling said. 'You gave everything he asked for. So much for your Federation.'

'We weren't ready then.'

'And are you ready now?'

'More than ready. We've been promised help from the Castle. The police will be used—the military if necessary. We've approached employers in England for financial assistance. They'll help if we call on them.'

Yearling smiled.

'I see you are learning from Larkin. Each for all and all for each. What will be the first step?'

'To outlaw Larkinism. The members of his union will be given the option of resigning from it or being sacked. Those who are not members of the union must give an undertaking never to join it.'

Bullman paused. He was coming to the crucial part.

'Before putting the matter to the Board I made a count of the firms involved. Almost four hundred will take concerted action. The Board was unanimous in giving a solemn pledge.'

'Who is to be the leader of the gallant four hundred?' Yearling asked. He was anticipating the answer and made a quick gamble with himself. A further, prolonged week-end in Connemara if he was right—a ten-pound note to Father O'Connor's fund if he was wrong.

'William Martin Murphy,' Bullman answered.

The undubbed knight. His guess had been correct. He would arrange to go the week-end after next.

'Why are you telling me this?'

'Because as a director you should know what went on while you were away . . . fishing. I also feel under a special obligation. After all, you are my brother-in-law.'

'Thank you,' Yearling said.

He smiled. As a brother-in-law he would hardly count. But as a considerable shareholder he could dissent and embarrass the Board's determination and unanimity.

In the yard below men were working to pile coal into a huge rick. In the houses they fed furnaces with long-handled shovels. How many of them were Larkinites, Yearling wondered? They would resist, of course—that was why police and military must stand by. The telpher glided past the window again, suspended from the arced track. Yearling watched. It would be like being in a balloon—or more accurately, one of those new flying machines. He remembered something Mrs. Bradshaw had mentioned to him a long time before and began to search in his wallet. He found a piece of paper with the name *Robert Fitzpatrick* written on it. The meeting was obviously at an end, so he rose.

'We've a man of that name on the staff,' he said, handing it to Bullman. 'If anything can be done to advance him it has the recommendation of a very dear friend of mine.'

Bullman was surprised, not at the request, but its source. He put the slip of paper under a weight and said, with a cordiality calculated to please:

'We'll be shuffling around the key men to get rid of Larkinites. I'll see that he's considered.'

They went down the stairs together and parted in the ground-floor office, where clerks on high stools, aware of their presence, wrote figures into ledgers with intense concentration. Yearling, left alone, surveyed the scene for some moments, tapping his stick lightly against his knickerbockers, enjoying the tense and artificial silence. He took a paper bag from his pocket and offered it to a bald stooped clerk whom he judged to be the senior.

'Have a Kruger's Soother,' he invited pleasantly. The man gaped at him. Yearling placed the sweet on his desk, took one from the bag for himself, bowed gravely and began to eat it as he went out.

In the morning, when they called to the hospital, the Italian was dead. They stood awhile beside him in the morgue, where he lay all unknowing, his hands joined on his breast. They crossed themselves and said a prayer.

'He won't be playing "Over the Waves" any more,' Hennessy whispered, when the prayer was finished.

'Unless they give him a harp with a handle,' Rashers whispered back.

'We should have brought the monkey.'

'What would we do that for?'

'To see the last of him.'

The sentimental note in Hennessy's voice made Rashers forget the presence of the dead.

'And have him screeching and roaring crying,' he shouted, 'is that what you want? Monkeys is notoriously highly strung and emotional. If he saw your man stretched out there in a late and lamented condition he'd go beresk.'

'Keep your voice down,' Hennessy pleaded, 'remember where you are.'

'When we get back home,' Rashers said, once again whispering, 'don't breathe a word about this in front of the monkey because if he gets word of it at all he'll go off his grub and die of a broken heart.'

They put their hats back on their heads.

'The question is,' Hennessy said as they closed the door of the morgue behind them, 'what are we going to do with the poor brute. And how will we dispose of the barrel-organ?'

It was a problem which occupied them during their journey home. At first Rashers was in favour of keeping both. Providence, with an unusual show of favour, had placed at their disposal an easily mastered instrument and a well-trained animal. It would be a means of livelihood, a self-contained business. He proposed a partnership, in which Hennessy's only responsibility would be to push the barrel-organ—the rest he would attend to personally.

'It's very tempting,' Hennessy admitted.

'We'll be set up for life,' Rashers urged.

'Yes—until the police catch up with us.'

That was the difficulty. The Italian may have said something to the hospital staff. If there was an inquest something might come out. Or the relatives might have the police searching high and low already for the barrel-organ and the monkey.

'It's too much of a risk,' Hennessy decided.

Rashers was forced to agree. There was hardly any way at all of earning an honest penny. The door opened and when you stepped forward with hope—bang—it slammed to again. Now and then, as when he was boilerman, it stayed open for a little while. But never for long. And the older you got, the less often it opened. Soon he would become too old to cope with poverty. What would he do then?

'We'll give it up to the police,' he said. 'Maybe there'll be a reward.'

They brought the monkey and the organ to College Street Station. Rashers recognised the sergeant who had once given him a shilling, Sergeant Muldoon. Often since then he had met him on patrol, and they would stop for a joke and a friendly exchange. Usually he came away a few pence the richer.

'Can you play it?' the sergeant asked, indicating the barrel-organ.

'I never tried,' Rashers evaded. It might not be legal to have borrowed it for a whole day.

'I'd imagine now,' the sergeant said, with a great air of ingenuousness, 'a man of your musical gifts would have little difficulty in mastering the likes of that. I'd nearly be able to knock a tune out of it myself. Hasn't it a handle—like the gramophone?'

Rashers pretended to examine the instrument for the first time.

'It has wheels on it too,' he said finally, 'like the motor car. But that doesn't mean you could drive it to mass of a Sunday.'

Hennessy withdrew a little. The movement caught the sergeant's attention.

'Who's your friend?' he asked suddenly.

Hennessy froze and said: 'Hennessy, Sergeant—Aloysius Hennessy.'

'Better known to his friends and well-wishers as the Toucher,' Rashers provided. He was at ease with the sergeant in any matter that was on the right side of the law.

'I see,' the sergeant acknowledged. His face, Rashers observed, had a grey colour and his body, suspended from once burly shoulders, was thinning. That was unusual in a sergeant. Usually they grew fat and had big, well-nourished bellies. The sergeant was showing age. Policemen, when they could work no longer, were given pensions. That was the great difference.

The sergeant, having thought about it, decided to put the monkey in one of the cells. They accompanied him.

'Would there be a reward, do you think?' Rashers asked.

'There might,' the sergeant said, 'and then again there might not. It depends on the relatives.'

He turned the key in the lock.

'I'm wondering now will I have trouble with *habeus corpus*.'

'Is that one of his Italian relatives?' Hennessy asked.

'It's a conundrum of the law,' the sergeant told him, 'which I never, in all my years, understood properly myself.'

They walked back down the corridor with him and stopped once again beside the barrel-organ. It looked incomplete without the monkey. The sergeant leaned against it.

'It's a funny thing,' he said to Rashers, 'but a young policeman the name of Gallagher, that you may or may not know, reported yesterday evening that he saw yourself playing a yoke like this at the corner of Bachelor's Walk. You were in company, he said, with a man unknown to him.'

'That's very strange,' Rashers said, for want of something better.

'It was probably someone like you,' the sergeant agreed, 'but not you at all.' He brought them to the door.

'Now—off you go—and good luck,' he said.

He stood to watch their passage down the street. The gait of Rashers reminded him—as always—of the little boy dying of meningitis. After a while he went in, turning away not from the street only but from young eyes fixed on him and his own helplessness, from love unable to intervene. Everything in life was alone; his child dying whom he could not help, the brute dog lying with bloodied nose and lolling tongue on the pavement that he had been called on in the course of his duty the day before to shoot. He went inside again and hung the keys on their familiar hook.

'He knew I was using the barrel-organ,' Rashers confided.

'I thought the same,' Hennessy agreed.

'In a way,' Rashers said, 'we have as much right to it as this relative—bloody *habeus corpus*.'

Hennessy shrugged. Blood, he felt, was thicker than water and had legitimate claims. As they turned at last into Chandlers Court, Rashers stopped and said:

'That was *my* cell he put the monkey in.'

Then he began to tell him, not for the first time, of his day in prison that marked the visit of Edward VII.

The blinding rain of a bad Sunday evening kept the three of them housebound. Father O'Sullivan, armed with pen and ink and writing material, entered the sitting room about eight o'clock and found Father Giffley there—a rare occurrence. Father O'Connor, arriving later, was equally surprised at Father Giffley's presence. Knowing an immediate withdrawal would betray uneasiness, he sat down.

'What terrible rain,' he remarked as he did so.

'I've been expecting it all day,' Father O'Sullivan said. He was now writing at the table, but left down his pen to raise his right arm and make a grimace which conveyed pain.

'Rheumatism?'

'Since early morning,' Father O'Sullivan said, 'it's an infallible sign.'

Father Giffley lowered his paper to stare at him.

'A little Kruschen salts, John,' he said, 'as much as will fit on a sixpence. Take it regularly each morning and you'll have no further worries of that kind.'

'You advised me about that before, but the pain goes away after a day or two and I never remember,' Father O'Sullivan confessed.

'Take the Kruschen,' Father Giffley admonished, 'or continue as you are—a walking weathercock.'

Father O'Sullivan smiled, picked up his pen and returned to his work.

After that the atmosphere was easier. The three settled down, great wind gusts sent the rain rattling against the window and made a dull roar in the chimney. But the fire burned brightly and the oil lamps—so disposed that reading or writing did not overtax the eyes—cast a soothing light.

It was a brown room, with heavy upright chairs in black about the great centre table, and heavy, comfortable armchairs, also in black, in an arc about the fire. Father O'Sullivan's biretta for some reason crowned the pile of magazines that stood near the end of the table on his left. The enormous painting of the Crucifixion which hung on one wall was beyond the effective range of the lamps, so that only the white zigzag of a lightning streak above the cross stood out and an oval of grey countenance sagged under its thorny crown. In daylight there was a cobweb interlaced with the crown, Father O'Connor remembered—a real one—too high for the servant's brush. Black letters on a brass plaque beneath said: *Consummatum Est*. On either side in daylight, but not now seen, were the Blessed Mother in a blue mantle, head bowed in grief, arms folded on her bosom; and the disciple beloved of Jesus. Son, behold they mother—mother, behold thy Son. John—same name as O'Sullivan.

The Kruschen worried Father O'Connor. Surely it was intended for the bowels. A little brandy, Giffley had once advised him, but he had refused. A wonder he had not recommended peppermints—his own unvarying physic.

Both prescribed for and prescriber were now lost in concentration, the one writing laboriously, the other reading. Father

O'Connor searched his pocket and found Yearling's letter. He began to read it again.

As a result of a wager with myself, which I had the good fortune to win, I am back here in Connemara. My intention was to fish, but in making the arrangement I overlooked a simple fact—that the fishing season had already closed. So, although I am determined to uphold my undertaking to myself by staying here for the promised duration, my rods are lying unpacked in the bedroom and there is no one left in the hotel to share the turf fire here in the lounge with me except the cat, an animal so overfed in the season on the left-overs of the best salmon and trout that he (perhaps she—cats always baffle me) is a phlegmatic egocentric who sleeps most of the time. What night life is there for a cat in Connemara, especially outside the holiday season? What Can It Do? Being one of the lower animals, not yet advanced sufficiently along Mr. Darwin's evolutionary path, its accomplishments are limited. In centuries to come, I have no doubt, its descendants will vie with each other in the compilation of histories and the elaboration of philosophies, like Anatole France's penguins. Meanwhile it yawns and waits.

Have you read Sketches of the Irish Highlands *by Rev. H. McManus? Do you know of him? I think he may have been a friend of my father's but I am not sure. He was the first missionary of the General Assembly of the Presbyterian Church in Ireland to learn the Irish language in order to spread his particular brand of enlightenment among the Connemara peasantry. I am reading him at present from a mildewed copy which I found in the bookcase here on a wet afternoon some few days ago. How he ever hoped his parsimonious bore of a God could succeed with these naturally gentlemanly and generous people I cannot imagine. I am entirely behind them in their rejection of a Deity disinclined to gaudy images, incantations, Holy Water and plenty of drink.*

Autumn is not so noticeable here in Connemara as elsewhere, I think because there are so few trees (a stone wall is a stone wall, winter or summer). Yet I feel the melancholy of the season just as keenly. The glow of the fire, the smell of the

336

turf smoke, the quality of the light which is now beginning to fail outside the window, all speak as certainly as any scurry of brown and yellow leaves of the turning of the year. Soon they will light the lamps and call me to my meal. Mutton. No possibility whatever of a surprise. In Connemara it is always either salmon or mutton.

Have you seen Bradshaw lately? He and I are not firm friends. When I dared some time ago to suggest that he ought to do something about repairing those tenement houses of his by the railway line, he concluded that I had become an honorary emissary of Mr. Larkin. You should speak to him if you get the opportunity. Some day they'll collapse on the unfortunate tenantry. I know your main concern will not be whether they are killed but whether being killed, they are all in a fit state of saving grace to ascend straight to heaven to fill the vacant places left by Lucifer and his fallen angels, which, as you once so picturesquely explained to me, is the reason why your God creates his populous conglomeration of verminous and underprivileged slum-dwellers. Why can't He make more angels on the spot, instead of taking such a roundabout means of filling the vacant celestial mansions. Look at the trouble and expense he puts good-living and well-to-do Christians to (including our friend Bradshaw) bribing the City and Borough Councillors to stop them serving an order on them to have their wretched hovels made habitable. And look at all the failures, whom he sends to hell to swell the enemy ranks and make Lucifer feel the revolt was well worth it. I was about to ask if you had read Anatole France but I seem to recollect that he is on the Index—Omnia Opera, lock stock and barrel.

Oh dear, I could go on in this vein for many pages, but they have come to tell me my meal is ready. How far away this little place is from your strike-tormented city; Larkin and Syndicalism, Carson and Home Rule, Griffith and his Sinn Fein desperadoes. By the way, did I ever tell you what I heard G. B. Shaw saying at a lecture several months ago in the Antient Concert Rooms, when he was asked what he had to say to the menace of Sinn Fein? He said: 'I have met only one Sinn Feiner since I returned to Dublin. She is a very nice girl.'

337

Despite all this agnosticism, my continued regard and good wishes.

Father O'Connor left the letter down and sighed. It was cynical, like Yearling's conversation, reflecting the attitudes of the authors he so often spoke about: this man France, that man Butler, the sceptic Shaw. The great thing was not to be clever but to have Faith. Faith was a gift from God, freely given, not earned. Without it the human mind questioned even its own efficacy and lost itself in the darkness. The slum-dwellers for whom he expressed concern were richer in real treasures than Yearling, despite his money and his education, for they had Faith and with grace they would merit Heaven. Yet Yearling was a good man, who gave generous financial help when Mrs. Bradshaw approached him for the collections for the poor of St. Brigid's. His combination of generosity and culture could not go unacknowledged by a merciful and forgiving God. Yearling would be rewarded in due season.

The clock above the mantelpiece, a heavy affair, too, in black marble, gave out a single, musical stroke. Father O'Connor rose.

'Are you off?' Father O'Sullivan asked, looking up. It was his form of politeness.

'I have the early mass tomorrow,' Father O'Connor reminded him, 'so it's early to bed and early to rise.' Both smiled. The cliché displeased Father Giffley, who frowned behind his newspaper. When the door had closed he lowered it slowly and said:

'John—be a good fellow and get me my early-to-bed nightcap.'

Father O'Sullivan left what he was doing to get the bottle and a glass. There was a jug of water, which he examined dubiously.

'Would you like me to get you some fresh water?'

'It will do well enough. Sit down and join me.' Father O'Sullivan said he would—a small drop to make him sleep. His arm was still troubling him. Writing with it had not helped.

When the glasses had been filled, Father O'Sullivan protesting at the over-liberal measure which the other poured for him, they raised them ceremoniously to each other and Father O'Sullivan said, without meaning anything more than a customary Dublin greeting: 'The first today.'

'I wish I could say the same,' Father Giffley responded with a sad smile. He looked over at the manuscript which lay open on the table.

'Is it still the same devotional pamphlet—the one about the Holy Family and the humble Catholic home?'

'I am trying to revise it.'

'I once promised to read it for you and failed.'

'A man of your experience,' Father O'Sullivan said, ' . . . I quite understand.'

'I found I couldn't. There are already far too many pious homilies addressed to the poor.'

'I've never worked among well-to-do people. I don't think I'd know what to say to them.'

True. Looking over his glass at the grey face of his curate, Father Giffley thought there were few priests in whom humility and a sort of common or garden holiness were combined to such excellent purpose; he gave and, as admonished in the famous prayer, he did not count the cost; he fought—and did not heed the wounds; he toiled—and did not seek for rest; he laboured and looked for no reward save that of knowing that he did God's Holy Will.

Amen. So be it.

To wear the yoke without complaint. To be busy. Not to raise the eyes too high or too long from the work surrounding you. Not to look inward for too long nor to quest beneath name and occupation for the *you* that had been born hopefully of woman so many years ago. To ask continually Whither am I going? but never Who Am I? for there began the war of individual appetite with circumstances and the sanctions of the community and the Laws of God.

Yet if all refused the challenge to explore, the world would still be flat, suspended on the ageing shoulders of Atlas, or on the tortoise swimming eternally in an eternity of sea.

Revolt was better, even at the risk of damnation. To examine His Universe with the eyes of the critic and His Order with an eye to its improvement. The meek shunned Thought to save their souls; the reckless went forward knowing that a slip might send them to the furnace.

'Thank you, John,' he said, suddenly holding out his glass.

When the other poured gingerly, he raised his voice sharply. 'Don't stint.'

Father O'Sullivan, avoiding the eyes, poured again. He left the bottle on the table. The face disturbed him, its hard, staring eyes, its lips set thinly, the veins thick and blue in the temples.

'And yourself?' Father Giffley invited.

'No, thank you,' Father O'Sullivan said, indicating what was still left in his glass. 'I have more than enough here as it is.'

'Please yourself.'

That afternoon he had walked through the parish. The mood took him after lunch as he stared from the window of his room. At that time the tall, decaying houses, rising against a sky black with cloud, were waiting for the rain to begin. The gloom outside drew him. He went on impulse, without his overcoat or the walking-stick it was his habit to carry. He went through the streets with his hands clasped behind him, noting with a bitterness no longer new to him the signs of deprivation and poverty. Every rotten doorpost and shattered fanlight reflected his own decay. He had a craving for alcohol that made him no better than the dogs and the cats that nosed about the bins and the gutter. His hopes lay littered with the filth and the garbage of the streets. They were responsible, those pious superiors who had planted him in the middle of all this because he was proud and refused to fawn. The others drank afternoon tea and were at one with solid, middle-class people; he had refused to flatter the merchants. The others thought themselves of consequence, my lords the Reverends Pious and Priestly, the publicans' sons from the arsehole of Ireland. Ho!—but vulgarity released pain, you with your silk hats for the respectable; soft, pitiless comfort for the destitute.

It began to rain, great blobs of sooty water that fell reluctantly, disturbing the dust and with it the malignant odours of street and sewer. Then the wind freshened and the rain started heavily, until even the dogs and the cats disappeared and he had the street to himself. He walked alone, coatless, his hands still clenched firmly against the small of his back.

He had been too long in the wasteland, at war with his superiors, deprived of the company of his intellectual equals. Not much, these equals of his, but equals, such as they were, and as such, necessary. Their absence had dragged him down. His pious superiors had anticipated that too. It was part of their plot against him. Had he been stronger, he might have triumphed over his surroundings. If he had less compassion he might have ignored them. Compassion—that was his undoing. He could be selfish and do little or nothing for people for whom nothing could be done anyhow. But he could not be blind, like the others. He felt. He saw. That was more than the Silk Hat Brigade had ever been capable of.

The rain increased until his clothes clung so tightly against his body that it was hard to walk. All their spite hung over him, trapped between rain-soaked houses, leaking roofs, gutter gurgling, wind-tormented streets. As he walked he looked about for shelter, passing door after door endlessly, until above gas-lit windows and frames of blackened paint he saw, reading laboriously through the rain: 'Choice Wines James Gill & Son. And Spirits'. And went in.

He had never been in a public house before and hesitated to find his bearings. The floor was bare wood, covered with a layer of sawdust. Three gas-lamps suspended in a row from the ceiling lit it. At the far end a group of men were in conversation. The man behind the counter had noticed him and stood transfixed with shock.

'A glass of whiskey,' Father Giffley said.

The man recovered a little and said: 'Certainly, Father.'

He went away.

Father Giffley examined the fittings behind the bar. There was an oval mirror, with the words 'Three Swallow Potstill Whiskey' encircling it. From the middle of the oval his face looked back at him. The grey locks of hair were flattened about it by the rain. His clerical collar looked ridiculous. When the barman brought the whiskey he leaned forward and suggested:

'There's a snug at the back, Father.'

'Snug? I don't understand. Snug?'

'A private room.'

'Leave it there,' Father Giffley insisted. The barman left the whiskey on the counter.

'Certainly, Father.'

'Bejasus,' one of the men told the group, 'but it put the wind up me.'

'Why didn't you clatter it?'

'With what might I ask?'

'With your belt.'

'A mad cow coming at me down the gangplank?' the man asked. 'Oh no bejasus—none of that for yours truly.'

The barman moved anxiously towards them.

'What did you do?'

'Jumped into the water.'

'You were right,' another said. 'Better a watery grave than a gory end.'

The thought of his friend taking to the water before the charge of an enraged animal amused one of the company so much that he spluttered over his drink and said :

'Well, Jaysus, Mary and Joseph but that's a good one.'

The barman with signs and whispered admonishments drew their attention. Then they all turned round and lapsed one by one into silence. One of them said sheepishly :

'I beg your pardon, Father.'

Father Giffley removed his eyes from the caricature in the mirror and said :

'Why apologise to me. My name is not Jesus.'

An astonishing thing happened. When he said the name 'Jesus' the men automatically raised their hats. That was habit. He had said the Name. Not at all the same thing as swearing with It. What were they? Dockers, cattle-drovers, seamen back home from voyaging? Dublinmen anyway. The raising of the hats proved it.

He looked again at the caricature; the oval advertisement, the grey, drowned locks, the priestly collar, aware as he did so of the unease which his presence was causing. He was a Catholic priest in a public bar. He was giving scandal. That could be put right.

'I was caught by the rain,' he explained, 'don't let me disturb you.'

After a moment one of them, more courageous than the rest, said heartily. 'Divil the disturb, Father.'

Then he called to the barman :

'Why don't you offer a towel to his reverence. He's soaked to the skin.'

But Father Giffley held up his hand and forbade it.

'This is the best towel of them all,' he said, finishing the whiskey. 'And now,' he added, 'give me another for my journey, so that I won't take pneumonia. And give the men here whatever they fancy.'

They protested, but he insisted. They had a consultation of some sort while they waited for the drinks. At the end one man left. Then the drinks came and they vied with each other to be agreeable to him, saying what a terrible evening it was and how easy it would be to take a sickness out of such a wetting and how wise he had been to take the right kind of precaution. They told him they were dockers. He noticed the buttons in their coats.

'Followers of Mr. Larkin, I see,' he remarked. They said they were. Then, to their surprise he said firmly : 'You do right.'

At that moment the door opened and the man who had left earlier reappeared. He was now almost as wet as Father Giffley.

'Did you get it?' they asked him.

'It's outside the door,' he said.

'What's this?' Father Giffley asked.

'He went to find you a cab, Father, it'll save you another drenching.'

For the first time in several lonely years someone had done him a kindness. Father Giffley was moved.

'I am extremely obliged and grateful.'

'For nothing, Father,' the men assured him, 'you're more than welcome.'

They saw him to the cab, which brought him home to a warm bath and a change of clothes. That was why he had taken the unusual course of using the general sitting room. His jacket and trousers were drying at the fire in his own room.

'I think my presence here made Father O'Connor uneasy,' he said.

'He always retires early when he has the early mass,' Father O'Sullivan explained.

'That is not what I meant. He forgot this.'

Father Giffley rose and picked up Yearling's letter from the arm of the chair that Father O'Connor had been using. He took it back to his own chair with him; then, holding it up, he asked: 'His Kingstown friends—do you think?'

Father O'Sullivan avoided reply by rising to put the whiskey bottle back in the press.

'Leave it where it is,' Father Giffley commanded sharply.

'I am sorry,' Father O'Sullivan said. 'I thought you were going to bed.'

'We'll see what his friends have to say first,' Father Giffley said. 'Listen.'

As he deliberately opened the letter Father O'Sullivan advanced quickly towards him and said: 'Please—I beg you not to.'

Father Giffley looked up at him. 'You will sit down, John. Over there, opposite me. Do as I tell you.'

Knowing there would be a scene if he refused, Father O'Sullivan did so. As the other read the letter aloud, deliberating on it sentence by sentence, he gripped the arms of his chair and strove to keep the horror from his face. Opposition of any kind would precipitate a storm. His parish priest, he realised, was very near to madness.

In the morning, when Father O'Connor and Father O'Sullivan were at breakfast, Father Giffley joined them briefly. He took the letter from his pocket and pushed it towards Father O'Connor.

'Your property, I believe.'

Father O'Connor stared at the pages; Father O'Sullivan lowered the cup he had been raising to his lips.

'I am sorry your friend finds difficulty with the doctrine of the Fall,' Father Giffley said, 'his sympathies otherwise are admirable.'

He turned to Father O'Sullivan. The skin of his face was blotched and taut, a pulse beat in the black vein which showed as a knot in his left temple.

'Of France I know very little,' he continued, 'but Darwin, I believe, holds that we are descended from the apes. Isn't that so, John?'

Father O'Sullivan remained frozen, with nothing at all to say, until at last Father Giffley turned away from him and went to the door, where he paused and said generally:

'It is possible—I think it eminently possible.'

The door closed. They looked at each other.

'He read it,' Father O'Connor said, 'he read my letter.'

'The man is not well.'

'My private correspondence—how dare he!'

'He's become very odd. You must try to understand him.'

'I understand him very well,' Father O'Connor said.

'Father Giffley is sick.'

Father O'Connor rose angrily and pushed back his chair.

'A drunkard,' he said, 'who hates me.'

He had almost reached the door when Father O'Sullivan's quiet voice stopped him. 'Your letter, Father.'

Once again he had forgotten it. It lay on the tablecloth where Father Giffley had thrown it. This second oversight embarrassed him. He put the letter in his pocket without thanking Father O'Sullivan.

'I am beginning to consider seriously what I should do,' he said.

'Forgive him,' Father O'Sullivan suggested gently.

'It is no longer a question of forgiveness only,' Father O'Connor said bitterly. 'There are other considerations.'

He closed the door.

CHAPTER 8

IT was raining. Mulhall, taking his breakfast by candlelight, heard the sprinkling of drops against the window as
he ate.

'Is it bad?' he asked.

His wife went over to peer out. In windows down the length
of Chandlers Court the light of candles wavered above a pitch
black street. A squall rattled the window pane as she looked,
taking her by surprise.

'It'll be bad enough,' she said.

He filled his pipe, feeling the cold of the morning in his
fingers. It would be two hours to the first of the light and by
that time he would have the horse yoked and the cart loaded for
the first delivery of the day.

'Wear the sack about your shoulders,' she advised him.

She was now on her knees in front of the fire, preparing to
light it.

He puffed at his pipe.

'Call Willie,' she said, busy.

'In a minute.'

He was thinking of the day ahead; yoking up, driving through
wintry streets, hoisting wet sacks and labouring up and down
stairs with them. He was in no humour.

'There are times,' he said, 'when I think Hennessy above has
more sense than any of us. He only works when the weather is
fine.'

'Call Willie for me, like a good man,' she urged.

'It's too early to call him.'

'No it isn't,' she said. 'He wants to practise for half an hour before he goes out.'

'Wouldn't you think he had enough of it last night,' he grumbled.

He took the candle and went into the small room at the back. His son was deeply asleep. On a chair beside the bed was the music he had been practising the night before. On top of the music lay his fife.

'Willie,' he called.

There was no stir. He leaned down until the candle lit up the sleeping form. The boy was nineteen now, tall. If all went well he would be as big in the body as well. He shook him by the shoulder.

'Get up. The fire is lit and your breakfast is ready.'

The boy sat up, shaking his head to get rid of the sleep.

'Playing that damn thing all night—and then not able to stir in the morning,' Mulhall grumbled to his wife when he came back to the main room.

'He's anxious about the competition,' she said.

It was to be held in the Queen's Theatre that night—a Grand Fife and Drum Band Competition. They were going together to it. She would have her husband's navy serge suit laid out airing for him when he came home, so that he could change quickly. She herself would wear her best dress, and in addition Mrs. Fitzpatrick might have something nice to lend her. They were friendly and she would call over during the course of the morning to enquire. The thought made her happy.

'Be home early,' she told him. 'it's not often we get out together.'

He pinned the sack about his shoulders and took his lunch parcel from the table.

'Have you everything?'

She had asked the same question every morning of their lives—on weekdays as he went out to work, on Sundays when he made ready for mass. As he settled his cap on his head he smiled at her and said: 'When me hat is on, me house is thatched.'

But as he went down the steps his moment of good humour

left him. He was dispirited and reluctant to face the day, and wondered if he was starting a cold. The hall smelled dankly; on the steps the wind lifted up the sack so that he had to take his hands from his pockets to hold the ends in position. He bent his head against the rain and went down into the street. There were footsteps in the darkness ahead of him and behind him, echoing with the lonely sound of early morning. They were his mates and fellow-workers, a multitude moving through a dark dawn to earn their bread. In all the meaner streets of the city they were turning out to face the winter day.

In Brunswick Street, where the lighting was better, and he could see as well as hear the hurrying figures, a placard outside the Queen's Theatre announced the evening's attraction:

'Tonight
Grand Fife & Drum
Band Con . . .'

That was as much as he could read. Rain had loosened the lower portion, which made a flapping noise in the wind. Was it 'concert' or 'contest'? Not that it mattered. The tickets were at home and he knew all about it. No wonder, with Willie practising night after night for a full week.

Further down the street the Antient Concert Rooms promised music of a different kind. Holding the sack ends across his chest like a cloak he stopped to read:

'Tonight (Friday) 13th December 1912
Dublin Philharmonic Society
Hymn of Praise
Athalie
(Mendelssohn)
Conductor Charles G. Marchant Mus.D.
Madame Nora Bonel
Miss Edith Mortier (Feis Gold Medallist)
J. J. Maltby (Principal Tenor, Chester Cathedral)
Full Band and Chorus

Prices : Reserved & Numbered seats 4s.
Balcony 2s.
Area 1s.
Booking at Cramer's, Westmoreland Street'

Swanky stuff. Women in white and men in evening dress, reading the words out of books. He had seen them once, though not in full regalia, when he went in during a rehearsal to ask about delivering a load of coal. He had stood at the back, wondering whom to approach, while the voices of the chorus and the orchestra filled the hall with music. That was not in the Antient Concert Rooms, but in a hall attached to a convent school. A nun told him to sit and wait until the interval, but he felt self-conscious and slipped out again when she left him. Despite the convent, he felt they were a very Protestant-looking crowd.

A cold wind raked the quayside, driving the rain in squalls. Above the loading yard the windows of Mr. Doggett's office and those flanking it were blank. It was too raw and early as yet for the owner and his henchmen. The air in the stables, comfortingly warm, smelled strongly of horse urine. The stableman greeted him. He was tossing hay by the light of a paraffin lamp, a shadowy presence in its inadequate glow.

'Seasonable weather.'

It was seasonable, all right, and set now to go on being seasonable through January and February and early March, the most godforsaken months of the year.

'I thought she was going lame on me yesterday,' Mulhall said, stroking the mare.

'A little stiffness,' the stableman said, 'nothing much. I gave her a rub.'

'Rheumatism, maybe,' Mulhall suggested.

'A twinge' the stableman said, 'she's only flesh and blood— like the rest of us.'

Sure of a bed and a bit to eat while she could work, Mulhall thought, and a bullet to end it all when she was past labour. If she didn't die in harness, like many another. The stableman started to cough, checked it, then began more violently. He had to lean on the rake until the fit passed. He was a long, thin man with a haggard face and consumptive frame, who lived on the premises. In the daytime he cleaned out the stables and in the evenings he examined the horses for any signs of injury or ill-health. If an animal was sick he stayed up at night to tend it. His father and his grandfather before him had done the same thing in their time.

Mulhall continued to stroke the horse.

'Less than a fortnight now to Christmas,' the stableman said, when he had got his breath back.

'You'll be going abroad for it, no doubt,' Mulhall joked. The neck muscles of the horse were quivering delicately under his hand.

'I was talking to the missus about that,' the stableman said, 'she has a fancy for the Riviera.'

'My own was thinking of one of them spas,' Mulhall said.

'Right enough,' the stableman said, after a moment of consideration, 'you meet a nicer class of people altogether at a spa.'

'That's my own experience too,' Mulhall agreed.

'Did you think of Lisdoonvarna—or must it be abroad?'

'Abroad,' Mulhall said. 'Herself always insists on the sea trip.'

'Well—have a nice time,' the stableman said, beginning once again to rake up the straw. But as Mulhall was leading the horse across the yard another thought struck him and he shouted after him: 'And don't forget to send us a postcard.'

Mulhall yoked up and went over to the hatch for the bundle of dockets which would make up his delivery duties for the day. He checked through them. They were all city business premises, which meant very little stair-climbing, a relief. Then he noticed that there seemed to be less of them than usual.

'Is this the lot?' he asked.

'There's one more,' the clerk said. 'It's a very special one so I kept it separate.'

He handed out another docket. It was for a house about six miles away, on the other side of Phoenix Park. It had the word 'Priority' inscribed and underlined on the top corner.

'Holy Jaysus!' Mulhall exclaimed when he saw it.

'Some friend of Doggett's,' the clerk speculated.

'It'll take the whole morning.'

'I know. That's why I've given you less of the others.'

It would mean a long slow journey across the city and by the high, unsheltered road that led through the Park. On a fine day he would have welcomed it; today it meant freezing with inactivity and being soaked to the skin. Mulhall stuffed the dockets into his pocket and went across the yard again, this time to load up.

The long mirror of the wardrobe showed her the transformation. The dark coat, with the pleated cape at the shoulders, completely hid her house clothes. The feather on the black velvet hat nodded at her from the glass, with such an air of elegance that she became uneasy. It was too good for her. It would embarrass her husband. She said so to Mary, who stood behind, admiring her.

'Nonsense,' Mary said, 'it looks just right.' She turned to Fitz for confirmation.

'He won't know you for style,' Fitz said encouragingly.

Mary, busy helping Mrs. Mulhall to adjust the hat with the feather, asked him to look in the box on the sideboard for a white medallion which was yet another of the odds and ends Mrs. Bradshaw had sent to her over the past several months. The articles came regularly; now a chair, or curtains perhaps, cast-off clothes that were far better than any she could have bought in the second-hand shops. The latest gifts were two ornamental dogs which now stood on the mantelpiece on either side of the clock Pat had given them on their wedding day. Mrs. Mulhall had noticed them the moment she called to borrow the coat.

'You have everything,' she said, looking round a little enviously at the comfortable room.

Fitz found a cameo brooch among the litter of buttons and safety pins.

'Wear it on your blouse,' Mary said to Mrs. Mulhall, 'it will look very nice.'

The older woman hesitated. It was one thing to be clean and

tidy, but another to dress above your station. The brooch was meant for a lady.

'I couldn't,' she protested, 'it wouldn't be right.'

But in the end she took it away with her. It was a long time since she had been to a theatre. It would be a long time again.

She left the clothes in her bedroom and put on her shawl to shop for Willie's lunch. She wore it over her head and shoulders, holding it tight under her chin with her hands. It was Friday so she bought herrings. When a carter drove past her, huddled against the cold and wet of the morning, she was sorry for him and thought of her own husband. Bernie was a big man. He was strong. But he was not getting any younger. Strength was no use against the wettings and the colds of winter. You needed youth as well. When she got home, before she started to prepare the dinner for her son, she took her husband's suit from the cupboard and spread it in front of the fire, which she built up with reckless extravagance, until its glow showed on each wall of the room. His clothes would be aired and warm for him when he came home. Then she peeled potatoes. That too, made the day unusual. Normally the men did not get home until evening. But today Willie was taking the afternoon off to attend a final band practice before the competition. She set the table for him and prepared the pan. It was donkey's years, she told herself, since she had done that in the middle of the day.

'What did you think of her?' Mary asked.

'Who?' Fitz said absently. He was taking his dinner before going to work.

She sighed and said: 'Mrs. Mulhall—of course.'

'I thought she looked very nice,' he said.

'She'll enjoy her little outing.'

'So will I,' Fitz said. 'I've been listening to those same three tunes on the fife for the past six weeks. How Bernard Mulhall sticks it I don't know.'

'Willie is their son. That makes all the difference,' Mary said.

She took away his plate and poured tea into a mug she had bought for him when she was staying with her father. It had the words 'A present from Cork' engraved on it. He looked at the inscription and then at the rain beating against the window and thought how long ago that had been. She had returned in July, and after that it had been their best summer together in their four years of marriage. Steady work and the occasional assistance from Mrs. Bradshaw made them modestly comfortable. Having the second-hand pram they got down most Sundays with the children to Sandymount Strand. There must have been wet days, but he could not now remember them. He could only remember blue skies and level stretches of sand. If the tide was fully ebbed it took half an hour to reach the edge of the sea, and when you turned around the houses along the coast road were tiny with distance, and the beauty of the mountains of Dublin and Wicklow encircling the bay would take your breath away. Even now the thought of that strand moved him. He had played on it as a child, and many a long evening he had walked across it from the Half Moon Swimming Club, a young man made melancholy by the breadth of a summer sunset, or perhaps passing the time by trying to count the lights that had begun to appear through the dusk along the coast road.

'Cork by the Lee,' he bantered, taking the mug.

'Caherdermott's on the Lee too,' she said, 'but it's only a small stream you could wade across.'

'So is the Liffey near Sally Gap.'

'Where's Sally Gap?'

'In the mountains. We'd need bicycles to get there.'

He used to cycle there too in the summers of long ago. Once he had lost his way and an old man who lived alone in a cottage made him have tea and bread and butter and boiled eggs for both of them. It was strange, all the memories of summer a mug with 'Present from Cork' on it could call up. He told Mary about it as he finished the tea, but it didn't sound very interesting. Then he took his supper parcel and went out to work, meeting Willie Mulhall on the way. Willie had on a bandsman's hat and wore a patent leather strap across one shoulder like a Sam Browne. The fife was sticking out of his pocket.

'Good luck tonight,' he said, as they parted in the street.

'We'll need it,' Willie said fervently. He was nearly nineteen now. Competitions were important.

'There's Willie Mulhall with the cap on him,' Hennessy said. He was sitting in the basement with Rashers and could see the street above through a section of the window that the cardboard was not wide enough to cover.

'What cap?'

'The bandsman's cap.'

'Bandsman how-are-you,' Rashers said, letting a great spit into the home-made brazier that stood in the fireplace. It was an old bucket pierced with holes and full now of glowing charcoal he had gathered laboriously from the beach the day before. It was to be found along the high-tide mark when the water had receded, especially after stormy weather.

'That was a wathery one,' he added, as the spit continued to sizzle among the protesting coals.

'You nearly put the bloody thing out,' Hennessy reproved.

'I can't abide amateurs,' Rashers said.

'There's some band competition on,' Hennessy explained, 'and he's been practising for weeks. I used to hear him as I came in and out. He was talking to me about it.'

'I know,' Rashers said, 'going over and over a couple of scraps of tunes, with music stuck up in front of him in case he'd forget. I never had to do that '

'You have the head for it,' Hennessy flattered, 'a memory plus a natural aptitude.'

'That's what you need,' Rashers agreed, 'that's the difference between the amateur and the professional. The amateur has to have his music—but the professional plays by ear. Supposing, every time I went to play at a race meeting, I had to stick a music stand up in front of me, what'd happen?'

Hennessy smiled. 'The crowd would get a right laugh out of you.'

'They'd knock the whole shooting gallery over every time they rushed to the rails.'

'Can you read music yourself?' Hennessy asked.

'I don't have to read music,' Rashers said, 'isn't that my point.'

'What I mean is—did you ever learn how to read music?'

Rashers felt he was being pinned down.

'In a class of a way,' he evaded.

'Who learned you?' Hennessy persisted.

'How do you mean—who learned me?'

'Who was your teacher?'

'I taught myself.'

Hennessy rooted from pocket to pocket until he found a collection of cigarette butts. He offered one to Rashers, who made a paper spill and inserted it into one of the holes in the bucket. The butt was so small that Rashers had difficulty trying to light it. He growled suddenly and slapped at his beard.

'Jaysus,' he said, 'I'm in flames!'

'What's wrong with you?'

'Me beard went on fire.'

Hennessy frowned, wrinkled his nose and sniffed.

'It did,' he said, 'I can smell it.' He took the butt from Rashers, lit it and handed it back to him.

'It's a complicated thing—music,' he pursued, when Rashers had drawn a few pulls without any further accident. 'Willie Mulhall was trying to explain it to me. He says there's seven notes, called A.B.C.D.E.F.G.'

'There is,' Rashers said, 'and a hell of a lot more. What about H.I.J.K.L.M.N. and all those?'

'He didn't mention those ones at all,' Hennessy said.

'Of course he didn't mention them,' Rashers said, 'because he doesn't know them. Them amateur bands never teaches them further than G. But a professional like myself wouldn't get very far with seven notes. Wait till I show you.'

He took the Superior Toned Italian Flageolet from his pocket, blew through it to clear it of fluff, and he played a chromatic scale in two octaves.

'How many notes was that?' he asked when he had finished.

'I didn't count them,' Hennessy confessed, 'but it was nearer twenty-seven than seven.'

'And that's without the help of a bandsman's hat,' Rashers boasted.

'Natural aptitude,' Hennessy repeated, convinced. His admiration was genuine. He thought it a perfect example of the Divine principle of Compensation. Rashers had been afflicted with a bad arm and a bad leg, but God had thrown in the gift of music as a make-measure.

'Play us something,' he invited. Rashers shook his head in refusal, but almost immediately changed his mind. He fingered a few notes thoughtfully, then he began a long, slow improvisation, decorating the air with frequent shakes and trills. Hennessy, staring into the brazier, thought it sounded very sad. The wind was driving the rain once again against the cardboard in the window. He could feel the cold of it on his back, although the fire was hot on his face and hands. There was no fire in his own flat upstairs, but the children had gone out to search for cinders and sticks and in due course, he hoped, would come back with something. Winter was a bad time always. For a whole week now he had searched for odd jobs but without success. In another week perhaps, when the Christmas spirit began to stir in the hearts of those who had the giving of it, there would be something. Christmas usually brought him a bit of luck.

The basement was in semi-darkness, partly because cardboard occupied such a large part of the window, partly because of the rainy skies.

'That was very nice,' he said when Rashers had finished. 'What's it called?'

'It's not called anything, because I was making it up as I went along,' Rashers said.

'Composing?'

'Following my own thoughts,' Rashers qualified. Then he said:

'What's young Mulhall doing when he's not suffering from musical delusions?'

'He works as a messenger boy in the despatch department of the Independent Newspapers.'

'Hairy oul messenger boy,' Rashers said.

'I expect he'll get the push one of these days. They have to at a certain age.'

'He won't knock a living out of music anyway,' Rashers said. But almost immediately he felt he was being over-severe. He gave a great sigh.

'What is he, when all's said and done, only a boy. It's all before him.'

Hennessy approved the change to tolerance.

'Live and let live,' he said.

'You're right,' Rashers said. Then he repeated it. 'You're right.'

Unanimity reigned. There was no use in rancour, they both now felt. Be patient. Endure. Willie Mulhall was only a little less advanced on the road to infirmity and loneliness and God knows what tribulation.

'Play something else,' Hennessy prompted.

Rashers, after an interval of thought, complied, resuming the meandering air with its trills and turns while Hennessy, staring into the red coals, let his mind wander. They had sat like this on another occasion, in the boiler room under St. Brigid's Church, he recollected, drinking port and eating turkey and ham. That was around the Christmas time too. No, after it, he now remembered. Rashers was misfortunate to lose a good job like that. He had thought of going to the parish priest and applying for it himself, but as he considered it, it began to seem a traitorous sort of thing to do. Rashers, rightly or wrongly, felt he had been dealt with harshly. It would be disloyal to offer to work in his place. But Rashers was a stubborn and bitter oul oddity too, refusing to chance the effect of an apology, refusing even to go to St. Brigid's for mass. They said the parish priest was kindly enough, although a bit abrupt. He could have gone to him. But no. Pride.

It would have been nice to walk in through the door and say: I've landed a steady, respectable job. Seasonable, but steady while it's there. With the clergy. That would impress. The clergy. As boilerman. St. Brigid's. She would respect him then . . . as she used. You could make a career out of a job like that if you minded it. Aloysius Hennessy, Boilerman to St. Brigid's.

'A nice morning, Mr. Hennessy.'

'A lovely morning, ma'am, thanks be to God.' And then, when he had passed, but was not quite out of earshot: 'Who's that, Alice?'

'Who?'

'The man in the overalls you just said hello to?'

'Oh, that's Aloysius Hennessy, the boilerman from the church.'

The charcoal had grown so hot that the sides of the bucket glowed with a pinkish colour. He turned up his collar against the draught at his back. Firelight and meandering music interweaving in the half-light drew him dreaming into their labyrinth. He heard her voice remotely. He heard it a number of times before he realised with a shock she was in the room beside him.

'So this is where you are.'

It was his wife, arms on her hips, a small, emaciated woman with a strident voice. The music had stopped.

'Idling and gossiping while your children go hungry.'

'A few words with a good neighbour and a friend, Ellen,' he said. 'I was on my way up in a minute or two.'

She began to scream at him.

'A nice article I married. Sitting on his arse while he should be looking for work.'

'I searched high up and low down,' Hennessy said earnestly, almost in tears. 'I'm going to try again in the evening.'

'You will. When every gate is closed and they're all gone home for the day.'

Her voice was so loud that the dog began to bark.

'And this article beside you,' she said, referring to Rashers. She turned her anger fully on him.

'You're no better than he is,' she shouted at him. 'There's a pair of you well matched.'

Rashers began to rise to his feet. He did so, as always, with difficulty because of his leg. He was stiff from sitting and had to hold on to the fireplace for support. He stared at her and she moved back a little, afraid of him; afraid of his eyes, his unkempt beard, his infirmity.

'Ma'am,' Rashers said, 'he's your husband and I suppose he has to listen to you. I don't. Now clear off out of my premises and conduct your barney on your own battlefield.'

'Ellen,' Hennessy pleaded, 'we'll go upstairs and leave Mr. Tierney in peace.'

'That's what you'll do, ma'am,' Rashers said, 'because if you delay another second I'll set the dog on you.'

'You would too—you bloody oul cripple.'

'Rusty,' Rashers called.

The dog came to his side.

'Ellen,' Hennessy appealed, 'leave when you're asked.' He was distressed and took her by the arm, but she pushed him away.

'Bloody oul cripple,' she screamed.

Rashers raised his good arm threateningly above his head and immediately the dog snarled.

'Jesus,' she said, in terror of its bared teeth.

'Go with her,' Rashers told Hennessy. He was holding himself very straight. His anger and hatred made his beard stiff and his eyes malignant. She backed through the door, Hennessy following. When they began to climb the stairs Rashers shouted after her:

'Blame God for the cripple part of it—not Rashers Tierney.'

His voice set the dog barking furiously.

'Do you hear me, ma'am,' Rashers shouted after her again, knowing she was terrified to answer. 'The cripple is God's handiwork. Criticise Him.'

He heaved violently against the door with his shoulder so that it slammed. Then he leaned against it, trembling with rage.

'Once upon a time,' he said to the dog, 'that was a comely young girl with a gentle voice. She was all pink and milky white. Now she's as yellow as a drain.'

His rage overwhelmed him once more. He jerked open the door and bawled up the stairs.

'Do you hear what I said, you consumptive oul bitch—you're as yellow as a drain.' His voice beat on wall and ceiling. It carried his anguish through all the passageways of the house.

The rain became heavy sleet when he reached the Park, and the road climbed until there was no shelter from the gale, which drove the sleet against him until his hands were locked about the reins with cold, and the flakes took a long time to melt on his eyelids and left him travelling blindly. When at last he reached shelter he found he had either forgotten, or lost, his lunch. The load was delivered and the docket marked 'Priority' signed without anyone in the house offering him a cup of tea. But a tip of sixpence had been left for him. He was tempted to spend it on something hot when he got back into the city. He resisted. It would provide a treat tonight for his wife when they went to the theatre. He worked through his city loads until three o'clock and returned to the loading yard to find his lunch parcel waiting for him at the checker's office.

'The stableman found this after you'd pulled out,' the clerk said, 'you left it behind you.'

Mulhall took it without saying thanks. He was too tired.

'There's one more load for you,' the clerk said, 'a near one this time—Morgan & Co.'

'Nothing after that?'

'Nothing at all.'

An early finish would suit him down to the ground. He stuck his lunch in his pocket. It would be better to get loaded and complete the job and make for home. He could sit in comfort at the fire.

'Here goes,' he said, his mood brightening for the first time since morning. He delayed to light his pipe before leaving the shelter of the office. A smoke would help to keep his hunger at bay.

The winter dusk was settling as he passed through the gates and into the yard of Morgan & Co. It was large, with gas-lamps at intervals which a man was lighting with a rod.

'Single load,' he said to the gateman.

'That'll be for office use,' the gateman answered.

'I know,' Mulhall said. A single load was always for the fires in the offices. For some reason they liked to keep their office heating expenditure separate.

'You know where to leave it.' It was a statement, not a question.

'I do,' Mulhall said. He had been delivering to Morgan's most of his life. But when he pulled up outside the office block the caretaker stopped him from carrying the sacks through the hall-way.

'There's a Board meeting on up above,' he explained. 'They'll be coming down any minute.'

Mulhall understood. The passageway was unusually spick and span. It would not do if the departing directors found it marked with a trail of coal-dust.

'Where will I leave it?'

'I'll show you,' the caretaker said. He led him to an open space by the further wall of the building. Then he got three men to give a hand.

'Is Bob Fitzpatrick on shift?' Mulhall asked, when the unloading was completed.

'He's in No. 2 House,' the caretaker said. Then, conspiratorially he asked: 'Union business?'

'That's right,' Mulhall said.

'Good stuff,' the caretaker approved. 'We'll keep the Red Flag flying. I'll get him for you.'

'Tell him I'll wait for him beside the new mechanical hoist.'

There was accommodation beside it for tethering horses. He would be less conspicuous there.

The men working at the hoist recognised him and hailed him. Since his gaol sentence he was one of their leaders, a militant Larkinite. He acknowledged with a wave of his hand. Communication was too difficult. They worked on a platform about the machine. Steel ropes, biting into the grooves of great wheels, kept an endless chain of steel buckets moving, charged with coal on their upward journey, empty and ready to be refilled as they descended. The noise of rattling steel was continuous.

Mulhall heard his name being called again and peered for some moments through the dusk and the drizzling rain before fixing on a man at the winch who was beckoning to him. He climbed on to the platform and went across to him. It was a man named O'Mahony.

'How's tricks?' Mulhall said.

'I have a bit of news for you about the Tram Company,' the man said, 'I can't tell it to you here because it's a long story, but

I'd like to meet you outside and have a talk with you. Are you free tonight?'

'Not tonight,' Mulhall said, 'I'm going to the Queen's with the missus. How about tomorrow night?'

'I'll see you at Liberty Hall,' O'Mahony agreed.

'Can you give me the gist of it now?'

The Tram Company was of very special interest. William Martin Murphy, its chairman, had refused to meet Larkin.

'I heard the tram men will be invited by the management to a secret meeting and they'll be bribed to leave the union. It was all discussed in a certain house.'

'How did you hear this?'

'I can't tell you now, but it's reliable.'

'How reliable?'

'It's from my own sister—she's in service.'

'Good man,' Mulhall said, and turned to go.

The man, pleased with his approval, grinned and stepped back towards the wheel. It was a careless movement that brought him too close to it. He stumbled against it, threw out his arms to find balance and shouted. Mulhall ran back and found him groaning with pain. His right arm was pinned firmly between the steel rope and the winch, which, despite the obstruction, continued very slowly to rotate, gripping the arm more and more tightly as it did so. Mulhall threw all his weight against it and shouted for help. No one seemed to hear. The buckets continued to rattle as they descended and the slack rope, no longer being drawn in by the winch, began to pay out about the platform. Mulhall, exerting all his strength, kept the winch from moving and shouted again. No one responded. The dusk had grown deeper, the rain heavier, the jingling of buckets seemed to increase every moment.

'Jesus,' the man beside him said. Mulhall's strength was failing and the winch had moved a fraction more.

'Switch off,' he shouted, 'switch her off.'

Fitz, arriving a moment later, found Mulhall agonised with effort.

'Tell them to switch her off,' Mulhall said to him. Fitz went to the middle of the platform and shouted up to the control cabin. At first they failed to understand. Then the message reached them. The buckets ceased to move. The wheels stopped. There was silence. The other men gathered about the winch and forced it backwards until the rope slackened and the man's arm was free. They took him down from the platform.

'Are you all right, Bernie?' Fitz asked Mulhall.

'Gameball,' Mulhall said. He leaned against the winch. Every muscle in his back ached; his lungs laboured for air.

'Rest a bit,' Fitz advised. He went down to examine O'Mahony. The arm was badly bruised but otherwise it was sound. Somebody shouted down from the cabin above and a voice shouted back.

'All clear now. Start away.'

The sound of the buckets beginning to move again drew Fitz's attention. He looked back at the platform. What he saw horrified him. Mulhall had moved away from the winch and was swaying with exhaustion. The winch, with no weight dragging against it, was hauling in the slack rope that lay in coils about the platform at a pace that increased each second. Fitz saw the danger and shouted out: 'Bernie—watch the ropes. Jump.'

Mulhall straightened and looked out at him. Fitz shouted again. It was too late. The loop of steel rope that Mulhall was standing in rode up about his legs at a terrifying speed, tightened, and pulled through. When Fitz reached Mulhall he was lying in blood.

'What happened, Fitz?'

'Lie still,' Fitz said. But Mulhall raised himself with a great effort and saw lying beside him his own dismembered feet. They had been amputated from just below the knees.

'Lie back,' Fitz said gently. He took off his coat and began to tear his shirt. With another man he made a tourniquet for each leg. They wound them as tight as their strength allowed. They knelt there in the rain, under arc lamps that the men had rigged up, holding on doggedly until the ambulance arrived, and Mulhall, now unconscious, was carried away. Fitz picked up the two feet, grotesque and horrible, and wrapped them in a sack. An ambulance man took them from him. When they had gone Fitz leaned against the side of the platform, shivering.

'Are you all right?' a strange voice asked him, very gently.

'In a moment,' Fitz said. Suddenly his stomach turned over and he was violently and repeatedly sick. A hand gripped him by the shoulder and when the bout of sickness had exhausted itself the same strange voice said:

'Where do you live?'

Fitz automatically gave his address.

'I have a motor car at the gate. I'll take you home.'

Fitz looked round and found his companion was Yearling.

'I've to finish my shift.'

'Nonsense,' Yearling said, 'you will come with me.'

He led Fitz down the yard. In the car he found that Fitz was trembling and produced a silver hip flask.

'Take some of this,' he said, 'good stuff for shock.' Then he gave the address to the driver, who said he would need directions.

'Yearling is the name—I'm a director.'

'You're very kind,' Fitz said.

'It was a dreadful accident. How did it happen?'

Fitz described it as they drove. As he talked he realised it would never have happened only for the fool who had signalled the cabin men to restart the machine. But he said nothing of this to Yearling, in case it might implicate one of the men. The damage was done. Mulhall, whether he died or lived, was finished. At Chandlers Court he got out, and thanked Yearling again.

'Never mind that,' Yearling said. 'Have a rest when you go in. And don't come to work tomorrow. I'll see you don't lose anything on that account.'

When he got in Mary knew already. Word had been brought and the house from top to bottom was astir with the news.

'I was just going over to Mrs. Mulhall,' Mary said, 'she'll need somebody with her.'

'I'll go with you for a moment,' he said.

They knocked on the door and a quiet voice said, 'Come in.
She was sitting at the table, dry-eyed and shocked. On the bed in the corner lay the clothes Mary had lent her earlier in the

day. At the fire, spread out to air on two kitchen chairs, were Mulhall's good suit and a clean shirt, awaiting his return. She rose as Mary came across to her and the two women embraced.

'My poor Bernie,' Mrs. Mulhall said in a whisper, 'my poor, darling Bernie.'

She began to cry. Mary held her tightly. There was no other comfort she could offer.

Over a fortnight later, on New Year's Eve, while Mulhall in hospital still hovered between life and death, Fitz came home with news that he had been made a foreman. Mary knew it was Mr. Yearling who had done it and that it was Mrs. Bradshaw's influence. She spent a long night writing a letter of thanks. Fitz went up to the hospital to see Mulhall. Carrington, who had been promoted to superintendent and whose place Fitz was filling, had said to him:

'You'd be well advised to leave the union. It's no longer in your own interest to meddle about with Larkinism.'

'Thanks for the tip,' Fitz said, 'but I'm not opting out now.'

'Well, keep quiet about it anyway,' Carrington said. 'I'm not trying to get at you. This is just a friend's advice.'

'I know that,' Fitz said, 'there's no misunderstanding between us.'

He was allowed in briefly to see Mulhall, who was asleep. He peeped behind the screens at the great body that would march in no more processions and battle no more through cordons of police. He would never let down the trust of that ageing and wounded man.

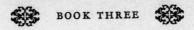

BOOK THREE

1913—1914

CHAPTER I

CHRISTMAS brought Hennessy a little work, a job as porter to a butcher. Rashers saw him pushing a delivery bicycle through the streets. It had 'A. Rattigan—Choice Meats' written on the enormous basket in front. He was not very expert at bicycle-riding and the basket in front made him wobble a lot, but Rashers waved encouragingly. The children in the poorer areas were less sympathetic.

'Ay—mister . . .' they yelled after him, and then, when at the risk of wobbling over altogether he looked around to find out what was wrong, they pointed and said:

'Your back wheel is going around, mister.'

When he cursed at them they had an answer too.

'Get down and milk it,' they yelled.

He soon learned not to look back at all. After a week the wobbles were noticeable only when he was starting off or stopping. A publican, by arrangement with the butcher, decided to use him in the night hours to deliver and collect bottles, so that he had two jobs. On Christmas Eve the butcher, a kindly man who knew there were several children, gave him a round of meat for the family dinner. The publican, not to be outdone, threw in a bottle of whiskey and a bottle of Tawney wine. Before going home Hennessy spared a little of each for Rashers, topping up the bottles with water so that his wife would not know.

For Mary it was the best Christmas she could remember. She bought holly to put around the walls, she had mottoes over the fireplace which read 'Happy Xmas' and 'God Bless Our Home'. They were painted in green and red and yellow on rectangles of

369

glossy black oilcloth. Mrs. Bradshaw sent a cake and a sovereign. For the first time she made Fitz play Santa and put little six-penny toys in the children's stockings. She had a sprig of mistletoe hung up too, which Pat took advantage of when he called to wish them the compliments of the season. He stayed for the meal, with Mrs. Mulhall and Willie, whom Mary had invited over because for them it was a sad time. In the evening Joe called. So, too, did Mr. and Mrs. Farrell. Farrell looked very much older, but he was still working on the docks and Mary was very much moved to see them again, remembering the time she had stayed with them in the first months before her marriage, remembering too the wintry seas almost outside the house and the driftwood on the strand brought in by the tide after the dreadful storm. They had drink too and sang songs. Pat persuaded Mrs. Mulhall to sing, but in the middle of it she began to cry, because she knew only one song and that was the song Bernie loved, and the thought of it all became too much for her.

'You'll have him back home soon,' Pat comforted her, 'and isn't that something to look forward to.'

'If God will spare him to me, that's all I ask,' she said, 'we'll manage the rest somehow.'

Pat said there could be no doubt about it now. The shock was the worst thing and once he'd weathered that, he'd weather the rest. Fitz said so too, though he knew that Mulhall was still lying in the shadow of death and felt it might be better, when all was said and done, if God decided to take him. She was reassured and asked them not to mind her and said she was sorry to spoil their pleasant evening.

Then the Christmas season had gone. Mary took the mottoes from the wall and threw the holly on the fire. As it blazed and sent its aromatic smoke about the room, she dreamed of what the year might bring. Fitz was a foreman now, with a foreman's wages. They might get a little cottage of their own somewhere, away from the squalor and tragedy of Chandlers Court. Mrs. Bradshaw was her friend, generous, thoughtful, a person of influence in Fitz's employment. That was the important thing, to have a friend in high places. The future was going to be happy. She sat down in the lamplight and began to write another letter, this time to her father, telling him how well the children were, how nice Christmas had been and all the great news that he would be so delighted to hear.

For others there was less to look forward to. First the publican decided the time had come when there was no longer any need for an extra porter; then the butcher, despite a kindly sympathy, had only three days a week to offer; then week-ends only; then, with regret, nothing. The city, its spending over, closed its purses to Rashers. January spread its dark skies above the children whose little bodies were bent daily over the ashcans. A series of shipping strikes marked the resumption of the dogged fight against long hours and inadequate wage packets. People who had overcoats kept them buttoned to the chin. In the mornings their eyes saw nothing except the lighted windows of their business places and in the evenings nothing but the lighted windows of home.

'The supports are moving,' Bradshaw said, leaving the letter on the breakfast table. She waited for him to continue, but he had huddled back into his chair.

'What supports, dear?'

'Good God—the supports they put up to strengthen the walls of the houses—what other supports?'

'Is the letter from your agent?'

'Who else do you imagine would write to me about the damned supports?'

'How could I know,' she said gently, 'you didn't explain who the letter was from. You simply said: "The supports are moving." '

He had picked up the paper. It was February. The shipping companies, he read, had settled up with the men. It was an unusually generous settlement. It amounted, Bradshaw considered, to a complete and abject surrender.

'The supports of the whole world are moving, if it comes to that,' he said gloomily.

She clicked her tongue in sympathy. She had no idea what this latest remark was about, but he seemed so miserable. The room was cold and he disliked cold intensely. Agents' letters always made him miserable too. Why he did not sell the houses she could not imagine. It cost so much simply to keep them standing that no matter how many he crammed into them there seemed to be very little money left over. She had dared to hint her view to him once or twice, but when he growled back at her she had to confess that she knew little or nothing about such things. He dropped his paper for a moment.

'I think it a very odd thing.'

He said nothing further, so that in the end, although she was quite afraid to do so, she asked:

'What is that, dear?'

'About Yearling.'

'Is there something odd about him?'

'He hasn't called to see us for several weeks.'

'I noticed that too.'

'That's what I think very odd.'

'I was thinking so too.'

'You never said so,' he said, accusingly.

He was working himself into a state of misery and ill feeling which, if she allowed him to go on, would last all day. That would be very bad for his health.

'I thought perhaps I was only imagining it,' she said, hoping to humour him.

'I don't see how you could imagine that Yearling *hadn't* called. You could imagine someone *had* called even if someone *hadn't*. But to think you imagined someone hadn't called seems . . .'

'I know dear . . . that was a stupid thing to say.'

'Preposterous. However, I suppose I shouldn't worry.'

'You mustn't.'

'Did you ever notice the way he treated my whiskey?'

'I remember he used to drink rather a lot.'

'Guzzled it,' Bradshaw said, 'What's the use of making excuses for him?'

'He played the 'cello very nicely,' she remembered. Sadly. If the summer would only come quickly. Then at breakfast they could look out on the flowers in the garden, gay and full of colours. In winter the french windows showed you too much of the desolate skies and let in draughts all the time.

'His tone is very rough at times,' Bradshaw objected, 'and when he becomes engrossed he breathes very heavily. I always found that very distracting.'

'He doesn't realise it, of course.'

'In addition, he's too Liberal—far too Liberal.'

'He likes a generous measure,' she agreed.

'I mean his politics—not the whiskey,' Bradshaw exploded. He was sick to death of these misunderstandings. He tapped the newspaper. 'He has liberal opinions which lead to *this*. If it goes on Mr. Larkin will be cock-o-the-walk.'

She had not read the paper as yet and so could not know what latest villainy of the labour leader Bradshaw had in mind.

'He expresses strong sentiments,' she said, 'Sometimes I think . . .' She hesitated.

'You sometimes think what?' he demanded.

'Sometimes I think . . . it's the whiskey.' It was such a dreadful thing to say that she was covered in confusion. At the same time, it seemed to please her husband.

'Yearling is easily deceived. He can't see that all this modern blarney about betterment of the workers' conditions is a mere stalking horse for Red Republicanism.'

He took out his watch. It was the hour for his walk along the front. The prospect, on such a morning, was not at all pleasant. Nevertheless, regular exercise was essential to health. Putting back the watch with an air of resignation he added: 'I think I might write to him.'

'But won't you be seeing him?'

'Good God, Florence—I don't mean the agent, I mean Yearling. I think I might write to Yearling.'

Then he said, deciding firmly:

'That's what I'll do, I'll write to him. He's getting as odd as two left feet and I know why. It's living all alone for so long in that enormous and empty house. Don't you think I should do that?'

She saw now that he had missed Yearling. The grumbling was only a cloak. She saw, too, that he was uneasy about writing, for fear of a rebuff.

'Suppose I invited him for a musical evening,' she suggested. 'I could ask Father O'Connor as well. I'm sure he'll be delighted to come.'

She knew that this was what her husband had hoped for.

'Excellent,' he said, 'write to both. Yearling is a nuisance, but we've known him such a long time. We mustn't watch him become an old oddity of a bachelor and do nothing at all to help him.'

He put on his heavy muffler, his greatcoat, his hat, his gloves. He went out into the raw morning air. It made his ears tingle and smelled bitterly of the sea.

They met on St. Patrick's Day. Yearling brought a fresh sprig of shamrock for his hostess. Mrs. Bradshaw praised it, found a pin and put it on her blouse. Then she said:

'It seems a shame in a way. It withers so quickly.'

'There's an honoured custom, ma'am,' Yearling reminded her, 'and it's called drowning the shamrock.' He meant with spirits, of course. She smiled indulgently because no matter what her husband might say, he was jovial and yet thoughtful and that was nice. Bradshaw took the decanter from the sideboard. The glass was already out in readiness.

They sang Moore's melodies because it was fitting to the occasion. They expressed national sentiments. It was altogether a very pleasant evening which concluded when Father O'Connor sang 'The Dear Little Shamrock' and they all joined in the chorus. The last tram had gone when they broke up but Yearling said he would leave Father O'Connor back to town in his motor, it was no trouble at all. After he had wound all the clocks and put the chain on the door, Bradshaw was in very good humour and sat at the fire for a while. She sat with him.

'You played very nicely, Florence,' he said.

'I'm afraid I was out of practice.'

'No,' he insisted, 'you were in excellent fettle. Most pleasing.' He poured himself a small measure of port for a night-cap. 'What was your opinion of Yearling?'

'He seemed very well disposed.'

Bradshaw nodded agreeably.

'Warm. Unusually so. Whatever was troubling him, he seems to have got over it. I think the evening did him good. It took him out of himself.'

On the way home Yearling and Father O'Connor spoke of Ireland in a sentimental way, of her sad history, of her hopes of nationhood so often and so bloodily thwarted, of the theatre of Mr. Yeats and Mr. Synge. Father O'Connor confessed that he had not seen any of the plays, but he had heard that they were in tone and language somewhat immoral. How much better Tom Moore had served Ireland through the medium of music and literature. He quoted:

'Dear Harp of my country in darkness I found thee
The cold chain of silence had hung o'er thee long.
When proudly, my own Island Harp I unbound thee
And gave all thy chords to light Freedom and Song.'

Yearling agreed. He said he wished often that he could have been present when the brave Tom was bringing tears to the eyes of pretty ladies in early nineteenth-century London drawing rooms by singing them songs that were sweetly seditious. Then he threw back his head and sang defiantly:

'Dear Harp of my Country, farewell to thy slumbers
This sweet wreath of song is the last we shall twine.
Go—sleep with the sunshine of fame on thy slumbers
Till touched by some hand less unworthy than mine.'

He paused to say, 'Come now, Father, join in,' and continued, helped timidly by Father O'Connor, who was not happy about the seemliness of singing at the top of the voice in a motor car on the public street:

'If the pulse of the patriot, soldier or lover
Have throbbed at our lay, 'tis thy glory alone
I was but as the wind passing heedlessly over
And all the wild sweetness I waked was thine own.'

'Very beautiful,' Father O'Connor said, when Yearling had adjusted his hat, which had tilted askew during his lusty chorus.

'Did you know, Father, that Byron praised Moore's verses highly?'

Father O'connor confessed that he had not known.

'It's a fact,' Yearling said. 'The same Don Juan had a reputation for practising more than his poetry, but he had the magnanimity to acknowledge another man's genius.'

'Admirable,' Father O'Connor said. He had to raise his voice. The motor, in the dark, deserted streets, was making a lot of noise.

'Home Rule, of course, is a mirage,' Yearling said, surprisingly, since the Bill had been passed in January by the House of Commons.

'But the Lords can no longer veto it,' Father O'Connor objected, 'it must automatically become law in two years.'

'It will be stopped.'

'Surely not.'

'Carson,' Yearling said. 'Carson will stop it. He has a hundred thousand volunteers drilling to fight it.'

'I understand they have nothing but dummy rifles.'

'They'll get the real things when the time comes. If the British Unionists don't supply them, our splendiferous and grandiloquent cousin—I refer to his Imperial Sublimity the Kaiser Wilhelm—will oblige. Do you know who Carson's grandfather was?'

Father O'Connor could not say.

'An immigrant Italian who resided in Dublin called Carsoni. The name of the present bould Orange blade is an abbreviation.'

Father O'Connor was astounded.

'True bill,' Yearling said.

'Now that you mention it,' Father O'Connor said, 'his skin is very dark.'

'A combination of liver trouble and the pigmentation of the Middle Sea,' Yearling said. He turned a corner with a flamboyant twist of the wheel. A moment later he slowed to a standstill.

'Your destination,' he announced.

'I've brought you very far out of your way.'

'A pleasure. Think nothing of it. By the way, what did you think of Bradshaw?'

'He seemed anxious to be agreeable.'

'That's what I thought too. I knew him at school, you know.'

'So you've told me.'

'He should never have married,' Yearling said. 'He's becoming quite odd. I've noticed the change over the years.'

'In what way?' Father O'Connor asked.

'Well, for one thing, the peculiar way he looks at me when I raise my glass to him and say "Good health". Almost inimical.'

'I think you exaggerate.'

'No indeed. It happens almost every time. Still, I'm glad we went. I think the evening took him out of himself. Well—good night.'

'God bless you,' Father O'Connor said.

The railings were black and forbidding and the bulk of the church rose darkly against the sky. Yearling honked the horn in a friendly way and went off. The noise was ear-splitting.

In June again there was a shipping strike, followed by a building strike, followed by a strike of engineers There were Larkinite processions, Larkinite banners, Larkinite slogans scrawled on the walls and footpaths of every street in Father O'Connor's parish. Throughout the weeks of summer he watched them. The weather was fine and yet the air that lingered over evening thoroughfares seemed heavy not with the sun's aftermath but with veiled and terrible anger. Men, no longer awed by his cloth, shook collection boxes under his nose at street corners; the little children begged coppers from him whenever he passed them. He had made a rule not to give charity because it only prolonged and encouraged discontent, yet he broke it on many occasions because the children had a pinched and hungry look in their faces. It was his duty, he felt, to harden his heart, but it was impossible not to have pity for the young and the innocent. These were not at fault. The air of the city told Father O'Connor that it must end badly. He could smell evil in the streets.

Pat and Joe were involved, and then they were back at work —then once again they were called out. Farrell stood idle for some weeks when the dockers refused to handle cargo. Fitz alone escaped. He set out to work each morning with growing uncertainty, yet when he returned each evening nothing had happened. The foundry workers had the rumour that a general strike was imminent, that the workers in Britain were waiting to join them in a complete close down in every part of the British Isles. In July Mulhall, back home from hospital and bedridden, sent across for him one evening and told him Willie and the rest of the messengers in Independent Newspapers had been dismissed for being members of Larkin's Union. Mulhall was still weak. His face had a grey and bloodless pallor. But he clung tenaciously to the subject and the steps that should be taken and they sat talking until a late hour. The next day Independent Newspapers were black-listed, shops and even railway kiosks that sold it were picketed. The distributors' vans went about their business under police escort. The arrangement, only partly successful, added to the general tension.

The newspapers that continued to be distributed claimed that the shipping strike was a flagrant breach of an agreement only one month old. Mr. Larkin protested that he could not get the men back to work.

'If an army rebels,' he was reported as saying, 'what is the commander to do?'

'He should be hanged for a rogue,' Bradshaw said furiously, when he read it.

'He's a very wicked man,' his wife agreed, 'think of all those poor, suffering children.'

'And a liar,' Mr. Bradshaw added, as though she had not allowed him to finish.

Yearling noted at the beginning of August that the men in the parcels department of the Tramway Company had been dismissed because they refused a managerial instruction to relinquish their membership of the Larkinite union. The dismissals were an obvious challenge. There would have to be a counterstroke. Both the men in the parcels department of the Tramway

Company and the boys dismissed from Independent Newspapers were employees of William Martin Murphy. He began to follow events with considerable interest, but without passion. He had no special feeling about the social order. It bored him. But he could understand the hatred it inspired in the many who suffered the brunt of its inequalities. Hunger was a great irritant. One day when a copy of the Larkinite paper *The Irish Worker* was offered to him in the street, he bought it and found the style fascinating. He read:

'Every dog and devil, thief and saint, is getting an invitation to come to work for the Dublin Tramway Company. Every man applying is asked: Do you belong to Larkin's Union?— if so, no employment.

'Well, William Martin Murphy will know—I hope to his and Alderman Cotton's satisfaction and the shareholders' benefit—who is in Larkin's Union, and who will have to be in it. Every man he is employing is known to us. What say Howard and Paddy Byrne? What say scab O'Neill? What say Kenna and Lawlor & Co.?

'We have Them All on The List.

'Mr. William Martin Murphy's satellites, Gordon and Tresillian, have discharged some ten men for being in the Union.

'Right, William the Saint. We have not moved yet and will not move until we are ready.

'Woe betide Scabs then!'

He made a point of calling on his newsagent. There was a picket outside.

'I wish to add an extra paper to my weekly list,' he said.

'Certainly sir—which one?'

'*The Irish Worker.*'

'I beg your pardon?'

'I said—*The Irish Worker.*'

'I'm afraid it is not a publication we can obtain through any of the usual distributors.'

'In that case you'll have to get it through the unusual ones, I suppose.'

'It may be difficult.'

'Not a bit,' Yearling said. 'At least twenty of them were stuck under my nose in the course of half an hour's walk through the city. There are some men prancing up and down outside your shop at this minute who, I am sure, can put you in touch with the most reliable of sources. Anyway, I am assuming you will see to it.'

'We'll do our very best, sir.'

'Thank you. In that case I know I may expect it regularly.'

'Of course, sir. Regularly. You may rely on it.'

As he passed through the picket on his way out he paused to speak to the leader.

'Interesting paper you get out,' he said conversationally. 'I like the style.'

They stared in unison after him.

Fitz had news for Mulhall during the same week. He went across each evening when he was not on shift work. He would bring a little tobacco and light Mulhall's pipe for him, so that he could enjoy his one smoke of the day. He now occupied Willie's bed, in the little room just off the living room. There were only two beds, so Willie now slept on the floor. He did not mind. Crippled, stricken, unable as yet to attend without help to any small, personal need, his father was still something of a god to him, a hero of great strength, gentle and good at home, without fear or price in the world outside it.

'I've news for you this evening,' Fitz said.

'Pull over the chair,' Mulhall invited.

'On Saturday William Martin Murphy called all the tram men to a meeting in the Antient Concert Rooms. It started at midnight.'

'They shouldn't have gone,' Mulhall said, getting angry.

'Wait now,' Fitz said. 'Let me finish. He offered half a day's pay to anyone who went to the meeting and when they went he offered them a shilling a week rise.'

'Their demand is for two shillings.'

'Wait now. The shilling was to be on condition that they'll remain loyal and refuse to come out if Larkin calls them. He said if they go on strike he'll spend a hundred thousand pounds to fight them.'

'Had it any effect?'

'I don't think so,' Fitz said, 'The tram men will do what Larkin tells them.'

'They'll have to come out,' Mulhall said, 'not for the sake of the two shillings, but to stand by the messengers and the men in the parcels department.'

He remained quiet for a time. Then he stirred with impatience and said : 'If only I could be out and about.'

'If you're going to talk like that,' Fitz said, 'I'll never give you another bit of news.'

He found Mulhall's pipe, filled it with tobacco and lit it for him. The small window let in so little of the evening light that he could see the tobacco reddening in the bowl. Then he helped to hoist up Mulhall so that he could smoke it.

'Do you think Larkin will move?'

'Certainly Larkin will move,' Mulhall said, 'he never drew back yet.' Mulhall's belief was unshakable.

'I knew Jim,' he said, 'when we had nothing. We started the union in a back room in Townsend Street and two candles stuck in bottles was all the light we could afford. We were fighting the employers and we had to fight Sexton and the National Union of Dockers at the same time. Jim won't draw back.'

'You fought hard,' Fitz said, 'all your life.'

'While I could,' Mulhall agreed. 'Now I'll fight no more.'

'You did your bit—and more than it.'

'Never any more,' Mulhall repeated.

He did not want comfort and his tone rejected Fitz's offer of it. As they sat in silence and the dusk deepened he stared straight in front of him. The room became even smaller. It had a closed-in air. Even when he was not smoking it smelled of tobacco, of successive pipes lit and smoked and laid aside on days that looked at him with expressionless eyes. No gaoler was necessary now. He was its prisoner for ever.

✿ CHAPTER 2 ✿

T HE bustle was familiar—and yet there was something odd
     about it, something that made it seem not quite the same as
     in previous years. It puzzled Yearling, this strange differ-
ence in an annual event he had looked at year after year since his
childhood days. The ingredients were the same; the stream of
hackneys and motor cars on their way to the grounds of the Royal
Dublin Society, the foreign visitors, the military, the strings of
horses, the riders in black caps and scarlet coats and tightly cut
breeches. The ladies as usual engaged his special interest. Most
of them were at their best; fashionable and feminine and agreeably pretty. A hefty and horselike few displeased him. That
was as usual too. He had once described the ladies of the Dublin
Horse Show as a mixture of Sweeties and Tweedies. The remark
came back to him from his remote student days. Perhaps youth
was the missing ingredient. He was getting old. He sighed
and consulted his pocket watch again. Father O'Connor was now
half an hour late. It was uncharacteristic and puzzling.

His interest in the traffic flagged. Yearling returned his watch
to his pocket and walked as far as the bridge, in the hope that
the name on the parapet would restore his good spirits:

'Balls Bridge
Erected 1791
Rebuilt 1835
Widened and improved
1904'

Henry Grattan, he remembered, had fought a duel here when

382

Ireland still had a parliament of her own. Self-government had been sold in return for place and pension. Pitt's fear then had been a French invasion. Now England's anxiety was that the same old Home Rule question would cause a civil war between the Redmondites and the Carsonites with weapons supplied to both sides by courtesy of the Kaiser. A distressful country. Napper Tandy was right.

It was an August morning of bright sunshine. When he lifted his eyes to the water and then upstream towards Herbert Park its beauty filled him with pleasure. The trees crowding over the river from either bank broke the sunshine into gleaming shafts; the water was a living floor of black and gold in a tunnel of green. At a point where the bank sloped gently into the water a little girl was washing a handkerchief. The sight put him in mind of a street rhyme which he was trying hard to recall when Bradshaw tapped him on the shoulder and said urgently:

'Where on earth is Father O'Connor. Hasn't he arrived?'

'I can't understand it,' Yearling said.

'But you were to meet him on the corner. What are you doing on the bridge?'

'Trying to remember a street rhyme,' Yearling admitted.

'I wouldn't be surprised if you've missed him.'

'I missed something,' Yearling confessed, 'but not Father O'Connor. Youth, probably.'

Bradshaw stared at him.

'Yearling,' he said seriously, 'you are becoming distinctly odd. Florence and I sometimes worry about you. Do you realise that you're talking a lot of incomprehensible nonsense?'

'Is it incomprehensible that a man should mourn over his youth?'

Bradshaw fumbled impatiently for his watch.

'It's half past eleven,' Yearling informed him, 'I've just looked at mine.'

Bradshaw pushed his watch back again.

'I am anxious about Father O'Connor. And you take it all so lightly.'

'I can see the corner perfectly well from here. Besides, I

like the name of this bridge. It amuses me.'

Bradshaw hesitated, saw what he meant and said:

'I am not entertained by undergraduate bawdiness.'

'I remember now that you never were.'

'Some day,' Bradshaw added, 'it will land you in trouble. It comes out sometimes in the wrong company.' Yearling turned again to the parapet, sorry to have roused the other to ill temper. It was an easy thing to do. Bradshaw did not mean it. Blood pressure was responsible. Or some abiding anxiety about society and the world.

The child was still gravely at play.

'Look at the little girl.'

'What's she up to?' Bradshaw asked, peering.

'She's washing her handkerchief.'

'That's an odd thing.'

'She's playing at being a mother, I imagine. The instinct comes out, even at that age. Don't you find it moving?'

Bradshaw peered more intently.

'She'll fall in,' he decided.

'Now I've remembered the street rhyme,' Yearling said, 'it goes like this.'

He closed his eyes, digging deep into his memory for the words.

> 'Down by the river where the green grass grows
> Where Mary Murphy washes her clothes
> She sang and she sang and she sang so sweet
> And she called for her sweetheart down the street
> Sweetheart, sweetheart will you marry me?
> Yes love, yes love at half past three
> Half past three is very very late
> So we'll have our party at half past eight.'

With guarded politeness Bradshaw asked:

'Where do you hear these things?'

'From the children of the back streets when I'm on my way to the foundry. They play these singing games. I find them fascinating.'

'I'm sure.' Bradshaw was fidgeting again.

'It's nice to have seen Mary Murphy,' Yearling said. 'I wonder will I ever meet her sweetheart?'

Bradshaw turned suddenly away from him and waved.

'There he is.'

'I beg your pardon?'

'Father O'Connor, dammit, he's crossing the street.'

Yearling turned from the river too and saw the priest, with quick glances to left and right, hurrying through the traffic. When he joined them his face was red with exertion. He tried to shake hands with both of them at once.

'I'm so sorry to have kept you.'

'Something happened, Father,' Bradshaw said, 'I know by your manner.'

'Something dreadful,' Father O'Connor said.

'Rest for a moment,' Yearling advised.

Father O'Connor leaned against the parapet.

'I had to walk,' he said, 'there were no hackneys available. Everything hirable has been snapped up.'

'But . . . the trams?' Bradshaw asked.

The truth flashed suddenly into Yearling's mind. Of course something had been missing, something so large and obvious that he had not thought of it until now.

'The trams have stopped working,' Father O'Connor said. 'Mr. Larkin stopped them at ten o'clock.'

They saw for themselves afterwards, while on their way to the Imperial Hotel for lunch. Tramcars lay abandoned all along the route, left at whatever spot they happened to have reached at the appointed hour of ten o'clock. Their numbers grew until at Nelson's Pillar a whole fleet stood driverless, surrounded by an excited crowd. There were more policemen than Yearling had ever seen before. They had surrounded the drivers and conductors.

'What are they up to?' Yearling wondered.

'Arresting them, I hope,' Bradshaw said.

'They can't arrest them for going on strike.'

'They can arrest them for causing obstruction,' Bradshaw answered. 'I've heard it argued very convincingly.'

So Mr. Larkin had carried out his threat. Yearling pulled up his motor car some distance from the hotel. It would be better to walk the rest of the way. A police inspector, seeing them approach, called two policemen to escort them to the hotel.

'Too bad this should happen during Show week,' he said to them.

'Is it a total stoppage?' Yearling asked.

'Seems to be,' he said, 'they've left the cars lying all over the routes. We'll be making an effort to bring them in very soon.'

'Plenty of your chaps around.'

'Enough to keep the situation under control, I would hope,' the inpector said, smiling.

'I wonder,' Yearling said.

Mrs. Bradshaw found lunch a disappointment. She had looked forward so much to a day of elegance, fashion, interesting conversations, pleasant encounters. Instead the sole topic of the dining room was the situation. Men kept rising from their tables to stare through the windows at the crowded street below. Late-comers brought further news.

'The company is organising a skeleton staff,' one of them said to Yearling, 'but the police say the cars won't be allowed to run after dark.'

She knew nothing of these matters and found the last remark quite frightening.

'This is only giving in to them,' Father O'Connor said.

Bradshaw looked at Yearling, who raised his eyebrows.

On their way back to the car they saw the police at the Pillar clearing a pathway through the crowd. A tramcar rattled past them. Two policemen stood on the front platform, guarding the driver. Later, in Mount Street, they saw the same tram. All its windows had been shattered, glass and woodwork littered the street. The driver and the two policemen were not to be seen.

The incident made a deep impression. Father O'Connor, who was to have gone to the Bradshaws for dinner, decided it would be better in the circumstances to go straight home from the Show grounds. There would be no trams after dark to take him from Kingstown, hackneys would be uncertain, it would be unfair to let Mr. Yearling drive him. Darkness might well ring serious trouble. He decided to walk back on his own, so that Mrs. Bradshaw would not be obliged to travel into the city with them. All agreed with reluctance that this was wise. There might be unpleasant scenes. He hoped they would enjoy their evening and set off.

It was strange to walk back alone. A few trams were now running, each guarded in front and at the back by a policeman. Impulse brought him towards Mount Street. The shattered tram had gone. What had happened, he wondered, what outbreak of back-street violence had ambushed and wrecked it? He examined the fragments of wood and broken glass which had escaped whoever had tidied up. There was blood on the ground. The clotted stains made him feel sick. He remembered the night, years before, when a torchlight procession and the thunder of socialist speeches affected him in the same way. He had thought at first it was the wine Yearling had pressed on him, but it had not been that at all. Anger and violence and blood unmanned him, yet some morbid need now sent him searching the streets aimlessly for further evidence. Perhaps it was the need to look them in the face.

He crossed back over Mount Street Bridge and found himself passing Beggars' Bush Barracks on his way to Sandymount. At first the roads were busy with Horse Show traffic, but at Irishtown this was left behind. He saw no additional signs of violence and when a tram approached at last he signalled it to stop. The police sergeant at the back saluted and helped him to mount.

'Sit near this end here, Father,' he advised.

Father O'Connor noticed his unfamiliar badge.

'You are not a member of the Dublin Metropolitan Police, are you?' he asked.

'No, Father. Royal Irish Constabulary. We've been drafted in to give a hand.'

'Will it be as bad as that?'

'It could be bad enough.'

'A terrible state of affairs,' Father O'Connor said. His hands were trembling.

He took his seat. He had barely done so when the tram,

turning the bend that led to Ringsend Bridge, ran into the out
skirts of a riot. The driver stamped his foot continuously on the
bell. They had got only a little way when the crush became so
great that it brought the car to a standstill. The focus of atten
tion lay somewhere on the route in front and at first no one
seemed concerned about the tram. The sergeant dashed upstair
to survey what was ahead. When he came down he called hi
younger companion to him.

'Is that a tram depot in front?' he asked. He was new to the
city.

'It's Ringsend power station,' the Dublin policeman said.

'Whatever it is there's bloody murder going on around it,
the sergeant said, 'go up and look for yourself.'

Father O'Connor followed the young policeman upstairs
The street was jammed tight with people. In the distance a soli
mass of police and people were at grips. Batons flayed abou
above a tumult of heads.

'It's an attack on the power station,' the young policema
confirmed. They went downstairs.

'Get the passengers off,' the sergeant said to the conducto
But it was impossible. They stood in the tram and waited, sur
rounded by a wall of bodies, until pressure from far in fron
began to pack the crowd more tightly. It began to retreat, step
by step. Hundreds of faces passed slowly by the windows a
Father O'Connor watched. For the most part they were me
with cloth caps and women with shawls. The movement back
wards increased. They jostled and began to claw at each other
Then in a swirl of faces and writhing bodies the battle betwee
police and the rioters came abreast and surrounded them. Stick
and batons beat at each other in a desperate mêlée. He saw fore
heads running with blood and sweat, torn hands and faces
hatred and brutality in hundreds of pairs of eyes. The thumpin
of bodies and sticks against the bodywork of the tram was te
rifying. He stood in the inner doorway of the cabin, as far fror
either window as the small space allowed. The rioters fell bac
until he could see only policemen's helmets through the win
dows on both sides of the tram. They were rescued.

'Keep steady,' the sergeant said, 'we'll be able to move soon

The tram driver went up front again, waiting for the police to be clear of the line. He stood ready, fear and eagerness to be away making his hand tremble on the control lever. The last line of policemen passed the conductor's platform.

'Now,' the sergeant shouted, 'get her away—fast.'

The driver made a clumsy and eager movement and the tram jolted forward, but after a few yards it stopped again.

'Keep her moving,' the sergeant shouted. He went up forward.

'I can't,' the driver said, pointing. Several men, remnants of the battle, lay bleeding on the line.

'Come on,' the sergeant said to the young policeman, 'you and I will get to work.'

'I wouldn't advise it,' the young policeman ventured.

'The street ahead is clear.'

'The street is clear,' the younger man agreed, 'but the houses aren't.'

The sergeant looked about him. They became aware, for the first time, of the tenements. On either side windows mounted above rows of windows, silent, watchful, menacing the now isolated tramcar.

'You know more about this city than I do,' the sergeant conceded.

If there was danger behind those windows two uniformed police alone in the street would be the right provocation.

'Our lads will be back to guard that power station,' the sergeant added, 'we can clear the street then.'

They stayed in the car and waited.

'No need for alarm now,' the sergeant assured the passengers, 'there's plenty of help at hand.'

'Here they come,' the conductor called.

The police were returning in marching order. They too had suffered severely, Father O'Connor saw. Many of the faces under the protecting helmets were bruised and bloodied. The sergeant stepped down off the platform to consult with them. The column came to a halt. They talked for some moments before anything happened. Then Father O'Connor saw one of the upper windows being raised. A missile, aimed at the sergeant, flew wide and shattered the glass in the tram. The passengers began to panic and the sergeant, breaking off his consultation, climbed back on to the platform.

'Keep your heads down,' he instructed, 'use your coats to protect them.'

The police outside, turning their attention to the houses, found window after window opening and had to crouch back under a rain of bricks and bottles. Father O'Connor felt the glass tumbling about his shoulders and heard the volume of the ambush filling the street outside. After a while the noise of missiles gave way to shouting. He looked up to find the police had been driven off and the car was surrounded again, this time by the rioters. They were pulling the sergeant and the conductor off the platform. The driver and the young policeman had already disappeared. He got to his feet in sudden panic and shouted at the crowd.

'How dare you molest these people. I instruct you to behave yourselves.'

A piece of brick grazed the side of his forehead and he fell back. He felt blood on the stiff, white ring of his collar.

'Hooligans,' he said, staggering towards the platform, 'you must stop at once.'

Those nearest reached out to take his arms.

'It's a priest,' they appealed, 'let him off the tram.'

'He shouldn't be on it,' an angry voice shouted.

'None of them should be on it,' another yelled. There was an angry roar of agreement. Nevertheless Father O'Connor was helped down. They did not handle him ungently. He began to push his way through them. What had happened to the two policemen and the other passengers he did not know. The seething crowd had swallowed them up. Rough clothes that smelled of dirt and poverty brushed against him but made way when his cloth was recognised. The crowd thinned as he reached its outskirts and he found it possible at last to take his handkerchief from his pocket to staunch the blood that was oozing from the cut on his temple. At a great distance behind him, the tramcar was being hacked to pieces.

In the morning, while he was at breakfast, Father O'Sullivan made a point of joining him for a cup of tea.

'How does it feel now?' he asked with sympathy.

A thin bandage surrounded Father O'Connor's head. Cotton wool and sticking plaster made a bulge over the wound.

'It's nothing,' Father O'Connor said, 'some scratches and a little bruising.'

The blow did not matter. The gravity lay in the insult to his cloth.

'Have you seen the morning paper?' he asked.

Father O'Sullivan had. But he picked it up and found again, prominent among the accounts of strike incidents, the headlines Father O'Connor was referring to.

Assault on Clergyman
Priest Manhandled
Sacrilegious Incident at Ringsend

'It is heartbreaking to be insulted by our own flock,' Father O'Sullivan said.

'These people have always insulted me,' Father O'Connor answered, 'since first I came to work for them. When I organised what little charity I could they rejected it and assaulted my helpers. The truth of the matter is they have been taught by scoundrels to covet what is not theirs.'

'I've never known them to lay a finger on a priest before,' Father O'Sullivan said. 'Perhaps it was an accident.'

It had been no accident. The brick had been thrown in answer to his command to them to disperse. The situation was deplorable. Father O'Sullivan did not understand its gravity.

'There are new elements who will stop at nothing,' he said, 'and they were present in that crowd.'

The door opened and Father Giffley came in.

'Are you well this morning?' he asked.

'Quite well, thank you.'

'No ill effects?'

'None at all—thank God.'

'Excellent,' Father Giffley said. He turned to address Father O'Sullivan.

'The incident is causing quite a stir,' he said to him. 'I've been coping already with an outburst of clerical fury. They all seem to be adopting Mr. Larkin's slogan: "An Injury to One is the Concern of All". Father O'Leary of *The Messenger* wants to print an article about it and the editor of *The Irish Catholic* wishes to have the full details for editorial comment. I told them we wanted no more about it.'

'That was best,' Father O'Connor agreed.

He hoped Father Giffley would not see the morning paper. It lay open on the table. With unusual complicity Father O'Sullivan picked it up as he rose from the table.

'May I?' he asked Father Giffley.

'Take it, John. The Dublin press has become a ragbag of lies.'

'Thank you,' Father O'Sullivan said.

He left, taking the paper with him. Father O'Connor looked after him with gratitude.

'I am glad you agree with me,' Father Giffley said.

'I have no desire for notoriety.'

'I should hope not,' the other acknowledged. Then he added:

'It was unwise in the circumstances to board the car at all.'

'I had to get home.'

That was not quite true. But how could he give a true account of something so inexplicable.

'It only serves to inflame the people,' Father Giffley added. 'In the past we have usually managed to say the wrong things but contrived quite often to do the right ones—at least the more humble clergy, such as ourselves. In this unfortunate business we must not appear to take sides.'

He was being rebuked again—this time for being assaulted and humiliated. He would say nothing. Nor would he give interviews. He would bend his will to that of his superior.

'As you wish, Father,' he said.

The following morning a letter from Mr. and Mrs. Bradshaw sympathised with him and conveyed their warm concern, while one from Yearling expressed his feeling of deep guilt at not having insisted on leaving him home. They, at least, held him in respect and affection. He was not altogether forsaken. During the next few days he followed the newspapers with close attention and wandered through the streets, watching and listening. He saw trams running under police protection and squadrons of police parading through the streets. The papers told him that Mr. Larkin had publicly burned Magistrate Swifte's proclamation forbidding a mass meeting in Sackville Street on the coming Sunday and promised his followers the meeting would be held. 'I care as much for Magistrate Swifte', they reported him as saying, 'as I do for the King of England.' But they also reported that there was a warrant issued for his arrest, that all the police had been mobilised and that police pensioners were being recalled to do duty as gaolers. The military, too, were in readiness and standing by. For most, the battle to be fought was between Capital and Labour. For Father O'Connor it was one between Godlessness and God.

ALOYSIUS HENNESSY, replete after a breakfast of fried bread and tea, counted the stairs as he descended light-heartedly from his room to the hallway and emerged from its darkness into warmth and sunlight. The bells of Sunday were sounding over the street, the time was wearing up to mid-day. At a distance ahead of him a figure hobbled in the same direction. The gait was unmistakable. Hennessy quickened his pace and caught up without difficulty.

'Going to mass?' he asked.

'I am,' Rashers said, 'and damn nearly late, at that.'

'Whereabouts?' Hennessy asked.

'The Pro-Cathedral, along with the Quality.'

'So am I,' Hennessy said, 'I'll walk along with you.'

'After the week's carry-on you'll hardly want to take a tram, anyway,' Rashers said. 'How's tricks?'

'Things is looking up. I have a few weeks work with Cramptons above in the Park. Pushing an oul barrow here and there for them.'

'That's good,' Rashers said. 'I'm glad for the children's sake. Are they well?'

'All on the baker's list,' Hennessy said.

'And yourself?'

'Gameball,' Hennessy said.

There was no enquiry about Mrs. Hennessy. Rashers had asked deliberately after them all in order to leave her out.

'Have a cigarette,' Hennessy offered, to show that they were still the best of friends.

They stopped to light up. The air was sultry, the sound of bells and mass-going traffic intermingled.

'I like Sunday,' Hennessy said, leaning on the railings to inhale his cigarette, 'A man can take his legitimate rest.'

'Come on,' Rashers urged.

'What's your hurry?'

'I'm bad enough without the addition of a mortal sin. We'll be late for mass.'

They resumed. Hennessy, suiting his pace to Rashers, noticed how painfully slow it had become. He had money in his pocket and that made him want to step it out. The bowler on his head, though a bit too big, was a source of pride. He began to whistle.

Rashers, irritated, said:

'Tie a bit of string around it—will you. You're like a bloody canary this morning.'

'It's the bit of work,' Hennessy apologised.

'If you want to keep it, I advise you to give over the whistling. It's unlucky in the morning. Whistle before your breakfast and you'll cry before your supper.'

'I had my breakfast,' Hennessy said.

'That's more than I had,' Rashers said.

Hennessy felt abashed. He was full himself and had not thought that Rashers might be hungry. He searched in his pockets and found a shilling.

'Take that,' he said.

Rashers stopped to examine the coin.

'You're a decent skin,' he said, putting it in his pocket. 'I'll pay it back to you when the ship comes home.'

Hennessy waved this aside.

'Time enough,' he said.

But Rashers was moody. Ill fortune had been dogging him.

'I always made plenty during Horse Show week,' he explained, 'but this time the tram strike ruined me. The gentry was too busy ducking bricks and jamjars to have ears for a bit of music.'

'The commotion was terrible,' Hennessy agreed.

'It killed the trade,' Rashers said.

They turned into D'Olier Street and met the first section of police.

'The Larkin Reception Committee,' Rashers said.

'Do you think he'll turn up?'

As Hennessy asked, the vista of the street opened to them. Rashers stood still. Sections of police were placed at intervals up its entire length, from the bridge to beyond Nelson's Pillar. They had never seen so many policemen before.

'If he comes down in a balloon,' Rashers decided.

They made their way cautiously up the street. Others, on their way to twelve mass too, walked in front and behind them. There were the usual Sunday strollers, young men in their Sunday best, girls in their finery. The police were keeping them on the move, but otherwise there was no interference.

'I'll tell you this, though,' Rashers added, when they had seen the full strength of the preparations. 'If he does turn up there'll be Holy Slaughter.'

As they joined the people who were thronging into mass, Hennessy fumbled and produced two pennies. He slipped one to Rashers.

'You'll want that for the collection plate,' he whispered.

'Thanks,' Rashers said.

Hennessy removed his bowler, wiped it carefully with his sleeve and dropped his own penny on the plate. He entered ahead of Rashers, the bowler clasped piously against his chest. Rashers passed by the collection plate with an air of abstracted fervour and put the penny beside the shilling in his pocket.

After mass Hennessy wanted him to walk through Sackville Street again.

'Not for a knighthood from the King himself,' Rashers said.

'I'd like to see if Larkin turns up,' Hennessy said.

'You've the full use of both your limbs. But poor oul Rashers would be a sitting target for any murderous bowsie of a Peeler.'

'Ah—come on,' Hennessy urged.

'Go by yourself, with my blessing and full consent,' Rashers said, 'but Rashers is home by the back lanes.'

They parted. Hennessy adjusted the bowler and made his

way back to Sackville Street. Others came with him. The crowd in the street was enlarged by the after-mass strollers. A cab driver who knew Hennessy reined in for some moments to pass the time of day.

'You're looking very spruce,' he said.

'I can return the compliment.'

'Are you taking your constitutional?'

'A bit of a ramble after mass to work up an appetite for the plate of pigs' feet and cabbage.'

'I'd ramble somewhere else,' the cabman said, leaning down from his seat. 'Do you see them stalwarts beyond?'

He meant the body of the Dublin Metropolitan Police drawn up in ranks outside the Metropole.

'I'd want to be blind to miss them,' Hennessy said, marvelling at their numbers.

'Half of them bowsies is drunk,' the cabman said. 'I've passed six platoons of them already and the waft of bad whiskey from each made the oul nag stagger between the shafts. Do you know what some of them is up to?'

He leaned down even further and beckoned Hennessy nearer so that he could whisper in his ear.

'Smoking,' he said, 'smoking on jooty. There's a quare one.'

'That's shocking,' Hennessy said.

'Half of them hasn't been in bed for three days and nights because of the riots. They've been bombarded from the winows with everything from flower boxes to chamber pots—full ones. The result is their nairves is gone. Every one of them is itching to get a belt back at someone—anyone. So I'd advise you to get out.'

One of the policemen had crossed over as they spoke. He rested his hand on the driver's rail.

'Are you going to anchor there for the day?'

'A few words on a matter of business with my friend here,' the cabman explained.

'Take him with you or break it up,' the policeman said, 'you're causing an obstruction.'

'I've said what I want to say,' the cabman answered, giving a jerk to the reins. As the cab moved away he turned and shouted back at Hennessy.

'Have regard to what I was talking about,' he advised.

Hennessy waved and moved on. The crowd had increased during their conversation. There was a small Larkinite element near the G.P.O. wearing the Red Hand union badge in their coats. Young couples promenaded as they always did on Sundays, looking in the shops and pausing to greet their friends. There were men swinging light canes and wearing buttonholes, the more respectable classes. Hennessy mingled with them. Near the Imperial Hotel a stranger said to him:

'I don't think he'll turn up. Do you?'

'I don't see how he can,' Hennessy agreed.

'Even the Quality follow him around now,' the stranger said. 'There's plenty of them about this morning.' They surveyed the street together, noting the number of well-dressed citizens in the crowd. Cars and carriages passed up and down. Despite the efforts of the police, groups were gathering and swelling at various points in the street. There was an air of holiday.

'What time is it?' Hennessy enquired. The man produced his watch.

'Wearing up to half past one.'

'Time for a bit to eat,' Hennessy said.

'Have a look at his jills,' the man said.

Hennessy looked. A stooped, frock-coated old man with a beard and a tall silk hat was being helped from a cab by the coachman and a young lady. He leaned on her arm and paused to look about the street.

'Wouldn't you think he'd have a bit of sense,' the man remarked, 'at his age.'

They watched as the old man, still leaning heavily on the arm of the girl, was led into the hotel.

'The niece . . . would you say?' Hennessy speculated.

'I would. With an eye on the money, waiting for God to see fit to call the poor oul fella.'

'He looks the sort that would have plenty of it.'

'That's what keeps them alive. No worries and plenty of money. Ah well.'

'The good God made a queer division,' Hennessy said. As they moved away people detached themselves from the crowd on the far side of the street and began to move towards them. Others joined in, until the whole street seemed on the move. Hennessy looked behind him. The figure of the frock-coated old man stood on the balcony above the street. Hennessy saw him straighten up and pull the beard aside. He flung out his arms in a gesture that by now was unmistakable.

'It's Larkin,' the man beside Hennessy shouted. The crowd roared its recognition and surged forward. Larkin on the balcony shouted in triumph.

'I promised you I'd speak to you in this street today. I've kept that promise. I'll leave here only when they arrest me.'

Hennessy gazed upwards, thunderstruck, but in a moment the police had reached the balcony and Larkin was seized. He saw him being led out of the hotel and marched towards College Street Station. At the window of the cab in which Larkin had arrived, a woman screamed: 'Three cheers for Jim Larkin.'

'It's the Countess Markiewicz,' the man with Hennessy said. Police surrounded the carriage, ordering it to turn about. They began to manhandle the driver. The countess was forced back into her seat and the crowd surrounding the cab began to heckle.

'Trouble,' the man with Hennessy said, 'let's get out.'

But the pressure of the crowd tightened suddenly and lifted Hennessy off his feet. Over their heads he saw the first wave of police, their batons drawn, coming at the double towards the crowd. His heart jumped with horror. He thought of his bowler. A belt of a baton would ruin it forever. He tried to raise his hands to take it off his head but they were pinioned to his sides. His ribs were caving in, every breath became an agonising struggle. He was almost unconscious when the impact of the baton charge turned the crowd and it began to break up. Hennessy dropped to the ground. He lay there for some moments, gasping, until the thought of his hat galvanised him once more. He felt his head. The bowler was gone. He searched about frantically on his hands and knees and found it again. Then, clasping it tightly to his chest, he stood up. He began to move down the street. There was no escape that way. Furious battles were being fought around O'Connell's monument and across the length of the bridge. The victims of the first charge lay everywhere about him. He moved up the street cautiously, but only for a few yards. There was another charge in progress and hundreds of people, trying to escape, were running in his direction. As he set off diagonally towards Princes Street those in front of the fleeing crowd were already about him. He made Princes Street and slowed down, gasping for breath. For a moment the street seemed deserted and he thought he had found an escape route. He put the bowler back on his head, spat to clear the heavy phlegm from his gasping lungs, then suddenly snatched the bowler off again. Another section of police had appeared at the head of Princes Street and were preparing to charge. With police in the narrow street in front and police behind, there was now no escape. Police began to beat their way through from both ends. Hennessy dodged several blows before he was hit. He backed away from one policeman only to bump into another. The second struck him a blow on the shoulder which paralysed the right side of his body. The first raised his baton and, as Hennessy was falling, brought it down hard on the side of his head. Hennessy, the bowler still clutched firmly against his chest, went down like a log and lay still.

The ambulance men brought him round. They lifted him up and found the bowler under him. It was dusty, but intact.

'Is this his?' one of them asked.

'Shove it in along with him,' the other said. When Hennessy could speak he claimed the hat and thanked them from his heart.

'It would have been better on your head,' one of them said, examining the jagged wound.

Hennessy tried to smile. It wouldn't. The head would mend, with the help of God. The man attending to him touched the right shoulder and Hennessy gave a gasp of pain.

'Better bring him in,' he advised.

The news was bad that night. Two workers had been killed, hundreds were hurt. The hospitals were thronged all day. At night the gas-lamps were extinguished and the side streets were loud with pitched battles. In one place the West Kent Regiment was called out to help to restore order. Hennessy was able to limp his way home around five in the evening. His shoulder was dislocated but the bowler still fitted. He was able to raise it with his left hand, exposing the bloodstained bandage, to salute Father O'Connor when they met near the corner of Chandlers Court. Father O'Connor raised his hat automatically in return.

The sight of a similar bandage on the priest's head transfixed Hennessy.

Father O'Connor, flushing slightly, passed on. Hennessy remained rooted to the ground.

'Holy God!' he exclaimed at last. The world had turned upside down.

Yearling, making his way across town to a meeting of the Board, was held up by a procession. It was the funeral of a dead striker. It passed him slowly, with bands and torches and stewards with crêpe-covered staves who marshalled the thousands that followed into uneven ranks. At the front marched members of the British Trade Union Congress, including Keir Hardie, whom he recognised immediately. He would make the oration, Yearling surmised, in place of Larkin, who was now in gaol. At the very back a force of mounted police kept a watchful eye on the mourners. The music affected Yearling, as music always did, and the dense rabble marching in time to it looked to him like figures from the French Revolution. Most of them were ragged and many had bandaged heads and limbs. They were out in force once more, drawn from their lanes and warrens by a now uncontrollable discontent. He stayed to watch, even when the way was clear for him to continue with his journey. The thought that they were so many appalled him. He had a drink and read with particular care the newspaper reports of the disturbances. When he reached the foundry of Morgan & Co. the meeting was over. His brother-in-law invited him into his office.

'I'm sorry you missed it,' he said.

'I was held up by a trade union demonstration,' Yearling said.

'More rioting?'

'No. A funeral of one of the strikers. I'm sure it was the largest since Parnell.'

'We've decided to move,' Bullman said.

'I beg your pardon?'

'We're going to put a stop to all this immediately,' Bullman explained. 'No more Larkinism and no more broken contracts. I've reported to the Board on the meeting of the Employers' Federation. They've agreed to a man to support the proposal.'

'What proposal?'

'The proposal of the Federation to outlaw Larkinism. We are issuing this tomorrow. Four hundred other employers are pledged to take the same action.' He took the top copy of a form from a bundle on his desk and handed it to Yearling.

'All employees must sign it—whether they belong to Larkin's union or not.'

Yearling took the form and read it. It ran:

'*I Hereby Undertake* to carry out all instructions given to me by or on behalf of my employers, and, further, I agree to immediately resign my membership of the Irish Transport and General Workers' Union (if a member); and I further undertake that I will not join or in any way support this Union.

> Signed.................................
>
> Address ....

Witness.................

Date ....'

He handed it back and said:

'Who drafted this?'

'Our chairman—William Martin Murphy.'

The undubbed knight was moving openly at last.

'Suppose they refuse to sign?' Yearling suggested.

'That's what we hope they'll do,' Bullman said, 'when the Larkinites refuse we'll get rid of them.'

'But you're giving this to both Larkinites and non-Larkinites,' Yearling said. 'Suppose the non-Larkinites refuse to sign also?'

'That's unlikely,' Bullman said. 'Why should they fight Larkin's battles for him?'

'Why do they take sympathetic action and why do they refuse to handle goods they regard as tainted?' Yearling pointed out.

'Are you against the proposal?'

'Isn't it indiscriminate?'

'Why didn't you attend the meeting?' Bullman asked irritably.

'Fate,' Yearling said. 'I seem to miss the few important occasions.'

'You'd have been in a minority of one,' Bullman assured him.

'Possibly. But I would have frightened them.'

'I doubt it.'

Yearling recovered his hat from his brother-in-law's desk.

'You yourself would have been the hardest nut to crack,' he said, 'and you are frightened already.'

Rashers lit the candle and lay down between the rags he had accumulated during his long occupation of the basement of Chandlers Court. The dog stretched itself at his feet, the candle cast familiar shadows, all was as usual in his cellar below the city. In the street above him the day was still waning, although the hour was almost eleven. The weather of August was being kind that year, the light reluctant to quit the sky. But the cardboard in the window kept out what was left of it, making the candle a necessary expense.

Rashers drank water from a jamjar and chewed some dry bread from the rusted biscuit tin at his bedside. He was tired from tramping the streets and he was afraid of what might happen. The police were carrying out raids on the tenements, smashing furniture, breaking delph, beating up the inhabitants. They were wreaking a savage revenge on those who had ambushed them continuously from the windows of dark streets. Every tenement was an enemy now, a fortress furnished with bricks and bolts and chamber pots. It was unlikely they would visit a basement, but the stories he had heard were not reassuring. The police were angry. They were determined to spread terror wherever they could.

'A gang of bowsies,' Rashers said to the dog.

At the sound of his voice it stood up. It watched him as he ate, its eyes begging for its share. If they came Rusty would protect him. If he heard their feet coming down the stairs he would whisper, 'Get them, Rusty.' The barking was a protection in itself. But if they were too incensed or too drunk to be put off by that, then let them break in the door and face the music. Rusty would take them all on. Without hesitating to make a count of the helmets.

He called the dog to him and said: 'Here, Rusty,' and shared his bread with his bodyguard. The dog gulped it down and then licked his hand.

'No more, Rusty,' he said sadly. The biscuit tin was empty.

The poorer streets were keeping a wary eye on the possibility of disturbances. In the more respectable areas his rags marked him out as a representative of the hooligan element. People closed their doors on him or turned aside from him. He had thought of writing a ballad about the arrest of Larkin, but the words refused to come. The pockets he'd compose for were now likely to be as empty as his own.

'What'll you and me do if it becomes a general thing, Rusty?' he asked.

If job after job closed, and beggar after beggar invaded the streets, until the city became a vast hunting ground of unemployed?

'So far as you and me is concerned,' he said to the dog, 'God never shut one door but He closed another.'

He lay back and tried to be calm about the threat of the dark hours and the uncertainty of the days that were coming.

'Go to bed, Rusty,' he ordered.

Once again, the dog stretched himself at his feet. Rashers blew out the candle.

The bundle of forms was taken from Mr. Bullman's desk for distribution. On the appointed day he waited, with anxiety, for their return. None came. He addressed enquiries of a discreet nature through the hierarchy of control. The answer was that his workers, Larkinites and non-Larkinites alike, were refusing to sign. He held council again with his Board. They decided to be resolute. The next day instructions were given to reduce the furnaces gradually and to set up slow fires. The men refused the instruction. Bullman, knowing that his supervisory staff could do this much for him, took the necessary steps.

In the morning Fitz entered as usual through the office and signed his name in the book left there for foremen. When he reached No. 1 furnace house the night shift was leaving. No one came to replace them. After half an hour or so he left and went across the works yard. He found the main gates closed. He heard the voices of men outside and let himself out through the gateman's hut. A large poster on the gate declared a lock-out. Work would be available only for those who reported first to the office to sign the Federation form. No one went to the office. They stood about for a while or slipped in by the side gate to collect some personal belongings from the company's lockers. They returned after a brief interval carrying teapots or cracked cups or overalls and working shirts bundled all together. Then they drifted away. Fitz, returning to No. 1 House to check if anything remained to be seen to, found Carrington waiting for him.

'Do you think they'll change their minds?' Carrington asked.
'Hardly,' Fitz said.

He surveyed the empty house. The line of furnaces, charged by the night workers before they left, glowed dimly down its length. The silence was oppressive.

'We've to bank down all the fires,' Carrington said. 'You'll know what's to be done. Take the heats down slowly. We'll have to do that over two or three days or the brickwork may crack. The office staff will be down in an hour or two to give a hand.'

'You'll need more than the office staff.'

'Some of the workers will come back to sign,' Carrington said. 'We'll put them at it. Then we'll recruit casual labour.'

'If you do that,' Fitz said, 'there'll be serious trouble.'

'The police will give protection. We can't let the bloody plant get damaged. That wouldn't be in anyone's interest. Your job will be to direct operations in here. You'll have a crowd of clerks working under you and they won't know what they're supposed to be about. You'll have to keep a sharp eye on them.'

'What time will the office staff report at?'

'In about an hour—or even less. They're being rounded up at the moment.'

'I'll be here for them,' Fitz said.

'We'll boil up a can of tea while we're waiting,' Carrington suggested. 'Have a fag.'

'No,' Fitz said. 'I'm going up aloft to look after the reserve water supply. It may be needed and I've found nobody else has ever been able to put it in working order.'

He climbed laboriously up steel ladders and felt his way by handrails that were covered with a thick coating of dust. Below him the light from the untended furnaces threw tiny pools of red along the empty floor. He felt his way along the galleries, the handrails guiding him where the gloom was thick, an occasional rooflight easing the strain with a dusty shaft of sunlight. He trod gingerly through the remote and intricate web of steel until he found the water reserve which was located above No. 4 House. He remembered testing it many years before, when the coal-stack went on fire and Mulhall was one of the carters called in to help. He went through the same drill with it now, until the pipes began their agitated dance and the gallery trembled with the sudden outburst of noise. Satisfied that the reserve would work if called on, he followed the catwalk until it led him through a doorway and on to the roof.

He looked about him, grateful for the fresh air. Below him the works yard was empty. There were no carters leading their horses, no labourers piling coal. The telpher, its arcing rail empty, no longer sent blue sparks flying from its trolley. The new loading machine, to which Mulhall had sacrificed his legs and his manhood, was abandoned and untended and bathed in lonely sunlight. Beyond the yard, at a distance of a few intervening streets, was the river. Here and there smoke curled from the funnels of ships. None of the cranes was working.

Either it was the hour between tides, or the lock-out had spread to the riverside. He delayed for some time, looking at the empty yard and considering his own position. He had not been issued with a form. Probably they assumed that he had left the union when they made him a foreman. Carrington then, had been decent enough to keep his mouth shut.

When he got back the office staff were assembled already in No. 1 House.

'You organise this lot,' Carrington said. 'I'll look after No. 2 House. There's a cup of tea ready for you when you get them working.'

'Right,' Fitz said.

He divided them, putting some on the skips and giving shovels to others. Then he explained what was to be done, and at what times. He appointed a senior clerk to direct the rest. He watched them charging the furnaces and showed them how to dress the fires lightly. The heat was to be brought down, he told them, a little at a time and with care. They understood what was at stake and grasped the system quickly. When the initial confusion and awkwardness had been evercome, he left them at it and went to find Carrington.

Carrington's gang had not yet arrived. He poured tea from a billycan for Fitz and asked:

'How's it going?'

'Smoothly enough,' Fitz said. 'They'll get the heats down without damage.'

'Fine,' Carrington said.

Fitz took the tea. It was thick and brown. Carrington made tea in the way of the workers: tea leaves and sugar all in together, with a lacing of condensed milk. It had the taste of the job off it, of coal fumes, of sweat, of furnace-house gossip. Carrington said:

'You'll have to keep an eye on them, just the same.'

Fitz drank his tea, thinking his way ahead.

'They'll fold up after a while, of course,' Carrington pursued. 'Enthusiasm is no substitute for experience.'

He took his tea.

'Muscles too soft,' he explained.

'They'll manage,' Fitz said.

'With a bit of guidance,' Carrington said, indulgently.

'Well,' he added, when Fitz did not seem disposed to talk, 'better get back on the job I suppose.'

Fitz examined his cup. There was a residue of liquid in it, enough to wash the tea leaves from the sides as he tilted it about and about. He considered carefully and said:

'I won't be going back to the job.' He had the feeling of pushing a bolt on a door firmly home, or making a will. Carrington said nothing for some time. He, too, was feeling his way.

'You realise what you're doing?' he said at last.

'Perfectly,' Fitz said.

'There's a chance, sooner or later, they'll show a little mercy to the others. But they'll never forgive a foreman. If you quit now you'll walk through that gate for the last time. You'll never get back.'

'I know that.' Fitz said.

'Then why do you have to be such a fool?'

Why? Personal pride, or the hope that at the end of so much travail, somewhere in the unseeable future, there would be a change in the world. He had seen a man suffer and afterwards he had picked up two dismembered feet and wrapped them in a sack.

'I couldn't leave the union now,' he said. 'People who were never in it and never intended to be in it are locked out because they won't sign a bit of paper promising never to join it.'

'They've the prospect of getting back,' Carrington said. 'You've none.'

'We'll cross that bridge when we meet it,' Fitz said. He pushed the cup away from him and stood up.

'See you sometime,' he said.

Carrington offered his hand. Fitz shook it.

'Thanks,' he said.

He left the house, crossed the empty yard and went through the gateman's hut into the street. The notice of the lock-out was still posted on the main gates, which were closed.

By the end of the week Bullman had assembled the facts for his Board. The four hundred firms in membership of the Employers' Federation had stood firm, thirty-two trade unions had joined with the Larkinites in refusing to sign the form. The lock-out was general throughout the city. They must act from now on in consort with the rest of the employers. They would have financial support from employers in England. Gates closed, machinery came to a standstill. The city of Dublin was practically paralysed. It was reckoned that about twenty-four thousand men were involved. In a matter of days the streets filled with the hungry hordes Rashers had feared.

M ARY, alone with the sleeping children, sat at the window overlooking the street and felt the dusk growing in the room about her. At first she had been occupied by the children playing in scattered groups below, until in twos and threes they were called away and there was nothing left to watch except the changing tones of pavement and housefront as the shadows of late evening began their transformation. It was September and already the dusk came perceptibly earlier. Soon the women, meeting each other, would remark: 'God bless us, but aren't the evenings closing in.' Soon would come the colder weather and the need for fires. With half the city idle, what was to happen then?

The thought remained to trouble and preoccupy her. Fitz's promotion to foreman had brought not only extra money and a little more comfort but a place in the world that was better and more secure than any of her neighbours. He could have left the union when he was promoted. Foremen, she had thought, were above unions. Yet he had come out with the rest, and in doing so put everything she had and all she hoped for in jeopardy—her children's future, the possessions she had gathered to make a home with, the small weekly amounts she was beginning to save. It was not in her nature to question his decision, yet the consequences of it distressed her. Hunger and want were again part of her world, twin possibilities that threatened in her moments of solitude and were now calamitous presences in the shadowed corners of the street.

A tapping at the door roused her. She realised that someone was calling her.

'Mrs. Fitzpatrick, are you within?'

She recognised the voice and for a moment hesitated. Then she called, reluctantly.

'Come in—Mrs. Hennessy.'

The woman opened the door and poked her head around it, peering into the gloom.

'Your husband is out?'

'He is,' Mary said.

Mrs. Hennessy, entering the room, let the shawl down from her head and settled it in folds about her shoulders.

'Them oul stairs has me killed,' she said conversationally. She was small and thin, with dark hair that was greying and a drawn and yellow face. Her eyes, inquisitive and watchful, challenged the word to do its worst.

'Can I help you?' Mary said, waiting for the customary flow to start.

Mrs. Hennessy produced a jug from beneath her shawl.

'I was wondering if I could borrow the loan of a sup of fresh milk for the baby,' she said, 'she's too young for the condensed.'

Mary went to the press.

'Wait till I tell you what happened,' Mrs. Hennessy said. 'There was a terrible commotion some hours back. Some bowsie put a brick through the window of Kerrigan's dairy and there's not a sup to be had there. Only for that I wouldn't trouble you at all.'

Mary poured milk into the jug. Mrs. Hennessy, watching the operation closely, said: 'The blessings of God on you.' Then, as a quick afterthought, added: 'You might lend me the loan of a cupful of sugar as well.'

Mary took the cracked cup which also appeared from under the shawl and filled it with sugar.

'You're far too generous,' Mrs. Hennessy said, 'and you'll have it all back as soon as the tide turns.'

'It's nothing,' Mary said, 'don't think of it.' The quick and inquisitive eyes were taking in the room.

'Did you hear what the police is up to?'

'I did, indeed,' Mary said.

'Depredation and damage—that's their programme now,' Mrs. Hennessy said. 'They're breaking into the houses and smashing things and manhandling defenceless women and children. I know several this night that hasn't a stick of furniture left whole—everything the poor souls ever had smashed into smithereens.'

'God forgive them,' Mary said. But she got no chance to say anything more.

'God forbid they'd ever break in here,' Mrs. Hennessy continued, 'and you with everything a body could want for. Sofas and chairs and tables and nice pictures. They'd make short work of it all. Thanks be to God they'll find little of value to damage in Ellen Hennessy's caboosh, and what little there ever was is safely stored by now in The Erin's Isle Pawnbroking Establishment. That's the advantage of having nothing. You can't lose it.'

Then, after a breath she said: 'Still—God is good.'

Mary said sympathetically: 'Your poor husband is out of work again, I'm told.'

'Is he ever *in* work,' Mrs. Hennessy broke in. 'He had a nice little job and, as usual, wouldn't mind it.'

'It was unfortunate,' Mary said.

'Wait till I tell you,' Mrs. Hennessy said. 'He goes off to Sackville Street a few weeks ago to see will Larkin turn up and comes home to me with his head in a bandage and his arm dislocated. 'What happened to you Hennessy?' say I, when he came in the door. "I was caught in a charge in Sackville Street," says he, "and got a belt of a baton. And when I fell I think I was walked on be a horse." Right enough, when he took off his shirt he was black and blue all over. "That's what you get," says I, "for playing the Red Hand hayro. Now your wife and your unfortunate children can go hungry".'

She gathered her shawl about her head once more.

'I'll go up now,' she said, 'And look after them. They're all alone and like a bag of cats for want of a bit to eat. I'm more than obliged for the loan of the milk and the sugar.'

Then she surveyed the room again. Her eyes went from item to item, assessing each.

'You have enough here to stave off the hunger for many a long day,' she assured Mary, 'and if the time ever comes when you have to start shifting some of it, just give me the word. Ellen Hennessy will see you get the right price in any pawnshop in the city. Don't forget now.'

'I won't forget,' Mary said.

She closed the door after Mrs. Hennessy and stood for a moment to wonder whether kindness or envy had inspired the other woman's offer. God help her, she had little in her life to prompt her to generosity, with her husband who seldom worked and a family that kept increasing. Her life was a succession of childbirths, her days dependent on the pawnshop and reluctant little charities wheedled from her neighbours. If she was envious or grudging she had every reason to be.

Mary sat down at the window again, determined to be patient while she waited for Fitz to return from his meeting, trying not to lose hope among the ever deepening shadows of the street. What Mrs. Hennessy had looked upon as her guarantee against misfortune would be the misfortune itself, to part with the things she had gathered, to break up the home she had made through personal sacrifice and with the sympathetic help of Mrs. Bradshaw. That help, at least, would continue. Mrs. Bradshaw was a kindly woman. When she knew of the trouble she would do little things to help. For Mrs. Bradshaw had everything except children. That was the strange way the world worked. Mrs. Hennessy had too many. But that was the Will of God.

Sometimes she had tried to imagine what it would be like to change places with Mrs. Bradshaw, to sit in a beautiful house looking out at the garden, with a bell near at hand to summon a servant to open the windows when the room grew warm with the sun, or to close them when the evening air became cool. To give orders about the meals. And to arrange the flowers— saying this should go here and that should go there. To play the piano when there was company. To dress elegantly for the theatre. To wash with delicate soaps. To carry a pretty purse of notes and sovereigns. And she would have education. And she would speak with a beautiful accent. But she would have to have been born differently, never knowing her father, or her mother who was dead. And she would have no children. And she would have Mr. Bradshaw. No.

She heard Fitz on the landing outside and heard him opening the door.

'You're sitting in the dark,' he said.

She looked round, noticing for the first time that by now there was hardly any light falling into the room. She rose and said: 'I'll light the lamp. How did your meeting go?'

He left his cap on the dresser, a habit she had given up trying to cure him of. He saw her hair falling forward across her cheek and saw the outline of her features in the lamplight and remembered their wedding night.

'They're releasing Larkin,' he answered. 'The Government have stepped in.'

That was probably good news. She did not know the ins and outs of the trouble.'

'That's good,' she said.

'And the strike pay will be ten shillings a week—for a while at any rate.'

'Is it going to go on, do you think?'

'They say it can't,' Fitz answered.

She was aware of him watching her as she bent over the lamp. She knew he was watching her closely. He was troubled. She felt that too.

'But you think it will,' she said, knowing by his tone.

'Yes,' he said.

She put the chimney back on the lamp and adjusted the wick.

'What are we to do, Fitz?'

He had been thinking about that for some days. The only hope had been that the general refusal would lead to a withdrawal of the form and a return to work until the whole thing had been argued out. But that had not happened. Instead the employers had hardened in their attitude.

'As well as releasing Larkin, the Government have promised an inquiry,' he said.

'Please God something will come of it.'

'I doubt it,' Fitz said bitterly. 'If they want the thing settled why don't they withdraw the help of the military and the police. We might have some chance of making the Federation listen to us.'

He had not answered her question. What were they to do if it dragged on? But she knew the answer. She had seen it happen to others countless times before. The homes, piece by piece, would go to the pawnshops. That was what Mrs. Hennessy had meant. The grocers, for a while, would give a little credit. The moneylenders would step in, taking a profit in keeping with the risk.

When the chimney had heated and there was no danger of cracking it she turned up the wick to its full strength. It made the transition from evening to night seem quite sudden. But the yellow glow of the lamp was more cheerful than the dusky half-light. She began to cut bread and to make him cocoa.

'Maybe you should spare it,' he suggested.

'We still have our savings,' she said, 'and I shouldn't complain. We're better off than most poor souls.'

They sat down to table together. He had been over with Mulhall to tell him the latest and now he told Mary about Mulhall, how he looked, what he said, what Mrs. Mulhall had said, how he thought she would fare now that Willie and her husband were both idle. It was the small talk they always indulged in over supper. But tonight the full meaning of what was happening seemed to sit along with them. He had to say something about it.

'You've never asked why I wouldn't leave the union,' he said.

She surprised him by saying: 'It's because of Bernard Mulhall. I didn't have to ask.'

Her voice was gentle and sympathetic and he knew she was thinking not of the accident only but of what the Mulhalls were left to face.

'Mulhall was a tower of strength,' he said.

He would never betray Mulhall's trust. But it was not altogether that. There were Pat and Joe and the men who worked with them. There were Farrell and the dockers and thousands of others throughout the city, some long resigned to perpetual squalor as to the Will of God, others rebelling with recurring desperation whenever there was a leader to lead them. Never before had they stood so solidly together. He said to Mary:

'The men in the despatch department of the Tram Company were dismissed simply for belonging to Larkin's union. There was no other reason. The tram men had to support them. Then this form was issued to everyone all over the city. The rest of us had to take our stand with the tram men.'

'I thought you wouldn't be asked to sign it?' she said.

'I wasn't,' he admitted, 'but I couldn't stay in when the others were locked out. I couldn't do that.'

'I know you couldn't,' she said.

'Are you angry?'

'No. I'm glad you wouldn't do something you knew you shouldn't do. In the long run it wouldn't work out.'

The gratitude in his face moved her deeply. She came to him and kissed him. Then she said:

'The children are the real worry.'

'I know,' he said.

'I was thinking about it before you came in. If we put a little of what we have aside—and never touch it, no matter how bad things may be—we'll know that if the worst happens we'll be able to send them to stay for a while with my father.'

'We'll do that,' he agreed. Then he thought about it and added:

'You could go with them yourself too. That'd be better still.'

'I wouldn't leave you here alone,' she said.

He held her to him and said no more. If things became very bad he could talk to her again about it. They must wait. The gates were closed. The keys that could open them were in other hands.

'You've taken a weight off my mind.'

'I'm glad,' she said.

She knew he would have acted as he did whether she approved or not. But she was happy she had spoken. She was close to him and part of him. That was what she wanted.

Rashers set out with the determination to try everything he knew. He was hungry. He had been hungry for weeks. It was a miserable kip of a city at the best of times. It had gone to hell altogether now. Day in and day out he stood in the gutter and played his whistle. Nobody minded him. Occasionally, when he had made certain there were no police to see him, he begged. They turned aside from him. He knocked at door after door for odd jobs. There were none, or some locked-out unfortunate had got there before him. Once he met Hennessy. He was aggrieved at the perversity of fate, the obduracy of the employers, the supineness of the Government, the stubbornness of the strikers, the deadlock that looked like paralysing the city for ever.

'Is there any moves at all—or what?' he asked irritably.

'Not a damn thing,' Hennessy answered. He too was gloomy.

'Jaysus,' Rashers exploded, 'are they going to let the whole bloody population starve!'

'That seems to be the programme,' Hennessy confirmed.

'You're not working yourself—I suppose?'

'No. I'm living on the expectations.'

'Sit down a minute,' Rashers said.

There were two abandoned buckets on the piece of waste ground. They upended them for seats. Grass and nettles surrounded them and in front of them, against the gable of a warehouse, a hoarding displayed its advertisements. One had been put there by some religious-minded body. It read:

'Ask—and you shall receive.
Knock—and it shall be opened unto you.'

'Me arse,' Rashers said, when he had read aloud this message of hope.

'Some Protestant crowd puts them up,' Hennessy explained.

'Yes, telling a pack of bloody lies. They shouldn't be let,' Rashers said.

Hennessy, prepared as always to be reasonable, said: 'I suppose it gives employment.'

Then, in an effort to be cheerful he asked; 'What do you think of the one beside it?'

Rashers studied the picture of a man with a ruddy, smiling face, dressed in blue striped pyjamas, straddling a Bovril bottle, that tossed on the waves of a blue ocean. It said: 'Brovil—prevents that sinking feeling.'

He spat elaborately and glared fiercely at Hennessy.

'Ah now,' Hennessy protested, 'it makes you laugh.'

'It makes me hungry,' Rashers said.

'It was no use trying to humour him. So Hennessy said: 'The Government inquiry might bring this lock-out to an end sooner than we think.'

But it did nothing of the kind. When the inquiry pronounced and said the Federation form should be withdrawn, the employers refused, so the only result was a further spread of the lockout. It set more and more pacing the streets, and there were fewer still in a position to give anything to Rashers. He walked through streets that were empty of any promise of help. The collecting boxes rattled, the pickets paced up and down, long convoys of carts and wagons moved through the city, always under escorts of police and military; the trams and the power stations were similarly guarded. Sometimes he went down to the monster meetings at Beresford Place, mingling with thousands of the out-of-works and listening, as the great orange sunsets of early October stained the waters of the nearby Liffey with colours of green and red and gold, to the speeches that thundered from the lighted windows of Liberty Hall. He heard the wild cheering and now and then the great outpouring of thousands of voices in song. He watched the startled gulls rising from grimy parapets and hovering with loud cries about the iridescent river. And as he did so he became conscious of belonging to nothing in particular. The thought increased his desperation. There was a time when he could have put a brick through a window and earned a few days in gaol, where there would be shelter and food of a sort. Now they would treat him as a rioter and beat him until he was half dead. He watched hungry faces that looked up at the speechmakers from under the peaks of caps. He saw the light of hope in thousands of eyes. But he was not one of them. The respectable and the good-living in neatly kept clothes passed him on their way home. They glanced at him quickly and turned away and wanted nothing to do with him. When the well-to-do looked at him they did not see him at all. That was in early October, when the days were drawing in and the evenings were coming early, making the pavements damp and the streets cold. His spirits sank lower. He was constantly hungry. He was always cold. Then, for the first time in many months, his luck changed.

He was looking into a shop window in which he saw nothing but his own reflection, his long, ragged coat, the grey beard, the hat that had lost all semblance of shape and fitted over head and ears like a bowl. He was thinking of food. He had thought of little else for days. A hand tapped him on the shoulder.

'Using the head?' said the voice.

When he turned around it was Pat Bannister. A generous skin, Rashers knew, but unlikely to have anything to give away.

'I'm thinking about hard times,' he said.

'It's a general complaint,' Pat said.

'I don't suppose you have anything you could spare?'

Pat shook his head.

'Why aren't you playing the whistle?' he asked.

'Because no one has the inclination to listen,' Rashers said. 'Some is too stingy and the rest is just too bloody hungry. Music is out of fashion.'

'Did you ever try advertising?'

'It isn't one of my accomplishments,' Rashers confessed.

'There's nothing to it,' Pat said. 'Come on for a walk with me and I'll show you.'

They went through back streets that both of them had known since childhood. They now looked different. There were too many men moving about and there was too little traffic. Nothing was happening. Rashers thought it was like Sunday without the bells. As they walked Pat said there was little hope of the strike finishing soon. It would go on through the winter. They were setting up food kitchens for the women and children in Liberty Hall. The Countess Markiewicz was going to serve the meals with her own hands. He asked Rashers if he had ever heard of her. Rashers grunted. She was one of them high class oul wans that were sticking their noses into a hundred and one things nowadays. Trouble-makers. Like Madame Despard and Maud Gonne. Acting the hooligan about votes for women when they should be at home looking after their husbands and their unfortunate children. Mad Gonne and Mrs. Desperate, the people were calling them. No wonder the city was starving.

The distant ringing of a handbell interrupted his thoughts and Pat said: 'Now you'll see what I mean.'

They turned the corner. The gleam of the three brass balls outside Mr. Donegan's shop caught his eyes first, then the long queue of women, each laden with ornaments or bundles of clothes, then the figure of the bellringer. He was a man of Rashers' age, but more hale. His body was hidden beneath two sandwich boards which were suspended by straps from his shoulders. The boards announced:

'Donegan's for Value
Best Prices
All Welcome'

'There you are now,' Pat said. Rashers stared, puzzled.

'What about it?'

'The advertising business. A job like that would suit you down to the ground.'

'What the hell use is that when this fella here has nabbed it already.'

'If Donegan finds it worth while to take on a man, so will somebody else,' Pat explained. 'The thing for you to do is to persuade one of the other pawnbrokers. What about Silverwater in Macken Street?'

'The Erin's Isle?' Rashers said. 'I'd have a hope.'

'Give me a minute,' Pat said.

He went across to the man with the bell. They talked for a while. Then he rejoined Rashers.

'Now we'll make our way to The Erin's Isle,' Pat announced.

It took them about ten minutes to reach Mr. Silverwater's establishment. It was an unusual building. Beneath the three brass balls the figure of Ireland, with golden tresses reaching down the green mantle about her shoulders, wept over her stringless harp. The scroll at her feet spelled out in white letters: 'The Erin's Isle'. A queue of patient women had formed outside.

'Now what do we do?' Rashers asked.

'We wait,' Pat said firmly.

Rashers wondered why. But it did not matter. There was nothing else to do.

'That's an occupation you get used to,' he said.

The pawnshop had once been a public house. Rashers remembered having a drink in it as a young man. About forty years ago, he thought. In those days it had not been so hard to find a crust to eat. Or so it seemed now.

'Do you remember Jeremiah Brady?' he asked Pat.

'Who was he?'

'He owned The Erin's Isle when it was a public house.'

'I don't remember it as a public house,' Pat confessed.

'Jeremiah had three faults that make a bad publican,' Rashers said. 'He stocked only the best, he kept too easy a slate and his best customer was himself.'

'A good man's failing,' Pat said.

'It put Jeremiah in Stubbs,' Rashers finished, 'and in the heel of the hunt it put him in Glasnevin.'

The sound of a handbell attracted the attention of the waiting women as the man from Donegan's turned the corner into the street. He nodded over at Pat. Then he began to parade up and down. The noise brought one of The Erin's Isle clerks to the door. Eventually Mr. Silverwater himself appeared. He found the bellringer parading up and down, bawling out the claims of Mr. Donegan to the patronage of his own customers. Mr. Silverwater was astounded.

'Hey, you,' he shouted, 'get to hell out of my street.'

The bellringer ignored him. Mr. Silverwater read the board in front and when the bellringer turned he suffered the shock of reading the same message on the back.

'Donegan's for Value
Best Prices
All Welcome'

'My customers,' Mr. Silverwater yelled at Pat, who had crossed over to sympathise with him. 'He wants my customers.'

'That's shocking,' Pat said.

'What's the matter with Donegan?' Mr. Silverwater asked. 'We're good friends. We often play poker together.'

'Maybe you beat him too often,' Pat suggested.

'We've been playing for maybe fifteen years,' Silverwater said, 'it couldn't be that.'

'He's taking advantage of the times to extend his trade,' Pat suggested. 'Business is business.'

'Business be damned,' Mr. Silverwater said.

Then he yelled again.

'Hey, get back to your own streets.'

'You won't shift him that way,' Pat said, 'let me talk to him.'

He went over to the bellringer. They held an animated discussion out of earshot of Mr. Silverwater. Pat returned. The bellringer went off.

'How did you do it?' Mr. Silverwater asked.

'I told him you're a friend of Mr. Donegan, and it wasn't very nice to cause trouble between you. I said you played poker together.'

'That was it. That was exactly my very strong emotions,' Mr. Silverwater approved. 'We are poker friends for years.'

'The trouble is,' Pat continued, 'he'll keep away from your shop all right—but will that stop him from parading the streets your customers live in?'

The villainy of it made Mr. Silverwater speechless. He nodded his head several times, unable to find words.

'I could tell you what to do,' Pat added. Mr. Silverwater clutched his arm.

'You speak,' he invited. 'I like you. You tell me.'

'Get a bellringer of your own. Send him around the neighbourhood every day.' Pat pointed to Rashers. 'There's a man over there that's popular and well known.'

He called to Rashers, who shuffled over. Mr. Silverwater looked him up and down.

'Can you ring a bell?' he asked Rashers.

'Everything from a door bell to a church bell,' Rashers confirmed.

'And you know the neighbourhood?'

'Born and reared in it—man and boy.'

'Do you want a job?'

'Lead the way,' Rashers said.

Mr. Silverwater did not hesitate.

'Come to me in the morning. I'll give you a start.'

Rashers said he would consider it an honour.

'I'll fix Donegan,' Mr. Silverwater swore.

They parted.

'You're a decent man,' Rashers said to Pat as they walked back towards Chandlers Court.

'It worked like a charm,' Pat agreed.

'If I'd the price of it I'd stand you a drink.'

'We'll take the wish for the deed,' Pat said. He went off smiling.

Rashers made his bargain with Mr. Silverwater. The job was worth ten shillings a week to him. He was furnished with sandwich boards which had the advantage of keeping out some of the cold. He was given a handbell and instructed to parade the neighbourhood during mornings and afternoons. One of his perquisites was a glass of milk and a bun on Saturdays when the shop closed and he had helped to put up the shutters. Life was a little better, but he was not happy. He found it hard to get about. Sometimes, especially on wet days, his bad leg ached and made him hobble. Sometimes his chest pained abominably and dizziness made the streets spin and spin about him. He began for the first time to be troubled by the hunger of others. The men who joked as he passed were gaunt and dispirited, the women he rang his bell at were hollow-eyed and worn. Little children pressed their faces to the glass on Saturdays to watch him eat and made the bun stick in his throat. He trudged through the streets and rang his bell and made up cheerful jingles to cry beneath the windows. But his heart was full of anxiety and his spirit was beginning to bow in defeat.

FOR two months Father O'Connor ministered in his stricken city. It had become a world of picket lines, thundering speeches, convoys that moved under police protection, bitter outbreaks of street fighting that were followed by day after day of apathy and misery. They were reaping now the fruits of their disobedience. They shook collection boxes at him: 'Help the locked-out workers.' God helped those who helped themselves. If they signed the undertaking to obey the lawful instructions of their employers there would be an immediate end to collection boxes and violence. But no. They listened only to Larkin. Pride it was.

Hunger was in the sky. Rashers, limping on his rounds, read it above him in large letters. As the weeks of the lock-out passed it continued to surprise him that a condition he had grown to regard as exclusively his should have become so general. Even the Fitzpatricks were selling their sticks of furniture. He had spotted the wife of a couple of times already in the queue at The Erin's Isle and that yellow-faced bitch of a Hennessy one with her. Giving her a helping hand with the bargaining, moryah—in return never doubt it for a cut out of what was coming.

Yearling, walking the city too, found it all as he had predicted. The challenge of the employers' ultimatum had been taken up, as he had known it would be. Now there was deadlock. They would fight it out through the Autumn; perhaps into winter. By banding together to break Larkinism the employers had turned an industrial struggle into a crusade. That, of course, was what William Martin Murphy had wanted. He heard the revolution call from the lips of the little children as he walked to the foundry. They had new songs about it and they sang one of them for him to the air of the latest ragtime thing about Alexander's Band.

> 'Come on along, come on along
> And join Jim Larkin's Union
> Come on along, come on along
> And join Jim Larkin's Union
> You'll get a loaf of bread and a pound of tea
> And a belt of a baton from the D.M.P.'

They knew him well now and were no longer in any way afraid of him, and when he shared his loose change with them they gathered about him and they all talked at once. They told him their mammies got food packs from Liberty Hall where a countess and other ladies were making up parcels of bread and cocoa and giving them out to them and they said there were ships full of food belonging to Jim Larkin and they were coming from England today, all the people had marched down to meet them. He asked them if they knew where England was and one of them said yes it was over the sea in Liverpool and the rest said yes that's where it was. So he said he would go down to see the food ships too if they would tell him the way and they led him along. But at the outskirts of the crowd he stopped them and said they must all go back now so as not to get hurt among all the people and he pushed his way through on his own.

The crowd was tightly packed. But his height gave him the advantage over most of the others and because he was well dressed and carried a cane under his arm and said excuse me with a voice of authority they made way for him.

The ship was covered from bow to stern with slogans and coloured bunting. Along the rails, smoking and talking and watching the activity, leaned several men whom Yearling recognised. They were members of the British Trade Union Congress. Jim Larkin was among them. He was a fine-looking man, full of confidence. There had been the usual speeches, you could feel it in the air. And whenever the men guided the laden trolleys down the gangplanks and pushed them through laneways of people to the waiting floats great cheers broke out. All this could be related with excellent effect to Ralph Bradshaw. Better, in a way, than that horse tram. The crowd cheered again and the bowler-hatted figure immediately in front of him joined in wildly. When it died away he tapped his shoulder. The head turned slightly. He had a glimpse of a thin excited face. Under the bowler a bandage showed bloodstains that were being gradually effaced by time and weather.

'Has Mr. Larkin spoken?'

'He has, sir.'

'Pity . . .'

A conversational opening occurred to him and he said: 'You've been injured recently, I see.'

Hennessy stiffened. He turned around as fully as the crowd permitted. The broad shoulders, the light cane tucked firmly under the well-tailored armpit, convinced him. He hedged.

'Just a little knock, Superintendent.'

Yearling hid his surprise.

'A baton charge, no doubt?'

Hennessy thought quickly.

'Ah no, Superintendent, nothing like that. A wardrobe I was moving for a lady fell on me.'

Yearling looked severe and squared his shoulders.

'I hope so,' he said. 'Take my advice and keep well away from the other thing. Our chaps are well equipped to deal with trouble.'

'I know that,' Hennessy said. 'I seen it often enough.'

The crowd cheered again. This time Hennessy remained silent.

'What name has the foodship?'

'*The Hare*, Superintendent.'

'*The Hare*,' Yearling repeated. 'And your own name?'

'Hennessy. Aloysius Hennessy.'

The face looking up at him reminded him of a small dog waiting to be struck. Yet there was refinement in it. And the eyes, large, long suffering, had liveliness and intelligence.

'How did you know I was a superintendent?' he asked, dropping his severity and becoming conversational.

'The build,' Hennessy said immediately, 'and the cane. Sure what would you be doing here otherwise?'

As he spoke Hennessy smiled. Yearling responded. His deception shamed him a little. Had he not enough advantage, without this. The crowd cheered again, still without help from Hennessy. Yearling, troubled a little by what he had done, said in a friendly tone:

'Cheer away and never mind me. There's no law in the book against cheering.'

'I suppose there isn't,' Hennessy agreed. But he stayed silent. It would be unmannerly, to say the least, in front of a plain-clothes superintendent.

That evening on the train to Kingstown he met Bradshaw. Opening his paper and sitting beside him he said:

'Do I look like a superintendent?'

'I beg your pardon?'

'Today I was mistaken for a superintendent of police. It's a useful thing to know.'

He spread out the paper. There was a long report about the ship and the speeches. Larkin, thanking the workers of England for their magnificent support, had said.

'You have broken the starvation boom.'

'An odd name—*The Hare*,' Yearling remarked.

'I've been reading about that,' Bradshaw said, 'why don't they mind their own business over there and leave us to mind ours. They are only prolonging the thing.'

'It cost five thousand pounds.'

'And a ship. Surely from their own point of view that's a criminal waste. Why not send the money?'

Because a name on a subscription list meant nothing. But a ship sailing in with food while the bands played and the flags and the slogans waved above cheering crowds, that was poetry. Dublin—a besieged city. 'You have broken the Starvation Boom.'

'Do you remember Mary Murphy?'

'Mary Murphy?' Bradshaw repeated.

Yearling quoted:

'Down by the river where the green grass grows
Where Mary Murphy washes her clothes . . . you remember?'

'Ah,' Bradshaw said, mystified.

'She's found a new sweetheart,' Yearling confided. He re
turned to his newspaper and became engrossed, unaware i
seemed, of Bradshaw's occasional, anxious side-glances.

At the food kitchens of Liberty Hall Catholic families wer
selling their souls to self-professed socialists for a bowl of soup
Father O'Connor saw them frequently, for he found it difficul
to stay away. They stood for hours, some of them from his own
parish, with mugs, jamjars, anything at all that would serve t
carry away what was being given out. Sometimes, instead o
soup, they got small parcels of bread and tea and sugar. Ther
was the usual joking, most of it vulgar, as was to be expecte
from them. He leaned on his umbrella at times to listen. H
would have admonished them publicly, but he had been for
bidden to intervene. He was not even allowed to give then
counsel in his sermons.

'I want no pulpit-thumping,' Father Giffley had replied whe
he spoke to him about it. 'Let them fight it out between them.

That was early on in the trouble, when the three of them wer
seated, as was customary on Sunday evenings, in the depressin
common room with its great centre table and heavy black arm
chairs and its enormous painting of the Crucifixion. The even
ing was warm and the fire made the air in the room stifling.

'The situation is so critical,' Father O'Connor pressed
'should they not be instructed in the dangers of socialism?'

'They are very fully instructed in the dangers of socialism
The press instructs them daily. The Catholic papers do s
weekly. The Jesuits have all relaxed throats running retreats
Every half-baked sociologist with a Roman collar thinks he doe
a service to Christ by upbraiding the destitute.'

'I do not pretend to be a sociologist,' Father O'Connor sai
coldly.

'You must find it very lonely,' Father Giffley snapped.

His face was red and the telltale vein in his temple was purple

He had been drinking heavily again. Father O'Connor struggled with his anger. It turned to contempt. He fought that too. The man was sick. In a reasonable tone he said:

'If we learned that proselytisers were distributing food and preaching in the parish we would take action. The socialists are doing the same thing.'

'No, it is not the same thing,' Father Giffley said. 'They do not pretend to show the road to heaven.'

'Their principles are a danger.'

'To whom—to Kingstown?'

Father O'Connor mastered himself.

'To souls,' he said quietly, after a brief pause.

'There is a more real danger to souls and to religion than any socialist,' Father Giffley said, rising. He walked over and stood above Father O'Connor. 'And it is my present duty to tell you what it is.'

Father O'Connor dropped his eyes.

'A heavy-handed pastor,' he finished and strode away.

Father O'Connor kept his eyes on the fire, anticipating the violent slam of the door. He waited, confident. But there was nothing further until he felt a hand on his shoulder. It was Father O'Sullivan.

'Has he gone?' he asked, looking up. Without waiting for the answer he looked around at the door. It was wide open. Beyond it he could see the hallway, which was empty. He looked back to Father O'Sullivan and said:

'Was I in any way unreasonable?'

'No, no indeed,' Father O'Sullivan said, 'not at all unreasonable.'

'Then why am I treated like this?'

'He is unwell. Please don't let it upset you.'

'I can endure the insults—they don't matter. But what of our duty. If every parish and every Catholic publication is warning against Larkinism, surely it is our duty to give guidance to our own parishioners. Is that being a heavy-handed pastor—as he calls it?' He appealed directly to Father O'Sullivan.

'Are you yourself satisfied to remain entirely silent?'

'His mind is better than mine,' Father O'Sullivan answered

simply. 'I am content to leave it to his judgment.'

'Judgment,' Father O'Connor repeated. He looked up. 'Is i
judgment—or John Barleycorn? The man is half crazy. And
you know it.'

Father O'Sullivan made a quick signal, cutting him off. The
parish priest stood in the doorway. He had a hammer and a
sheet of cardboard in his hands.

'Am I?' he said to Father O'Connor. He strode into the room
'John—a chair, if you please. Over here.'

Father O'Sullivan fetched the chair and placed it against the
wall.

'Now—your hand.' He helped Father Giffley, who climbed
on to it and swayed unsteadily for a moment.

'This will serve to remind others, John, of my instructions.'

He placed the cardboard to the right of the picture of the
Crucifixion and began to nail it to the wall. His shoulders hid
it from their view. He grunted as he drove each nail home
Then he turned and said :

'John—your hand.'

But while Father O'Sullivan was moving to his assistance he
swayed and fell from the chair. The impact of his fall made the
floor shake. They both rushed to him. There was a small cu
above his eye, which bled a little. His face had gone pale. Then
he opened his eyes and said :

'I fell, John.'

'Are you all right?' Father O'Sullivan asked, distressed.

'Perfectly.' He summoned his will, levered himself on his
elbows and smiled.

'The just man of the Scriptures never touched a drop, John
yet we are told he fell seven times a day.' They helped him to
his feet. He would not allow them to see him to his room. To
Father O'Connor he said :

'If I am crazy, then I am crazy in good company.'

He held out his hand to Father O'Sullivan for the hammer
took it, and left them. His gait was unsteady. Father O'Connor
looked at the cardboard on the wall. Father Giffley had written
on it in large letters with the red marking ink they used for
parish notices.

Notice

The Great St. Gregory has Said:
It Is Not Enough
To Have Learning. These Also
Are My Sheep.

They both looked at each other. Father O'Sullivan said:

'I'll open a window, if you don't mind.'

'Please do. The air is stifling.'

The frame screeched and bumped. When Father O'Sullivan returned to the table neither could find anything to say, until Father O'Connor, as though repeating an earlier question, said:

'What are we to do?'

'I don't know,' Father O'Sullivan said.

It was the first time he had ever admitted there was a question to answer. He tried clumsily to change the subject.

'The fire is my fault,' he apologised, smiling. 'I should never have complained about rheumatism. Whenever he finds me working in here he immediately orders the fire to be lit. There were times throughout the summer, I can tell you, when I was almost stifled to death.' He continued to smile, inviting Father O'Connor's participation.

'That is what I mean,' Father O'Connor, unsmiling, said. 'He is not . . . *compos mentis.*'

Father O'Sullivan gave up pretending to smile.

'I think I should go to his room and see how he is now,' he suggested.

Father O'Connor nodded. 'Of course,' he said.

The weather soon made the fires in the heavily furnished room welcome. The queues at the food kitchens became less talkative. The jokes, worn thin by repetition, fell out of currency. No one found new ones. It was work enough to keep alive.

She stuck her head around the door of the little room to see that all was in order; on the small table at the bedside two candles, as yet unlit, a basin with a clean towel, a delicate glass bowl lent by Mary and now containing Holy Water and a sprig of Blessed Palm which would act as a sprinkler, a white cloth also loaned by Mary, a crucifix. Was he sleeping? She called quietly:

'Bernie.'

'What is it?'

'You won't forget that Father O'Sullivan is coming?'

'Huh.'

The room smelled of stale tobacco, but there was nothing she could do about that. Father O'Sullivan was not one to notice

In the afternoon gloom of St. Brigid's the candles on either side of the tabernacle wavered into life as the clerk tipped each with the taper. One—a pause and it lit. Two. Both now. He genuflected. He knelt on the bottom step, the felt hammer now in his hand, the brass gong within reach. Father O'Sullivan kissed the stole and lifted it over his head and about his shoulders all in one movement, inserted the key in the door of the tabernacle, removed a communion particle from the ciborium and genuflected. The clerk struck the gong once, a warning that Jesus Christ, Body and Blood, Soul and Divinity really present under the appearance of Bread, was exposed on the altar. Father O'Sullivan placed the wafer from the ciborium in a pyx and put the pyx in his inside pocket. He locked the tabernacle. His boots, which were new, creaked as he genuflected again and removed the stole. In the vestry the clerk handed him his street coat, black, faded by age, and his hat, a shapeless one. All this was in silence. There would be no unnecessary speech or gesture while Father O'Sullivan carried on his person the Living Presence.

The streets were sunlit and had a lazy air. Trams and commercial vehicles passed him, guarded by policemen who were bored or by soldiers who were embarrassed. It would take about fifteen minutes to reach Chandlers Court. In a fixed mood of recollecion, his mind bent to the custody of eyes and ears, he passed the cab rank near the station, a public house, a series of garbage bins at the rear of an hotel. The smells were successively horsepiss, stale beer, decaying vegetable matter. The new boots squeaked at each step. They hurt him. The pain he could ignore. But the squeak, unseemly, incongruous, persistent, dragged his attention time and again away from his inward dialogue of veneration and love. In the end, being a simple man, he mentioned the matter apologetically. It became a joke. No longer embarrassed or distracted Father O'Sullivan for a while made fun of squeaking boots as he and Jesus Christ went together through the back lanes of the city. He never once mentioned the pain.

Patterns of October sunlight shimmered on the ceiling, holding his gaze for long stretches of unremembered time, trembling when a curtain stirred in a faint airy current or when a door somewhere down the afternoon house opened and slammed; delicate they were and voiceless, embodiments of drowsy things, of long past insubstantial summers. His mind in contemplation forgetting for long stretches his body without feet, forgetting pain forgetting the sentence of perpetual immobility, roamed among remote memories. In warm sunlight he stopped his horse and cart and jumped to the ground at a public house in a country lane where hedges brought the wild roses almost to the whitewashed wall and insects were busy about them everywhere. He kept goal for Liffey Wanderers between white uprights in a sunny field and stretched and touched his toes to pass the time because for several minutes the play had stayed away down at the other end. He picked blackberries on a warm Sunday and when a butterfly settled on his boot, beautifully white against the polished black leather, he kept very still and let it remain there. He came out of the sea at Williamstown and walking to his clothes the deep footprints in the soft oozing sand behind were summer too, summer of childhood of youth of manhood. With a swift movement of his hand he knocked the wasp from Ellen's neck and that was at the Scalp. It was the Liffey Wanderers' outing when the coloured streamers flowed out in the breeze or sometimes drooped down and tangled themselves and broke in the wooden spoked wheels. How many drags were there? Nine. Who was present that he could now recall? Mick Reynolds, George Brierley, Jack O'Connor, Cap Callaghan,

Alex Carr, Joe Kinsella. Others forgotten. Paddy Kelly the secretary he now remembered who had arranged the lemonade for the women, the sweets, buns, sandwiches, not forgetting the main thing which was the firkins of porter for the men. Winners of both the League and the Metropolitan Cup that year. Ellen yelled and the yellow-hooped body spun to the ground. He crushed it under his foot. Hard. Like that!

A dog barked in the basement. Father O'Sullivan went up the steps to the open halldoor, limped now through the hall, climbed the stairs, one landing, two landings, the third. The smells successively were woodrot from the basement, a privy odour in the hall, a conglomerate malodorousness of living as he climbed, individual stale airs, carbolic evidence of recent scrubbing. Limping still he came to a halt, rested briefly and knocked.

'This way, Father,' Mrs. Mulhall said in a whisper, reticent of speech and gesture, a lighted candle in her hand because of Christ Bodily Present. She led them without delay but also without haste across the scrupulously scrubbed and tidied room, knocked on the inner door to warn her husband, opened it, lit the candle on the table from her own and left her own on the table to companion the now lit candle on the table. Then without delay but also without haste because His present business was not with her she made her genuflection and withdrew, closing the door. She made a quick survey of the larger room for any impropriety of detail which might reflect on the thoroughness of her preparations. All seemed in order. She took out her rosary and knelt to pray. It was in no way remarkable to her that Jesus Christ Son of God the Father Creator of Heaven and Earth and of All Things should be one of the three people in the adjoining room or that He should come in person to the two pair back Three Chandlers Court. She had known Him a lifetime now and He was not by all accounts greatly taken with the Rich and He had been born in a humble house Himself. She was only sorry that He could not have seen her two china dogs. They were no longer on the mantelpiece. She had had to pawn them.

Having received Christ, Mulhall made his devotions quietly.

After an appropriate interval of prayer and meditation Father O'Sullivan crossed himself, waited unobtrusively until Mulhall had done likewise, and snuffed the candles. Hearing sounds again in the room Mrs. Mulhall busied herself and brought in on a tray (also borrowed from Mary) two cups of tea and some biscuits.

'This is trouble . . .' Father O'Sullivan began.

'What trouble, Father,' she answered and left them alone again.

He drank. He was glad of the tea but the biscuits distressed him. They were a delicacy rare in his parish and meant sacrifice.

'Ah—the women,' he said to Mulhall, and elaborately selected a biscuit.

Mulhall selected a biscuit himself and he was at once amused and tender.

'Biscuits, no less,' he remarked, 'she'd die or have style.'

'Isn't it a strange thing,' Father O'Sullivan said, 'I haven't had a biscuit this long time—and they're an item I'm very fond of. I must tell the housekeeper.'

'What you lack is a wife, Father.'

'It's a great lack indeed,' Father O'Sullivan acknowledged, 'but then again—suppose I got a cranky one?'

They both laughed at that and Father O'Sullivan took another biscuit. Then he became grave and said:

'Tell me, Bernie, are you at peace now with God?'

Mulhall hesitated and considered.

'With God—yes, Father.'

'I understand,' Father O'Sullivan said. 'Times are bad.'

'Times is very bad.'

Father O'Sullivan nodded his agreement.

'And I'd dearly love to be abroad—doing my bit.'

'To strike a blow,' Father O'Sullivan said, to show he understood.

'Do you condemn us, Father?'

'I go here and I go there,' Father O'Sullivan said, 'and the things I see would melt a heart of stone.'

'Yet some of the priests is never done condemning us.'

'And some don't,' Father O'Sullivan reminded him, 'but at

the same time you'd be the last to want them marching in procession with you.'

'I want them all to keep out of it—that's what I want,' Mulhall said vehemently. Then he added: 'That's what I meant, Father. I'm at peace with God, but when I hear reports of what some of them say, I'm far from at peace with certain of his clergy. Is that sinful?'

'Do you think you know better than they do?' Father O'Sullivan asked, but not offensively.

Muhall set his face.

'I do, Father.'

'You have first-hand experience of it, anyway,' Father O'Sullivan agreed. Then he said:

'But do you think you're a better person than they are?'

'No,' Mulhall said, 'that's another matter entirely.'

'In that case,' Father O'Sullivan said, 'I wouldn't worry unduly about a difference of opinion with them.'

'I'm glad you say that, Father.'

'The only danger I see in it is that it might lead you into hatred. Differences of opinion often do. First bitterness—then hate. That's the fellow I'd watch—Hate. That would be very sinful:'

'I see, Father,' Mulhall said. He was listening carefully.

'No matter what a man—or a priest for that matter—says or does, you can oppose him certainly, but you must love him all the same.'

'It's asking a lot,' Mulhall said doubtfully.

'Don't I know it is,' Father O'Sullivan agreed. 'And in times like this particularly. But there's no way out of it.'

'I know,' Mulhall said. It was the truth. Neither priest nor bishop had invented that one. It had come from Higher-up.

'That's the one I'd watch,' Father O'Sullivan concluded.

Mulhall frowned.

'Ah well,' he said, 'so long as we're not expected to give in to them.'

Father O'Sullivan carefully gathered the tea things on to the tray.

'I'll leave these with herself,' he said, taking his leave.

It was easy enough to give counsel, he told himself when he was again in the street, but an ounce of example was worth a ton of advice. Clothe the naked, feed the hungry, visit the sick. Well, he had done the last. But what of the first two. Father O'Connor had argued that charity only made things worse by prolonging the struggle without doing very much to relieve the suffering. The work was there for them; they were idle—destitute through their own choice. That was too glib and pragmatical. You had only to visit the tenements.

His feet hurt, his boots still creaked. He was limping noticeably. A cab driver drew in alongside him and hailed him.

'Are you going back to St. Brigid's, Father?'

'I am,' Father O'Sullivan said.

'Then hop in. I'm on my way back to the rank.'

'God bless you. Isn't it Tom Mangan I'm talking to?'

'That's right, Father.'

He got into the cab. It was a relief to be driven. It was also something of a novelty. He was not a man to spend money on cab fares. He had visited Mangan's wife about a month before, a sick call. The cab passed the rank and stopped at St. Brigid's. Mangan was going out of his way.

'You shouldn't have done that, Tom, the rank would have done fine,' he said when Mangan opened the door for him.

'A few yards—what's that,' Mangan said. 'Besides, your call brought us great luck altogether.'

'Is she coming on?'

'Famous,' Mangan said. 'I mentioned your visit to a regular passenger of mine, a doctor, and he said he'd come along and have a look at her. He's been calling twice a week since and whatever it is he gives her she hasn't had pain or ache since. He says she'll be fit to get up and about in a week or so. And it won't cost me a ha'penny.'

'I'm delighted to hear it.'

'You might know him, Father. He's a head man in the Rotunda, Dr. Hayes.'

'I don't then,' Father O'Sullivan said, 'but he's a good man to do that.'

'There's few like him,' the cabman agreed.

Father O'Sullivan waved his gratitude as the cab went down the street. The thought of the doctor's charity edified him. It was not, after all, a city of unrelieved bitterness or indifference. A man of learning regularly brought his skill to the bedside of a poor woman in the slums, and did so out of pity alone. He creaked his way towards the house. Father Giffley met him at the hall door.

'I see you came home in style, John,' he said. The tone was humorous.

'I did. A good Samaritan offered me the lift.'

Father O'Sullivan groaned without meaning to.

'I'll have to take off the boots for a while. They're killing me.'

He creaked his way through the hall. Father Giffley laughed. It was sympathetic at first but it grew too loud. He stood still in the hall, frightened for himself, as its echo died away.

CHAPTER 6

A LL day the high wind from the sea raked the streets of Kingstown. It slackened in the late afternoon, but as dusk came it began to freshen again. After dinner, while Father O'Connor played the piano for them and Mr. and Mrs. Bradshaw listened attentively, Yearling noticed that the oil lamp beside him was flickering from time to time. Taking care not to disturb his guests he searched quietly with his eyes for the source of the draught. The heavy curtains of the windows were stirring slightly. He sighed. All that was left to him of yet another of his diminishing store of summers was a warped window pane. He would have it seen to. In common with the rest of Kingstown he must take stock and prepare for the rigours of winter. He disliked doing that. It was always sad to bury a season.

The music was hypnotic but not inspiring. Ralph Bradshaw, he suspected, was in a torpor; Mrs. Bradshaw less so. He secretly appraised the comfort of the room. Soon he would have to surrender to fashion and science by abandoning his beloved paraffin lamps. He admired their soft light, the patterns of their beaded shades on floor and walls, their luminiferous elegance. But Progress had outmoded them. Soon they must go.

A gust of wind carried the sound of an ambulance bell into the room. It lifted to a peak, compelling their momentary attention, then the wind bore it away again and they returned to the music, the Bradshaws automatically, Yearling with an effort of will and only nominally.

He was so restless. His trip to London had been no help at all, except for the relief of stepping off the mailboat again at

Kingstown Harbour. Should he have married? Not as things had happened. Now youth had gone; manhood almost. And the old order he had been expensively brought up in was being bitterly assailed. It too would go. In London a great meeting of locked-out dockers had gathered about the platform of Ben Tillett and chanted over and over again in thunderous chorus: 'O God, strike Lord Davenport dead.' In Dublin Larkin flung his terrible phrase at the employers. 'You'll crucify Christ no longer in this town.' The streets were shaking with the sound of his voice, the burden bearers were straightening their backs. They were multitude. There would be no escape from them. In Moore Street he had watched the ragged urchins crawling beneath the barrows of the vendors in search of rotten fruit.

The music ended. Mr. and Mrs. Bradshaw said it was very nice. Father O'Connor apologised for the inadequacy of his technique. The music of Mozart was always more difficult than it looked. Yearling said the performance had been very accomplished and asked if anyone had noticed a draught. Mrs. Bradshaw and Father O'Connor assured him they had not. Bradshaw said he thought he had felt something.

'I think the window-frame has become warped,' Yearling said. 'It seems to happen every summer.'

They both went over to examine it.

'It's the sun,' Bradshaw pronounced. 'I have the same problem myself. And there isn't a competent carpenter in the country.'

'The windows opening on the garden give constant trouble,' Mrs. Bradshaw supplied.

'That's what I said,' Bradshaw told her impatiently. With the shortening of the days he always went over them, carefully sealing them with sticky paper which never failed to become unstuck again after a couple of weeks.

Father O'Connor had vacated the piano stool.

'Someone else,' he suggested. His tone was dispirited. His own performance had disappointed him. Sensing this, Yearling became jocular and went to the piano.

'There's a new music-hall song in London,' he announced, 'which amused me. It goes like this.'

He was not a pianist but he could vamp a bass to a melody in the right hand. He did so now, discordantly at times but with infectious enjoyment, half turning to the company as he sang to them:

> 'Joshua, gosh you are
> Sweeter than lemon squash you are.'

His imitation of a music-hall artiste made even Bradshaw smile. The atmosphere became more alive. When he had finished they applauded and he said:

'There were quite a few new songs. "Who were you with last night." "Hold your hand out, you naughty boy." "Hitchy Koo." "It's a long way to Tipperary." I went a lot to music-hall.'

'Can you remember any of the others?' Mrs. Bradshaw prompted. But her husband, alarmed at some of the titles, cut in quickly.

'What else did you do?'

'I went to gape at some suffragettes who had chained themselves to railings. They're burning empty houses now and setting fire to letter boxes.'

'Disgraceful,' Mrs. Bradshaw said.

'And everybody I met expects a civil war in Ireland.'

'Because of the Home Rule Bill?' Father O'Connor asked.

'Carson,' Bradshaw supplied grimly. 'He won't give up the North.'

'Tory hostesses are refusing to entertain members of the Government,' Yearling continued. 'And in the House someone flung his copy of Standing Orders at Winston Churchill's head.'

Another ambulance bell rang furiously outside, rising and fading as the wind caught it and carried it away. The conversation stopped.

'That's strange,' Yearling said eventually. 'I thought I heard one earlier—while Father O'Connor was playing.'

'I heard it too,' Mrs. Bradshaw said.

'Could it be a fire?' Father O'Connor wondered.

'I would hope not,' Bradshaw said, 'not in this wind.'

'Perhaps we should look,' Yearling suggested.

He and Bradshaw went to the hall door. They had to hold it against the wind as they opened it. Outside it was dark. Trees in the garden tossed wildly. They searched the sky. When they returned they could report nothing unusual.

'I've been wondering if it could be a baton charge,' Father O'Connor said.

'In Kingstown?' Mrs. Bradshaw exclaimed, horrified.

'Kingstown has its blackguards too,' her husband said, 'make no mistake about it.' He looked very grim. Father O'Connor agreed with him.

'Violence is everywhere,' he said, raising his hands a moment to deplore it.

'As Father O'Connor has good reason to know,' Bradshaw reminded the company.

'Yes, indeed,' Mrs. Bradshaw said—reminded.

'You are quite recovered?' Yearling asked.

'Quite recovered,' Father O'Connor's tone acknowledged their solicitude, begged them modestly not to be reminded.

'We live in terrible times,' Mrs. Bradshaw said. The ambulance bells, the gusting wind, filled her with foreboding. Outside the cosy circle of lamplight lay all the uncertainty and hardship of the world.

'I went shopping in town last week,' she told them. 'It was terrifying. There were little children everywhere and they were begging for pennies.'

Her husband regarded her sternly.

'I hope you kept your purse closed,' he said. She did not reply, but looked hopefully at Father O'Connor. He wore a sad look.

'The children are hungry,' Yearling said.

'They are hungry because they are on strike,' Bradshaw insisted.

'The children are not on strike,' Yearling challenged.

'Their fathers are,' Bradshaw said.

Yearling in turn looked enquiringly at Father O'Connor.

'What has religion to say to that?' he asked. He was smiling and conversational in manner, but his eyes were cold. Father

O'Connor became uncomfortable.

'We must all have compassion for those who are hungry,' he said at last, 'but this is not by any means a simple matter. It is the duty of the parents to feed their children. If through misfortune they are unable to do so, then it is our obligation in charity to help them. But in the present instance their hunger is not due to misfortune. It is the result of a deliberate decision not to work. If we help them we are doing at least two things that are unjust; we are encouraging them to defy their employers and we are prolonging a most distressing situation.'

Bradshaw looked approvingly at Father O'Connor and then turned to Yearling.

'I think that answers you very adequately,' he said.

'There is a third objection, to my mind the most important,' Father O'Connor continued. 'If Larkin and his colleagues win their fight it will be a victory for socialism. And socialism, as a very eminent Jesuit has clearly shown, is the worst enemy of the working man. It uproots his confidence in hierarchical order. It preaches discontent. It makes him covetous of the property of his social superiors, and impatient with the trials and obligations of his own station in life. If it does not destroy altogether his belief in God's Fatherhood, it certainly cuts him off from the graces and spiritual fruits which are the rewards of poverty cheerfully borne and which flow from humble resignation to God's Will.'

Father O'Connor was now very grave and looked unhappy.

'For these reasons,' he concluded, speaking directly to Mrs. Bradshaw, 'and I know how cold and even cruel it must all sound to a nature that is tender and maternal, we must harden our hearts.'

Her husband set his mouth and nodded approvingly. She lowered her eyes.

'I see,' Yearling said quietly.

He had read Father O'Connor's arguments in newspaper reports and leaders on countless occasions since the lock-out had begun. He probably preached that way too. Now they had an extraordinary effect on him. He found his sympathy to be completely on Larkin's side. The discovery filled him with good humour. In future he would help them whenever he could. He would not be the only one of his class to do so. George Bernard Shaw had spoken for them. George Russell, the mad mystic, had written a scathing letter against the employers. William Orpen, the painter, and several highly respectable intellectuals were denouncing William Martin Murphy and his policy of starvation.

He offered drinks to his guests and then said:

'Now, Mrs. Bradshaw, ma'am—something from yourself first—and then both of us will oblige.'

She smiled and went to the piano. His 'cello lay in the corner with new music he had bought in London in readiness beside it. It included a selection from *Il Trovatore*, arranged for 'cello and piano, which he looked forward to trying with her. As though she had guessed his thought, she said:

'I know you're just dying to try your new purchases.'

But he shook his head.

'Later,' he said.

She began a selection for piano from *The Merry Widow*. She had only started when a servant entered. After a moment of uncertainty he crossed and whispered in Yearling's ear.

'There is a sergeant of police at the door, sir—he says he must see you at once.'

Yearling nodded. He signalled to the others to excuse him and left quietly as Mrs. Bradshaw continued to play. In the hall a policeman whom he knew quite well saluted him.

'We've been searching everywhere for Mr. Bradshaw, sir. I understand he may be here.'

'Something has happened?' Yearling asked. Then he said: 'Step in here a moment.'

He opened the door to a waiting room and turned up the flame of its low-burning lamp.

'Is it a death?' he asked, when he had finished his business with the lamp.

The sergeant removed his helmet to wipe his forehead.

'It's them houses he owns down near the harbour,' he said.

'A fire?'

'No—not a fire, sir. We enquired at his house and were told he was here. Two of them collapsed about an hour ago. We don't know how many of the poor creatures is dead.'

As he spoke another ambulance bell beat violently above the roar of the wind and receded. From the room Yearling had left *The Merry Widow* waltz tinkled remotely. Yearling sat down for a moment to consider the news. Then he said:

'He is below with his wife. We mustn't shock her more than is necessary. If you give me just a moment I'll send one of the servants to fetch him here to us.'

'That would be best,' the sergeant said.

He waited while Yearling composed himself. He saw him rise and go to a tasselled rope woven of red and yellow threads. He saw him pull it.

They left Mrs. Bradshaw home and then went to the harbour side. Bradshaw was unable to say how many inhabitants the two houses had held, but his agent reckoned between forty and fifty. The death roll was seven when they arrived; within twenty minutes it had risen to nine.

'Was there no warning?' Yearling asked the sergeant.

'It seems there was,' the sergeant said. 'A man in the first house saw the wallpaper suddenly tearing across. He rushed around knocking at doors and warning people. They left as fast as they could.'

Rescue workers were everywhere among the pile of rubble. Above them, in the light of the acetylene lamps, Yearling saw the skeletons of the two houses, their rooms and stairways laid naked by the collapse of the wall. Twisted beams and broken floors and masonry hung at dangerous angles. From time to time pieces of brick and wood were wrenched loose by the wind and raised a cloud of dust as they fell. Among the ambulances and fire brigade engines were vans from the Gas Company and the Waterworks. Firemen had rigged the hoses in readiness against an outbreak.

'But not fast enough, it seems,' Yearling said, when two more bodies were released from the debris.

'Old people,' the sergeant said, 'or a mother trying to save her children.'

Father O'Connor had gone in among the injured. Two other clergymen were already busy. They said to him:

'The dead have been attended to.' He went down the line to a young woman whose dark hair was matted with blood. He gave her absolution. But she was barely conscious and kept saying over and over again: 'The children . . . the children.' As the rescuers worked, a guard with each party kept watch for signs of a further collapse. Bradshaw shuddered and touched Yearling's arm.

'They were passed as safe only a month ago. I have the inspector's letter.'

'Of course,' Yearling said. Then he said: 'You should go home.'

'How can I leave?'

'There's nothing further you can do. When they want you they'll call on you.'

They were rejoined by Father O'Connor.

'I'm telling Ralph he should go home.'

'Of course,' Father O'Connor agreed. 'Mrs. Bradshaw will need you.'

'It's the railway being so close,' Bradshaw said. 'I've written several times to them. The vibration affected the foundations.'

They brought him home. Yearling insisted on driving Father O'Connor back to town.

'Do you think it was the railway?' Father O'Connor asked.

'It was neglect and old age,' Yearling said grimly.

'But they were passed as safe.'

'They were condemned long ago—and then reprieved because Ralph knew the right people.'

'I refuse to believe it,' Father O'Connor said. He thought of the young woman who had been calling without cease for her children. Would they be found?

'If there's an investigation and the truth comes out,' Yearling said, 'Bradshaw and certain other gentlemen will be in trouble.'

Father O'Connor said nothing, his mind still occupied with the badly injured woman. He had ministered to her impulsively, without his usual horror of suffering. Pity and compassion and his priestly office had filled his thoughts. For the first time in his life the sight of blood had not frightened him.

The papers said:

'Appalling Disaster
Tenements Collapse
Families Buried in Debris
Several Killed And Injured
Ruins in Flames'

The fire, Yearling gathered, had broken out after midnight when a tunnel made by the rescuers let air into the smouldering ruins, but the fire brigade kept it under control. A boy of seventeen, Eugene Salmon, who had rescued several children, was killed himself while trying to carry his little sister to safety. A reporter of *Freeman's Journal* wrote: 'The two houses numbered 66 and 67 were owned by Mr. Ralph Bradshaw who is also the owner of extensive property elsewhere in the city. His agent, Mr. H. Nichols, informed me yesterday that about two months ago an official inspection of house No. 66 had been made and he had been directed to carry out certain repairs. This he had done and he states that the improvements were effected to the satisfaction of the inspector.'

At the inquest, the inspector confirmed the agent's statement. Yearling, reading it, knew that the collapse had been so complete that there could be no evidence left to prove or disprove the inspector's assertion. Later he received a letter from Bradshaw. He had been too shocked to attend the inquest, he said. He was taking Mrs. Bradshaw abroad for an idefinite period. His agent would handle all that was necessary. He would write soon.

The news headlines of the same day announced the opening of a relief fund.

'Freeman-Telegraph
Shilling Fund
For Relief of Sufferers
Homeless Families
Destitute Orphans
An Urgent Appeal'

Yearling put Bradshaw's letter aside and subscribed a thousand shillings. Then he thought again and sent on another thousand shillings, this time with the specific request that it should go to the family of the boy Eugene Salmon. After that he took a walk by the harbour, passing the ruins of the collapsed houses, about which the workmen were building a hoarding. It was a grey day, cold, with a mist blowing in from the sea. He walked towards Sandycove, remembering an October sunset of an earlier year, when the sea had drawn his thoughts towards England and a remote past and Father O'Connor had offered him God as a consolation, as though Christ could be passed around like a plate of sandwiches. The sea again compelled his attention, pounding in now through its grey mist and breaking on its grey rocks, an age old motion, dragging the pebbles after it in its backwash, full of terrible strength but not a brain in its vast bulk, a slave played on by every wind. The wind too was a slave, compounded out of combinations of hotness and coldness. What was there left now of school or university? No wisdom, little companionship, and memories only of an odd escapade. Two sentences ran in his head without relevance, mnemonics taught to him by his music teacher when he was a child of about twelve.

'Good deeds are ever bearing fruits'—the sharp keys.

'Fat boys eat and drink greedily'—the flat keys.

The information had been useful.

On his return journey he made a slight detour in order to pass the Bradshaws' house. It was boarded up and he stood to look at it. He regretted the piano inside, now silent, and the absence of the gentle woman who had played it. There was no longer anyone to bring flowers to.

Mary saw it boarded up too. She came to it, unsuspecting, at dusk on a Sunday afternoon. The gate creaked as she opened it, the carriage way was littered with leaves that had been left to rot. In places the wind had piled them into black hillocks. The window that had once framed a view of the splendours of Edward VII was shuttered. She knocked at the side entrance as a matter of form, knowing there was no one at all to answer and knowing too that its clamouring would fill her with terror. There were ghosts inside, ghosts of the Dead, left-behind ghosts of the Living. She forced herself to wait a little while, feeling a shutter might jerk open and that Mr. Bradshaw would glare at her from a curtainless window. She did not dare knock again at the basement door. She feared Miss Gilchrist's face.

Lamplight and candles showed in the windows of Chandlers Court when she returned home. Rashers limped into the hallway just a little ahead of her, his sandwich boards laid aside because it was Sunday.

Fitz was reading by lamplight. He had the kettle boiling for her on the fire. When he saw her face he left down his book.

'What is it?' he asked.

'They've gone.'

'The Bradshaws?'

'The house is all boarded up,' she said. Her voice was very quiet.

She began to prepare the tea. For the first time since the lock-out had begun she had returned empty-handed. The consequences troubled her.

'It never crossed my mind they'd go away,' she said to him.

'It crossed mine,' Fitz confessed.

'We're going to miss their help,' she said.

He knew that. The furniture, the flooring even, all had come from Mrs. Bradshaw. Food too and at times, he suspected, money. She took down the mugs the children used and put them on the table. Then she sat down suddenly and began to cry. He went to her.

'Mary,' he said, 'we'll manage. Don't let it upset you.'

'You know what's going to happen,' she said.

'I know,' he said, 'but we'll weather that. Others have gone through it already.'

She meant that now the furniture would begin to go, piece by piece, the pictures off the wall, the ornaments she prized because they gave the room an air of comfort and sufficiency.

'What will we do?' she asked.

'We'll have our tea,' he told her, 'it's not the end of the world.'

He took over the laying of the table and began to cut the bread.

'Where are the children?' she asked after a while. She had stopped crying.

'With Mrs. Mulhall.'

'I still have the money for their fare . . .'

'Well, then,' he said, 'that's the only real worry looked after.'

'Yes. My father would take care of them.'

'If it comes to that,' he said, 'but it may not.'

'You wouldn't mind?'

'When you feel the time has come—say so. Is that all right?'

'Yes,' she said. She took over the making of the tea again.

'This will be ready in a moment,' she told him.

'I'll go up and call the children,' he said.

When he had gone she paused for some time to measure their new situation. She turned down the lamp a little to husband the oil. Then she resumed her work.

When it became necessary Mrs. Hennessy conducted her to the pawnshop. They packed the pram with two chairs and a small selection of ornaments. Rashers was ringing his bell and entertaining the queue. His sandwich boards announced to the world that the value obtainable at The Erin's Isle Pawnbroking Establishment was superior to any other in the city. He had a rigmarole which he repeated over and over again. As Mary and Mrs. Hennessy joined the queue he rang his bell and called out to them.

'Now ladies step along lively with no shovin' and no pushin'. First come first served. Don't give the polis the impression that The Erin's Isle Pawnbroking Establishment is the scene of an

illegal assembly.' Then he rang his bell louder and bawled out
generally. 'Hay foot straw foot, Step along and see a live lion
stuffed with straw, Eating boiled potatoes raw. Have yiz e'er a
blanket to pawn or sell—e'er a table or e'er a chair? Best prices
in town for pairs of ornamental pieces.'

'That fella has a slate loose,' Mrs. Hennessy decided.

'I heard that, ma'am,' Rashers challenged her.

'It matters little to Ellen Hennessy whether you did or not,'
she said.

'But I'll not take issue on it,' Rashers told the queue, 'because
her husband did his bit in Sackville Street on Bloody Sunday.'

'What happened him?' a voice asked.

'He was walked on be a horse,' Mrs. Hennessy told her.

'Which is not half as sore as being walked on be an elephant,' Rashers said generally. He went off, ringing his bell in
triumph.

They queued for over two hours. The women discussed the
food kitchens and the arrival of scabs from England. They talked
about the health of each other's children and the way to drive
a good bargain with Mr. Silverwater and his assistants. 'Don't go
near the son if you can avoid it,' they advised Mary, 'he's worse
than the oul fella.' She waited and listened and tried to forget the
two chairs and the other articles that were lying in the pram. In
bits and pieces from week to week her home would be eaten
away. She was standing in line for the first time with the half
starved.

'Your poor children will begin to feel the pinch now,' Mrs.
Hennessy said.

'If it gets worse I might send them away,' Mary said.

'And where would you send them?'

But Mary was sorry she had spoken at all.

'It's something I'd have to speak to my husband about first,'
she said.

Rashers limped his way through the poorer streets of the city,
ringing his bell and giving out his rigmarole to keep his spirits
up and fight the fatigue and the monotony.

'Step up and see a live lion stuffed with straw, Eating boiled potatoes raw. Have yiz e'er a blanket to pawn or sell, e'er a table or e'er a chair? Best prices in town for pairs of ornamental pieces.'

A policeman threatened to take him in for disturbing the peace. For a while a gang of children followed him, attentive and curious. When he got back to Chandlers Court it was dark. He met Hennessy and sat down wearily on the steps.

'Sit down and have a chat.'

'I can't,' Hennessy said. 'I've to go out to do a bit of a job.'

'At this hour of the night?'

'It's a class of a watchman's job,' Hennessy said.

'Whereabouts?'

'Cramptons near the Park.'

'You're well got there.'

'I know one of the foremen.'

'I thought Cramptons men were locked out?'

'This is only a casual class of a thing,' Hennessy said uneasily, 'a watchman's job.'

'I'd be careful, all the same,' Rashers warned him. 'You don't want to be dumped into the Liffey for being a scab.'

'There's no picket,' Hennessy said. 'I'm not passing any picket.'

'Are there polis guarding it?'

'Not that I've noticed.'

'That's an ill-omened brood, the same polis,' Rashers said. 'One of them threatened to run me in today.'

'What for?'

'For ringing me bell in the pursuit of me juties. He asked me did I think I was a bloody fire brigade.'

'A smart alec,' Hennessy said with sympathy. 'I've met that kind myself.'

Rashers became enraged.

'In this kip of a city it's regarded as a crime for a poor man to go about his lawful occasions. The rich can blow factory hooters and sirens and motor horns and the whole shooting gallery. But when a poor man rings a bell for his livelihood it's regarded as illegal.'

'I'd a brush with one of them myself some weeks ago,' Hennessy said. 'A fella in plain clothes that was watching the food ships arriving. Asked for my name and address.'

'I hope you gave him his answer.' Rashers spat from the steps into the basement and peered into the darkness as the glob of mucous made its silent descent. It relieved his hatred of policemen. Hennessy decided it was not the moment for the whole truth.

'I took him very cool,' he told Rashers. ' "Who are you," I asked him—"and may I see your credentials, if you have any." '

'Did he show them?'

'He produced them for inspection right enough,' Hennessy lied. 'He was a superintendent.'

'That's where the public's money goes,' Rashers complained, 'paying thick-looking gougers from the country for spying on native-born Dublinmen. Did he try to interfere with you?'

'He was objecting to me cheering,' Hennessy said, 'but I took him up on it. "So far as my knowledge of the matter goes, and correct me if I'm wrong, Superintendent," I said to him—"but I'm not aware of anything on the statute books that makes it a crime for a man to cheer." '

'That was right,' Rashers approved, 'the nerve of the bloody rozzers in this city is appalling. Did he take it any further?'

Hennessy felt his powers of invention flagging.

'No,' he said, 'the matter rested at that.'

'Jaysus,' Rashers said, 'it bates Banagher. First they open your skull with a cowardly blow. And then they want to know your name, address and antecedents.'

He tried another spit, which sailed in a graceful arc between the railings. It pleased him.

'Were you down at the food kitchens at all?'

'Once or twice for curiosity's sake only,' Hennessy answered. 'I've no union card.'

'Did you ever see the Right Reverend Father Vincent Holy B. O'Connor down there?'

'I can't say I have.'

'Well—I did,' Rashers said, 'three times.'

'What brings him to those parts?' Hennessy wondered.

'It's not the soup anyway,' Rashers decided.

'No,' Hennessy agreed.

'It's no charitable thought that moves him—that's a certainty; a long cool drink of holy water is the most you'd ever get off that fella.' Rashers screwed up his eyes. 'It often struck me he might be a spy for the archbishop.'

'Ah, I don't know,' Hennessy said, 'Dr. Walsh is a decent man.'

'They're all the wan in this city,' Rashers said, 'condemning the poor and doing the unsuspecting Pope out of his Peter's Pence. I suppose you wouldn't have a cigarette to spare?'

'Not till Friday—payday,' Hennessy said.

Rashers nodded in sympathy.

'The same as myself.' He rose from the steps. It cost him so much effort that Hennessy had to help him.

'Don't get into any trouble over that job,' Rashers warned him. 'Watch yourself now. And make sure it's above board.'

'I'll do that,' Hennessy assured him.

But he was worried and decided to say as little about it as he could. Crampton's men were locked out. But there was no picket and he was not replacing anybody. He brooded over it as he walked along the quays, the river keeping him company for almost a mile. When he turned eventually into the back streets they were dark and unusually quiet. They oppressed him with their air of misery and hunger. His own children were sleeping on the floor and his wife had only an upturned box to sit on because the last of their few chairs had now been sold. The stump of a candle that guttered in the centre of the table could not be replaced until payday.

The neighbours were no longer able to spare anything. Something had to be done.

In the foundry Carrington, with the help of the clerical and supervisory staffs, was still managing to keep the furnaces on slow heat. An unanticipated problem was rust. It attacked idle machinery with a persistence that defeated all his efforts. Where he discovered it, he got the staff to treat it with sandpaper and oily rags, yet it threatened always to gain the upper hand. The overhead wires that fed the Telpher became slack after a stormy night and had to be left that way. A faulty gutter caused a patch of dampness to disfigure the wallpaper in the boardroom. He could do nothing about it despite Mr. Bullman's repeated instructions. There were ladders, but nobody who could be trusted to work at such a height.

Doggett, for the first time in his life as managing director, saw grass springing up between the cobbles in the loading yard. Winter would now arrest its growth, but its presence convinced him that, so far as he was concerned, things had gone far enough. The financial assistance he was getting from employers' organisations in England helped him with the cost of keeping his staff locked out; it could not protect his premises and equipment from the ravages of disuse. He spoke about it at a meeting and framed a resolution calling for a determined plan to recruit free labour from England. There was no lack of support. He had the satisfaction of seeing his proposal adopted without having to stick his neck out by moving it himself. In the matter of militancy Doggett's philosophy was to let others have the credit.

TIMOTHY KEEVER now toiled from seven in the morning until seven in the evening in the back portion of Xavier Broderick Sons & Company, Church Furnishers and Chandlers, Merchant's Quay, for a weekly wage of fifteen shillings. After two weeks of the lock-out Father O'Connor had used his kindly interest to secure the position for him. It was a non-union shop and the money was smaller than he had earned in Nolan & Keyes, but he was locked-out with the rest and had no choice. There were compensations. He was in out of the weather and the labour in the stores was mitigated by simple clerical duties which required him to carry at all times a heavy marking pencil and a fountain pen. These he displayed prominently in the breast pocket of his shop coat. There were disadvantages also. The clerical work, although it filled him with pride, took its toll in concentration and anxiety. His overseer was a foul-mouthed little man of atheistic and anti-clerical views and blasphemous observations to which he was provoked most frequently by the Holy Statuary that thronged both the stores and the shop. He passed discreditable remarks to Keever about the pious effigies of St. Joseph, the Little Flower, Blessed Martin of Porres, the Infant of Prague, The Virgin and even Christ the King. He suffered from stomach trouble and treated it by eating the charcoal which was sold for use in Thuribles for the burning of incense, his belief being that charcoal was very good for flatulence. Keever shuddered at his talk and felt there could be no luck in a place where charcoal destined for a holy purpose was pilfered and consumed in such quantity. But he feared to risk his own security by objecting and had to be content to close his eyes and shut his ears.

457

Sometimes when Father O'Connor came in on business he was called into the shop to speak with him. These were proud moments. The lady assistants looked on with respect and even the floorwalker smiled and said: 'Here is Mr. Keever for you now, Father.' So among the statues and the priedieus, the ciboria and chalices, the lamps of brass and the vestments hued according to liturgical ordinance, Keever enjoyed for brief moments a world that could have been a cluttered anteroom to the real heaven into which, his duty earnestly done and his earthly life over, he hoped by the Mercy of God and the intercession of the Saints to be eternally translated.

Mostly they spoke of the affairs of the parish, who was on strike, who had given in, what was the prevailing temper of the people. With Mr. Hegarty he still visited certain of the aged and the poor, dispensing on Father O'Connor's behalf what relief could be afforded out of the remnants of the fund. Father O'Connor had given up the hope of a regularly operating charitable society. The issues had become too complicated. It was impossible to distinguish between those who were suffering because of circumstances beyond their control and those who were hungry because they were in revolt against lawful authority.

But Keever could report that the suffering was spreading and growing more intense with each week that passed and that neither the strike fund nor the food kitchens could keep the condition of the mass of the people from deteriorating. One afternoon he told Father O'Connor that there were rumours of a new move, a plan to send the children of the strikers to working-class homes in England. The effect on Father O'Connor was quite astonishing. He began to tremble and had difficulty in speaking.

'Are they out of their minds?' he asked.

Keever was appalled at the effect of what he had reported.

'Maybe it's only talk, Father,' he said contritely, 'I shouldn't have repeated it to you.'

'No, no,' Father O'Connor assured him, 'this is an extremely grave matter. You did right to tell me.'

'I hope so, Father.'

Father O'Connor became very serious.

'Mr. Larkin may see nothing wrong in sending Catholic children to homes which are almost certain to be of the Protestant faith. But I'd expect Catholic parents to understand the grave danger. If you hear any further talk of this—even a whisper, make it your business to let me know immediately.'

'I will indeed, Father,' Keever said.

He returned to the stores, where, among the smells of colza oil and benzine, paraffin and brasso and beeswax, he made up parcels and filled cans and pondered on Father O'Connor's reaction to what he had reported, until the overseer interrupted him to draw his attention to a new consignment of statues and gave him a price list.

'I want you to mark these up,' he said. 'Put a price code on one of each kind and bring it up to the shop for display.'

Keever took the list and unpacked the first of the statues. It was St. Michael the Archangel. He looked at it in some doubt and said : 'Where will I mark it?'

The little overseer screwed up his face.

'On the right cheek of his arse,' he said.

Shock paralysed the hand in which Keever held the marking pencil. It refused to move.

'Go on,' the overseer said after a while. 'Do what you're told. There's no fear he'll sit down on it.'

Mulhall's face, once powerful and ruddy from the open air, grew smaller and became silver coloured. The bulk of his body under the bedclothes grew smaller too. More frequently now, as he lay between sleep and wakefulness the patterns on the walls cast by sunlight or lamplight drew him into the half-world of imagination, where he drove unearthly horses and humped weightless sacks in streets that were shadowed and soundless. He squared his great shoulders and led processions and listened at vast meetings to voiceless speeches. The bands played in dumb show, the torches waved wildly to noiseless cheering, faces mouthed words at him that he could not hear. But the exultation ended always, whether he was carrying sacks up a stairs or marching with his comrades, when he looked down in sudden agony to discover that he was walking on stumps. Sometimes he wept, but only if he was sure he was alone. At times it was for pity of self. At times it was because of the things he could no longer do for Larkin and the union.

Whenever they visited him he was still militant. Pat he liked best to talk to, because Pat was one of the strong-arm element engaged in ambushes on the police and in teaching scabs that strike breaking would not pay.

'That's my man,' he would say approvingly at the end of each account of a victorious clash, 'into the river with them.'

'That's the motto, Barney,' Pat would say. 'The prospect of a watery end is a great deterrent.'

Once, when Fitz said: 'One of these days you'll find your-selves had up for murder,' Mulhall grew angry.

'There's a lot of ways of murdering people,' he said, 'and one is to starve them.'

'That's not the law,' Fitz pointed out. Mulhall tried to pull himself up in the bed and roared at him:

'Whose side are you bloodywell on?'

But Fitz took the outburst quietly. Mulhall's anger with him was always brief.

When they got outside it was Pat who said: 'He won't last.'

'No,' Fitz said.

'How are they managing?'

'On Willie's strike pay. That's all they have.'

'Christ help them,' Pat said.

They went down the stairs together.

'What do you know about Hennessy, the fella with the bowler hat?' Pat asked.

Fitz became cautious.

'What should I know about him?'

'That he's got a job somewhere.'

'I didn't hear that.'

'To be precise,' Pat said, 'that he's watching at night for Crampton's.'

'He could be,' Fitz said.

'A few of us intend to find out. We'll lie in wait for him. If he turns up we'll let him have it.'

They were walking down the street now. Fitz stopped.

'I don't think you should do that,' he said.

'Crampton's men are locked out. It's a scab job.'

'He's an inoffensive poor devil with a crowd of young children,' Fitz said. 'I'm sure he doesn't see any harm in it.'

'He's replacing a watchman.'

'I don't think Crampton's ever employed a regular watchman.'

'I don't care whether they did or not,' Pat said truculently, 'if he isn't replacing a watchman he's helping the police by taking a job off their hands.'

'I'm sure he doesn't see it that way.'

'Then it's time it was made clear to him.'

'Look,' Fitz said, 'I don't want Hennessy beaten up.'

'He's got to be stopped.'

'All right. But leave it to me,' Fitz said, 'I'll have a talk with him.'

'Will it do any good?'

'He'll stop if I ask him,' Fitz said.

Pat was reluctant. His comrades had been killed and maimed. Lily, too, had pleaded with him to keep away from trouble and personal danger but he had refused. Force was the only answer. Sentimentality had to be discarded. He said to Fitz:

'When will you talk to him?'

'Now—if you like.'

'Right,' he said.

They turned back together and entered the house once more.

'Fetch him down,' Fitz said, 'I'll talk to him in here.'

'It's a pleasure,' Pat assured him.

Fitz went into his own flat to wait while Pat climbed to the next landing. He listened outside the Hennessys' door. He could hear the voices of children. A woman's voice was raised above the bedlam, scolding them. When he knocked the voices stopped at once. There was silence for a while, then the woman opened the door.

'I want Aloysius Hennessy,' he told her.

'He's getting ready to go out,' she said.

'Tell him he's wanted now. Down in Bob Fitzpatrick's apartment.'

Mrs. Hennessy examined the stony face. It frightened her.

'What's he wanted for?'

'He'll find that out when he comes down,' Pat said. He looked beyond her into the room. She had been giving the children their meal. There were jamjars with tea in them and some bread on the table. A sour smell flowed through the half-open door and mingled with the already fouled air on the landing.

'I'll tell him,' she said. 'He'll call in on his way down.'

She slammed the door.

There was something wrong. Pat knew the signs. He had knocked several times on doors like this one, calling out husbands who were breaking the lock-out. Sometimes when they refused to show themselves Pat and his butties broke in and dragged them out, while the womenfolk and the terrified children screamed and pleaded for another chance. It was necessary to close the ears to that too. Scabbing was infectious.

He decided to wait inside the hall door in case Hennessy tried to get out without meeting them, but it was unnecessary. In a few moments the thin figure with the oversized bowler descended the stairs and knocked at Fitz's door.

'Are you within, Mr. Fitzpatrick?' Pat heard him ask. He went up and joined Hennessy in the room.

'It's a cool class of an evening,' Hennessy ventured. He looked uneasily from Fitz to Pat.

'You don't know how cool it's going to be,' Pat said. The remark made Fitz angry.

'I'll do the talking,' he said. Then he turned to Hennessy and said: 'There's no need to be upset. It's just a few questions we'd like to ask you.'

'Certainly,' Hennessy said. His face had grown pale and his hands were trembling.

'You're working for Crampton's?'

'I am,' Hennessy admitted.

'For how long?'

'For the past four weeks.'

'What kind of work?'

'As night watchman.'

'How did you get the job?'

'There's a gaffer up there knows me. He gives me small jobs from time to time.'

Fitz was beginning to find his role unbearable. He pitied the thin figure with its stamp of lifelong suffering.

'What are they paying you?'

'Ten shillings a week.'

'A scab rate, too,' Pat put in.

'For Christ's sake shut up,' Fitz shouted at him. 'The man is being honest.'

Then he said gently to Hennessy: 'Did you know that Crampton's men are locked out?'

'I did,' Hennessy said, 'but I'm not replacing anybody. They never used a night watchman before.'

'It's a scab job,' Pat insisted.

'There was no picket,' Hennessy said, turning to him. 'I didn't think there was any harm in it. I mean . . . a night watchman.'

'If there was a picket would you have passed it?'

'No, gentlemen,' Hennessy said, 'I wouldn't pass a picket.'

'I'll save you a journey,' Pat said, 'there'll be a picket on Crampton's in the morning.'

Hennessy's features quivered and he had to struggle to speak.

'Whatever you say, gentlemen,' he answered.

'When are you paid?' Fitz asked him.

'On Friday nights.'

'Carry on until Friday and then quit,' Fitz said. 'If you promise to do that no one will interfere with you.'

'I promise,' Hennessy said.

'That's all I wanted to say,' Fitz concluded. 'Now go ahead and attend to your work until you draw your week's money. No one will interfere with you in the meanwhile.'

When Hennessy had gone Fitz warned Pat.

'There's to be no rough stuff,' he said. 'Is that clear?'

'You're too bloody soft,' Pat said. But his tone conveyed that he would do as he was told. It was not in his nature to go against Fitz.

Hennessy took his usual route by the river, to watch Crampton's premises from eight at night until eight the following morning. He had nothing with him for supper, not even a cigarette to dull the hunger or give a moment's illusion of company during the slow hours. At the end of the week he would draw his last ten shillings. He wondered what he would say to his wife. The thought of his numerous children was so unbearable that he pushed it in panic from his mind. Instead he kept his eyes on the path and the gutter, watching diligently for a discarded cigarette end that might be retrieved. But he had little hope of that either. Rain had begun to fall and path and roadway glistened damply.

When Mulhall died some days later it was Mary who went for the priest. First Mrs. Mulhall called over to her and said, in a voice which made Mary anticipate what was coming:

'Is your husband in?'

'He's not,' Mary said. 'Can I do anything for you?'

'It's Bernie,' Mrs. Mulhall said. 'He's been rambling in his mind and then sleeping. I don't like the look of him at all.'

'You want the priest for him?' Mary said.

'I've been waiting for Willie but he hasn't come home.'

'I'll go immediately,' Mary said.

'The children?'

'They'll be all right on their own for the while it takes,' Mary said. 'I have a guard for the fire.'

She hurried to the church. It was the hour when those who were lucky were finishing work. The streets were full of impatient people, the tramcar trolleys made blue flashes against the night sky and the wheels made a continuous rumble. She went to the vestry and gave her message. The last time she had been inside it was with Fitz just before their marriage. There had been a funeral, she remembered. Almost five years ago.

Father O'Connor was on duty. The clerk found him having his evening meal with Father O'Sullivan.

'What is it?' Father O'Connor asked.

'A sick call,' the clerk said. 'A Bernard Mulhall, of Chandlers Court.'

'Is it urgent?'

'The woman says he's dying.'

'Oh,' Father O'Connor said. He looked uncertainly at his unfinished meal. Father O'Sullivan had risen.

'I'll go, Father,' he offered.

'Oh no,' Father O'Connor said, rising in his turn, 'it is my responsibility.'

'I know the poor fellow very well,' Father O'Sullivan explained. 'I'd like to attend him—if you will allow it?'

He said it anxiously, as though afraid of giving offence.

Father O'Connor said: 'But of course—if you wish to.'

'Thank you,' Father O'Sullivan said. He threw his napkin on the table and indicated to the clerk that he would go immediately. Father O'Connor felt he should at least have finished up what remained on his plate. The clerk went out to tell Mary the priest would come at once. She hurried back to help Mrs. Mulhall to prepare.

So it was that Father O'Sullivan made his way once again to Mulhall's room, this time to administer the final sacrament, to forgive him his sins, to anoint his five senses with holy oils. He found the room prepared as before, though this time with signs of haste and this time without the fine glass bowl and without the white linen cloth, which had been sold. A cup held the holy water, a sheet of clean paper covered the table. Mulhall's breathing made the room shudder. His mouth gaped open, his cheekbones looked as though they would burst through the taut skin. His Spirit had already surrendered to death. Only the body continued the struggle, going through the repetitious motions, mechanical, instinctive, unaware. Father O'Sullivan signalled and Mary led Mrs. Mulhall from the room. The sound in it terrified her. She was glad to be able to leave.

Father O'Sullivan bent over the labouring body. He spoke to it, but knew there would be no response. He then began to administer Extreme Unction, blessing with holy oils each eye, each ear, the lips, the palms of the hands. From long habit he loosened the bedclothes at the foot of the bed, then as he did so remembered that there were no feet to anoint. He tucked the clothes back under the mattress again. The breathing suddenly became quieter, although when he looked the mouth still gaped open. He took the lower jaw in his hand and closed it firmly. For a while the face remained in repose, the cheekbones no longer threatened to burst it asunder. He watched, thinking for a moment that Mulhall had come through his crisis of unconsciousness into natural sleep. He may have done so. But as Father O'Sullivan was about to call to him again Mulhall sighed, stirred a little, and died. Father O'Sullivan knew immediately. For a moment Death was a presence. He felt it enter the room. He prayed. In a brief while Death ceased to be a presence and became merely a state.

He went to the door and summoned Mrs. Mulhall. Mary was still with her and her son Willie, who had just come in. He avoided saying her husband was dead. Instead he said: 'I was just in time.' His face and the gentleness of his tone told her the rest. She went past him into the room.

'Everything has been done that should be done,' he told Willie. To Mary, as he was leaving, he whispered: 'Stay a little while with her and comfort her.' Mary nodded.

Mrs. Mulhall was standing at the bedside. Her world of girlhood and womanhood lay there. She would listen no longer in the nights for the furtive signals of distress. She would rise no more in the hours of darkness to calm a man suffocating in nightmares. It was at an end now. She said to Willie:

'You'll have to go down to Mrs. Henderson in Townsend Street and tell her. Tell her to come and attend to him and lay him out. We must have everything arranged and decent before the neighbours begin to call.'

'I'll do that,' he said, 'I'll do it now.'

His voice was very like his father's and as he went Mary noted the same deliberate movements, the confident set of his shoulders. He was almost twenty now, she reckoned. She went to the older woman and put her hand about her shoulders.

'We reared a good child,' Mrs. Mulhall said. She was speaking not to Mary but to her dead husband. She sat on the bedside chair and reached out her hand to touch his forehead. 'Bernie,' she said to him. 'My poor Bernie. This is what their machines have done to you.' She turned to Mary a face that became contorted as she struggled to speak. At last she said: 'What am I to bury him with?'

Her grief mastered her. She stretched her body across that of her husband and sobbed.

The meaning of the question at first evaded Mary, then shocked her. Mrs. Mulhall had no money. There was nothing to pay for the decencies of death and burial, for the shroud and the coffin, the carriages and the undertaker. Mrs. Mulhall, looking at her husband's body, had seen a pauper's end for him. It was a shame too terrible to bear thinking about.

Mary waited for Mrs. Mulhall's grief to exhaust itself. Then she said: 'Whatever happens—that won't happen.'

'Where can I turn?'

'The neighbours will see to it.'

'How can they,' Mrs. Mulhall said, 'when they've nothing themselves?'

'Have you no insurance?'

'I had to stop paying it. There were things over and above that had to be got for Bernie. Every week I did my best to pay it up but always there was something. Then it lapsed altogether.'

'You're not to fret yourself about it,' Mary said, 'we'll think of something.'

Already she had thought of something, a thought which frightened her and which she tried to push away. She struggled with it as she kept vigil beside Mrs. Mulhall, until at last Willie and the woman whose customary work it was to wash and prepare the dead of the parish arrived.

Mary went across to her own rooms and found Fitz with the children. He had heard the news.

'How is she?' he asked.

'She'll be all right for a while,' Mary said. 'Willie is with her. I want to give her some candles.'

'Can I do anything?'

'Not at the moment,' Mary said. She found the candles. There were six of them, her own reserve supply. They would help to furnish the wake. She was about to bring them across when she changed her mind. She put them on the table and sat down.

'Fitz,' she said, 'I want to talk to you.'

'What is it?' he asked.

'The Mulhalls have no money and no insurance. Unless they

467

get help the poor man will have to be buried on the parish.'

'We could try to organise something among the neighbours,' he said, but not very hopefully.

'The neighbours haven't enough for themselves.'

'I don't know of any other way,' he said.

She made up her mind as he was hesitating and said quickly, 'I do.'

He stared at her.

'There's the money we laid by for the children's train fares,' she reminded him.

The suggestion took him by surprise.

'And you'd lend them that?' he asked.

'If you think it would be the right thing to do,' she answered.

He thought of Mulhall, his independence, his pride.

'Yes,' he decided. 'I think that would be the right thing to do.'

His tone reassured her. She went to the hiding place where the few pound notes had been lying since the lock-out began. She counted them. Then, as though she must get it done before prudence tempted her to change her mind, she said: 'I'll give these to her straight away, before the neighbours begin to call on her. It'll relieve her mind of that much at least.'

He nodded in agreement. It was a hard decision. But it was right. There was no option.

Mulhall had his wake. There was no tea to pass around and no drink for those who called. They did not expect it. No one nowadays had anything for hospitality. But he had candles and a habit and, when the customary two days had passed, a coffin and a hearse. The grave belonged to Mrs. Mulhall's mother and father, whose bones already occupied it. The neighbours and his trade union colleagues walked behind him and men with hurling sticks on their shoulders escorted the procession, forming a guard of honour. The sticks were an innovation, defensive weapons against police interference, now carried at all trade union processions by men who called themselves soldiers of the Irish Citizen Army. It was a new body and its members drilled and studied military tactics. They knew they were an army of scarecrows but they did their best to keep their backs straight and to walk in step. They had been formed to protect trade union meetings against police interference. If the police charged it was their job to strike back.

Willie Mulhall was one of them and already a veteran of a number of engagements. The hurling stick on his shoulder, which had the shape and feel of a rifle, filled him with pride. So did the huge turn-out of workers and the fact that a detachment of police followed the procession all the way to the church. It showed that his father had been recognised as a leader by the authorities too.

The police followed but kept their distance. The procession was big, but orderly. There was no band and there were no speeches. But there were blazing torches to carry which filled the air with the smell of pitch. Streamers of sparks were plucked from these by the wind and went scattering above the heads of the marchers. As Willie Mulhall watched them pride and grief struggled for supremacy in his heart. Fitz watched them too. Love, he thought, was better than prudence. The flaming torches were telling the city that the people of his class would not be starved for ever.

CHAPTER 8

THERE had been a time, Yearling remembered, and it did
not seem to be so long ago, when he had wished to be
forty again. Now, re-lathering the face that stared back
at him from the mirror, he would have settled cheerfully enough
for fifty. But the morning sun which had found a chink in his
bedroom curtains had announced it and the calendar in his
pocket diary had confirmed it; another birthday was upon him.
He was fifty-three. If he ever saw fifty again, he told himself
(pouting the under lip and removing an area of lather and hair
with a deft upward stroke of the open razor) it would be on a hall
door. That was the way life went. You closed your eyes a while.
You opened them and the thief had been and gone. What could
one do, except go on shaving. There was a time when he had intended to grow a beard because it seemed a pity not to give
expression to one's total potentiality. He would never do so
now. It was too late for revolutionary changes. Procrastination
had undone him. If, in the next life, the Master chided him for
burying one of his talents, he would point to the moustache as
an earnest of his good intentions.

With his fingers he explored minutely his face for areas that
might have been skimped, but the job was satisfactory. He
emptied the shaving mug (the water had grown tepid) cleaned
his razor, stropped it, put it away. As he did so he whistled 'Is
Life A Boon?'

The sun sent a finger of light into the hallway and the house
smelled agreeably of bacon and eggs. The barometer, an
habitual liar, declared for wet and windy. Like the barber's
cat, Yearling decided, tapping it from habit. A solitary post-

card on the breakfast table had a basket of flowers worked in crochet on the front and on the back it said: 'Many happy returns—Florence Bradshaw'. She had not forgotten. There was no address but the stamp was Italian.

'Robert,' he said to his servant, 'you may wish me a happy birthday.'

'Many happy returns, sir.'

'Thank you.'

'Will there be anything else?'

'Nothing that you could provide, Robert. Isn't that unfortunate?'

'Indeed it is, sir.'

'You'll find some envelopes on my dressing table, Robert, with something for each of you. I've also ordered some refreshment which will arrive in the evening. It's addressed to you. Share it out and drink my health.'

'You're very generous, sir.'

'But please watch Mrs. Lambert. Last year she wanted to come up and play the piano.'

'I'll certainly guard against any repetition, sir.'

'Thank you—you could bring me the marmalade.'

'I'm sorry, sir—I thought you had made a ruling against marmalade.'

'It gives me indigestion. But it's my birthday and I'll risk it.'

'Yes, sir.'

Sunshine gleamed on the roofs of the town and the sea lapping on the rocks was as gentle as summer. A gull on the wall stared intently at the horizon, as though expecting a ship. In the streets women with empty shopping bags were hurrying to ten o'clock mass. The Pope's green island. Carson was fearful of it. No Home Rule for Signor Carsoni. Home Rule is Rome Rule. Ulster will fight. And Ulster will be Right. A Protestant Parliament for a Protestant People.

The poet William Mathews met him as arranged at the Merrion Row gate of the Green. They lunched in the Shelbourne. Yearling drove his new motor car and found comfort in being rich. It was a Straker-Squire 15.9 horse power, price four hundred and sixty-eight pounds. It took them afterwards by Bray and Kilmacanogue, where Parnell had changed horses and sometimes slept on his way from Avondale to Dublin, then across the brown expanse of Calary bog and eventually to Glendalough. They parked and entered the ruined monastic city on foot. An ancient gate gave them access. The Round Tower rose into a clear sky. Beyond it the lake was a mirror for blue, precipitous mountains.

'Very lovely,' Mathews remarked.

'I was here with my father exactly forty years ago,' Yearling said. 'It was my thirteenth birthday. That day, too, was sunny and beautiful.'

'Were you fond of him?' Mathews asked.

'Very,' Yearling said. 'He was one of the few human beings I have ever loved. This is a little pilgrimage to honour the past. I hope it doesn't bore you.'

'On the contrary, I am surrounded not by the past but by the literature of the immediate present. Round towers, seventh-century saints, harps, legends and shamrocks.'

'Mother Erin,' Yearling suggested.

'Two divine persons in one,' Mathews said. 'A mother lamenting her children in bondage. A girl ravished by the Saxon, who weeps over her stringless harp. But her young champions keep watch in the mountains, awaiting the dawn of the bright sun of Freedom. They will gather around her with pikes and swords.'

'I thought they were waiting to do that at the rising of the moon.'

'There are two schools—the nocturnal and the matutinal,' Mathews conceded, 'but one basic thought. Arm. Rise. Cast off the Saxon yoke.'

'We are great dreamers,' Yearling said. Pensive, indulgent, he poked with his stick the grass about the base of a gravestone. Monastic Ireland lay broken about him. St. Kevin's kitchen, St. Kevin's cell, St. Kieran's church, a Celtic cross. Beyond the wall was the deer stone, in the hollow of which by command of the saint, a deer had shed its milk each day to nourish a baby whose mother had died in childbirth. Illuminated manuscripts of the tonsured saints, bronze bell and tallow candle, latin text and colloquy in the soft tongue of the Gael, these upon the rising of a mysterious sun or in a night of full moon would all be restored. A shepherd walking in the dew of morning would find milk again in the hollow of the stone. Young men, taught by old men, believed it.

On the gravestone a horseman and Roman soldiers followed Christ to his Crucifixion. The horseman, he noticed, wore a cocked hat and eighteenth-century costume. He looked closer. The Roman soldiers carried guns. He drew Mathews' attention.

'Do you notice anything?'

Mathews peered for some time.

'Ah,' he said at last, 'a latter-day Saviour.'

'The stone is by Cullen,' Yearling told him, 'a local mason, if I remember rightly. There should be other examples.'

They went searching. At the end of half an hour they had located three. It was quite enough.

The path took them by the shores of the lake, with the forest on their left. The day remained calm and beautiful. As they walked Yearling returned to an earlier thought.

'Do you consider the removal of the Saxon yoke possible?'

'Everything is possible,' Mathews said.

'Desirable, then?'

'Carson doesn't think so, but then he doesn't regard it as a yoke.'

'The Gaelic League?'

'A confused body. They had a clash the other day over whether the Portarlington Branch should have mixed classes.'

Yearling stopped, relished it as a titbit. Then he pursued:

'Arthur Griffith?'

'A formidable man—in the tradition of Swift. Burn everything English except their coal. Have you read his *Resurrection of Hungary*?'

'No. But I've heard his Sinn Feiners referred to as the Green Hungarian Band.'

'Don't underestimate them,' Mathews said. 'Their policy is national self-sufficiency. And there are young men with him who will keep vigil on the mountains. Dangerous young men, from the Saxon point of view. That suit you're wearing—where was it made?'

'In London.'

'And your shoes and your shirt?'

'English.'

'And your new motor car?'

'You could call it a Saxon yoke,' Yearling admitted.

'If you spend all that abroad,' Mathews said, 'what hope can there be for Irish workmen.'

'Are you a Sinn Feiner?'

'No,' Mathews said. 'I'm a follower of Jim Larkin.'

Yearling, examining the elegant figure beside him, smiled. Larkinism was the fashion now among the writers and the intellectuals. Moran in the *Leader* had suggested that Liberty Hall ought to form a Poet's Branch. Russell had written a moving letter in the *Irish Times* on the strikers' behalf. Shaw had championed them at a meeting in London.

'You should write them a marching song,' he suggested, 'something bloodthirsty, in dactylic pentameters.'

'I've done a little more than that,' Mathews said, 'I've helped in Liberty Hall.'

Yearling stopped smiling. Mathews, he realised, despite the light manner, was in earnest. With delicacy he asked: 'I am interested to know in what way a man of letters can help?'

'There are several ways. By canvassing editors to publish articles for instance. By sending testimony about conditions here to writers in England and asking them to speak and write about it. It all helps.'

'Do you know Larkin personally?'

'I've conspired to hide him when there were warrants for his arrest. I've done the same for others among the leaders too. I've even gone out at night with buckets of paste and pasted notices of meetings.'

'I see. Are you not afraid I might have you'—Yearling searched for the expression—'*turned-in?*'

'Not at all. The police know already. They won't arrest a gentleman. The Castle, I imagine, has told them not to. It creates the wrong kind of reaction.'

Yearling stopped again.

'Mathews,' he asked, 'do you intend to renounce riches?'

'Never,' Mathews said, 'Riches and I will remain inseparable.'

'Good,' Yearling said. 'Now I know I am in the company of a true poet. You must take me down to Liberty Hall sometime. I'd like to see it at work.'

'It will be a pleasure,' Mathews assured him.

They reached the end of the lakeside path and stood again to remark the quietness. They could see the Round Tower, now far away to their right, a finger of stone that men had built a thousand years before. It rose now above their bones and the rubble of their dwelling places. There was no stir on the lake nor among the reeds at its edge. White clouds hung without movement in a blue sky. The sun was warm. It drew an Autumn smell from the bracken. There had been a day like this forty years before and there had been days like this when men were putting stone upon stone to raise their tower; there would be days like this in years to come when he himself would have joined the dreamers under the monument and the nettle.

He shouldered his walking stick and remembered the barometer in the hall. It had never been so wrong. As he walked back he said to Mathews :

'Do you know the expression—wet and windy, like the barber's cat?'

'I know it well,' Mathews confessed.

'Why the barber's cat, I wonder?'

'A consequence of frugality,' the poet explained. 'Its staple diet is hair and soapsuds.'

The explanation was unexpected but, on reflection, curiously satisfactory.

'I see,' Yearling said.

The day which filled Yearling with nostalgia for the lost world of boyhood found Mr. Silverwater in a contrary mood. He was not a lover of sunshine. At the best of times it hurt his eyes. When unseasonable its unexpected warmth was uncomfortable. He was a man who regulated the weight of his underwear in accordance with the calendar on a rigid basis calculated over a lifetime. It was his misfortune to have a constitution intolerant of cold and an occupation which obliged him to work in what he was convinced was the draughtiest shop in Dublin. The unseasonable day caught him in two sets of vests and underpants, in addition to the usual jacket, waistcoat and woollen cardigan. The result was a feeling of prickly suffocation. He endured it. The alternative of taking something off would expose his health to the mercy of more seasonable temperatures likely (at the drop of a hat) to return. But the discomfiture preyed on his spirit. He snapped at his customers and drove ruinous bargains. He was not sure that he wanted custom. His shelves and his storerooms were choked with paraphanalia which, if the lock-out went on very much longer, would never be redeemed. On an already glutted market their present value was negligible. At lunchtime he discussed it with his senior clerk. They went through the storerooms together. There was too much in goods and too little in capital.

'From Monday, Mr. Johnston,' he decided as they were both opening the doors for the afternoon trade, 'from Monday, business with regular customers only.'

Mr. Johnston approved by nodding his head until it was in danger of flying off.

The sound of Rashers' bell in the distance held them listening for a moment in the shop door.

'That's another thing, Mr. Johnston,' Silverwater said, but did not finish his thought.

'Of course,' Mr. Johnston answered, as though there could be no possible doubt about whatever it was.

Rashers, who had no underwear at all, praised God for the heat of the sun. It would do him good; his cough, the creaking in his bones. He rang his bell at gatherings of men and women, at dogs that barked back in fury at him, at terrified cats that arched their backs and then shot away from him. He rang it for the amusement of the children. They no longer jeered at him. His sandwich boards and his bell had transformed him into a person of consequence, someone they wanted to be when they grew up. Their admiration filled him with pleasure.

At lunchtime he went to the waste lot where the man in the striped pyjamas still smiled from his perch on the unsinkable bovril bottle. The religious text had been changed. It now read: Take up your Cross, and follow Me.

Rashers took off the sandwich boards and made a seat of an upturned bucket. He began his lunch. He had bread and dripping and a bottle of water. It was quiet and sunny. Three birds were dozing on a nearby chimney. They were silhouetted against the sun. He failed to determine whether they were gulls or crows. The grass at his feet and the warmth of the sun set him thinking of race meetings he had attended long ago, when he was active enough to walk long distances to play his tin whistle for the crowds and hardy enough to sleep at nightfall in the shelter of a ditch. Officers and their ladies, gentlemen with tall hats and binoculars, three-card-trick men, tipsters and fruit vendors. He had often bought himself an orange from one of their trays. If he had one now he'd eat it skin and all. A ditch was well enough in summer if you remembered to bring plenty of newspaper. One of these days, when the summer came, he'd buy himself an orange. To hell with the money.

He put on his boards again and tested his bell. The birds rose from the chimney stack in fright. He was stiff from sitting. He put one foot carefully before him and then the other and after a few difficult steps walking became a simple enough matter. More or less. The bloody boards were a weight. Take up your cross was right. Here I come, Jesus, one front and back.

At doors in the unexpected sun the old and the cripples had been left out to air. He greeted each of them. A Grand Day, he shouted. Thanks be to God, they shouted back. Or gave no answer but smiled. Or made no response whatever, neither hearing nor seeing him nor anything else, habituated to separateness, aware only of being put out and taken in like clothes off a line with each change of the weather. When I can no longer fend for myself, Rashers prayed, then God, let me die.

The thought stirred him to activity. His voice resounded in the street that had opened its hall doors to let in the sunshine.

> 'Have yiz e'er a blanket to pawn or sell
> E'er a table or e'er a chair
> Best prices in town for pairs of ornamental pieces.'

He worked contentedly through the afternoon, until at half past six or thereabouts his bell was heard once again outside Mr. Silverwater's shop. By that time he was weary. He wondered about his dog, which had been locked up all day. He wanted to get home to it, to make himself tea with water which Mrs. Bartley wouldn't mind boiling for him, to take off the boots which were crucifying his feet. There were no customers at that late hour. The interior of the shop was dark after the light of the streets. Mr. Johnston looked up from a ledger, blinking at him.

'Tierney,' he said, 'Mr. Silverwater wants to see you.'

'Where is he?'

'In the store at the back.'

Rashers, used to the place now, lifted the counter panel and let himself through. He groped his way down a dim passage. Mr. Silverwater was trying to make sense of the conglomeration which had built up as a result of the lock-out.

'You wanted me,' Rashers said.

Mr. Silverwater dragged his thoughts from the problem of his stock with some difficulty. He stared at Rashers.

'I did, Tierney. Let me see. Yes. You can leave the boards and the bell here tonight.'

'And what about the morning?'

'You won't need them. I've decided to stop this advertising.'

'Are you not opening tomorrow?' Rashers asked.

'Our arrangement has come to an end,' Mr. Silverwater said. He was still preoccupied.

'Do you mean I'm sacked?' Rashers asked. He was rooted to the ground.

'You finish up tonight,' Mr. Silverwater said, 'Mr. Johnston will put away the bell somewhere. Give it to him on your way out.'

'And my money—what about what's due to me?'

'Call at the end of the week for it,' Mr. Silverwater said. 'We'll settle whatever you're entitled to then.'

Rashers felt an ache inside him, as though something were eating at the wall of his stomach.

'Could I not finish out the week?' he asked.

'Not another hour,' Mr. Silverwater said to him. He waved at the junk which surrounded them.

'Do you think I can afford to take any more of it. The half of it will never be redeemed and there's no one I know who would buy it. It's regular customers only from this out. I'm busy now. Call back on Saturday for your money.'

He turned his whole attention to his stock. Rashers tried to piece an appeal together. It was useless. The ache wouldn't allow it. He stared foolishly at Mr. Silverwater's back. He could think of nothing. In the end there was nothing to be done except to take off the boards and leave them against the wall. He went back through the passage and into the shop. Mr. Johnston was still engrossed in his ledger, staring hard at it in the poor light. Rashers put the bell on the counter beside him. He looked up at that but Rashers made no effort to talk to him. He opened the door of the shop and stepped out into the street. Dusk was settling over it and the pavement was giving back a little of the heat it had stored during the course of the beautiful, unseasonable day. Its ghost still haunted the sky. As Rashers limped his way slowly towards Chandlers Court, it faded away. The sick and the dying had been taken in again from the steps.

In the night time hatred kept Mrs. Hennessy awake. She heard her children whimpering with hunger and cried out to God to curse those who had stopped her husband from earning. By day, though it tormented her unceasingly, she kept it hidden away. She searched out small charities and showered blessings on every giver. Her mouth seemed to have no lips at all, her eyes were those of a bird of prey. She borrowed daily and sent the older children out to beg. When hope of borrowing was exhausted she went into remote neighbourhoods where people would not know her and begged herself, until a policeman terrified her by asking her name and address.

He made a great show of taking out his notebook and examining the point of his pencil.

'Is your husband on strike?'

'No, sir. He's a decent man and they stopped him from going to his work.'

'Who stopped him?'

'A bad neighbour, sir.'

'What name?'

She hesitated. The notebook and the helmet terrified her.

'A man named Fitzpatrick—and a butty.'

'Where does Fitzpatrick live?'

'In the same house as myself, sir.'

'I see.' She watched as the policeman wrote the information into his book. He closed it with a snap.

'Be about your business now,' he said to her. She hurried away. It was some time before it occurred to her that she had given information about her neighbours to the police. The thought brought her to a stop.

The evening sky drizzled rain, leaving fog patches in laneways. She was more terrified now and still without food. The Protestant charities she could go to would want her to turn away from her religion and deny the Blessed Virgin. That would bring worse luck still. Temptation began to trail her through street after street. At the gates of St. Brigid's she stopped again. She peered through the rain at the church. If her own clergy refused her, there would be nothing else left.

The door of the vestry was opened to her by Timothy Keever.

'Is Father O'Connor within?'

'What name?' he asked.

'Mrs. Hennessy.'

He thought he recognised her.

'From where?'

'Chandlers Court.'

It was a street that was barred to him for ever.

'And your business?'

'I want a little help. I have a houseful of hungry children and my husband was stopped from working by a gang from the union. Don't turn me away empty-handed.'

'Who stopped him?'

'Bob Fitzpatrick and Pat Bannister.'

She had informed again. It was too late now to turn back. She heard Keever saying:

'I may be able to help you. Come inside.'

In the waiting room set apart for the altar boys he listened attentively to what she had to say.

'Your husband is not in any union?'

'No, sir.'

'And the neighbours are against him?'

'The most of them is, sir.'

'Have you heard any talk among them about a scheme for sending children to England?'

'There was a meeting about that only yesterday.'

'Where?'

'In Liberty Hall.'

'Father O'Connor has been hearing rumours of this for some time past,' Keever said, 'and if it's true he'll want to know everything about it.'

'It's true enough,' she said, 'the mothers were told that homes could be found in Liverpool for hundreds of the children.'

'Do you know of anyone who agreed to take part?'

'A few weeks ago Mrs. Fitzpatrick told me she was thinking of sending her children away.'

'To Liverpool?'

'She didn't say where. She said she'd have to ask her husband about it.'

'I see,' Keever said. It was his duty to keep Father O'Connor informed. The woman would be useful in the future.

'I can't assist you now,' he told her, 'because I've to wait here for Father O'Connor myself. But if you call to my house later—about nine o'clock—I'll see you get a share of whatever help we can afford.'

'The blessings of God and His Holy Mother on you for that.'

'Say nothing to others about it,' he warned her, 'in case there'd be more blackguardism.'

'I'll say nothing at all,' she assured him.

He saw her to the door. He felt sympathy and pity for her. She closed her shawl against the rain and walked the streets aimlessly, wearing the time away until it was nine o'clock. She refused to think about what she had done. The hours stretched endlessly. She bore them rather than face her children empty-handed.

Father O'Connor found Keever's news confirmed in his newspaper. A Mrs. Rand and a Mrs. Montefiore had been organising accommodation for the children of the strikers in the homes of workers in England. The report said they had three hundred and forty offers already. The headlines and editorials reflected his own horror. Little Catholic children were to be sent to Protestant or even socialistic homes, regardless of the risk to their faith and their immortal souls. The scheme would be used as a trap by the proselytisers. Larkin had finally shown his hand.

Father O'Sullivan admitted the danger. The Catholic press seemed certain of it. There was little to be hoped for from Father Giffley. All he could expect from that quarter would be a snub. The notice hanging on the wall to the right of the picture of the Crucifixion still commanded him to be silent. He put the matter to Father O'Sullivan.

'I think perhaps if you were to approach him.'

'I wonder if I should?'

'We have a duty. Surely you agree?'

'Yes,' Father O'Sullivan said, 'I think we must at least ask for a direction.'

But he returned to report failure.

'There is to be no preaching. We are still forbidden to take sides.'

'Did you stress the danger of apostacy—that souls may be lost to us for ever?'

'I told him I believed that possibility certainly existed.'

'And what was his answer?'

Father O'Sullivan hesitated.

'He is a hard person to understand. He said it would be a poor religion that couldn't stand up to a few weeks' holiday.'

'If that is the view he takes,' Father O'Connor said, 'we will be forced to act in spite of him.'

Press reaction justified him. The editorials worked up a public outcry. A priest from Donnybrook led a picket of Catholic militants to patrol the quays and the railway stations, determined, he declared, to prevent the move by force if necessary. Other clergy joined with him. The archbishop addressed a letter to the mothers of the children. He asked them if they had abandoned their faith and put it to them that they could not be held worthy of the name of Catholic mothers if they co-operated. The headlines made a display.

> *'Workers' Children*
> *to go to England*
> *Catholic Mothers*
> *Archbishop's Warning'*

Father O'Connor now knew where his duty lay. If he was forbidden the use of the pulpit, he could still make a physical protest. The souls of little children were at stake. His way was clear.

The controversy took a dramatic turn which caused Yearling to consult Mathews. He wrote:

My dear Mathews,

I have just read that Mrs. Rand and Mrs. Montefiore have been arrested (!) and are to answer a charge of KIDNAPPING!!

Can you throw any light on this? It seems quite preposterous. Is there anything I can do?

This public pandemonium about Proselytising is beginning to irk me, pallid Protestant though I am. There was a verse in the Leader *the other day*

> *'Where naked children run and play*
> *Oh, there we find the wily*
> *The slum soul-snatching bird of prey*
> *At work for Mrs. Smyley'*

Is it yours, by any chance?'

B. Yearling

Mathews answered:

Dear Yearling

It is true that the two ladies in question have been arrested and are being held on the charge which you rightly describe as preposterous. It cannot possibly stand up, but it will keep them out of the way and I suppose the authorities find this a convenient device for upsetting our plans. It shows the lengths they are prepared to go to support the employers. To hell with them. I have volunteered with some others to conduct the children to the ships and the railway stations. Would you care to join us?

The verse you quote shocks me. Naked children?

Here is one from the pen of a humble, working class scribe. I read it in The Worker *the other day.*

> *'A toiling and a moiling*
> *O what a life of bliss*
> *They'll promise you heaven in the next life*
> *While they're robbing you in this.'*

Robust and down-to-earth—isn't it? He has all this religious hocus-pocus in shrewd perspective.

T. Mathew.

Yearling thought about it. He decided to write again:

My dear Mathews,

Yes. I will join you. But as an observer. Let us arrange it.

Yearling

FATHER O'CONNOR, having fortified himself with a substantial lunch against a day that he felt was going to be exacting and distasteful, went out into the streets of Dublin to do battle for God. He had rehearsed his motives meticulously to make certain they were sincere. They were. Catholic souls needed his intervention. Although the children of his parish might be of little consequence to the world they lived in: lowliest of the lowly born, illiterate, ill-used even, each was as precious to God and had as much right to salvation as the highest and noblest in the land. In that belief he would play his priestly part. He regretted only that Father O'Sullivan had not seen fit to join him.

Proselytism was rife. He had known cases of it personally, where families attended bible-readings because soup and bread were given in return. One child had told him of being enticed into the house of a lady who had the servants put him in a bath and scrub him with carbolic soap before feeding him and handing him tracts which, fortunately, the child could not read. Perhaps God had His own purpose in the general illiteracy of the poor. A more experienced colleague had made that shrewd observation to him. Father Giffley wouldn't listen to stories of that kind. But then Father Giffley was in the grip of an addiction which had already gone far towards unbalancing his mind. These people had money and leisure. They had even learned the Irish language to spread their heresies among the peasantry in the remote wildernesses of Connemara. During his novitiate a friend had shown him one of their bibles in the Irish language.

His first call would be on Mrs. Fitzpatrick. If it were true that she intended to send her children away he must take every step to dissuade her. She had been trained in a good house and was intelligent enough to understand the harm that must follow. Through the kindness of Mrs. Bradshaw she had had plenty to be grateful to God for. Would she repay the debt in this way? That was the question to put to her. His line of approach was clear.

The next thing was to remember where she lived; not the house, which he knew fairly well, but the particular room. He did not want his presence to be known to everybody. That would be indiscreet, even unjust.

He picked his way through streets which were threatened with an assault against the Motherhood of the Church and citizens who by and large did not seem particularly to care. They pursued their own lives and bent their thoughts to their own narrow affairs. They raised their hats briefly to him as they passed him on the pathways. They held up public house corners and spat at intervals to pass the time. They thronged the shops and carefully counted their change. And every so often a tram passed guarded by police, or a convoy of lorries guarded by police, or simply a cordon of police on the way to guard something not as yet equipped with the protection applied for. That was the pass the city had come to: hatred, strife, hunger, ambush, disobedience.

There were men now who made violence their everyday concern. They planned assaults on the police and attacked those who were replacing them at their work. In the county of Dublin farm labourers who had been locked out were burning outhouses, spiking fields, maiming cattle and forcing the farmers who had once employed them to go about armed. The socialists were the instigators, but the masters themselves were not without blame. They had been wanting in justice and, above all, in charity. He had told them so from the pulpit before he left Kingstown, warning them that Christ Himself had said He would not be found in the courts of Kings, where men were clothed in soft garments, but in the desert. The slums about him were the desert. Among the poor who inhabited them must Christ be sought out. That was where the masters had failed.

And because of that failure the devil had now taken possession.

His parish engulfed him, spinning its web about him of malodorous hallways, decaying houses, lines of ragged washing. His work had not been very fruitful. He had failed to learn how to love them as brothers and sisters. But he could love them as a father by instructing them and protecting them against temptation and weakness. At least he had walked their grim streets and entered their unsavoury rooms. In time he would learn to communicate with them.

Chandlers Court acknowledged his presence. Here and there a head appeared at a window; the children stopped their play to stare at him; one or two men saluted him. He stood still, recollecting. Number 3? While he tried precisely to remember, two figures whom he recognised emerged from a hallway. One was the scarecrow of a man he had had to dismiss from the post of boilerman. He felt reluctant to approach him. They came nearer to him. Tierney, that was the name. Father O'Connor, detecting pride in his attitude towards a poor, crippled oddity, put himself to the test. He waited, his stance one of enquiry and irresolution, until they came near him.

'Good evening, men,' he said.

Hennessy raised his hat and said, 'God Bless you, Father.' Rashers said nothing.

'Tierney, my man,' Father O'Connor said, 'I would like you to show me to the room in which Mrs. Fitzpatrick lives—if you can spare the time.'

'I can do that, Father,' Hennessy volunteered.

'Just a minute,' Rashers said, 'I'm the one that was asked.'

'I'm sorry,' Hennessy said.

'And I'd like to tell Father O'Connor what he can do,' Rashers continued.

Hennessy looked at his face and became alarmed.

'Now, now, Rashers,' he pleaded. He put his hand on Rashers' arm.

'Shut up,' Rashers said. He turned his attention to Father O'Connor. He leaned forward on his stick to be closer to him.

'That's the first civil question you've addressed to me in a number of years, Father,' he said, 'and I'm not going to answer you. But I'll give Hennessy here a message he can deliver to you.'

'Now, now,' Hennessy implored. 'Remember Father O'Connor is one of God's holy anointed.'

'He is indeed,' Rashers agreed, 'and I'll tell you what to answer him on my behalf, because I wouldn't insult one of his cloth up to his face.'

Rashers looked back at Father O'Connor.

'So you can give the Reverend Gentleman this message from Rashers Tierney. Tell him to ask my proletarian arse.'

He turned and hobbled away. When Hennessy found his voice he said : 'For God's sake, Father, don't pay any heed to him or take any offence at all.'

'I am not offended.' Father O'Connor said quietly.

'The poor man has been out of his wits this long time.'

'I am not angry,' Father O'Connor said. His face was white.

'Then let me do what little I can by showing you the Fitzpatrick's apartment,' Hennessy offered.

Father O'Connor kept his voice under control.

'Thank you,' he said. He followed Hennessy, who continued to apologise. Father O'Connor made short but quiet replies to all he said. The insult had found its way to his stomach. He felt chilled.

'Do you intend to drive all the way?' Mathews asked. He was uneasy.

'I have been wondering should I,' Yearling answered.

'Not quite to the hall door, perhaps.'

'A bit ostentatious, you think?'

'Well . . . Better not.'

'Pity. If I had thought of it, we could have rigged up a Red Flag on the bonnet.'

'Just as well you didn't.'

Yearling looked disappointed. 'For a poet,' he said, 'you lack a taste for the dramatic. Shelley scattered pamphlets on the heads of passers-by from his lodgings in Grafton Street.'

'The pamphlets were in support of Catholic Emancipation.'

'Oh—that's rather different.'

'In fact he later gave great offence in his speech to the Friends of Catholic Emancipation by arguing that one religion was as good as another. Both Catholics and Protestants were outraged.'

'Quite understandable,' Yearling said. 'To be persecuted by a fellow-Christian is understandable. To be liberated at the hands of an agnostic, unbearable. I think I'll park here.'

They stopped near St. Brigid's.

'Do you plan to pick up the children at Liberty Hall?'

'Yes.'

'Have we time for a drink?'

'Plenty,' Mathews said. But when they were ordering he would only take a ginger beer.

'A hint of alcohol on the breath and Larkin would ask me to go home,' he explained.

'Oh—and what about me?'

'Perfectly all right,' Mathews said, 'the children won't be in your charge.'

'You sound smug, Mathews.'

'To tell the truth, I'm just a bit frightened,' Mathews answered.

They strolled down to the North Wall. A large crowd had gathered at the Embarkation sheds, respectably dressed men and some women too, with a sprinkling of priests. Their banners read: 'Kidnapper Larkin': 'Save the Children': 'Away with Socialism'. When a car approached they spread across the road and stopped it. They questioned the driver and searched inside before letting him drive on, then grimly resumed their watch for God. One of the priests moved constantly from group to group, a purposeful man with a heavy face.

'That reverend gentleman is Father Farrell of Donnybrook,' Mathews remarked, 'an actionist if ever there was one. Yesterday the children were seized when they tried to board the mail boat at Kingstown. In fact some of the children were with perfectly respectable parents who had a deal of trouble getting them back into their custody. I'm told that one lady was obliged to open her box to show her marriage certificate.'

Yearling had read of these things and found them rich in human absurdity. Now he looked at the reality. It was shoddy. It was worse. It was unbelievably ugly. He took Mathews by the arm and both turned away.

'Let us get on to Liberty Hall,' he suggested. Humour had deserted him.

Father O'Connor climbed the stairs and knocked on the door Hennessy pointed out to him. He waited. At first Hennessy's footsteps, sounding on the stairs, filled the house with noise. When they had receded Father O'Connor became conscious of a great stillness. There were children's voices somewhere above him, but at a great distance it seemed, so faint and intermittent that they made the stillness about him hard to endure. He knocked a second time and knew from the sound that the room was empty. Was he too late? The thought that the Fitzpatrick children might be on their way to the boat already, alarmed him. He began knocking again, this time with his umbrella, with such force that the handle broke off. It rebounded off the door and made a clattering noise on the wooden floor. The sound brought him to his senses. He must control himself and think. As he searched in the half-light to recover the handle of his umbrella a door on the other side of the landing opened and an elderly woman came out. She was frightened until she recognised him.

'It's yourself, Father,' she said, reassured. He searched for the handle and found it before answering her.

'Who have I here?' he asked.

'I'm Mrs. Mulhall, Father,' she said. He peered at her.

'Ah yes—of course.' He remembered her now as the woman whose husband had recently died. She might be able to give him the information he was looking for. He stuffed the umbrella handle into his pocket and said: 'I'd like to have a word with you, if I may—immediately.'

'Certainly, Father.'

She led him into a room in which upturned boxes were serving as table and chairs. The linoleum showed unworn and unfaded patches here and there in places once occupied by furniture. An easy chair at the fireside stood out in incongruous luxury. She dusted this and offered it to him. He sat down. She was, he remembered, a good and devout woman. Father O'Sullivan had spoken most highly of her. The death of her husband must have been a cruel blow. He would have to refer to it. Presently.

She sat on one of the boxes opposite him and he found an opening.

'You are going through hard times,' he said, looking about at the evidence of the room.

'We're all having the bad times, Father,' she answered. Although he was agitated he found time to have pity for her, an ageing woman sitting on a box in a home without a fire. Whoever might be responsible for the evils of the times, it was not she. Exercising patience, he said:

'Your husband's death was a sad blow, I'm sure.'

'It was at first, Father, but now I'm happy God took him when He did. He was lying there all those months breaking his heart because he couldn't be out and about with the rest of the men.'

'You are very brave.'

'If nothing could ever give him his two legs back to him, why should I wish God to keep him lying there fretting and suffering.'

Father O'Connor nodded. He remembered more precisely now. They were speaking of the man who had assaulted Timothy Keever and whose conduct he had deplored from the pulpit. The woman was not embarrassed. Father O'Sullivan, no doubt, had made it his business to reassure her in her time of trouble. It was a gift which most puzzled him in that humble and otherwise very ordinary priest. 'Your resignation is a great credit to you,' he said. 'It is indeed.'

'God was good to me,' she answered, 'and I had the kindest of neighbours.'

He could now move nearer to the enquiry he wished to make.

'One of your neighbours is Mrs Fitzpatrick—isn't she?'

'The kindest and best of them.'

This made it more difficult. He deliberated.

'You have a very high regard for her—I can see.'

'With good reason, Father.'

'Then if I tell you I'm here to help her and to persuade her against making a very grave mistake, you'll assist me?' The woman hesitated. He sensed her uneasiness. Conscious suddenly of his own isolation in this poverty-haunted parish, he set his will to the duty before him.

'You must trust me,' he urged.

'I was never much hand at meddling in another's affairs.'

'Sometimes it becomes our duty,' he told her, 'I'm sure you'll understand when I explain to you.'

She nodded. He took up the umbrella to lean forward on it and rediscovered its lack of a handle. That upset him. He pushed it aside.

'You know that there is an attempt at the moment to send children to England. And you know, I am sure, that the Archbishop himself has written to deplore it. God knows what sort of homes these children will end up in; Protestant homes, for all we know—or homes of no religion at all. I am told that Mrs. Fitzpatrick intends to let her children go. And I want to persuade her to remember her Catholic duty.'

'Who told you that, Father?'

'I am not at liberty to say. But it is a person I place trust in. Have you any knowledge of it?'

'I know it couldn't be true, Father. I'm the closest to her in things of that kind, and I've watched the children for her many a time. If the thought had ever entered her head, I'd know it.'

'Where is she now?'

'She's out walking with her children, a thing she always does when the afternoon is fine.'

'Did she ever speak to you of sending her children away?'

'She did, several weeks ago. But it was to her father in the country she was thinking of sending them.'

'I see,' Father O'Connor said. The woman was very sure of herself. He knew she was telling what she believed was the truth.

'Did she say this to anyone else?'

'She may have, Father, but not to my knowledge.' A thought occurred to him which he knew he must express delicately. He found it hard to spare the time to do so. The children might at that moment be on their way.

'Times have been so very hard with all of you,' he suggested. 'Could it be that she intended to send them to her parents if the necessity arose, but found when the time came that she could no longer afford to do so?'

The woman hesitated again. It took her some time to answer.

'It could have happened that way,' she said at last. She appeared upset. He felt he was near the truth.

'In that case, she might well have been tempted to take part in this Larkinite scheme instead.'

The woman began to cry.

'Please don't be upset,' he said. 'I have to say such things because of what is at stake. Do you know if she had money to send them to her parents?'

'She had indeed, Father . . . but she gave it to me.'

The woman was weeping bitterly now. Suspicion of the cause made him rise and go to her. She was not telling him all she knew.

'Are you holding something back?' he asked, 'If so, I command you as your priest to let me know the truth. Is she taking part in the scheme?'

'No, Father, I'm certain of it.'

'We cannot be certain.'

'She'd have told me.'

'She might not. Why did she give you the money?'

He was now standing over Mrs. Mulhall. Suspicion and anxiety had swamped his pity. She turned her head away from him.

'When my husband died I had no money in the world. She gave me hers.'

'Why?'

The woman struggled to answer. He repeated himself.

'Why?'

'So that I could bury him with decency,' she said.

The reply took him by surprise. He understood now why his questions had upset her. But the fact remained that he could still not be sure that the scheme was not the desperate alternative.

'What she did was edifying and Christian,' he said, 'but if it has led her to such despair that she has allowed her children to be taken away from her, then it would have been better for all of us if she had kept her money.'

The woman's sobbing became uncontrollable. He took the broken umbrella under his arm.

'Forgive me for the upset I have caused you,' he said. He went to the door. What he had said struck him as bald and unpitying. He had not meant it that way.

'Please don't feel I am too harsh,' he added. 'The fate of these little children is an urgent and terrible charge on all of us.'

He closed the door and strode across the landing to knock once again at the Fitzpatrick's apartment. There was still no answer. Enough time had been lost already. He went down quickly into the street.

Merchandise cluttered the South Wall of the river. At the berth of the one shipping company which had remained open by refusing to join the Employers' Federation a single ship was working. To the right and left of it idle ships waited through flood tide and ebb tide. Larkin had said they would be left there until the bottoms were rusted out of them. Across the river, about the Embarkation sheds of the North Wall, crowds had gathered. Father O'Connor made for Butt Bridge. There were crowds at Liberty Hall also, he noticed. If there was to be a battle for the children, his help would be even more important. No room for shirkers now.

He reached the demonstrators excited and out of breath. Their numbers reassured him, their banners roused his admiration. He sought out the priest who was obviously in command.

'Good evening, Father,' he said. 'I'm Father O'Connor of St. Brigid's.'

'A parish in which there has been a lot of activity,' the other said. 'Your assistance will be most welcome to us,' They shook hands.

'How can I help?'

'By keeping your eyes open. You may recognise some of the parish children. Or their parents may be known to you. Your presence in itself will be an invaluable addition.'

'What can I do?'

'I'd like a priest with each lay contingent. It reassures them. You could take charge of the group over there. Come and I'll introduce you.'

They went over together to some twenty men, members of a Branch of the Ancient Order of Hibernians. He was asked to assist them by scrutinising any children who might arrive as passengers. There was little conversation. After a polite exchange the leader turned to the others and said :

'Now, men—a hymn while we're waiting. Let's have "Faith of our Fathers". All together—One . . . two . . . three.' They assumed grave expressions and lifted their voices in unison.

> 'Faith of our Fathers living still
> In spite of dungeon, fire and sword
> Oh, how our hearts beat high with joy
> When e'er we hear that glorious word
> Faith of our Fathers, holy faith,
> We will be true to thee till death
> We will be true to thee till death.'

The gulls rose in alarm from roofs and the rigging of ships, and the other groups, as the voices rebounded off corrugated iron and sheds and the walls of warehouses, took fire and joined in, swelling the sound of the second verse.

> 'Faith of our Fathers, guile and force
> To do thee bitter wrong unite,
> But Erin's saints shall fight for us
> And keep undimmed thy blessed light
> Faith of our Fathers, holy faith
> We will be true to thee till death
> We will be true to thee till death.'

The hooter of the one ship that was working across the river at the South Wall gave a long wail which swamped the voices and for a moment shattered all tonality. Its echo ran the length of the river, a groan of anguish which surged past Ringsend and the empty marshalling yards, spreading between the strands of Dollymount and the Shellybanks and Merrion, until it passed the estuary and became a ghost above the lonely lightships far out in the Irish Sea. Father O'Connor, unused to the procedures of the riverside, felt the sudden anger that mounted in the groups about him and wondered if it had been blown derisively.

There was the usual queue at the soup kitchen. Yearling spared the waiting women a glance, noting the jamjars and bottles and tin cans in their hands, then followed Mathews through the door of Liberty Hall and up the stairs to the second floor. It was dirty. The mud of countless feet had dried on the wooden stairway and on the landing. It smelled of people. Poverty, he had noticed before, had its own peculiar smell. A man's station could be judged by what the body exhaled. Expensive odours of brandy and cigars; sour odours of those who nourished nature with condensed milk and tea. In an outer room were two men he recognised. One Orpen the painter, whom he knew well; the other Sinclair, an art dealer, who was said to love the fine things in his shop so much that he was constantly refusing to sell them.

Mathews excused himself and went into the inner office. Yearling approached Orpen.

'My dear Orpen, what are you doing here?'

'Some sketches,' Orpen said. 'Have you been to the food kitchens?'

'No,' Yearling confessed, 'this is my first visit.'

'Then let me show you these.'

Yearling examined cartoons of faces and figures. They wore skull-like heads and raised skeleton arms towards a woman who was ladling out soup.

'How do you find them?' Orpen asked.

'Depressing.'

'You should see the reality.'

'Do you come here a lot?'

'Every other day. One meets everybody here.'

'So I gather,' Yearling agreed. 'I read a suggestion in *The Leader* that there should be a branch for intellectuals in Liberty Hall.'

'Larkin is working night and day,' Orpen said. 'He expects to be summoned before the court any day now to answer a charge of sedition. They're bound to convict him.'

Mathews returned to the room and joined them.

'The children are on the next floor. Will you come up?'
Yearling followed him. The air was pungent with the smell
from the cauldrons in the basement. They entered a room where
about twenty children were being prepared for their journey.
Some women were helping them to food. There were two men
among them whom Mathews consulted.

'There are pickets on the North Wall,' he said, 'there isn't a
hope of getting through if they are determined about stopping
us. We've got to distract their attention by sending some of the
children to Kingsbridge Station. The plan is to give them time
to follow. Then we rush the rest of the children to the North
Wall and try to get them aboard while the way is clear.'

'I don't think it will work,' one of the men said, 'there are
thousands of them.'

'Are you willing to try?' Mathews asked.

'Of course,' the man answered.

'So am I,' Mathews told him. He looked at his watch.

'If you will take the decoy party now,' he suggested, 'I'll go
with the others in an hour's time. Later on your group can go
by train from Amiens Street to Belfast and we'll ship them out
that way.'

'You'll need help,' the man said. 'Skeffington here could go
along with you. The trouble is he's a pacifist and not much good
in a fight. He just stands still and lets them hammer him.'

Skeffington smiled.

'Perhaps your friend . . .?' the man suggested.

'Strictly a non-combatant,' Mathews said.

They all looked at Yearling.

'Not now,' Yearling said. 'I'll go with you, Mathews.'

'Good for you,' Mathews said.

The children who were to act as a decoy were got ready.
Yearling recognised one of them, a little girl. He went over
and crouched to talk to her.

'And how is Mary Murphy?' he asked. 'And is she still washing her clothes? And did she marry her sweetheart after all?'

The child became shy.

'I don't know, sir.'

'Tell me another of your songs,' he said.

'What one?'

'Any one,' he invited. The child considered. Then she said: "Applejelly lemon a pear"?'

'That'll be very nice.'

She drew a deep breath.

> 'Applejelly lemon a pear
> Gold and silver she shall wear
> Gold and silver by her side
> Take Mary Kelly for their bride
> Take her across the lilywhite sea
> Then over the water
> Give her a kiss and a one, two or three
> Then she's the lady's daughter.'

'That's nice,' Yearling said when she had finished. 'I like the lilywhite sea bit, don't you?'

The child smiled at him. He went across to Mathews.

'I know that little girl there. Could she come with our party?'

'She *is* coming with our party.'

'Good.'

He returned to the child.

'Applejelly lemon a pear,' he repeated. 'I must learn that one. Tell it to me again.'

He went over and over it with the child, until the decoy contingent set off and they moved over to the windows to watch. The group of men about the doorway parted. The contingent passed through. From the height of the third floor they looked very small and vulnerable. The people who passed by were indifferent. Soon they were lost to his view. Some twenty minutes later the jeering of the men at the door brought him to the window again. Several cabs were passing in procession. The familiar banners were being held through their windows and the horses were moving at a smart pace. Their route was towards Kingsbridge Station. The plan was working.

'We'll move off in fifteen minutes,' Mathews decided, 'get everything ready.'

They began their final preparations.

When Hennessy caught up with Rashers the incident with Father O'Connor was still weighing on his mind.

'What did you want to speak to him like that for?'

'Why shouldn't I?' Rashers answered.

'Because there's no luck will come of it—that's why.'

'I haven't noticed much of that commodity lately anyway,' Rashers said.

'Things is deplorable,' Hennessy agreed, 'but why make them worse by insulting the clergy?'

'To hell with the clergy.'

'Are you not afraid he might turn you into a goat?'

'I wish to God he would,' Rashers said.

'You have the beard for it anyway,' Hennessy decided, after scrutinising him sideways.

'I have. And what's more, enough spirit to puck Father O'Connor in the arse,' Rashers answered. His good humour returned. But only for a while. He was not a goat. It was highly unlikely he ever would be. He was simply a man without employment, without health, without a friend of substance to turn to in his native city. That was the sum total of the matter.

'What the hell are we to do?' he asked.

Hennessy had no ideas. Except to walk about and keep their eyes and ears open, to let the mind imagine possibilities, to fasten the attention on the moment and not to try to look too far ahead. His eyes, searching along the footpath, fixed on something.

'Here's a sizeable butt we can share,' he said, stooping to pick it up. They examined it together. It was a long one.

'God bless your eyesight,' Rashers said. 'I'd have missed that.'

They had no matches. Hennessy, storing it away for later, suggested doing the round of the public houses to see if a porter's job might be going, or some work washing bottles. They passed the queue of children waiting outside Tara Street Baths to be scrubbed and fitted out with clean clothes. It engaged them for twenty minutes or so. Half-heartedly they went on with their search. They had no luck, but they continued to wander the streets.

'Did you hear Mrs. Bartley and the family is going to America?' Hennessy asked.

'I did,' Rashers said.

'A brother of hers did well out there and sent her over the fare.'

'She's a woman was always good to me,' Rashers said, 'and I wish her the height of luck. I'm going to miss her.'

They begged a match from a passer-by and stopped to light the butt Hennessy had found. They leaned on the wall of the river, sharing it puff for puff. Hennessy remarked the procession of cabs on the opposite bank. Rashers was unable to see that far.

'It's the demonstrators,' Hennessy told him, 'the crowd that want the children kept in Ireland.' He became conversational. 'Supposing we were chislers again,' he said, 'being cleaned up and dressed in decent clothes and sent off to England to be looked after. We'd have no troubles then.'

Regretfully Rashers passed back the butt. There was about as much chance of becoming chislers again as there was of being turned into a goat. Hennessy's vein of fantasy was beginning to irritate him.

'We'd make a hairy pair of chislers,' he told him.

The children walked in pairs with Mathews leading. He held his stick under his arm and strode purposefully. Yearling kept to the side. His job was simply to see they did not step out under the traffic. Three other men followed behind him and two more took up the rear. Yearling had counted thirty children at the beginning of their journey and threw his eye over them at intervals during their march to count them all over again. Although nothing much was expected of him, he felt anxious and responsible. The little girl who had recited the street rhyme was talking to the child beside her, unconscious of any tension. If they attempted to use her roughly, Yearling decided, he would take a chance on violence himself.

At the Embarkation sheds they found a cordon of police

waiting for them. Behind the police the demonstrators had spread out in a line across the road. Traffic was being held up and searched. There were hundreds of them. The contingent that followed the decoy party had been easily spared.

Warning the children to behave, he went up front to Mathews.

'It looks rather bad,' he suggested, 'do you think we should proceed?'

'Personally, I intend to.'

'Oh. Very well.'

'But there's no obligation of any kind on you.'

'My dear Mathews,' Yearling said, 'please lead on.'

'You're quite sure?'

'Glory or the grave.'

They moved again. Yearling kept to the steady pace set by Mathews. The police parted to allow them through. Then they came up against the front ranks of their opponents, were forced to a stop and quickly surrounded. Yearling, doing his best to shield the children, was aware not of individuals but of bowler hats and moustaches in unidentifiable multitudes. Bodies pressed about him and exhaled their animal heat. The priest in charge made his slow passage towards them. He was red-faced and trembling with excitement.

'Who is in charge of these children?' he demanded. Mathews stepped forward.

'I am,' he said.

'And where are you taking them?'

'You know very well where I'm taking them,' Mathews said.

'I know where you would wish to take them,' the priest said, 'but we are here to prevent it.'

'By what right?'

'By God's right,' the priest shouted at him. There was an angry movement. The slogans were raised and began to wave wildly. 'Proselytisers,' 'Save the Children.' Someone bawled in Yearling's ear: 'Kidnapper Larkin.'

'I am not Mr. Larkin,' he said.

'You're one of his tools,' the voice said. 'You're all his henchmen.'

A loud cheering distracted him and he looked around. The cabs which had set out earlier for Kingsbridge were returning. They cantered in single file along the quay, their banners waving in response to those surrounding the children. At a distance behind them a group of Larkinites from Liberty Hall followed. Yearling saw the police parting to let the cabs through, then closing ranks again against the Larkinites. The situation was becoming explosive. He said so to Mathews.

'These children will get hurt.'

'Hold steady,' Mathews said.

They both watched the Larkinites, who had now reached the police cordon and were parleying. An Inspector waved them back but it had no effect. The crowd about Yearling began to sing 'Faith of our Fathers' once again. Almost immediately the battle between the Larkinites and the police began. The priest became excited once more.

'I command you to hand over these children,' he said to Mathews.

'Have the parents of Dublin no longer any rights?' Mathews asked.

'If you persist in refusing, I'll not be responsible for what happens.'

'But of course you'll be responsible,' Mathews said, 'and if they suffer hurt it will be your responsibility also.'

'Seize the children,' the priest shouted to his followers.

Father O'Connor, dismounting from one of the cabs, saw the mêlée about the party of children but failed to distinguish the figure of Yearling. When his attention switched to the police he found the Larkinites were breaking through. He gathered his contingent about him and began to shout instructions at them.

'Stand firm men,' he ordered. 'Stand firm for God and His Holy Faith.'

As the Larkinites broke through the police guard he mounted the footstep of one of the cabs and waved his broken umbrella above their heads. All about him bodies heaved and tossed. Police and people struggled in several groups. He stood clear of the fighting himself but kept up a flow of encouragement for his followers. He felt no shame or hesitation. This was a battle for God.

Hands seized Yearling and pulled him away from the children he was escorting. He saw Mathews some yards ahead of him being manhandled in the same way.

'Damn you for zealots,' he shouted and began to fight back. The fury of his counter attack drove them back momentarily, but they were too many for him. They crowded about him on every side. Hands tore the lapels of his jacket, his shirt, his trouser legs. He lashed out blindly all the time until at last, exhausted, he fell to the ground. Mathews and the other men and the children had disappeared. He was alone in a circle of demonstrators. He felt blood in his mouth, explored delicately and discovered a broken tooth. Blood was running down from his forehead also, blinding one eye. He found his pocket handkerchief and tried to staunch it. He had no fear now of the faces leaning over him. A wild anger exhilerated him.

'Damn you for ignorant bigots,' he shouted at them, 'damn you for a crowd of cowardly obscurantists.'

Father O'Connor saw the police gaining control once more. The Larkinites were driven back up the quays, his own followers regrouped and began to cheer. To his left he saw the priest from Donnybrook leading the children away. The demonstrators were grouped solidly about them. He got down from the footstep and went over.

'We succeeded,' the priest said to him.

'Thanks be to God,' he answered. He searched the faces as the children passed but could find none that answered to his memory of the Fitzpatricks. For the moment at any rate they were safe. He thanked God for that too and began to push through the crowd. They gave him passage and he acknowledged grimly.

'Who have we over there?' he asked, his attention caught by a dense ring of men.

'One of the kidnappers,' a man told him. He pushed his way into the centre and recognised their prisoner with horror.

'Yearling,' he said.

Yearling had difficulty in seeing him. The blood was still

blinding his right eye. He dabbed again with the handkerchief and realised who it was.

'My poor fellow,' Father O'Connor said, 'let me help you.'

'Call off your hymn howling blackguards,' Yearling demanded.

Father O'Connor motioned the crowd back.

'Let me take you home at once,' he offered, 'I have a cab just across the road.'

'No,' Yearling said, 'I intend to walk to a cab myself.'

'You're in no condition.'

'I am in excellent condition,' Yearling assured him, 'let the city look at your handiwork.'

'Please,' Father O'Connor begged, 'let me help you.'

'I don't need it.'

Yearling raised himself to his feet and tried to arrange his torn clothes. He had the appearance of a bloodied scarecrow. Father O'Connor offered his hand in assistance but Yearling stepped away. He stared at Father O'Connor.

'I see you've been on active service,' he remarked.

Father O'Connor, following Yearling's eyes, found they were fixed on his umbrella and remembered its broken handle.'

'You misunderstand completely,' he said, 'let me explain.'

'You have been beating some unfortunate about the head, I suppose,' Yearling said. 'Do you regret it wasn't me?'

'Yearling, please. This is dreadful. You must listen to me.'

But Yearling turned his back. He began to limp his way towards Liberty Hall.

'Don't interfere with him,' Father O'Connor said to those around him. 'Please don't interfere with him in any way. Let him pass.'

He began to cry.

'Let him pass,' he repeated.

The priest from Donnybrook marked the occasion with an address to his followers. He reminded them that the demonstration had been unorganised and unprepared. 'It shows the love you have for the Catholic children of this city,' he told them. The great crowd cheered him. Then they formed in processional order and marched bareheaded through the streets, singing 'Hail, Glorious St. Patrick'. Rashers and Hennessy watched them passing and saw Father O'Connor marching with them. They looked at each other silently.

Father O'Connor tried to join in the singing but found his thoughts pulled elsewhere. He had lost a friend for the sake of the children. He was prepared to sacrifice more. But it was hard. He offered to God the ache in his heart, the humiliation which made his cheeks burn. He offered to God also the coming loneliness and isolation.

The newspapers carried another letter from the Archbishop. It read:

Archbishop's House
Dublin
28th October 1912

Very Reverend and Dear Father,

In view of the exceptional distress resulting from the long continued and widespread deadlock in the industries of Dublin, more especially in some of those parishes that are least able from their own unaided resources to meet so grave an emergency, it occurs to me that the case is one calling for an exceptional remedy.

The children, innocent victims of the conflict, have a special claim upon us, and I think the best way of helping them is to strengthen the funds by means of which food and clothing is provided for the thousands of schoolgoing children who, even in the best of times, are in need of such assistance. Those funds, fairly adequate in ordinary times, have now been subjected to an excessive strain. In a number of cases they are practically exhausted. As usual in times of distress, the proselytisers are energetically active. If they are to be effectively combated, it must be by a combined effort, each of us doing what he can to help the poor in their hard struggle.

Although no public appeal has as yet been made, I am already in receipt of a number of subscriptions, from £25 down to 2s. 6d., sent to me by generous sympathisers, rich and poor, in England and Scotland.

It would be strange, then, if an opportunity were not afforded to the people of our own diocese to give practical expression to the sympathy which they must feel with the children suffering from hunger and from cold.

I am, therefore, asking the Parish Priests and Parochial Administrators of the various parishes, and also the heads of religious communities in charge of public churches in the diocese, to arrange for a special collection to be held in their Churches on next Sunday in aid of the fund that is now being raised.

A small Committee, consisting of some of the city clergy and some members of the St. Vincent de Paul Association, will take charge of the collection of the fund, and the distribution of it in the parishes where it is needed will be in the hands of the local clergy and of the local Conferences of the Association of St. Vincent de Paul.

I know that I can count upon your cordial co-operation. I ought perhaps to add that if there is any local reason why next Sunday may not be a convenient day, the collection can be held on the following Sunday. But you will kindly bear in mind that the case is one of real urgency.

I remain,
Very Rev. and Dear Father,
Your faithful servant in Christ,
✠ William
Archbishop of Dublin
Etc., etc.

P.S. The amounts received are to be sent to W. A. Ryan Esq., Treasurer, Special Committee, Council Rooms, Society of St. Vincent de Paul, 25 Upper O'Connell Street, Dublin.

Yearling read it in his bed in the Nursing Home where he was recovering from a dislocated shoulder. He was enjoying the rest. Mathews had escaped with bruises which still discoloured his face. Yearling read him the letter.

'So that's what we are,' he said, 'two proselytisers, energetically active.'

'I forgot to tell you,' Mathews said, 'Mrs. Rand and Mrs.

Montefiore have been released—on condition that they leave the country.'

'They'll miss the collection,' Yearling said.

'They can take the credit for it,' Mathews pointed out, 'and so can we. If we hadn't moved, the Hierarchy wouldn't have noticed any exceptional distress whatever. I wonder will the faithful stump up?'

When the bells of Sunday rang out above the city the collection boxes rattled in the streets and outside the church porches. The Faithful, instructed by their Archbishop, dipped into fob pocket and muff for loose change. There was exceptional distress, now officially recognised. The local clergy in consultation with the laymen who were Brothers of St. Vincent de Paul decided on the distribution. When their duty was done and Sunday was over they read of the arrival in the city of a large contingent of British Blacklegs. They saw nothing wrong in this, although it was designed to take the bread out of the mouths of the men and women and children they had just been collecting for. It was a crime to deport children in order to feed them, but no crime to bring in adults to see that they continued in starvation. When the workers organised a protest, the local clergy and the Brothers of St. Vincent deplored mutually the grip the Atheists held on the city.

CHAPTER 10

THE man who lit the gas-lamps told Pat where the scabs were quartered. It was near Mountjoy Gaol. He also told him where they drank. Pat knew the pub. It was an out-of-way place not far from Drumcondra Bridge. They were escorted there, those who wanted to go, by police. The snag about any attempt to attack them was, the lamplighter pointed out, that the bloody police stayed on all the time to guard them. And incidentally, needless to remark, said the lamplighter— remarking it just the same—to wet their own whistles with more than a law abiding modicum. He himself had seen four of the police having a murderous fight among themselves, with the scabs helping the rest of the police to separate them. A disgraceful scene.

'There's example for you,' the lamplighter said. He was a small man with a pale face and bushy moustache who, it was said by those who should know, wore his bicycle clips in bed.

'Thanks for the information,' Pat said to him.

'Up the Republic,' the lamplighter answered.

Pat reported to Liberty Hall at a meeting of the Actionists, who had no official existence as such within the union, but who were regularly in session just the same. The problem was how to get rid of the police in order to attack the scabs. They spent some hours deliberating. A diversion was the obvious answer. There was another public house about a hundred yards from the one in which the scabs drank. A mêlée there and the use of a couple of stolen police whistles might do the trick. Joe and Pat, with two of the others, undertook to create the diversion. They would work out a line of retreat for themselves so that they could disappear before the police caught up with them.

After surveying the ground in the course of two morning rambles they were able to propose a plan which had prospects of success. Those who were to attack the scabs could assemble in the early afternoon in a friendly house from which the scabs' pub could be kept under observation. With Pat and Joe were another carter called Mick and an enormous docker usually addressed as Harmless. Joe would arrive in the pub first. The others would come separately.

The night was suitable. Fog hung in laneways and made the streets damp and uninviting. Pat set off early so that he could check their escape route. He passed the pub where the scabs would assemble later for drink and recreation. The pub he himself would visit looked almost empty. He turned the corner and followed a laneway which led, after a number of intersections, to the banks of the Royal Canal. Some yards along the towpath a barge was tethered. He went aboard. The door of the cabin was open as had been arranged. It would hide them from the police. The next morning, if the search continued, they had only to stay put and the bargeman would take them downstream and let them off at one of the city bridges. It should work smoothly.

Satisfied, he followed the towpath towards the bridge. It was miserably cold and dark. The fog made his hair wet and found its way up his sleeves, chilling him. He was hungry. He lived a lot of the time on bread and tea. Hunger was a state that was constant, yet seldom critical. But it depressed him. The mud on the towpath squelched under his boots, the withered grass at its edge was still tall enough to wet his trouser legs as he brushed past, the waters of the canal were oily and shrouded in mist. At a distance, like something seen through a tunnel, was the main road bridge with its gas-lamps and traffic. He walked towards it; but without enthusiasm.

When he reached it there was still time to kill. He leaned on the parapet. The water cascading through the lock gates made a deafening sound, scattering spume that smelled of rotting vegetation. His thoughts, not for the first time, contemplated defeat. The lock-out was now in its fourth month. Winter would be an ally of the employers. Beating up scabs had become a mere gesture. It provided an outlet, but could no longer achieve anything. There were too many of them and the employers, helped by their cross-channel colleagues, still had plenty of money. There was no real hope. Expropriating the expropriators was a lifetime's work. Or the work, maybe, of many life-times. The boss class stuck together.

'Pat,' the voice behind him said. He swung around.

'Lily.'

She was smiling at him, a slim, familiar figure against the lamplight.

'I've been watching you for ages.'

'I'm only here five minutes.'

'Where are you off to?'

'A bit of business,' he said. 'Union business.'

'At this hour?'

'It's a bit of night work,' Pat said grimly. She guessed what he meant.

'Is it making trouble?'

He smiled.

'You're not to,' she said.

'A cartload of scabs,' Pat said. 'We have a plan to get at them.'

She came to his side and tried to argue with him, but found it difficult to pitch her voice above the roar of the water. She put her arm through his and drew him away. They walked.

'Have you time?' she asked.

'A little,' he answered.

She said she was angry with him for not coming to her for something to eat. He had promised to do so at least once in the week.

'You look half famished.'

'I've been doing all right.'

'I know. Bread and tea. Or pints of porter. That's no way to go on. Come home with me now and I'll make something hot for you.'

'I can't, Lily.'

'All right. Walk into town with me.'

'I have this job to do.'

'Pat. Suppose you get hurt. You're not to go.'

'I have to go.'

'Then let me come with you,' she suggested.

'You know I can't do that.'

'You'll get beaten up one of these days,' she told him. 'Why don't you let the others do something for a change. Why is it always you?'

'It isn't always me, Lily—there are plenty of others.'

'I haven't met them.'

'They don't go around wearing badges,' Pat said.

'Pat, if you don't come with me now, you needn't ask to see me ever again.'

She was angry with him. But she was frightened too.

'You don't mean that, Lily.'

'I do mean it. Try it and see.' He disengaged his arm.

'If I don't go,' he said, 'about twenty decent men are going to be let down.'

'Then, goodbye.'

'Lily.'

'I'm sorry I met you tonight.'

'So am I,' he said. She walked away. He had no alternative but to let her go. It was time to be about his business.

He pushed her image from his mind because the hurt it caused made it impossible for him to concentrate on his plan. Joe would be seated already in the pub; Mick and Harmless would be already on their way. His hand, exploring his coat pocket, closed about the stone he had hidden there. He would need it later.

There were two policemen on patrol duty, which meant the scabs had begun their night's drinking. The other police were probably inside. He passed at an easy pace and a little later turned into the public house where Joe was sitting in a corner drinking on his own. Harmless was leaning on the counter, a pint in front of him. Giving no sign of recognition to either, Pat took a position near Harmless and ordered a pint.

'Hardy night,' he said generally, while he waited.

'Fog on the river,' Harmless said.

'I heard the groaner at it,' Pat answered.

'Bad for the ships,' said Harmless. The publican, who was drawing the pint, listened.

'Are you a docker?' Pat asked.

'I used to be,' Harmless said, 'but it's a long time since I worked.'

'Locked out?'

'That's right.'

'Same here,' Pat said.

The publican brought the pint. Pat paid him.

'You're not busy tonight,' Pat said, drawing him into the conversation.

'There's not much business anywhere this weather,' the publican complained. 'No money.'

'There's a big crowd down the road,' Pat told him.

'That crowd. I wouldn't let them cross the door,' the publican said. 'Scabs.'

'Is that a fact?' Pat asked.

'With policemen guarding them,' the publican continued. Harmless indicated that he wanted the same again and the publican went to the taps. He turned around to make a correction.

'Did I say guarding them?' he asked. 'No. Drinking with them would be more correct. And after hours too.'

'Is that the game?' Pat said.

'That's the carry-on,' the publican confirmed. 'Bobbies how-are-yeh. It's a bloody disgrace.'

'Imagine that,' Harmless said, shocked.

The publican brought the pint.

'Your man that owns the place has one son in the police and another in Holy Orders,' he said, putting the pint on the counter, 'and if you were wondering why, out of all the pubs in this vicinity, the police should choose to patronise that certain particular premises—that's your answer: the Clergy and the Castle.'

'Influence,' Pat remarked.

'Pull,' the publican asserted.

Someone knocked at the glass partition of the snug and he excused himself.

'The scabs are in possession,' Pat said softly to Harmless.

'And the police?'

'Two on duty outside. God knows how many inside.'

'What about our own lads?'

'They're all ready. They gave the signal when I passed.'

'Then we'd better get to work.'

'We'll call another pint first,' Pat said, 'if anything goes wrong, let it go wrong when I've had my few jars and not before.'

Harmless took a tolerant view.

'That's very reasonable,' he said.

They chatted and drank for about half an hour. The money had been given to them for the purpose by the Actionist Committee when Pat pointed out that having some spending money for drink was essential to the plan.

'With regard to our mutual butty—his jills with the apron,' Harmless began.

'You mean the publican?'

'Just so,' Harmless confirmed. 'With regard to his views on serving scabs . . .'

'He'd serve every scab in the country if he got the chance,' Pat said, 'all that oul talk of his is sour grapes because his neighbour down the road got the business.'

'I know that,' Harmless agreed, 'but it's a good lead-in to what we intend to do next—if you follow me.'

'I was thinking that myself,' Pat confessed, 'but leave the talking to me.'

Harmless nodded benignly.

'No better man,' he said.

'Joe,' Pat said, while the publican was still absent, 'the next time you call a drink, come up to the counter and stand beside us.'

Joe nodded and held up his right thumb.

When the publican returned they ordered again. Joe rose and came to the counter.

'You can do the same for me,' he told him.

They waited in silence. The publican whistled tunelessly as he operated the pumps. Above his head a gas-lamp made a hissing noise which was incessant yet barely audible.

He gave drinks to Pat and Harmless. Then as he was placing a third on the counter for Joe, Pat took it up and moved it so that it stood between Harmless and himself.

'What's this?' Joe asked.

'I wouldn't take that money from him,' Pat told the publican.

'And why not?'

'While you were away, this gentleman and myself had a little conversation.'

'Just so,' Harmless said.

'And we found we both knew this man here. He's a scab.'

'Who's a scab?' Joe demanded.

'You are,' Pat said, becoming belligerent.

'Now gentlemen,' the publican appealed, 'no violence—for the love of God.'

Harmless was polite about it.

'We'd like him removed,' he suggested to the publican.

'Let him try,' Joe said.

'I can't remove a man that's not under the influence and is paying for what he orders in accordance with the requirements of the Innkeepers Act,' the publican said.

'So give me back my drink,' Joe demanded.

'That's right,' the publican said, 'give him back his drink and let there be no more nonsense.'

He appealed to Harmless.

'You're a civil spoken class of a man,' he said, 'and I'm asking you now to control your friend.'

Harmless tapped Pat on the shoulder and said :

'Give him back his drink.'

'Certainly,' Pat said. He lifted the pint glass and emptied it over Joe's head.

The publican yelled and began to climb over the counter. Harmless grabbed him by the shoulders, holding him in a grip of iron. Meanwhile Pat and Joe, locked together, were rolling about the floor.

'Get the police,' the publican yelled wildly to whoever was

514

hidden in the snug. 'Go out and shout for the police, before they break up the place.'

Harmless lifted him bodily, held him poised for a moment while he took aim, then pitched him neatly on to the shelf behind the bar. A shower of bottles and glasses scattered as he landed, littering the floor.

'Out,' Pat whispered to Joe.

Harmless followed them as they ran outside. Mick appeared from nowhere and began blowing a police whistle.

'With regard to the front window there . . .' Harmless remarked.

'I'd better let go at it,' Pat agreed, 'otherwise the Bobbies mightn't consider it worth while giving chase.'

Mick gave a few more blasts at the police whistle.

'Just so,' Harmless said, with regard to the window. They heard the sound of running feet in the distance.

'You boys break for it now,' Pat said, 'I'll hang on until they're in sight.'

'Right,' Mick said.

'Come on,' Harmless ordered.

'I'm bloodywell destroyed with porter,' Joe complained.

'A good run will warm you up,' Harmless told him, 'and prevent you taking cold on account of the wetting.'

'Hurry,' Pat said.

The three of them ran off. He listened to their footsteps receding. He listened also to the footsteps which were approaching. At what he judged to be the right moment he took the stone from his pocket and heaved it at the plate glass window. Although he was expecting it, the crash of breaking glass startled him. He turned to run.

'Pat.'

It was Lily again. He almost fell over her as he turned.

'I followed you,' she said, 'I was afraid you'd get hurt. Why do you do things like this?'

He hesitated. Her presence threw him into confusion. For several precious moments he could not think what to do. Then he realised the police were dangerously close.

'I have to run.'

She gripped his arm and screamed.

'Pat . . .'

He did the only thing possible. Grabbing her hand, he began to drag her along.

'Run, Lily—run like hell.'

But he had allowed the police to come too close. If he made for the canal barge now, he would lead them to the others. He turned off the route he had planned, using the laneways in an attempt to lose his pursuers. He took a wrong turning and found himself stopped by a wall.

'Try to climb over,' he said to Lily. He helped her but she lost her grip each time.

'Go yourself,' she begged him, 'they won't harm a woman.'

'Wouldn't they,' Pat said.

He was trying to lift her a third time when the police reached them. A hand grabbed him by the collar and a fist smashed into his face. He fell back against the wall, blood spurting from his broken lips. Lily sprang forward to defend him but was swung off her feet by one of the policemen. He flung her to the ground. Her head struck against the wall and her arm buckled under her as she fell. The police grabbed Pat.

'Where are the others?' one of them demanded.

'The woman,' Pat said, 'pick her up. She's hurt.'

They twisted his arm. 'The others . . . where are they?'

'What others?' Pat asked.

'Clip him,' one of the police advised.

He was struck across the mouth again. He could feel his arm twisting in its socket. The pain was excruciating.

'Bastards,' he yelled.

A fist again struck him in the face and the world went black.

'That was a mistake,' one of the policemen said, 'you've bloody well knocked him out.'

'Take him in,' another said.

'What about the woman?'

'She's bad enough. We'd better get her to hospital.'

'They'll want to know how she got hurt.'

'That's easy,' one of them said, 'we'll tell them this bloke here was beating her up.'

'So he was,' another agreed.

They took Lily and Pat from the laneway. The chase was abandoned.

CHAPTER 11

FATHER GIFFLEY, stretching out his left hand, drew the lace curtains of his bedroom window gently aside. Beyond them was a green and yellow world. He blinked his eyes several times. It remained. The sky poured out a green and yellow light; the roofs reflected it back. In the street it was the same. People and conveyances floated with a swaying motion between a green and yellow sea. A bell somewhere struck the hour. He became rigid until it stopped. The notes boomed inside him, with a din that almost burst his chest. He was the clock. A metal-shod wheel bounced so loudly on the cobbles that it broke away and was propelled towards him, a coloured Catherine wheel of cold light. He ducked back in terror. The curtains fell into place again. He turned his attention to the room.

The light was subdued, the air was easier to breathe. It stank, he was sure, of peppermints and whiskey. There was nothing he could do about that. It was too late now. His course was set. The whiskey bottle by the bedside was empty. There was nothing immediately to be done except to get more. He looked about him.

The bookcase in the corner regarded him accusingly. The black notebook on the chair moved of its own accord, very stealthily, hoping he would not notice. But he had. He pounced on it. Then he recollected himself and it resumed its inanimacy. He opened the pages and forced himself to concentrate. He read:

'Call often to mind the proverb—the eye is not satisfied with seeing, nor the ear filled with hearing.'

That was familiar. A friendly voice repeated the words into his ear. He nodded his head. Yes.

The green and yellow light was coming from inside him. He knew that. A condition of the liver. Exercise would drive it away. Or might. He put on his coat and hat, took his walking stick, wound his black scarf about his throat. If he could bring himself to eat, that would help too. But his will refused to entertain the idea. Eating, it said, would kill him. Don't eat.

Images hung in his mind with the weight of a stone; first the threadbare hole in the hall carpet, then the green slime on the edges of the holy water font, after that the cupped depression worn in the granite flag at the entrance gate by countless churchgoing feet. They clung behind his eyes like a picture gallery until the repetitive movements of arms and legs, the swinging of his walking stick, the quickening of the sluggish juices of his body, dislodged them. One by one, at spaced out intervals, they crashed from their pegs. He was free of them. His body quivered uncontrollably and he was forced to stand still. When that in turn passed he felt better and thanked God. He could now find his way to another drink. It did not trouble him that it must involve in the end nothing less than his own doom. There was no longer any practical alternative. He found a public house and entered without shame. The customers stared at him. He asked for a glass of whiskey and lowered it at his ease, ignoring them. He felt better. That was the essential thing. He paid what was due and went out, noting with relief that the streets now wore their habitual winter grey and the things that passed him made the sounds of everyday.

They were drab streets, these streets of his. He was parish priest to a community of beggars. Their windows were broken and their abodes stank. No one considered them. No one cared for them. He had failed in care himself. It was not his nature to love rags and filth or to believe that suffering ennobled the illiterate. Yet he pitied them. It didn't do them any good of course, but it was better than contempt. O'Connor was contemptuous. And a prig. Ought to shave himself in holy water.

To add to the drabness, rain began. It caught him unawares and made him angry. He had not reckoned on the possibility of rain. Rain was another part of the drabness of the world, the greyness of all Creation. It brought soot and dirt down out of the air and made a cesspool of the broken street. He looked about, saw a railway bridge and took shelter.

It was gloomy and cheerless. Drops of water dripped on him. A chilling wind inhabited the place. Through the eye of the arch he saw the vista of the street; grey, the rain beating on it so fiercely that the drops rebounded. He could find no single thing, outside him or within, to fasten on to in hope against the void and the absence of God. He looked at his walking stick.

'Good evening, Father.' The voice startled him. He did not look around immediately. These bodiless voices had troubled him before. He would not be tricked. Still looking at the stick he said, in a matter of fact way, in order to reassure himself.

'I should have brought my umbrella.'

'You don't remember me, Father,' the voice said. This time he looked around. He saw a bent and bearded figure with a haggard face. He stared.

'Who are you?'

The figure wore a sack about its shoulders and a coat tied about the middle with a piece of rope.

'Rashers Tierney, your Reverence. I used to work in the church. A boilerman.'

'Tierney,' Father Giffley said. He pondered. He remembered.

'Tierney,' Rashers repeated.

Father Giffley studied the face closely.

'You look ill.'

'I'm not in the best, right enough.'

'Are you working?'

'Divil the work.'

'Your chest was bad,' Father Giffley remembered, 'and you had an animal—a dog.'

'Rusty.'

'I beg your pardon?'

'The dog's name was Rusty.'

'Quite. For the moment the animal's name had escaped me.'

'That's terrible weather to be caught out in.'

'It is,' Father Giffley said. He looked again down the vista of the street, finding it still empty, still without God, still with no gleam of grace or of hope.

'I could go off and search for a cab for you, Father,' Rashers suggested.

'You could,' Father Giffley said firmly, 'but you won't.'

'As you please, Father.'

'Don't be disappointed, however, I'll give you something just the same.' He searched in his pocket and found a half-crown.

'Almighty God's good luck to you,' Rashers said, when it was handed to him. Almost immediately the sound of wheels and the trotting of a horse caused them both to look around. A cab was coming towards them through the rain.

'He seems to have heard you,' Father Giffley said, smiling. They stopped the driver at the bridge entrance and Rashers, thanking him again, went off into the rain.

Father Giffley watched his bent figure and slow gait. After a moment he said to the cabman.

'Turn about. I want to speak with that old man again.' When they drew abreast Father Giffley ordered the cab to stop, and called to Rashers to get in with him.

'Where do you live?' he asked.

'Chandlers Court, Father.'

'Take us to Chandlers Court,' Father Giffley instructed. Rashers looked astounded, but the driver flicked his reins and the cab lurched forward.

The wet sack and the coat smelled abominably. Father Giffley undid the leather strap and opened the window an inch or so. Then the swaying motion of the cab began to draw him back into the half-world he had been fighting to keep away. He felt it flowing noiselessly towards him, a tide of darkness creeping across a dim strand. The leather-buttoned upholstery was regarding him with sea-creature eyes, expressionless, heavy-lidded. He sweated, sat up straight, forced himself to collect his thoughts. He opened the window a little more.

'Tell me what happened to you since you were dismissed,' he said to Rashers. 'The whole story. Don't be afraid. I am most interested to know.'

He leaned on his walking stick, gripped its knob tightly,

listened. He was determined to attend meticulously. It would keep out the void that waited moment by moment to engulf him.

'I'll tell you that, Father,' Rashers said, 'and I'll tell you no word of a lie. I have the ill fortune to live in the most misbegotten kip of a city in the whole wide world.'

Father Giffley nodded. The word kip engaged him. It meant, to the best of his knowledge, a common lodging place. He had heard it used in the Confessional to mean a resort of ill fame, a whorehouse. It was a fitting word. It pleased him.

'Proceed,' he said.

The bearded figure began to enumerate its misfortunes. Father Giffley, the better to aid concentration, categorised them under certain headings: The waning popularity of the tin whistle and the erosion of technical standards due to infiltration of the profession by charlatans and chancers; the inevitable, because hereditary, crookedness of Jewish pawnbrokers; The inability of once kind neighbours to be kind any longer: the fierce competition for the contents of all dustbins and in particular the assertion by the strong (to the complete exclusion of the infirm) of sole right to the refuse outside certain well-to-do houses where the leftovers reflected the high living standards of the inhabitants.

Father Giffley attended, gathered, itemised, as the cab jolted its way through rain-swept streets. The smell grew steadily worse. It was the breath of Destitution itself.

Father Giffley said:

'If you call to me on Tuesday next I'll see you get work to do, either about the church or elsewhere. Go to my housekeeper for something to eat and wait for me until I am free.'

'The blessing of God on you, Father.'

'You'll do that?'

'Let anything try to hinder me.'

'Good.'

The cabdriver leaned down and shouted to them.

'Chandlers Court, Father. Was it Number 3?'

'Number 3,' Rashers answered.

'There's something very peculiar going on there,' the cabman said. He slackened pace and drew in to the footpath. As

Rashers stepped down the cabman said to him:

'Have a look.'

Father Giffley poked his head through the window. A crowd had gathered about one of the doorways.

'It's the police,' Rashers said, 'A police raid.'

'Take my advice,' the cabman offered, 'and keep away from there until they leave.'

'And let them ill treat the poor oul dog,' Rashers said, 'not bloody likely.'

He turned to salute Father Giffley and limped away.

'What would the police want?' Father Giffley said.

'Breaking up the homes of the unfortunate people,' the cabman said, 'that's a regular game of theirs.'

'For what reason?'

'To terrorise them. There's another shipload of scabs came in from England this morning and Larkin is holding a protest march and a meeting about it tonight. So the police is getting in the first blow.' The cabman gathered in the reins and added: 'I know you condemn Larkin and the people that follows him, but it's no bed of roses for any of them.' He flicked the reins.

'One moment,' Father Giffley ordered. He stepped down on to the path and surveyed the crowd.

'Wait here for me,' he added, when he had made up his mind.

The rain had eased, leaving behind it oily puddles along the cobbled street. He had condemned nobody. On the contrary. And he would not have the Church represented as an oppressor. Some women in the crowd ouside Number 3 were weeping. Neighbours comforted them. The children, who cried simply because their mothers were crying, were dirty and dressed in rags. As he pushed his way through the crowd they gaped at him in surprise. 'It's Father Giffley,' he heard them say. He acknowledged their salutes grimly. A woman cried out:

'Stop them, Father, stop them.'

It was a despairing cry. He pretended not to hear it, but something in his heart leaped in answer. He was not, after all, entirely useless.

He strode into the hallway and up the stairs. The first landing was deserted. He listened. Heavy sounds came from somewhere above him. He climbed to the second landing. The noise was coming from behind the door on his left. He pushed it open and stepped in. He stood speechless.

In one corner a young woman with her children gathered about her was crying with terror. Two policemen held a man who had been beaten to the floor. His face and shirt were covered in blood. A dresser of delph had been overturned and the shattered debris was scattered over the floor. Chairs and boxes had been broken. Three other policemen stood around while a fourth was using a heavy bar to smash a table. At every blow the children screamed. His anger fought against his speechlessness until at last it surged out thunderously.

'Stop,' he shouted.

They all turned together to look at him.

'What devil's work is this?'

It was the voice of the Pulpit. They stopped. Their eyes fixed on his priestly collar, then moved almost in unison to their spokesman. The sergeant squared his shoulders.

'We're only doing our duty, Father.'

'Duty.'

'This man here intimidated another and prevented him from attending his work. When we called to question him in the course of our duty he became violent and refused to co-operate.'

'Indeed. And for that reason you terrify his wife and deliberately destroy his property.'

'That was in the course of the struggle.'

'Was this hulking brute here breaking up a table in the course of the struggle?'

'That was in the heat of the moment, Father.'

'You're a glib-tongued, lying rogue,' Father Giffley said. He crossed the room and stood over the two policemen.

'Release that man,' he ordered.

The policemen obeyed him. Fitz straightened his arms. The agony of doing so was almost worse than what he had endured when they had twisted them behind his back. Mary rushed over to put her arms about him and then to wipe his face. She was sobbing uncontrollably.

'Now, get out,' Father Giffley said to the police. The sergeant began to bluster.

'We have our duty to do . . .' he said.

Father Giffley strode across to him.

'If you delay another moment,' he said, 'I'll have you put behind bars yourself for what you have done to these people. I intend to report everything I've seen.'

'I mean no disrespect to your calling, Father . . .'

'Go,' Father Giffley ordered.

The sergeant signalled to his men. They left.

Father Giffley took a handkerchief from his pocket and handed it to Mary.

'Use this,' he said, 'attend to your husband's injuries. What's your name?'

'Fitzpatrick, Father.'

'Fitzpatrick. I intend to report what has happened. Perhaps we should call an ambulance?'

'I'm all right, Father,' Fitz said.

'Very well.'

Father Giffley took a pound note from his pocket and left it on the mantelpiece.

'A little assistance,' he said, 'you'll need it.' He turned about at the door and said to them:

'Have courage.' Then he left.

The people had come back into the house and were crowding the staircase and the hall. He went grimly through them, neither turning his head nor acknowledging what they said to him. When he reached his cab he said to the driver.

'Take me to Liberty Hall.'

'Liberty Hall?'

'Isn't that Mr. Larkin's headquarters?'

'It is, Father.'

'Very well. Take me there.'

The void was forgotten, yet the streets that moved past the narrow window of the cab were not altogether real. There was too little of them to be seen at any one time; a patch of cobbles, an open door, railings from which a child, seated on a rope swing, bobbed once into sight and was whipped away. He opened the window wide and leaned nearer to it and that was better. The smell of sea and shipping came to him. He saw the surface of the river tormented by the wind, the funnels of ships against the threatening sky, gulls rising against it and being whirled backwards; and at last, the squat building by Butt Bridge with the words over the door that appeared in the papers day after day: Liberty Hall.

'Wait for me,' he said.

There was the unfailing queue for food and soup. He passed them. In the hallway and on the staircase the smell of cooking and of ill fed bodies intermingled. He knocked on a door which was opened by a man in the working class uniform of cap and knotted muffler.

'I wish to speak with Mr. Larkin.'

'Who shall I say, Father?'

'Father Giffley of St. Brigid's.'

'Please wait here, Father.'

He stepped inside. It was a long room overlooking the river. There were rough benches about the walls and a long table in the centre. In anticipation of the outcome of the forthcoming trial for sedition men were preparing rough posters and fitting them to poles. One lot read 'Release Larkin'. And another 'Larkin gaoled by Lloyd George'. There was a third:

'British Comrades
No Larkin
No Lloyd George'

The man returned and said, 'This way, Father.' He opened the door of an inner room, nodded to Father Giffley to enter, closed the door behind him.

'Father Giffley,' Larkin said, 'please sit down.'

'I would rather stand,' Father Giffley said.

'Suit yourself.'

Father Giffley, face to face with the most talked about man in the country, remained silent. He saw a man of about thirty-five years of age, big physically, with a face which had a strong jaw and deep circles of tiredness under the eyes. A lock of brown

526

hair fell across the forehead and had a streak of grey running through it.

'Don't hesitate,' Larkin Said, 'I get at least three of your cloth here each week—all warning me of the devil and hell's fire. What complaint against me have you?'

'I have no complaint against you.'

'You've come to offer to help me?'

'I have,' Father Giffley said.

'A number of priests have done that, too. For their own sakes I send them away.'

'There is something I need advice about,' Father Giffley said. 'Today, in one of the houses in my parish I found a body of police who were acting like blackguards. They had beaten a man and terrified his wife and children. When I arrived they were wantonly destroying every stick of furniture.'

'Didn't you know that it happens all the time?'

'Perhaps I did. But I had never witnessed it before. I intend to lodge a complaint and if necessary, give evidence. I want advice on how best to go about it.'

'It would do no good.'

'It can be tried.'

'It has been tried countless times already,' Larkin said, 'By eminent men who have courage and sympathy. And by a few men of your own calling too, Father. Nothing is ever done, because the Government is committed to the employers and the police can indulge in any lawlessness they like so long as it's aimed at the poor.'

'Then I'll take part in your protest march,' Father Giffley said, 'and condemn it from your platform.' It was the voice of the Pulpit again, determined, authoritative, loud enough to fill a church. But there was a note in it which brought Larkin to his feet. Father Giffley's face was red and its muscles were no longer under his control.

'Father,' Larkin said, 'I'm grateful for your offer, but it wouldn't be wise for either of us. Now let me thank you and see you safely down the stairs.'

Father Giffley did not move. He was angry. He was ashamed. It was a shame he had never experienced before, a dark tide of

shame from the half-world he had tried to defend himself
against all day. It flowed noiselessly into him and filled him,
engulfing everything. He began to sob, but without tears. Larkin
put his arm about his shoulder. Father Giffley said :

'Don't come with me. Please continue with your work.'

The cabman was still waiting for him. There was no rain
now. The wind had bundled it away. They set off once more
through streets that were growing dark with evening, so that
their disconnected fragments jolting past the window were too
dim to have any impact. He was grateful for that. He listened
to the grinding of cobbles, the swish of puddles beneath the
wheels. The need to drink again became pressing. He tapped the
glass.

'You may let me down,' he said, 'I'll walk a little.' He paid
off the cabdriver, then took his bearings. He was on the riverside again. The waters, still tormented by the wind, were criss-
crossed with laces of foam and slapped angrily against the berth-
ing walls. They stretched before him, drawing his eyes with them
as they widened and outran the massive confines of the quays
and merged into the darker, undisciplined spaces of the bay.
It was a vista of cold, grey tones. A lamplighter, moving at a
distance ahead of him and to his right, lifted his long stick with
its taperlike flame and added bead after bead to a chain of softly
glowing lamps. The melancholy became unbearable. He hastened his steps. The windows of a public house relieved the gloom
of a side street. He passed the large swing doors and found
what he wanted, the small, discreet entrance marked—Snug.

There was a slide in the wall which opened when he tapped
on it.

'Whiskey,' he said.

'I'll put a match to the gas for you,' the barman offered.

'No, no—leave it as it is.'

The partition dividing the snug from the bar did not rise
all the way to the ceiling. The light that spilled over was enough
for his purpose; it was insufficient to betray his features or his
calling.

'Very good, sir,' the barman said. He brought a glass of
whiskey which Father Giffley raised to his lips, then lowered

528

without tasting to say quickly before the barman could turn away: 'Bring me another.'

Some time later he sat down. He slept a little and seemed to dream. He heard the door open, heard a scuffle and smothered laughter and then a woman's voice said:

'Oh Jaysus, stop, look, there's someone there.'

Or thought he had. He could not be sure. There were three glasses of whiskey on the table in front of him, little yellow points of light in the semi-darkness. The bar had grown noisy, a persistent but sleepy noise that was now that of rough, confused voices, now the far off murmur of a church full of people at prayer. He took one of the glasses and swallowed. One little yellow point of light went out. He placed it sadly between the two that still glowed. He regarded it.

Bloodied faces begged him to have pity on them, not to beat them, not to forget he was a man of God. A puppy that had been given to him in his father's house when he was seven years old came and barked at him and wagged its tail and asked him to play. It was white with brown markings. The sister of the bishop threatened to report him. She was as hateful as ever. She told him he was a disgrace to the priesthood, one who consecrated Christ only to crucify Him. No wonder there was blood on everything he saw or touched.

As she said this the the two yellow points of light became red. He was about to shout at her. A voice advised him not to; he would be heard by others. Instead he raised one of the glasses with a sudden, defiant movement and swallowed. Thick, clinging, sickeningly warm, the taste of blood transfixed him. He spat out what he could. It was no use. The odour spread outwards and thickened the air about him. The semi-darkness became unbearable. He left down his glass and groped his way out to the street.

A band was playing in the distance. At first he could hear only the rhythmic beating of the drum. He tried to ignore it, suspecting that the sound came from inside his head. But as it grew louder in volume and the brass and reed instruments added their voices he realised what it was.

The footpath, still wet from the rain, glowed a little in the light of lamps and shopwindows. It had a tilt. He leaned sideways to balance, decided his direction, lurched forward. The wind caught him full in the face. It was the blow of a fist. He endured it. He was used to beatings; from superiors, from anonymous letter writers, from friends of the days of studenthood who had found it more prudent to forget him. The parish he ruled over beat and bruised him, with its hovels, its ignorance, its hunger, its filth. It had broken him with beatings. It had filled his mouth full of blood. He stopped at the corner, leaned against a wall, braced himself against the sudden lurch of the unstable street. The band approached.

He would go immediately to his church. That was his refuge. But first the band. The bandsmen wore peaked caps and wide bandoliers of shining black leather. The brassy notes battered against the wall he was holding, making it beat like a giant pulse beneath his hand. The din grew and the bandsmen multiplied, until they spread in fanlike waves from the centre of the street to the wall he was leaning against. With shining bandoliers and sounding instruments they passed over and through him. The wall offered no resistance to them, they brushed by him without impact, they filled the street and the sky. The banners followed and whirled above his head like shrieking birds, the torches tossed and sparked and flared in long processions down corridors of his mind, boots pounded in streets of his being, the citadel in which he had barricaded the last of himself was assailed and shaken. He hid there, awaiting dissolution. Then the band passed.

'Help the lock-out, Father.'

Someone was rattling a box at him. He wiped the heavy sweat from his face, pushed the box aside, lurched forward in his effort to get quickly away.

'Jaysus,' the shocked voice said, 'will you look at his Reverence—drunk as a lord.'

The words cut into him like a knife thrust. He recollected himself, posed cunningly as an invalid, made use of his walking stick, simulated a limp. It took him, unnoticed for the most part, through the remaining streets. They were not, at that hour, populous. He crossed the granite flag with its worn depression, passed the holy water font with its green slime and found himself in the dimness and quietness he had desired. His church.

He sat down. A woman, deep in prayer, knelt some distance from him. At shrines and side chapels candles, like gossips, bobbed numerous heads and held mischievous conversations. The sanctuary lamp, sign of the Real Presence, houseflag of the Lord God, showed a tiny point of flame above the high altar's sacrificial slab. Christ was in residence. What was an altar, then? A monument to the world's cowardice, where Holy men cringed to and propitiated God's anger with the blood of others; saving their own skins with slaughtered bodies; with lambs, with doves, with the innocent blood of Christ Himself. The World—not Christ—judged, mocked, derided; the world trampled on the weak and battered in its rage at the faces of the defenceless; the world—not Christ—crucified, maimed, chastised with rods, demanded sacrifice. What priest could take the body of the world and break it between his fingers? How many desired to?

The woman in front had forgotten his presence, if she had ever been aware of it. Her prayers had stopped. He listened carefully and knew she was weeping. Her grief was soft and controlled, her sobbing barely audible. He raised himself with the help of his stick and went to her. He felt steady again. His mind was clear, untroubled, reasonable. He touched her shoulder.

'For whom do you weep, my poor woman?' he asked. His voice too, he was glad to discover, was entirely under his control again. He felt extremely well.

'For my poor husband, Father.'

'Has he died?'

'He died on me two days ago.'

'And have you buried him?'

'He'll be buried tomorrow after the ten o'clock mass.'

'Then his body is in the mortuary chapel?'

'It is, Father, we brought him here this evening.'

'Then dry your tears and follow me.'

She rose obediently. They went into the mortuary chapel where the coffin rested on trestles between four tall candles.

Beads of holy water still besprinkled the lid. Father Giffley turned to her and said gently.

'I'll raise him up for you.'

He smiled as he did so. It was a terrible smile. The woman backed away from him. He raised his voice to its pulpit pitch and shouted:

'Lazarus—come forth.'

The woman began to scream. Her terror echoed through the whole church.

'Jesus,' she screamed, 'Jesus, Jesus, Jesus, Jesus . . .'

He lifted his voice once more, so that their shouting intermingled in a nightmare of noise.

'Lazarus—come forth.'

Then he stretched out both hands and pushed the coffin from its trestles. It fell thunderously on the stone floor. The lid burst open. The corpse tumbled out and lay in a grotesque bundle on the ground. The woman's screams became wilder.

'Jesus, oh Jesus,' she kept calling, 'Jesus, Jesus, Jesus . . .'

Father O'Connor and Father O'Sullivan arrived together. It took them a long time to quieten her and then to persuade her to go into the house with the clerk to rest and recover. When she left they looked for Father Giffley. They found him eventually at the foot of the high altar. He was lying prostrate, his face downwards and his arms spread wide in formal veneration. He was either heavily asleep—or unconscious.

On Tuesday morning at eleven o'clock Rashers knocked on the basement door and asked the housekeeper if he might speak with Father Giffley.

'Father Giffley is not here,' she said.

'That's all right,' Rashers told her, 'he said I was to wait for him.'

She looked at him peculiarly.

'But Father Giffley isn't here at all, at all. He's gone away.'

'Gone away?' Rashers repeated. The housekeeper nodded. He hardly dared to ask the next question. He waited for some time, but the housekeeper volunteered nothing further. He said, fearful of the answer.

'And when do you expect him back?'

'He's very sick, the poor man,' the housekeeper said. 'God alone knows when we might hope to have him back with us.'

Rashers absorbed the information slowly. The pain in his heart made it difficult to speak. She closed the door.

He went back again towards Chandlers Court. The streets were warm with unseasonable sunshine. It did not comfort him. A parade passed him but he paid no attention whatever to it. There was the usual band and the usual whirl of banners.

'Larkin gaoled
by
Lloyd George'

'British Comrades
No Larkin
No Lloyd George'

The court had sentenced Larkin to seven months' imprisonment. The news meant nothing to Rashers. He had no further interest in anything. Nothing mattered.

CHAPTER 12

I N December defeat became a certainty. It afflicted the streets
and peered through the windows of tenements with a cold,
grey eye. The grates were often without fire, the rooms
without furniture. Hope flickered for a moment when the Archbishop of Dublin, moved by their hunger and distress and the
nearness of Christmas, succeeded in assembling a Peace Con-
ference. It failed almost as soon as it began. In London the
British Trade Union Council met to consider a plea for
sympathetic strike action. It was refused. They promised instead
to increase the subsidies so that Dublin's strike pay could be
improved. The opposite happened. The subscription lists in the
Labour papers grew shorter, the central strike fund dwindled
almost to nothing.

Mr. Doggett, fixing his new calendar for 1914 to the wall of
the office overlooking the idle marshalling yard, looked beyond
it and noted that the ships at the quayside were working normally. Free labourers now glutted the port. The police were there
to guard them, of course, but he took heart. It could not possibly
be long now. In January also Fitz attended a closed meeting in
Liberty Hall at which the members were advised to go back to
work if they could do so without signing the document that had
started the whole thing. Joe, who was standing beside Fitz,
looked around at him. They were beaten. For the present anyway. No one had said so, but everybody knew it. They would
have to get back to work now as best they could.

'That's that,' Fitz said. They stood at the river wall to talk
awhile. The food kitchens in the basement were already closed.
There were no longer queues with jamjars and cans.

'What are the chances?' Joe wondered.

'None for me,' Fitz said.

'Still—no harm trying.'

'No harm in the world,' Fitz said.

Mary said the same thing. She had never criticised or complained, but she had grown thin and looked unwell. The police had wrecked what little remained in the room which once had been her source of comfort and pride. It had only the broken table now and, incongruously, the clock that had been Pat's wedding present to them. The police had overlooked it. Or perhaps Father Giffley's unexpected entry had saved it. She said he should try his luck. Maybe they would remember that he had always been a good workman.

He went down to the foundry with the rest. They were presented with a form which was not quite the same as the original. It demanded an undertaking that they would not take part in sympathetic strikes but it made no mention of relinquishing membership of their Union. They discussed it and decided to sign.

'There'll be another day,' Fitz told them when they consulted him. He himself was called aside by Carrington. They walked in silence down the yard to an empty storeroom. At the door Carrington took a whistle from his pocket and stopped to blow two blasts. A boy appeared from one of the houses.

'Get my sandwiches from the locker,' Carrington told him, 'and bring a can of tea.'

'Yes, Mr. Carrington,' the boy said.

They went inside. There was a stove lighting in one corner and from the window they had a view of the wintry yard. It looked desolate enough. Exposed machinery had gathered rust, grass had rooted in the spaces between the cobbles, the paint on doors and woodwork had faded and peeled.

'We'll have a cup of tea when the nipper comes,' Carrington said.

'I'm not here to drink their tea,' Fitz told him.

'The tea is mine. Don't be so bloody shirty.' His tone was friendly. But he was embarrassed.

'I'd like to know what the news is,' Fitz said. Carrington

opened the shutter of the stove and stirred the coals until they flamed.

'We might as well be warm,' he said.

He offered Fitz a stool to sit on and gave him a cigarette. It was so long since Fitz had smoked that the first pull of it made him dizzy. For a while Carrington's face became a blurred disc.

'The news isn't good,' Carrington said at last.

'I thought it wouldn't be,' Fitz told him.

'I told you they wouldn't re-employ a foreman who went out with the rank and file, and that's the instruction they've sent down. You're not to be taken on.'

'Am I the only one?'

'There are two others.'

'Shop stewards?'

'One is a shop steward. The other is just an incurable trouble-maker.'

The boy came in with the sandwiches and the tea. Fitz rose to go but Carrington gripped his arm.

'We're not enemies, Fitz.'

'No.'

'Then stay where you are. I want to talk to you.'

'Is there any sense in talking?'

'Sit down.'

Fitz hesitated. But he took the mug of tea which Carrington pressed on him and accepted a sandwich. The feel of the sandwich in his hand roused reserves of hunger that had been building up for weeks. It had meat in it. He forced himself to delay before eating it. It took an enormous amount of will. After a decent interval he began to eat it. Once he began it was impossible to stop. He worked away steadily at it until it had gone. Carrington immediately offered him another, but Fitz waved it aside.

'No shame in being hungry,' Carrington said, 'take it.' He was smiling. Fitz gave in and took it.

'Thanks,' he said.

'There's one way you might get back,' Carrington said, 'but you're probably going to be stubborn about it.'

'Tell me what it is.'

536

'If I could tell them you'd leave the union and give an undertaking never to join it again, it might make them change their minds.'

'Is this your idea or theirs?'

'Mine. I don't even know if it would work. But I'm willing to put it to them.'

'I'll do anything within reason,' Fitz said, 'but not that.'

'Fitz,' Carrington said earnestly, 'I have respect for you as a person and as one of our best foremen. If you do what I ask it'll all be forgotten about in a few months anyway. What's the sense in being stubborn?'

'No,' Fitz said.

'Do you realise the position you're in?'

'I've a shrewd notion.'

'I don't think you have,' Carrington said. 'You're the only foreman I know of who walked out with the men. It's not just a matter of the foundry refusing to employ you. You'll be blacklisted in every job in the city.'

'How do you know?'

'Because I've been given the general list drawn up by the Federation with instructions to follow it, when I'm taking men on. Your name is on it. You don't believe me?'

The information was hard to accept. As he reflected on it he felt panic beginning to stir in the back of his mind.

'I believe you,' Fitz said.

'Then let me try what I suggested.'

Fitz hesitated. He shut his mind to speculation about the future.

'No,' he said.

'You're a stubborn bloody man,' Carrington said. He offered another cigarette and they smoked in silence. Then Carrington said:

'There's something else I wanted to speak to you about. I'm thinking of that friend of yours who lost his legs here a couple of years ago. Mulhall—wasn't it?'

'Bernard Mulhall,' Fitz said. 'He died.'

'I know that. Had he a family?'

'A wife and an only son.'

'That's what I was told. How old is the son?'

'About eighteen. He might be more.'

'I think I can help him.'

'I seem to remember Bernie Mulhall being on your blacklist too.'

'I know. But there was a lot of admiration and sympathy for him higher up. I can offer him a job.'

'Have you been told to?'

'Not in so many words. But one of the Directors expressed interest in the case and sent word down the line. A bit mad in his way—Yearling.'

Fitz made no comment.

'He's the man that left you home on the evening of the accident,' Carrington supplied.

'I remember him,' Fitz said.

'Will you send young Mulhall down to me?'

'I will,' Fitz said.

'And keep in touch with me. There's nothing I can do here, but I get to know of odd jobs here and there. They might help to keep things going for you while you look around.'

'Do you think there's any point in looking around?'

'If you can stand up to being sent from pillar to post. Don't let them beat you.'

Fitz smiled at him.

'I'm wondering whose side you're on.'

'Not on Larkin's anyway,' Carrington said. 'Yours—I suppose.'

'That's something,' Fitz said.

Willie Mulhall started in the foundry a week later. It was his first adult job. His mother came over to thank Mary the moment she got the news.

'Now I'll be able to pay back what I owe you,' she said. She embraced Mary and began to cry.

There was nothing for Fitz. He went from job to job but was turned away time after time. In February the Strike Fund closed down altogether. When that happened Mary put the clock in the pram and wheeled it down to The Erin's Isle Pawnshop. Mr. Silverwater refused to look at it. He was open for people who wanted to redeem the articles they had pledged, not to take in more. She returned home and Fitz put it back in its place on the mantelpiece.

'What are we to do?' she asked him. He had no answer for her. Except to offer to try what Carrington had suggested. That, too, was impossible.

'We'll keep trying. Things will be better as the rest begin working again. Something is bound to turn up.'

That evening he borrowed from Joe, who was back at work in Nolan & Keyes.

'It'll be a while before I can pay you back,' he said.

'Don't be worrying,' Joe told him. But he worried just the same. He had never before borrowed money without knowing how he was going to return it. He was starting at the bottom again—a scavenger for odd jobs.

$\mathbf{P}$AT was passing the shop with its display of religious goods
when the little foreman stopped him on the pavement
and said:

'I don't seem to have seen you around lately?'

'I've been in gaol,' Pat said.

'When did you get out?'

'This morning, about two hours ago.'

'And what was it like?'

Pat considered.

'A bit confined,' he decided.

'Come over here with me, for the love of God.'

'What is it?' Pat asked.

The little foreman insisted on dragging him over to the window.

'Have a look at that,' he invited, pointing at it. Pat looked in.

'Well—I'll be damned,' he said.

Inside the window, with a pencil behind his ear and a roll of
dockets peeping from the breast pocket of his shop coat, Timothy
Keever was struggling to put a statue of St. Patrick on display.
The statue was heavy and the window space already crowded.

'Watch this,' said the little foreman. Pat had met him from
time to time in various bookmakers' shops, where his fellow-
punters knew him as Ballcock Brannigan. He now banged with
his fist on the glass to attract Keever's attention. Neither could
hear the other because of the thickness of the glass, so Ballcock
began to convey his instructions in dumbshow. Keever, indicating that he understood, moved first a statue of St. Christopher
and another of the Little Flower. But the rearrangement was

unsuccessful. He looked out for further instructions.

'Move the other stuff first,' Ballcock shouted in at him. Keever shook his head.

'Did you ever see such a thick?' Ballcock asked Pat. He gave the instruction again, this time in dumbshow. Keever acknowledged and set to work again. He shifted a heavily mounted candle, Paschal in design; then a set of purple vestments, appropriate liturgically to the seasons of Advent and Lent; then a shroud which would provide for the last sartorial decencies of some deceased Brother of the Third Order of St. Francis. In his struggle with these complexities he banged his head severely against a sanctuary lamp, a pendulous one with a red bowl and a brass container.

'Holy Jaysus,' Ballcock said. Keever, reaching up to steady the lamp which was swaying from the blow, nearly toppled the statue nearest to him. Ballcock hammered furiously on the glass.

'You clumsy bastard,' he shouted. Keever looked out, puzzled.

'Deaf as well as everything else,' Ballcock decided. He turned his back to the glass and lit a cigarette.

'That's what you get for employing ex-scabs,' Pat said.

'No choice of mine,' Ballcock said. 'Clerical influence—that's what has Keever in his job. Here, have a cigarette.'

'Thanks,' Pat said.

'I suppose you haven't been doing the horses lately?'

'They didn't encourage it,' Pat said. 'What's any good today?'

'I'll tell you what's good,' Ballcock confided. 'Packleader at Leicester in the two-forty. It's information which I got from a priest that's a customer—a most Reverend punter.'

'I haven't done a horse for months,' Pat told him.

'Nor nothing else neither,' Ballcock said, 'not if gaol's the same as in my day.'

'That's right,' Pat agreed. 'Nothing else.'

'Well—be true to the Church and back Packleader. Follow your clergy. Have you a job?'

'I don't know. I'm on my way down to Nolan & Keyes to find out.'

'If you don't pick it up right away,' Ballcock offered, 'drop back to me. I have three days casual I can give you.'

'I'd be glad of it.'

'Welcome,' Ballcock said. He flung away his cigarette butt and looked again at the window. Keever was doing his best to rearrange the display.

'Excuse me,' Ballcock said, 'I have a few things to discuss with mahogany skull there.'

He strode in and called Keever from the window. They both disappeared into the back of the shop.

It was a cold, blustering day, with a sky that was too bright and too wide after his months in prison and streets that were noisy and suddenly unfamiliar. The shop window was better. It was neatly framed and, now that Keever had left, comfortingly devoid of speech and movement. St. Patrick, the National Apostle, occupied a central position. In green robes and bishop's mitre he gazed past Pat at the streets of the capital city. Snakes at his feet cowered in petrified terror of his golden crozier and in his right hand a stone shamrock symbolised the mystery of the Unity and the Most Holy Trinity. St. Patrick's Day, Pat calculated, was almost exactly a week away. He was glad to make the calculation. It brought him into touch with everyday life for the first time since his release.

There was a second fact to be absorbed. Tonight, all going well, he would sleep in the House of the Boer War Heroes. Lily's letter to him had said so. While he finished his cigarette he took it from his pocket and read it again.

. . . you will have nowhere of your own to stay after all those months will you but don't worry the landlady here is away I have the house all to myself and I can put you up for the night which will give you a bit of a chance to look around for somewhere but don't come until after seven o'clock so as I will be home from my work. Everything with me is all right hospital was a great rest and I have good news for you Pat which is why I want you to come as well but watch out for the neighbours if they as much as well you know what I mean be careful for God's sake or we are both sunk . . .

At seven o'clock, about ten hours away, he would see her and be staying with her again. The thought made him restless. He returned the letter to his pocket and began to walk. There was his job to be enquired about. There was this suddenly unfamiliar city to be considered. They were not the streets of a few months before. No collection boxes rattled, no pickets were on patrol, the trams ran without police protection. It seemed a tame end to eight months of struggle. He wondered how his mates on the job would feel about it. He quickened his pace.

Gulls circling above the river gladdened his heart. That and the strong smell of the sea. His spirit now welcomed all sounds, those of crane and ship, dray wheel and bogey. The width of the sky exalted him. He stopped and was overjoyed at the sight of the unloading gangs along the wharf. To men he did not know he shouted.

'Hi, mate—more power.'

They grinned and waved back. There was no defeat in the faces he passed. They sweated familiarly, were dust-coated, had ready answers. They had spirits that recovered easily from adversity. A few weeks work and everything was as it had always been. More or less. There was little to be lost that was worth pining about.

The gates of Nolan & Keyes stood wide open, a sunlit space where the air smelled of tar from the nearby gasworks. It was noonday now. The carters were either off on their rounds or gathered in the shed near the stables having their midday food.

Suddenly unsure, he stepped into the gateman's hut and found the yard foreman drinking tea and smoking his pipe by the gas fire. The foreman looked around, then rose slowly.

'Pat Bannister,' he said. To Pat's surprise he held out his hand.

'Back again,' Pat said, taking it.

'When did you get out?'

'This morning.'

'You should have let me know.'

That was hopeful.

'They weren't greatly in favour of letter-writing,' Pat said.

'You're looking for a start?'

'I came down here first thing.'

'Certainly,' the foreman said.

'When?'

'Right now, if you like. There's a half-day left.'

'That'd suit fine.'

'Quinn has your horse I'm afraid,' the foreman said, 'but Mulcahy's out sick so you could yoke up his. Come on the scales with the rest of them after the meal break and I'll have a half-day made up for you.'

Pat hesitated. He wondered about the form, but there seemed to be nothing else.

'No formalities?'

'Not here,' the foreman said. 'Nolan & Keyes and Doggetts want to get on with the bloody work. But don't go shouting out loud about Larkin. Give it a rest for a while.'

'Are the lads below?'

'They are,' the foreman said, 'you'll find them chewing the rag—as usual.'

'I'll be glad to do the half-day,' Pat confessed.

'It'll be waiting for you,' the foreman assured him.

He thanked him and made his way across the yard. He was hungry and the light but pungent smell of tar aggravated it. He strode out and began to sing. It was a great joy to be able to walk freely. He knocked ceremoniously on the door of the men's shed and then pushed it inwards.

All the faces turned around. There was Joe and Harmless, Quinn and Mick. There were three or four others as well. Mick jumped to his feet and came forward.

'Pat,' he shouted and threw his arms about him.

The others stood up.

'Well—I declare to God,' Joe said as Mick dragged him over to the fire, 'they let him out.'

'And bloody nearly time,' Quinn told them.

Harmless expressed agreement.

'Just so,' he said.

They shook hands with him in turn. Then they all settled down to fire questions at him.

'When are you starting?'

'What was it like?'

'Did you do the full stretch?'

'How do you feel after it?'

Pat looked at the cans of tea and the food.

'I'll tell you how I feel,' Pat said, 'I'm starving with hunger.'

They plied him with sandwiches. Harmless made a special show.

'Take this one,' he said, 'there's two nice rashers in it.'

'Showing off,' Mick said.

'By reason of the missus taking in two lodgers recently,' Harmless explained modestly, 'they don't always finish their breakfasts.'

'I'm starting this afternoon,' Pat said, answering an earlier question.

'Dammit,' Quinn said, 'I'm using your horse.'

'It's all right. I can yoke up Mulcahy's. The yard foreman said so.'

'I wish you luck with it,' Joe told him, 'it won't pass a pub.'

'A sagacious beast,' Harmless remarked. 'I seen Mulcahy and that animal many a morning—and both of them with a hangover.'

The food tasted real for the first time in a long score of weeks. The tea was strong and sweet and hot. The stove blazed with familiar cheerfulness. There was an all pervading smell of horses.

'What's all the news?' Pat asked.

'Terrible weather. Floods all along the Shannon. You were well off to be inside.'

'There's bad foot-and-mouth disease down the country too. We've been keeping a sharp eye on the horses.'

'That's why Mulcahy's out.'

'Mulcahy hasn't got foot and mouth,' Harmless objected.

'I mean the rain,' Quinn explained, 'too many severe wettings.'

'They say Home Rule is coming.'

'So is Christmas,' Harmless remarked, looking sceptical.

'I'm going by what's in the papers every day.'

'And I was remarking with regard to Sir Edward Carson.'

'You think he'll get Ulster excluded?'

'Just so.'

'Home Rule or no Home Rule,' Joe said, 'you and me won't notice any great difference.'

'Certainly,' Harmless agreed.

'And the union?' Pat asked. 'What about the union?'

'Down, but not out,' Quinn told him, 'we'll rise again.'

'When the fields are white with daisies, we'll return,' Mick prophesied.

'We've the members and the Hall still, anyway.'

'All we're short of,' Joe commented, looking cynical, 'is the money.'

'Like myself,' Harmless added.

The yard foreman blew his whistle.

'Yoke up mates,' Quinn said, shaking the wet tea leaves from the can into the fire, which sizzled and hissed and spat out angry spurts of steam at him.

He took his afternoon easily because he had to. The knack of shouldering sacks had not deserted him—after three or four journeys he was back again into a rhythm of lifting and turning that had been perfected over a lifetime. But his back and shoulder muscles gave him trouble and his legs, after a couple of journeys up narrow stairways, protested painfully at the weight of the load he had to carry. He also discovered that it was no slander to put it around that Mulcahy's horse was fond of its beer. It stopped outside three public houses where it had come to regard itself as a regular and refused to budge until one of the curates brought out the dregs of porter from the pan.

'A grand animal,' one of them said, stroking it while it drank, 'cute as a Christian.'

'Cuter,' Pat remarked, 'a Christian would be expected to pay for it.'

He remembered Ballcock's tip and tied the reins to a lamp-post.

'Watch her for me,' he said, 'I won't be a minute.'

The bookmaker's office smelled of sweat and stale smoke. He studied the board over the shoulders of several others, then decided on a double—both at Leicester. He wrote, laboriously as always, a slip which backed two shillings win on Packleader and decided to double it with Revolution in the three fifteen, both at Leicester. Revolution took his fancy. He put the docket which the clerk gave him in his pocket and felt that the day was now normal.

Mulcahy's horse was tonguing its lips appreciatively. He untied her and she moved off contentedly. He let her take her own pace while he rested his aching muscles and observed the ordinary life of the streets with affection and tenderness. He felt kinship with his city; with his fellow carters who always waved a greeting, with the trams and their hissing trolleys, with the ramshackle houses and the humble people who trudged on humdrum errands. At the end of the day he unyoked in the stables by lamplight. He was back now in the place fortune and habit had ordained for him. It was more than bearable. It was desirable. Joe came to him and said:

'If you've nowhere to stay tonight, you could doss down with me.'

'Thanks. I'm fixed up already.'

'Sure?'

'All arranged.'

'What about money?'

'That's a different matter.'

Joe fumbled in his pocket and put a two shilling piece into his hand.

'I can spare it,' he said.

Pat watched the glint of it in the lamplight.

'You're a brick.'

They left the stable yard together and Joe told him about Fitz.

'We were luckier here,' he said, 'there was never any mention of signing any form.'

'Poor Fitz,' Pat said, 'he gets the rough end of everything.'

'If we ever reorganise, it's someone like Fitz who will have to do it,' Joe said. It was one of the few ungrudging thoughts Pat had ever heard him express. He nodded agreement and decided he must see Fitz, if only to mention the possibility of three days casual work with Ballcock Brannigan.

At Chandlers Court his mood changed. There was a deadness about it now that evening had fallen. He hesitated to face the reproach of the bare room. Optimism had come easily to his mates. They had had more time in which to adjust to the collapse, more days of routine to get used to streets without placards announcing meetings and flaunting the name of Larkin. In their company his renewed contact with the bits and pieces of everyday had filled him with joy. Now, in the evening light and the emptiness of the familiar street, pity possessed him for the people of his city and their defeat.

A dog shambling along the opposite pavement caught his attention. It was the first he had seen in months. It was old and wore the look of defeat too. A bent and bearded old man followed at a distance. He did not recognise Rashers until the dog had mounted the steps and disappeared into the hallway of Number 3. The name floated like a ghost into his memory.

'Hi—Rashers,' he shouted.

The bearded figure made no response. He peered more closely to be certain he was not mistaken. The change in Rashers shocked him. He shouted again. Rashers mounted the steps slowly and unhearingly.

'How's the Bard of the Revolution?' Pat yelled.

It had a momentary effect. Rashers, now in the open doorway, paused briefly. Then he turned his back and with the same slow gait disappeared into the house.

'Do you know him?' the lamplighter asked. He had pulled up in front of Pat and was parking his bicycle against the footpath.

'Rashers Tierney,' Pat said.

'That's the label.'

'Has he gone deaf or what?'

'Not deaf,' the lamplighter distinguished. 'Disinclined. I've known Rashers this many a year.' He reached upwards, expertly engaging the gas tap with the hook on the side of his long stick. He pulled downwards, then touched the mantles with the thin blue flame which danced at its tip. The gas popped. A pool of light surrounded them.

'Do you know the people in Number 3?'

'The most of them,' the lamplighter answered, appraising his handiwork, professionally critical.

'The Fitzpatricks?'

'Two pair front,' the lamplighter said immediately.

'I've a message for them but I don't want to go in with it myself. Will you oblige me?'

'Certainly,' the lamplighter said.

Pat found the stub of a pencil but nothing he could write on. He took out the betting docket.

'Half a minute,' he said.

He wrote on the back of the docket:

Just out this morning and back at work in Nolan & Keyes. There is three days' casual going with Brodericks of Merchants Quay. Ask for Mr. Brannigan say I sent you. This docket is a Double Packleader and Revolution good name at Leicester if it comes up collect and use the cash. I'm fixed all right. See you on the Christmas tree. Pat Bannister.

As he read it over a thought struck him and he added: *I warn you Keever is working there but what about it.*

The lamplighter took the docket and promised to leave it up immediately.

'I'm greatly obliged,' Pat assured him.

He watched him crossing the street and climbing the steps. As he entered the hall its gloom engulfed him so that there was nothing to see except the flame at the tip of his stick floating like a little star in the darkness. It too disappeared. It was time at last to visit Lily. He stood for a while looking up at the window of Fitz's apartment, still tempted, still afraid. He turned at last and headed for O'Connell Bridge. He was sad. Once again the streets were too spacious. He wanted shelter and companionship.

The footsteps of the lamplighter echoing in the hall and on the stairs above caused the dog beside Rashers to stir restlessly.

'Easy,' Rashers whispered.

He lay on the floor on his bed of straw and accumulated rags.

A little of the light from the street lamps found its way through the broken window. It touched the ceiling and the upper part of the wall, leaving the rest of the basement in darkness. The dog settled briefly but stirred again, a fidgeting movement that for The moment was unbearable.

'It's nobody for us,' Rashers told him. Silent, cold, pale yellow in colour, the reflection on the wall compelled his attention. It had appeared quite suddenly some moments before. It had a soporific effect. He let his eyes dwell on it in the hope that it might soothe him into sleep. But the dog whimpered again, dragging him back to the dampness and darkness, reminding him that they were both sick and cold and hungry. He did not want to move. It had been a mistake to lie down the moment he got in. It made it harder than ever to resume responsibility.

'In a minute,' he pleaded, 'give me a minute.' He groped without enthusiasm for the sack which was somewhere in the darkness beside his bed. He failed to find it.

'Sweet Mother of Jaysus,' he moaned.

He sat up and located it near his feet. There was some bread in it he had retrieved from a bin. It smelled a bit from contact with other garbage but he was past caring about that. It was the best he could do. He broke some off and held it towards the dog which sniffed at it for an unbearable length of time and kept turning its head away. Losing patience Rashers flung the bread on the floor.

'Like it or lump it,' he shouted.

The shout exhausted him. He lay back and began to nibble at what was left. It tasted sour but his body demanded it. His bad leg and his arm were becoming numb with the damp and the cold which was rising through the straw. It would be better to move about, to light a fire with the few sticks he had foraged, to boil a can and beg a few spoons of tea from someone in the house above him. No. Not from those who lived with him. If they gave—well and good; he would not ask. He returned to contemplation of the pale yellow strip of light on the ceiling.

It brought him down green lanes to race meetings of long ago. He saw white railings and coloured shirts and tents and three-card-trick men; the Curragh with its short grass and bushes of yellow gorse; the Park with its shading trees and the river to be glimpsed far below; Leopardstown by the railway line surrounded by blue mountains. He had been able for it then. A little luck and another summer and he would be able for it again. What was it Hennessy sometimes said? We never died of winter yet.

He bit again at the loaf but had to spit it out. The taste was abominable.

'I'll light my bit of a fire,' he decided.

But he was so numb and weak that he was unable to rise. He tried different positions for leverage, grunted, gave up, forced himself to try again. There was no sound at all from the dog.

'Rusty,' he called, as terror overmastered him for a moment. The dog ambled across to him. He dragged himself along the floor until he reached the wall, which he used to lever himself at last into a standing position. He waited to get his breath back.

'You were watching for them rats again,' he accused the dog, 'do you want to get yourself poisoned. How many times have I to speak to you?'

He had paper and sticks and two wooden setts saturated in tar which he had stolen from a pile where men had been digging up a road. When the fire had taken the tar in the setts bubbled and blazed furiously. The dog left off his vigil by the rat holes and came over to heat himself. Rashers boiled water, which warmed him and was better than nothing. Tomorrow he would beg at a few houses for sugar and tea. He took out the tin whistle and regarded it regretfully. The air hole at the mouthpiece was bent inwards, so that it was impossible now to get anything out of it beyond a shrill squeak. That had happened two days before. First he ran into trouble with a younger man called Morrissey when he went to search the bins on Pembroke Road. Morrissey had been there before him.

'It's my road,' Rashers had said, 'I've had this road since you were in petticoats.'

'It's mine now,' Morrissey said.

'You're only an unprincipled bowsie,' Rashers said. Morrissey gripped him by the beard, jerked him forward and struck him in the face with his free hand. The blow sent Rashers sprawling.

'Clear off,' Morrissey warned.

Rashers, his head reeling, refused to be silenced.

'You're only a bowsie,' he said again. The dog snarled but it was an empty threat. It too had grown too old for fighting. He left Pembroke Road to Morrissey and tried playing his tin whistle outside the Church at Haddington Road. Here a policeman moved him on. In fury and impotence he dashed the tin whistle on the ground. When he cooled down sufficiently to pick it up, he found it was bent.

He drank the hot water and dwelt on the world's misuse of him. Then he lay down again in the hope of falling asleep before the fire went out for want of fuel. It glowed on the walls, making grotesque shadows. He was glad he had stolen the setts.

'We never died of winter yet,' he said to the dog. But his heart told him it was a lie.

'Who is Keever?' Mary asked.

'The one Mulhall went to gaol for,' Fitz told her, 'he used to work as a carter.'

She remembered. 'Will you try for the job?'

'First thing in the morning.'

'I'll call you early.'

'If I get three days with Brodericks and the week Carrington told me about, that won't be so bad.'

She was putting coal on the fire from a bucket Mrs. Mulhall had sent across to them earlier.

'We'll knock it out somehow,' she said.

For how long, he wondered. There seemed no hope at all of anything permanent. He had been trying without any sign of success for three months. If he could get to England there would be some hope, but it would mean finding some way to keep Mary and the children alive while he looked around. He decided against mentioning it again. They had talked enough about it in the weeks that had passed. He turned the betting docket over and examined the message again. Packleader and Revolution : the combination amused him.

'If this double turns up,' he said, 'we'll buy a little place in the country.'

She smiled.

'I wonder why he didn't call himself,' she said.

The House of the Boer War Heroes was unchanged and unchangeable. Souvenirs in the china cabinet still spoke of comings and goings that had ended at the turn of the century. The same uniformed groups occupied the mantelpiece and the top of the piano. Queen Victoria's portrait on the sitting room wall stared down at Lily and Pat with longstanding disapproval. They had their tea at the fire and ignored her. With the landlady away the house was their own. Pat lay back on the sofa and smoked. To see a fire again was an adventure; to be with Lily a piece of good fortune he would never have dared to hope for. He watched her now as they talked and found her looking better than ever. Living in a house which was comfortable with an old woman who appreciated her as a companion rather than as a lodger had changed her. Her speech was less sharp, her manner more subdued and reticent. Life was no longer something to be fought.

'I hated you being in gaol,' she said, 'all those criminals.'

'There didn't seem to be any criminals,' Pat told her. 'From the account of themselves they gave to me, every one of them was innocent. So far as I could find out, the only one guilty of the crime he was locked-up for was myself.'

'In that case it's just as well they let you out,' Lily decided, 'you might have corrupted the rest.'

'It used to worry me,' Pat admitted.

'And you have your job back?'

'Started right away.'

'I'm glad.' She came over and sat beside him.

'Pat—you must take it easy from now on. No more fighting and getting into trouble. Or heavy drinking.'

'I'm not a heavy drinker,' he objected, 'you need money for that game.'

'You seem to manage—somehow,' she told him.

'Are you going to nag?'

'Listen to him,' she begged, addressing Queen Victoria. But she relented and said, gently:

'I thought you didn't look well when you called. Gaol was no cakewalk, was it?'

'It's nicer to be out,' Pat admitted.

'It's nicer for me too,' she said softly. The tenderness that had been denied for so long overwhelmed him. He took her in his arms and she yielded warmly to him. His heart quickened with happiness.

After some minutes she moved a little away from him and said:

'You didn't ask me about my good news.'

'I thought I'd let you come to that in your own time,' he said. He was a little bit apprehensive, wondering if she had got a job which would take her away, or if she had met somebody who meant more to her. He was not certain that he wanted to hear.

'It's about that thing which used to worry me.'

'What thing?'

'Oh, God!' she exclaimed. 'Do I have to use the deaf-and-dumb alphabet?'

He knew then what she meant. It had become so much a part of their knowledge of each other that he had not considered it.

'I'm sorry,' he said.

'When I was in hospital there was this nun. She was very kind and I think she took a fancy to me. Anyway I screwed up the nerve to mention it to her and she insisted on me having all sorts of examinations.'

He waited. It was a subject he had learned not to discuss.

'Pat,' she said, 'there's nothing at all wrong with me. I've got a clean bill.'

He reached out and took her hand. But he knew it was better not to say anything. He was never sure on this score.

She said: 'So—if you still want to marry me—everything seems to be all right.'

'Lily,' he said.

She laughed and came close to him.

'I was a bit of a fool in those days, wasn't I?' she said. 'I was going to be smart and make easy money. That's what I thought.

554

A bloody little fool. It's just as well I got a fright that knocked a bit of sense into me.'

'It's a long time ago, Lily. I wouldn't go on thinking about it.'

'I suppose we're both fools. That means we ought to suit each other.'

'Down to the ground,' Pat agreed.

'Well—are you going to ask me?'

'Ask you what?'

She appealed again to Queen Victoria.

'Listen to him,' she begged.

He realised what she meant and made amends.

'Will you—Lily?'

'Yes,' she answered.

He looked in his turn at Queen Victoria and a thought struck him.

'Do you want to ask her permission?'

'I don't recognise royalty any longer,' Lily decided.

'A Sinn Feiner?'

'No,' Lily said, 'Workers' Republic.'

'Grand,' Pat pronounced, 'we'll get on together like Siamese twins.'

He kissed her and they became serious again. There were no more barriers. Love and tenderness engulfed both of them.

Rashers moaned in the darkness. The fire had burnt itself out. The streak of light had left the ceiling. A chill dampness filled the basement and settled on his beard and on the rags that covered him. The burning agony in his bowels was turning his insides into vapour and water. He tried to raise himself but found that in one arm and one leg there was no sensation at all. They hung with an immovable weight, pinning him down.

'Sweet Christ,' he repeated over and over again. 'Sweet Christ.'

He listened for sounds that would tell how near it might be to morning. There were none. The house above him slept, the streets outside were empty. He felt his bowels loosening and ground his teeth as he fought to control them. If he fouled what he was wearing there was nothing he could change into. He made another desperate effort to get to his feet. It was useless. He had no power over his limbs. He was held by the weight of his ailing body.

'Rusty,' he called. The dog came to him.

'Lie down,' he said, 'lie down.'

In the dense darkness he could see nothing, but he felt the weight of the dog as it settled against his side. For a moment there was comfort in that. He could hear it breathing in the darkness and feel the warmth of its body. The world was not entirely empty. Then the pains became worse. He felt his bowels melting and loosening in spite of his will. A burning hot liquid trickled incontinently. He made an agonising effort to stop it but failed. With a sudden rush his bowels voided their contents of foulness and gas. He felt his buttocks sticky and saturated. But he still could not move. He had an interval of complete numbness, without pain or thought of any kind. Then the slow agony inside him flickered into life and began its mounting torture all over again.

In the morning Pat slipped out of the house when Lily signalled to him that the way was clear. At the loading yard he found he had his own horse back again. He was pleased when it greeted him with signs of excitement. His first stop was at a bookmaker's office, where he found his Double had turned up, Packleader winning by four lengths from Romer and Enoch at seven to two—Revolution by a length from Duke of Leinster and Prince Danzel at nine to four on. The collapse of the aristocracy was a good omen. Fitz, he reckoned roughly, would draw about fourteen shillings. He did not grudge it. Securing the sack about his shoulders with a large safety pin Lily had supplied he strode out to face the work of the long day. There would be other and better doubles. His heart told him he was on a winning streak.

CHAPTER 14

O N St. Patrick's Day, the newspapers reported, the weather was somewhat sharp—but for the robust, healthy and invigorating. The display of the chosen leaf was universal. In the Pro-Cathedral and other churches the ceremonies were specially devoted to panegyrics of the national Saint and sermons in Irish were preached to crowded congregations. A visiting English priest reminded the Irish Faithful that it was fifteen hundred years since Ireland's great Father and Friend had passed away to the music of the spheres. Another referred to Home Rule and prophesied that the hour of National deliverance was at last at hand. The shop windows of the city, including the one Keever had dressed, devoted themselves to displays of home-manufactured goods while the citizens, most of whom had a holiday, went to the races at Baldoyle or made extended excursions by train, tram and outside car. From the flagstaffs of the Town Halls from Dublin to Bray the green flag was floating, Kingstown being the only exception. It was the exception that proved the Rule.

At the Mansion House the Gaelic League denounced the Post Office for refusing to accept parcels addressed in Irish. At the Castle there was a St. Patrick's Ball where the excellent music of the band, the gaily moving dancers, the beautiful costumes of the ladies, the bright and varied military uniforms of the officers and officials, the stately Court dress of the gentlemen, all blended in a pleasing kaleidoscope of colour and harmony. Earlier his Excellency the Lord Lieutenant had attended the trooping of the colour in the Castle yard, where he inspected the parade of the Second Battalion West Riding Regiment. It was thrash the beetles and God Save the King; Hail Glorious St. Patrick for Brittania Ruled the Waves.

Hennessy inspected a parade too. It was the procession of the Irish National Foresters in their plumed hats and tight breeches, marching on their way from Parnell Square to Donnybrook Church, headed by members of the Ladies' Section in their long cloaks. In order to do so fittingly he bought a buttonhole of shamrock with a penny and told the vendor to keep the change. He found the day robust and sharp, but not invigorating. He had continuous trouble with a drop on the end of his nose due to the wind and an attack of chronic catarrh. He wiped it away several times but it kept on turning up again. Like a bad ha'-penny, he decided.

It did not affect his humour. He had had regular work for some weeks that paid modestly and was full time. It would continue for another fortnight at least. After that it would be time enough to worry again. For the present he had a little money, the National Festival to celebrate, a band to listen to and a parade to gawk at.

It was a good parade. The Foresters stepping it out in their ostrich-plumed hats, their frilled shirts, their top boots, their green coats and plentiful gold braid brought back the age of Erin The Brave. In line upon line the proud brotherhood passed him, imperishable, glorious, while with erect soldierly bearing and eyes flashing under the rim of his bowler hat he reviewed them rank by rank—Robert Emmet Hennessy; Aloysius Wolfe Tone. The band made his heart beat hard and sent his blood racing. It played (but in march time, he noted) 'O Rich And Rare were the Gems She Wore', which told of a maiden who adorned in costly jewels and without escort of any kind walked the length and breadth of Ireland unafraid of robbery or assault.

Hennessy repeated to himself :

> 'Kind sir I have not the least alarm
> No son of Erin would offer me harm
> For, though they love women and golden store
> Sir Knight—they love honour and virtue more.'

So too did Son of Erin Robert Emmet Hennessy, the Honour and Virtue loving Aloysius Wolfe Tone.

The parade passed, the music of the band faded away on the somewhat sharp but healthy and invigorating March air. He had been to holy mass already. It was time to wet the shamrock. A hot whiskey, he thought.

'Sharp weather,' he said as he asked for it.

'It's healthy,' the publican said.

'Better than the rain,' a customer put in.

'Invigorating,' the publican agreed.

Hennessy removed the drop from his nose and wondered if the publican would be as enthusiastic if he had to be out in it. But the golden colour in his glass and the steam rising from it mollified him.

'Here's the first today,' he said, raising the glass in salute.

'*Slainté*,' the publican returned.

The other customer approved.

'That's what I like to hear,' he told Hennessy, 'an Irishman using his native language—matteradam whether he knows much or little of it.'

'I know damn all about it,' the publican confessed honestly, 'except that *slainté* bit and Conus Tawtoo. And—oh yes—slawn lath.'

'There you are,' said the customer encouragingly, 'you know a fair bit just the same.'

'If I had to confess my sins in it,' said the publican, 'I'd stay unshriven.'

He was a man who refused to be flattered.

'Are you an exponent yourself, sir?' Hennessy enquired, adopting a tone of gentility in deference to the other's air of education and good manners.

'In a modest way,' the other confessed, 'I've attended classes.'

'At mass this morning the sermon was in Irish,' Hennessy told them. 'It was a grand thing to hear.'

'And did you understand it?' the publican asked.

'Well—no,' Hennessy admitted.

'I fail to see the sense in that,' the publican decided. He was counting empty bottles into a crate.

'In honour of the National Apostle,' Hennessy explained.

'And did St. Patrick speak Irish?'

'Fluently,' the customer said.

'I didn't know that, mind you,' the publican admitted.

'Irish and Latin,' Hennessy confirmed.

'Latin, naturally,' the customer agreed, 'it was the language of the Universal Church.'

'If he didn't know Irish,' said Hennessy, pressing his point, 'how could he have explained our holy religion to the Irish princes and chiefs. There wasn't one of them knew a word of English.'

'French,' the customer corrected.

'I beg your pardon?'

'French,' the customer repeated. 'St. Patrick's native language was French.'

'Well—French then,' Hennessy amended. 'I doubt any of the Irish princess spoke French.'

'To be fair now,' said the customer, 'some of them might have. There was a lot of trade with the Continent, if you remember.'

'That's true,' Hennessy said, with an educated nod.

The publican hoisted the full crate on to the counter and exclaimed blasphemously as he jammed his thumb in the process. Then he apologised and said :

'That's one kind of language the Saint wouldn't know, I'll warrant.'

'I wouldn't be so sure,' the customer said, 'he could be crusty enough.'

'Giving out oul lip to God at times, I believe,' Hennessy said.

'That's true. When he was fasting up there on Croagh Patrick and wrestling with the devil. He hammered hard at God to get the privilege from him of being allowed to be the judge of the race of the Gael on the Last Day.'

'He got that promise—I understand,' Hennessy said.

'I take a lot of that stuff with a grain of salt,' the publican told them. He was cooling his bruised thumb under the counter tap.

'Ah well,' Hennessy said, 'whoever it is does the judging, I hope he won't be too hard on any of us.'

'Right enough,' the publican said, relenting, 'the only difference between any of us is that if one of us is bad, the other is a damn sight worse.'

'Amen to that,' said the customer.

They had another in honour of the day that was in it, the publican, despite initial reservations about the earliness of the hour at length consenting in deference to the demands of true patriotism, to join them. They toasted the cause of Ireland which was Holy and their kin both at home and in exile. They then shook hands and said slan leat several times and went their various ways.

Hennessy was a little light in the head. He was also very happy. He liked things going on about him and welcomed the holiday bustle in the streets. The public buildings were gay with flags, men and women wore their sprays of shamrock pinned to their coats or pushed jauntily into their hat bands. The little girls had green ribbons in their hair, the small boys wore harps and St. Patrick badges on their jerseys. He was glad he had got mass on his way from his night work and that he had had the foresight to bring something in with him so that he could have his breakfast on the job. It left him free to enjoy the celebrations without the inconvenience of feeling hungry. Later he would arrive home with little gifts to distribute. For the moment the church bells and the traffic and the sounds of parading bands were blending together in a wave of welcome excitement. It was Ireland's Great Day.

As the bell of St. Brigid's boomed across the forecourt to summon its shamrock bedecked parishioners to last mass, Father O'Sullivan pushed open the door of the common room. He found Father O'Connor waiting for him. The fire was blazing away satisfactorily, the great centre table was set for lunch. They would dine later than usual today in order to accommodate their guest, the Reverend Father Ernst Boehm of the Society of Jesus, who had consented to lead the rosary and deliver the sermon in Irish at afternoon devotions. He was, they understood, a Gaelic scholar of distinction.

The housekeeper seemed to have done very well. The napkins were tastefully arranged, a dish of shamrock made a pleasant display of green against the white tablecloth.

'Mrs. O'Gorman has excelled herself—don't you think?' Father O'Sullivan remarked. As senior curate he was responsible for parish affairs in Father Giffley's absence. The entertainment of so important a guest caused him anxiety.

'She has forgotten the finger-bowl,' Father O'Connor said.

'The finger-bowl?' Father O'Sullivan repeated. He surveyed, inexpertly, the layout of the table.

'Thank goodness you noticed,' he said, 'we can have that put right.'

'Without difficulty,' Father O'Connor assured him. His manner was grim.

'I have been wondering what we should offer him. Beforehand—I mean. Whiskey, do you think?'

'Sherry would be better.'

'Sherry, of course. I'm the world's worst at this sort of thing. . . . Have we got any?'

'I saw to it.'

'Grand. I'm glad you thought of that.'

'I also took the liberty of ordering some wine. For the meal. I felt you would agree.'

'Of course. That was very farseeing. These S.J.s . . . Besides, he's a Continental, isn't he?'

'German.'

'Boehm. Yes, indeed. Thank God you thought of the wine. We'd be put to shame altogether.'

Father O'Sullivan rubbed his hands together and chuckled at his thoughts.

'Do you know,' he said, 'it's comical when you come to think of it. When we need someone who is able to preach in Irish on the feast of our National Apostle, we have to ask a German.'

He noticed that Father O'Connor declined to be amused.

'Is there something amiss, Father?' he asked, his anxiety returning.

'With great respect,' Father O'Connor said grimly, 'I think there is.'

He turned and stared at the notice on the wall. It still hung to the right of the enormous painting of the Crucifixion, its bold red letters and its improvised air clashing with the heavy respectability of the rest of the room. It had no place there above the upholstered armchairs, the hospitable fire, the great breadth of the tastefully laid table. The cardboard had warped and yellowed but the message was still large and legible:

'*Notice*

The Great St. Gregory has said
It is not Enough to have Learning
These Also are My Sheep.'

'We have discussed this before,' Father O'Sullivan said gently. He was embarrassed.

'We have,' Father O'Connor conceded, 'and I am sorry to speak about it again.'

'If we removed it and Father Giffley returns, he could rightly feel that we took advantage of his illness to flout his authority.'

'Father Giffley won't return.'

'I can only hope you are wrong.'

'Besides,' Father O'Connor pressed, 'All that is over. It no longer serves any purpose whatever.'

'I agree with you. But it will do no harm to leave it there until he returns.'

'Among ourselves—no. We are both used to Father Giffley's extraordinary . . . habits. But what about our guest?'

'Perhaps he won't notice it.'

'He won't,' Father O'Connor said irritably, 'if he happens to be blind.'

Father O'Sullivan said unhappily, but with no sign of changing his mind: 'I am sorry it should distress you.'

'I am concerned about Father Boehm,' Father O'Connor answered. 'He will suspect us of harbouring some madman with a passion for scrawling on walls. However, I will say no more. After all, he will be right.'

He went off to remind the housekeeper about the finger-bowl.

In the hallway Hennessy debated with himself whether to

visit Rashers first or the Fitzpatricks. He decided to leave Rashers until last. He had a drop of whiskey and would stay to share a drink with him and to gossip about the goings on in the city. After that he would go up to his own place and his dinner. There would be a bit of bacon and cabbage to mark the feast day. He looked forward to that.

Fitz himself opened the door to his knock. Mary and the children had gone to mass and to look at the parades. He invited Hennessy to step in.

'Am I disturbing you?'

'Not a bit,' Fitz said, 'I'm all on my own.'

The room was still bare of any real furniture. But there was a fire in the grate and the table which had been cracked by the raiding police was serviceable. Fitz had improvised chairs out of wooden boxes. He waved Hennessy to one of them.

'We're a bit short on decent chairs,' Fitz apologised.

'The depredations of the militant months,' Hennessy remarked sympathetically. 'I still see them everywhere.'

'I think things are getting better,' Fitz said.

'For some,' Hennessy agreed.

'For yourself—I hope.'

'Yes, indeed,' Hennessy admitted. 'I fell on my feet. A steady job as night watchman.'

Fitz smiled.

'You seem to be a great draw as a night watchman.'

'It suits my peculiar temperament,' Hennessy said. 'I can stay up all night, but early rising never agreed with me.'

He took a cigarette packet from his pocket and offered one to Fitz. He kept talking as he did so. He was anxious to share his riches without drawing any notice to the fact that circumstances had for the moment reversed their respective roles of giver and receiver.

'It's a tidy little job and of course—all bona feedy and above board. No trouble about the union. In fact I called to ask you about joining up.' He thought a moment and then aded, 'Of course it would have to be on the Q.T.—for the moment.'

'There's no trouble about that,' Fitz said, 'just call down to number one branch in Liberty Hall. Say I sent you. You'll get a card right away.'

'And I can keep it quiet for the moment so far as the job is concerned?'

'A lot of us have to do that,' Fitz told him.

'That suits up to the veins of nicety,' Hennessy decided.

He had left his bowler on the table. He now stood up to retrieve it. It was, Fitz remembered, a size or so too large for his head, the overcoat too broad for his light body. Hennessy fumbled for some time in the pocket of the overcoat and produced a paper bag.

'It's a few sweets for the children,' he explained, handing the bag to Fitz.

'You're a strange man,' Fitz commented, 'spending your few shillings on these.'

'Now, now,' Hennessy said, 'they cost nothing. A little treat for St. Patrick's Day.'

'They'll be delighted,' Fitz assured him.

Hennessy put the bowler back on his head, using his ears as wedges to prevent it from falling down over his eyes. He had completed his business. Fitz saw him to the door.

'Hennessy,' he said, 'I'm glad to see you fixed up. It wasn't a pleasant experience having to stop you in your last job.'

'All's fair in love and war,' Hennessy said agreeably.

'Your wife didn't think so.'

'She was a bit put out,' Hennessy admitted.

'I didn't blame her.'

'Women seldom appreciates a principle.'

'A lot of men have the same failing.'

'That's why I hope I can claim a modest place among the trusted and the true.'

'You can,' Fitz assured him.

Hennessy looked pleased.

'Well, then. I'd better be leaving. I've to see Rashers and then go up to my dinner. I have a few sweets for him as well. You'd be hard set to decide which of them has the sweeter tooth—himself or his dog.'

Fitz smiled and held open the door. A thought struck him.

'By the way,' he said, 'what sort of a place is it you're doing the watching in?'

Hennessy hesitated. Then, with an air of apology he said: 'Well—as a matter of fact—it's a sweet factory.'

'I see,' Fitz said gravely.

He had been right. The expropriators were being expropriated.

Hennessy checked his pockets to be sure he had the sweets and that the drop of whiskey was still safe. It was. He anticipated a complaint from Rashers for not having visited him for so long. The new job and the night work had upset his routine. The whiskey would heal the breach. Maybe Rashers would be out in the streets, selling badges or playing his whistle to the crowds. If so he could go up for his dinner and call on him later. He went down the stairs into the hall again. A cold blast of air flowed from the streets through the open door. He went through the hall towards the backyard where a sack hung in place of the original door of the outside privy, then turned to descend the stairs that led down to the gloom of the basement. He expected the dog to start barking. There was silence. He hesitated in the half-dark, convinced now that Rashers was out. As he waited he noticed, for the first time, a heavy smell. It was not the usual smell of damp earth and decaying woodwork. It was sweet and sickly and, it seemed, intermittent. A thought struck him which made his blood turn to ice. He groped for his matches, lit one, held it above his head. The door to Rashers' den was closed. He lit another match and slowly opened it. A stench of decay flowed out and choked him. He was certain now.

'Jesus protect us,' he said.

Through the window with its broken sheets of cardboard that flapped in the wind a feeble light entered the room. He forced himself to investigate, crossing the floor fearfully, step by step.

The Reverend Ernst Boehm proved both amicable and talkative. He said nothing at all about the notice on the wall. Perhaps he did not see it. He wore the thick glasses of the scholar with lenses that looked like the bottoms of twin jamjars. But he remarked appreciatively on each course as it was served and he praised the wine without reservation. Father O'Sullivan was delighted, Father O'Connor was proud. The huge fire blazed cheerfully in the grate, the dishes and the glasses reflected its red and yellow flames. Their faces above the shining white tablecloth were slightly flushed. St. Brigid's was enjoying a rare moment of elegance.

Father Boehm spoke interestingly of St. Patrick and early Irish monasticism, referring frequently and often confusingly to the *Annals of Innisfallen*, the *Annals of Clonmacnoise*, the *Chronicum Scottorum*, the *Book of Leinster*, the *Annals of Tigernach*, the *Annals of the Four Masters*. He mentioned Plummer's *Vitae Sanctorum Hibernia* and paused to offer some penetrating comments which, however, were difficult to follow. In a lighter mood he praised Kuno Meyer's recently published *Ancient Irish Poetry* and, offering them a quotation, pursed his lips and wrinkled his massive forehead as he explored his labyrinthine memory. An abrupt and triumphant exhalation of breath signalled that he had cornered one. In a deep voice which had a slight accent he began a poem of the ninth century called 'The Hermit's Song'.

> 'I wish, O Son of the Living God
> O Ancient eternal King
> For a little hut in the wilderness
> That it may be my dwelling
>
> Quite near, a beautiful wood
> Around it on every side
> To nurse manyvoiced birds
> Hiding it with its shelter'

The mention of birds and woods caused Father O'Sullivan to glance automatically at the shamrock in the bowl. It was withering fast from the heat of the fire. He quickly returned his attention to the poem, a little puzzled because it did not seem to rhyme.

'A pleasant Church and, with the linen altar cloth
A dwelling for God from Heaven
Then, shining candles
Above the pure white Scriptures

Raiment and food enough for me
From the King of fair fame
And I to be sitting for a while
Praising God in every place.'

Father Boehm beamed at them. Father O'Connor praised its
simplicity and grace.

'What a pity we cannot all follow the poet,' he remarked,
regretting the need to be involved with the world.

Father Boehm said his sermon would treat of the three great
saints of Gaelic Ireland: Patrick, Brigid and Colmcille. Brigid
was peculiarly appropriate, he suggested, since she was the
patron saint of their parish. Did they know there was a legend
that she had once hung her cloak on a sunbeam? That was amusing, of course. But beautiful too. Had it not charm? Father
O'Connor agreed to play for benediction on the harmonium.
He hoped it was serviceable. It was so long since it had been
used. Father Boehm wanted the final hymn to be 'Hail, Glorious
St. Patrick'.

'With a thunder,' he enthused. 'Grandioso. An Anthem of
triumph.'

Father O'Connor, thinking of the harmonium, promised to
do his best.

It was at that moment the clerk knocked on the door and
opened it with a look of anxiety and apology. Father O'Connor
was displeased. But the clerk remained fidgeting and looking
uneasy so he excused himself and went out to see what was
amiss. When he returned Father O'Sullivan asked:

'Is something wrong?'

'A child has brought a message and it is somewhat garbled.
Someone has been killed—or has been found dead, I cannot be
sure which—in Chandlers Court.'

'Do you know who it is?'

'No. The message is very unsatisfactory.'

'One of us had better go,' Father O'Sullivan decided.

He rose automatically. But Father O'Connor knew his place. He was the junior. There was an important guest to be looked after.

'No, no, Father—please,' he said, 'the duty is mine.'

'Dear me,' Father Boehm said.

'I'll go immediately,' Father O'Connor decided.

'Take a cab,' Father O'Sullivan advised.

'Yes. I'll do that. It will mean I can get back in time for benediction.'

He made his apologies to Father Boehm who waved them away. He quite understood. He consented to a little more wine but studied the exact amount scrupulously and then motioned its sufficiency to Father O'Sullivan.

'Wine is a blessing in moderation, an imperfection in excess,' he explained. His genial smile pleased Father O'Sullivan, the attentive host. He listened with meticulous interest while Father Boehm discussed the early Irish Penitentials, referring initially to Zettinger on Cummean, but later and in more detail to Finnian of Clonard.

News of something wrong spread through Chandlers Court like a fire. A body found; a woman drunk, a suicide. By the time Father O'Connor arrived the details were known. People were spread on the pavement outside. They lined the hallway. They leaned over the basement bannisters. Down below it was dark, but neighbours had provided candles which gave a wavering light. A man found dead. This was better than the parades and the make-believe. This was the drama of death. They had passed time and again along the street above the cardboarded window. Little knowing. A woman told another that only that morning she had remarked it to her husband. She had wondered, she said. There were women with shawls, subdued children, men with grave faces.

'This way, Father,' Hennessy said. He assumed a natural precedence, having been the discoverer. The people made passage.

'What exactly has happened?' Father O'Connor asked.

'I called down to see him about an hour ago. He was dead.'

'Called down to see whom?' Father O'Connor asked shortly.

'Rashers Tierney,' Hennessy said.

Father O'Connor stopped.

'It's not a pleasant sight, Father,' Hennessy said, 'he's been dead for some days.'

Father O'Connor had remembered a figure in candlelight lying on a coke heap. He could smell urine and the reek of spirits. The memory was arrestingly vivid.

'Show me the way,' he said, after a moment.

As he passed all their eyes were fixed on him, depending on him. For what, he did not know. It was as though they expected him to do something about Death. He shook off the lingering influence of the white cloth, the wine, the learned talk that had so transformed the common room of St. Brigid's. These were his parishioners. This was the true reality of his world. He was here of his own free choice. He had demanded to be allowed to serve them.

Led by Hennessy he passed between the candles they had set along the stairway and into the dimly lit room. The smell of corruption was overpowering. In the corner furthest from him sacking covered the body. They had decided for decency's sake to hide it from him. He searched the faces of the few men in the room and recognised Fitz. He looked at the bulging sacking.

'Is that he?'

Fitz nodded.

'He's been dead for some time?'

'Several days, Father, by the look of it.'

'Then there's little I can do,' Father O'Connor said. He meant it was too late for the administration of the last rites but they would know that already. Presumably. They nevertheless continued to regard him. Expecting what? The smell was sweet, sickly, unbearable. He could not minister to carrion.

'Have you notified the police?'

'We have,' Fitz said.

There would be an inquest. They would take it to the morgue and bury it God knows how or where. The sooner the better. In the interest of health, if nothing else.

These were the ones who refused to trust him because they thought he had tried to break their strikes when all he intended was to give a little charity to the old and the destitute. They expected him as a priest to lead a prayer for the dead boilerman. That was their right. But he would do more than that. He motioned to Hennessy.

'Remove the sacking.'

They had not expected it. He saw them looking uneasily at Fitz, waiting for him to answer for them.

'He's in a very bad way, Father,' Fitz said, 'the rats . . .'

Delicacy stopped him from finishing. Hennessy hung back. Father O'Connor removed his hat and handed it to one of the men. He had decided what to do. He went across the room, bent down, began gently to pull down the sacking. He sweated, strangling his impulse to cry out.

The head had been savaged by rats. The nose, the ears, the cheeks, the eyes had been torn away. The hands had been eaten. He forced himself to be calm.

'Is this Tierney?' he asked quietly.

'It is, Father.'

'And what is this?'

Hennessy came over obediently and looked. His face was a silver-grey colour.

'It's his dog, Father.'

For the moment they had forgotten all about that. The animal's ribs were etched starkly against the taut skin of its carcass. Its discoloured teeth from which the lips had fallen away, wore the wide grin of death. The rats had ripped open its belly and exposed its organs.

In a voice that had found a new tone of gentleness Father O'Connor said:

'It isn't fitting to lay the brute beast and the baptised body together.'

Hennessy understood. He bent down and took the dog by the forelegs, dragging it slowly across the floor and steering it into the darkness of the far corner. Father O'Connor went down on his knees. The rest knelt one by one. He took a small bottle from his pocket and, making the sign of his blessing, gravely sprinkled with holy water what decay and the rats had yet left of the boilerman Rashers Tierney. He prayed silently once again, aware of how often he had failed, for the grace to know how to serve without pride and without self. He prayed, as was his way, to a crown of thorns and a pair of outstretched palms, his Christ of Compassion who always looked like the statue that had once stood in Miss Gilchrist's ward.

It was some time before he remembered the others. He had excluded them from what he was about and that was wrong. Taking the mother of pearl rosary from his pocket he said:

'Let us pray together for the repose of his soul.'

He began the usual decade of the rosary. At first only those in the room responded. Then to his surprise, for he had forgotten they were there, he heard the responses being taken up by those outside. The sound grew and filled the house. From those lining the stairway outside and the landing and the hallway above, voices rose and fell in rhythmical waves. The sound flowed about him, filled him, lifted him up like a great tide. He looked down at the ravaged body without fear and without revulsion. Age and the rot of death were brothers, for rich and poor alike. Neither intellect nor ignorance could triumph over them. What was spread on the straw before him was no more than the common mystery, the everyday fate, the cruel heart of the world.

The prayers finished. There was one more thing to do. He did it without hesitation and without reasoning why. He joined what was left of the two half-eaten hands across the body and wrapped his mother's rosary beads about them. He pulled the sack back into position. He rose to his feet.

The man who had been minding his hat returned it to him and he put it on. There was nothing further to be done.

'God bless you all,' he said to the assembled men. They made a way for him through the crowd and saw him to his cab. At St. Brigid's he had time to be sick and then to wash his hands and face before climbing to the organ loft to play for benediction.

While he was still playing they arrived with a stretcher and a tarpaulin and took Rashers to the morgue. A policeman took the dog away in a sack and saved himself a lot of unnecessary trouble by quietly dumping it in the river. Hennessy went up to his dinner but when it was put before him found he was unable to eat it. His wife had a rare moment of understanding and took it away without reproof. Hennessy said nothing further either but went down to the backyard and hid himself behind the shed of the privy and wept because he felt his own good fortune had led him shamefully into neglect of Rashers.

By that time the congregation in St. Brigid's, urged on by a gesticulating Father Boehm, were singing 'Hail Glorious St. Patrick' with great fervour and piety. Father O'Connor, doing the best he could with the wheezing instrument at his disposal, listened and felt he had drawn a little nearer to them and, through them, to the God and the way of eternal salvation he so earnestly believed in.

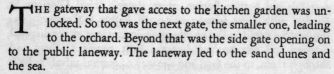

CHAPTER 15

THE gateway that gave access to the kitchen garden was unlocked. So too was the next gate, the smaller one, leading to the orchard. Beyond that was the side gate opening on to the public laneway. The laneway led to the sand dunes and the sea.

It was sometime in September. What date, Father Giffley did not know. What day he was not quite sure. Thursday perhaps. But the route from the main grounds of the Nursing Home was by now quite familiar. It was also forbidden. That did not bother him. The orchard was heavy with sunshine and the odours of apples and pears. They lay at intervals along the grass-grown pathway, they bent in profusion over him as he searched in the broken water butt by the wall. It was there. He looked about him to be sure there was no one to see. Then, with the bottle of whiskey hidden in his coat he let himself out the side gate and set off for the sand dunes. It was three o'clock. He was quite certain of that. His pocket watch was the one thing in the world that was always right.

Wasps were busy among the blackberries in the laneway. Soon they would die. He admired their yellow-and-black-hooped bodies. They were delicate, cruel, innocent. As he walked sand that had been blown from the sea dusted his broad black toe-caps. It lay along the bottom of the hedges too in little grey and silver mounds, left there by the wind. Sand was like spirit, unconfinable. It would get into his socks soon.

The laneway dipped under the railway arch. The arch itself was scrawled with messages of love and obscenity. His feet sank in powdered sand. He climbed among hillocks of wiry seagrass and scattered shells. Beyond was the sea, calm now with a thin edge of foam. It was wide and sunlit. He found a hollow which gave him privacy. The horizon was far away and sea noises spoke to him of changelessness and unalterability. He sat down. He opened the whiskey bottle.

In Kingstown, which was a little nearer to the city, Yearling put his latchkey in the lock and let himself into his house. He had been away for over two months. Now he wondered why he had bothered to return at all. His servants had been let go. Accumulated mail littered the hall. The air was stagnant and unpleasant. He too, felt like a drink. But there was none in the house. He gathered up the letters and automatically inspected the rooms. Nothing had been disturbed. Nothing was out of place. He drew the curtains from the window. Sunlight flooded in. He opened the window and the room seemed to stir. It was as though it had taken a deep breath. He sat down at the table to examine his post.

By six o'clock the whiskey bottle was empty. Father Giffley did not mind. He had had the foresight to fill his hip flask with enough to meet the needs of the night. For the moment he was happy to contemplate the empty sea, to explore at leisure the notions of immortality and eternity. The rocks, the sand, the sea, the declining sun, these were eternity. No doubt they had changed a little in all their billions of years and conceivably they would not last for ever. But they lasted a long, long time. Long enough to satisfy any reasonable mind. Human beings changed from era to era, indeed from minute to minute, but mankind remained. It, too, lasted. For long enough. For more than long enough. That was immortality, or as much of it as he could burden his long-suffering and often overtaxed imagination with. Above and beyond that eternity and this immortality was God, or That which was Greatest. Should the Devil ever become greatest then he would become God in turn and the order of creation would be changed in an instant. Not changed simply as from that moment, but right back to wherever and however it had had its beginnings. But in God and Divine Order there is no Becoming, no passive Potentiality. All Is. No Was or Shall Be. The Devil hadn't a hope. Poor devil. Amen.

He decided to commit something to the sea, a thing he had been fond of doing as a child. He found a pencil and tore a page from his pocket diary and scrawled:

Time takes all away. This was written by a madman on the shores of a mad island.

He put the note in the bottle, pushed in the cork, and threw the bottle as far as he could into the sea. Not very far. He could see it bobbing up and down. He had to squint to do so. His eyes were not very good.

By that time the troopship had cast off from the North Wall, the civilians had finished their cheering and waving, the band on the quayside had come to the end of its brassy music, Mary and Mrs. Mulhall were already on their way back to Chandlers Court. Fitz, the leavetaking over, leaned on the rail of the ship while below him the water of the river whirled past. On the quayside every single thing was familiar, every shed, every crane that raised a bony finger along the South Wall. He saw the gateway of Doggett & Co, the gateway of Nolan & Keyes, the Gas Company gasometers, the corrugated shelter that housed the emergency water supply on the roof of No. 4 house in the yard of the foundry. He hoped they had found someone who could work it. At the Pigeon House, where the river widened out, he saw the strand he had walked with Mary and the Shelly-banks where he had proposed to her. Children were exploring its seapools. He wondered if they were still searching for a crab that had money in its purse. Away inland he could see the Martello tower and the houses along Sandymount Strand.

Another soldier said to him:

'Got a match?'

He took out his box. The soldier offered a cigarette. He took it. The wind whipped at the match. He cradled the flame between his palms. They lit up.

His heart was full of Mary. Each moment that passed was putting its extra little piece of world between them, each twist of the propeller carried him further and further from her. But she would have the allowance. The children would eat. The rent would be paid. In the Royal Army Service Corps he would learn to be a motor mechanic or a car driver. He would be sure of a job when he came back. If he came back. That was as would be.

The soldier seemed lonely and leaned beside him on the rail. He was from Dublin too. He said:

'Funny feeling—isn't it?'

He was looking at the mountains that surrounded the bay. They were floating dreamily on sea and sunlight. Multi-coloured.

The two of them smoked together. The Black Lighthouse loomed up and fell behind them as the ship cleared the river at last and swung into the bay. Bells tinkled remotely. Their speed increased. Ireland slipped away behind. Before them lay England and training camps, beyond that the Continent. Foreign tongues, unfamiliar countries, shattered towns. War.

The bottle kept returning to Father Giffley. Three times he flung it into the sea. Three times the sea, after long intervals of indecision, brought it back and left it lying again on the shore. The third time it deposited it almost at his feet. He picked it up angrily and smashed it against a rock. Then he became conscience stricken and carefully gathered together the broken pieces. He took them back among the sand dunes and stowed them in a place where they could inflict no damage on bare feet. He cut his own thumb in the process. Blood ran down his coat sleeve and stained the cuff of his shirt. He wrapped his handkerchief around his thumb. The pain set his nerves on edge. He allowed himself a measure from his hip flask, enough to soothe, but not so much as would leave him short for his need later on.

The letter from the Bradshaws dated 19th July told Yearling they had been to Portsmouth to view the test mobilisation of the Fleet on a day of perfect weather when the whole place had been en fête and the seafront packed with people. They would both be returning to Ireland in September but not to Dublin. They would stay with Mrs. Bradshaw's family in Kilkenny while they looked around for somewhere permanent. They hoped to see him.

The letter was two months old. It read already like something from twenty years before. He stuffed the remaining correspondence in his pocket and rose to his feet. He knew now he would go to London. Not because of the war. The war was irrelevant. The war was neither here nor there. He had been uneasy and restless for such a long time. Among the lakes and rivers of Connemara where he had fished and dreamed for two not very memorable months, among people he had met in clubs and hotels, among the streets and byways of Dublin. Nothing would ever happen in Ireland again. Not to him anyway. Nothing ever had. But in London, for a little while and impossibly long ago, life had revealed briefly its dangerous dimensions. Perhaps in London it would do so again. In some other way, of course. And without heartbreak.

He went over to his piano and lifted the lid. It looked lonely too. Very gently he pressed one of the keys. A single musical sound startled the room. It was sweet toned, luminous, sad. He shut the lid again. It was time to go. There was nothing to stay for any longer. He closed the window and let himself out the hall door. It clicked shut behind him.

As Father Giffley made his way back up the lane a train crossed the bridge. He heard its rumble in the distance, stopped, decided to look. Two children at a window saw his black-coated figure and waved their handkerchiefs at him. He waved back. The sky had filled with a pink light which tinted the inland fields and spread its glowing stain on the sea. They continued to wave at each other, the children with their white handkerchiefs, he with his bloodstained one, until the train had gone a long way and looked like a giant black caterpillar against the fields and the pink sky.

Father Giffley made his way up the lane again. The wasps were still busy about the hedges, the blackberries shone in the evening light. He could hear still the never-ceasing movement of the sea.